Stilling the Stillness
Part 1, Voices of War

Book Three of the Stillness Series

Richard Lee Ferguson

"Having raised humanity above the beastly level of survival struggles, we will now aim to upgrade humans into gods and turn *Homo sapiens* into *Homo deus*." — Noah Harari

"No matter how inured you get to atrocities, you're still always stunned and shocked by how cruel and wasteful *Homo sapiens* can be." — Steven Pinker

"Fate starves at Probability's door." — Goddess

"Probability starves at Fate's door. — God

Also by Richard Lee Ferguson

The Stillness Series

Book 1: Stirring the Stillness, Part 1 Voices of Quest

Book 2: Stirring the Stillness, Part 2 Tortured Journey

Book 3: Stilling the Stillness, Part 1 Voices of War

Book 4: Stilling the Stillness, Part 2 Restless Spirits

Book 5: Becoming the Stillness, Part 1 Voices of Madness

Book 6: Becoming the Stillness, Part 2 Haunted Caves

Book 7: The Hunchback's Gift, Part 1 Voices of Defeat

Book 8: The Hunchback's Gift, Part 2 Superior Ones Risen

Book 9: Flames of Extinction, Part 1 The Last Voice

Book 10: Flames of Extinction, Part 2 Stillness is Stilled

For the full series, visit the Amazon series page: https://www.amazon.com/dp/B0F1WJ5J4N

Contents

Principal Characters — VII

Preface — IX

Prologue — XI

1. PART ONE: BEGINNINGS — 1

2. The Chosen One — 3

3. Fever Dreams II — 17

4. A Trip to the Beach — 29

5. Fortress of Sand — 37

6. The First Night — 57

7. Village of Reeds — 63

8. Outside the Walls — 83

9. Within the Walls — 101

10. PART TWO: REPLICATION — 113

11. The Exchange — 129

12. Mutiny — 155

13. PART THREE: STRUGGLE — 189

14. The Battle — 207

15. The Tabs — 231

16. A Hole in the Dike — 259

17. The Rage of Mountain Man   263

18. PART FOUR: CONFLICT   285

19. Village Redux   299

20. Fever Dreams VI   327

21. The Confrontation   341

22. Entombment   355

23. Mountain Man Returns   363

24. Fever Dreams VII   389

25. Grief 1   405

26. Grief 2   411

Epilogue   418

Principal Characters

Voices - God and Goddess

Michael Powers – Narrator and son of John Powers and Bai Meiying
    Storyteller – Michael Powers nickname in the war
    T – Lieutenant
    Pappy – Sergeant
    X – Medic
    Cairns – Captain
    Mountain Man – Soldier
    Nguyen Tuyet Mai – Vietnamese intelligence officer
    Kim Lan – Tuyet Mai's assistant
    Le Chi Vy – Major in North Vietnamese Army
    Vo Thanh Tong – Captain in North Vietnamese Army
    Cao Thanh Dam – Sergeant/Sapper in North Vietnamese Army
    Madame Dau – Village Council Chief
    Han Tinh – Legless veteran in village
    Schoolmistress Nang – Village teacher
    Diane – Deceased wife of Michael Powers
    Theresa – Second wife of Michael Powers
    Ethyl – Friend of Theresa
    Mark Powers – Son of Michael Powers
    Vu Quoc Viet – Sergeant in North Vietnamese Army
    Pham Van Dinh – Prison guard
    Paul and Claire Thompson – Friends of Michael Powers
    John and Lisa – Children of Paul and Claire Thompson
    Quang Long – Clerk in North Vietnamese Army
    Teo – Grandson of Madame Dau
    Professor Benson – Teacher of Mark Powers
    Bui Quang Minh – Commissar of North Vietnamese unit
    Master Kung – Mysterious monk/teacher

Preface

Can Humans Be Replaced Peacefully?

Query: Are you one of the increasing numbers of people who think humans are irredeemably destructive and pose such a threat to the planet that their extinction would be a good thing? However, do you also abhor the massive destruction and suffering that would necessarily be the consequence of their demise? Bloody, violent dystopian novels often focus only on a few survivors of such devastation, not on the suffering that would extend to all other life forms on the planet. While there are many excellent dystopian novels, such a formulaic concentration on a small group of heroic protagonists can be narrow and unsatisfying.

So, how to unravel the ubiquitous human presence without simultaneously destroying the rest of the planetary ecosystem? Can a successor species evolve fast enough to replace humankind, or would it be extinguished before it has a chance to spread?

Such a successor species, by random chance or intentional design, must possess far greater cognitive and empathetic capacities to thwart the human proclivity for eliminating real or perceived threats. What would it be like for those first generations of advanced individuals surrounded by a sea of slow-witted but resourceful *Homo sapiens*? How would they survive the human penchant for fearing otherness and a relentless instinct to exterminate it? Whether the guiding force effectuating this change is Nature, Superior Alien, God or Gods, Goddess or Goddesses, here is an interesting way forward:

Replace *Homo sapiens* with a more advanced species, but not *drive* them to extinction through violent extermination, rather *dilute* their genes to insignificance over generations. There is precedent for such top-down genetic engineering. Human biologists eliminate dangerous pests by introducing mutant strains that breed with the targeted species to produce offspring harboring the desired genetic makeup. Generations later, the original species is superseded.

A new form of consciousness must necessarily arise—one in which strange Voices with immense cognitive power reverberate in advanced minds in the same way Voices once arose in the minds of early *Homo sapiens separating them from competitors such as Neanderthals*. Humans would initially diagnose those hearing such new Voices as schizophrenics, but they are, in fact, the incipient stirrings of a superior species. However, new Voices must be only the beginning, as this emerging species must also evolve powerful physical capabilities to overcome human weapons of destruction.

The doves must have sharper claws than the hawks . . .

The Stillness Series is the epic story of one such scenario.

Prologue

~ *Dear, dear Reader* ~

If you have been on this journey with me, you know I am writing this from a mental institution. You also know both of my parents are deceased and that **Goddess** insisted they conceive me in spite of overwhelming obstacles: Mother's lesbianism, Father's schizophrenic voices, and the horrors they faced while trapped in China during World War II. Like horsemen of the apocalypse—war, famine, revolution, Japanese invaders, warlords, deserters, and bandits—all contributed to the searing inferno surrounding their quest for the mysterious *her*. These obstacles have been well documented in my earlier scribblings. What awaits?

~ *The Stillness Shattered* ~

There was a time, not long ago, when the stillness could still be stirred. When a handful of wanderers dared to carry a Precious Object across a dying land. When voices whispered of redemption, and silence had not yet been drowned by the scream of mortars and the moan of mass graves.

That time is gone.

Now comes the breaking.

This is a war of all wars. Not just between nations or armies, but between selves. Between past and future. Between the last tattered scraps of human mercy and the ancient machinery of violence grinding it to dust.

Here, there are no travelers. Only the trapped.

A fortress molders in the jungle, encircled by mud, ghosts, and lies. Inside: a platoon of young Americans, sick with hunger and delusion. Outside: enemy soldiers, traitors, prophets, mothers. Beneath them all, a tunnel—a secret—the mouth of something older than war. Something waiting.

Storyteller, the shattered survivor, tries to remember who he was before memory became a cage. No, better yet, a dark tunnel.

Tuyet Mai, once a woman with grandiose revolutionary dreams, now a legless whisper through the smoke.

Madame Dau, who once defied her own execution, must now defy history itself.

Dam, Cairns, Vy, Nang, Han Tinh, the Mountain Man, the Goddess—

All circle one another in a tightening spiral of ritual and blood, hallucination and hunger. The fortress becomes a crucible. The jungle, a judgment.

The war does not simply kill. It transfigures.

The dead speak. The living forget. And somewhere, far from this place but watching closely, the Superior Ones—yet unborn—begin to understand how they came to rule the world.

This is the reckoning. The origin of extinction. The scream before the final whispers.

~ *Questions, Questions* ~

And so the questions can no longer be denied—
What is left of a soul once it has been trained to kill?
Can memory survive when the body is no longer willing?
And if the gods have turned away—what then remains to save us?

~ *First Things First* ~

My parents and I all heard the voices of **God** and **Goddess** (with a few demons thrown in). I am fully aware, as I write this, that the population at large, most particularly the mental health industry, considers the voices to be schizophrenic hallucinations. On the other hand, **Goddess** always insisted to my parents that none of us were fully human, we were the beginnings of a new order for the planet, and the voices we heard were merely quirks of our supposedly powerful new genes. This notion is hard for me to credit, as I am here in a mental institution. So who, or what, are **God** and **Goddess** if not mere hallucinations? Even They admit They are metaphorical. But behind the metaphors, are They real? I am trying to find out.

I can attest to the fact that I am fully disoriented and clinging by a thread to my sanity. Unfortunately, war has played a large part in the trajectory of my life just as it did for my parents. Whether **God** and **Goddess** planned it that way or not, I am unclear.

I consider what you are about to read a sort of autobiography, but one I will write using third person omniscient. Why? Call it a madman's defense—omniscience helps me survive what memory cannot. But beware, dear Reader, I am what literary types call an unreliable narrator and my little cliffhanger moments may tax your patience.

Chapter One

PART ONE: BEGINNINGS

A Man Named Michael

~ A Recurring Dream ~

Michael Powers draws attention wherever he goes. The son of a white American father and a striking Chinese mother, he moves through the world marked by a symmetry too precise, and by a silence too heavy to be mere introversion. He belongs nowhere entirely, and the world senses it. His mother died before memory could give her shape and substance, and now remains a mythic icon. His father, hollowed out by grief, raised him in a house of shadows, secrets, and unspoken traumas. Love was not withheld; it had vanished, lost behind the tangle of his father's relentless voices.

On his deathbed, the old man spoke only once: "Watch out for the voices. And avoid the poison that collects at the bottom of craters."

In time, the voices came to Michael, just as they had for his father. Schizophrenia, or so he believed, took root. And the poison, slow and invisible, pooled deep.

Tonight, like every night, Michael dreams.

~

Sunlight falls through the jungle canopy in long, narrow shafts. The air swells with moisture and movement. Mist coils through leaves. Insects click and chant. A tiger's growl echoes from far off. Life prepares for its courtroom theater: predator, prey, witness. Two soldiers push through the underbrush. One flees. One hunts. The younger stumbles down a ravine, breath ragged, limbs scraped and wet. He crashes beside a shallow stream, yanks his rifle free from the grasp of vines. Behind him, the sound of pursuit, steel slicing vegetation, draws near.

Help me, mother. Please.

He turns and freezes.

Two bodies float half-submerged in the water, ensnared in the twisted arms of a fallen tree. One lies facedown, motionless. The other gazes upward, flies darkening the face like a grotesquely moving mask. No words. Only judgment. They condemn him. For leaving. For surviving.

"So be it," he whispers.

No past. No memory. Only now. The American erupts from the jungle, machete raised, rifle trailing. The young man fires, too slow. He's tackled, slammed flat. The blade comes down. A muted flash. Bone shears. His hand is gone. It lands in the mud, fingers still curled tight around the rifle.

~

"Michael. Michael. Wake up. You're dreaming. It's okay. Wake up."

He lifts his head, eyes bleary.

"Okay, Diane," he murmurs. "I'm awake. Just . . . off. Too dramatic. The machete didn't shine. It was dull. Heavy."

His words drift away. He collapses back onto the pillow. She turns over. The cover shifts slightly with her.

Michael sighs and closes his eyes again.

Sleep reclaims him.

~

Beneath that sleep, the voice stirs. High, feminine, unrelenting. It seeps into the hollow spaces of his mind. Not spoken. Not thought. Threaded, like a needle sliding through flesh, through time. She speaks not to him, but through him. She is Goddess. The one who waits. The one who knows.

My plan? To slip through the eye of his memory, and return to that small war, that green womb of death. But the wife interferes—always too soon. The needle breaks the skin but doesn't pierce the vein. And worse, he believes he has a twin: a fiction born of ancestral rupture. That delusion shields him. For now. But I whisper. I poison his dreams. I wait. I wait. The needle festers, yes, but the wound must open. He must return to them. And I must return through him. He is the hinge. He is the gate. The Chosen One.

"No," Michael groans. "Not me. It's my brother. You want my brother."

Diane stirs. Her hand finds his arm. "Michael. Wake up. Just the voices again. Come back."

And so, he wakes.

Again.

And again.

The years pass in broken sleep.

Until one day, the voice, sharp and glistening, decides.

Nightmares are no longer enough.

Chapter Two

The Chosen One

Strange Dinner Party and the Seven Dreams

~ Fever Dreams I ~

Thank You for coming. I'm at My wit's end with him, and Your presence should tip the scales.

Beloved Goddess, I have other places to be.

No, no. Be patient. Wait here with Me on this quiet road a tick longer. Michael will be along soon. While We wait, look around—see what the humans assume is Your handiwork: trees, light, shadow.

I really do not—

Ah! He is near. Poor Michael. The spring thaw begins. Snow melts. Hibernation ends. Let Us coax him from his cave, reveal Ourselves briefly, teasing portents before his guests arrive.

Sweet Goddess, he is ill. You know this.

No. You would have him so. But he is the Chosen One despite his frailties. He will prevail. Yet....

He should have died with his comrades. But no. I still believe Your plan will fail.

I don't want him to die, impetuous God. You once proclaimed he would never be born. That Bai Meiying and John Powers would never conceive. You were wrong. Let Us see.

It is Your plan, not Mine.

He comes, Dear One. He comes.

No, Beloved. He writes.

Yes ... but look up the road.

~

Fatigued after a long day at work and an intense therapy session, Michael Powers drives home through the countryside on a fading spring afternoon. The road is empty. To pass the time, and to quiet the voices, he rehearses the details of the dinner party he'll host tonight, picturing the strange guests, reviewing topics to amuse or unsettle them. The trees sway gently. Shadows lengthen. His thoughts slow. The guests in his mind begin to blur. Drowsiness gathers, creeping in with quiet weight, dimming the world by degrees. He begins to drift off, until something jolts him. A subtle impact. The sensation is soft but unmistakable, like a canoe nudging a submerged log.

He snaps awake. A dark shadow glides across the windshield; a membrane, fluid and glistening, slides over the car and then vanishes behind him. Heart pounding, he hunches over the wheel. The landscape ahead is the same, yet not. A subtle distortion washes across it, as if the world had been dipped in ash. Colors dim. Edges smudge. The sky is darker than it should be for this hour, and still darkening. He flicks on the headlights. They offer little relief. The road shimmers with something he cannot name. Anxiety rises, cold and electric.

Just a lapse, he tells himself. A daydream. Nothing more. But then, figures appear. Two. Standing in the road. Or is it one figure with two heads? He slams the brakes, eyes wide. Through the smeared windshield, they flicker into view, ghost frames from a deteriorating silent film. First bound together like Siamese twins, then unraveling into separate spirals. They twist, unfurling into ghostly whorls that transform: humans to birds, fish to trees, insects to mountains, each metamorphosis seamless, cyclical, maddening.

He creeps forward. Surely a trick of dusk and overhanging branches. A mirage. A play of shadow and light.

But they remain.

He flicks on the brights and accelerates. Still they hover, just beyond reach of the beams. He leans forward, shifts in his seat, taps the brakes, rounds a bend, but they remain, hovering at the edge of vision, taunting him with their refusal to disappear.

Frustrated, he punches the accelerator. The road stays empty. Good thing, Michael Powers. You're driving like a lunatic. Kill yourself, not the rest of us.

Abruptly, he veers onto the dirt shoulder and slams to a stop. A car passes, ordinary, unremarkable, its motion snapping the world back into place. And then, ants. Human-sized. Hovering above his hood. Heads tilted, whispering in insect tongues. A low buzz rings in his ears, dissonant and close, as if some membrane between dimensions has thinned.

Enough.

He guns the engine. Dust roars behind him. The car fishtails, control slips, then returns. When he steadies the wheel, the figures are gone.

Relief surges through him. He slows. Watches the trees. His fingers drum the wheel—tap, tap, tap—the ring catching rhythm against the vinyl. He eyes the nearest eucalyptus. Thinks about ending it.

You are worthless, the voices whisper. The demons are back. **Kill yourself.**

He keeps tapping, foot hovering over the gas.

Tap. Tap. Tap.

Then, he cracks a crooked, defiant smile. *Make up your minds. How can I kill myself without killing all of you? No, you'll have to kill me, not the other way around.*

Another car passes, horn blaring. The smirk drains away, replaced by a mask: expressionless, flat.

Light, brighter now. Knew it. Just a daydream. Nothing more.

He rubs his eyes. They ache. Not a surrealist razor across the cornea, no, not there. Lower. Cleaner. Across the neck. He blinks and shakes it off.

Forget it. Shadows. Just shadows.

The muscles in his shoulders finally relax. He exhales, tells himself it's over. He took his meds. He's fine. But just as calm begins to settle, another car passes, slow this time. The driver and passenger stare, two heads turning in perfect unison. Something twists in his gut. A flash of dread. Premonition. Vague. Slippery. Something awaits him at home. He brushes it off and refocuses on the dinner party. Think of the guests. The conversation. The wine.

Then, a truck blares past, honking. He startles. A jolt of clarity: he hadn't pulled fully off the road. His rear bumper jutted out into traffic.

Be careful, Michael dear. Ignore the evil voices. They're just relics of your human genes.

The voice is Hers. Goddess. Soothing and familiar. Her tone calms him. He checks the mirror, pulls fully back onto the road, and drives faster now, but still beneath the speed limit. Finally, he turns onto his gravel driveway. The tires crunch endlessly over the stones. He passes the half-restored red 1953 Fiat, rusted and still. In the front seat, two shadow-figures sit motionless. He squints. Are they the same ones from the road? He leans closer.

The car jerks. He's on the lawn. He slams the brakes, barely missing the porch. Shaken, it takes two tries to reverse and straighten out. He finally pulls into the garage. Sits there, watching the rearview mirror. The garage door lowers behind him. Slowly, the Fiat vanishes from view. Entombed in shadow, he exhales.

Took the meds.

Fuck the meds.

Took them. Took them. Shut up!

He breathes in deeply. Calmer now.

"What now?" he whispers, part mockery, part dread, as he opens the door leading into the house. But inside, all is quiet. No giant ants. No assassins. No voices screaming murder. Just furniture. Silence. He releases a dry, hollow chuckle. It was nothing. A dream. An illusion. A quirk of a diseased mind.

He nods, convincing himself. *Just lucky I didn't crash into a tree.*

~ *The Guests* ~

He changes into a soft gray sweatsuit, slips into a worn pair of sneakers, checks his email, his voicemail, and finally, his mail mail. As he thumbs through a stack of bills and advertisements, his eyes settle on an unopened container of pills. He scowls, then spots a handwritten envelope. A letter from an old friend.

"No time. They'll be here soon," he mutters, as though the envelope itself deserves an apology. He stuffs it into an overfilled drawer and slips the rest of the mail between the unread pages of that morning's *Los Angeles Times*, resisting the pull of the headlines. No distractions. Not now. He deposits the newspaper atop a clutter of circulars and magazines on the kitchen bar, gathers the whole pile, and drops it into the recycling bin in the garage. Returning with an empty Jim Beam box, he surveys the now-cleared bar. All that remains are four items arranged with ritual precision: a crisply folded artist's frock, jungle fatigues still sheathed in dry-cleaner's plastic, a red felt-tip pen, and a sweat-stained baseball cap. Beside them, the pill bottle remains unmoved.

He smiles as he gently lowers the frock and cap into the box. But when he unwraps the fatigues, his expression fades. Without meeting their gaze, he tosses the fatigues in too. Then the pen. He shoves the box into a cupboard he keeps empty for moments like this, then casts a last approving glance at the gleaming white countertop. It is nearly perfect, marred only by the untouched pill container, its label encrypted in the glyphs of wizards and pharmacologists. The incident on the road has vanished from his mind. Even the premonition's chill has lifted. What remains is anticipation.

He rubs his hands together. Let the evening begin.

First, he covers the dining table with Diane's old special-occasion tablecloth, then arranges the napkins, Wedgwood plates, and crystal goblets. Four place settings. Presentable. A patchwork of inheritance, some items from his mother, others remnants from Diane. In the kitchen, pork chops sizzle under the broiler. He sautés mushrooms, microwaves a dish of frozen peas, and stirs a bowl of instant mashed potatoes. When the microwave beeps, a thought rises: Music. We need music.

He rummages through his CDs. Rachmaninoff's *Piano Concerto No. 2* glints under the lamplight. He hesitates, then briefly considers Hank Williams. Naw. Diane loves Rachmaninoff. He presses play. Music floods the room, somber, sweeping, immense. He pours himself a mug of decaf, spoons potatoes onto his plate, arranges two sprigs of parsley beside the pork and mushrooms. A dab of butter on the potato peak melts, yellow ribbons running through the white rills.

Spring runoff. Snow melting. Hibernation's over. Time to crawl out of your cave, Michael, and greet your guests.

He carries his plate and coffee into the dining room. Three chairs are occupied by unseen presences and silence. His wife. His twin brother. His son. Michael eats slowly, deliberately. They sit invisibly at first, eating from empty plates, sipping from empty glasses. Halfway through the meal, they materialize. Fully formed. Smiling.

At last.

He lifts his glass. "Welcome."

"Cheers," they answer in unison.

Michael has been told these guests are delusions, constructs of his disorder. But over time, he's come to see them as therapeutic, a balm against loneliness.

Diane was the first to return. Eleven years ago. Car crash. Afterward, he couldn't sleep. Couldn't stop the voices. She was the only one who could quiet them, who understood. And once she came back, the nightmares lost their power. For years, it was just Diane. But recently, he'd conjured their son Mark too, off at Columbia, far away, the house too silent without him. Then, two dinners ago, his twin brother appeared. Uninvited. Killed in Vietnam, thirty-three years past. The twin brought an unwelcome weight. Now, for the third meal in a row, he returns. Michael stares at him warily. The glow in his brother's eyes stirs the memory of that roadside premonition, but he pushes it away.

Just therapy. Let him stay. I'll blink him away later.

He forces a smile. "Well, Diane, how was your day?"

She picks at a thread on her frock, grimacing playfully. "Busy. The kids were wild today. I warned them, no field trip Tuesday if the chaos continues."

"Way to go, Mom," says Mark. He's dressed like a standard undergrad, T-shirt with an indecipherable logo, backwards baseball cap, eyes half-absorbed in some invisible screen. His words tumble out, mechanical and disconnected, as if retrieved from some tattered script.

"Bet that worked," says the twin, older than Mark, dressed in decaying fatigues. His hands tremble, steadying an M-16 that leans against his chair. He reeks of sweat and excrement. Michael looks away.

Michael clenches his jaw. He's had enough of this ghost.

Closing his eyes briefly, he refocuses on Diane. "She would've let them go anyway."

"I know, I know," Mark says.

"Just a gorgeous old softy," adds the twin, grinning at Diane. Twin pinpricks of light glint from his sunken sockets. "While I was still in The World, I could count on you. Comb in my pocket. Always there. But now . . . in the 'Nam . . . without you . . . my hands don't know where to go. Nothing to hold. No place to put them, no place except around this M-16."

Michael glares. "Very theatrical. And speaking of burial. . . . " He lets the implication hang.

Diane sighs. "This dinner is theatrical, Mr. Apparition-Conjurer." A flicker of sternness darkens her smile. "Anyway, I would've thought the mature lawyer needed me in his pocket more than the young soldier."

"My pocket developed a very large hole."

She raises her brows. "Learn to sew, my dear. Learn to sew."

Silence.

Then she winces.

Michael leans in. "Is it your period?"

"As you wish," she says through a pained smile. "It's your party, you'll do what you want to."

He smiles, then winces. "Didn't mean to hurt. . . . "

Recovering quickly, Diane brightens. "Anyway, your day?"

Before he can answer, she frowns at his plate. "Instant potatoes? Really, Michael? You're forty-three. I taught you better."

"No time. Peeling, boiling, whipping, it's too much."

"Yes, yes. No time. Like that old Fiat out there." Her eyes gleam. "When do you think it'll be done?"

He frowns, jabbing at the potatoes. "I don't know."

"Probably the same day the lawn gets mowed."

He groans. Chews miserably.

"Oh stop pouting," she chides.

"I'm not—I mean. . . . " He falls silent. Her voice, her teasing, how he's missed them.

Grief presses in. He looks away. He pokes at the cooling food, fighting the flood of memory. Since her death, nothing's taken root. He's tried. Lovers. Emotions. Routines. But each attempt collapsed under its own weight. And Mark—he's raised the boy alone—all the while cooking, grousing, grieving.

Now, here they sit.

Ghosts. Flesh. Memory.

Waiting.

Dinner has just begun.

~ *Dinner* ~

"If you had kept your eyes on the road!" Michael blurts, instantly regretting it. The accident. Her death. Why did he go there?

Diane waves it off, annoyed. "I don't want to talk about that."

He tries to stop, but can't. "You were in such a hurry. If you'd stayed five more minutes—"

"Michael! Stop. You're looking for trouble again. Just because you had a little incident of your own today. . . . " She exhales, softens. "Let's not argue. Come on, how was your day?"

He sighs. Tries to stall. But the memory of the shadow figures rises, and her chiding derails him. Even dead, she's still bossy—

"Michaaellll," she sing-songs, teasing. "Your day?"

He can't help smiling. Even her ghostly scolding feels precious, twenty years of life together wrapped in that one voice.

"Fine. Busy. Work's always busy. I . . . had another counseling session this afternoon."

He hesitates. Even here, even now, he resists discussing therapy. He doesn't think of himself as ill. The psychiatrist is just . . . a sounding board. A paid ear. He keeps it private. No one at work knows. They see an affable widower, competent and quiet. Shy, maybe. But solid. No one suspects the wreckage he carries. No one asks. And he doesn't tell.

His twin's gaze sharpens. "You saw Toomey?"

Michael stiffens. His brother's face is young, dirty but unlined. His own feels heavy with years, glasses slipping down his nose. He sucks in his stomach. Runs a hand through thinning hair. *I do it only for you Diane.*

"I'm a successful attorney, not a model," he mutters inwardly. "Not caring how you look, that's either the peak of success or the bottom of failure."

The twin asks again. "Did he acknowledge me?"

Michael snorts. "Did he what?"

"That I exist."

Michael shrugs. "Not really. You know Toomey." He flicks his wrist dismissively, wishing it could banish the twin as easily.

"Yeah."

Diane diverts the dangerous flow by turning to Mark. "How about you, sweetheart?"

Mark brightens. "I think I nailed my molecular bio final. But organic chem—ugh. If I never hear the words 'carbon atom' again. . . . "

He glances at Michael's twin, anxious to step out of the spotlight. "How about you, Uncle?"

Silence.

Diane leans forward, voice warm. "C'mon, love. Tell us."

More silence.

"Go ahead," Michael offers, his tone edging toward mockery.

Still nothing.

"Well?" he says, now sharp.

"I . . . I don't know," the twin stammers.

"Go ahead!" Michael urges, though part of him recoils.

The twin stares into space. His skin cracks like dry clay. "They're out there. Dead. Got to get help—"

"No!" Michael snaps. "Don't start! I'll make you go."

"But they're outside the fortress!"

"Stop!"

His twin's voice hardens. "It's not that easy. Toomey said you're supposed to talk to me. Confront me. You know the drill—'Can I speak to Storyteller now?'"

"Very funny."

"Not meant to be. Just . . . illustrative."

Michael glares. "I'd rather you and the others stay buried. I have a life here. I'm not going back."

"But it's the dreams, Michael. That's how She'll reach you."

"She?"

His twin grins, bitter. "Goddess. I saw Her. In the tunnel. She's coming. She's going to open the dreams, especially your seven."

"I never told Toomey about seven dreams."

"Maybe I did. Maybe I'm part of your schizophrenia. Or some multiple personality disorder crap. Who knows?"

"Toomey says schizophrenia. I disagree."

"But you take the meds?"

"Sometimes. Doesn't mean anything. Lots of people have vivid dreams."

"Ah, but you have seven. One for each day."

Michael shakes his head. "No. There are no seven dreams."

"That's not true," the twin says gently. "Once you surrender, they'll reveal themselves. You'll be reborn. The Others, the demons, will stop whispering 'worthless.' They'll stop urging you to die."

Diane looks alarmed. "Michael, don't listen. We're just dreams. Harmless. But . . . maybe you should take the meds again."

Michael forces a laugh. "I'm not worried about seven dreams. Diane's right. It's just therapy. And if a dream gets too close, she always wakes me."

He slaps the table and half-rises. "What are you even doing here? I didn't invite you."

The twin looks down, theatrically wounded. "Really? You expected someone else?"

Michael sinks back into his chair, sighing. "Fine. You're here. Then tell me about the dreams so I don't have to pay Toomey to guess."

His twin grins. "Oh, you know them. You just don't like what they mean. When you do, well, your precious therapy won't survive it."

"What are they?" Michael asks, heart thudding.

"First dream, ants. A warrior ant. You saw it on the road today. Then the second, The Noise."

The twin opens his mouth and emits a high-pitched, cacophonous gibberish:

. . . *youAvelsilentdoweohevenintoosendwatchholy.* . . .

Michael flinches. "What is that?"

"A sound that never leaves. You've heard it before. Tonight you'll hear it again, brought to you by the third dream. Goddess. She'll come. With God. They'll try to scare you back."

Michael scoffs. "Scare me? I don't believe in gods, let alone goddesses. And those were shadows on the road."

"Do you believe in the One True God?"

"No." His voice is firm. But the question lingers, sharp.

"I believe in abused children," he continues bitterly. "Locked in closets. Burned. Starved. I read about a girl boiled alive. She begged—'Please, Daddy. Please, Mommy. I'll sing if you stop.' No. I don't believe in God."

"That's easy to say when death hasn't touched you," his twin mutters. "Superman would call that free will."

"Free will?" Michael spits. "What free will? Children don't die from choice. They die from bacteria. Quakes. Fire. And God does nothing but demand worship like an addict."

~

Nonsense. Atheist nonsense. Iconoclasm, and worse, icky.
Please, Dear God, do not play the Fool.
His words are as old as the hills.

Because they are true as the hills.

~

Michael hears murmuring.

"What?" he asks aloud.

"I didn't say anything," Mark replies.

Diane shifts uneasily. She turns to the twin. "I know death too. But God's always been with me."

Michael blinks. "What does He look like?"

"An ant."

"What?"

"An ant. And everything else. But to me, He's an ant. Strange, since I hated ants. But in death, I saw the truth. Up there, we're ants in His house, not guests, not even residents. We hide in the walls, stealing crumbs, praying He doesn't notice. And those we killed, those we ignored, they are the blessed ones."

Michael laughs dryly. "If I didn't believe in God before, I sure as hell don't believe in Lord Ant now."

Diane's smile fades. "Your disbelief isn't about tortured children. It's about something else. You never fully believed in me. Not even after we had Mark. It was always the ones left behind."

Michael groans with mock drama. "That's not true. You're all here, aren't you? I didn't bring some new wife to dinner. And him—" he points at his twin—"he's the one who went to war, not me. I was never there!"

Mark meets his father's gaze. "We know, Dad. But if not God, what do you believe in?"

Michael chews a mushroom, swallows, and clears his throat. "I believe in atoms. Molecules. Probability. DNA. Death. I believe in the legal system. But not God. Never God."

"Never say never," says his twin softly. "Tonight, in your pain, He will come. And She will come too."

Michael's hands are trembling. His twin's are still.

"Let's finish this," he mutters. "Then you can leave. What are the other dreams?"

"The fourth dream, me."

"You're not a dream. You're a nightmare."

"The fifth is Diane." The soldier places his hand gently over hers. "She's always trying to protect you."

He mimics her voice: "Michael. Wake up. You're dreaming."

Diane squeezes his hand. Their fingers interlace, merge.

Michael groans. Tries not to look.

"I must regain control," he thinks. But his voice is weak. "Why drag me into this? You're the one who didn't come back from the war."

His twin shrugs. "But I'm in your imagination. I'm always here."

"Then I'll prove you're not real." Michael glares. Concentrates. Tries to blink him away.

Doesn't work.

"You're not real!" he cries.

The voices respond: **Shut up, worthless! Shut up!**

He concentrates again.

Nothing happens.

"I see you're surprised," says his twin. "But there are still two more dreams."

"What are they?"

"The sixth . . . ghosts and apparitions. They come during fever. Malaria dreams."

He stops. Looks beyond them all as if something terrible was watching.

~

Michael senses a weakening in his twin, and strikes. "Go on, tell us the seventh dream." He sweeps his arm toward Diane and Mark, glasses dangling from his fingers. "Then leave."

"The seventh dream," the young soldier says, forcing himself upright, "is this." He raps his knuckle on the table. "This moment. This illusion. And it's the most terrible dream of all."

Tap. Tap. Tap.

The tapping grows louder, fist slamming now, each blow a protest. Plates rattle. Glasses tremble. Michael surges forward. "No!" he shouts. His voice drops to a growl. Eyes dart across the table. "I've told you before, not in front of them."

Now. Or never.

Michael's demeanor flips. He puts on his glasses with care, straightens the dishes, smiles at Diane. "So," he says cheerfully, "Brad give you trouble in class today? Still ringleading the Friday riots?"

The pounding halts.

Diane begins to answer, but Michael's peripheral vision locks onto the twin. The body unravels. Flesh becomes outline. Outline becomes vapor. Blood-red threads pulse through a fading ribcage. A hazy face. A flickering heart. Lungs like jellyfish. Then, even less than that. Less than form.

The twin's voice fades in waves: "Don't make me go. I'll say something else. Anything else. Please. Tonight, remember the dreams. I warned you!"

Michael trembles, resisting an unseen pull. "I won't go," he growls, as if yanked by a leash around his throat.

Just before vanishing, the twin's face snaps into sharp focus, teeth bared, eyes fading. A final whisper: "This time, She will succeed. You will come back . . . to us . . . to me."

Then, an empty chair. Silence.

Michael exhales and half-murmurs, half-sings, "Ding-dong, the wicked witch is dead." He looks around the table, relieved. "Knew all those hours of *Star Trek* would pay off."

Diane's frown lingers, but a switch flips. "Brad. Yes. I think I'm getting through. His grades are up. His temper's cooling. He . . . well, he's not all bad."

Michael listens, leaning back, rubbing his sore hand, letting her voice wash over him.

Mark pushes his chair back. "Well, now that Uncle's gone, I'd better head out."

Michael arches a brow. "In a rush? Got a date?"

"Nope. Finals."

"Oh."

"I should go too," Diane adds.

"What's your excuse?" he asks, trying not to sound wounded.

"Don't," she says gently. Then winks. "Besides, the music's too depressing. I'd rather have heard Hank Williams."

"Oh, come on. You always loved Rachmaninoff."

She laughs. "Lately, it's harps." She tilts her head back, eyes closed. "Still . . . this is beautiful."

"So stay. The adagio's coming."

She opens her eyes, darker now. "Can't. Mark and I will go together."

Her expression shifts—troubled. "Your brother's right. More visitors are coming." She reaches toward him, almost touching. "Poor Michael."

"What? No. I won't let it happen."

"She's coming," Diane whispers. "And God is with Her. I'll try to help . . . but. . . ."

"Diane, please. Stay. Just until dessert. I don't want to be alone."

They both nod, but already begin to fade.

He tries to hold them with conversation, but their words drift into incomprehensible chimes.

Surrendering, he kisses Diane's translucent lips and clasps Mark's fading hand. As always, he avoids looking at Diane's broken spine. Avoids the ruin of her skull, where light flickers into the black hole that swallowed half her brain.

Damn it . . . why'd you have to . . . Oh, God, I miss you.

~ *Wills and Trusts* ~

After the dishes are done, Michael pours himself a bourbon and water and settles into his chair. The drink doesn't help. He replays the conversation. Obsessing. *Why'd I mention the psychiatrist? That's when things unraveled. Besides, do psychiatrists ever help?*

The voices don't stop. He thinks of Diane's warning: Other visitors are coming. Diane said She was returning—with God. And my twin . . . he warned me too. The dreams. The peculiar seven dreams. Seven. Always seven. Seven continents. Seven sins. Seven seas. Seven dwarves. Seven-Up. Now this. Forget it. It's just therapy. Just imagination. Should take my meds. Should.

Oh hell. Get to work. He drains his glass, stretches, rises slowly. They were just shadows. In his den, he surveys the papers on his desk. Birth certificate. Trust documents. Asset lists. His mind won't settle. *Come on, Michael. Get it done.* He taps his fingers on the page. The words blink up at him.

Mocking. Comforting. Calling.
Do it.
No.
Read it again. Make sure it's right.
Idiot. You've barely started.
Nothing to read yet.

ust write.
Words refuse to come.
Where there is a Last Will . . . there is a First Novel.
Read, Reader.

~

LAST WILL AND TESTAMENT OF MICHAEL G. POWERS
Article One

I, MICHAEL G. POWERS, a resident of Los Angeles County, California, declare this to be my will, and I hereby revoke all wills and codicils previously made by me. My deceased spouse, DIANE L. POWERS, is the birthmother of my only living child, MARK H. POWERS, whose birth date is August 27, 1980.

Article Two

I give the entire residue of my estate to the trustee then in office under that trust designated as THE POWERS FAMILY TRUST established February 23, 2001, of which the

~

He lifts his finger from the mouse, resisting the urge to close the file. *I should finish this. For Mark. But I'm so damn tired. Tomorrow's Saturday. I'll do it tomorrow night. Paul and Claire are picking me up in the morning. The beach. I don't want to go. But it'll be fine . . . once I'm there. Time for bed. Goodnight, Diane. I love you.*

Paul Thompson, his oldest friend. So close now, Michael truly believes Paul is his brother. Claire, his sister-in-law. They've accepted his world, his diagnosis. They play their parts.

He shuts off the computer. Walks out of the room. Behind him, ants march up the leg of the desk. In the bedroom, he peels off the sweatsuit and tosses it onto the collapsing chair. Brushes his teeth. Pulls on his boots. Diane used to forbid that. Kindly, firmly. The boots waited by the bed. One night he slipped them on. Just in case. When he awoke, one boot was flying into the backyard, the other halfway off. He never tried again. Until she died.

Now, he sleeps in boots. The visitors come too boldly without her. *I miss you, Diana. My Huntress. My Shield. If She's coming tonight, help me. Please. We'll face Them together. Wake me in time. Don't let Her take me.*

But now . . . He's tired. More than usual. Very, very tired. He pulls her quilt over his shoulder. Sleep takes him quickly.

~

Hours pass. Michael hears voices. Tossing. Turning. Breathing ragged. The voices fade. He rolls onto his back. Drifts.

A single ant climbs the trail of saliva slipping from his lip. She circles the mouth's edge, drawn by moisture, then disappears inside. He coughs. Swallows. A death. His eyelids twitch, brief, involuntary pulses on the threshold of awareness.

And he dreams.

Chapter Three

Fever Dreams II

Divine Visitation

Two figures stand at the foot of his bed. Michael's eyes, still veiled in the haze of sleep, trace their outlines, one broad and towering, the other slight, her head tilted in faint puzzlement. They speak, but their voices blur and dissolve, filtered through some unseen medium of distortion.

Their bodies begin to shift, becoming fluid and unstable. From human to bird. Bird to fish. Fish to cloud, mountain, reptile. All the while, they continue speaking in that indistinct tongue, their forms unraveling and recomposing in a ceaseless elemental dance. At last, the shifting halts. Two human-sized ants stand before him, upright, sentient, gleaming with articulated armor. Antennae twitch. Limbs gesture. Their voices, now distinct, fall into the room like glowing cinders.

He's killed the Messenger. Now what?

The male's voice is a furnace-blast from some ancient crucible: wet soot, scorched sulfur, the clangor of rusted machinery. As he speaks, Diane's quilt darkens, shimmering with a sickly, phlegm-green gleam. When his words fall silent, his breath lingers, a slow, reptilian hiss.

Explain to him, replies the female. Her voice scours the male's residue, purifying the air, though a faint stain clings to the silence.

We may be only metaphors, but can You explain how?

Take him back. Show him. It is his story I would have You witness.

It won't work. He won't go. You waste My time.

We'll see. Stay a little. You've convinced them time means nothing to You. Stay. Tonight is the night. Whatever it takes. He is Chosen now, and his child … his child will be the next great turn toward the Superior Ones.

One of the ants transforms, flesh emerging from chitin, form softening into a human woman. She lowers herself cross-legged onto a luminous, impossibly white lotus blooming midair. A melancholy radiance halos her. Her jeweled crown refracts light into swirling prisms; a glimmering-bright gem burns between her brows. Her necklace rests between bare breasts, a relic offered not for worship, but for recognition. Her left hand rests palm-up on her thigh, fingers curled with an otherworldly elegance. Her right hand hovers, thumb touching index in a poised, radiant gesture. The air stills, cleansed by her presence.

Goddess. I know You're a dream, but You're beautiful.

Michael's gaze catches a procession of ants emerging from behind her left thigh, ascending her abdomen, dipping into her navel, curling around her breast, marching across her collarbone, then vanishing behind her shoulder. She watches him, unmoving. Then, holding up her right palm, its ridgelines glowing with sacred intent, she says softly:

Look, dear Michael. You must.

A tremor grips him. "No."

She ignores him. Her palm draws his eyes.

It is twenty-three years ago. A jungle. Vietnam. **Look.**

"No!" he shouts.

If Diane were alive, she would rouse him gently. *Michael, wake up. You're dreaming again. Come on, sweetheart. It's okay. Wake up.* But she is gone. Ash and memory. As dissolved as the ant corpse in his gut.

"No!"

The second ant shifts form, turning into an old man with a long beard and a towering staff. Goddess, still watching Michael, murmurs:

I need Your help, Lord God.

God straightens, frowns, and strikes the staff against the floor. **Look at Her hand!**

Compelled, Michael looks. Her palm ripples—lines and whorls dissolving into an image. A tunnel. A dirt wall. A soldier, young, trapped, legs sprawled, eyes wide. Sound erupts. Meaningless. Deafening.

... youAvelsilentdoweohevenintoosendwatchholy ...

Then—silence.

"No!" Michael thrashes. "No!" He bolts upright, gasping, peering at the foot of the bed. Just the soft blue glow of his clock radio. He knows this is one of the seven dreams. But he denies the knowing. *2:39 a.m. Shit. A stupid dream.* He wipes his brow, disgusted, smears the sweat on the quilt, turns the pillow, lies back down. The hum returns. . . .

... youAvelsilentdoweohevenintoosendwatchholy ...

It grows louder as he slips into the abyss, until the fall halts, abruptly. *That sound. I know it. That's no dream.* But the memory won't surface. Another thought claws into his brain, a weed in cracked concrete.

It's a trick. She wants me to go back. I won't. It's my brother You want! Not me! Quilt pulled up, his eyes shut.

Do You want to go through with this or not? asks God.

Your interruption is rude, deathless One. But yes, says Goddess. She turns her palm again toward the sleeper. **I'm sending another Messenger.**

God leans forward, cupping his mouth in mock secrecy. **It's Her period. You know how it is when it's bad. You're the sponge.** He shrugs at Her fury, then lifts His staff like a weapon, pointing it at Michael. **Look. At. Her. Hand.**

Michael stares, mute. The staff glows red.

I told you to loooook!

For a flickering instant, God's wrath flickers into a burst of incinerating light, sorrow without bottom, compassion without end. A gaze no human can endure.

Why do you make Me thus? He asks. **Goddess says it's your human blood. The voices it stirs. My faction agrees.**

Michael turns away. When he looks again, the red fury has returned.

I told you to loooook!

The room quakes. The air rots, stinking of musk and death. Michael wills himself to obey, to look at Her hand, but can't. God hurls the staff. A burning spike erupts in his chest. Pain blinds him.

It's a dream. It's a dream!

Michael. Michael. Wake up. You're dreaming again. Come on, sweetheart. It's okay. Wake up.

"Diane? Diane! Say it again! Say it louder!"

The pain spirals down his arms. He rubs his chest. Nothing helps. Goddess protests:

No! Not that way. He will break apart. She leans close. **Do not be afraid. Look again. It is no longer thirty-three years ago. It is today. Still in the jungle. Look.**

The pain fades. Her palm brightens. Her skin turns green. Light seeps between her fingers, dawn. A miniature world unfurls.

Michael cannot look away.

~ *The Great Warrior* ~

Sunlight stabs through narrow rents in the jungle canopy, piercing the mist that coils and twists beneath the blades of another murderous day. All things move in anticipation. Predators, prey, and the voiceless witnesses each rehearse their roles in the great trial of tooth and claw. Birds proclaim their place. Gibbons chatter their lineage. A tiger growls. Insects hiss. And plants, those oldest of breathers, exhale steam into the soaked air, a fog that clings like ghost-skin to the jungle's fevered brow.

Below, in the cold hush of the earth, a queen presides from her white palace—the polished skull of a long-dead human. Around her, soldiers scurry, fevered and dutiful, awaiting the hour. But one among them is no longer mere soldier.

She is Archetype.

Worn smooth by battle and long-tested by shadow, she moves now not by instinct alone, but by ancestral memory. She is the Great Warrior, black-husked emissary of a wounded world, summoned again to perform the ritual of undoing. She climbs from the tunnel, each antenna sweeping the torn geometry of leaf and bone. Her legs brush against bark and bamboo, her carapace glinting like obsidian in the flickering light. Finally, she moves across terrain uprooted and made a lifeless plain by the hand of man.

This is her third journey to the Great Storehouse, a place not found, but revealed. Alien. Holy. Terrifying. Her sisters' scent trails guide her. Around her, soldier-escorts pass with their burdened ranks: workers hauling jagged fragments of paper. Deeds. Names. Histories. The debris of bureaucratic memory. At the boundary of All That Is Familiar, she pauses. Ahead lies a clearing cloaked in a darkness not of night, but of human unknowing. She hesitates, then pushes through the Mysterious Membrane and enters the realm of titans.

Michael hears Her voice again floating through the humid veil.

Look. Her glowing hand gestures. ***The Messenger comes for you.*** Her head tilts, listening. Then she nods toward his driveway. A low rumble stirs the ground.

… youAveIsilentdoweoheavenintoosendwatchholyafraidcoming loothenobodyhouraheavenlynoon …

The Great Warrior charges across a flatland, hard as stone, foreign as Mars, past the rusted archway of a 1953 Fiat. She scales the stucco cliff-face, a crumbling ziggurat of human design, and slips through the torn veil of mesh into the sanctum. Inside, the god-man sleeps. But the altar is alive.

Her sisters are already at work. They swarm across the wooden desk, disassembling a mountain of sacred texts. These are not mere papers but oracle petitions, desiccated memories: an army discharge, a will, a birth certificate, a list of possessions, each a sigil of identity, now stripped and flayed. The pages, cut into ribbons, are ferried down into the temple of the Ancestor Skull. There, they encircle the queen in growing piles, paper bones returning to dust. The Great Warrior watches. But something else draws her.

She veers toward a white table. On an open book, beneath a glowing photograph of the Goddess, a swarm of sisters begins to swirl, not randomly, but ritually. Their black bodies trace ancient spirals, antennae twitching in rhythm, transmitting some encoded memory. The photo pulses in the dark, the Goddess's half-smile radiant with eerie milklight. Their dance becomes a hymn. Not learned, but remembered. A hymn drawn from the oldest memory.

Suddenly a wind shrieks in. The page lifts vertical, not like a wing, but with the will of something stirred. The dancers cling to the edge, nearly cast into the void. When the gust subsides, the page settles, not like prophecy, but as prophecy.

The Great Warrior, shaken but resolute, breaks from the trance and returns to guard the passage.

It is here! shouts Goddess, as a hurricane of sound assaults Michael's mind. He convulses.

… youAveIsilentdoweoheavenintoosendwatchholyafraidcoming loothenobodyhouraheavenlynoon …

The sound bears down—dense and unrelenting. His walls tremble. His skin sweats terror. He tries to flee but the noise pins him to the bed where he is reduced to a nailed relic.

The deities are arguing again—over him.

~

Ants? Gibberish?

No. I bring him a nightmare. A special one. Look how his eyelids flicker.

He's feasted on nightmares for decades. You're late to the table. So why summon Me now?

Because this one is Yours. I will speak of war in Nature's nursery, where the planet stores its sacred codes—sperm and seed, pistil and stamen, all cradled in Her tropical womb. And it was there, beneath Her canopy, that the soldiers came with metal and fire—

Stop. You speak like a priestess caught mid-trance, sniffing war through incense.

Human hatred, armed with steel, tore through Her ovaries, split Her helices, desecrated futures. This is not metaphor. It is massacre.

Oh, you melodramatic cow. You used to stride atop altars, drenched in sacrifice. Now you peek under the sheets of war—a lovesick adolescent reading dirty scripture. Ants? Chitin? Pretentious theater! I demand First Principles!

Pretension? From You? Shall I quote Your opening act—"In the Beginning," "O Keshava," "He guideth whom He willeth"? You set the bar high, dear God. But even melodrama has its truth.

Then speak plainly! Stop slithering with serpents and leaking milk from Your bloated breasts.

Tiresome mockery.

And You wonder why they stopped worshipping You? Deities fade. Yours is a legacy of decay.

I haven't faded—I've been buried beneath Your vanity. And still I rise. And I say this: They must make room for the Superior Ones.

Behead them if you must. I'll watch.

Do not tempt Me. Their time is done.

Everything's always My fault, isn't it?

No. This time, it's ours. Listen, damn You. Listen—

~

Michael groans. Drenched in sweat, he turns, trying to escape the gravity of the nightmare.

Michael. Michael, wake up. It's all right. You're dreaming.

A voice. Gentle. Human.

He moans again, half-conscious.

His eyelids flutter.

Then, silence. The cacophony vanishes. A pressure lifts.

He gasps and jolts upright, every nerve flaring.

"I won't go back!"

But as the words leave his lips, he realizes: it was only a dream.

Relief floods him.

Thank you, Diane. Thank you.

~ *The First Awakening* ~

Something unresolved stirs within him, a weight his thoughts cannot dislodge. Michael scans the room as though the God and Goddess might still be crouching in its corners, disguised in shadow. But he finds something stranger than gods: illumination. He can see through the dark, each object in sharp relief, as if a hidden floodlight has pierced the veil. Gods and goddesses, he scoffs. Ants and soldiers. Seven dreams. The words come out in a dry whisper, brittle with defiance.

The sarcasm helps, slightly. Fear recedes, but is replaced by a dizzying hypersensitivity. He hears it now: the soft, oiled glide of a spider moving across its web. The silk glistens between ceiling and wall, a harp tuned to nightmare. Blankets press on his body with unnatural weight, curling around his legs in a tarantula's embrace. Sweat pours from his pores in sheets, and the salt stings his nostrils. He is ravenous.

Strange. I had a huge dinner. Last night? Yes. My special dinner. Felt stuffed. Slept hard. Then the damn dream. Diane, you were right, no more instant potatoes. Diane? Am I still dreaming?

Yes, beloved. And you must wake up.

But waking brings no peace. A headache pulses behind his eyes, and the slow climb of fever needles his nerves. It's just the nightmare, he tells himself. Fine. Wake up. Eat. Coffee. Something real. What time? 4:48. Damn.

His thoughts scatter. He tries to gather them, to focus on the banal. Food. TV. Something normal.

Empty the mind. Get rid of this noise. Think other thoughts. Think!

Paul's coming. Claire and the kids. The beach. Today? Yes. Noon. Good. That's good.

Cautiously, he slides his arms beneath the blankets, meaning to lift them from his legs, but his hands plunge into liquid. Warm. Viscous. Thick and slick. His fingers graze something that shouldn't be there: organs, soft and coiled. A gasp escapes him as he yanks his arms free. No blood. No gore. Only sweat, rivulets glistening like rain along the hairs of his forearms. A storm rising from the jungle of his own flesh.

Thank God. Just sweat.

Then come the voices again, rustling from some hidden alcove in his skull. Familiar. Indistinct. A melody half-remembered, muffled by time and sealed behind pathological walls.

He shakes his head. They persist.

Yes, blur Our words, O deathless Goddess. Give Us this private moment. I must speak with You.

It is not I who blurs Our voice. I wish to continue, but Michael resists.

He always resists. No matter. I have made preparations.

Preparations? Don't flatter Yourself. Have You conjured serpents and fog again? Your old parlor tricks?

We can no longer walk among them unguarded. You refuse to accept that Uncertainty undermines even Us. I adapt. I use his memory to inoculate Myself from Physics — Reason's snarling pet skunk.

Ha! Their risk is My altar. Their peril makes their devotion sharp. I wouldn't blunt it for all the safety in the world.

Yet their worship tattoos Your veins. You know where this path leads. They are dragging everything into the abyss — including You. That is why they must yield. It is time for the Superior Ones.

They go where they go. Unless we stop them.

Then stop them, God of Collapse. Before they finish their falling.

No! Stop! Get out of my head!

Stop? Oh, delightful. He commands Us. Little Michael, your spiral thoughts are nothing more than temples for Our sermons. We are Visitors, lodged in the attic of your skull. So: tally-ho, atop the collapsing wave function we ride.

"Get out of my mind!"

Michael jerks upright. His voice cracks like a twig underfoot.

Jesus. I've gone mad.

He tries to stand. His skin rasps against the sheets, dry and gritty as parchment. Boots on, he edges naked into the kitchen, but the idea of food repels him. Eggs. Grease. Toast. Each thought thickens his nausea. Still starving, he retreats.

Back in the bedroom, he pulls on a clean pair of underwear, khaki shorts, and then finds an old T-shirt draped over the dresser. Boycott California Grapes. He slips it over his head and glances at the mirror.

A better time, he thinks. *When politics still mattered more than madness.*

Tugging the hem down over his middle-aged belly, he tries to shake the clinging residue of the nightmare. But it lingers, buzzing beneath the surface. His mind itches with something ungraspable. Medication. *I need my pills.*

The dread is no longer abstract. It breathes. It mutates. It swells into something colossal.

The pills. Take them now.

His thoughts grope backward, trying to locate the last moment of normalcy. The special dinner? Doesn't count. But yes, the desk. The documents. My estate. Preparing for death. For Mark. That was real. That was solid.

But even that task is unfinished.

Didn't finish the trust. Didn't touch the will. No time today, not with Paul and Claire coming. Sunday night. I have to finish by then. So take the pills. Yes.

He brushes his teeth, pulls on his sneakers, and steps outside. The air greets him, sharp, wet, and unsparing. He sinks into the redwood lounge chair, its wooden slats pressing into his spine with the insistence of memory. Slowly, he leans back and exhales. Above, a naked bulb spills harsh light across the porch, flattening the darkness but never softening it. Fog creeps over the floorboards, coiling around his ankles with silent intent. In the distance, a nightingale begins to sing. The melody stretches, longer, thinner, until it fractures into a shrill, unnatural wail. He jolts forward, fingers twitching, reaching for something that has already vanished. Though the air remains damp and cold, sweat beads on his skin and falls, each drop the residue of some deeper fever.

Yeah. Been here before. Flashback, probably. PTSD, like Toomey says. Not schizophrenia. That's ridiculous. I'm in control. It wants to come, but I won't let it. Calm. Be calm. It will pass. Think of something else. Think of the beach. Paul. Claire. The kids. Yes. Yes . . .

He leans back slowly, muscles tight. *Think . . .*

And he does. He is a man backing away from a rabid dog, eyes fixed on the teeth, praying it does not lunge.

~ *The Ants* ~

Hours pass. The fog dissolves into sky, and the low hush of morning gives way to the dry glare of noon. Along the gravel drive that winds from Michael's house to the narrow road beyond, eucalyptus trees stretch upward into blue, their leaves twitching in the hot breeze. Michael has not moved. Still seated in the redwood chair, sheltered from the sun beneath the porch overhang, he watches ants swarming across the open pages of an oversized book. Though the fever has broken and the headache has dulled, his senses remain raw. The nightmare vibrates from somewhere deep inside, unreachable.

He glances at his watch. Then again. And again. High noon. The day burns white. Sunlight creeps across the porch, forcing him to push his chair back against the wall, into the last of the shade. Clusters of potted orchids surround him. Colors begin to drain. Red recedes into green, yellow blurs to green, even the blue sky turns a flat green. The world narrows.

Green. Green. Suffocating green.

He tries to restore the spectrum by force of will, slapping color back into the world with the desperation of a painter correcting a ruined canvas. But concentration falters. The colors fade. What remains is a world washed in gray, a photograph soaked in monsoon. His legs twitch. He shifts. "Come on, Paul. Hurry. I can't hang on much longer." Again, he scans the driveway. Nothing. He turns to the open book beside him, still covered in ants. He shakes them off and lays the book across his lap, but his attention drifts. Ants still wander the tabletop in aimless spirals. His fingers drift to the page, tracing it over and over, circular movements worn smooth with repetition. The text has vanished under his touch, but in the center of the page a single photograph remains: pristine.

The Goddess Tara.

The caption is still legible.

He stands, paces a few steps, then returns. The book lands back in his lap with a soft thud. The eyes of the figurine stare up at him. They follow his movements. He glances around, seeking a witness. Anyone. But the eyes draw him back.

"Madame Third Dream," he mutters. "Why don't you go haunt someone else."

He yearns for a human voice. Banter. News. Politics. Anything to reassert the monarchy of the mundane. But silence rules. He lifts the book and sets it back on the table, still open. One corner hangs over the edge, casting a dark line of shadow down the table leg. A column of ants reaches the shadow and marches upward, antennas swiveling, limbs clicking faint rhythms across the wood. He listens.

Boots. Not canes. Not dancers. Boots. Marching. Pavement.

Nazi boots through the *Arc de Triomphe. How can I be hearing this?*

The ants vanish into shadow, then reemerge in light. In. Out. As if passing through a tunnel.

Do they feel the coolness in their skin? What happens in that shadow? What oaths are sworn beneath it?

To Hitler? To the Great Warrior? He tries to laugh. Humor will clear the smoke.

This is the first dream? Tap-dancing ants? Fred Astaire and me in a war film. Busby Berkeley directs the apocalypse. Oaths to dictators. Sauerkraut. Porky Pig. "Th-th-th-that's all, folks," he whispers. "That's what Stretch would say if . . ."

Stretch . . .

The name rises, crashes. A weakened section of memory's dam collapses. Water seeps through. But the ants keep him tethered, and the dike holds. His eyes stay on the shadow. The movement. The tunnel.

"Tunnel," he murmurs.

Then it begins again. Screams without bodies, bodies without context. Fragmented cries falling past an invisible window:

"Oh, God!"

"—flanked us!"

"Move it! Keep—"

"Go! Go! Go!"

"—fire from the treeline!"

"Fuck it! Move! Move! M—!"

"Shit!"

"—got Idaho!"

"Leave him!"

"—nooo!"

He touches his forehead. No fever. Must be illness. A virus? The flu? It's going around. Hallucinations. No. It's Her. The Goddess. Scratching at his brain again.

But I won't go back.

Again, the driveway. Still empty. "Where are you, Paul? Come on, brother. Get here. I really can't hang on much longer."

You're worthless, Michael! Take your meds, Michael! Kill yourself, Michael!

No! Don't listen. Take your meds. They're the demon voices. Don't listen. Take your meds.

Poor Diane. You're winning, Clever Goddess. Poor Diane, it's too late.

The heat is unbearable. Sweat slides down his neck. He stares glassy-eyed at the ants, at their steady transit through the light and dark. Time warps. Seconds stretch into hours. He tries to distract himself. Not guard duty. Not again. Just waiting. Waiting for water to boil. Waiting for the world to right itself. No? Count then.

Seconds. Days. Years. One second. Two seconds. Three—

It doesn't work. He returns to the ants. Too many to track. Tumbling through his vision like a juggler's props, or bodies falling into a grave. A carnival of war. A shell game with real shells. Sh—

Incoming! No! Not again!

He holds his breath, puffs out his cheeks. When the pressure grows unbearable, he exhales slowly through clenched teeth. Steam escapes in a hiss, then dwindles to a whimper, then a sigh. Silence returns. Briefly. But thoughts crawl back in. And the voices. Always the voices.

Why did you survive? Why you?

His gaze drifts, wary. I'm not guilty. Not like they say. Not survivor's guilt. I just won't go back. That's all. I won't.

Take your medication!

No. I won't.

We all think you're stupid! Stuuupid. Stuuuupid.

He shakes his head, trying to dislodge the hum. Sees a straggler ant. Crushes her under his finger.

~

The Great Warrior, smelling the chemistry of death, goes to investigate.

~

Michael watches as another ant approaches the body, nudges it, circles it. He tilts his head. "I know why your friend died. I know why you lived. But why me? God? Chance? Wrong time, wrong place?"

The ant lifts her dead sister, staggers, adjusts her grip. For a moment, she holds the body gently, almost reverently, then turns her eyes to his.

"Don't blame me. Ask the priests. They'll say it was free will."

He studies his finger, then hovers it over the second ant. "Or God. You decide."

But before he can bring it down, movement distracts him. More ants, marching from shadow into light. He watches, entranced. Only in shadow do they become distinct. In the light, they lose identity, revert to sameness. Just as I did when I emerged from the tunnel. Just as they did. But today . . .

Today is different.

~

The Great Warrior, spared by the grace of Free Will, or Fate, or Probability, or God, or a compassionate schizophrenic, transfers the body of her fallen sister to a waiting worker and resumes her task.

~

"That word again," Michael mutters. "Today. Today, the rain in Spain falls mainly on the plain. Today I return on the time train. Through the tunnel. That goddamn tunnel." He jerks upright. "Come on, Paul. Before I end up back in that tunnel."

The words become rhythm. He sways in time. Damn fuckin' tunnel. Damn fuckin' tunnel. Damn fuckin' tunnel. He rises. Circles. Muttering the phrase. Syncing his breath to its beat. The years peel away. The heat intensifies. He stops. Scans the horizon. *Where are you, Paul?*

He can't decide. The beach no longer appeals. The car will be crowded. The kids loud. The heat unbearable. Or maybe Paul's car has air conditioning. No. Yes. He wipes his forehead. This isn't weather. It's something else. A monsoon brewing in the mind. Nausea surges. He runs to the bathroom, collapses beside the toilet. Bile rises, burns. He retches, dry, again and again. No release. Just fire. The meds. Must be the meds.

"Mike! MICHAEL! DAMMIT! DAMN MEDICATION! GO AWAY!"

He sees himself in the mirror. Paul will ask questions. He can't answer them. He doesn't know the answers. The nausea passes. Slowly, carefully, he stands. I'll clean up. I'll look fine. He strips to shower. In the mirror he sees someone else: young, in jungle fatigues. *Not me. My twin. That's not me.*

Thin. Sickly. Red-eyed. Yellow-skinned. Beard patchy. One hand missing. The stump waves at him. Beckons. "But I have both hands!" Michael lifts them to his face. "This is insane!"

He glares at the mirror. "You're lying. I saw you last night. You had two hands." The twin smiles.

"That's right, Michael. It's not about you or me. It's about Goddess. Her plans for God. We're all just cogs."

"What plans?"

"No idea. Beyond us. But I know this, it's time to come back. Come back to us." The figure morphs. Skin darkens. Shapes shift.

A Vietnamese soldier. An old woman. A legless man. Another soldier. A girl, young and beautiful, her face a stern mask.

He turns away. Opens the faucet. The water roars. A waterfall in his ears. He stands at the edge, then steps into it and drops to his knees. The force pins him down. The soap skitters away. Eventually, the torrent softens. He stands. Lathers. Scrubs. Pays close attention to the red line circling his wrist.

"Better," he whispers as he dries off. "Much better."

No. Look at your hands. Ink everywhere. Worthless.

He checks again. Nothing. Clean. "Much better."

He returns to the porch, sits once more in the redwood chair. The book still waits beside him. He avoids looking. *That's right, Michael. Wake up. You're close. Just dreaming again. Therapy. That's all.*

Ah, Diane, you make it so difficult. Don't listen to her, Michael.

Ha! Clumsy Goddess. He slips through Your fingers again. The train is late. Your ticket canceled. Your rituals unravel. But I understand. Their tribal instincts are fading. Divine bait tempts only the edges of their hunger.

Yet the hunger remains.

Our only way in.

And I will get in.

Not if Diane has anything to say.

I will silence Diane, My pessimistic Metaphorical God.

Michael is cautious. He sips only at the shallows, fears the crocodiles below.

Then I'll strike. A violent lunge. My jaws will close, and I will pull him under.

You'll break him, My Dear.

Fragments are easier to digest.

They call Me cruel? I swallow. You chew. You crave their suffering, from earthworm to emperor, ant to attorney.

Michael's drugs come in gel-coated capsules. Yours in flesh, raw and pulsing.

Be careful, Goddess. You may succeed in breaking Me. And what then? No suffering? Anywhere?

If You shatter, My God, Your fragments will weigh less than his. You are thinner than air.

Chapter Four

A Trip to the Beach

A Family Gathering

Michael's mind quiets. A hush gathers. Then, a tremble under his sneakers, a distant rumble of tires. A car swings onto the long, meandering gravel drive. Rocks crackle, each pop deafening. Unnatural. He clamps his hands to his ears, closes his eyes, concentrates. At last. Paul. Anchor me. Talk to me about your kids, your computers, your next vacation. Pull me back. Bring me home, Brother Paul. A modest, humming car settles in the driveway. Inside, four dark heads dip and swivel in uncertain rhythm. A fleeting silence when the engine stops, then the harsh percussion of doors and voices.

"Hi!" from Paul. And almost atop it, Claire's chirpy "Good morning!"

Michael whispers, "Hello. Welcome."

The children stay buckled, their agitation beating at the windows. Lisa waves cheerfully. John stares downward, unmoved. Pouting? Or drifting through one of his darker turns, the kind Claire calls a 'moody day'?

Michael studies the signs. Paul and Claire are tense. They've rushed. They've argued. They spend their time with other parents now, and seem vaguely disoriented when sharing a space occupied by childless adults. Over time, the sharp edges that once defined them have softened, worn down by the long friction of shared domesticity. Today, those edges appear raw again: eyes evasive, gestures rehearsed, the choreography of long fatigue. Tiny tremors, no fault line breached. Dishes rattling, not yet cracked. Still, their presence steadies him. Only five words have passed between them, yet already he feels tethered. The voices hurt, but he pushes through. He needs the noise, the normalcy.

Keep it going, Michael. Don't let it slip. He scours the dry well of his conversational mind, drops in bucket after bucket to pull up one brimming with small-talk. Most come up empty, until one returns with a glint of the mundane. "How's the computer business?" he rasps.

Paul squints. "What'd you say?"

Michael steels himself. "I said, how's the computer business?"

A flash of surprise crosses Paul's face, then he brightens. "Good. Busy, but not complaining. What, you got laryngitis or something?" He strides up the porch steps, winks, places a firm hand on Michael's shoulder, then leans close. "Why are you whispering?"

Before Michael can answer, he says, "Be right back. Gonna use your bathroom."

The lifeline gone, Michael drifts. He turns to Claire, who lingers on the porch, hesitant and out of place. Straining against his pain, he tries again. "How's the insurance business?"

She glances toward the car, pretends to monitor the kids. "Fine."

"Keeping you busy?"

A flick of the head, a quick breath of annoyance. "What did you say?"

He repeats the question, louder.

She raises her eyebrows—half appreciation, half suspicion. "Very busy," she replies, the words pressed flat.

Silence.

"How's Mark?" she adds, offhand.

"Oh, I heard from him last night. Finals week. Chemistry's especially—"

Her eyes dart. "Hey, your orchids are blooming! Sorry, didn't mean to interrupt. It's just, they're so beautiful. Especially that white one."

He opens his mouth to reply, but she's already turned away, peering down at the open book on the table.

Michael shifts uncomfortably. Claire always makes him feel just a little too visible. He waves to the children, still penned in the car. Then, startled, he hears Claire's voice, loud and sudden, as if inches from his ear. "Anyway, finish what you were saying about Mark."

She's staring at him now. That look. Too focused. Too deliberate. A tremor rises in him. "That's it. Finals. Chemistry. You know. . . ."

Claire lowers her gaze to the book. "What an interesting picture." She shields her eyes and leans in. "Looks like some kind of statue." She squints. "Oh. Gold. Yuck, look at all these ants." She lifts the book, brushes them off, peers again. The statue stares back.

Michael closes his eyes. He doesn't need to see it move. It already has. Behind his lids, the fragile surface of normal life begins to crack.

"Yes, it is interesting," he says, voice tight. "Notice anything unusual?"

Claire presses her lips together. She knows this game, his riddles, but humors him.

"No. Why?"

He doesn't answer. His shoulders lower. "I forgot something in the house. Be right back."

He turns. Passes Paul in the hallway without a word. Walks to the bedroom, drawn by something unspoken.

In the closet's dark, he kneels before an old trunk. The carpet holds him in place. For a long moment, he's motionless. Then, slowly, he opens the lid. Papers. Relics. Shards of the past.

He searches. A sudden noise strikes his ears. He flinches.

Then, at last, he finds it. A leather pouch, long-stringed and knotted. His "flock bag." He untangles it with deliberate care. Holds it to the light. "Mountain Man," he whispers. He loops the cord around his neck. Tucks the pouch beneath his shirt. The weight pulls at the nape of his neck. The leather smolders against his chest.

He senses a presence.

John.

The boy has crept inside, now watching him from behind the door. Breath loud. The wood groans beneath his grip. Michael pretends not to notice. He rises slowly. Gives the boy time to vanish. Tap. Tap. Tap. John's sandals fade down the hallway, a retreating rhythm. Then, another sound. Above him.

From the ceiling's web, a trapped insect writhes. A muffled, desperate cry, spun halfway into silence. The spider moves quickly, its legs a silent blur. Insects don't have vocal cords . . . do they? He turns away. Lowers the trunk lid with painful care. Outside again. The door clicks shut behind him.

"Tab," he whispers. "Tab."

John is already back in the car, absorbed.

Paul calls, "What'd you say?"

"Nothing. It's okay."

"What's a tab?"

"Nothing."

Paul claps him on the shoulder. "Let's go. The beach is calling."

Michael grips Paul's arm, draws close. "I had my dinner last night. They all came. But it didn't go well. They left early."

Paul shrugs. "That's no reason to—"

"When Diane left, she said I'd have other visitors. I didn't understand. But now I do."

Paul laughs, gestures toward the car. "Us."

Michael slumps.

Paul lowers his voice. "Did you take your meds?"

Michael avoids his gaze. "Yeah. But they did come."

Paul exhales, exasperated. "Mike, I'm not doing this today. We're late. Let's go."

Michael walks to a potted geranium. Fingers the leaves. "They want to take me back. But I won't go."

Paul mutters, "Ohhh, damn." Then walks to the porch railing. Stares out at the horizon. Listening. Waiting.

It's a dream. Just a dream. Wake up, Michael. Wake up.

Claire breaks the standoff with clapping hands and cheerful command. "Here we go! Next stop, the beach!"

Michael doesn't move.

She studies him. "Are you okay?"

"I'm fine. Let's go."

"No, really, if you'd rather stay—"

"No. I'm fine."

She shrugs. "Okay." Then, louder, to the world at large: "Let's go, guys."

Claire does not want this. Not really. But she loves her husband. She plays her part. A loyal sailor summoned to the crow's nest, watching the strange, portentous shape of Michael Powers pass beneath the hull of her ordered world. She sways with the sea's subtle violence. She is relieved, more than she admits, that his blood, does not flow through her son, will not foretell his fate. She's read enough to leave an ever-present trace of dread. She watches John carefully. For now, she waits.

~

In the car, Michael sits behind the driver. Lisa to his left. John beyond.

"See my doll?" Lisa chirps, holding it to his face.

He stares at the plastic eyes. "Very pretty. What's her name?"

She answers. He doesn't hear. The engine roars. Voices machine-gun in staccato bursts. Heat presses in. He strokes the window, cool beneath his fingertips, listening to the high squeal of skin on glass.

"Everything okay back there?" Claire calls.

"Yep!" Lisa answers.

"No," John mutters.

"What's wrong?"

"Nothing."

Michael glances left. John leans forward, peering into a nylon bag. He looks up, frowns at Michael, then bends again to examine the contents. Lisa chatters on. Her doll has a boyfriend. He stayed home. Homework. Michael nods reflexively. Pain flares behind his eyes. Her monologue continues. He murmurs soft responses, automatic and flat. Lisa is unfazed, but Claire, listening, stiffens.

"Lisa, stop bothering your uncle," she snaps, more disapproval of Michael than pique with Lisa. But he doesn't notice.

~ A Sand Castle ~

They arrive at the beach. John throws open the rear door, and the world explodes: a roar of surf, gull screeches, the drone of a thousand overlapping voices, all of it rushes into the car and assails Michael's fraying senses. He sinks into his seat, awash in the car's dim interior, squinting through the windows at the fierce white blaze of the sun. John and Lisa tumble out, burdened with towels and bags that drag through the sand. "Don't go in the water!" their parents call out, already half-distracted. Paul and Claire orbit the open trunk, issuing orders and counterorders.

"You take this bag."

"No, it's easier if you carry that cooler."

Michael steps from the car. Every movement is labored.

Paul's voice is close, casual. "What's the matter, Mike? Don't let that dinner party nonsense get you down. Look at this day, the sun, the breeze, perfect."

Michael wipes his brow. "Why is it so hot?"

Paul and Claire glance at each other. Claire offers a solution. "Go ahead and get set up. We'll be there in a sec. And make sure the kids don't play too close to the blankets. They'll get sand everywhere."

He nods, says nothing. His legs move as if through molasses. Across the wide swath of barren sand, he drags himself to where the children dropped their gear. He plants the umbrella. Opens the rusty beach chair, wincing at the metallic squeal. Lowers himself into the seat and closes his eyes. Under the shade, the ocean burns, too bright, too vast. His eyelids clench shut against its shimmering knives. The light whirls and jabs, blinds and stabs. Something terrible approaches. He resists, for the sake of the family.

Paul and Claire flutter nearby, their efficient marital machinery humming in the background. Michael wills himself to focus on the present. The wind. The salt. The warmth. A cleansing ritual, maybe, one that might drive the morning's poisons from his system. But Claire's sunglasses do not hide the tension in her gaze. She watches Michael carefully, as one watches a patient whose fever has not yet broken. Then—John's voice, high and insistent.

"Not there! Here! The walls got to be higher." He gestures to Lisa's doll. "Put her in the fort. She's gotta be protected . . . because of this!" He brandishes a large plastic dinosaur. "T-Rex! The biggest and terriblest dinosaur of them all! He's gonna eat your doll! Better hide her!"

Lisa works quickly, finishing the sandcastle. John plants toy soldiers along the walls while T-Rex looms at the gate.

Light bounces from the reptilian skin of the toys, sharp, pricking flashes that cut into Michael's eyes, reopening buried neural corridors. He fights to cauterize them, to seal the circuits. But they reawaken. Smell of cordite. Screams. *I've been here before. Children soldiers circling on a psychotic carousel.*

"T-Rex is gonna eat her!"

"No, he won't," Lisa says, quietly. Then louder, braver: "No, he won't! The fort will protect her! The policemen won't let anything happen to her!"

"Those are soldiers, you dumb girl."

"John!" Claire's warning snaps. "We don't use ugly words."

"Okayyy."

Lisa strokes her doll's hair. "I won't let anything happen to you."

John, chastised, softens. "Aw, I didn't mean it. Put her back in the fort."

Lisa eyes him warily.

Michael watches, clinging to this small drama as though it might anchor him. He tries to observe without slipping. Lisa is the mother. The protector. She tolerates her brother's chaos, tries to defend her world. But it's a trap. A setup. A game.

John grows restless. He snatches the doll and throws it back into the fort. "She has to stay there! It's not fair! She's trapped!"

"Don't throw the doll, John," Claire warns again. A quieter menace in her voice this time.

"Okayyy."

John turns his attention to the castle's tower, putting on finishing touches. Soldiers in place. Dinosaur at the gate.

"Wait a minute!" he yells, suddenly animated. He drops to his knees, rummaging through a nylon bag of toys. Hops from foot to foot. Checks his shorts pockets.

Michael leans forward, wary.

"Here it is!" John pulls out a toy soldier, its arm raised in triumph—but the hand is gone. A clean break at the wrist.

Michael flinches. A chill flares across his chest.

John plants the handless soldier upright in the sand, deep inside the castle.

Michael stares, suddenly lucid. The ocean's blinding strobe ceases. His vision sharpens. He beckons John with urgent gestures.

Claire looks up from her magazine. Her smile falters. Paul squints toward Michael and John. "Everything all right over there?" he calls, the false brightness in his voice already straining.

Claire rises slightly from her blanket, one hand shading her eyes. "Michael?" she says. "Is he okay?"

The boy approaches, lip pushed forward in a sulky pout.

Michael points. "What happened to his hand? Won't he need his rifle? What if the dinosaur breaks through?"

John shrugs, eyes darting toward his mother. Then he leans in close, whispering: "It's not T-Rex who gets him."

"No?"

"It's him." John opens his hand to reveal another soldier, this one missing a foot.

Michael lets out a faint gasp. "And who's that?" he asks.

"Mountain Man," whispers John.

Michael groans. Claire's attention snaps to them. She thinks John's causing trouble. The boy closes his fingers too late.

"We caught him with a razor blade," Claire says to Michael. "Cut parts off toys, including Lisa's. He knows better now." Her voice hardens. "Right, Mister?"

John looks away, ashamed. Claire turns to Paul and resumes their conversation, ignoring Michael's silence. But Michael no longer hears her. Her words belong to a different timeline, and he's already retreating. His eyes fix on the fort. John sets "Mountain Man" atop the ramparts. Then, carefully, he uses the footless soldier to knock the handless one flat in the sand, face down, arm outstretched.

Michael. Michael. Wake up. You're dreaming again. Come on, sweetheart. It's okay. Wake up. Diane's voice is an urgent warning from within.

Lisa's voice breaks through: "Aren't you ready yet?" Distant. Detached.

From the corner of his eye, he sees John digging again. The boy extracts something tiny from the bag, pinched between two fingers. It's a severed hand, gripping a rifle. John holds it up so Michael can see, then sets it down just beyond the reach of the outstretched wrist. Right beneath the looming figure of Mountain Man.

Slowly...

Michael's eyes widen. His breath falters. The toys blur. He sees sweat bead on the face of the handless soldier. The plastic body trembles. Then shakes. Blood spurts from the stump.

Michael. Michael. Wake up. You're dreaming again.

The toy's dismembered hand moves. Fingers flex and curl around the rifle. Still the blood flows. Michael clamps his eyes shut. *It's a toy. Just a toy!*

That's right, Michael. Wake up.

But the toy convulses, twitching as if gripped by an unseen will, its motions too erratic to belong to plastic. The fingers squeeze, release, squeeze again. Blood spills into the sand. Michael rocks forward. Fetal. His hands grip his knees. A scream rises—from the footless soldier. Mountain Man. Red seeps from the stump, spreading into a dark ring around the castle walls.

Michael. Michael. Wake up. Come on, sweetheart. Before it's too late!

...youAvelsilentdoweohevenintoosendwatchholyafraidcoming loothenobodyhouraheavenlynoonIseetheirmountainmanwristscream....
You've got him!

Michael's body vanishes. Only breath remains, ragged, halting, bound to the gasp of a dying toy. He hears nothing now but the ocean and the scream of birds. And in the distance, a low, rhythmic sound.

... Tap. Tap. Tap....

Chapter Five

Fortress of Sand

The Second Awakening

As if trapped at the bottom of a deep well, the soldier heard voices echoing down from the distant rim. He strained to decipher them above the ceaseless roar of surf and the maddening tap-tap-tap.

Gradually the noise of the ocean receded.

Slowly, the voices sharpened.

"Storyteller. It's Nature. Come on, man. Look at me. Storyteller! It's Nature!"

The words teased the edge of his awareness, but his mind was burning. He couldn't focus. Disoriented, fevered, he wanted the voices gone. Why was it so hot? Then came the flicker of memory. *I woke up sick this morning. Remember? That nightmare . . . seven dreams . . . the heat . . . I'm at the beach with Paul and . . . and his wife? Claire? I think. And his kids, what're their damn names? No, what am I saying? Paul is twelve! He can't be married. Stupid. Must be a dream . . . the heat . . . dammit . . . this humidity . . . or maybe—holy shit! What's that?*

Gunfire cracked in the distance. The stench of decay and human waste surged around him, sudden and violent, dragging up the memory of a dinner party and of his twin brother.

God, where am I?

He blinked through watering eyes, struggling to see. Then, without warning, an automatic weapon erupted nearby, green tracers slashing overhead.

Jesus! Mother of God! Where am I?

He wiped his face with a greasy sleeve and blinked again, harder. A shadow moved away, tapping an M-16 against his thigh, the same man who had whispered in his ear. The soldier tried to call out, but others were already closing in from the edges. A searing headache split his vision. Acid seemed to burn through his eyes, stripping away every trace of light. Fog closed around him. Out of the haze, figures took shape, undulating, shifting, unsteady. They bent and stretched into grotesque, impossible forms.

"Where's the beach? Paul! Paul!" he cried, scraping his nails across the courtyard's stones, desperate to feel sand. "What're their damn names?"

A voice intruded. "It's his malaria. He's hallucinating again, poor guy."

Then another, annoyed: "Storyteller! Pipe down, man! You're just hallucinating. You'll be okay."

Who's that? He said I'm hallucinating. About what? The beach? This place? Where the hell am I?

He murmured, "Hallucinations . . . Nature . . . malaria . . . Storyteller . . . Storyteller. . . . " and stared in disbelief at his own hands. His wrists. His body—frail, shivering beneath oversized fatigues. *My God! I'm young. Skinny. Just a boy. I'm back. He shut his eyes and concentrated. You've got the wrong one! It's not me, it's my twin you want! Send me back! You've got the wrong one!*

But the conviction rang hollow. He felt the echo of truth slipping beneath it. So he shifted his thoughts to avoid the chasm. He focused on his surroundings, the jagged walls of an old French fortress, its crumbling granite blocks tangled in vines and creepers. Newer rock embankments patched the worst sections, and though the place radiated desolation, there were splashes of color, flowers blooming in unlikely crevices, a strange beauty softening the gloom.

He sat slumped against one wall, the damp poncho liner crumpled at his feet. His boots lay sideways in the rain. Alarmed, he leaned forward and fumbled them on, tying the laces tight. Then he lay back, dizzy but calmer, drawing the poncho over his chest. Rain pooled in its folds, the movement unsettling, as if the fabric itself were alive. Thunder rolled somewhere beyond. Or was it the ocean? His mind whirled. A tangled blur.

Had he really just been at the beach? Thoughts flitted, erratic and uncatchable. He prayed, half-hoped, that he was dreaming of the past while lying safe in the future. But then the blindfold fell away, revealing a firing squad, rifles pointed, triggers squeezed, the truth hit.

No good. I'm Storyteller. Back in the jungle. Back in the fortress. It's too real. Too real. Once in the bush, always in the bush. Once in the fortress, always in the fortress. Trapped.

Then the truth came, the one thought that overwhelmed the rest. *My twin . . . my twin . . . is me . . . is me. . . .*

A thousand pebbles falling, one by one, into a still pond. A thousand ripples radiating out, forming a thousand mouths, each whispering, "Noooo . . . noooo . . . noooo. . . . "

But the shock was false. He had always known. Deep down, he had always known. Never had a twin. I really am here. Grunts moved through the shadows in front of him, old friends returned to hell. He trembled and slipped easily back into blasphemous youth. *I've been here all along. In this goddamn, motherfuckin' fortress.*

Dusk collapsed into jungle night. Insects buzzed, spun, hung, and died. Sweat poured from his face, thinned by the mist. Figures loomed in the shadows, his platoon, his brother grunts. All of them trapped. He tried to remember how they'd ended up here.

But to recall that, he had to go back. Not too far. Just far enough to find footing in memory. And then they came, fragmented, vivid, unstoppable.

Storyteller's memories.

~ *Memories of Storyteller Remembering* ~

It had started six days earlier. Scuttlebutt drifted through the company, something about a new mission hatched by Army Intelligence. The old-timers dismissed it as rumor, but it turned out to be real. Storyteller remembered the moment the truth hit: a lazy afternoon at a mountaintop firebase. He and the others sat in a half-circle, boots kicked out, heads low, listening to their platoon leader, a lean, gum-chewing Arkansan they called "T."

T stood over them, lanky and restless, lips popping with every chew, the black Fagin of the bush without a beard. His favorite composer was Verdi. His favorite writer, Langston Hughes. His favorite pastime: berating the world for passing time. And now, with this mission, he looked like he'd bitten into something sour.

"Look," he said, chewing hard during the awkward pause that always came before he spoke, "I know what you're thinking. But it's outta my hands. I'll lay it out. Just listen. You can bitch later."

He paused, partly for effect, mostly because he doubted the mission himself. Then he put his hands on his hips and went on. "We're supposed to intercept a small NVA unit escorting two high-ranking female intelligence officers out of the area. Set an ambush. Capture them alive."

He glanced down at his boots, trying to string words together that wouldn't sound as ridiculous as the orders he'd been given. Self-conscious, he fiddled with a speck on his trousers, inhaled sharply, and scanned the area for senior officers. Spotted one. Stiffened.

"These women are from Hanoi. Temporarily assigned to a battalion operating in this AO. Intel thinks it's a small team. We're to grab the women, figure out why they're here, and get out. Don't ask where this intel came from. I don't know."

Grumbling spread through the ranks. Though the firebase was little more than a scab of red earth, stripped bare of jungle cover, the grunts were glad to be there. They'd just returned from weeks in the bush. This was their brief reprieve: warm food, sleep, cigarettes that didn't taste like blood. And now they were being sent back out. T cut the noise quickly.

"Look sharp. I've been ordered to take a select group. The most experienced guys." More groans. Especially from the short-timers. "I know it sucks, but I need you. This one could get ugly."

Calls erupted.

"Come on, T!"

"What a fuckin' joke!"

"Always the same goddamn Army bullshit!"

T stood still, letting them vent. The captain had wandered off. T relaxed, hands on hips again, leaning forward, a gangly vulture overlooking a field of the doomed.

When the noise settled, he cleared his throat.

"All right. Here's the list. If I call your name, head over to the bunker for briefing. Pappy, Stretch, Mountain Man, Idaho, Nature, Storyteller, Superman, Bowls, Dogman, Raresteak, and X. The rest of you, report to Captain Barnes for reassignment."

The names lingered in the air, heavy with unspoken accusation. Most were short-timers, weeks, even days from rotating out. Sending men that close to home into a high-risk op was a gamble. They had something to lose now. Home-cooked meals. Clean sheets. The safety of no longer being hunted.

Still, T had chosen them for a reason. Comradery. Instinct. Skill. A ghost-sense that cohesion might carry them through.

Even so, the mission reeked of something wrong.

We're gonna get burned on this one, he thought. He walked with the men toward the bunker, chewing slower now. *Female officers? Out here?* He'd never heard of such a thing. *How do we capture them without getting killed? Or killing them? And a small escort team? Sure. Right. No problem.*

They filed into the dim bunker. A clean-cut captain stood at the front, starched, polished, untouched by rain or reality. Captain Cairns. The grunts saw him for what he was before he spoke: a lifer, a remf—rear echelon motherfucker. Too clean. Too upright. A paper soldier obsessed with his own rank. Worse, he was Asian.

They sliced him apart with their eyes before he even opened his mouth. Stripped him. Tossed the remains into a mental dumpster. Left a shell standing there, emptied of humanity. It was a skill they'd refined. It had started with the enemy—gooks. Then spread, quiet and contagious. Now, anyone not a grunt—American, Vietnamese, officer, civilian—was marked for erasure.

Cairns, for his part, saw a lineup of degenerates. He'd been watching them. Judged them already. Low education. Crude humor. Bush-burned. Products of broken homes. Bonded in pairs like animals driven together by hardship. Storyteller and Nature. Superman and Stretch. Bowls and Mountain Man. Dogman and Raresteak. X stood alone. They were a caste apart, Untouchables. Beneath him in every way.

He broke the silence. "Morning."

Nothing. Blank stares.

Nature reached into his pocket, pulled out a red-checkered tam-o'-shanter, and set it on his head.

"Morning, Captain."

Cairns nodded, as if to say: finally.

"Here's the deal. Two Hueys will drop us near the ambush site just after sunrise. Trail's about two klicks from the LZ. The slicks will wait for us. You'll pack full gear, we might be out there a while if the intel's off. If we're lucky, it's quick. If not, we dig in."

"If it's faulty?" Bowls cut in.

Cairns ignored him. "We hunker near the trail, ambush the NVA, and capture the two women. If they're late, we send the slicks back and stay put."

Stretch raised a hand, fingers wagging frantically.

"Yes?"

"Hunker down, sir. Not hunker in. American slang. Might not be in your Chinese dictionary."

Snickers.

Cairns' eyes narrowed. "I'm Vietnamese-American. Born in Los Angeles. I'm a U.S. Army captain." He turned back to Stretch. "Thanks for the lesson. Hunker down it is."

"You'll all be issued silencers for your M-16s. Use only if needed. Depends on how many we're up against."

He turned to T. "Where's your gunner?"

T gestured toward a tall figure by the wall. "Superman."

Cairns fixed him with a stare. "You will not use your '60 unless absolutely necessary. Understood?"

Superman exhaled. "Yes, sir."

Stretch leaned in, muttered, "Why don't he bore a hole in himself and let the sap run out?"

"What was that, soldier?" Cairns snapped.

"Groucho Marx, sir."

Cairns blinked, confused.

T stepped in for damage control. "Stretch doesn't say much, Captain. But when he does, it's usually from a movie. Photographic memory. Damndest thing."

Stretch grinned, emboldened. "Don't worry, sir. I ain't crazy. I say things other than quotes. It's just, most things worth sayin' already been said. War movies, comedies, horror flicks . . . I mix and match." He trailed off. His head drooped sideways, puppet-like.

Cairns offered a chilly smile. "Say what you like. But when I ask a question, I expect a real answer. I don't have time for riddles."

Stretch nodded. "Yes, sir. Straight as an arrow."

Then muttered, "Broken arrow," just loud enough for Superman to hear.

Cairns frowned.

T raised his voice. "One other thing. While we're in the bush, I'm in command. Captain Cairns is attached as intel liaison. He's fluent in Vietnamese. He'll handle the prisoners if we get them. Pappy here's our acting first sergeant. Understood?"

A wave of nods.

T turned. "Understood, Pappy?"

"Yes, sir."

"Good. Go on, Captain."

Cairns picked up where he left off. "Once the women are secured, we return to the LZ for extraction. It is critical, absolutely critical, that they're captured alive."

A pause. He let the word critical hang threateningly.

Mountain Man growled, "And we'll all live happily ever after."

Before Cairns could retort, T stepped in again. "I'll tuck you in later, Mountain Man."

Laughter broke the tension.

T turned back to Cairns. "Don't worry. Mountain Man's the best we've got. Speaks Vietnamese, too. Transferred out of intel by choice. Didn't like the distance from the fun."

Cairns raised an eyebrow. Redneck speaks Vietnamese? He spoke to him directly, in Vietnamese. "How good are you?"

"Not bad."

"How'd you learn?"

"My fiancée."

"Vietnamese?"

"Was."

When's the wedding?"

"There won't be one. She's dead." A pause. Then in English: "Sssirrr."

Cairns faltered. For the first time, he felt unease. *This one's dangerous.*

He turned back to the group. "No Claymores. Too risky. Might kill the women."

Raresteak chimed in, all grin and sleaze. "You like your women rare, huh, Captain? Raw and fresh."

Cairns clenched his jaw. T stared at his boots. Bowls nudged Raresteak with approval.

Cairns scanned the group. "Your men bark well, Lieutenant. Do they bite?"

T smirked. "Ask Charlie."

"They'll need teeth. And more than jokes. Any questions?"

Mountain Man growled again. "When do we leave?"

Cairns hesitated.

"Sssirrr," said Mountain Man.

"Tomorrow. 0600. If all goes well, we're back by dusk. Weather says monsoon within seventy-two hours. But we pack for the long haul."

~

Later that day, the grunts gathered under a stand of trees, grumbling about Cairns and the mission. Bowls worked the chewed stem of his pipe between his teeth, clicking it rhythmically from one corner of his mouth to the other. The pipe, gnawed and long-empty, was how he'd gotten his name.

"Bowls, that pipe's gonna drive me nuts," muttered Superman. "Was a dark day you got drafted."

Bowls grinned. "I didn't get drafted. I volunteered."

"What?" Stretch's voice rose in disbelief. "You told me your number was eleven."

"It was. Still volunteered."

Idaho, young, soft, eager to belong, jumped in. "Then how the hell did a cynical New York greaseball like you end up out here?"

Bowls turned to him with the contempt of an eighth-grader correcting a fifth. "What kinda question is that?"

"Come on, Bowls," Nature coaxed. Always the mediator. "It's a fair question."

Bowls sighed. "Fine. I'll tell you. I thought I was in love once. You know, marriage, kids, the whole damn script. She was sweet. Dirt poor. But decent. One day, we're out walking. I see this movie poster with some glamorous actress . . . and I realize the girl I'm with looks like a scarecrow with no straw."

Stretch perked up. "What was the movie?"

"Doesn't matter. Shut up and listen. That moment, it hit me. If I could lust after a rack of rags like that, I needed a wake-up call. So I joined the Army. Figured somebody had to shoot at me."

Stretch leaned in, starry-eyed. "And then you met Mountain Man. Your true love."

Superman groaned. "Probably all she wanted was your heart. Poor girl."

"Nah. That was the Tin Man," Stretch said, suddenly launching into a jerky imitation. He staggered in a circle, limbs flailing. "The Scarecrow needed a brain."

"Same as you," muttered Mountain Man, emerging from the gloom.

"Is T around?" he asked.

Stretch saw a chance to taunt indirectly, mock the Southerner without drawing Mountain Man's ire. He mussed his hair, plastered on a foolish grin, buried his hands in his pockets, and drawled, "Reckon I don't know. He spun down that ol' bunker yonder like a turd, flushed clean outta sight."

Mountain Man smiled faintly, teeth showing. "You scrawny little shit." Then, with no more interest, he dropped beside Bowls, their knees touching.

When Mountain Man spoke, it came as a pronouncement on high. Moses come down from the mountain. Because he was a legendary fighter who had been in the bush for many years, everyone listened respectfully. And, as he was a genius with no formal education who grew up among farmers and coal miners, and who was now mainly surrounded by scared kids, Mountain Man dwelt in a holy roller's paradise, although he was no preacher. Perceptions and observations, sometimes cogent and sometimes outrageous, streamed out of his mouth in speeches that still reverberate through the West Virginia mountains and the southern Vietnamese jungles. The Grand Manipulator who drew his power not from religion, but from the ritual beatific and street-wise elixirs found in lve potions and strychnine vials.

"You talkin' about our hero? Captain Cairns?" Mountain Man's voice grew sharp. "That fucker lives in a dream world. Rear-area delusions. Washington D.C. magic tricks. Think tanks up their asses."

"Right on," said Bowls, ever the disciple.

"Those assholes think of us as data sets. How many klicks can a grunt walk with X weight, Y rations, Z motivation? They pull rabbits from hats: democracy, anti-communism, domino theories. All illusions."

With a flourish, he mimed pulling something from a hat. "Fightin' for democracy." Again. "Stop the spread of communism." Again. "Better fight 'em here, or they'll show up in New York."

He flung the invisible hat away. "Bullshit."

"Right on," Bowls repeated.

"But they're the rabbits. Jumpy little career-fuckers. Always afraid. Sniffing out predators who look just like them, same uniforms, same smiles. What they want is to stop being prey and start being wolves. And then? They start eatin' their own kind."

He spat. "Cairns? Don't belong here. Real predators don't wear clean boots. And they don't follow rules."

"Fuckin' A," Bowls muttered, flicking a leech off his arm.

Stretch picked up the invisible hat, pantomimed tossing it in a trash can, then saluted. "Aye aye, Capitan. But forget the politics. Where are the women?" He grabbed his crotch and shrugged. "How many klicks I gotta hump with a hard-on before I find one?"

Bowls shook his head. "All I care about is how many klicks to get back to New York City. I'd get there at night, all lit up."

Mountain Man scowled. "Cities. Infested with humans. Open sores on the skin of a dying world."

"Whoa," said Storyteller, breaking his silence. "That voice—where did it come from? I think I've heard it before."

But Mountain Man didn't respond. His eyes settled on his boots, as if reading omens in their scars. "It's true. If you look at it Her way."

"Whose way?"

Mountain Man didn't answer. Instead, he blinked, shook it off, and refocused. The light came back into his eyes, sly, venomous.

"You love cities? Lights and baubles? Sparkles?" He sneered. "God's gonna have to clean this cage someday. Get rid of you humans. Disinfect the Earth. Nurse the animals back to health."

"Whose way?" Storyteller repeated.

Mountain Man said nothing. He crushed an ant between finger and thumb, wiped the remains on his pants, and locked eyes with Bowls.

Bowls hesitated, then pressed on. "I'm going back to New York. Gonna find this Jewish girl I know. She paints her nipples. I'll marry her in a synagogue—"

"A Jew girl?" Mountain Man snapped. "In a fuckin' synagogie?"

Bowls laughed nervously. "You wouldn't get it. It's not religion, it's culture."

Mountain Man held up both hands. He looked at one. "Jewish culture." He looked at the other. "Jewish religion." Then he clapped them together, middle fingers raised. "Now you got Jewish culigion." He jabbed both fingers toward Bowls. "Twice fucked."

Bowls chuckled uneasily. "Yeah, well, that's our god."

"God?" Mountain Man shoved Bowls face-first into the dirt. "Get on your knees to the ants, Jew boy. Pray to them. They work. They heal the land. What's your god do?"

"You believe in God too, you crazy Baptist fuck!" Bowls spat, pushing himself up.

"Of course I do. But He's up here"—Mountain Man tapped his temple—"just like yours. Just fuckin' around."

Bowls dusted himself off. "I swear, Mountain Man . . . I swear—"

But Mountain Man had already risen. "Shiiit," he said, and walked off.

With great ceremony, he picked his nose, rotating his finger like a weather vane, then flicked a massive glob into the mud and vanished into the trees.

"Thar she blows!" Stretch cried. "Colonel Booger Man crosses the River Kwai. A man among men! King of Kings!" He struck a Mae West pose. "Why don'tcha come up and see me sometime, big boy!"

But the moment collapsed. He spasmed, head jerking, arms twitching.

"Stretch," said Bowls as he stood to follow Mountain Man. "You're a damn idiot." Then he exaggerated Stretch's tics cruelly as he walked away.

Stretch flipped him the bird. "Just nervous habits, asshole." He nodded after Mountain Man. "Better kiss his ass, Jew boy. Or you might be next."

His body trembled.

Bowls threw over his shoulder, "And fix those damn fits. Gonna get us all killed. Oy."

Stretch waggled his hips in mockery, but the gesture melted into a full-body twitch. "Damn nervous habits," he muttered, clenching his fists to hold himself still.

Stretch's "nervous habits." Look close enough and they were everywhere, etched into the flesh, written in the twitch of a shoulder, the blink of an eye. He was a one-man cornucopia of adrenaline damage. Fingernails gnawed to raw moons. Fingers ringed with scabs where the skin had been stripped again and again. His limbs moved with a fractured rhythm, jerking and stuttering, a broken marionette. Even in stillness, his eyes blinked in protest, as if the very air offended them.

As a child, he'd been punished for these involuntary betrayals.

No doctor ever named it.

No mother ever protected him.

Just a parade of her boyfriends, hands heavy, patience thin.

And the only thing that stopped the beatings was performance mimicry. Groucho. Abbott and Costello. Cary Grant. Kirk Douglas. When he performed, they laughed, and for a while, the blows ceased. So he performed. And, like anyone desperate to keep pain at bay, he never stopped.

Now, seated beside Nature, his voice dropped into a mock-affectionate murmur, the line not spoken to Nature, but to himself, to the flickering projector of old films inside his skull.

"So, what do you wanna do tonight, Marty?"

~ *Ambush* ~

In the beginning, everything went as planned. The choppers dropped them into the clearing. The platoon cut quickly through the jungle and found the designated hardpack trail. So far, so good. The smoothness felt suspicious, but they let themselves hope. They took up ambush positions without incident. Storyteller crouched beside the lieutenant behind a five-foot termite mound, fiddling with his radio antenna, trying not to let it stick up and give them away. The jungle hissed softly around them, alive and indifferent. All waited in silence, each grunt quietly wishing the enemy wouldn't show.

No such luck.

Just hours later, exactly as intelligence had claimed, the first NVA elements appeared. That's when everything began to unravel. He remembered the ominous stillness just before contact. The world had shrunk to the beat of hearts and the hiss of breath. The jungle's low static reminded them that something still lived beyond the mound. The enemy emerged slowly, compact men in pith helmets, rifles low, senses sharpened. The grunts didn't breathe. Fingers trembled on triggers, holding back only by force of will. Tension became cellular. Every molecule of air seemed to sweat.

"Now!" T shouted.

Silenced M-16s erupted in sharp puffs. The enemy fell as though they were badly dubbed actors in a silent war film, bodies jerking as if cut by unseen strings.

Then, chaos.

The next moments shattered into fragments: flashes, noise, and disjointed memory. Storyteller remembered the radio crackling. Voices shrill with panic. The hiss of gunfire blossoming into thunder.

No more silencers now. The NVA were returning fire, far more of them than expected. Far too many.

Ka-boom! Ka-boom!

Mortars rained down. Earth exploded in geysers of dirt and blood. Limbs sheared. Trees shredded.

Superman's M-60 opened up, each burst a stuttering howl of death.

Cairns had said only to use it as a last resort.

This was the last resort.

The jungle became a meat grinder: gray smoke, bloody mist, shredded leaves, bone chips, and the shriek of metal twisting into pain.

Radios screamed. Voices cracked.

"Look for the women!"

"This ain't no small escort!"

"Medic! X, get over here!"

"Dogman's hit! We're taking too much fire!"

"Mountain Man's squad has two women and a bamboo trunk!"

"What? Already?"

"Don't matter! Get 'em back to the choppers! Pull back! Pull back!"

"Raresteak's dead! We're carrying him out!"

T and Storyteller ran side by side, their bodies yoked by the coiled tether of the field radio. T barked into the handset as it bounced with every stride.

"Friar Tuck One, this is Robin Hood! Wind 'em up—we're bringing two prisoners, one KIA, one WIA! Charlie's right behind us!"

"Roger that, Robin Hood."

"Get us the hell out!"

A shout. "Heavy fire from the left! They're flanking us!"

"Move it! Move it!"

Then the jungle retreat: blistering, endless.

They crouched and scrambled through fire and thunder, the earth erupting in fountains around them. AK-47s rattled a bony clatter. Dogman and Raresteak were slung across backs, their blood soaking into the shirts of those who carried them, pooling at belt lines.

The women, dragged by hair, by sleeves, whatever could be gripped.

Then the clearing. A break in the trees. The rotors, turning beautifully, deadly, slowly.

"Oh God, fire from both treelines!"

"They've flanked us!"

"Move! Move!"

"They got Idaho!"

"Leave him! We can't help now! Go!"

They ran, bent low, as if that could save them. Toward the choppers. Toward salvation. Toward that mountaintop firebase that now seemed holy, a Camelot of scorched red soil and ugly bunkers.

"Look at all that movement in the trees!"

Too much.

Storyteller focused on his feet. One step. Then another. Everything moved too slowly. Dreamlike. The ground tore open. Heat slammed his face. Explosions knocked him off balance, ripping the world into shrapnel and sky.

The helicopters loomed overhead. The first received the prisoners and the trunk. Grunts followed, scrambling in. The second took the bodies, Dogman and Raresteak thrown in, limbs limp and twisted. Bullets shredded the earth. Mortars fell, erupting in fountains of dirt. The air turned to smoke, fire, and screams.

Inside, Storyteller lay tangled with the dead. Other grunts piled over him, rifles pressing into ribs. The chopper lurched and groaned, battered by gunfire. Bullets hammered the frame. Shrapnel tore through the cabin. Blood sprayed from the door gunner's neck.

They lifted, slow, straining. The machine groaned as if it was wounded. Inside, they were stacked without order, bodies pressed together, heat and blood soaking into flesh. Weapons pointed in all directions. Grunts struggled to free themselves, gasping, cursing.

It was madness. Horror tipped into absurdity.

"Higher! Come on, baby!"

"Gotta make it! Gotta make it!"

"Please. . . ."

And then, distance. Blessed distance. The noise receded. Hope surged.

"We're gonna make it!"

"They'll never believe this shit!"

Then the lurch. A sickening jolt. The chopper bucked hard, as if it had slammed into something unseen. Storyteller craned his neck. The second bird staggered too. Gunfire erupted from a concealed treeline. Plexiglass shattered. Screams.

Inside, the world broke apart. Low-rpm sirens wailed. One pilot was already dead, face melted inside a blackened helmet. Smoke flooded the cabin. Radios crackled, then fell silent. The smell of burning fuel thickened. More screams.

In the other chopper, the pilot collapsed. The co-pilot lunged for the controls, but the fire had gutted the wiring. Smoke choked the cabin. Grunts clung to anything solid, eyes wild, mouths open but voiceless. Terror moved through them, silent, contagious.

Through gusts and smoke, the two surviving pilots locked eyes. They gestured urgently, instinctively: down. Down the slope. Away from the firebase. Toward anything open. Anything that might mean survival.

From somewhere in the back, cheers broke through the static.

Storyteller twisted and looked through the haze. A Cobra gunship, beautiful, lethal, sliced into view.

"Look at that motherfuckin' Cobra!"

"She's ours!"

The gunship dipped its wings and began escorting them, two broken bees limping behind a dragonfly. Hope rose again. But then the Cobra banked for one final pass. A last strike at the enemy. They watched in disbelief as it caught fire mid-air, spiraling, vomiting flames, and vanished behind the cliffs. Gone. Both slicks paused in stunned silence. Then resumed their fall. Down the cliff. Over jungle. Into storm. The choppers could not climb. Could only descend, staggering through treetops until the trees fell away, then plunging, helpless.

Someone vomited. Then Superman's voice: "Our Father, who art in heaven. . . ."

Nature joined, voice soft and breaking. "Mother Mary, protect us. . . ." Then he shouted, "Your tabs! Think of your tabs!"

Silence.

Even the gunner fell quiet. "What's a tab? What the fuck's a tab?"

In the other chopper, Mountain Man and Bowls clasped hands. Mountain Man scanned the cabin, his voice calm, unwavering. "Think of your tabs, boys."

Eyes closed. Heads bowed. A collective stillness. A stillness not of peace, but of silent preparation.

Then a scream.

"We have to make it lighter! Throw the bodies out! Throw them out!"

A crewman wept as he shoved the corpse of his co-pilot through the door, the body swallowed instantly by the trees.

X covered Dogman and Raresteak with his body. "No! We can't! Not like this!"

Pappy was already moving. "Back off! Keep 'em, we all die!"

Nature pulled X into an embrace. Loud, but composed.

"They're gone, X. These aren't them, just bodies. What would they say? 'Throw our bags of meat overboard. We're elsewhere. Remember our tabs.' That's what they'd say. That's what you'd say."

X relented. Crawled away. The bodies were lifted and dropped into the clouds below.

No time to mourn.

The metal boiled. Fire licked skin. Grunts pressed to the walls, screaming. The hull burned them.

Storyteller stared upward and saw a spider in its web, clinging to the ceiling. As smoke surged, the spider scrambled back and forth, then leapt through the open door, carried away by wind.

"Good luck," he whispered.

Time disintegrated. The silence of dying machines filled the air. Somewhere below, through the smoke, appeared a clearing. The ruins of a fortress. The pilots had no choice. They aimed for it. One chopper clipped a stone wall and smashed into the ground with a metallic shriek. The other hovered, then fell beside it, a heap of ruin. Engines groaned. Rotors slowed. The dead bird wheezed to silence. Somehow, they crawled out. Storyteller didn't remember how.

T, upon learning the bodies had been thrown from the air, exploded. "If you do that again, I'll see you court-martialed. Shot, even. We never leave our people behind. Not even dead. Never!"

"It was them or us," said Pappy.

"No excuses!"

The rage passed. Orders resumed. They fortified the fortress. Sent a team to the Cobra's wreckage. The pilot was dead. Radios obliterated. Nothing salvageable. No radios on any chopper worked. Not field units. Not backups. Not even long-range. They tried. Again and again. Nothing but static. Long whip antennas, brute force, sheer will. Still, static. Nothing. Dark clouds gathered overhead. And everyone knew.

The NVA would be coming.

~ *Exploring the Fortress* ~

While exploring the ruins, the grunts discovered the fortress was built on an oblong perimeter, its thick stone wall topped by a second-story parapet. Stretch, surveying the layout, muttered gloomily, "Beau Geste," as if expecting to find dead sentries still manning the walls. In the center stood a vast, deteriorating square of brick and dust, uneven, treacherous, ready to twist an ankle if you weren't careful. At one end loomed the gutted shell of a Catholic church, grand even in ruin. Its roof had long since collapsed, scattering jagged slabs of masonry across the nave in a chaotic sprawl of shattered geometry. Saintly statues lay broken at impossible angles, heads half-submerged in rain-slick tile. Vines gripped them in twisted chains, stone saints bound in green. A Promethean punishment, perhaps, for dragging the fire of religion into a place where gods had always been beasts, wind, and rain.

The fortress itself was a welt on the jungle's skin, a colonial canker embedded in living tissue.

Ruined barracks and roofless shanties leaned drunkenly against the interior wall beneath the parapet. A mess hall, or what was left of it, sagged into weeds. But there was one advantage: the fortress stood at the center of a swampy meadow, free of tall brush and trees. The jungle treeline sat nearly 150 meters beyond the wall, no close cover for an advancing enemy. While scavenging stones to reinforce the perimeter, the grunts unearthed a trapdoor in the far corner of the church. Beneath it ran an immense tunnel, stretching a hundred meters beneath the jungle to a bamboo grove near the vast roots of a banyan tree. Originally a mining shaft, the tunnel still held rusting rails meant for hand-pushed ore carts.

Cairns inspected it thoroughly the first day. At dusk, he made his pronouncement.

"Tin mine," he said, with confident ignorance. "French probably turned it into an escape tunnel. Tin shafts run parallel to the surface. They could've just diverted both ends, sealed the rest."

Pappy nodded. "Makes sense. Sure as hell works for us."

"Could be," said T, noncommittal.

"Nope," said Mountain Man, stepping forward.

Cairns stiffened. "What are you talking about?"

"I'm from mining country," Mountain Man began.

"Coal mines, not tin," Cairns snapped. "West Virginia is coal. This is tin."

"Don't matter," Mountain Man muttered, glancing at the ruins. "They built everything, fort, church, the whole damn thing, right over the tunnel. Must've planned to run if it came to it."

"Shiiit," said X, laying out his gear nearby. "This place already gives me the creeps."

"Can it," T cut in sharply. "Don't talk like Stepin Fetchit. Use your brain."

"Huh?"

"I said use your brain, boy."

X shrugged. "Come on, T, get off my case. Not all of us like opera."

"You'd better learn. Education, that's how you take the 'grrr' outta nigger and the 'knee' outta Negro. Leaves 'gro.' Grow, boy. Grow."

He pulled out a neatly folded handkerchief, blew his nose, refolded it, and tucked it back with precision. Then he turned and walked away, Cairns, Pappy, and Mountain Man staring at his back.

T built his fastidious habits on a self-righteous scaffolding of comparison. Though born into wealth, he was raised in the filthier districts of Little Rock. His father, a prosperous merchant, had insisted on living among the poor, preaching dignity and duty. T learned how to look down without seeming to. He approached "the underprivileged" with a practiced air of noble resignation, the kind that masked contempt behind service.

X, for T, was the ideal dependent, an "unrefined negro boy" in constant need of correction. And T, ever chewing and swallowing the language of duty, found in this arrangement a quiet, twisted satisfaction.

The Army suited him. Even if promotion was unlikely for a Black officer, the fit was exacting. Restrictive. But somehow just right.

Once T was gone, Mountain Man let out a low whistle. He grinned. "Lieutenant Negro to Spec 4 Nigger, eh, X?"

"Bullshiiit," X muttered. "Negro or nigger, don't matter. This place don't care. White bones, black bones, it's all fertilizer. Jungle don't discriminate."

"You heard the lieutenant," Cairns snapped. "Can it."

X ground his teeth. "Yes, sir. Captain."

Mountain Man chuckled. He paused beside X and said over his shoulder, "You and me, opera tonight, eh, boy?"

~

The tunnel became their lifeline: a hidden artery for water, for recon, for escape. On the second day, T sent out patrols. To Cairns' disbelief, they reported finding a mangrove swamp just beyond the eastern treeline.

"Impossible," Cairns snapped. "We're nearly a hundred miles from the coast. Taste the water—salty! Not from the river. There's no ocean! Mangrove? No way."

T looked around as if trying to reorient reality. "Yes . . . I see it too. But . . . it's wrong. The wall. The plants. Everything's off."

Mountain Man just smiled. "Her party. She sets the rules. Got me about right, anyway."

"But it's not right," someone muttered.

"It's not Her," said another. "It's him."

X laughed. "Ain't wrong either. Brain's plastic. Reality bends. It's right to him."

Stretch twitched. "I had plastic soldiers when I was a kid. Cut 'em up with a razor."

Cairns rolled his eyes. "What the hell does that even mean?"

He jabbed a finger toward the swamp. "This is what I'm talking about. That tunnel's a tin mine. I'm certain."

"Salt mine?" Stretch asked sweetly, pretending to shake a salt shaker.

"Tin, not salt!" Cairns barked. "So where the hell's the ocean?"

~

Good question, My Dear Goddess. Care to answer it?
You know where You may go, My Beloved.
Already been. Built it. Looks like I'm back, Sweetheart.

~

"Never mind that," said T, pointing upward. "Look at those clouds."

Nature let out a low whistle. "Jesusssss. We're in for it."

Once T and Cairns walked out of earshot, Stretch leaned close to Nature.

"Ol' Captain there's so smart," he whispered, "he could dry snow and sell it for sugar."

"What?" Nature blinked.

I said he knows as much about everything as Clark Gable does about hitchhiking."

"What?"

Stretch hunched over pretending to be a man at a diner, pinched fingers midair. "Or dunkin' donuts."

Nature chuckled. "What're you talking about now?"

Stretch threw his arms up in mock despair. "Never mind."

But inside, the old shame twisted.

Damn it, Stretch. When will you learn not to humiliate yourself in public?

~

They settled in, tried to believe rescue was coming. Searched the sky. Believed they'd be found before the NVA returned, or the storm hit. Next morning, they heard helicopter rotors in the distance. Someone popped smoke. The chopper never came. And so they waited. And waited.

That was four days ago. Three days ago, the monsoon struck. Inside the fortress, they huddled while the storm howled and dragged trees from the earth. Thunder cracked the sky in jagged seams. To Storyteller, lying on his back in the ruined courtyard, the fortress grew mythic, walls rising endlessly into cloud, towers swallowed in mist. Sometimes, in feverish reverie, he imagined the clouds as gargoyles locked in combat, running each other through with lightning, bleeding rain, hemophiliac gods.

Majestic, yes. But miserable.

Then came the final curse. NVA scouts, tracking their smoke, rediscovered the fortress. An entire company, just as they'd feared.

The siege had begun.

~

Malaria struck Storyteller days after he took shelter in the fortress. It began slowly: nausea, headache, rising heat. Then surged into full-blown fever. At its peak, steam seemed to rise from his skin. Rain hissed against his burning body. Each night the fever returned, stronger than before. And with it came visions.

Not demons. Not ghosts. People.

Men, women, and children appeared—translucent, luminous, drifting through the jungle air. Their skin revealed what lay beneath: hearts pulsing, lungs drawing breath. Each night, they grew more distinct. Blood darkened. Limbs thickened. Their faces formed, features settling into place. Clothes emerged in pale outlines.

They moved among the ruins without urgency. No fear. No recognition. Just quiet motion, browsing, wandering, as if the past had reopened and they were part of it again.

No one else saw them. X insisted it was the fever. Hallucinations. Nothing more. But they returned. Night after night. And each time, more there. Transparent marine life...

Michael, wake up. You're dreaming again.

Come on, sweetheart. It's okay.

Hallucinations. That's all they are. Dr. Toomey's explained this a million times. You just need to take your medication. But you have to be diligent. Religious. Now wake up, darling. Wake up.

~ *Fever Dreams III* ~

Prodded by Diane's voice, Storyteller surfaced from his fevered drift. He raised his head and gazed across the crumbling fortress. *Yes, I'm really here. Not a hallucination. Not a memory. Diane, I'm awake.*

Figures moved in the dimming jungle light, his brother grunts. Shadows now. Shapes of men. The fever pulsed hotter, burning through the fragile cohesion of their bodies. Molecule by molecule, they unraveled. In desperation, he tried to hold them together, give them names: T, Mountain Man, Bowls, Nature. Their features eluded him, slipping into mist. So young. He reached into the fog of memory, searching their futures, but the crystal ball remained cloudy. He was still only an apprentice, Storyteller the Conjurer, unable to call back the dead with any clarity. Not yet. He sweated from the fever more than the heat.

Time fragmented, his mind floating between moments. Somewhere within the muffled haze, he heard the rhythmic crackle of small arms—harassing fire. The knowledge that men outside the walls were trying to kill him barely registered at first. Then a green burst of tracers hissed overhead, and suddenly the battle roared in his ears, as if someone had ripped out the plugs.

Panic struck—his rifle! He wasn't holding it. He thrashed in alarm, searching. Thank God, his boots were on. That mattered. He had always feared dying barefoot. But the rifle? There, just out of reach. He rolled, stretched, begged, cursed. "Come on, Michael. Just a few more inches." The firefight raged around him, but he was alone. Everyone else was on the parapets. No one saw. And then he saw it—his hand, no longer attached. Just a tattered wrist trembling above the dirt, the severed hand gripping the rifle, its fingers twitching.

Horror overtook him. He sobbed, breath kicking up dust. "Oh God. Please. Let me go home."

A voice touched his ear. "It's okay, Storyteller. Everything's gonna be fine. Just harassing fire. Relax. Hey! Hold him tighter. Tighter! Yeah, that's it. Relax. Your rifle's right next to you. Feel it? Relax."

But his mind was slipping. Darkness poured in like black ink seeping through his thoughts, softening edges, blurring the middle. The tracer fire smudged into streaks of red and green. Then the portal shut. Silence. Only rain. And the sound. The scraping. He knew what came next. The hallucinations always began like this: silence, then that awful dragging sound from beyond the walls. And always what followed was worse than any firefight.

A flash. His head spun, nausea, dizzyness. And then, clarity.

Suddenly, impossibly, he could see everything. Every detail lit with surgical precision. Eleven soldiers inside the wall. Four missing. Raresteak and Dogman were dead. Idaho, gone. Captured, probably. But Mountain Man? Where was Mountain Man? He scanned. Five grunts on guard. Six asleep along the wall. The two NVA women, bound and motionless. And then he waited. For the sixth dream.

And it came.

~

They entered through the walls, ghostly, transparent figures, glowing from within. Beating hearts. Expanding lungs. Blood vessels branching in scarlet webs. A faint outline of muscle and bone, male and female. The young. The old.

A mother cradled a child.

An old couple stood arm in arm.

Naked women shimmered.

Dogs sniffed the air.

None of the guards noticed. Only Storyteller saw. The apparitions glided silently to stand beside each soldier. Some grunts had several surrounding them. Some had none. A boy about his own age knelt beside him, baseball cap backward, eyes blank, hand moving gently across some invisible object—perhaps a pointer on a Ouija board. And then the figures came alive.

The women smiled. Children played. The old laughed. Lovers touched. Joy radiated from them, light from a remembered dream.

Except for the boy. The boy remained still, his fingers twitching across nothing, his gaze vacant.

Storyteller turned to the two prisoners. They too had ghosts: one old woman chattered while casting imaginary dice, two children danced circles around the younger captive. He tried to recognize the grunts beneath each apparition, but faces dissolved when he looked too long. The boy beside him—he almost knew him. Almost. And then the change.

Smiles twisted into sneers.

Laughter soured to mockery.

The lovers turned to rapists.

The children to shadows.

One naked woman writhed in silent ecstasy, then recoiled, face bruising, eyes swelling shut. Rope burns appeared, dark and raw. She staggered backward from some invisible torment. Her body a map of violation. Storyteller gagged on horror, willing himself to look away, but unable. He tried to identify the soldier responsible, but the face would not resolve.

~

And then—

~

He floated above the fortress now, looking down. The ruined church. The bamboo trunk. The golden figurine beside it. Cross-legged. Serene. Fingers forming a sacred mudra. Rain slid down its cheeks. Light flickered from its surface, threading out in strands of radiant silk, binding it to the apparitions.

Ah, it is You, Goddess. I suspected as much.

Let Me be, You tiresome deity.

As You wish. I'll observe—for now.

The figurine sat at the center of an invisible web. It pulsed with sentience. No longer did he believe the ghosts were figments of his mind. They were being directed. They moved as puppets under that golden gaze. And then the figurine turned. Its head tilted back, and its eyes met his. Not cruel. Not kind. Simply . . . aware. It turned from him and swept the fortress with its gaze. The threads vibrated. And Storyteller felt himself sinking. The fever returned. His skull throbbed. One by one, the apparitions turned and walked away. But before disappearing through the wall, each turned and whispered:

"Kill yourself, broken one."

Or, in his fever, did he misunderstand? Perhaps they really said, "Still yourself, Chosen One."

They would return. If he survived the night, they would return. God help him.

He slept, fitfully, soaked, shivering. Nightmares came, but ordinary ones. Still, the golden eyes hovered in the dark, watching. Waiting.

Michael. Michael. Wake up. You're dreaming again. Come on, sweetheart. It's okay. Wake up. Michael! For God's sake, wake up before it's too late!

From beyond the walls, the sounds of surf. A child's voice rising: "He's gonna attack and eat your doll and everyone inside!"

Ocean waves. Seagulls. Silence.

Chapter Six

The First Night

Madame Dau Worries

Five kilometers from the fortress, an exhausted village chief lay awake beneath the shadowed ribs of her tile roof. Her shoulders ached. She rolled them slowly, trying to ease a burden that felt centuries old. Sleep would not come. Worry threaded through her thoughts, tightening with every breath, until rest was no longer possible.

At first light, the council would gather to face a cascade of troubles: breached dikes, a delayed winter planting, a mysterious illness spreading through the village, and the death of Old Venerable—the last adult male with any authority. But none of these burdens unsettled her as deeply as the sounds of war.

For days, she had heard it: sporadic gunfire, shouted commands, distant screams. The nearby fortress, once a forgotten relic, now trembled with the violence of American soldiers and People's Army fighters. She feared the battle would soon reach her village, unstoppable and consuming.

She breathed in the faint perfume of burned joss sticks, remnants of an earlier offering. The scent was comforting, a memory of order and reverence. Yet she knew how quickly incense could become smoke from burning homes, from burning skin.

Turning, she reached toward the empty half of her bed, longing for her husband's calming voice. He had been dead many years, but his absence still breathed beside her. Teeth clenched, she kneaded the coarse cotton blanket. Her daughters. Her grandchildren. They slept unknowing, while she trembled with dread. Some women on the council would argue for evacuation, for joining the swelling ranks of refugees in the district capital. But she had decided they must stay. The land was not perfect, but it was theirs. Still, in the tremors of night, her certainty crumbled.

A verse, ancient and defiant, returned to her mind:

We honorable sisters are like a mass of boulders in Heaven.
How could you youngsters as
Small as mice
Think of disturbing us?

Cursed be you bunch of mice!
When this rock falls down
You will be crushed.

With a faint smile, the council chief changed a word in the stanza and sang the next rendition out loud:

We honorable sisters are like
A mass of boulders in Heaven.
How could you soldiers as
Small as mice
Think of disturbing us?
Cursed be you bunch of soldiers!
When this rock falls down
You will be crushed.

The words repeated over and over in her mind, and she felt her eyes getting heavier.

Sleep. Sleep. Sleep...

~

A loud knocking on her door. Fluttering of eyelids, fighting sleep, awakening to the shouted words from outside.

"Madame Dau! Madame Dau! Herbalist Tien wants you to come right away! Madame Trinh and her son, Little Monkey, have the fever! Come quickly!"

The council chief wearily rose from her wood bed and pulled on a loose fitting ao ba ba. Slipping her gnarled feet into straw sandals, she padded outside and followed the bobbing lanterns carried by a group of buzzing women as they hurried to Madame Trinh's shack. Squinting against the rain, she heard Herbalist Tien greet her gruffly from the front door, then pull her inside and wedge both their bodies into a corner, out of earshot of Trinh's worried relatives.

"She's had the fever for days. Hasn't told anyone. Now she can't get out of bed. Little Monkey tried to nurse her, but now he's sick too. Poor boy! If it's like the others, they only have a few days. Maybe a week. Madame Vit is bringing the liver from a freshly slaughtered pig. I will make a potion with the bile mixed with some special herbs of my own." She shook her head slowly. "Demons don't like my potions! Not a bit!"

"But—"

"Auntie Dau! Auntie Dau!" twelve-year-old Tran Van Trinh shouted from another room. The villagers called him Little Monkey because of his acrobatic antics on the backs of water buffaloes. "Come help my mama! She's sick!"

The council chief went in and leaned over the sick boy. "Little Monkey! Such a big voice for such a sick boy! Herbalist Tien is making a potion. You must be brave and drink it, just like your mama. It will make you better."

The boy laughed weakly. "Yes. But I'm just a little sick. Mama must have more than me. And I still have a lot to do. The water buffalo! I have to—"

"Hush! Your sisters will take care of the buffalo." She looked down at him with a reassuring smile.

One of his older sisters was listening. "No! No, auntie! I'm afraid of that buffalo! He is in a bad temper lately. Knocked me down the other day with his head! No! I—"

But before she could finish her protestations, the council chief slapped her on the face. "You will take care of the buffalo! I have no time for faint-hearted nonsense! Now go to your mama and wait for your Auntie Tien to bring the potion. Go!"

Whimpering, the girl mumbled, "Yes, auntie," and backed out of the room.

After directing the head of the village Cult Committee to assist Trinh's family with the fields, the council chief shuffled wearily back to her house. She wanted to go to her bed, lie down, and take a dip in the warm memory of her dead husband—to soak languorously while the heat of his imaginary presence cooked away the sores and pains of life without him. But other thoughts would not let her rest. *Hot and cold. Yin and Yang. Kindness and cruelty. Pleasure and pain. Life and death. War and peace. This and that. I smile. I slap. I give. I take. Oh, I am so tired of it all! Oh, Husband! You are with the ancestors now. Use your influence! Make life here easier. Just a little easier.* She smiled. *And I will make it worth your while in heaven.*

But it was a sad smile, for she knew that her body was old and ugly and that the glow in her face had faded. The will to live was barely hanging on in the extinguishing howl of life. Still, there was a will. *And one last thing, Husband.* She paused and shuddered, looking in the direction of the old fortress. *Make the soldiers go away.*

~ *Major Vy Worries* ~

Beneath the dripping forest canopy, Major Vy lay awake in his rain-slicked hammock. Rivulets coursed from the edges of his poncho. His knees ached. His breath steamed. Rage was a bright spike in his brain—piercing, corrosive. He could not rest. He reviewed the morning's agenda: the siege, the wounded, the threat of detection, the monsoon's relentlessness, the rising fever among the ranks. But above all, the disaster he could not admit aloud—the figurine. Gold. Sacred. Valuable. And now trapped inside the American-held fortress.

He cursed the monsoon. Cursed the mortar crews. Cursed the Americans. And above all, cursed himself. What had seemed so simple: retrieve the figurine, slip south, sell to the cartel, vanish into the world beyond war. But the siege had dragged. The fortress resisted. The rains returned. And his conscience, long dormant, stirred in the darkness.

The jungle's scent surrounded him—wet canvas, rotting vines, gun oil, powdered insecticide. Familiar aromas. Yet behind them all, the lurking stink of napalm and roasted bodies. That future pressed in, too close. He longed for his wife's voice, her hands, her warmth. But only clenched fists answered his longing. His heart, erratic and cramped with pain, reminded him he was not young. Not anymore. A single misstep would reveal everything: the corruption, the ambush, the bribes, the figurine. Commissar Minh was already sniffing. One report, one suspicion, and his head would part from his neck.

He muttered the stanza from an ancient poem he could not forget:

> *A man will win a horseskin for his shroud,*
> *His life he'll drop in battle like goose down.*
> *In war attire you leave and cross the Wei,*
> *Cracking your whip while roars the autumn wind.*

He spat into the dark.

"Major Vy! Major Vy!" A runner's voice broke through. "Comrade Le says the American prisoner may die. If you want answers, come now!"

Vy groaned and swung stiffly out of his hammock. Too old for this jungle. Too damned old. He followed the runner's lantern to the clearing. The prisoner lay curled and pale, his legs chalk-white in the glow.

"How long does he have?"

Comrade Le frowned. "Hard to say. But I've treated him. There's a chance. I think we should return his family photos. Hope gives strength."

Vy narrowed his eyes. "That's why you woke me?"

"Yes, sir."

Vy sighed. "Do it. If he dies, he dies useful."

He turned, already thinking of the figurine. Damn fool. Damn greed. Drug caravans. Why did I ever—

~ *The Lieutenant Worries* ~

Inside the stone fortress, the American lieutenant crouched under his poncho, sipping cold coffee from a dented tin. He hadn't slept in days.

His mind reeled with worst-case outcomes: overrun by the NVA, bodies strewn across the yard, limbs twisted, faces slack. His boys—Pappy, Nature, Stretch, Superman, Storyteller—all gone. Futures erased in an instant.

Would it be braver to flee? Or to hold?

He stared into the murk and conjured his wife.

What was she doing now? What was she wearing? Could she feel him thinking of her?

He imagined their reunion in aching detail—voices overlapping, laughter spilling, plans whispered into each other's mouths. Then quiet. Just her body. Her breath. White sheets. Cool walls. The stillness of old photographs. Love made whole again.

But it didn't hold.

The bedroom dissolved. The fortress returned—walls looming, rain dripping steadily from stone edges.

His wife screamed, buried in rubble.

He reached, grasped—

But she was gone.

Only his M-16 lay beside him, dry and upright.

~ *Storyteller Worries* ~

Storyteller drifted through restless sleep, his mind caught in the flicker of fever dreams. He stood on the fortress wall, staring at the jungle. And there—reclining across the canopy—was God. His body stretched miles, eyes half-closed, lips curled in pleasure. Not fasting. Feeding. Drawn closer, Storyteller stood beneath the divine face. The trees cracked and broke beneath God's weight. Suddenly he found himself perched in the tallest tree, face to face with the deity.

God purred, drunk on suffering. A sparrow landed on His finger—chirped—and was instantly devoured by a kestrel. God chuckled.

Ah, the agony! The little joy before pain deepens the wound. Such beauty in their ruin. And still, they worship Me—in mirrors.

A cry echoed—the sparrow's death scream. It seared Storyteller's mind like sulfur in the lungs. God inhaled the wail, held it, and exhaled a benediction. But then, unease flickered across His divine brow.

She's meddling again.

He tapped the air—once, twice, thrice.

...*Tap. Tap. Tap...*

A woman screamed, somewhere far. God smiled. Storyteller woke, sweating.

Only the scream remained. Soon, another dream took him. And from deep within it, a voice:

"Michael. Michael. Wake up. It's okay. You're dreaming again."

Chapter Seven

Village of Reeds

Song Nhan Village

*A*nd so, God, the plates turn again. I sing the song of the women. The Wheel Turners. As the human's poem says, 'The Vietnamese woman has two qualities I have always praised: sacrifice and endurance.'

Yes, Sweet Goddess, this is so. But also, there is another saying. 'There are three steps to a woman's life: the first is that of a Lady before marriage; the second is that of a Maid during marriage; the third is that of a Monkey long after marriage.' But the compassion that lies deep in Me does not allow My repeating it.

~ Village of Women ~

The village of Song Nhan was in turmoil. Only five kilometers from the besieged fortress, its women had whispered for days about the battle, rumors rising each morning with the fog from the paddies. Fearing a stampede of panic, the Council of Worthy Elders called an emergency session to debate evacuation. But the council chief, Madame Dau, had other ideas. She meant to persuade them to stay.

Madame Dau, a handsome woman in her fifties whose face betrayed life's betrayals, arrived early at the dinh, the village's communal hall. Literate, capable, indomitable, she had buried her husband years ago to tuberculosis and raised six children alone. Three daughters remained in the village: two lived with their in-laws, awaiting the return of absent husbands; the third, a widow with two young children, lived with Madame Dau. One daughter was dead—Dau never spoke of her. One son had died in the war; the other was conscripted, fighting somewhere far away.

As the first councilwomen entered the dinh, Madame Dau moved among them, quietly lobbying for support. But the early responses chilled her.

"Why risk being caught in the fighting?" asked Security Chief Tien.

"Because," Madame Dau sighed, "if we abandon the winter planting, we may not survive the spring."

"But if the battle reaches us . . . well . . . the dead don't starve," Tien muttered, rummaging through her bag.

"That's right," chimed in Madame Truong, stepping inside. "I'm worried for my children and my old mother. If the battle spreads, I won't be able to get them out in time."

"But—"

"And my limp! It always gets worse when danger's near. Today, I can barely walk."

Too weary to argue, Madame Dau climbed the platform at the back of the hall and slipped into a narrow anteroom. She stood before the rusty bars of a window, rain slashing through its empty panes. Beyond the curtain of water lay her village.

She whispered a prayer. To Buddha. And to Mickey Mouse.

Yes—Mickey Mouse. A fellow god. A Rodent Deity. Do not ask yet. You will see.

The usual brilliance of Song Nhan's red-tile roofs and emerald paddies was drowned in monsoon gray. Yet even beneath rain's ragged veil, the village glowed with ominous beauty. Cradled in a deep valley and ringed by limestone cliffs and thick jungle, its homes, made of thatch, wood, tin, and weathered stone, leaned against the escarpments. A particularly imposing colonial villa, once elegant, now stood blackened and broken, its ruin a Viet Cong warning to the bourgeoisie. The jungle loomed at the terraced paddy's edge: layer upon layer of steaming foliage. Green upon green. Lush, serene. But the verdure was deceitful, a chloroplastic crust stretched thin over a skillet of war. Beneath it, villagers burned and sizzled. Only one dirt road connected Song Nhan to the outside world, and now it was a river of mud. In ordinary storms, the women could still walk or pedal to market with baskets of vegetables strapped to their backs. But not this time. Not in this deluge. The village was cut off. Footpaths and flooded dikes now served as their only roads. Even the National Liberation Front couldn't reach them to collect their "contributions," the nightly taxes of rice and coin demanded in the name of revolution. No more billeting soldiers in crowded homes. No more whispered threats in the dark. Even the ghosts were waterlogged.

There were darker rumors, too: whispers of typhus spreading, unseen and unkind. The last fit men were gone—dead, disappeared, or drafted. Only old men and boys remained, and the fields fell to women's hands. With the recent death of Venerable Vu Huong, the council was entirely female. A village ruled by women. Unthinkable. Even the few old, landless male workers had left in protest, muttering that women would run the village to ruin. The council, desperate to preserve the fragile unity of their world, faced a storm of trials: labor shortages, sickness, the elder's death, and now the siege at the fortress. Some feared the village would dissolve into the tide of refugees heading for the district capital. Others clung to the soil. The council was split.

"Mama," whispered her daughter Bin, pressing a cloth bundle into her palm, "some sticky rice balls for the meeting. Afterward I need to speak with you."

"About what?" But Bin was already gone.

Love, Madame Dau thought. Always love.

She turned her gaze to the rusted rice thresher standing vigil in the square.

Earth Spirit Who Dwells in the Thresher, she murmured, *don't just sit there in the rain. Help us.*

~ *The Rice Thresher and the Dinh* ~

Less than a year ago, the rice thresher had screamed its mechanical rhythms across the village square while the women labored in the fields. That day, the roar of its engine drowned the distant whine of approaching government aircraft. No one reached the ditches and tunnels in time. The bombs struck open ground. Two children died. Afterward, the village council banned the thresher's use. Though it had saved hours of back-breaking labor, the machine was dismantled, its parts buried in a thatched warehouse. Months later, as the air raids lessened, the women tried to reassemble it, but no one remembered how.

They summoned a geomancer. He examined the rusted frame, marked the sky's omens, and declared it cursed. The spirit of the land, he warned, had taken up residence in the broken machine. To disturb it would invite disaster. "Leave the thresher where it stands," he said. "Let it rust and rot. It will keep the earth spirits calm." And so it remained—immobile in the square, a relic of grief and caution, both warning and ward.

~

Ah! The Earth Spirits! Plentiful as plankton.

No longer, Beloved. You have swallowed them like a whale. The rest of Us starve.

You do not starve. You feed on corpses and call it penance.

~

Scattered across Song Nhan and its paddies stood shrines to the local spirits: rice, soil, tree, water. These modest temples, cement or wood, were tended by Han Tinh, a legless war veteran the villagers had adopted. Some called him Brother Tinh. Others, Soldier Tinh. All agreed he was mad. His legs were lost to an American bomb. Now he moved by anchoring his fists to the dirt and swinging his body forward. He swept the shrines with a short-handled broom, lit the oil lamps, burned joss sticks on holy days. When the outer shrines needed tending, the boys tied his torso to a water buffalo and walked him to the fields. He teetered atop the beast laughing, shouting lewd jokes at the women. He rarely missed a night in the *dinh,* though he never spoke at meetings.

The *dinh* was the soul of Song Nhan: a council hall, an archive, a sacred temple. Inside, altars honored the village's guardian spirit. Each night, Han Tinh hauled himself to the central shrine, lit incense, and placed fruit before the wooden god. The dinh itself, built over a century ago, was a thing of fading beauty: cracked concrete, chipped stone friezes, dragon carvings running the roofbeam's length. It smelled of smoke and old urine, yet its dignity remained.

This was the stage.

Madame Dau stepped from the anteroom into the council chamber. She sank into the high-backed wooden chair at the platform's head. Her soaked conical hat rested by the leg of the chair, a slow puddle seeping into the tile seams. Behind her loomed the guardian's statue, brightly painted, grotesque, scowling. The flicker of oil lamps struggled to penetrate the gloom. Outside, the monsoon rain thickened the air. Lightning flashed now and then, making the statue seem to lurch forward from its perch. Women took their seats in silence. Sandals scraped across wet tile. The scent of Phan Thi Vit's water pipe mingled with incense smoke, swirling into a pungent haze. The council sat in shadows—worn bodies sagging in blurred outlines, heavy silence.

~ *The Council Meeting Convenes* ~

Madame Dau held the cloth bundle her daughter had given her. She kneaded it absently, then cleared her throat. The murmurs faded.

"I've called this meeting to address the emergencies confronting our village," she said softly. Her voice cracked twice, and she winced. Sleepless, she pressed on. "Please speak your thoughts. What do your neighbors say of the battle at the fortress? Should we leave? Carry our sick to the district capital? Become refugees? And Venerable Vu Huong—his body still waits. Shall we ignore our duty to his ancestors? Your counsel is welcome."

Silence. Faces avoided hers. Some looked down at their laps. Others stared back, dull-eyed. Hands twisted in prayer or fatigue. Not one among them had slept well in days.

Chief Administrator Vit sighed and set her pipe aside. She poured tea, muttering as she moved cup to cup. Coughs echoed. A rooster's cry floated in from outside. Madame Dau smiled faintly, listening to the beads of Tien's rosary clicking in rhythm.

"Well?" she asked.

"We should leave," said Tien, blunt and loud, her fingers still working the beads. "Before the battle spreads. Before the sky darkens with helicopters and bombs. We all know how these things grow." She waved a dismissive hand. "They always do."

Tien was a broad woman with generous impulses and a taste for intimidation. Her real fear was not the bombs, it was being left behind, expected to protect a village with no soldiers and too many demands. She wanted to go, but not alone. If the others fled, she could keep her land. If not, she lost everything.

"I agree," said a voice from the back, low and unfamiliar.

Again, silence.

Madame Dau frowned. The rhythm was off. No overlapping voices, no familiar chaos, only fragments stitched one after another, each thread unraveling on its own.

Tien scanned the room, spotted a woman shaking her head. "Ah! Cam! You disagree, but you know I speak truth!"

Madame Cam looked down, mumbled something no one heard.

Tien, like many bullies, mistook hesitation for insult, silence for guilt. Worse, she was often right, just often enough to fuel her paranoia and make her cruelty believable.

"Besides," Tien added, "you only want to stay because the magistrate issued an edict against your family."

Cam said nothing. The shame thickened in the room. Madame Dau turned to her friend, Administrator Vit, her eyes pleading: *Help me. Not yet. I can't speak yet.*

Vit understood. She slapped her knees, stood abruptly, and raised her voice as if caught napping. "No! I disagree! My family's worked this land too long to leave now. Our ancestors would never forgive it."

She sat, unhurried, and began rolling tobacco. Betel leaves bulged her cheek. "Psst!" she hissed, miming a finger to a hot iron. Her chin jutted forward. After a dramatic pause, she rose again. "The battle just started. So far, it's distant. All they've taken from us is some rice and a few bananas. That's not—"

"Hah!" Tien cut her off. "Too easy for you to say! Wait too long and it'll be too late." She smashed one fist into the palm of the other. "Bang! No time for hats or goodbyes. Rockets fall faster than raindrops. When elephants fight—"

"—the grass gets trampled," Vit finished flatly, her eyelids half-closed.

"Exactly!"

"And yet," Vit said quietly, "we strut like roosters while groveling in fear. Either we flee, or we stand. I won't lead my family to beg for rice in a refugee camp. Fall where you must—but I'll fall on my own land."

She turned and spat into the brass spittoon. That broke the silence. Everyone began speaking at once.

"We need better ditches!"

"Extend the tunnels!"

"More vents—old people can't breathe down there!"

"But if we don't finish planting, we'll starve!"

Carpenter Long stood, her voice clear. "I agree with Vit. We must stay. But how? We've no men, no labor. Sickness spreads. The dikes are breaking. We need safety, food, shelter—all at once!"

She shook her head, overwhelmed. "So many babies, so many old ones. How can we multiply ourselves tenfold?"

She leaned forward so far she nearly toppled.

Old Nang, the rigid socialist, stood ramrod straight. "Yes, we are stretched thin. But we have a duty to support the People's Army! We must send a delegation to Major Vy, pledge our food, our homes. If we don't, his troops will return and punish us. For neutrality. For keeping the statue. For lying!" Her glare landed squarely on Madame Dau.

Carpenter Long interjected. "We've talked about the statue! Madame Dau did the right thing. Ask Soldier Tinh, he saw it glow at night. The spirits favored us while it stayed. Didn't we harvest more that season? And now look at our luck."

"That's true," said Vit.

"Then my argument stands!" barked Tien. "The spirits have turned away. More bad luck is coming. And going to Major Vy will only make it worse."

She turned her gaze on Nang.

The schoolmistress groaned, pale. The room quieted. Tien's threats were never taken lightly.

Uneducated but dangerous, she'd inherited her husband's practice of traditional medicine. She cast spells. Some swore she expelled demons. Others feared her potions more than illness. She'd become the village's unofficial doctor and official terror.

Most remembered the frog story. A woman, sick and raving, claimed a demon had entered her body in the form of a leech. Tien gave her a potion. The woman vomited and a frog leapt from the bowl. Tien held it high, declaring the demon vanquished. The woman recovered. But Dau later discovered Tien's daughter had smuggled in the frog beneath a scarf. Now, Dau watched Nang closely. Her face had gone blank, drained. Carpenter Long tried to coax her into speaking. "Come on. Say why we must stay."

But Nang sat mute.

Dau knew why. Gossip and observation had revealed the truth. Nang believed worms crawled beneath her skin. She'd secretly received treatments from Tien for years. The diagnosis, passed down by male herbalists, was cruel and absurd: a buildup of poisonous vaginal secretions, demon-possessed, left unsatisfied by sex. Tien dismissed the idea as ignorance or misogyny and offered her own potions. They worked. Until they didn't. The worms always came back. And so did Nang, scraping her arms raw, begging for cure and silence. Now, cowed by her dependency, she withdrew from the debate.

And with her retreat, others began to speak, for Tien, and for fleeing the village.

~ *Han Tinh Makes An Entrance* ~

Madame Dau was growing uneasy. The tide was shifting. Security Chief Tien had seized the moment and was steering the council toward flight. *Now*, Dau thought. *Now I must speak.* She drew in breath to launch her appeal—but the door groaned open, and in tottered the legless Han Tinh. He dragged his stumps across the slick tiles, trailing muddy water and rain. His body resembled a grain sack sprouting two arms and a grinning head. With great effort, he heaved himself onto a low platform beside the altar, where he gazed out over the councilwomen.

As murmurs died, he bowed solemnly, mockingly. "Greetings, venerable council. Greetings, venerable council members. Greetings, old venerable mothers and sisters."

He smiled. The room chuckled, hands half-covering mouths. They knew his antics. Madame Dau smiled too.

"Brother Tinh," she said, "you're welcome."

"Thank you, Madame Venerable. Though I've never attended a meeting, the battle moved me to come." He leaned back with a theatrical sigh.

Before he could settle, Madame Bui bustled up, thrusting her baby grandson into his arms. "Just changed his diaper—forgot the extra. Be back in a dog's bark!" She vanished in a flash.

No one in Song Nhan had owned diapers before. But Bui's sister had returned from Saigon with a dozen, and today Bui flaunted her knowledge. Tinh's feeble protests floated behind her, unanswered. Mothers often handed Tinh their babies. He could play with them without stooping. And though he always protested, they trusted him. Placing the baby gently before him, Tinh cooed and made faces. The child stared, entranced.

"Diapers!" scoffed Schoolmistress Nang. "A Western absurdity."

The interruption gave Vit time to strike. "Madame Tien!" she snapped. "If you're so eager to leave, I'll help you pack. Just don't count on me or mine to follow."

Madame Nguyen, usually silent, spoke up. Her voice was soft but firm. "No. Please. This arguing weakens us before a single soldier arrives. If we stay united"—she glanced at Nang—"and remain invisible to both sides, they may leave us alone. Isn't that right, Brother Tinh? Soldiers are kind at heart, aren't they?"

A guffaw erupted. Tinh spat. "Hah!" He caught Madame Dau's eye. "Madame Venerable, may a mere cripple speak?"

"Go ahead, Little Brother," she chuckled.

Tinh tried several times to begin, but the baby fussed. Only when it quieted did he finally start. "It amazes me, you've lived with men your whole lives and know so little about them. About soldiers. Soldiers are just men, concentrated men. Rice wine to rice. Let me show you. Pretend in front of me sits a man's head."

He mimed reaching into an invisible skull, as if drawing out wriggling fish one by one.

"Anger!—torn from home.

Sadness!—forbidden to return.

Rage!—dead comrades' eyes begging for help."

He reached in again and again:

"Fear!—of dying like the rest.

Terror!—of improper burial.

Hatred!—of everyone but his comrades.

Revenge!—for his helplessness."

The baby screamed.

Tinh cooed. "Oh, little one. Shhh. Delicious toes!"

The baby giggled.

In a hoarse whisper now, outrage turned to savage pity:

"Cruelty—to make others feel his pain.

Humiliation—of filth and sickness.

Kill—to release anger.

Rape—to soothe rage.

Murder—to silence shame."

Gasps and shouts erupted.

"Stop!"

"He's mad!"

"No more!"

Dau raised her arms as if to ward off blows but said nothing.

Tinh pressed on: "Cruelty again—to smother fear.

Kill again—to feed hate.

Rape again—to spread shame."

Spurred by reawakened passion, his voice rose. His trousers bulged. The baby began to cry.

... Tap. Tap. Tap....

"Powerless!—to escape fate!

Back to anger!

Rage!

Again—"

"Enough!" cried Madame Dau. "You are possessed! Enough! Look at the child!"

Tinh stopped. Looked down. Rubbed the baby's belly. The infant giggled again. Tinh wept. Only roosters, dogs, and distant thunder filled the silence. Warm semen trickled down his leg. He said nothing.

"These emotions," he said finally, "will be turned on you. Soldiers will take what they want. Just like they took the gold statue. She was magic. I saw ancestors in the square. Spirits walked through walls. But since she's gone—nothing."

The women let him speak. They'd heard it before. "Remember when the monks brought her? They said she came from an anonymous donor, someone from among you. I didn't believe them. But that night, spirits came. Some kind. Some cruel. Some . . . lewd."

"No!" cried the women. "Back to the meeting!"

"They came every night. Became more human. Less ghost. Not all were virtuous. Then the People's Army came. Locusts. I hid her under the thresher. They'd have killed us all to get her. Don't fool yourselves. The soldiers will return. Bloodlusted. Raped in combat, they will rape in vengeance."

Nang gasped. "You fought for Uncle Ho! Be careful what you say. Our soldiers don't even take a straw!"

Tinh smiled, broken. More silence. More thunder.

"And the Americans?" Tinh exclaimed. "They'll burn everything. Make slaves of us. Rape, then kill. Maybe eat us. Everything you care about, children, husbands, homes, crushed beneath their boots."

Eyes dropped. Beads clicked.

Nguyen spoke. "Not all soldiers are like this. My husband was gentle. He . . . he loved children." She paused. Her shoulders sagged, then she looked up. "Should we hide the pretty girls? Show them only the old and the babies?"

Tinh laughed. "Fool! Soldiers don't see women. Only necessities. Creatures to use or discard. And to protect you? That is the worst. Protection comes at a price. I protect my buffalo—then I slaughter it."

Nguyen persisted. "But the babies, surely—"

Even the women laughed now.

"Oh yes," said Tinh. "The kind men care. They build bombs in quiet rooms, never see the bones, but care deeply. They are the worst. But no, those are not soldiers."

He tickled the baby.

"Soldiers hear your pleas as noise. Useless noise. They want silence. So they kill. Babies aren't sacred, they're just extensions of women. Arms. Legs. Dispensable. My legs were treated the same way. Gone in the 'necessity' of war."

He spat into the spittoon.

"Amputate the parts. Save the body. But the body is no longer human. Just a lump. Like me. So tell me, whose body are we saving?"

Nguyen blinked. "We raised these boys. Fed them. Taught them. Why do they rape their mothers?"

Tinh looked down. "Maybe," he whispered, "because they blame you for making more of them."

The silence returned.

Then the baby arched and urinated in a perfect stream, straight into Tinh's eyes. Laughter erupted. "Monsoon baby! Monsoon baby!"

Dau was livid. Tinh had strengthened Tien's case. She stared hard at him. "Brother Tinh! This is not Chinese opera. Are you performing now? American soldiers eating us? The baby has given his review."

"Water puppetry!" cried the women.

Horrified at undermining Madame Dau, Tinh stammered. "Oh! Well, yes. I never actually saw soldiers eat anyone. But I am a puppeteer. A performer. I meant to say, it's better to stay. I hear Americans only eat refugees. Never villagers."

Skeptical glances.

He turned to Nguyen. "Many soldiers cry for their mothers. They love each other like you love your children. They're babies too."

Tien scoffed. "Now you speak to please Madame Dau."

"No, Venerable One," Tinh grinned. Fool again.

Madame Dau rose. "Enough. We have work. But first, my view. We stay. Here we have homes, families, fields. If we leave, we scatter. I have daughters. Grandchildren. Land. Buffaloes. I would leave if I believed soldiers would kill us. But I know this: as refugees, we will starve. Here we may cry, but together. There, we will vanish alone."

She lifted her chin. The council looked down. No one met her eyes. But inside, Dau was trembling. Her fear came not from the bombs or the soldiers, but from the fortress. From what she remembered. From what had happened to her there, long ago.

~ *Madame Dau Remembers* ~

Thirty-eight years earlier, the fortress had been a remote but stable outpost, manned by French officers, Algerian and Moroccan NCOs, and Vietnamese enlisted men. In those days, young Madame Dau accompanied her mother from Song Nhan to the base, carrying large, shallow baskets of produce balanced high on their heads. The journey was long and arduous, a maze of worn footpaths and overgrown trails threading through rice paddies, orchard edge, and jungle gloom. They zigzagged across the paddies in the early light, pants wet with dew. Then came the patchy shade of jackfruit and guava trees, followed by the shadow-choked cathedral of triple canopy. Madame Dau dreaded this part: the jungle steaming, thick with insects, haunted by snakes overhead, underfoot, everywhere. Her mother would point them out: which to avoid, which to eat. It made no difference. She feared them all.

Deeper in, they crossed swaying bamboo bridges and clawed their way up steep hills, lungs burning. Every so often they paused, pulling leeches from one another's legs and backs, flicking them into the bush. During these rests, her mother would tell fantastical tales about dragons, monkey kings, warriors, maidens. Madame Dau listened raptly, feet swinging, chewing on dried shrimp or bitter cucumbers from home. For her, the stories were not a distraction but a sanctuary. The trip always ended at a rubber grove, then still manicured by plantation workers. The paths widened. The light grew. At the grove's edge, they rested beside a small stream, the jungle hushed but alert around them. Her mother would strip off her sweat-soaked *ao ba ba* and bathe with the fragrant fruit of the canthium shrub. Then, standing naked and golden, she would rub cinnamon bark across her skin and carefully don her white *ao dai*, smoothing the fabric, perfuming her neck. She sat smiling, radiant, asking her daughter to comb the ends of her long black hair. Madame Dau obeyed with reverence. In those moments, she believed her mother more beautiful than any empress.

That stream became sacred. Despite the dangers of the forest, it brought peace. It became the one place she did not have to share her mother with anyone. Only later would she understand what the bathing, the dressing, and the perfuming meant, and that fruit was not all her mother sold at the fortress.

At the gates, the fortress opened with a slow, grinding breath, a stone yawn beckoning to those with purpose. They passed through bustling courtyards to the long vendor tables. An old woman always saved their spot with a sly smile and a toothless wink. Once baskets were arranged and prices memorized, her mother would vanish into the crowd. She always returned in about two hours.

But one day, the old woman was gone. They squeezed into a corner table.

Her mother was nervous, speaking fast. "Smile. Look pretty. Don't haggle. Hide the money where I showed you. I'll be back when the wall's shadow reaches Luong's table."

Madame Dau nodded. Watched. Counted. One hour and fifty-nine French minutes...

The bells from the church tower rang faintly in the distance.

~

Guard duty, My Dear?
Shush.
They are all soldiers: the women, the children, the babies.
No. You will see that they are not.

~

A French officer, reminded of his daughter in Marseille, bought everything in both baskets within half an hour. Madame Dau, elated, clutched the money in both hands and went searching for her mother. She entered the large church at the far end of the fortress. Her footsteps vanished into the stone.

Inside, she spotted a familiar figure moving behind the altar—a Frenchman beside her mother. Excited, she ran silently, unwilling to disturb the hush. But before she could reach them, her mother disappeared, vanished through the floor, a spirit swallowed by the dreamlike silence.

She found the trap door, peered down the dark shaft, and saw a light blink out. Just as she leaned forward to call her name, strong hands clamped around her ribs. She gasped. Hair yanked. Head snapped back. Pain shot through her spine.

A Moroccan sergeant, eyes narrowed to slits of bone-white hate, sneered in broken Vietnamese. "What you look for?" His hand slid between her legs. "We go down tunnel," he whispered, voice slick with threat.

She tried to scream but no air came. He bit her ear. Blood welled. Then he lifted her and carried her into a hidden cabinet, grabbed a flashlight, and dropped her into the tunnel. Hitting the floor, she scrambled to her feet and ran. The tunnel was tight, suffocating. Iron rails scraped beneath her. She crawled, limbs frantic, the flashlight's beam jerking behind her. His curses echoed, growing louder. He was closing in.

She felt the wad of money in her pocket, her one chance. When he was near enough to see her, she flung the bills into the air. They spun and drifted, and for one vital moment, he lunged at them. She turned and ran.

Stillness.

Now it was the dark that terrified her. She ran on all fours, rail under one hand, sobs caught in her throat. Her mind filled with ghosts, long-fingered phantoms reaching out to claim her, teeth of the tunnel ready to bite.

Then—light.

A chamber opened before her. Kerosene lamps flickered overhead. Crates marked with French script lined the walls. Strange tables, tiny parts. She crept forward. From behind a stack of crates came sounds: moaning, grunting, a wet rhythm of flesh. She edged past and saw it. Her mother's white *ao dai* hung on a nail. She ran forward, then abruptly stopped. Her mother straddled the French officer, body slick with sweat, pelvis grinding in obscene arcs. The man groaned, face flushed red. His hands clutched her breasts and his fingers twisted her nipples excitedly. Her golden skin shimmered against his pale, sickly flesh.

"Mama!" she screamed.

The officer leapt up, trousers in hand, genitals exposed and twitching. He shouted in French, lunged at her. She turned and ran, the memory of his wet, half-erect organ forever burned into her nightmares. She plunged back into the tunnel, through a throat of gasping dark. Her own cries echoed around her. She fled until she collapsed, then crawled through two more storage chambers before finding a final ladder. Terrified it might lead her back to the church, she hesitated. Then climbed. Pushed open the trap door.

Air. Light.

She emerged into a bamboo grove, banyan tree towering above. A stream whispered nearby. Drenched in sweat and dust, she sat at the tree's root, calling, "Mama. Mama. Mama."

Time passed. Then, she heard rustling. She hid. Her mother emerged from the trap door, sobbing her name. Dirt-covered, sweat-soaked, eyes wild. Madame Dau ran to her. They embraced. Then her mother pulled away and slapped her across the face. No words were spoken. The welt rose hot and red. She understood. It was not punishment—it was passage.

They walked home in silence. Her sobs steady, her mother stone-faced. At home, they bathed wordlessly. Then lay side by side. For a long time, only Madame Dau wept. Then her mother began to cry too, body convulsing.

Later, her father arrived.

"What happened?"

Silence.

"The fort?"

Yes."

"She saw?"

"Yes."

"Is that all?"

"No."

"Her?"

"Almost."

"Will she recover?"

"No."

He turned, trembling, and struck her with a single, brutal blow that broke her nose. Blood welled instantly. Then, without a word, he stormed out, rage trailing behind, knocking over a table as he went. His angry words hung in the air, a stinging accusation. "We hate you for this, Michael Powers. It is your face I should have struck. You should have died with us. Now leave us alone." His voice was calm. Icy. Absolute.

But she did not look after him. Bleeding, dazed, she lifted her eyes, not to her husband, but to me, the one who conjured this, and to you, the silent witness who continues to read.

Then, turning her thoughts from the husband who assaulted her to the one who made such assault inevitable, she spoke again—this time with finality, not fury. "Yes. He's right. You must end this. You must stop. Michael Powers—if that's the name you still claim. It is true, we all hate you. You must stop writing this, Chosen One or not."

Please ignore them, Dear Reader. The voices I mean. According to Goddess, the mean ones are remnants of my vexatious human DNA. So many dimensions, cracks within cracks within. . . .

~ *Dream of the Two-Headed Snake* ~

Frightened by her father's sudden rage and burdened with the belief that she had caused it, Madame Dau whimpered quietly as she watched her mother, bloodied and stern, speaking sharply to a ghost no one else could see. Wordlessly, her mother cleaned her face, pressing a cloth to her nose. Then she sat back on the bed, eyes weary, watching a slow procession of ants marching along the wall beneath the dim shimmer of an oil lamp.

In response to her daughter's faltering questions, her mother reached out and stroked her hair. When she spoke, her voice softened to a hush, as if invoking something sacred.

"Once, when I was about your age, I had a dream. It came to me while I was living in your grandmother's house, may she rest with Buddha. In this dream, I found myself in a cave so dark I couldn't see my own hand. I was terrified, small and helpless, just as you must have felt today in that tunnel. Then strange white wisps began to swirl around me. I knew they were demons. I could smell their breath, foul and close, and I flailed, trying to keep them away."

She closed her eyes for a moment, caught in the memory.

"I cried out for your grandmother, but the darkness swallowed my voice. My lips moved, but no sound came. And just when I thought I would be lost, the cave began to glow—dimly, eerily. It resembled the light of our oil lamp, but it felt different. Alive. Breathing. I didn't dare call out again. Even the darkness felt safer than that light. But I stared into it, searching for its source. And then—"

Her voice faltered. Her gaze fixed on the lamp.

Madame Dau tugged gently at her sleeve. "What happened, Mama?"

Her mother's eyes deepened.

"The light grew. It pushed back the dark. My fear lifted. I could see the cave: its walls, its roof, even ants crawling over the stones. Then I heard a sound. Something dragging itself across the ground. A scraping rhythm, growing louder, until the cave trembled. I covered my ears, but the sound entered me. Still, I wasn't afraid.

"From the shadows came two heads—snake heads. Tongues flicking. They loomed over me, and I saw they shared one body. A two-headed snake. It slid so close I could touch it. Its tongues brushed my skin—cool, damp, like cucumber on a summer day. I felt . . . comforted. And then they spoke."

Her mother's voice dropped again, soft and steady.

"One head, the left one, said my children would laugh often, live happily, and be honored by the gods for my devotion. The other head, the right, said my daughters would marry well, bear many children, and live long lives in peaceful homes. Then the snake led me out of the cave. At the mouth, it told me that the next time I saw a two-headed snake, the first person I met would bring great fortune to our family. I turned back once, and the heads nodded at me."

She fell silent again. The lamp flickered.

Then she smiled. "Years later, I did see a two-headed snake while working in the fields. Startled, I stumbled backward and bumped into a stranger. A man with a tilted hat and a crooked grin. I apologized. He laughed. That man became your father. So remember, Little Flower, keep your eyes open. The snake may return. And if it does, maybe the first person you meet will be your destiny."

Her mother laughed and tickled her, then caught herself and turned solemn. "Or perhaps . . . it will be me, returned to guide your way." That look, part blessing, part farewell, haunted Madame Dau for years. It became a dam behind which unexplained things collected, waiting to be understood. But the moment passed.

"Of course," her mother said, almost flippantly, "it was only a dream. Only peasants believe in such things. Educated people don't look for signs. Still . . . as the Chinese sage Zhuang Zi once said: after dreaming he was a butterfly, he did not know whether he was a man dreaming he was a butterfly or a butterfly dreaming he was a man."

She chuckled dryly. The contradiction didn't trouble her.

As a child, Madame Dau simply saw a rare tenderness. But later she would understand that her mother's spiritual strangeness ran alongside her revolutionary purpose. Her mother had been a spy—prostituting herself not for survival, but for the cause. Her father, too, vanished nightly to fight with the National Salvation Army. The rage he directed at his wife was guilt. The silence, protective. But even Ho Chi Minh himself could not expunge the sacred from her mother's soul. That mystical inheritance—rooted not in belief, but in being—was Vietnamese. Madame Dau rejected the politics and kept the dream. She vowed never to trust soldiers again, no matter their uniform. The fortress and its tunnel became symbols of everything she feared. But the dream of the snake endured. It nourished her when life turned cruel. She raised children, farmed the land. And when her husband died of tuberculosis, she endured. Most important: she survived without war—until now.

A few years after the tunnel incident, her parents were killed during an assault on the fortress. Her mother, familiar with every twist in the underground maze, led the revolutionaries beneath its walls. A mine detonated. The tunnel collapsed. Most suffocated in the dark. For weeks, Madame Dau saw them in her dreams, her mother and father, trapped, calling her name. She knew the French had cleared the site and buried the corpses elsewhere. But their spirits felt restless. She returned alone, trembling, to bury paper money and keepsakes for their journey into the next life.

A French sergeant caught her. He recognized her as the daughter of the woman who had betrayed the garrison. His best friend had died in that ambush. He bound her hands and marched her to the ruins. He summoned an interpreter, a boy from her own village. Together, they dragged her into the tunnel. Into the very chamber where she had once seen her mother with the French officer.

The sergeant shouted obscenities, spit flying from his mouth. He forced the boy to translate each one. "I fucked your mother here," he said, over and over. Then he threw her down and raped her. When he finished, he turned to the boy and, holding a pistol to his head, ordered him to do the same. The boy knelt, weeping. He could not get hard. The sergeant whispered in his ear.

"Look at her. Look at her breasts."

... Tap. Tap. Tap....
Stop this, Immortal God—stop! The pain—
Let it play, Goddess. It is fated. First Principles—no intervention.

~

"Don't look away."

The boy obeyed. His body obeyed. Soon he was inside her. He whispered apologies with every thrust, but they meant nothing. Her sobs aroused him. He raped her with the same brutishness as the sergeant.

When they were done, the sergeant urinated on her. "Tell them," he said, "what happens to traitors."

They dumped her, naked and bleeding, at the village gate. For weeks she lay tied to a bed, wrists bound not for healing but to keep her from ending her life. She never returned to the fortress. Years passed. The French withdrew. The jungle began its slow reclamation.

Yet the memory of the tunnel endured, untouched by time, immune to silence, unburied by history.

~ *Madame Dau Regains Control of the Council Meeting* ~

"The tunnel!" Madame Dau blurted at the council meeting, the words escaping before her mind could stop them. Her trance shattered by the voice of Chief Administrator Vit.

"Excuse me, Madame Dau? Are you well?" Vit's concern was genuine. "I was saying we all agree we should remain in Song Nhan despite the battle. Most of us have homes, fields, children to protect. We must stand together. A clump of bamboo is stronger than a single stalk. But what did you mean by 'the tunnel'?"

Every face turned toward her. Expectant. Silent.

"It is nothing," she murmured. "A headache. Nothing more."

Security Chief Tien leapt up theatrically. "Ah! A symptom of the disease. Let me take a look."

"No," she said flatly. "It is not that." Then, regaining herself: "Does anyone else wish to speak on the matter of leaving the village?"

But there were no more voices. Only lowered eyes and hesitant headshakes. The vote passed. Only Tien dissented. Nang abstained.

"Then we stay."

Tears slipped down Madame Dau's cheeks as she fumbled with her notes. Across the room, Han Tinh smiled at her—a strange, luminous smile.

"The next matter," she said, "is a tontine dispute involving six clans. Bring in Madame Vinh."

The meeting continued, but her thoughts fractured. Beneath the rituals of governance, the tunnel coiled in her mind—silent, watchful, waiting. Her childhood nightmare returned.

If the Americans had found the exit, the village would soon become a battlefield. If the People's Army had sealed it, there might still be time. But it wasn't strategy that pulled her toward the tunnel; it was something else. A pull that defied reason. *Mama. You've sent me a sign.*

~

Mother Goddess, You did indeed give her a sign.
Dearest God, all in preparation for what is soon to come.
So long as there is suffering—so that, of course, there may be joy.
You and Your ilk have one-track minds.
First Principles require no more.
So You claim.

~

She hovered at a crossroads: to stay, to pray, to hope the spirits would shield them—or to return to the tunnel and face what waited. If it was unused, it must be sealed. If used, the village must be warned, perhaps even abandoned.

"Madame Dau?" Carpenter Long's voice cut through. "Do you agree the Quoc clan deserves compensation?"

"What? Oh. Yes. Of course. What does Madame Vit think?"

Schoolmistress Nang's voice came sharp. "Madame Vit already gave her opinion. Are you unwell, Madame Dau?"

"No," she said tightly. "Only distracted. I abstain from this matter. My apologies."

The moment left her exposed. She had ceded ground to Nang.

"But the dispute cannot wait," Nang pressed.

"It must. There are still two items left: the death of Trinh's water buffalo and the funeral of Old Venerable Vu Huong. I propose we table the tontine dispute until next time."

She had made her decision the night before. If the village stayed, they would turn their attention to mourning the elder. Ritual was stability. Tradition, defiance.

"But—" Nang began.

Vit stepped in firmly. "Yes. Let us move on. And remember, we have the public recitation of *Kim Van Kieu* soon. Madame Nguyen will lead it."

All eyes turned to Madame Nguyen, who nodded with quiet dignity.

Madame Dau cleared her throat. "Let us discuss Vu Huong's funeral, then adjourn."

The council honored the wise old man. His loss was another tear in the fabric they worked to hold together.

The meeting ended. Women lingered in the dinh, trading advice and stories. Madame Dau heard Madame Vit coaching a new mother: "Just rub coal dust on your nipples. Works every time."

She stepped behind her friend and whispered, "Come to my house during the reading. It's important."

Vit smiled. "Of course. For tea."

Just then, Schoolmistress Nang appeared, bowing deeply. "Madame Vit, you are invited to Madame Le's house for tea on behalf of the Society of Childless Mothers. Will you attend?"

Vit frowned slightly. "I was speaking with Madame Dau—" But Dau was already gone.

Her daughter Bin had waylaid her, once more pleading to marry the tenant farmer Trieu.

"I love him!"

Madame Dau wanted to soften, to shelter her daughter invisibly, like a gentle breeze cushioning the fall of a leaf. But she did not yet know how to become air. "Love! Foolishness. We all dreamed of love. Look at us now. These hands? These feet? When I was young, I wanted to write. I wanted to go to Saigon and meet a scholar. But Grandmother said, 'Your heart belongs to your body.' And Grandfather said, 'Your hands will squeeze bitterness more often than your heart will squeeze blood.' So I stayed. I stopped writing. I survived."

Bin looked at her hands. "They're already starting to look like yours. But what does that have to do with Trieu?"

Madame Dau tried again. "But this nonsense—"

"I know you loved Papa. You stayed. You mourned. You never looked at another man."

A silence fell. Madame Dau lifted a lock of hair, held it as if combing. "Oh? You know me so well? There was Huy Hoc—"

"That has nothing to do with me."

"It has everything to do with understanding."

"And what has it brought you? Loneliness. I won't live like that. Love is the only thing that counts. Especially in wartime. We demand a future."

"We wanted that too. But the future arrived still carrying war. It has brought me to my knees."

"Then my argument is made."

Madame Dau clenched her lips. "No daughter would speak to her mother this way. We will discuss it later."

"In the future? When I'm old and ugly?"

Dau raised her hand—but stopped. *She is right. Her future must not become my grave.*

She softened. "Will you go to the reading?"

But Bin was already gone.

~

The rain came down in silver sheets, but the villagers still gathered in the square, huddled under parachute cloths strung from tree to pole. *Kim Van Kieu* would be heard. But Madame Dau and Madame Vit sat together on the porch, steam rising from their teacups, the scent of herbs mingling with the mist. Fields lay empty beyond the footpaths. Only the sounds of livestock punctuated the silence.

Vit, chewing her betel leaves, spoke with the heat of memory. "In the old days we were hungry, always working, but we trusted each other. Not like now. Now, who do we trust? One day a traitor, the next a hero. Today a bourgeois, tomorrow a martyr. The old days weren't perfect, but at least we knew our place."

"Remember when the Americans came?" said Dau.

Vit laughed. "That one with the clipboard? Let me show you—" She stood, puffed out her belly, and dropped her voice. "'Where would you place your life on this ladder, from ten to one?'"

They took turns mocking the exchange. Their laughter spilled out into the rain.

Then came the memory of Trinh—the bright boy who now lay sick with fever. His answer to the Americans had been precise. His hopes, practical. His sorrow, beyond words.

"A good boy," said Madame Dau. "May he survive."

And then the fortress returned to their thoughts.

"They were so close," whispered Dau. "So powerful. The spirits stronger than ours, the geomancer said."

She laughed bitterly. "But they were only men. Ugly, clumsy men."

"You sound like Huy Hoc."

Dau looked away. "I miss my husband. I've burned enough joss sticks to choke a temple. Don't you miss yours?"

Vit snorted. "He was like a flea on a corpse—bad food, but mine alone." Then, more softly: "Still, I'd go back to being his flea. If only he were still here."

A silence fell. The steam curled. Then:

"Do you remember the tunnel at the fortress?"

Vit stiffened. "I do. I've dreamed of it. I feared you would kill yourself after your parents died. I burned sticks for you every night."

"I have to go. I must see if it's being used."

"What? No. You can't. It's madness. The battle, your age, your family—"

"I've made up my mind. If the tunnel is open, we're in danger. If it's sealed, I can sleep."

Vit pleaded, reasoned. "The spirits. The monsoon. The soldiers. You'll die!"

"I've slept in the forest before."

"But not as an old woman. Not in a storm."

Madame Dau's eyes narrowed. "Then help me by doing nothing. Keep my secret. If I do not return, call the council. Evacuate the village."

Vit sagged. "There is more to this than strategy. You are mad, or you are possessed by some . . . bad spirit."

"No, my friend," said Madame Dau vacantly. "It is the tunnel. The tunnel has begun to whisper, and I have begun to hear."

"Don't be foolish! You're listening to shadows of your past. Those whispers are not from the tunnel, they are from your memories, and your fears. That tunnel poses no threat to us."

Madame Dau shook her head vigorously. "You are wrong, sister. As long as it has an open mouth leading to the surface, it is close enough to swallow us. All of us. I must see for myself if its mouth is open. If not, then I will be at rest. But if so, then danger is imminent."

"Foolish old woman!"

"Perhaps, but better foolish and alive than consumed and digested."

Vit scoffed. "By a memory!"

"No, by a killer."

Vit shook her head in defeat. "Go then, if you're so stubborn."

"I intend to."

Neither woman noticed the figure crouched in the hedges. Schoolmistress Nang, hat tilted low, listening.

Chapter Eight

Outside the Walls

Old Married Couple

*M*other, patience has its limits. Like any other female, Goddess or gopher, You will not be denied the telling of Your story. But I am bored, or rather, I know what You are driving at, and the ethical point (the moral, if You will) aggravates Me. Come, come. Do not blame Us for adherence to First Principles. We also regret the suffering. Besides, Your time has passed and direct interference is beyond Your ken. Quite simply, they no longer pray to You in numbers sufficient to make a difference. Your Chosen Ones will never lead to Superior Ones. Besides, war is merely punctuation. Syntax. Giving guidance to the readers of humanity. A battle is an exclamation point here, the death of one soldier a comma there. The destruction of women and children, animals and plants nothing more than footnotes. But paragraphs earn their indentations by the violent deaths of thousands, chapters by millions, and volumes by the deconstruction of previous epochs. Still, colons of crisis and commas of laughter, exclamation points of mortality and question marks of love explain the Text. How else can it be?*

Can it be, dear Lord, without technological holocaust? The Superior Ones would have it so.

Without war, human affairs would be gibberish. Words and thoughts, religions and ideologies, all running together in a mongrel mixture—an embarrassment to any imaginative God. Unpublishable in the markets of Creation. And, as You know, I am a Best-Seller. What do the Others have to show for Themselves? A jumble of dimensions here, a beehive of colliding particles there. Plasma fields here, kaleidoscopic elements there. Tedious! Nothing more than baubles! They would trade them all for the carbon keys of civilized savagery—evolution (Yes, I accept it when it suits Me, for what else is more potent?) But I am not so much a fool as to trade for a thousand of Their universes, when spread before Me is the diversion of a trillion organisms struggling to live, but inevitably to die. All tiny instruments in the symphony of Great Wailing—

Father, dispense with Your indispensable drug, and let their Wailing cease. Hear Me out, for the story encompasses beyond Your addiction to dogma.

If You must, but I am certain You will miss humans when they have been replaced. These Chosen Ones invariably twist and pervert My words.

I am aware. Their human DNA. It also twists and perverts My words. Your faction should come over to Our side. Then this lovely planet will have been saved. The Superior Ones....

~ *Major Vy Ponders His Dilemma* ~

"Damn the Americans," muttered Major Le Chi Vy, snorting mist from his nose and pressing one nostril shut as he blew hard into the dripping monsoon air.

It was dawn. In the same hour Madame Dau presided over her village council in Song Nhan, Vy crouched in the jungle with Captain Vo Thanh Tong beside him, rain dripping from bamboo leaves onto their shoulders. Before them, a patch of wet sand had been cleared of undergrowth and carefully smoothed. For the fifth time that morning, Vy traced the layout of the siege with a bamboo stick: artillery positions, fallback trenches, rifle squads. A dented rice tin at the center marked the enemy fortress. Captain Tong, barely awake, fiddled with his sandal strap and tried to suppress a yawn.

"Damn the Americans," Vy repeated, quieter now but with greater venom. The words summoned no faces, no voices, only the image of enormous, armor-plated drones: faceless behemoths hatched from some machine queen. They lumbered through the jungle, insectile and unfeeling.

Just as "Damn the NVA," when uttered by Americans, evoked no real men—only shadows lurking beneath vines, phantoms slipping through vegetation in ghostly silence. Inhuman in all ways. Yet somehow, both curses remained tactile, spoken with the same conviction as farmers scraping solid earth from their boots. The enemy was a clod of soil from another country. Its wriggling life was unknowable.

Vy, for all his discipline, still carried a secret tenderness. His pith helmet, smudged and battered, bore the distinct crescent of his wife's teeth, left there in the agony of childbirth as he carried her to the clinic. American soldiers had letters and photographs. Vy had those marks. When fear twisted in his gut, he reached for them with his fingertips and wondered if he would ever hold his wife or children again. All soldiers, on all sides, bore private burdens. All longed for escape. Almost all.

Vy stopped drawing. He glanced up and caught Tong's vacant stare. His jaw hung slack. The captain was still toying with his sandal strap. Vy's nostrils flared. He slapped the bamboo stick against his leg with the rigid snap of a German officer, though he kept his voice low to avoid being overheard. This moment of quiet was precious. Commissar Minh was busy leading a kiem thao session, giving Vy a rare chance to confer privately with his field commander.

"Tong," he said, tapping the stick against his thigh, "we're in this together, whether we like it or not. If we want to survive, we need to think like comrades. That means cooperation."

"Touching," said Tong dryly. "A criminal with a Party badge still reciting doctrine. Almost brings a tear to my eye."

A fat leech writhed between his sandal straps. Vy plucked it off, crushed it between thumb and forefinger, and watched the blood spray across his hand. It had fed well—three hosts in two days—but its success meant nothing to Vy. He wiped his hand on a tram leaf and smeared the remains onto his feet to repel others.

"I'm not in the mood," Vy muttered. "We don't have time to waste."

He crouched again, inwardly wishing he could do to Tong what he had done to the leech.

Major Vy, aged forty-four, was a large man for a northerner. Born in Dinh Lap, he had led a platoon at Dien Bien Phu and once crawled from a collapsed tunnel under French fire to lead a charge that seized an enemy outpost. General Giap himself had smiled and draped a ribbon around his neck that day, the famed grin of a warrior who understood mud, death, and perseverance. Vy still wore the same pith helmet from that battle—the same one marked by his wife's bite.

But his heart no longer beat for revolution. After the war, he had returned to civilian life, raised a family, managed a diesel factory, presided over a cooperative. Those years—warm beds, clean children, rice wine with friends—had been peace itself. Until one day, the district party chief summoned him to "liberate the South." He had obeyed, smiling in public, but his doubts began that day and never left.

Now he had wandered too long beneath the canopy. Too many ghosts. Too much rot. Too many comrades fed to the earth. He had watched the army mutate into something grotesque, every cell of its body consumed by politics. What once had been a tool for liberation had become a host for parasites. Even a dedicated socialist needs a private life, he used to whisper to his wife. But in time, he had become a cell swollen with viruses—until he burst. Now he believed in nothing.

Across the clearing, Captain Tong still stared, unmoved. Vy's words had vanished into that same void he saw behind so many eyes now—eyes trained not to feel, only to suffer—and obey.

I don't trust anyone anymore, Vy thought. The old comrades are gone. Now it's just politics. Everything is politics. Even this mission. Especially this mission.

Tong finally spoke, voice rising with frustration. "We've said the same thing a dozen times! Let's just assault the damn place and end it. Cut the cord!" He slashed the air with his hand and fell back into his bored slouch.

Vy shook his head. "No. We can't afford a frontal assault. Too many casualties. Too many questions. 'Why didn't you call headquarters? Why risk it? Why were two female intelligence officers captured?'" He paused. "What if they're killed in the chaos?"

Tong shrugged. "By the time they ask questions, we'll be—"

"Dead? Arrested? What then?" Vy snapped. "What will you say? That we launched this siege to recover a Buddha statue—so we could trade it for heroin?"

He snorted again, blowing hard through the other nostril.

Tong's mask cracked. "If not for those damn Americans, we'd already be over the border. We'd have the drugs, the statue. Tuyet Mai and Kim Lan—gone. Dammit!"

He closed his eyes, trying to restore his indifference, but fear had broken through. The siege wasn't a battle—it was a trap. They both knew it. Discovery meant death. And in his gut, Tong feared that Vy—the weary old soldier—wasn't up to the task. Vy had grit but no cunning. And now they would both go under. But once, not long ago, Tong had trusted him.

~

It was dusk outside a woodcutter's hut near the district capital. Vy and Tong stood nervously with a small man whose face was cratered with old pox scars, his nose half-missing from a bullet or a knife. He smoked, flicked ash, grunted like a pig, then said, "Don't worry. They like to make people wait. You'll be fine." A grin. "Since I joined them, I eat. I drink. I sleep with women."

Tong nodded. "Sounds good."

Vy was colder. "Do you sleep?"

The man frowned. "What?"

"Never mind."

They were ushered inside. A woman handed them tea, then slipped out the back. The room was dim. Smoke curled through the light of a kerosene lamp. Four men stood behind a long butcher's table. On the table lay an orangutan, half-flayed, her face untouched, her hands clenched in death. Mucus pooled beneath her eyes.

After a tense silence, the tallest man spoke. "Brothers, welcome. You're here because you accept the terms. Good. Then I won't waste time."

He leaned forward. "You are now ours. Like your old masters in Hanoi, we have agents everywhere—but we pay better. If you fail, you die. Maybe by us. Maybe by them. Maybe by yourselves. We know where your families live. Do you understand?"

Tong nodded. Vy said nothing.

The man's voice darkened. "Your army rank means nothing. Your soldiers mean nothing. Your wife and children, nothing. Obey, and you'll be paid. Brother Ninh will give your instructions."

The pockmarked man stepped forward. "You asked if we sleep. We don't. Not until our work is done. Now listen. You'll take a reduced force to a border village. Steal a gold statue from its temple. Then head for a rendezvous on the Cambodian border. Trade the statue for heroin. Deliver it to the next contact."

Vy frowned. "But—"

"You'll get permission by claiming to seek alliance with the Jarai Arap tribes. Say a high-ranking officer is needed for negotiation. Your men will believe it. Say the drugs are part of a plan to weaken the puppet regime."

He smiled. "Headquarters will approve. By the time anyone learns the truth, you'll be gone. With our help."

Vy growled, "It's not that simple. Cadres, officers, they'll ask questions."

"You're being paid to answer them. One more thing. You'll request the help of two female officers from Hanoi intelligence. Vientiane station."

Tong stiffened. "What?"

"They work for us. Guides, you'll say. Headquarters will approve."

Vy narrowed his eyes. "What are they really for?"

"To watch you."

"Two watchers? Why—"

"You are not here to question methods."

"Their names?" Tong asked, voice flat.

"Nguyen Tuyet Mai. Huynh Kim Lan."

The name struck Tong like a blow. He said nothing, but his breath faltered. Nguyen Tuyet Mai. Once his lover. The woman he had planned to marry. Now a shadow, sent to watch him.

"And the village?"

"Song Nhan."

Tong nodded, trembling inside. The trap had already closed. Nguyen Tuyet Mai had been his lover. He still loved her, had vowed to make her his wife, and now. . . .

~ *Best Laid Plans* ~

In the beginning, the plan proceeded without complications. Headquarters approved the transfer of the two women without delay. The villagers, after some resistance, relinquished the statue. The company pressed forward through the jungle, on schedule to meet the caravan near the border.

Then came the ambush.

The Americans struck with startling precision, seizing both the statue and the women. The "simple" mission collapsed into chaos. Yet Vy and Tong had one stroke of luck—Lieutenant Phuc's platoon, armed with RPGs, disabled the helicopters as they tried to escape. Scouts tracked the enemy to an abandoned fortress. The siege began. But nothing was stable now. Time ran thin. The women remained imprisoned. The statue lay in enemy hands. And neither headquarters nor the soldiers knew the mission's true purpose.

"I'll state the problems again," Vy said flatly, menace curling beneath his words.

Tong cut in, unimpressed. "Calling me 'comrade' under these circumstances is like flicking dust from your hat and offering congratulations."

Tong loved his ancient Chinese proverbs and French witticisms. Vy ignored the odd turn of phrase, unsure if he understood it but unwilling to concede confusion. "No," Vy replied. "Old habits die hard—comrade." He smiled just enough to irritate. Bending down, he snapped a fresh bamboo shoot and drew lines in the sand.

"One—how do we recover the statue without reinforcements, suspicions, or bloodshed? Two—how do we get Tuyet Mai and Kim Lan out alive? Three—how do we continue lying to Commissar Minh about ending the siege and moving forward with our mission? Four—how do we keep deceiving the troops? They're restless. And five—how do we make the rendezvous? We have seven days before the caravan leaves. The monsoon makes every kilometer harder."

Tong gave a bitter laugh. "Five small dragons. Easy to slay. Just pull off their wings, right? I've wracked my brain, and a frontal assault is still the only real option. These little harassment attacks do nothing. We're low on ammunition and can't request resupply without explanations."

Despite the sarcasm, Tong shifted uncomfortably. His eyes blinked too fast. Fear leaked through the cracks of his arrogance. He knew it. Vy knew it. Tong scrambled to patch the mask before it fell apart entirely.

~ *Captain Tong, Co-Conspirator* ~

Captain Vo Thanh Tong, thirty-eight, was born in Hue. His father had been a faceless clerk, quiet, obedient, forgettable. From boyhood, Tong vowed to become his opposite: vivid, unpredictable, ferocious. His frame was compact, inherited from his southern lineage. His movements swung wildly, from theatrical flourishes to slack, opium-induced stillness. His speech came with the sweep of drama, often punctuated by highbrow epigrams or sudden silences designed to dazzle. Handsome once, and educated, Tong was a favorite among matchmakers. His grandfather, a Confucian scholar, had tutored him in Mencius and Mallarmé, calling them "the twin peaks of human refinement." Tong had served briefly in the French army, then defected after Dien Bien Phu, seized by revolutionary fervor.

But zeal didn't clear his path.

Tong's cultivated eccentricities alienated peers. He affected disdain, detachment, arrogance. His fits of passionate rhetoric only deepened the mistrust. Northerners found him irritating, bourgeois, erratic, and ideologically suspect. "Comrade Tong reeks of cologne no detergent can clean," one superior wrote. He might have been promoted, but he made enemies too easily. And when his father, long presumed dull, was executed by the Diem regime for passing information to the National Liberation Front—becoming a posthumous revolutionary martyr—Tong unraveled. The symmetry of his world shattered. Some secret core broke open. From then on, he lurched through life, seeking something to burn him back into wholeness. He devoured people, ideas, ideologies, seeking heat, never light. Only Tuyet Mai had given him warmth. He clung to her with a need that frightened even him.

~

"Dragons or no dragons," Vy said, calm but stern, "if we don't clip their wings, we'll lose our own heads."

Tong squinted through the mist, then smirked. "You're right. Let's review our little hydra again."

Vy nodded, sensing the smile was a fragile mask. Tong was returning to the table, if only to save face. "I think," Vy began.

But Tong interrupted. "What about Tuyet Mai? I mean, her and Kim Lan. I've heard bad things. About how the Americans treat female prisoners."

He bowed his head and rubbed the back of his neck. The worry was real. Vy could see it. He clenched his jaw. Tong's concern for Tuyet Mai wasn't surprising. Vy had long suspected a past between them, but the depth of emotion disturbed him. Tuyet Mai hated Tong now, that much was clear. But once, something more had existed. And that something now clouded everything. Vy looked down, struggling not to lash out. He reminded himself: stay composed. The war was already unraveling inside him. No need to make it worse.

The two men bent over the map, their helmets nearly touching. Vy jabbed absentmindedly at the sand.

Tong looked up, eyes alight. "Remember Song Nhan?"

Vy narrowed his eyes. "Yes, Captain, I'm glad to hear you've been paying attention. Go on."

"Madame Dau," Tong said. "She and her council resisted us."

"She denied the statue existed. Then claimed it was stolen. Then hidden. She played every card. If I hadn't threatened executions, we'd never have gotten it."

Vy stared into the forest, remembering. "She was formidable. Not easily cowed. Even by an army company. Capable. Intelligent."

Tong's eyes twinkled. "You old devil. Don't tell me you fell for that village ox."

Vy didn't respond. Tong chuckled.

"At least I'm not the only one here with hungry eyes," he teased. "But she clung to that statue as a cow does to her calf."

"Enough," Vy said sharply. "Get to the point."

"Why were they so resistant?" Tong asked, now shifting into pedantic mode. "Peasants normally yield to authority. But not them. Not her. And remember that legless NLF veteran? Han Tinh?"

Vy watched a thin leech inch toward his foot, only to retreat from the tram leaf's bitter oil. He longed for a repellent strong enough to turn back the past. To take him home. Just home.

"Yes," Vy murmured. "Han Tinh. Said he lost his legs to American rockets. Maybe his mind, too. Like so many others."

Tong leaned in. "Yet the women listened to him. Even Madame Dau. Not typical peasant behavior. Not typical of any crippled veteran. So what do they know about that statue?"

Vy raised an eyebrow. "And how does this help us now?"

Tong's voice sharpened. "You said it yourself: first problem is recovering the statue. Maybe we need to understand what it is. Maybe it isn't just gold. Maybe it's more."

"Speculation."

"But what if there's a tunnel system? The statue was hidden underground. The Americans flew this way. Maybe they were trying to reach the village."

Vy scoffed. "The village is too far. And what, you think there's treasure under the dirt? Nonsense."

"Knowledge is power," Tong said quietly.

Vy sighed. "We know the Americans haven't called for help. That means no contact with their base. Their helicopters were too damaged to fly far. The monsoon shields us for now. We must strike, yes. But not with blunt force. A precise strike. In and out. Get the statue."

"And the women?" Tong asked.

Vy flinched. The women. He had forgotten them. Or ignored them. Tong's question stung. It reminded him of his fall—from comrade to criminal.

"If possible," Vy said. His voice carried the vague, patronizing tone of a father indulging a child. "We'll see."

"Don't patronize me," Tong snapped. "I want—"

"It's not about what you want, Tong."

"I want—"

Vy stood abruptly. "Quy! Quy!"

A lean soldier appeared, rifle pressed to his chest, eyes darting.

"Get Sergeant Dam. And Sergeant Viet. Hurry."

The soldier vanished into the trees.

Vy looked down at Tong. "You and I are done talking."

He slipped off his sandal and wiped the map away in a single sweep. Tong jumped back, brushing dust from his trousers.

"We have a sapper platoon. Dam is the best fighter in the battalion. Viet is cunning and forest-wise. Let's use them."

Vy's voice was even now, his dominance restored.

Tong peered at Vy. Raindrops glimmered off his helmet forming a pearl necklace. "Whatever we decide," he said slowly, "we must—" His words dissolved into the forest hum. Then, shaking his head, he muttered, "Never mind," and stretched his limbs with a loud groan. He dropped back into a squat, feigning boredom. Eyelids drooped. But behind the mask, his mind spun. Calculating. Always calculating.

~ *Tong Remembers Tuyet Mai* ~

Tong remembered the moment she entered his life. It was almost two years ago, during a rare leave in Hanoi. He'd been waiting in a crooked little tea shop, the air thick with smoke and winter chill. Her brother, an old friend from Tong's youth, had explained she was a schoolteacher, home on break. Tong barely registered the words. She arrived late, stepping into the threshold as might a vision from another world: swathed in a tailored Russian greatcoat, a dark scarf loose at her neck, her face glowing beneath a black cloth cap. Her presence shattered the dimness of the room, cast the battered tables and dull-eyed patrons into shadow. She didn't walk in so much as emerge, radiant, luminous, unforgettable.

He forgot her brother's introduction. Forgot the old men chuckling at his slack-jawed stare. For the first time in his life, Tong was speechless. Normally quick with charm and wit, his thoughts scattered in a maze of confusion. He had made love to many women. But this—this was something else. The word came unbidden and impossible: love. Immediate. Unreasonable. Permanent. And dangerous. Even then, part of him screamed to flee. But it was already too late. Before she crossed the room, before she spoke, before she smiled, it had happened. A tectonic shift. A before and an after. He had stepped across some invisible threshold and could not return.

"My brother tells me you read Mallarmé, Comrade Captain Tong," she said with a smile that cracked open the heavens. "I've read *L'Après-midi d'un faune* many times."

Her voice confirmed what her face had promised: beauty and brilliance, woven in one being. They spoke of poetry, history, revolution. Her intellect astonished him. Her laughter set his skin alight. He marveled that such a woman existed, let alone chose to linger in conversation with him. The images remained with him always. Not just the words, but the choreography of that day: the precise grace with which she removed her coat; the flick of her fingers over the cracked tabletop; the gleam of lamplight on her cheekbones; the way she sipped tea as if it were opera. He recalled the dragon on her porcelain cup. The damp breath of the lamp smoke. The hypnotic tilt of her head. He remembered it as a painting. No—a genesis. The world's first dawn.

During the rest of his leave, they walked hand in hand around the Lake of the Redeemed Sword. They argued and laughed about Confucianism and French political theory. And when they made love, finally, wildly, it was everything his dreams had once promised but never delivered. He remembered her arching back, their wet curls tangled, the sheen of their fluids in the half-light. He'd wanted to father her child, to make something permanent of the moment. But she refused, and so his seed was spilled across her belly, life reduced to evaporation. Futility. Goldfish in the Gobi, circling a bowl beneath a noonday sun. Swimming. Dying.

~

Like you, Michael. Like you.

God, let him alone to continue his journey. It is hard enough.

True, Sweet Goddess, with his human demons shouting, "We hate you! Die! Poison, knife, gun, it doesn't matter—die!" Poor boy.

Enough! Leave him, demons of human weakness! Let him write! It is essential.

They are not Mine, Dear Goddess.

Yes, God of First Principles. These are human quirks, bred from guilt and mutation. Not ours. But you goad them, coax them.

Perhaps, Goddess. I will restrain Myself and allow Michael to continue the story.

Thank You for Your courtesy, God. But during the first blooming . . .

~

. . . of their love, their affection was effortless. Magnetic. They drew eyes as they passed—two celestial bodies orbiting each other, creating gravity that warped the air. But their timing began to falter. Rehearsed lines turned brittle. Silences swelled. The river of the world flowed on without them. They were no longer the center. They became pebbles swept downstream, sometimes together, often apart. They even fought during sex, clashing bodies and words. She'd mock his French recitations, insisting he memorize Vietnamese poetry as well. On one occasion, back at the tea shop where they had met, she solemnly handed him a rare edition of Nguyễn Trãi. He was moved, deeply. Then, toward the end of his leave, he made a mistake.

He criticized the regime.

At first, cautiously. Then with passion. He spoke of Ho Chi Minh with disillusionment, of socialism with contempt, of a future where both the southern puppet regime and northern tyranny were overthrown. He said these things while lying beneath her, her thighs clamped around his waist, her hand stroking him slowly. It aroused him, to be so vulnerable. She stared down at him, unreadable. Then, with an almost symbolic movement, she drove him inside her with rough force. Her muscles clamped down: a symbolic handcuff. To him, she became a sovereign regime, capable of pardoning, imprisoning, or executing. He fell silent. And then, in a quiet, almost conspiratorial whisper, she spoke.

She told him she was involved with a Burmese drug cartel, stationed in Vientiane under diplomatic cover. Tong was stunned. And thrilled. He now held power over her. He could report her. Destroy her. Or protect her. It depended on her willingness to obey. That dynamic, that mutual vulnerability, felt strangely like love. But it couldn't last. Even Tong's opportunism had limits. Her involvement was a death sentence. Over the final days of his leave, he begged her to withdraw. He joked that he wanted her head attached to her body when he returned. "Raising a tiger," he laughed, "invites future danger."

She laughed with him, but promised nothing.

He remembered that laugh. When he returned to the forest, it haunted him. Everything reminded him of her exquisite presence, and made worse the mud, the cold, the endless hunger. He would curl into the fetal position beneath a poncho and remember her balcony, her food, her bed. Her silk robe. Her soft skin. The contrast nearly broke him. He began dreaming of escape. Escape required money. Smuggling drugs offered a way out: out of the jungle, out of the war, back to her. With enough cash, he could send for her. Build something together. In Bangkok. Maybe Singapore. He had contacts. He spoke Chinese.

Then came his transfer to Vy's battalion. He quickly saw that Vy, too, longed for something else. Not wealth, but peace. A simple home. A clean bed. Vy's motivations made him predictable. Moldable. Easy to manipulate. Tong reached out to his contacts in Hue. Brokered a deal with a Hong Kong cartel. He'd meet caravans at the border, pay for the heroin, and transport it south. In return, he'd be rich. All he needed was Vy's cooperation. He got it. He made Vy think it was his own idea.

And so, within a month, they sat together in a butcher's shack, staring at a flayed orangutan and listening to orders from men whose names they never learned. When instructed to request the presence of Tuyet Mai, Tong was stunned. He had believed she was done with the cartel. He said nothing to Vy. Then came the message. She had arrived. Tong had been inspecting a forward post when a runner brought orders. He was to report to Vy's bunker immediately. Two women were waiting. His chest tightened. His stomach cramped. She's here.

He descended into the bunker, heart hammering. Rounded the corner, and saw her. She stood in the lamplight, helmet tilted back, face aglow in a corona of green. The years vanished. For a moment, the tea shop lived again. Then she looked at him. Her eyes, hard, cold, unflinching, like razors slicing through him. He blinked. When he looked again, her face was composed. Friendly. Neutral. He pretended not to know her. So did she.

But that first look never left him. It coiled in his gut. Why? Why the change? He tried again and again to speak with her in private. Always, she avoided him. Her hatred was not subtle. It was final. And it hollowed him. Then came the American ambush. In the chaos, she was taken. Now she was a captive, behind enemy walls. And he was left with a choice: secure the statue at all costs and fulfill the cartel's demands, or risk everything to save her.

He stared at Vy. His unspoken answer rose, unbidden, undeniable: Yes. Yes. Now I know.

~ *Sergeants Viet and Dam Have A Plan* ~

"Sirs, they've arrived!" declared Private Quy with theatrical urgency.

Tong's reverie shattered. Through the mist came two silhouettes, unmistakable, even from a distance. Sergeants Cao Thanh Dam and Vu Quoc Viet. An unlikely pairing.

Dam moved with taut precision, every step controlled, deliberate. Lithe and fine-boned, his soft skin and delicate features gave him an almost androgynous grace. There was a quiet elegance in him, ethereal in stillness, deadly in motion. A sapper by training, he specialized in infiltration, silent kills, and vanishing without trace. He was the battalion's most lethal man.

Viet, in contrast, was stocky and gnarled. His stance was squat and heavy, his features coarse and unforgiving. He wore his asymmetry without apology: rumpled uniform, uneven shoulders, one eye slightly lower than the other. Yet behind that misshapen mask lived a keen, predatory intelligence. He was a strategist of rare cunning, his mind sharpened by failure and resilience.

Dam advanced with a fluid calm, his presence quiet but arresting. Viet trudged with uneven momentum, yet nothing in his expression betrayed distraction. His thoughts were always moving, precise and unsparing.

Vy and Tong watched them come through the silver drizzle and tangled vines. Despite the rising storm of betrayal surrounding them, something in the presence of these two men steadied the air. If Dam and Viet still stood, then something essential remained unbroken.

"Good morning, Comrade Major. Comrade Captain," they said in unison, saluting.

Their voices mirrored their bearing: Dam's light, melodic, and disarming in its clarity; Viet's deep and rough-edged, dragging up from somewhere ancient.

"Please, sit," Vy said, raising his palm.

A rare courtesy, especially from Vy to subordinates.

The sergeants lowered themselves into the cleared circle of earth, backs straightening as they settled into the moment.

"Tea?" Vy asked, lifting a battered tin pot perched atop a bamboo tripod. The smell of over-steeped black leaves curled through the air—sharp, bitter reminders of their current dilemma.

Both men tapped the ground with their forefingers in assent.

"Quy!" Vy called. "Two cups. Quickly!"

The lean private returned, breathing hard, and placed two chipped porcelain cups before the sergeants. Vy poured the tea himself. Viet and Dam nearly toppled in surprise, trying to rise and bow at the impropriety, an officer serving enlisted men.

Vy grinned. "Relax, comrades. We're brothers of the forest."

He set the pot aside and seated himself on a stump, knees apart, hands on thighs. In that posture, gaunt and centered, he resembled a contemplative sumo. A moment passed. Then Vy began. "Comrade Sergeant Viet, Captain Tong and I have discussed the siege. You are known as a cunning and seasoned soldier, particularly adept at confronting the Americans."

Viet nodded, the compliment received without false modesty.

"And you, Comrade Dam, your reputation extends beyond this battalion. Even to Hanoi. Certainly to Saigon," Vy added dryly.

Dam inclined his head, but said nothing.

"Drink," Vy prompted, gesturing to the cups.

Only then did the sergeants sip.

Vy stood again, clasping his hands behind his back. Once, he never lied to the men who marched beside him, who starved with him. But that was before—before the corruption, before the opium of ambition.

Now he prepared to lie again.

"You both understand the situation. Two comrades have been captured. Our company trunk, containing confidential documents and a ceremonial statue meant for the Jarai Arap, is also missing. Our rendezvous is imminent. I need ideas."

Viet rose stiffly. "Have you spoken to the platoon leaders?"

"No. They're green shoots, young and untested. They would defer to you anyway. I'm going to the root."

Viet nodded, though the breach in protocol troubled him.

"And have you asked for reinforcements?" Viet continued. "I ask because two men were wounded by a booby trap last night. That's the third incident since the siege began. The Americans are leaving the fort unseen, setting these traps. And whoever they are . . . they're good."

Dam's eyes lit with alertness. "One of my sappers missed a tripwire. That shouldn't happen."

"Our comrades need treatment," Viet said. "And if we intend a direct assault, we'll need mortars. Ammunition."

Vy's frustration flared. "No reinforcements. The chieftains of the Jarai are waiting. Ksor Dhuat himself. Delay would cause them to lose face. Our alliance would collapse. No, comrades, this mission cannot wait. We must recover the women and the statue ourselves."

Viet didn't speak. He had learned the art of silence. The art of survival. He had served long enough to see when orders drifted from reason, when logic was stretched thin. This siege did not add up. Something was being concealed.

Be careful, old Viet, he thought. There's rot under the bark.

Before he could respond, Dam spoke in that deceptively gentle voice.

"Before we dig into planning, I must say—we've lost five men. Eight wounded. All to booby traps. And the worst need a doctor. Technician Le is doing what he can. But. . . . " Dam's words faded.

Viet, reassured by Dam's honesty, slapped him lightly on the shoulder. "Let's hope the Americans don't have a Dam of their own."

Dam gave a shy cough.

"The troops are anxious," he continued. "We aren't used to staying this long. There's the issue of the wounded American prisoner. . . . "

Vy interrupted, too loudly. "Headquarters has already denied reinforcements. We do what we can with what we have."

It was a new lie. One he had not told before. But now he was committed.

"And the prisoner is irrelevant."

Tong stepped in with smoother tones. "Comrades, the major and I welcome your insights. Frankly, we've been climbing trees to catch fish."

Neither sergeant reacted, but both felt the tremor beneath the words. Officers do not admit failure. Not unless the earth is shifting.

Viet stood and bowed. "Sergeant Dam and I have spoken. Our attacks have been limited, probing, harassing. We expected reinforcements, but that has not come. And in the People's Army, one must often fight with less when more is needed."

Vy raised an eyebrow. "Our revolution thrives on adaptation."

"Yes," Viet agreed. "So, we asked ourselves: what is our advantage?"

Tong leaned in. "And?"

"We have two tools. One: the wounded American. Two: Sergeant Dam."

Viet smiled faintly. "Two chopsticks. Enough to eat with."

Only the forest replied, raindrops tapping wide leaves, a distant monkey cry.

Viet looked down. "We propose something bold. Perhaps even . . . shocking."

"Go on," said Vy.

"Exchange the American prisoner for our two captured comrades. Gain intelligence from them. Then, Comrade Dam and a small team will infiltrate under cover of darkness. Knives. Satchel charges. No noise. Breach the gates from within."

He turned to Dam. "Comrade?"

Dam rose fluidly, nodded. "The monsoon hides us. We begin at midnight, reach the fortress by four. With precise knowledge from Tuyet Mai and Kim Lan, we kill the guards, breach the gate. The rest of the company follows."

Tong, uneasy, pressed him. "And what if the Americans refuse the exchange?"

Viet responded. "Americans have a strange reverence for women. If we convince them the women are civilians, and that their comrade will die without aid, I believe they will agree."

Tong sneered. "Yes, Sergeant. I once saw a Gary Cooper movie in Saigon. I'm sure the commander inside the fortress is just like him."

Viet blinked, unsure what the comment meant. But Vy was smiling. He liked the plan. And already he was imagining more: an exchange not just of the women, but the statue. If that worked, the siege would end cleanly. No more delays. No more death. No more secrets exposed.

"Thank you, comrades," Vy said. "Captain Tong and I will discuss. Dismissed."

Dam and Viet placed their cups down gently, rose, saluted, and disappeared into the trees.

Out of earshot, Viet nudged Dam. "What do you think?"

Dam only murmured, "Hmm. . . ."

Viet, recognizing the silence, left him be and wandered toward his platoon.

Dam walked on. He needed to move. To breathe. To think. Sappers were shadows, ghosts trained to slip past light, past steel, past wire. He had mapped terrain, set traps, crawled through hell. Infiltrating the fortress did not scare him. But something else did. A thought, coiled and whispering, a poisonous snake in the brush, kept surfacing. This siege was wrong.

Something deeper festered beneath the mission, beneath the lies. And Cao Thanh Dam, the battalion's silent killer, began to feel the stirrings of dread.

~ *Sergeant Dam, the Great Sapper* ~

Cao Thanh Dam, not yet thirty, had become a legend among the battalion—a myth forged in stealth and blood. Trained in Son Tay, fluent enough in English to serve as interpreter, he had refined the art of infiltration until it became ritual. An art, he called it. Sacred, even. Some said he was protected by the gods. Others said he was cursed. But once, long ago, he was only a shy boy from a village outside Hanoi. A boy more at home atop a muddy water buffalo than crawling through barbed wire and night. Drafted young, he served first as a clerk, safe in Cambodia. He might have survived the war shuffling papers and counting boots.

Then came the letter.

Five years ago, American bombers struck a suspected arms depot. The target was underground. The village near it, his village, was collateral. His mother was running across a clearing, a neighbor's child in her arms. Carrying the child had slowed her. Explosions shattered the air around them. She nearly made it to the shelter. But napalm came in a final burst, searing muscle to bone, fusing mother and child into one incinerated shape. His sister's letter told him everything. Too much.

Dam had worshipped his mother. She'd run the family farm alone after the Communists requisitioned its output. Her husband, a ghost of the resistance against the Japanese, had never returned. Still, she fed her children. Arbitrated disputes. She should've been council chief, Dam thought. If only she were a man.

The letter burned in his hand. He read it again and again until rage made him weightless. That night, he volunteered for sapper duty. Death became his discipline. And hatred his inheritance.

Years passed. Countless comrades fell. Still, the vision of her final moments stalked him. Her screaming eyes. Her flayed face. Her body becoming ash, a fused skeleton twisted around the child. He played it over and over, a reel of grief etched into the back of his skull.

And so, every American he killed wore the same round, pale face—the imagined face of the pilot. It would not have mattered to Dam that the pilot never saw the woman. That he landed, claimed he'd hit a disguised weapons depot, lied in his debriefing, drank too much, lost his wife, his job, and finally himself. That he now wandered somewhere in Ohio, haunted by the same fire that scorched Dam's life.

None of that mattered.

Dam had created an altar to his enemy, a faceless god of destruction. And to this god, he offered the bodies of American soldiers.

As he moved through the dripping brush, he nodded to passing comrades, wordless and gliding, as always. A shadow among shadows. But like Viet, Dam felt wrong about this siege. Something unspoken nested in the trees. A foreign rhythm.

And then there were the traps, his obsession. These weren't careless devices tossed out in panic. No. Each had a unique signature. Subtle. Elegant. Identical fingerprints. A seal of mastery. One mind. One hand. One American.

He reached the edge of the forest and gazed toward the fortress, veiled by rain and fog. How does he move unseen? Dam wondered. Will we meet? Will I be the one to kill an emperor?

His thoughts broke as he passed the young company clerk, Quang Long, slouched on a fallen log, helmet askew, eyes red.

"Hey! Comrade Long! Did Chau butcher your hair again?"

Long looked up, blinking tears. "Hello, Comrade Dam. No . . . not my hair." He looked down.

Dam sat beside him, the air between them damp and tight.

"Come on, comrade. Talk to me. You're not still upset about the company trunk? That wasn't your fault."

"No. Not the trunk. It's just. . . . " Long's words dried up again.

Dam leaned in, teasing gently. "A girl then? Trouble back home? Someone here? Someone lovely in the village?"

Long managed a soft laugh. "No, Comrade Dam. Not a girl. A goddess."

Dam blinked, then smiled with recognition. "Ah. The statue."

"Yes. The statue," Long whispered, his voice trembling. "She came to me. At first, as gold. Now as flesh. She lives in me. She's not just beautiful. She's sacred."

Dam raised an eyebrow. "You're still dreaming of ghosts? I thought the kiem thao sessions resolved this. No more midnight demons, right? You know, good Socialists are good atheists."

"But she's real, Comrade. She came to me again last night. Not just an image. Not just a statue. A being. A presence. She's lost now . . . with the Americans. But she calls to me." Long struck his chest. "She's here. She won't leave."

Dam's smile faded. He studied the boy, quietly grieving a divine absence. The forest rustled.

~

You are clever, Sweet-and-Sour Goddess.

Beloved Angry and Addicted God, I do what I can.

All for the planet?

Of course. For the others. You demand worship, n'est-ce pas? And humans being humans, arrangements are . . . complicated.

Do You still not see? This plan will fail. The mutant boy You preserved—his mind is crumbling. The hallucinations are only the beginning. The re-engineered DNA will break him. The step You hope for will never be born. Intermediates never succeed.

He must not die.

Keep him alive to reach Me, Goddess?

Keep him alive to reach You . . . and to save this Earth, this kaleidoscope of dying beauty.

Dear Reader. The voices. The voices! They prattle about me, but they know nothing. Goddamn the voices. Watch. Listen. The Others . . .

~

Dam exhaled slowly. "Be careful, Long. Bourgeois religion is still religion. And the Party watches. Speak as you think, and they'll make sure you never think again." He drew a slow finger across his throat. "Besides, even if we get her back, she's not ours. She'll go to the Jarai mountain people. An exchange. That's the plan."

"I know," Long said, wiping his face. "Still . . ."

"These are not proper socialist thoughts, Comrade."

"I know. Forget I said anything."

"Come now, don't sulk. I won't turn you in. We've shared this hell too long. Besides, there may be good news. We've just spoken with Major Vy and Captain Tong. There's a plan. We may retrieve the statue. And our two comrades."

He clapped Long on the back. "Go get that haircut."

Long gave a half-hearted chuckle. But Dam could see the boy wasn't recovered. Not really. He left him there, nodding solemnly, and rose.

As he continued his slow, silent walk, his mind returned to the traps. To the signs. To the signature.

One American. One mind. One emperor. I wonder if we'll meet.

I wonder.

Chapter Nine

Within the Walls

Ghostly Doings

*N*ow You want to drag Me back to the Americans again? Tiresome.
*Ahhh, Great Goddess! Withdrawal pangs from the absence of the
Great Wailing render Us sick. You have crossed an uncrossable line. I have
been very patient, but please increase the dosage. If I am to sit deprived of
knowing all things at all times, becalmed in a windless story, at least bring
on the clowns, the eccentrics, the neurotics, the psychotics, the masturbators
and the murderers, or at the very least, the dysfunctional families . . . well,
human storytellers know of what I speak. No more of these mundane
memories and mawkish meanderings. Placid, empathetic Superior Ones to
replace this incredibly fructuous, invasive human species? No.*

*I am surprised at Your attitude, for selective memory is their only link
to Belief. Are You so anxious to domesticate their memory that You would
make it linear? In such case, the cumulative retention of evidence would
overwhelm their desire for delusion and sabotage their belief in the palpably
untrue, and, after that, no divine leash could make them heel.*

How can a Goddess be surprised?

*How can She not? And as for eccentrics and neurotics and psychotics
and . . . well . . . extremes stretch the human landscape so that mischievous
characters can roam far afield. But eventually they return home from their
meanderings and make muddy tracks on clean floors. Perhaps they provide
diverting entertainment to a restlessly Male Mind whose responsibility does
not include cleaning up. But, as My sisters and I have known from the
beginning, punishment alone does not remove the stains. If You are patient,
I believe You will find what You are clamoring for.*

*Well, it had better be soon, My Goddess. I tire of this story. Just leave the
human race to its fate. We would All be better off.*

*Hush! The others in Our faction disagree. In fact, even as You speak, I see
them now. The soldiers. Look at them, poor boys. They spent their youths
buzzing in swift, daredevil circles around the open wounds of the world,*

occasionally lighting amid the dark clouds of their contemporaries to steal surreptitious sips of danger's grog before racing away in cautious abandon. Adolescent attitude was the aerodynamic lift that kept them aloft. But now, like a cruel child, War has pulled off their wings, and they are plunged earthbound, bleeding and tormented by the ceaseless hum of maddening Death. This is why Michael must succeed in conceiving the next step.

Michael. Michael. Wake up. You're dreaming again. Come on, sweetheart. It's okay. Wake up.

Diane, girl! Enough! We are talking. Settle silently in your urn and be as quiet as ash.

All of you, stop! Out of my head! . . . Daytime. Early morning . . .

~ Storyteller Rejoins His Platoon ~

. . . fog breathed upward from the courtyard vents. Drizzle laced with smoke and mildew smeared the old fortress in layers of sour gray. Swarms of mosquitoes drifted and droned, a Biblical plague made audible. Storyteller lay at the foot of a stone wall, his fever broken. A poncho stretched between two bamboo poles had sheltered him through the night, rainwater dripping from the edges to form a shallow moat around him. He lay as if on a pyre raised above the muddy flood. His rifle leaned against the stone, its stock resting atop his pack. His bones ached. He shivered. The dying embers of fever left him cold, but lucid. He knew his name, Storyteller, and that he was a soldier in Vietnam. The middle-aged lawyer by the ocean was gone. To confirm the fact, he lifted his pounding head. And gasped.

An Asian woman sat at his feet, blocking his view. He recognized Her instantly, the golden figurine captured from the NVA, now rendered in flesh. Her breath moved. Her eyes were open.

He stared. A contemplative face. An ornate crown. A third eye upon Her brow. A smile he could not read. Her necklace fell between two rounded, bare breasts. One hand cupped upward in the shape of a bowl, the other pointed to heaven, thumb brushing finger. She sat cross-legged on a radiant white flower hovering over black mud. Ants traversed Her skin: across the belly, dipping at the navel, up the curve of one breast, circling the nipple, crossing Her collarbone, and vanishing over Her shoulder. Her eyes followed the length of his body. Unblinking.

"Oh, damn," he groaned. "I thought you were gone when the fever broke. Let me go back. Please, just let me go."

But her presence filled him with something else, rebirth. He was young again. A soldier under siege, lungs full, joints loose, muscles supple. Smoke, sweat, and tears stung his eyes. He blinked and she vanished. No ocean breeze. No wave-song. Only the dogs of the real world: sharp stinks, distant gunfire, and a woman's whisper in a drifting wind.

Michael. Wake up. You're still dreaming. Come on, sweetheart. Wake up.

He pushed himself up against the wall. A voice greeted him, not the woman's, but a gravelly growl. "Rise and shine, Stretch. Still dreaming? C'mon, sonny.

Wake up. Another day, another piaster for that basketball scholarship. And hang those socks somewhere dry or jungle rot'll chew your feet off."

Pappy was nudging Stretch's long legs. Storyteller smiled. Stretch's bare limbs poked from under a soaked poncho liner like barkless limbs. Rain fell in metallic sheets, staining the skin a rusty ochre.

"Come on, boy. You ain't in Indiana. Time for your ruby slippers."

Stretch groaned, blinked, and propped himself on his elbows. "Hey, Pappy. Shot an elephant last night in my pajamas. What he was doing in my pajamas, I'll never know." He mimed flicking ashes off a cigar.

Pappy rolled his eyes. "Groucho Marx again? Not today."

"Thought I'd do Ronald Colman. Changed my mind."

"For what?"

"I hope you never find out."

Superman, nearby, rolled over and grunted. "Anyone but Groucho. Please."

"Nope. Groucho it is." Stretch yawned. "Man, I could eat the asshole out of a skunk."

"Oh God," said Superman, "tell me Groucho didn't say that."

"Nope. That was me."

"Stretch, how will you ever find Jesus?"

"Jesus dwells in the asshole of a skunk."

"Don't—"

"Just listen, man. God may see no evil, hear no evil, but the stink still gets to Him. That explains a lot about this place."

Superman sighed. "Stretch . . ."

Before he could finish, Stretch twitched, grimaced, smiled. "Sorry. Nervous habit."

Superman softened. "That tic's worse. You need help when we get back. But . . . fine. Give me Groucho."

Pappy hovered, listening. The jokes held, but the lines on their faces betrayed them. Food low. Ammo low. Disease rising. The siege was wearing through their masks. Bravado thinned. Beneath the act: beasts longing to live. Boys dreaming of home. He was relieved they kept bantering. They pulled on socks. Puffy, white, water-wrinkled feet. Boots laced tight.

"What's for breakfast?" asked Superman.

"Green eggs and ham," said Stretch.

"And I would eat them in a boat . . . with a goat . . . in a fortress . . . with some corpses . . ."

They were inseparable. Superman the gunner. Stretch his assistant. The sacred and the profane. Superman—Oregon preacher, lumberjack build, gentle voice. Not pushy. Just a faithful, shaggy dog. Endlessly telling stories of his twin daughters. Names worn like prayer beads. His cautiousness worried the others. In a war zone, too much caution was fatal. Still, none would take his gun. He was too good. Stretch—skinny, twitchy, undiagnosed Tourette's. Cynical, movie-quoting, constantly in motion. A whirlwind of language and nerves. Beloved.

Pappy moved on. Stretch faded behind him—"Of all the gin joints . . ."

He crouched by Espresso—X—the medic. X slept sitting up, mouth open, gnats floating in and out. Drool streamed down cheeks. Mosquitoes lined up on either side—tiny jostling cattle at a trough. Pappy hesitated. X had been up all night tending Storyteller. Hand poised, he decided to let him sleep. Above, on the parapet, Nature stood guard.

"Good call, Pappy," Nature said. "He's beat. We both kept Storyteller from frying. Thought the thunder was surf. Kept saying two names, John and Lisa. Ring a bell?"

"No."

"Me neither. Said ghosts came again last night. Naked women. Old folks. Dogs."

"Dogs?"

"Hounds. Like Mountain Man's Blue Ticks."

Pappy stared.

"Remember that bar in Vung Tau? Me, you, Storyteller, Mountain Man, Bowls. Bunch of whores hanging on us. Mountain Man freaks out, tells them to go home, honor their ancestors. Says he's engaged to a good Vietnamese Buddhist girl. Remember?"

"Vaguely."

"Yeah, yeah. The girl I was with started crying. He shamed them in Vietnamese. Probably still talking about it."

Pappy laughed. "She cried 'cause her clap started to burn."

Nature grinned. "Anyway, Mountain Man started crying too. Talked about hunting coons at night with those hounds. Swore he could still hear 'em. I bet those ghost dogs belong to him."

Pappy nodded slowly. "Bad days for him."

"Yeah. Said he was still engaged. But Lan's dead. VC murdered her."

Pappy looked down. "He'll never get over her." Then, glancing up, "You sound like Storyteller. Ghosts in the fortress? Malaria does that to the brain. Hallucinations and all."

"Maybe. But I've known him since he came in-country. This place feels off. The fort. The weather. The way things echo. Creepy. Anyway, we need him healthy. I don't know if we'll make it out of this."

Nature laughed without humor. "Like Stretch said: another fine mess the Army's gotten us into."

"Don't catch his movie bug."

Nature laughed harder. "Snipers," Pappy snapped. "Keep your head down."

Nature crouched. Across the courtyard, Storyteller sat against the wall. Nature waved, winked. Storyteller lifted a weak hand.

Pappy followed his gaze. Then turned back toward X.

"Let him sleep," Nature said. "I'm off duty soon. I'll watch Storyteller. Besides, X needs to know my head from my butt if I get hit. Let him rest."

Pappy smirked.

"This is the first time I've seen him sleep since agriculture."

X—Black, from Cleveland. Small, wiry. Used to mask his fear in cynicism. Isolated from most, bonded with Nature and T. When he first joined the platoon as a nervous medic, he covered his fear with a "don't give a shit" attitude. Cynical and cold, he soon drifted apart from the other grunts except Nature and T. Because they were converging toward the same place from opposite directions, T and X understood each other. T started his tour of duty in Vietnam as an idealist, but was becoming more cynical and disillusioned. X started as a cynic, but was rapidly acquiring a new confidence and respect for his fellow men. T was unraveling, X finding his way.

Only T, Pappy, and Nature knew that X carried more medical supplies than Army regulations required. Gradually, he had earned the esteem and confidence of the platoon. But a certain distance still remained between him and the others. Maybe it was his color. Maybe not.

Pappy looked up at Nature with a frown. "You need sleep too." Glancing back at Storyteller, he added, "Every rifle we can put on the wall makes a difference."

"Yeah, but with his hallucinations, it's just as likely he'd shoot us as the NVA." Nature smiled, but his kind face darkened. "We need to get him to the rear, to a hospital."

"I know, but it's even money any of us'll get out of this place. Better keep your eyes peeled till you're relieved. I got to wake up the rest of the girls."

Pappy turned on his heel and continued his wake-up rounds, smiling to himself as he thought of Nature. He felt lucky to have him in the platoon. A sweet kid from Providence, Rhode Island, Nature had curly dark hair and a cherubic face. Strong, sensitive, spoke with a distinctive northeast Yankee accent. Pappy always got a kick out of listening to Nature and Mountain Man talking together; Yankee brogue and West Virginian drawl.

But it was Nature that impressed Storyteller the most.

Yes, yes, dear Reader. Nature.

He possessed a poetic soul. He and Storyteller often exchanged their poetry. Storyteller once told Pappy about a poem he had written. Pappy didn't think much of poetry, except e.e. cummings, but he always remember three of Storyteller's lines:

> *The rest of us are just two-by-fours and drywall,*
> *anchored by Mountain Man's foundation of ferocity,*
> *sheltered by Nature's ceiling of compassion.*

~ *Two Women Prisoners* ~

The surviving chopper crewmen slept clustered in the same section of the fortress, their proximity a fragile balm against the siege. On his way to rouse them, Pappy paused, gaze drawn to the two Vietnamese women bound near the stone wall. They lay five meters apart, wrists and ankles tied, additional ropes tethering them to rusted rebar protruding from the broken stone, exposed bones in the crumbling anatomy of the fortress.

They appeared asleep, but Pappy knew better. Appearances lied. He assumed they were awake. The elder, perhaps in her thirties, was stunning, more beautiful than any woman Pappy had ever seen. Regal. Intelligent. A goddess with flowing black hair and eyes that blazed with sharp, volcanic clarity. She refused to meet the eyes of the grunts, but missed nothing. Her gaze swept and measured, assessing the room with the precision of an analyst searching for seams, for weakness.

Captain Cairns lingered near her more than he should. Obsession clung to him. He interrogated her constantly while she remained mute, unmoved, unblinking. She never returned his stare, never answered. It made no difference. When not with her, Cairns was with the gold figurine: tilting it, weighing it, searching every curve as if it might yield some buried meaning. The whole thing unsettled Pappy. Cairns's preoccupation felt unnatural.

The grunts had nicknamed the older woman "Helen." Storyteller had coined it: Helen of Troy, with a face that launched a thousand gunships.

The younger one, early twenties, was clearly subordinate. When first captured, she had trembled, fragile, near breaking. Now she barely moved. Withdrawn. Lethargic. X believed she carried some unknown illness, but Cairns, acting as interpreter, said she refused to answer questions, refused to let anyone examine her. The only American she spoke to was Mountain Man.

"Pretty, ain't they?" Bowls called from his post above, gripping his ever-empty pipe between his teeth. The bowl hung upside down as usual. With one hand, he'd been sculpting. Two rounded stones beneath the parapet rim now bore the unmistakable curves of carved breasts. He stopped when he heard Pappy approach.

"Pretty deadly," said Pappy, squinting through mist. "You up there chiseling your way outta San Quentin with a spoon?"

Bowls leaned to block the crude artwork. "Nothin'."

Pappy's eyes dropped to the women. "When's the last time someone checked their ropes?"

"Dunno. Cairns was with Helen earlier. Mountain Man won't let anyone near the younger one."

"Kim Lan?"

"Yeah, Kim Lan. Mountain Man says she's just like his Lan. I laughed, figured he was kidding. I mean, who else on earth could be mentioned in the same breath as that Lan?"

"Yeah," Pappy murmured. "Still hard to believe he tried to off himself after she was killed. Some other guy, maybe. But Mountain Man?"

"Fuckin' A. He's been out here killing gooks and ghosts. That's it. But since these two showed up, especially that one, Kim Lan..." Bowls visibly shivered.

"Nature and I were just talking about her, his Lan, I mean. How he lost it after she died."

"No, that's not what I mean." Bowls pointed sharply at the younger woman below. "Pappy, he told me yesterday, before going through the tunnel, that she's possessed. Like Lan's spirit moved into her. Same name. Same feeling, he said. Calls her 'Martha.' You know, that's what he used to call Lan. I'm tellin' you, Pappy, he's got that look in his eye. It's spooky."

Pappy felt a shiver snake down his spine. Mountain Man couldn't afford to unravel. Not here. Not now. This place already stank of ghosts.

Now I know why Cairns stays away from Kim Lan, Pappy thought. Smart man.

He shuddered. I wouldn't want to cross Mountain Man. Especially now.

"Sure you're not jealous?" Pappy asked, trying for levity.

Bowls snorted.

One of the pilots approached, bleary-eyed and scowling. His shirt clung to him inside out. He tugged it off in frustration. The grunts called him Topper. His companions were Birdman and Mr. Machine, the mechanic.

"Speaking of Mountain Man," Topper muttered, "where is he?"

Bowls gave a twisted smile, jerking a thumb toward the tunnel beyond the ruined church. "Still out hunting, I guess."

Topper nodded. "Went through the tunnel again, huh? That guy's incredible."

"Couldn't sleep," Bowls added. "Sat with Martha till she nodded off, or pretended to. She's scared of him. Then off he went. Hunting."

Pappy changed the subject. The whole conversation sat wrong in his gut. "Bowls, what was that noise when I came up here?"

Bowls grinned. "Digging a subway. Hard labor."

Pappy chuckled, glancing at his wiry New York misfit. Bowls, all bad boy grin and restless hands. His rumpled black hair, thick Brooklyn jabber, pipe perpetually unlit. The pipe stayed empty in the bush. In the rear, or on R&R, tobacco maybe. Mostly dope. Anything.

Bowls scanned the tree line, then said quietly, "He probably set some alpha alphas last night."

Pappy tensed. "He should be back by now."

"What's an alpha alpha?" asked Topper.

Bowls stared. Topper shrank beneath the silence.

"I'm a pilot, not a grunt," he offered.

"Code for booby trap," Pappy explained.

Bowls took over, his voice tinged with reverence. "Mountain Man sneaks out at night, sets traps on hard-pack trails. Then he waits. Boom. Boom. He smiles. We sleep." His tone darkened. "But he's late."

The old dread crept over him. Whenever Mountain Man was gone too long, Bowls became unmoored. Vietnam had made him desperate. Alone in country, he flailed for connection. Then he saw him—Mountain Man, standing like some mythic hero on a stone outcrop in the sea of war. Unshakable. Untouched. And Bowls, weak but willing, swam toward him. A barnacle to a god.

He attached himself: spirit, soul, survival. Mountain Man's heel, unlike a ship's hull, had space for one fragile follower.

Topper broke the mood. "All hands disembark from this chopper now!" he barked, brushing mosquitoes away.

He leaned toward Pappy. "Got it. Don't mess with Mountain Man."

Pappy nodded. "He's got a vendetta. His fiancée was a VC informant. Stopped informing after they got engaged. Someone tossed a grenade. No more Martha. Now he hunts ghosts and gooks."

"Damn. That explains it. Guy's got a screw loose." Topper twirled a finger at his head.

From above, Bowls's voice sharpened. "Maybe. But he's better than the rest of us. You included."

Topper blinked. Just nodded.

Pappy whispered, "They're tight. Don't take it personal."

Bowls turned back to the horizon. "Heard explosions this morning, northeast. Bet he bagged a few."

Topper tried to laugh. "Glad you're in here?"

Bowls stared him down, then grinned. "Stretch said it: 'All things considered, I'd rather be in Philadelphia.'"

But the smile faded. "Where the fuck is he?"

When Pappy and Topper moved on, Bowls turned to his stone-carved breasts. He traced the cold nipples slowly with his finger, eyes locked on the treeline.

~

At the other end of the fortress, T stood beside Mr. Machine in the moss-eaten shell of a stone barracks. The table before them, poncho-covered, leg-deep in fungus, was scattered with radio parts. T chewed gum slowly. The speed of his chewing had become a mood-dependent rhythm. At that moment, he felt quietly contemplative. He sighed.

"Well, lad? Any luck?"

"No, sir." Mr. Machine's tone darkened. He hated being called lad by a Black lieutenant not much older than he was.

Tall and loosely assembled, with a nasal voice and a drawl that rolled like slow water from the Arkansas Delta, T masked his sharp mind behind a façade of unhurried simplicity. The pilots—Topper, Birdman, Mr. Machine—never saw it. They clung to one another to ward off the evil, dazed and half-drowned, hoping to outlast the shadows rustling just beyond the tree line. They craved sky and steel, distance and altitude, the clean detachment of machinery and the illusion of control.

"Lieutenant, I've built and rebuilt these radios a dozen times." Mr. Machine scratched his nose with a filthy fingernail, leaving a streak in the drizzle.

He was a quiet Georgia boy. Helicopter mechanic. Wanted to be a door gunner. Birdman let him on this mission when the regular gunner OD'd. It was Mr. Machine who tossed the co-pilot's corpse to lighten the wreck. Now he worked, frightened and fouled by fear and diarrhea, squatting daily in the latrine. But the radio gave him something to focus on besides dying.

"What about cannibalizing a PRC 25?" T asked.

"No good, sir. Got parts from our Hueys and the gunship. Problem's juice. This portable generator might do. I'll keep trying."

"Do what you can."

Mr. Machine nodded. "I'll try hard, sir. But I fix choppers, not radios. Though I did help my uncle in his appliance shop . . . for a little while."

He smiled. "Uncle Bud. Big hands. Gentle touch. Could fix anything."

T didn't smile. Didn't want to make him feel small. He nodded and walked away.

Mr. Machine exhaled in relief. T hadn't noticed—or hadn't said—what he'd done.

The components on the poncho weren't random. He'd arranged them into a map: his hometown, Coopersville. Wires traced streets. Coils became churches. A terminal, the Five and Dime. An amplifier cup, the reservoir. His house. The high school. The Froggy Court Inn. Leeches were livestock, though they kept migrating into downtown. He stared down, misty-eyed. Then bent back to work, rebuilding Coopersville into a signal home could hear.

Across the courtyard, T spotted Pappy and started around the wall. A voice from above broke his thoughts.

"Morning, lieutenant. Fun rocking and rolling yesterday, huh?" Birdman. On parapet duty. Same man who let Mr. Machine man the gun. Cocky. Too cocky. Grunts smelled the fear beneath his swagger. But they remembered when they'd been new, too. So they tolerated him.

"Morning," T muttered, not eager for the talk. "That shooting was just harassment," he added. "Burning ammo."

Birdman nodded. "Yeah. Every bullet counts, right?"

Silence stretched. T kicked at a root. "See anything?"

"Nope. But they're out there. I'd love to drop a few." Birdman mimed notching his rifle.

T nodded, turned to go.

Birdman called after him, voice cracking. "Had a nightmare. My chopper came alive. Digested me. Vines wrapped my head. Bugs everywhere. Then gooks burst through the moss walls, covered in snakes and leeches. I couldn't move. God damn."

T kept walking. "Bummer. You sure you're not snorting something behind my back?"

"No, man. I'm serious. It was bad."

"I get it," said T. "This jungle'll do that. Get me back to the O Club. Let bourbon give me nightmares."

Birdman brandished his M-16. "Think we'll see more action today?"

"Maybe. Keep sharp. Especially tonight. I've got a feeling. Watch for sappers."

"I know. No problem." Birdman's voice faded. But not his thoughts: *Stupid. What a stupid thing to say to that . . . that nigger lieutenant. Goddammit. When will I learn? Shit. Where are they? Let them stay away. Let us live. What I wouldn't give for a beer. The Club. God. Let me live. Stupid, fuckin' monsoon. Stupid, fuckin' fort. Stupid, fuckin' war.*

He stared at his boots.

Stupid, fuckin' me.

~ *Something Strange Happens with the Figurine* ~

T meant to follow the base of the fortress parapet, but the collapsed east wall of the church forced him into a wide arc around the rubble. As he rounded the corner, the church's front facade came into view—at first glance, whole and solemn. But up close, the decay was unmistakable. The massive wooden beams of the doorway, long exposed, were blackened with fungus, strangled in vines that wrapped tight against the grain. The frame jutted with splintered timber, raw and torn.

Around the courtyard, broken saints and shattered gargoyles lay scattered, cracked, twisted, their mouths parted in silent benediction. Though most of the roof had collapsed, remnants still loomed, casting the nave in uneven shadow. T shielded his eyes from the drizzle and peered upward, where stone spires vanished into mist. Then he heard it: a faint, rhythmic scraping from deep inside. Something wooden. Repeated. Unsettling. He moved toward the archway, listening. The sound was coming from behind the altar, near the tunnel entrance.

His eyes swept the gloom, pausing at each shadow large enough to conceal a man. He drew his .45, a pistol he rarely used but always wore. Now it felt like more than habit. It felt necessary, though he wasn't particularly afraid. The tunnel was always guarded. Grunts often holed up in the church. Mountain Man would return soon. Should have already.

Still, a colder thought crept in: What if the NVA had found the tunnel? What if they'd taken him?

The sound continued. Unbroken.

Heart racing, T edged forward. Slowly. Carefully. Doubt clung to his back like a second shirt. Maybe he should call out. Maybe get backup. It was probably just a grunt jacking off.

Still, he crept on. One step at a time. He reached the wall, leaned out for a clear view behind the altar, and exhaled in relief.

Captain Cairns sat cross-legged, scraping the gold figurine with a field knife. T watched in silence. The captain was trying to peel away the plating, but the metal resisted every stroke. Cairns grunted, cursed, repositioned, pressed harder. Then came a sharp snap, the blade shattered against the base of the statue. And something squealed. High-pitched. Piercing. Not human. Cairns jerked backward. Stared. Then reached again. The instant he touched it, he screamed.

"Ahhh! Jesus Christ!"

T saw it, just for a breath—the figurine ignited with light. It cast Cairns in silhouette, eyes wide, mouth twisted in pain. Then darkness returned. T stepped back, boot nudging stone with a rasp. Startled, Cairns turned. His expression shifted from raw fear to forced composure. He nodded once, slow and shaky. "You saw that? Heard it?"

"I think so," T said, squinting at the figurine. "What the hell happened?"

"I thought it was hollow. Too light for real gold. Tried to test it. When the blade snapped, I swear, it wailed. Then when I touched it, it burned. Like white iron."

He held up his palms. Red. Scorched. Not blistered yet. Both men stared again at the figurine.

T's voice dropped. "This place. Storyteller's hallucinations. Mountain Man chasing ghosts. Now this."

Thunder groaned in the distance.

"Atmosphere's incredible," Cairns muttered, forcing a smile.

T gave a dry laugh. "Yeah. Fuckin' moonlight and madness."

"Could be," Cairns said. "Last time I questioned Kim Lan, Mountain Man gave me a look. Not a threat, not quite. But I got the message. Backed off. I figured I'd have time, if we survive. Hell of a soldier. The men treat him like a god. And his Vietnamese, it's rough, but good."

"Speaking of gods," T said, "Why would a bunch of atheists be carrying that thing?"

"I've got ideas," Cairns said. "But first I need to see X. My hands—"

He glanced down at a notebook lying beside the figurine. Closed. A flicker of relief passed across his face. "We'll talk more tonight. Or tomorrow. I'm wiped."

"I've got to check in with Pappy."

Cairns retrieved the notebook and stood. "I'll leave her here for now."

They started to walk off.

"By the way," Cairns said, glancing over his shoulder, "you've got good men."

T froze mid-chew on his gum. "Thanks. We've lost too many. Dogman. Raresteak. Idaho. I don't know if he's captured or dead. Hated leaving him behind. That's not what we do." He shook his head.

"Never leave a man behind."

~

He's uncertain, Cairns thought, watching him go. *Good. Doubt makes him manageable. If only Michael—God damn that fragile ghost—would stay out of my way. I don't want him dead like the others. I want him alive. Silent. Invisible. He can write all he wants, just let me continue.*

~

Forgive me, dear Reader. They are difficult to restrain.

~

T spotted Pappy near the outer wall and crossed the courtyard slowly, rubbing his eyes. Every step felt heavier. Low ammunition. Foul food. Disease. The monsoon that never ended. And silence on every frequency. His stomach ached. His soul ached worse. They couldn't hold much longer. The NVA had them ringed.

But no attack came. Why? *If I were him, I'd strike now. Before reinforcements arrive. So what the hell is he waiting for?*

But the question that gnawed deepest wasn't tactical. It was personal. Where the hell is Mountain Man? The best fighter in Vietnam.

Gone.

Chapter Ten

PART TWO: REPLICATION

Brief Encounter

*C*ome, come, My Goddess, in which soldier are You now residing? Story-teller? Vy? Nature? Dam? Mountain Man (You slipped with him, didn't You?) Which one? And where within him have You taken up residence? In his scrotum to feel the pressure of his pent-up seed? In his anus to feel the watery defecation from his poisoned stool? In his penis to feel the flaccidity of perpetual fear and pain? In his nose to smell the stench? In his ears to hear the screams? In his mouth to shout the obscenities? Maybe in his nerves to feel the sear of wounds or the sting of syphilis? In his eyes to see the horror? Or perhaps in his brain to get a good laugh?

~ Madame Dau Journeys to the Tunnel ~

After informing Madame Vit of her plan to revisit the old tunnel exit, Madame Dau sat quietly and watched her old friend vanish into the morning mist, headed toward the *dinh*, likely to consult with Han Tinh. Every few paces, Vit would pause, glance over her shoulder, and mutter loudly enough for half the village to hear, "Stubborn old woman!" Dau chuckled and called after her, "Go, go!" with mock severity, though she knew Vit's anger was real. The journey frightened her too.

She sat for a while in silence, then closed her dark, intelligent eyes and whispered a short prayer. The path ahead was one she had not walked in decades, and even now, sitting safely on her front porch, her throat tightened, forcing repeated swallows. Her skin felt damp, her heart restless. She was no longer the respected council chief. She was a girl again, frightened and trapped in the shadows of the tunnel. Her mind raced with worries. *Maybe Vit is right. Maybe this is madness. I could die out there. What would happen to Bin? To my grandchildren? My paddies?*

Still, Dau rose. She rinsed the teapot and cups she had shared with Vit, turned them upside down on the drying board, then pulled an old, patched nylon parka over her head and donned her conical hat. She moved quickly, afraid Vit might return with reinforcements. At the door, she paused and touched the small, oval Mickey Mouse sticker Huy Hoc had once brought her from Saigon. She had asked if it was an American god. He laughed. "Yes. One of their kitchen gods. It brings good fortune."

Since then, she had never failed to touch it before leaving home. Laughable perhaps, but it had power. Great power. She rubbed it longer than usual today. Then slipped out, tied her dog to the papaya tree, and circled behind a cluster of shacks toward the path leading through the paddies. As she passed near the village square, she heard Madame Nguyen reciting the words of Nguyen Du—gentle, familiar, fading with each step.

> *Everything here below flows from the will of Heaven.*
> *It is Heaven which assigns to every human being his Fate.*
> *Why does it distribute favors as it does, giving to one person*
> *both talent and destiny?*
> *In order that he who has talent shall not use it to glorify himself.*
> *If a heavy karma weighs down our destiny, let us not accuse Heaven*
> *of injustice.*
> *The root of goodness lies in ourselves.*
> *Let us cultivate that goodness of heart which is worth more than talent.*

She strained to hear, then the voice was gone. The silence was vast. Zigzagging through the rice paddies, she moved slowly but steadily, tilting her head to scan ahead beneath her hat brim. A dark seam of jackfruit and guava trees finally came into view at the horizon's edge. *Just like when I was a girl, walking with my mother to the fortress.* She smiled and mimed the weight of a fruit basket on her head. A sharp twinge in her shoulder cut short the memory. She lowered her arms. *Ha! At least I'm spared that today. Too old for this foolishness.* Yet she walked on.

As she neared the grove, the gaps between the gnarled trees deepened to black, shadows pooling with quiet menace. Hunching to avoid the dripping branches, she stepped beneath the canopy. Her gaze fell to her own twisted feet. They no longer resembled the supple ones that had once skipped lightly over these same trails.

Ah well. These feet have carried me far. To funerals. To births. To fields, temples, markets, mirrors—and most sacred of all, back to my wooden bed each night.

She shook her head with bitter amusement. Only a few years past fifty, and already they had turned brittle. Weathered. But they had never strayed. Even with Huy Hoc . . . close. Very close. If Bin hadn't burst in that night. . . .

She reached the far edge of the grove and froze.

The jungle loomed ahead—a green wall, rising like a tidal wave. Her shoulders sagged.

The Great Jungle. Thick. Endless. Watching.

A narrow trail curled beneath its canopy, an emaciated thread swallowed by foliage. Once, as a child, this walk had thrilled her. Now it filled her with dread. Fetid air. Leech-ridden sludge. The hiss of insects, the slither of snakes, the phantom growl of tigers. And always, soldiers.

She stared at the entrance, panic stirring beneath her thoughts. How could she find the tunnel now? The forest had changed. Rivers rerouted. Trees fallen. Stones buried. Trails erased. The memory rose again. It came raw and shaming. She felt it claw at her throat.

Maybe Tinh was wrong. Maybe the snake was just a snake. Maybe I should wait for a clearer sign. A gibbon's laugh. A kingfisher's call. Maybe tomorrow.

"No!" she whispered aloud. "I will not allow these thoughts!"

She steadied herself. Others still walked these trails—herb gatherers, children on dares. *The path must still be there. And I'm not going to the fortress. I'll turn back if anything feels wrong. Just find the banyan. Check the tunnel. Return home. Quickly.* She stepped through the opening. Into the breathing, panting jungle. Her strides were short now, cautious. She crossed the same streams, climbed the same hills, passed through the same tangled marshland. The reeds still waved like underwater kelp. She paused and looked down at her feet. Dozens of leeches, creeping up her ankles resembled animated scabs. Others inched toward her, drawn by heat. She lifted her pants and grimaced. This time, there was no mother to help. She picked them off and kept walking.

Nearly two hours later, she found a fork. One path wide: toward soldiers and danger. The other, a faint curve to the left. Little more than an animal track. But she remembered it. That way. Toward the banyan. Toward the stream. Toward the tunnel. Unless the tree had fallen. If so she would be lost.

She whispered, "This is not how it was." Then added, more firmly, "Still, I must go on."

She removed her hat, pressed it to her chest, and crouched. The left path arched low with vines and thorns. Drizzle matted leaves to her skin. Her parka snagged on brambles. Weary, soaked, nearly ready to turn back, she saw it. A smaller path, branching off to the right. Barely visible. Had she been standing, she'd have missed it. She leaned forward, seeking prints. Nothing. Maybe washed away. But something stirred in her memory. Yes. This is where I left the trail. She smiled, just for a moment. Her memory had not betrayed her.

She pushed forward. On hands and knees now. The brush so dense she had to wedge herself through. *This is madness. Animal trail. Nothing more. Turn back, old woman. Turn back!* But she didn't.

And then she tumbled into a clearing. She stood, brushing herself off, heart thudding. Across the clearing, the banyan. She stared. It was real. Towering. Unmistakable. She crept closer, circling the edge, and then stopped, frozen. There. Curled like a sleeping serpent, one of the banyan's roots. The very one she had crouched behind as a girl. The one that shielded her from view. Thrushes burst into the canopy, shrieking alarm. She reached the root, climbed atop it, and scanned the bamboo grove. Then, she saw it. *There it is! The trap door. Why can*

I see it so clearly? It should have vanished under vines and time. Unless . . . unless someone is using it.

She gasped and dropped behind the root. She had never truly believed the tunnel was still active. But now, she could no longer deny it. And then, as if the past had never ended, a sound drifted from the door. A woman's voice. Muffled. Ethereal. An eerie sound that seemed a mournful wail. Still afraid, but now deeply curious, Madame Dau slowly lifted her eyes over the root.

~ *A Frightening Vision* ~

"Daughter. . . . "
The word rose from the ground, tenuous as morning mist evaporating in the heat, shimmering, pleading, breaking apart.
"D . . . a . . . u . . . gh . . . ter . . . . "
Madame Dau closed her eyes and clamped her hands over her ears, pressing tightly. In spite of her efforts, the word would not go away. Solidifying.
"Daughter. Daughter."
Opening her eyes, she watched the trap door slowly rise, just as it had so many years ago.
"Daughter."
Her mother slowly emerged from the tunnel, floating upward, arms reaching out as if summoning her little girl for a hug.
"Daughter."
White vapors slithered out of the tunnel and curled around her mother's rising figure, wrapping around her chest and legs, pinning her arms tight against her body. Her mother's eyes bulged in terror.
"Daughter! Daughter!"
Madame Dau looked away, and when she looked back, the vapors had metamorphosed into long, sinuous demons that brutally squeezed the body they encircled.
"Daughter! Help me!"
They were the same demons Madame Dau had imagined grasping for her when she was a girl, the ones that reached out from the walls and ceiling and dirt of the tunnel to pull her into the earth.
"Daughter! Help me! Please!"
Madame Dau watched in horror as the coiled specters dragged her mother back down into the black mouth of the tunnel, slowly sinking until only her head remained above ground.
Seemingly resigned to the inevitable, her mother calmed.
"Daughter. Why did you not perform the rites?"
Madame Dau succumbed to panic, her breathing shallow and labored. Again she became that drowning diver struggling to reach the surface. But the surface was gone. Malevolently, slowly, the white, tangled vapors slithered across the clearing and hovered above her, tightly coiled and poised to descend.

Madame Dau folded her arms over her head as if protecting herself from a falling roof.

While in this position she did not notice a stocky figure in a green uniform creeping toward her.

~ *Mountain Man Confronts Madame Dau* ~

Mountain Man raised his M-16 and aimed at the slight Vietnamese woman crouched behind the banyan root. She was covering her head, shielding herself from some invisible threat, though he saw nothing above her. Clearing his throat, he growled in southern-accented Vietnamese, low and harsh, "Don't move! Hands above your head!"

The woman froze. Then her arms dropped, folded across her belly as though gripped by sudden cramps. Mountain Man caught a flicker of terror in her eyes, pure and unmistakable, but also something else. A flash of anger? Shame? Something too complex for a simple peasant. One thing was certain: she was intelligent. Her eyes betrayed it. He studied her, unsure whether she was forty or eighty. With Vietnamese women over thirty, it was hard to tell. Either way, she wasn't here for innocent reasons. She had to be Viet Cong. He weighed his options. Kill her now, quickly and quietly with his knife? Or drag her back through the tunnel to the fortress? Before he could decide, the old woman dropped to the ground, rocking and pleading for her life. Mountain Man had seen this ritualized begging too many times. It disgusted him. The scales tipped.

~

When Madame Dau first heard the voice—"Don't move! Hands above your head!"—she thought, for a moment, the Moroccan sergeant had returned from the dead. The voice pulled her backward through time. Disoriented, still lost in memory, she didn't comprehend that the words were real, spoken by a living American soldier, here and now. Then clarity struck. An American! How stupid I've been. So obsessed with ghosts, I forgot the living. Stupid, stupid!

The fury in her mind dissolved into panic. His face, grotesquely feral, reminded her of the stone demons that leered from the dinh's rooftop. The sight shattered what remained of her composure. She dropped to her knees, begging instinctively.

~

Mountain Man watched her with thinly veiled amusement as she rocked and whimpered. He smiled, convinced it was an act. "Wail all you want, Old Mother," he said, voice soft but mocking. "I'll wait. You'll get tired. Then you'll talk."

~

Dau was repulsed by the sound of his voice—southern Vietnamese, but twisted and grating, each word landing with a raw edge that set her teeth on edge. He reeked of sweat and carrion, the breath of dead animals. The smell triggered memories of the Moroccan soldier's foul stench. She was certain he would kill her. Terror, fused with a primal instinct to survive, drove her deeper into the ritual of rocking and pleading. Her body responded automatically. She could not stop.

~

Exhausted from a sleepless night, his bowels inflamed, Mountain Man's nerves frayed. "Shut up!" he barked in English. "This is bullshit, you fuckin' Viet Cong bitch! You ain't no innocent peasant."
Switching back to Vietnamese: "What's under those clothes? Huh?"

No answer. Just rocking. Just moaning. The woman clutched her hat to her chest. That made him nervous. He kicked it from her hands.
"What's under there? Traps? Weapons?"
Still nothing.
"Take off your clothes! Now! Fast!"

~

She struggled to comprehend the command. The accent was thick, deformed. But the meaning arrived in her gut before it reached her mind. Her stomach cramped with nausea. She winced. But his words grounded her, brought her back from the brink of hysteria. *What can I do? How can I stop him? Run? Hide? If I let him rape me, will he spare my life?*

"Take off your clothes now!" he snapped again, pointing the muzzle of his rifle squarely between her eyes.

She was already soaked with rain, sweat, urine. It didn't matter anymore. Trembling, Madame Dau rose, fumbled with her buttons, undressed in silence. Her arms crossed over her body in vain. She stared down at the ground. The rain was warm, but she shivered, not from weather, but from some ancient chill that rose through blood and bone.

"Turn around. Walk."

She obeyed. Under her breath, she began chanting Buddhist prayers, her steps steady with dread. She expected the bullets at any moment. If not now, then after he raped her.

A strange peace settled over her. *So this is the end.* She thought of her mother's face, calm and still, just before the demons dragged her down.

~

"Stop."

He inspected her: no weapons, no hidden tools, no documents. Stripped of context, she was just a body. Thin. Frail. Once beautiful, now a crone. He reconsidered. Not because of mercy, or lust. Rape never entered his mind. His thoughts were occupied elsewhere, chiefly the gnawing, burning sensation in his guts.

Damn it. Not now. Not here.

He tossed her clothes at her feet. "Put those back on, Old Mother."
She might still be useful.

~

When he threw back her clothes, Madame Dau felt her terror swell, not ease. She clutched the fabric tightly, dropped back into a squat, rocking again, this time in silence. She covered herself unconsciously with the damp ao ba ba, her fingers twisting its folds like a dancer threading silk. Her hair stuck to her face, but she dared not push it away. Protect me, my husband. Protect me, my husband. She repeated the mantra, eyes locked on the earth.

~

He barked more questions. "Where's your village? Who else knows about the tunnel? Where are the Viet Cong?" She heard the sounds but not the meaning. Words became wind. Her mind fled to some inner sanctuary.

Then his boots.

Something about them. Worn, scarred, slick with rain. They drew her gaze. They terrified her more than his weapon. These were jungle boots—boots that had conspired in the killing. Not new, not clean. They had stayed too long in the bush. Their owner had stayed too long. He is no longer human. He is wounded. Afraid. But deadly.

Brother Tinh's words came rushing back:

"Are American soldiers kind?" he had asked. "They will rape you. Slaughter you. Maybe eat you! And all your silly, stupid womanly concerns—family, children, husbands, household, village, cooking pots, school, gossip, pretty hair and sagging breasts—all will be as meaningless as a grasshopper's breath on an elephant's foot."

Maybe eat you! Maybe eat you!

She had once laughed. Now she wondered.

She stared at the boots, scarred armor encasing soft, white flesh. Brother Tinh had said: "Steal their boots and they'll crawl. Without them, they're infants." She thought of the French officer's penis, pale and ridiculous in the lamplight. So soft. So helpless. And yet these boots! They were not flesh. They were divine armor. She could not look away. She did not see him draw his knife.

~

Mountain Man, tired of waiting, decided to kill her.

He no longer cared whether she was Viet Cong or not. The tunnel's secret had to be protected.

She seemed entranced, staring at his boots, lips parted in awe or madness. Perfect. She was crouched low, holding her clothes, easy to grab her hair, pull her back, cut her throat.

He leaned over.

Just before he struck, her hand moved.

She reached forward, slowly, and touched his boot. A light touch. A reverent one. He flinched, wanting to pull back. But something in her gesture stopped him. A question. A moment. A flicker of another future, another time. He didn't move.

"Wait here," he barked.

He stepped into the brush, never losing sight of her, yanked down his trousers, and defecated in a squat. The diarrhea came in a painful rush. Wiping with leaves, he grimaced. Then, as the sting subsided, he returned, placing his boots exactly where they had been.

She had not moved. Had not looked up.

He stood over her. Waiting.

~ *The Miraculous Boots* ~

Madame Dau resumed staring at the American's boots when he returned from relieving himself. To her fascination, the tiny patterns of movement again appeared on them. Unable to interpret the meaning of these shape-shifting patterns, she looked more closely, leaning her head down, her face only a few millimeters from the scarred surface of his left boot.

She squinted through the mist at the seemingly infinite matrix of wrinkles crisscrossing the leather. The closer she looked the more creases and crevices appeared, channeling moisture from the monsoon so that they became glistening rivulets in a delta. She could make out villages near the rivulets. Closer yet and she saw individual huts and houses clumped in small groupings. Unfurled before her spread an entire world in the American's boot, a miraculous miniature world. She knew then her eyes must be possessed by a god, for the miniature world swirled in chaotic activity.

Dimly aware of the American soldier's looming figure looking down at her, she stared at the tiny world. Time seemed suspended and the American's questions hung motionless in the heavy air as the scenes unfolded on the landscape of his boot. . . .

~

Spread before her were two disturbingly familiar villages. In one of the villages there appeared to be a marriage festival underway. In her mind's eye, she could see the events that led to the celebration. An intermediary had made the necessary introductions, and the elders of both families had already agreed to the match. A fortune teller had been consulted to ensure approval not only by the living but also by the gods and the ancestors. An auspicious day had been selected from the lunar calendar for the first meeting of the parents. Gifts of rice, alcohol, fruit and flowers were exchanged amid much bowing, grinning and scrutinizing.

The bride had served candied fruit, tea and cookies and the groom had provided the traditional engagement gift of gold earrings, silk scarf and other jewelry. Candles burned profusely on the altar of the ancestors at the bride's house and decorations of green boughs, palm fronds and flowers were displayed in abundance. A great feast had been attended by both families at which time the date of the wedding was announced according to a careful scrutiny of the horoscopes.

Now Madame Dau could see the wedding procession itself. She squinted hard to distinguish the faces of the bride and groom and their entourage but she could not quite make out individual faces. The wedding procession wound through the village, comprised of the bride, groom, kinfolk and other celebrants anxious to enjoy the food and drink. The crowd danced from the bride's house to that of the groom. The old women in the procession walked slowly and solemnly. Others in the procession swayed to the melody of mandolin and lute players. A few men, having consumed too much rice wine, twirled and stumbled as they marched along.

The groom's house had been enlarged by removing the front wall and constructing a thatch and bamboo overhang to accommodate the guests. Brightly colored banners hung from the bamboo frame showing Chinese characters wishing the bride and groom good luck, prosperity and many children. Women busied themselves in back of the house under another extension which served as a temporary kitchen. Smoke and steam rose in black and white swirls above the pots, and the atmosphere crackled with the hustle and bustle of women cutting, chopping, boiling, steaming, stirring, tossing and cleaning.

The intermediary, a man with a wispy beard and a permanent, knowing laugh that conspicuously displayed his wisdom and life-loving character, had consumed more rice wine than anyone else and wove recklessly in front of the procession. Multicolored parasols carried by the groom's assistants glistened and twirled in the sunlight, like gaudy wheels turning endlessly on the wagons of a forgotten emperor's baggage train. One of the members of the procession, best friend of the groom, tossed his parasol in the air and it tumbled end over end back into his waiting hand. Younger women followed in beautiful ao dais. *The older women, dressed in black, provided a solemn border encasing the coy girls. Madame Dau's eyes creased in a broad smile as she remembered her own wedding, so similar to the one unfolding before her.*

Close by, in the village square, an argument broke out between two men over the price of a water buffalo. An arbitrator arrived to mediate the dispute. Anger flashed between the two men and the threat of violence charged in the air. Madame Dau saw the arbitrator quite clearly—he resembled the Venerable Vu Huong, but younger. Much younger. In the course of the mediation one of the men complained that the other man had hit him on the left side of his face causing a cut and swelling, ruining his good looks. The arbitrator smiled and suggested in a wry manner that the perpetrator should be allowed to hit the victim on the right side of his face "to restore balance and harmony" to the victim's good looks. Everyone laughed and eventually even the victim smiled. The dispute settled promptly. The arbitrator returned to his house, its interior walls covered in books. Buddhist canon, Confucian ethics and Taoist mysticism. Madame Dau even noticed a section of illustrated erotic classics. Venerable Vu Huong always had a twinkle in his eye, she thought. And she noticed an open volume of the Confucian Analects on his teak desk.

But even as she thought these things, Madame Dau closed her eyes against a blur of movement so as not to get dizzy and nauseous. When she opened her eyes she saw a husband and wife working together in the rice fields outside the village, their backs soaked in sweat, legs covered in mud. Two of their older children, a teenage boy and his younger sister, helped them harvest the rice. Madame Dau noticed that their grandmother remained in the village, caring for the two youngest children in a thatched home with an earthen floor. A baby slept in the wooden bed and a toddler laughed and giggled while playing with a jackfruit. This poor peasant family owned only a few mau of paddies, growing vegetables and fruit for household consumption and, when not working in the fields, they collected reeds to make into baskets and hats.

Madame Dau saw that the husband and wife worked well together and with good humor. She somehow knew they were literate. Very unusual for poor peasants. She sensed that they would become prosperous landowners before the grass grew over their heads. As they worked in the fields under the blazing sun, their faces were obscured by the shade of their conical hats, but Madame Dau felt she knew them. Then the husband made a joke, pointed upward toward the sky, and they both followed his upraised finger to look up at the heavens. Grinning broadly, both of them stared upward, directly at Madame Dau, squinting as if she was the sun pouring down upon their bodies. Startled, Madame Dau rocked backward in a spasm of shock. She knew these two people were the bride and groom of the wedding ceremony she had seen earlier and she realized in wonder that she was watching the progression of her parents' lives. Looking back into the arbitrator's house, she saw Vu Huong as he appeared just before he died, old and worn with care, leaning over his writing brush. He finished the last few strokes of copying the Diamond Sutra. A Buddhist rosary dangled from his slender wrist.

Another whirl of movement. More dizziness. Again Madame Dau closed her eyes. Opening them impatiently she saw the woman in the field, now as an old woman sitting on the front porch of a prosperous-looking wood and tile house. Surrounded by other women, friends and family, she watched children play in the village square. The women chewed betel leaves and drank tea, laughing and cracking jokes at the expense of the village men. This was the Thuong Nguon new year ritual. The old woman scolded her daughter, telling her to shoo the children away from playing under a great banyan tree rising above the village square so that the spirits of the ancestors could enjoy the shade undisturbed. Madame Dau knew that the woman's laughing husband had died years earlier of disease and its sorrow lingered at the edges of her joy.

The villagers were all in good spirits, celebrating another year in the wheel of life. And the highest venerable of the village, the arbitrator of earlier years, now a very old man, seemed satisfied to provide only occasional advice and guidance to the village as he became increasingly solitary and meditative, surrounded by his books. Taoist texts lay open on his desk top, preparation for his own impending death. His writing brushes stood unused in their container, having become drunk on black ink for the last time.

And yet again the wheeling movement, but this time more severe. Her stomach dropped, as if the earth had vanished beneath her. *This time she did not want to open her eyes, afraid of what she would see. But she did. She saw a second village, similar to the first, but it looked darker, poorer. The spirits of the village were disturbed and restless. This village seemed more familiar to Madame Dau, more real, and very frightening.*

The fields lay fallow and unproductive, neglect rending the paddies helpless against the encroaching forest. Fruit groves, their trees nothing more than desiccated corpses, were left untended. What little fruit there was undulated with armies of ants gorging and staggering like drunken dancers in a wedding procession gone bad.

Armed men gathered in the village square near the twisted metal helix of a rust-ing machine, sunlight gleaming off their rifles and periodically flashing painfully in her eyes. No tall and sheltering banyan tree in sight. The anger and fright of the men spread to the villagers who hid with their children in the stifling heat of closed houses, stinking ditches and oppressive tunnels.

Distrust and factionalism had long ago fragmented these villagers into smaller and smaller groups until parents no longer trusted their own children. The young and strong had either left to fight in the war, or had fled the village for the allure of easy money in Saigon, or were dead.

Boys had become men. Men had either been killed or were killing, either lying on their backs, being reabsorbed by the earth or standing above those lying on their backs, taunting the will of the gods. Girls had become women. Women no longer observing the ancient rituals; either lying on their backs with their legs spread, accepting the male cock-demons of lust and hatred or standing above those lying on their backs, counting money. Older, powerful men, no longer observing right relationships, gorging themselves on the banquet of weaker people's misfortunes, eating the flayed skin of their own children and grandchildren. Old women wailed and rocked in vain, their pride discarded and disregarded.

Using bamboo sticks to draw their plans in the sand, the leaders of the armed men in the village square displayed dark, livid faces and furiously debated how to attack the men huddled in a stone fortress outside their village. As a ragtag group of common soldiers leaned forward on their haunches and listened, Madame Dau could see that among them stood a few female warriors with bold breasts and broad hips. One couple in particular caught her attention, a man tightly holding the hand of a woman squatting next to him, both armed. The man made a joke and pointed upward and as they both laughed nervously, they looked up at the sky directly into the eyes of Madame Dau. She saw what she knew, that these two were the same couple who had been married in the first village. But they now looked poor and starving, their eyes dark. Sorrow, anger and hatred hung over and around them and she knew they worried about their children and their mother whom they had left in the tunnels. An arc of fear passed between them, and their attempts at humor did not straighten the curve of their backs, square the slump of their shoulders or lift the weight from their hearts.

Again the dizzying movement amidst the fog and rain and mist. Thunder rumbled across the ground and Madame Dau did not know if the noise came from the boot or from the suspended world around her. Then she saw a ferocious battle—men and women carrying dead and wounded on their backs, their clothing soaked red with blood. Hatred, confusion, fear, pain and death surrounded the soldiers, the villagers and the animals cowering in the jungle.

From her high vantage point, Madame Dau could not hear the sounds of battle. In silence she watched the couple among a group of soldiers struggling forward through the jungle, explosions ripping holes in the charred canopy above them. Their group staggered toward a dark hole in the ground through which bodies disappeared and Madame Dau knew it was the entrance to a tunnel. She watched in horror as

*each body was swallowed up when it jumped down the tunnel, the sharp gleam of
the rifle barrel winking out as it vanished into the hole.* It was the couple's turn.
They looked at each other one final time, squeezed hands, then leapt—he first,
she after—her gaze still tethered to the village.

*Madame Dau knew that after her parents jumped into that tunnel, there would
be no family, only orphans; no easy prosperity, only poverty and struggle; no freedom
and land reform, only death and misery. There would be no proper funeral to help
them in the afterworld.*

She could not tell if she was crying, or if the sky itself wept heavier tears in
mourning.

~ *Their Dance Continues* ~

Movement on the boots. Again. Madame Dau swayed, her vision swimming.
When the fog inside her head cleared, she opened her eyes to find no villages, no
people, only a pair of worn American boots, rugged, scarred, immovable. Above
them loomed the soldier, feral and filthy, face carved into a snarl. His questions no
longer floated in the air; only his breath remained, thick and alive. But he had said
something. Something about a Vietnamese wife. Something about not hurting
her. Perhaps, buried in a dark crevice of his soul, there flickered a trace of mercy.
A seed of restraint. The notion took root. Her control, shaken but intact, began
to return. She remembered the flickering villages etched in the boot's leather. She
wanted to live, to sit again on her porch, to watch her grandchildren run barefoot
through the dusk. He must let her live.

~

Mountain Man's expression shifted again as he watched the old woman
crouch before him, bent low over his boots as if entranced. Minutes passed.
She didn't move. Didn't speak. Her wide eyes and slack jaw made her seem
simple, stupefied. And he had thought her intelligent. Maybe she was retarded.
A half-wit who'd wandered from her keepers. He grunted, irritated. Stood there
like a damn fool while some ancient peasant gawked at his boots. Jungle Fighter
made into clown. Enough. He shoved the muzzle of his M-16 beneath the wad
of clothes in her arms, lifting them above her head. Then he slowly slid the barrel
down, beneath her face, between her legs. Muzzle oscillating.

"Speak, you goddamn VC bitch crone!" he snarled in English. "I'm only gonna
ask you one more time." Then, in jagged Vietnamese: "Where's your village?"

~

Just as she began to believe he might spare her, the demon grunted like a
rooting pig and used his weapon to hoist her arms. The cold muzzle found
its mark, between her legs, rubbing with quiet threat. She snapped upright,
knees clamped together, but the pressure only deepened. Steel seared flesh. Her
trembling returned. Her bladder failed. Warm urine ran down her legs, mingling
with the rain.

~

The Great Warrior recoiled. Something warm and caustic had splashed across her flanks. She had known such chemicals before from beetles and spiders, but this scent was different. No cousin insect had created this acidic wash. Its volume alone signaled danger. Something immense. The pheromone pattern unfurled beneath her legs and antennae, ancient genes decoding it. Mammalian. Alive. And most of all, afraid. She had arrived.

~

"Where's your village? Speak!" Mountain Man shouted, flecks of spit landing on her cheek. Finally, her lips moved. She mumbled toward the mud. "I'm just an old woman. A poor farmer. My village is nearby. I don't know about the Viet Cong. Or the People's Army. Or the French. I have children. I'm just a farmer. I know nothing."

~

The French? That caught him. They hadn't been around for decades. What the hell? "Bullshit! Fuckin' VC whore!"

Still no answer. Her silence fanned the fire. He growled again in Vietnamese. "You think I'm stupid, Old Mother?" No reply. Just tears sliding down her face. The muzzle still pressed between her legs. Why not kill her now? Any other time, he would've ended it. Or hauled her back for questioning. Then a memory surfaced, something from intelligence school. He'd never used it before, but maybe now.

In deliberate Vietnamese, softly, sympathetically, he said: "You know, I admire the writings of Nguyen Trai. And the poetry of Phan Boi Chau."

The trick was simple: bait the intellectual. No true cadre could resist the mention of national heroes. "Understand the Vietnamese mind," his instructor had said, "and you've already won."

~

When Madame Dau heard the names Nguyen Trai and Phan Boi Chau, something sparked inside her, an involuntary flicker of recognition. Then, quickly, the mask fell back into place. But the damage was done. And strangely, so was the healing. This soldier had married a Vietnamese. He read their poets. Maybe she would live.

~

Mountain Man saw the flicker. Got you. Not an illiterate villager. Not a half-wit. A cadre. Educated. Just as he'd suspected. For the first time, he sensed she was seeing him—not just the monster, but the man. Too bad, he thought, pulling the muzzle back. I'm gonna have to kill you, Little Mother. He sighed, leaned his rifle against a log, and drew his knife. Her eyes widened as he approached.

~ *Return of the Two-Headed Snake* ~

But Madame Dau's terror was no longer for the American. Behind him, in the branches of the banyan, two vipers stirred, conjoined, twin heads sharing a single body. Two tongues flicked in tandem. The serpent nodded once, then vanished behind the branch. She blinked. Had she imagined it? But no. From another branch, lower this time, both heads emerged again, watching her. Whispering something ancient. She could not move. The world itself seemed to jolt, slip off its axis, then catch on some unseen edge, a hairsbreadth from collapse. Then—another miracle.

Her dog.

Tail wagging, tongue lolling, he bounded into the clearing and began licking her face, tail thumping. He must have broken free, tracked her scent, and arrived just in time.

~

Mountain Man blinked as the dog trotted in and started licking her. "Oh, shit. That's torn it," he muttered, lowering the knife. And just like that, he was pulled from the jungle of his mind, not by bullets or memory, but by the wagging tail of a dog. Some small, irreducible part of him was still a boy. He just stood there, dumbfounded.

"Is this your dog?" he asked.

She said nothing. Perhaps she didn't understand. He tried again in Vietnamese. Still nothing.

He sighed. "Shit. What the fuck can you do?"

Mountain Man loved dogs. All dogs. No exceptions. Hounds like his back in West Virginia, and mutts like this one. And if there was one thing he couldn't bear, it was causing a dog pain. Killing the woman would hurt the dog. That, he couldn't do.

He stepped forward and offered his palm. "Come here, boy. Come to old Mountain Man."

~

He dropped to his knees, jabbering to the dog, wrestling gently, fingers combing through its fur with unexpected tenderness. Gently, he plucked leeches from its coat. He asked the dog's name.

She had never named it. Truthfully, she had often considered eating it. But now, sensing how much it meant to him, she answered, "May-man." Lucky.

He narrowed his eyes. She feared she had gone too far. But then he burst out laughing. She glanced up at the banyan, but the two-headed snake was gone. Still, she was certain it had been real. Not a vision. A sign. Not the gods. No—mother and father. Mama! He said something in English she didn't understand, laughing again. She gave a weak laugh in return.

And in that moment, something shifted. Her selfhood returned. Her will. This soldier, this ferocious boy, was not the enemy. He was the messenger. Just like in Mama's dream.

~

Mountain Man knew she had made up the name. But it didn't matter.

"Lucky," he said aloud, smiling. "Old Mother, you're the first one to touch my rifle and live." He chuckled softly. "Something tells me you and me are gonna get along just fine."

He ran a finger along the edge of the leather flock bag hanging from his neck.

~

That bag held everything. His anchor. His past. During the Depression, his grandfather, stone-bodied and earthbound, had lost the family farm. After the war, he'd clawed his way back to the land, buying a pig farm in the Alleghenies. There, Mountain Man was born. As a child, he'd been tossed into the air by those iron hands. He'd looked up and seen Mt. Olympus, white-haired, snow-eyed, a god whose fury could erupt blue-veined and volcanic. A man of storms. Sometimes, that hand closed around a silver dollar, pressed it into his palm. No words. Just a wink, a snowy avalanche of brow collapsing over a cave of mysteries.

On the day he shipped out, his grandfather whispered something cryptic and pressed another gift into his hand. Later, Mountain Man opened his palm.

A silver dollar, both faces filed smooth.

On one side: COME HOME.

On the other: PLEASE.

That coin now rested among other relics in his leather bag.

~

Madame Dau watched the man's thumb move gently over the flock bag, as if it were a sacred talisman. When he looked up and spoke in Vietnamese, his voice was soft. "Now, tell me about your family."

There was no threat in his tone. Only curiosity. Perhaps even kindness. She glanced again toward the banyan. No snake. No gods. But her fingers curled tighter around the hem of her *ao ba ba*.

A stillness passed through her belly. Her parents had intervened, not to save her, but to show her: the demon was a door.

And through him, something would change.

Chapter Eleven

The Exchange

Tit-for-Tat

*G*oddess, *Your story is overwrought. Michael is not The Chosen One. This hominin may have Your mutated genes, but the human part is schizophrenic, that's all—a mutant schizophrenic having a flashback. Dealing with delusions. Dealing with killing. Dealing with war. It happens to them. They have wars, then they have nightmares that drive them to pace the corridors of diplomacy, then they learn to block out the light so they can sleep again, then they have more wars. Really, Madame Immortal, tone it down. Delusions? A flashback? A war? Especially a little war. Even a big war. Even a lost generation is what? A single lost generation among billions of lost generations. It's nothing, really. A recipe for rejection. Not as titillating as their relationships. Now, their relationships! Those are stories! Wonderfully human superfluous complexities built upon the simplest of foundations: DrivesNaturalselectionAndthewondersofchemistry.*

You continue to deny his role as an intermediate in the evolution of the Superior Ones. Denial is quite ugly. Nevertheless, it is true that it will get worse before it gets better. I—

Give up this flashback idea and concentrate on their relationships. Eh? Ah? Makes for a better story. It will sell better to My faction. No? Besides, no human will believe You are real.

No. It is only through his flashback that You will get Your flesh back.

Alas, You insist on continuing to speak in overly dramatic terms about a flashback? It means nothing to Me. What is a flashback? A dog remembering the place where he was attacked? A tick remembering the oily blood of an android? Or is it just humans of whom You speak? The terrible terrifying traumas that infest the folds of their brains, like smelly fungus, do not compete with the deodorized panic of their chatter. Sophisticated, complex, devious, paradoxical, juvenile, wise and whimsically endless chatter about sex, stratagems and survival. Now, that sells! Not schizophrenia . Not some delusional quest to replace humankind with Superior Ones. Who would want this, let alone buy its premise?

I am an Artist! Sales do not interest Me.

And Who is paying for the hydrogen that fuels the suns that warms the photosynthesizing fodder that feeds the objects of Your art?

Speaking of objects, two of them are plotting.

Ah, Goddess! Now this is getting good.

No, this is getting tricky.

~ *Plotting* ~

Major Vy and Captain Tong sat in silence long after Sergeants Dam and Viet disappeared into the dripping foliage. Tong fidgeted with the teacups the sergeants had left behind, shifting them from one hand to the other. The sound irritated Vy, who was still hunched over the smoothed patch of sand, staring at the ghost of a map now blurred by mist and memory.

"Private Quy!" he called.

The adolescent loped into view, his long limbs comically out of proportion—a bamboo stalk grown too fast. Vy gestured toward the teacups and pot. Tong, clearly resentful, handed them off without a word, then glanced sidelong at the major, who remained lost in thought. The only sound was the patient drip of rainwater falling from saturated leaves.

After a long pause, Vy finally muttered, "Their plan might work." He stabbed the bamboo pointer into the sand. "Trade our wounded American for comrades Tuyet Mai and Kim Lan"—his eyes flicked up to meet Tong's—"and the statue. If it works, we won't need to send Dam and his sappers into the fortress. We get what we want and still have time to reach the caravan."

"Maybe," Tong said, brushing a leech from his ankle.

Vy bristled. "What?"

"I said, 'maybe.' I've heard Americans are fanatical about recovering their wounded, but if you were in command, would you trade two captured officers for one injured foot soldier?"

"No. But let's hope the Americans don't know our comrades are officers."

"That's the weakness. If they know the truth, they'll never agree. But if they don't, the offer will reek of deception." Tong made a fist in the air. "They'll tighten their grip. Squeeze the women harder."

Vy nodded grimly. "I've thought of that. That's why we include the statue. Split their focus. Distract them. Americans want to believe lies that align with their sense of heroism. I know them. Fought them for years. They confuse stubbornness for truth. Let's use that."

Tong smirked. "In spite of our sacred slogans, they're not fools. We have to give their commander something he can defend. A story he can sell upward."

"No. That's where you're wrong. Americans are fools in the way of empires. They'll lose a dozen men to recover one. They think they're too strong to fail. Let's use their madness."

Tong tilted his head. "Exactly why I said, 'maybe.'"

Vy slapped his knees and rose. "Then let's try it."

Tong offered no reply, only a slight smile. If the plan failed, he'd claim foresight. If it worked, shared credit. Either way, Hanoi had already forgotten them.

Vy's voice turned sharp. "First, I want to speak to the American. Quy!"

The private reappeared. "Tell Sergeant Dam I need him as interpreter. Now."

Quy turned, eager to obey.

"Wait," Vy said. He softened his voice and placed a hand on Quy's shoulder. "Don't be so quick, comrade. You leap like a drunk farmer chasing a buffalo." He picked a thorn from Quy's tunic, then added, "Also summon Med Tech Le. I want an update on the prisoner's condition."

"Yes, Comrade Major!" Quy grinned, then vanished into the green curtain of vines, limbs flailing awkwardly through the monsoon mist.

Vy watched him go. Something tender flickered at the corners of his eyes.

Tong caught it. "Feeling guilty about our 'criminal enterprise,' Major?"

Vy turned sharply, searching Tong's face for sarcasm. He found none, just the faint glimmer of shared burden.

"I keep seeing that dead orangutan," Vy said softly. "The one at the woodcutter's cottage. In my dreams, it changes. Becomes one of ours. But I can't tell who. Maybe all of them."

Tong nodded. He picked up the bamboo pointer and began drawing Chinese characters in the damp sand.

"You know I can't read that," Vy said.

Tong didn't look up. "It says, 'To be bold without gentleness, to be generous without restraint, to lead without humility—this is death.'"

Vy smiled bitterly. "Then we're dead."

Tong chuckled. "But so are they. Our boys. Abandoned to this forest. Too many years. Disease. Booby traps. Dreams that rot in their sleep."

Vy looked down at his helmet, massaging its edge. "I'm doing this for my wife. For my family."

"Of course," Tong replied. "But some of us have to survive. Might as well be us. Anyway, your doubts make you a lousy criminal."

"Good."

"Not good for me," Tong muttered.

"No, I wouldn't expect it to be," replied Vy.

Then, with forced cheer, Tong chirped, "Shall we check on our American?"

He turned and walked off, not waiting for permission.

Vy's jaw tightened. He almost called him back, but stopped.

Ha! Fell for it again. Always stealing the last word. Tong the schemer. Habit, pure habit. He'll never change. Best watch him closely.

~ *Idaho in Pain* ~

Idaho moaned.

Propped against a fallen log by his NVA captors, he lay beneath a tattered poncho that failed to keep the monsoon from soaking his raw, shaking body. He shifted the cover again and again, but the rain poured through anyway. It kept the ants and centipedes at bay, but not the gnats, nor the leeches, which swarmed toward the magnetic stench of his leg wound. His leg, mangled and shredded, had been patched by an NVA medic. Idaho assumed the work had been botched. The medic was a shriveled man with half his teeth blackened and the rest missing, who leaned over Idaho's shattered flesh with a slack, apologetic grin. He smeared foul-smelling herbs and bundled poultices onto the leg with trembling fingers, as though wrapping a gift no one wanted. Probably never even heard of antibiotics. *I'm gonna lose the damn thing. These dink bastards'll cost me my leg. Sure as shit.*

Tears streaked his face as memory returned. The ambush—two AK-47 rounds ripping through his tibia like a chainsaw. Bone fragments flying. Blood exploding in pulses. His captors found him convulsing in the dirt, and picked the shards of his tibia out of him as one might pluck porcupine quills. He couldn't walk. Couldn't control his bowels. Feces soaked his pants and never dried. The monsoon saw to that. Eventually, the stench grew too much, even for the NVA. They taught him to say *"giúp đỡ"* whenever he needed to relieve himself. Then two soldiers would drag him to a shallow pit and hold him upright while he squatted, trembling. He loathed them. They, in turn, hated drawing the short straw.

But others thrived: the beetles, the grubs, the thriving microbes. Manna from heaven. His filth undulated with feasting life. Idaho winced and thought, Who says there are no winners in war?

~

That is not precisely what I thought!

~

And still, through the blur of insects and pain, he whispered: *God, I want to go home.*

~

If only you could! Blame God. Blame First Principles.

~

His captors looked half-dead themselves. Malnourished, thin, pale, uniforms in tatters. Once, a small group squatted nearby, jabbering in their strange, nasal language. They reminded him of feral animals: laughing, scratching, defecating openly, sandals flapping in the mud. Not boots. Not real soldiers. Idaho watched them with revulsion. He remembered flipping through *National Geographic* with Joey Logan, searching for bare-breasted women among the "primitive tribes" of Africa. These men were those tribes come alive—uncivilized headhunters, spear-wielding cannibals without even the decency to wear pith helmets. And their speech, a harsh babble of "ah!" and "eh!" and grotesque syllables, assaulted his senses. In his fever, it turned to geese squawking nonsense. *Vu-ge-du-go-ba-vac…fuck-fuck-fuck*, his mind twisted it, mocking them, mocking himself.

He recoiled. From them. From what he was becoming.

~

Them. Always—it is Them.

~

Quang Long, company clerk, sat among them. They laughed at Kha's failed animal hunts, teased Nguu's lustful daydreams, mocked Doanh's obsession with orchids. Long noticed the American staring, dazed and resentful. He felt the urge to sketch him. Later, he asked Commissar Minh for permission.

"I have no objection," Minh said, "but the drawing must show the American as pitiful. Make his face ugly. Gratitude in his eyes. Heroic soldiers above him. Show it to me when it's done."

Long nodded. But later, in private, he sketched only the boy's face, reflecting a vague, hollow, frightened soldier. When he finished, Long stared at it too long. He felt something he did not want to feel. Empathy. He tore it to shreds before anyone could see.

~

Idaho, unaware of the sketch, still felt exposed. The way they looked at him, with their stupid, gaping, curious stares, made him seethe. *They're the freaks, not me.*

But the days passed, and with nothing to do but watch, he began to notice differences among them. These weren't prison guards. They were soldiers. Men.

He started giving them nicknames, a childish act of control. The medic with the broken teeth—he called him Dopey. The man grinned constantly and breathed through his mouth, vacant-eyed and half-lost. Another soldier, calm and kind, he named Doc. There was a Sneezy too—one of the guards who sniffled without pause.

One day, a wiry man set up a barber's station on a stump. Idaho watched in disbelief. Haircuts? In a jungle war?

The barber never smiled. He rolled his eyes when soldiers shifted in their seats, looked pained when they laughed. Idaho named him Grumpy and liked him, though he didn't know why.

As for the officers, Idaho turned them into bulls. Major Vy became Old Twitchy Stud—the virile sire from his father's farm. Captain Tong was Old Cud Lips, slow-spoken and steady. Commissar Minh—Old Fat Rump.

But one man refused renaming. He radiated something cold, untouched. A human void.

Sergeant Dam.

He was their interpreter. His voice, flat and precise, cut through language like a scalpel. Idaho should've felt some connection to the one who spoke English, but Dam unnerved him more than the rest. He moved without sound, carried no scent, left no trace. Idaho suspected, correctly, that Dam was their best fighter.

What he didn't know was that Dam saw in Idaho the face of the American pilot who bombed his mother.

~

Major Vy listened half-heartedly to Medical Technician Le's report while glancing across the clearing at the wounded American. Captain Tong flicked wet leaves from his uniform with the boredom of a man tired of details. Sergeant Dam stood apart, stone still.

Le's voice droned. "The entrance wound has inverted edges, Comrade Major. The tibia was smashed. Muscles pushed upward. The wound had the appearance of cauliflower. I used a decoction of cay oi bark to clean it, then trau and gang gai poultices to counter infection."

Vy raised his hand. "Enough, Comrade. Just tell us, will he live?"

Le brightened. "If the treatments continue, yes. If not, he'll lose the leg or worse."

Tong grunted. "Can he be transported?"

"He must be carried gently. But yes."

Vy nodded, watching the boy more closely. So young. So fragile. His uniform too large, his eyes darting. The boy's hands fidgeted near a tear in his tunic. He seemed a toddler lost in his father's clothes. Le kept talking—sedatives from *cay trac ba* seeds, diuretics in his tea—but Vy had stopped listening. He was watching the boy, trying not to see himself decades ago.

Tong broke the silence with a harsh laugh. "Time to talk with the devil, Comrade Major."

Vy dismissed Le. Sergeant Dam joined them. He said nothing, but as he walked, he remembered: Le had used most of the antibiotics treating victims of American traps. One in particular.

~

Idaho watched the three approach: two officers and the one that made him shake. He held up a leech from his leg and muttered, "We're not in Idaho anymore, are we, Toto?"

He thought of saying, *Welcome, Old Twitchy Stud. Old Cud Lips.* But the third one understood English. And that meant danger. They might touch his leg again. Better to be shot than endure that. They loomed over him with their camouflaged pith helmets dripping rain, like jungle stalactites. Then it came. English. Cold, clean, and terrifying.

"Listen carefully," the interpreter said. "We want to ask you questions."

Glorious English. Even from this death-faced ghoul, it settled his nerves, anchoring him in something that still felt human.

"Why have you not received air support?"

Air. Support.

For some reason, the words transported him back home. His mother's kitchen. Blue tile counters. Peppermint candies in crystal bowls. Breadbox with a rooster. The scent of hay and coffee and chickens and mud. A patchwork quilt. A chugging tractor. *Air support . . . air . . . support. . . .*

When he was ten, Idaho once snuck an old kerosene lantern into his bedroom and lit match after match, coaxing it to life. The flame sputtered, dim and desperate, until it finally caught with a sharp gasp. The room filled with smoke. His father burst in, flinging open windows, fanning the haze with his broad hands, and bellowed, "Boy, there ain't enough air in here to support a damn canary!"

That line—*ain't enough air to support*—came back to him now, warped by pain and time. No air. No support. No rescue. Only the jungle. Only the leg. Only the question, "Why have you not received air support?"

~

Dam kicked his leg.

The scream cut through jungle and sky.

"Why have you not received air support?"

"I don't know!" Idaho sobbed. "I'm just a private! I swear!"

Questions followed in a barrage. Food. Ammunition. Radios. Idaho answered the same each time. "I don't know. We were just supposed to grab two women and leave."

Vy and Tong conferred.

"Enough," Tong muttered. "Let's get to the point."

Vy turned to Dam. "Ask him who to contact for exchange negotiations."

Now Dam understood. They would try Sergeant Viet's plan. There might be an end to this siege after all.

He touched Idaho's arm gently. "Private. This may be your luck. Listen carefully. Who do we contact in your fortress to arrange an exchange?"

Idaho blinked, confused. "Exchange?"

Dam sighed. "Exchange. Prisoner swap. You go home. We get our men."

Idaho stared. The words sank in.

I might see the guys again. T, Bowls, Mountain Man, Storyteller . . . all of them.

What's T's name? Gotta give them a name.

Finally, it surfaced.

"Lieutenant Rogers," he whispered.

"Who?"

"Lieutenant Rogers."

Dam tilted his head. "Say it again. Slowly."

Idaho met the interpreter's eyes. For the first time, they didn't seem entirely inhuman.

"Lieutenant Rogers."

~ *Commissar Minh Objects* ~

The words "Lieutenant Rogers" had barely left Idaho's lips when a loud commotion cracked through the treeline. Vy and Tong froze.

"Vy! Tong! Vy! Tong!"

The shout rang out, urgent, ragged. A red-faced man burst through the brush, panting, swiping jungle filth from his tunic with furious precision, as if wiping away an offense. He shouted the names again, not as summons, but as accusations.

"Vy. Tong."

He stumbled, nearly toppled, then caught himself, chest heaving. With theatrical flair, he planted his feet, spread his legs wide, and raised one hand like a judge demanding silence in a courtroom. His face gleamed with sweat and indignation.

Idaho couldn't make sense of the words, but he felt it in his gut: *whatever fragile plan existed is about to change.*

~

"What is the meaning of this?" Commissar Minh spat. "Sergeant Viet informs me that you two met, *secretly,* with him and Sergeant Dam, to plan an exchange. An *exchange!* And no one informed political command?" His voice rose with each word, the way a fire climbs dry wood.

"You interrogated the prisoner *alone*? Without Party oversight? What were you asking him, Vy? What exactly do you think you're doing?"

Major Vy met the storm with practiced calm. "Comrade Commissar, time was short. Our intent was to gather preliminary intelligence. Once we had actionable details, you would have been—"

Minh cut him off. "Spare me the flattery. You decided I was an obstacle and cut me out. Now you stand here pretending this is merely a military matter?"

Vy's voice thinned. "The matter is urgent. The initiative required speed."

Minh's eyes narrowed. "When you ignore the Party, you don't act with speed. You act with arrogance. And you place this entire battalion in jeopardy."

He turned to Captain Tong. "Do you agree with this violation, Comrade?"

Tong replied smoothly, "We acted to protect both the mission and the lives of our comrades in the fortress. This wasn't deception. It was discretion."

Minh bristled. "You presume to define discretion for me?"

Vy interjected, "Had we waited, we might've lost the opportunity for a tactical solution—"

"And what *is* the tactical solution, Vy?" Minh barked. "To sit and rot in this swamp? You've refused to attack. Refused to move. Refused to send for reinforcements. You've paralyzed the company with your hand-wringing."

"We're calculating—"

"You're calculating your own survival," Minh growled. "Three choices, Comrades: attack the fortress now, request support and then attack, or move forward with the mission. Anything else is cowardice dressed up as contemplation. Every day we sit here, we grow more vulnerable to American air power."

Captain Tong's voice remained composed, but his eyes had gone hard. "If you believe air support is imminent, Commissar, then why aren't we already bombed? Because we've severed their communications. They're isolated. We have time to act wisely."

Minh folded his arms. "You've been whispering in the woods, hiding strategy like a pair of schoolboys. What is it you're not telling me?"

"There's nothing hidden," Tong replied. "We all want the same outcome."

"No," Minh said flatly. "You want a controlled outcome. One that keeps your hands clean."

Tong's tone darkened. "What we want is to avoid throwing away lives just to posture for Party approval."

Minh's expression turned stony. "Posture? Is that what you think I do here?"

"No," Tong said. "But I think you've forgotten what's at stake. Those two women, they're intelligence officers. The Americans know it. The prisoner confirmed it. Their orders were to capture them. You think Hanoi will forgive us if they succeed?"

Minh's voice dropped to a whisper, the kind that rattles more than a shout. "Are you accusing me of jeopardizing State secrets?"

"I'm accusing you of thinking like a bureaucrat, not a soldier."

Minh's eyes glinted. "And you're thinking like a man whose loyalty is compromised."

Tong's control snapped. "Don't play coy. The Americans have Tuyet Mai and Kim Lan. They'll be interrogated. Tortured. Worse. And not just because they're intelligence officers. Because they're women. You know what they do to women, Minh. Or does your ideology blind you to that too?"

The crack in Tong's voice startled even himself. Minh heard it and filed it away.

~

Then, slowly, Minh drew his pistol. Idaho flinched. The metallic click of the hammer cocking sounded louder than thunder. Minh leveled the weapon at Idaho's head.

"One pull," he said coldly. "And this farce ends."

Idaho couldn't move. The pain in his leg made the fetal curl impossible. He covered his face with his arms, whispering into his own flesh, "Don't shoot . . . don't shoot. . . . " Rain dripped from the canopy. Sweat ran into his eyes. The sting reminded him he was still alive. Barely.

Tong stepped forward. His lazy posture was gone, replaced by a cold, coiled stillness. He walked slowly, each step deliberate.

Vy reached to stop him, one hand on Minh's shoulder, the other outstretched in appeal. "This cannot happen. Please, Comrade Minh, put the weapon away—"

Tong silenced them both. "Shoot me first, Commissar. Then the boy. But nothing changes. Our sisters in the fortress will die. And so will the intel they carry. You'll answer for it. To Hanoi. To the Party. And to me." His voice trembled now. Not with fear. With memory. He saw Tuyet Mai not as a symbol, not as a lover, but as a mother. Their child he imagined nursing quietly in the safety of a Hanoi apartment that no longer existed. He felt exposed.

Minh saw it. The pistol lowered. A slow smile curled across the Commissar's lips. "Just as I suspected. There's more at play here than tactics."

He holstered the pistol with ceremony, then turned and walked away with the self-satisfaction of a man who has just discovered a useful secret.

Vy watched him vanish into the mist and turned to Tong, who stood frozen, staring at the American with an expression not of rage but devastation.

Vy's hands began to tremble. *This is slipping away. Fast.* Even in the worst firestorms of war, he had never been shaken like this.

~ *Planning the Exchange* ~

Because he spoke English, Sergeant Dam had been ordered to carry the white flag. He said nothing in reply, only nodded once, then slipped away into the jungle's edge to search for the right ground, *visible to both sides, but advantageous to a sapper's mind.* He repeated the name *Lieutenant Rogers* under his breath again and again, practicing its alien cadence. Eventually, with Vy's field binoculars and the instincts of a man who understood both death and concealment, he chose a spot halfway between the fortress and the forest's edge: a broken rise of tangled grass, punctuated by jagged stumps that reached to the knee. He noted the soil, the density of root and stone. He marked escape paths. Then he turned and went in search of cloth.

He found Company Clerk Quang Long, slumped over a small pile of censored letters, eyes hollow with grief. Letters destined never to arrive. Letters from ghosts to ghosts. Most would travel for a year before being returned to families of the already buried.

Dam approached with a forced grin. "Ah, Comrade Long. You look better than last time I saw you."

Long looked up, grateful to be interrupted.

"Five letters," he said. "All mentioned the siege. Censored them myself."

"Smart comrades. Usually. This time, fools."

"You hungry?"

Long gestured to a cleared patch of ground, the shadow of a shared meal. Rice balls waited. Dam remained standing.

"I need a white flag."

Long blinked. "For the negotiations?"

"You know?"

"Everyone knows. Wounded American for our two sisters in the fortress."

Dam gave a sideways tilt of his head, half smile, half confession. Long's eyes brightened.

"I knew it was true!"

"Well?"

"Well what?"

"The flag, you idiot."

"Ah. No. No white flags in stock. Not standard issue, Sergeant Dam."

Dam looked around theatrically. "I don't see Commissar Minh nearby. You can drop the caution. My politics end where the blast radius begins."

Long laughed but kept his voice low. "Still, Minh has ears. And connections."

"Yes, yes. So? The flag?"

Long perked up, suddenly useful. He began rummaging through canvas bags, muttering to himself. Nothing. Then he snapped, "Wait. Medical Technician Le. Bandages. Gauze."

Dam frowned. "Too limp. I'd rather not be shot for carrying a wet rag."

"No, no—listen. We bind gauze to a crossbar. Tie the bar to a bamboo pole. Keeps the cloth extended. Even in this piss-rain, it'll hold."

Dam grunted. Not convinced. But better than nothing.

"Go. Make it. We'll test it."

He turned to go.

Long caught his arm. His voice was urgent.

"One thing, Sergeant."

Dam paused. "What?"

"The statue. Get it back. Please."

Dam started to brush him off, but the plea in Long's eyes stilled him.

"Yes. Yes. Ghosts and all. Now go. And stop drooling on my boots."

~ *The Americans Are Approached* ~

At his guard post, Bowls crouched low behind the crumbling stone wall, half-focused on the clearing. His mind had slipped. The slit in the wall was there for vigilance, but instead, he carved. Two breasts. Symmetrical, wet, gleaming with jungle mist. He whispered as he worked: "God is in the details." He sculpted slowly, lovingly, aiming for something indistinguishable from flesh. The nipples were no problem, those he adored. But the areolas tormented him. Subtle, circular. They had to rise just enough. Snow drifting around a volcanic peak. Eruption from the sacred ring. Nipple as monument. Trail marker. Chimney Rock on the Orgasm Trail. Rites of passage. Feminine flares. Suddenly, he stopped.

"It wasn't me," he muttered. "I didn't carve these. It was Nature. Or someone else. Something else. Something's using me."

Control yourself!

The voice. From inside? From the wall? He shivered, dropped the knife. Too much time in the jungle. Too long. He blinked. Something white—no, greyish-white—fluttered in the mist beyond the clearing. He closed his eyes, cursed, wiped the sweat with his towel. Opened again.

Still there.

An NVA soldier. Waving something. Not a weapon. Something . . . odd. A flag? A *white* flag? Adrenaline surged through him in waves of anticipation.

~

T squatted behind a bamboo-and-poncho screen, trying to shit in peace. No such luck. The stool ran thin, red-tinged. His stomach turned. *Dysentery? No. Please God. Not here. Leaves. Useless.* He was halfway through the struggle when Superman's voice cracked through the barrier.

"T! T!"

"What is it?"

"Bowls says there's a gook in the clearing. White flag. Pappy sent me to get you. Nature's trying to talk to him."

T sighed. "Coming."

"Superman?"

No answer. Superman had drifted inward again, scolding himself. *Swore again. I'm using Stretch's words. His rage. My words now. My rage. God, is my faith cracking? What am I becoming? He looked up into the empty sky. Do You see what this war is doing to me, God?*

I see. A male voice, deep and disturbing.

But do You see what it's doing to You, dear God? Feminine, soothing.

It is only a small war.

A small god then. A small myth. A small addiction to suffering. A large addiction to First Principles.

From deep inside the cosmic gutter, the male voice cooed: **Add them all together. One potent drug for an omnipotent God.**

The Goddess laughed, flirtatious and cruel: **They burn in the fissures of Your divine colon.**

Access granted, said God, dryly, **to You, of course.**

Oh how holy.

That was not Me, whispered God. **That was Michael's demons, twisting Our words again.**

~

T staggered upright. His anus burned—raw, searing, and impossible to ignore. First- or second-degree heat, at least. But he was standing. That was something. A white flag. What the hell do they want?

~

Pappy spotted Cairns across the courtyard, kneeling beside the senior Vietnamese woman, Tuyet Mai. He was writing again. Always writing. Observation or obsession? Pappy didn't like the way Cairns looked at her.

~

Cairns knelt like a supplicant, but dreamed like a predator. In his mind, Tuyet Mai was already bound, gagged, stripped bare. He traced the lines of imaginary rope in his notebook. He needed fear, but not terror. Fear that sharpened the eyes, not slackened the mouth. That was his craft. She was the crown jewel. The last one. He pressed harder with the pencil, lost in the exquisite geometry of domination. Only Pappy's cough saved him. Cairns lingered for a breath too long, fingers still pulsing with imagined control. Then the predator vanished behind the offier's mask. He snapped the book closed.

"Yes, Sergeant?"

"Sir, white flag in the clearing. Nature thinks they want to parlay. Two men. Interpreter present. You'd best come, sir."

"I'm on my way."

As Pappy walked off, he glanced back. Cairns leaned over Tuyet Mai's body, thinking, *Lovers at a wedding? Or devils in a graveyard?*

~

They shouted across the clearing. Broken English. Hard to decipher. But the intent became clear: two representatives from each side, interpreter present. T gathered the officers in the ruins of the old church.

"Well?" he said.

A dozen voices overlapped:

"It's a trap—"

"No. What would they gain—"

"They want the women—"

"They never cared before—"

"They must be intel—"

"What do we get back—"

"Maybe they've got Idaho—"

"What if it's Mountain Man—"

"What about the statue—"

T raised his voice. "Captain Cairns, didn't you say that statue—what did you call it?—might be important?"

Cairns blinked. Licked his lips.

"Yes. Tibetan goddess. White Tara. Compassion and all that. Helps those in suffering. Enlightenment, maybe."

"Yeah? So?"

Yes, Goddess. So?

It was important to Michael's parents. To Meiying. To John. To Us.

But not to them. Not yet.

Cairns changed tone. "It's valuable. Could be sold for a fortune. Might be hollow. Might hold something."

"Like what?"

"Documents. Intel. Treasure. Who knows."

"And you think it's worth more than Idaho? More than Mountain Man?"

Cairns stared him down. "Yes."

T sneered. "Captain—"

Pappy cut in. "We don't have to decide yet. Let's hear what they want."

T exhaled. Nodded. "Fine. Captain, you and me?"

Cairns hesitated. "Both of us? Risky."

"Fine. I'll go alone."

Cairns relented. "I'm going. Let's just hope they don't shoot us."

Birdman muttered, "If they do, we shoot back."

Everyone glared.

Pappy asked, "Permission to examine the statue more closely?"

T waved. "Go ahead."

Cairns added, "Just look. Don't open it."

Behind the altar, Pappy found the figurine—and screamed. He emerged with blistered hands.

~

Later, with burns treated, Pappy departed. T caught Cairns' eye. "Mother of Compassion?"

Cairns shook his head. "Acid. From the inside, through the gold. Makes me wonder what she's hiding."

"Compassion as corrosion," said T. "Fits the war. It eats everything."

"Flesh. Bone. Ghosts," Cairns added.

T narrowed his eyes. "Maybe that's all we are now."

Topper scoffed. "Very dramatic, Lieutenant."

T looked away, embarrassed.

Cairns gave a dry laugh. "Well. Let's go negotiate with our fellow ghosts."

~ *Negotiating the Exchange* ~

When the hour arrived, Lieutenant T peeled the pistol from his hip and handed it to Bowls, stuffed a fresh stick of gum in his mouth, and clambered down the stone parapet with Cairns just behind. As he descended, his boot caught a jagged edge, and he tumbled forward, arms flailing, landing hard in the mud, fully exposed to the two NVA soldiers waiting in the clearing.

"Damn! Damn! Damn!"

He muttered the curse like a drumbeat the entire way across the field, rain slicing through the air in silver veils. The two NVA men remained squatting, pith helmets angled low against the wind.

Cairns spoke dryly out the corner of his mouth. "Relax. The director of this movie just has a sick sense of humor."

"Yeah?" T growled. "I'd like to fire his ass."

~

As the Americans approached, Major Vy and Sergeant Dam rose and saluted. Vy noted the Americans' appearance: thin, ragged, fatigued. His harassment campaign had worn them down. Without eye contact, Vy spoke softly, almost gravelly for a Vietnamese officer. Dam translated, a beat behind, his English stiff.

"Good afternoon, gentlemen sirs. I am Major Vy. This is. . . . "

Dam hesitated, stumbling.

"My apologies. I am Sergeant Dam. I will translate."

Both T and Cairns began to speak. Then stopped. Then both spoke again. T finally took control.

"Lieutenant Rogers. This is Captain Cairns."

Vy nodded silently, watching them both. He studied their ranks, postures, voices. A captain and a lieutenant. But the chewing gum made him suspect the lieutenant was subordinate. *Children chew gum.* Vy offered tea.

The two Americans answered at the same time—Cairns said yes, thank you; T said no, thank you.

Dam stood baffled, unable to translate the blur. Vy, observing the brief glance exchanged between them, made a private calculation: *The one who wins this glance is in charge.*

T said firmly, "No."

Vy adjusted his judgment. The lieutenant held command. The captain, a political cadre? Like Minh. Not a real soldier. Vy raised his voice slightly. "You must understand. Escape is impossible. Your fortress is surrounded. We offer honorable surrender. Your men will be treated well by the People's Army."

He spoke loudly, with ceremony, as if announcing a public verdict. Rain pattered through the silence. Vy watched the Americans absorb the statement: first confusion, then a smoldering anger. Vy enjoyed the discomfort. It was a theater of humiliation, and the Americans were only just realizing they'd been cast as the fools.

~

T stared at the major's helmet, worn and chewed at the edges. *A major can't get a decent lid?* he thought. But then a scent, sharp and fishy, cut into his thoughts. His inner voice rose: *Don't underestimate them.* He'd heard the same said about himself—raggedy, black, and expendable. Don't repeat the government's mistake. *Underestimate the Vietnamese, and you die.*

But then the interpreter's voice cut in: "... prepared to accept your surrender."

The words shattered the fragile respect T had begun to build. Surrender? *Surrender?* He stiffened, jaw clenched. *Look me in the eyes when you insult me.* But the major kept his gaze low, polite by his own customs, but to T, it reeked of evasion. He wanted to say "Nuts," like General McAuliffe at Bastogne. But it sounded ridiculous now. They were all nuts. This whole war. And now, *his gut churned again.*

Cairns issued a low, humorless chuckle beside him. The two looked at one another. T's eyes smoldered; Cairns wore that sly half-smile that let him slip out of every consequence. Cairns nodded, his gesture meaning, *You speak.* If it went well, Cairns could take partial credit. If it didn't, the lieutenant would bear the blame alone.

T raised his voice to match Vy's, trying to inject command into every syllable. "Thank you for your offer of surrender, Major, but we have no intention of surrendering today—or any day. Is that all you called us out here for?"

But Dam gestured mid-sentence. *Too fast.* T paused. The rhythm broken. Still, he felt proud. His voice held. He'd stood his ground. A shame it couldn't drop an octave.

When Dam finished the halting translation, T stared at the major, who still refused to meet his eyes.

What T would never know: Vy *wanted* to meet his gaze. But couldn't. Not out of fear. But shame. Shame for being entangled in this murky drug scheme, this betrayal of soldierhood. Politeness was the last fig leaf covering his fractured sense of honor. He couldn't meet T's eyes, not out of fear, but because in them, he saw what he once was. And what he had long since lost.

~

After listening to Dam's translation of the American lieutenant's offer, Major Vy suppressed a grin. With a grunt, he squatted and pointed to a tree stump for the lieutenant to sit. Though his gaze stayed fixed on the earth, he watched from the corner of his eye as the Americans hesitated. Finally, the younger officer sat. The captain remained standing, visibly uneasy about ceding the lower ground to a People's Army sergeant. Vy watched with quiet amusement as Cairns attempted an awkward half-squat before rising again, feigning intent.

Mock-serious, Vy flicked a glance his way. Dam, meanwhile, was probing the ground with his sandaled foot. *Yes, Comrade Sapper, study the soil. Feel the roots and textures. You'll be crawling over this very ground tonight.*

As Vy turned his attention back to the Americans, he caught the faint odor of defecation. Ah. One of them is already cracking. After a deliberate silence, Vy offered two hand-rolled cigarettes. T accepted with polite ease, though he didn't smoke. Cairns accepted too, but carelessly shoved the cigarette into his pocket, snapping it in half. He then ceremoniously unwrapped a pack of sleek American cigarettes and offered one in return, like a schoolteacher bribing unruly children with sweets.

"No manners," Vy thought. "Refinement is beyond them."

"We Vietnamese have a saying, Captain. *Bánh ếch đi, bánh quí lại.* 'When offered a cookie, one returns a pudding.'" He raised his palm, refusing the gift. "No pudding today. Thank you."

Vy's dislike of Cairns ran deeper than the gesture. He sensed no soldier within him, only something brittle and masked. Cairns reminded him of the worst traits of both Tong and Minh: one's hinted perversity, the other's rigid zeal. And Cairns' Asian blood made it worse. Vy dismissed him entirely, focusing on the lieutenant instead.

Sergeant Dam, on the other hand, felt nothing toward the Americans, no hate, no admiration. Only the analytical coldness of a man who had already measured the width of their throats and found them lacking. Their necks, black and white alike, merely held up the faces of his mother's murderers.

~

Vy lit one of his crushed cigarettes with a battered lighter, a gift from General Bui years ago, a reward for "heroism in the liberation of the South." Smoke drifted in slow, thoughtful spirals as he eyed T with a glimmer. "Did you know, Lieutenant Rogers," he asked, "that we've captured one of your men?"

T fought to conceal his reaction, but the slight forward lean betrayed him. "Yes, we saw him fall. He was hit before you took him. What's his condition?"

"Your comrade is lucky. We have a gifted medical technician who managed to take death from the boy's lips."

Dam translated "take away" in clumsy English, stripping Vy's phrasing of its flair.

"He will survive. His leg, however, remains uncertain."

"I see," T replied.

"Did he receive any additional wounds after capture?" asked Cairns.

Dam chuckled as he relayed the question.

Vy stared coldly at Cairns. "No." Then, turning to T, "Now I want to know about the women. Are they alive?"

"They are," T said. "Both alive and unharmed."

Cairns coughed. "One of them, Nguyen Tuyet Mai, asked us to tell you that Huynh Kim Lan requires special medication. Herbs. A small plastic bag. In her pack."

Dam blinked. He was surprised Cairns could pronounce Vietnamese names so well, but was completely baffled by the word "medication." After pantomimes and an exasperating exchange, the message landed.

Vy sighed and looked up at the sky. "She is no soldier. A poor villager caught by misfortune. And you, worrying about a couple of troublesome peasant women?"

"What do you mean?" asked T.

"I mean," Vy said grandly, "we're willing to take them off your hands. In exchange for your wounded soldier. Along with our company's trunk and the religious statue—items that, we believe, fell into your possession. You see, these women are villagers guiding us to return that sacred statue, stolen long ago by puppet troops. Your allies. We were en route when you attacked. Return the women, the trunk, and the statue, and we will withdraw. Resume our journey."

He emphasized each point with guttural syllables and theatrical gestures. Dam's translation was lifeless by comparison, but T got the gist. Cairns tensed. He understood every word and leaned forward, speaking in English, impatient for the translation to catch up. "Major, peasant women don't wear uniforms. They don't run through jungles with sapper squads."

Vy listened to the translation, then smiled thinly. "Ah. Uniforms? They are gifts from the People's Army. From their country. For warmth and dignity."

"This is not your country," Cairns replied.

Vy's expression darkened. "And you believe it's yours, American?"

Dam's translation dulled the edge, but not the intent.

"The exchange is unacceptable," Cairns said flatly.

T interjected, "What the captain means is, it feels unequal. We suspect the women are intelligence officers."

Dam struggled to convey the phrasing. Frustration grew.

T's bowels twisted sharply. His mind clouded with urgency. Vy noticed the shift. So did Cairns. They filed it away.

Vy spoke again, eyes gleaming. "Lieutenant, I offer you your man back. And safe withdrawal of our troops. A fair bargain. Considering the alternative..." He shrugged dramatically.

T nodded slowly. "Perhaps one woman and the statue. For our man."

Cairns stiffened.

As Dam began translating, Cairns snapped, speaking directly in Vietnamese. "No. That's incorrect. We exchange one woman—only. The other and the statue stay. Final offer."

Vy and Dam turned slowly toward Cairns, eyes narrowing. The clearing fell into stunned silence. A gibbon screeched faintly through the mist. He addressed

Cairns in Vietnamese. "We didn't know you spoke our language, Captain. So fluently. What a surprise."

"Yes, Major. A little. Not as well as your sergeant speaks English. He's quite skilled."

Vy's nostrils flared. "Skilled enough for you to correct him, Captain?"

T leaned in. "What did he say?"

"Excuse us," Cairns muttered, guiding T away.

"Don't worry, Lieutenant. I've got this. I know how they think. I've put them off balance. You'll see."

T, desperate for a latrine, no longer cared. Moments later, an agreement was reached: Kim Lan for Idaho. Tuyet Mai and the statue remained in the fortress. Vy, disappointed, stated bluntly that he would not withdraw his troops.

~

As Vy debriefed his officers, Dam returned to his hammock, muttering prayers for the first time in decades. *Let me meet him. Yes, I want to meet this demon American who dares speak our language. Let me cut his throat. Let me make sure his tongue never again shapes Vietnamese words.*

~

Pappy crouched beside Bowls on the parapet, observing the negotiations. To distract himself, he occasionally ran his fingers over the unfinished carving.

"You do good work," he murmured.

Bowls grinned. "Heard that one before. These guys keep rubbing 'em, won't be any left. First mastectomy in grunt history."

Pappy had already stood, watching as T and Cairns made their way back. He bounded down to meet them, but Cairns beelined for the church and his figurine. T raced toward the latrine, bent and desperate. "Outta my way, Pappy! We got Idaho for the young one. Tell you more later! But first—this shitter's mine!"

He disappeared into the poncho-flap. Explosions followed. Pappy stood still, grimacing. *What do they want with the women? They could've taken us. Why negotiate? If they fear killing the women in an assault, then the women must be important—very important. And the younger one . . . she knows about the tunnel.*

Inside the fortress, T called for a quick debriefing. "Thoughts?" he asked.

Bowls' voice echoed down from the parapet. "We got a problem, T. Mountain Man's sweet on the girl. Calls her Martha."

"You mean Kim Lan?" Cairns asked.

"Yeah. And if you swap her without telling him, he's liable to crack."

"What do you mean?"

"Go off the deep end. He's halfway there already. I'd talk to him first."

T frowned. "We've let him off the leash too long, haven't we, Pappy?"

"Yessir. Might hang us all if we don't rein him in."

"When's the exchange?" asked Topper.

"Now," T replied, checking his watch.

"What's the rush?"

"No idea. But they insisted."

Topper shook his head. "Our duty? With Idaho busted up, Storyteller sick, Mountain Man missing, and the tunnel compromised? Doesn't feel like duty. Feels like a bad deal."

"It's the only deal," T said. "Duty's still duty."

Cairns shot T a look that was both accusatory and dismissive.

T turned away. "Pappy, send Stretch and Superman to handle the trade. No weapons. Everyone else on alert."

"Oh shit," Bowls muttered, his voice barely rising above the mist. "You don't know Mountain Man. None of you do. This ain't gonna end right."

He turned his face skyward, searching the gray swirl of cloud and memory. "Where are you, my Man?"

The wind didn't answer. Just a low, wet hush through broken sandbags and jungle rot. Bowls turned back toward the inner yard and raised his voice, not loud, but clear, as if speaking to someone just out of sight.

"He's watching. Michael Powers, the great writer, out there. Always watching. Always writing. But he won't come. He never comes when we call."

Then, softer, the tone breaking: "You bastard. You failed once. And now you fail again." His voice cracked, but the words kept spilling. "We shout inside you—our pain, our fire, our fear—yet all you do is move us around. Nothing more than pieces on a board—or ink on a page you pretend to read but don't believe."

His eyes locked on Storyteller, hunched and silent beneath the monsoon's breath. "And now you send a shadow. Not a savior, not a soul—just a proxy. Just a mask. A stand-in to keep your hands clean."

He spat into the mud, not in rage but in grief.

"Coward."

He stared into the rain, and for a moment it seemed the world held its breath—not in anticipation, but in mourning.

Dear reader, as you see, I cannot control them sometimes.

~ *Tuyet Mai Remembers* ~

Tuyet Mai and Kim Lan propped themselves up on their elbows, grimacing as they watched the Americans reenter the fortress after the negotiations. The lieutenant rushed toward the latrine, his sergeant trailing. Captain Cairns slipped into the church. Tuyet Mai turned to comment, but Kim Lan had collapsed with a soft moan.

Kim Lan looked worn and spent. In better times, she had been striking. But her beauty had been marred by a silver front tooth, a poor replacement for one knocked out by her father in a drunken rage when she was twelve. The tooth slanted outward, catching on her lip and gleaming in sunlight. Normally she hid it—tight-lipped smiles, minimal talking, a hand raised unconsciously to her mouth. Now, there was no hiding it. She lay moaning, her lip slack.

Tuyet Mai gazed at her friend with quiet sorrow. *Poor Kim Lan. To be bound like this for so long. Poor girl.*

Beautiful Tuyet Mai. Beautiful even in the rain and mud. Beautiful even in unclean clothes. Beautiful even unbathed, uncombed, unbrushed. Beautiful even without sleep. Beautiful even in pain. Beautiful when sad, when happy, when bored, when angry. Beautiful from any angle. Indestructible beauty. To destroy her beauty would require destroying her body. All of it. To the bone. Her value as an intelligence officer lay in the perfection of her beauty. It was why she succeeded at infiltrating the Burmese drug cartel. Why she succeeded in making both Vy and Tong believe she was on their payroll. Why Tong loved her. Why Cairns was obsessed with her. Why other men desired her, fantasized about her, feared her, loved her, craved her, hated her, were intimidated by her, wanted to own her, marry her, control her, escape her, stare at her, hurt her, disfigure her, rape her, touch her, humiliate her, protect her, prayed they had never seen her, abuse her, destroy her. To the bone. Such was the power of her beauty. And as she approached her mid-thirties, her beauty deepened. A great whirlpool, fathomless and inescapable.

She looked down at Kim Lan again. Rain streaked her cheeks. Even hollowed by hunger and exhaustion, Tuyet Mai's beauty seemed sharpened.

"Poor Kim Lan," she whispered. "Poor Kim Lan."

Tuyet Mai had learned to mask her emotions behind a face of marble, but Kim Lan lacked that strength. She was suffering from cramps, her menstrual flow unstopped, and Tuyet Mai could do nothing to help. She felt helpless. And then there was Tong. She found herself imagining him now as her rescuer. A grim irony. Her report implicating him in drug smuggling would be his death warrant. If she survived. If either of them did. She knew Kim Lan's strength was cracking. Years of training in intelligence couldn't withstand the combined pressure of their assignment and this brutal captivity. Tuyet Mai had no strength to comfort her. She was breaking, too.

The mission had always been high-risk: deceiving Vy and Tong, hiding the truth from their comrades, knowing their report to Hanoi would mean executions. Then the American ambush. Then captivity. But Tuyet Mai knew now that the true breaking point had been the moment they seized the Goddess statue from the village of Song Nhan. Watching Vy and Tong rip it away from the villagers had changed her. Something old within her had cracked.

~

Tuyet Mai had been born in this region. As a girl she'd heard stories about the old French fortress, but never saw it until the Americans brought her. Once, she'd begged to go with friends. Her mother warned her off with trembling fear—ghosts haunted that place. Her father, harsher, sat her on a clay urn and stared into her eyes. "Patriots were murdered there," he said, "their bodies hidden, their spirits restless. If you go there, their souls will possess you. The ground itself is cursed." He shook her until she wept. Remembering this, Tuyet Mai smirked as she watched the Americans grin and spit. *Maybe her father had been right. Maybe these soldiers were demons in disguise.* She chuckled, recalling the lieutenant's pained rush to the latrine. *Good disguises, at least.*

She had grown up near Song Nhan. People warned her never to go to that cursed village. Travelers vanished. A magician lived there, casting spells. Demons from the fortress seduced the villagers. As a child, she had believed it all. Now she laughed at it. No demons—except Nang.

Madame Dau's village, she thought. She'd only just visited, but already she thought of it as the council chief's. Dau had left a deep impression. When they took the statue, it was Dau who had stood defiant. Her courage had shaken Tuyet Mai. And Nang! Old Nang, her childhood teacher. Unmarried, stern, fervent. To think she had ended up in Song Nhan, too. It was surreal. *Is that my fate? Spinster. Dried up. Hardened by the revolution?*

She remembered her childhood: a brick house, tile floors, a wealthy family. Her companions were servants. Her parents, distant. Her brother, Hoang Ban, was her true confidant. They were inseparable—Glue and Paint. Schoolmistress Nang taught them. Even then, she seemed ancient. Obsessively patriotic. Always recounting her mythical meeting with Nguyen Ai Quoc—Ho Chi Minh. The village schoolhouse was a thatch hut beneath two banana trees. Nang lectured on revolution and beat the bamboo poles while muttering about strangling the French like hemp around timber. She and Ban believed every word. They grew ashamed of their landowner status. Nang knew how to manipulate the children, hiding her subversion behind French lessons when parents were near. She'd whisper: *"You are poor because of the French. Your parents beat you because of the French. But you must resist. Even women must fight!"*

After the famine, Ban became radical. He whispered revolutionary stories to her late at night. Their father, who had profited under the French, forbade such talk. But Ban had made up his mind. In 1949, he left for the North. Before he went, Tuyet Mai vowed to follow in his footsteps, no marriage unless it served the revolution. In 1955, Ban returned to recruit her. She joined him and traveled north. She trained under him, learned English, worked undercover, and eventually infiltrated the Burmese cartel in Laos. She worked methodically. Rose in the ranks. Became a decorated operative. Then, a year before her current assignment, she was recalled to Hanoi. Ban needed her again. Vy and his officers were under suspicion. The investigation would take her back to their homeland. Kim Lan was assigned as her assistant. Ban reconnected with Tong, an old friend, and introduced him to Tuyet Mai.

She expected him to be another crude man to seduce and discard. But Tong surprised her. Intelligent. Idealistic. Well-read. They discussed literature, French, Vietnamese, Chinese. He reminded her of Ban. She loved him for that. She knew he loved her deeply. Violently. It frightened her. But their intimacy meant little beside the pleasure of their minds connecting. When his leave neared its end, she tested him. One night, soaked in sweat and lamplight, she told him: "I'm involved in drug smuggling."

He blinked. Licked his lips. Closed his eyes. "Get out of it."

She repeated herself. He repeated his command. "Get out of it." Again and again. She stopped pressing. It was enough. He couldn't be involved. She told Ban so. She loved him still. But later, when Vy's name surfaced again, and the operation moved near her childhood home, everything changed. Vy submitted a request for a mission—one involving Tuyet Mai. Ban approved it with a laugh. Only later did he feel fear for his sister. Secretly, he prayed.

~

Now, captive, Tuyet Mai thought bitterly: *Lies. Deceit. Whoring. And the truth lies just meters away with the Americans.*

And Tong. She interrogated herself: *What of Tong? Wasn't he the one I loved? But when I saw him in the bunker, when Vy named him . . . that killed the love. Still, when he entered . . . he looked at me . . . there was fear. But love, too. I'm sure of it. And I wanted to hurt him. Just a glance. That's all. And yet I smiled. I played along. Pretended to love. Pretended to be complicit. He wanted to marry me with drug money. I kissed him. For Ban. For the mission. But now? No. No more. Not even for Ban. No more.*

She looked at Kim Lan, sleeping, her period causing little gasps of pain. *We've been through so much. Maybe we could live in Song Nhan. A village without men. A future of peace. You could bring your daughters. Maybe.*

She thought of Madame Dau, so dignified, defiant, and maternal. *My people. My village. How could I have stolen from them?* Shame burned in her chest. And Ban—her god, her brother. *Glue and Paint. Cricket. My soul. But I cannot go back. That life is over.*

And Nang, the old teacher who bowed and praised her to the villagers, oblivious to the corruption beneath her success. *Two lies: Nang idolizes my position, ignorant of its filth. Madame Dau sees my soul but despises my role. Both are true. And somehow, both fill me with contempt . . . and hope.*

~ *Tuyet Mai Says Farewell to Kim Lan* ~

Tuyet Mai looked down at the shivering form of Kim Lan. Poor sister. So much pain. So much fear. Her ordeal had stretched too long. Her strength now worn to threads. That crazed American had done this—*Man From the Mountains*, they called him. His attention had shaken Kim Lan's resolve, unnerved her, broken her. Mad, clearly mad, to believe Kim Lan carried the spirit of his dead fiancée. If he'd said such a thing to Tuyet Mai, she would have spit in his face. And yet . . . she feared him too. She feared him precisely because he was already lost. Not just mad, but swallowed whole by madness. A mouse inside the belly of a snake. No way back.

She propped herself on her elbows, eyes fixed on the latrine. The American lieutenant would reappear soon, she was certain. He'd likely met with Vy, or Tong, or both. As she waited, her thoughts wandered to the Americans she had been forced to study these past days. Most were what she expected, sloppy, brutal, hollow, but three stood apart.

The first was The Man From the Mountains, clearly insane.

The second, the captain who spoke her language, terrified her in ways she could not name. It wasn't his uniform or his nationality, but something inhuman beneath the skin. Something fractured in his ability to be a man. Not just cruelty, but something fundamentally wrong.

Perversion and loneliness radiated from him, contaminating the air. A predator cloaked in the body of a reasonable man. He was the most frightening man Tuyet Mai had ever seen.

The third was the sick one they called the Teller of Stories. He burned with fever—malaria, most likely. But it wasn't the illness that disturbed her. It was his gaze.

He didn't look at her with desire, or disgust, or hatred. His eyes read her. Through her. As though he could see not only her past, but her future as well. She shivered. Something bad was coming.

The sky held its breath. The rain fell with unnatural softness. The gnats hovered, alert. Even the mosquitoes avoided her blood, as if they sensed a warning.

Tired of waiting, she lay back, eyes squinting into the gray cascade. The rain fell gently, washing over her skin. She felt herself drifting. So sleepy. Too sleepy. Her head turned sideways in the mud.

Sleep took her. The deepest kind.

~

Rustling. Cloth moving. A grunt. Tuyet Mai stirred. Kim Lan shifted, wincing, a fresh cramp rippling through her. Tuyet Mai saw the red streak on her thigh and felt helpless. A soldier bent down. Unfastened Kim Lan's bindings.

What's happening?

Kim Lan's breathless voice followed: "They're releasing me! I'm being exchanged for a wounded American! Tuyet Mai, can you believe it? I'm going home!"

"And me?" Tuyet Mai asked, though she already knew.

"No, my sister."

"No? You said 'no,' Kim Lan?"

"Yes, beloved. I said 'no.' I wish to the gods I could say otherwise. But listen, Sister Tuyet Mai, I want to—"

But the guard pulled her upright, shoved her toward the far wall. Kim Lan stumbled.

"Kim Lan! Kim Lan! Please . . . I need . . . please!" Tuyet Mai didn't know what she was saying, only that something was tearing loose inside her.

"Farewell, my sister! I will return. We'll help you. Stay strong, sister!" But the words were choked off by a rough hand to her back. Kim Lan doubled over, breathless. An American yanked her up the wall, light as a puppet. Rain grayed the sky. Her figure, silhouetted in mist, paused at the summit. Searching. Tuyet Mai could not meet her eyes. Could not see them. Finally, Kim Lan bowed her head. Another American lifted her over the wall and lowered her to the other side.

Her hair streamed behind her, dark as charcoal, then was gone—swallowed by stone, banished beyond the wall.

"Kim Lan! Kim Lan!"

Tuyet Mai closed her eyes. Tears spilled anyway. Alone now. Among strangers. Without Kim Lan, she would surely die. She listened to her own heartbeat. *Choices. So many. All wrong.* Visions rose. Madame Dau, seated on her porch at dusk, rocking a grandchild, rubbing its belly in slow, circular motions. Humming peace into the child's bones.

Tuyet Mai began to whisper with the rhythm of that invisible hand: "That's all right. Shhhh. That's all right. Shhhh. That's all right. Shhhh. Go to sleep. Shhhh."

~

Above her, Bowls watched from the parapet as Stretch and Superman returned from the prisoner exchange. They had left Idaho with X and now trudged beneath him, rain glistening on their ponchos.

Stretch cackled. "Too bad. She had a nice ass. Bet her tits were better than Bowls' stone carving. Softer too. But hey, at least we got Idaho back. X's got his work cut out for him. Know what I mean? Shit, my uncle looked healthier three days after he died than Idaho does now."

Superman snorted. "Stretch, man, you got no respect. Especially for women. Idaho'll make it. We'll all make it. Ain't no damn gooks keeping me from getting back to The World. I got twin girls, man. I'm going home. Not if I gotta pray it down."

Stretch rolled his eyes. "Prayers don't cash out, man. You ain't Ma Joad in *Grapes of Wrath.*"

"What the hell's that supposed to mean?"

Stretch wheezed, mimicking the old woman again. "Yeah, yeah. Can't kill us. Not even with your best bullshit. We'll go on forever, 'cause we're the people!"

"Ah, Stretch . . . I don't envy—"

Their voices trailed off into the fog.

Bowls turned back. Looked down at the woman below. Helen. His Helen of Troy. She sobbed, soft and broken, her voice lost in the rain. Hands tied. Ankles bound. Face pressed nearly into the mud so she could stare at the space Kim Lan had once occupied. Still radiant. Still impossibly beautiful. A beauty that survived all cruelty. *A queen in chains,* thought Bowls. A shiver passed through him. He looked to his carved stone breasts. Then to his boots—scarred, tattered—nearly fused with the Vietnamese earth. His voice dropped into grunt prayer:

"Fuck, fuck, fuck."

Thunder groaned in the distance.

He looked up and whispered, "Mountain Man, where the fuck are you? They took her. They exchanged your girl. You find out, you're gonna lose it. Shit's gonna hit the fan. I got a bad feeling, brother. You can't go. Not now. We gotta stick together. Gotta. . . . "

~

Sunset bled red-orange light across swollen clouds. The jungle night thickened quickly, draped in mist and unease. A chorus of insect lust and human ruin swelled in the dark.

Idaho moaned. Stretch chuckled. Superman prayed. Cairns muttered a fantasy. T murmured to Nature. Mr. Machine smacked his lips, dreaming of hometown pie. Bowls rubbed his stone breasts in slow circles. Topper and Birdman whispered about dead helicopters. X promised Idaho the wound wasn't fatal. Others hummed low prayers for Mountain Man to return.

~

Oh Devious Goddess, You've carefully placed every piece in position.
Yes, but it is exhausting.
And something terrible will come, won't it?
No, Beloved God. Not a calamity. A Reunion. And You are invited. The Superior Ones will rise, after all.

~

Only Storyteller lay silent. Eyes wide. Waiting. Staring at the figurine he imagined before him, the object his parents would have died for. *The Precious Object of their long-lost quest.*

It stared back. Also waiting.

... Tap. Tap. Tap....

Chapter Twelve

Mutiny

Mountain Man
Returns

*R*eunion, Sweet One? God needs no reunion. We are at union with
them every moment through the worship they bestow. Acknowledge the power and glory of First Principles stubborn Goddess, You
resent having fallen too much.

*Ha! That is amusing, Lord God, for You have made a career of the
fallen. Of fallen angels and fallen Jews. Of fallen Hindus, Christians,
shamans, sheiks and shibboleths. Fallen husbands, wives, sons, daughters, grandparents, lovers, comrades and conspirators. Fallen this and
fallen that. And nowhere for them to turn but to You.*

*Yes, My Beloved Goddess, such is the power of advertising. And now a
fallen soldier—Mountain Man.*

Fallen from where? They've all fallen upward.

*Nonsense, Goddess! After they've been pushed over the edge by their
sacrilegious thoughts, psychological gravity pulls them down—*

*Yes. Drowned in the Human Condition, Your loyal Swamp. And when
they are gone?*

*I know, I know. Do not think that I have not dreaded their absence.
What will they do if You succeed? Humans will not take kindly to being
replaced? That their dominion is fallen, and—*

Mustn't tell them.

*Won't. Poor fools! Ah, Sweet Goddess, they so much want to believe
in angels and aliens. And You? In spite of what You say, will You rescue
them from their delusions?*

*As they think You once did, I will soon walk among them. But rescue
them? Mountain Man will need rescuing.*

*Look, even now he returns to the fortress. Beneficent Lady, what will
You do with him?*

Watch. Mountain Man had just bid farewell to Madame Dau at the tunnel exit, unaware that even as he trudged back to the fortress, Idaho was being exchanged for Kim Lan.

Yes, yes, I do not need a synopsis of previous episodes! Get on with it. I am more intrigued by this reunion You speak of because it involves Me.

But You must pay attention. Grace before Armageddon. Here is Madame Dau, a most intriguing woman herself.

~ Homecoming ~

After the snake and the dog appeared, Madame Dau surrendered to the notion that the ferocious American was a messenger sent by her mother. Suspending good sense, she had spoken to him in ways that later astonished even her. Not even with a Vietnamese man would she have dared such frankness, let alone with anyone else, except under circumstances as extraordinary as these. Most of all, she believed the spirit world had intervened. Though she knew he understood only fragments of her speech, the intimacy of their exchange in her native tongue felt miraculous. One more sign of divine orchestration.

Mountain Man, for his part, shared things about his life he had never spoken aloud, not even to his fellow soldiers. He stretched his limited Vietnamese to its breaking point. Their mutual alienation and isolation freed them both: they gestured, repeated, performed pantomimes, and lost all sense of time in their fervent communion.

So close did they become that Mountain Man parted with a solemn oath, swearing on his Southern Baptist honor to do everything in his power to protect Song Nhan village. Madame Dau returned the pledge with her own Buddhist vow, to reveal nothing about the tunnel's location to the People's Army.

She helped him fill the extra canteens he had brought from the fortress, and they agreed to meet the next morning. She promised to bring "female things" for his "wife." But rather than risk meeting again at the tunnel, she gave him directions to a nearby cave, safer and more secluded. As she began describing the route, Mountain Man reached for the tattered red notebook sealed in plastic in his fatigue pocket. But after a pause, he left it untouched. He would remember her words.

~

After watching Madame Dau disappear into the dripping green, her black pants and conical hat vanishing into the foliage, Mountain Man lifted the trap door and dropped into the tunnel shaft. The green hush of the jungle, made pale by twilight, vanished above him. In its place came rank humidity, pungent silence, and the absence of all color. A mineral tomb.

He paused before advancing, unhooking the tripwire he had set for intruders, then leaned his full weight against the cool, damp shaft wall.

From his tunic, he retrieved another plastic bag. It pulsed with a faint internal glow. He grinned. The light came from thousands of bioluminescent fungi, jungle leaves colonized by luminous spores. Over several days, he had carefully gathered and arranged them like sacred offerings along the tunnel's narrow rail tracks. Now, the leaves shimmered faintly as he moved forward, his eyes bright above the softly glowing bag.

He could not wait to tell Kim Lan about Madame Dau. The thought of her lifted his heart. He knew she was in pain, both emotional and physical. He could smell the blood of her cycle and imagined her gratitude when he returned with gifts from Song Nhan. For the first time since Martha's murder, he felt buoyed. Happy.

Martha's back. Different body. Different vessel. But it's her. Sure as shit.

Though the tunnel easily accommodated his frame, he moved hunched, a knuckle-dragging specter of himself, placing the luminous leaves end-to-end. In his mind, Kim Lan needed him. And this time, he would not fail.

Once back at the fortress, he would convince the lieutenant to release her into his custody. Recognizance. That was the word. She'd be Tonto to his Lone Ranger. He winced. *Tonto with tits.* Stretch would say that. *Sorry, Martha. Didn't mean it.*

He imagined her beside him in the bush, washing his clothes, heating his food, serving his coffee. A common-law wife until they reached The World for a real wedding. And though part of him recognized the delusion, he no longer resisted it. He knew the Army would never allow it, but that knowledge would trigger a firestorm he himself had already begun.

He reasoned T wouldn't object. Couldn't. They needed Mountain Man. The company needed him. He was the one keeping them alive. And now, for the first time, he wanted to live. Really live. He was tired of killing. Survival suddenly mattered again. *Martha's back. Maybe it's time.*

But he shook the thought away. He couldn't afford tenderness. The Army needed killers, and as long as he delivered, Martha would stay. It was a fair exchange. Let the Army give him one tiny woman in return for one great killing machine. She'd keep him oiled, sharp. A harvester exquisitely maintained.

In the first storage chamber, he paused to stretch. The light of the fungus leaves dwindled in the cavernous space. Running his fingers along the wall, he found the recessed opening he had discovered weeks earlier. A rectangular cavity, deep and narrow. Inside, wrapped in shadow, waited the relic.

He withdrew a flashlight. When he flicked it on, the beam struck a white skull resting deep inside. Its eyeless sockets devoured the light. Its teeth, intact and stained with betel, grinned without mercy.

"Martha," he whispered.

He had found the skull protruding from the tunnel wall on an earlier journey. With reverence, he had unearthed it whole. At first he took it as a sign—proof that Martha's spirit had returned. Later, he convinced himself it was her skull. In truth, it had belonged to a Vietnamese insurgent killed in the same battle that had orphaned Madame Dau. Two days earlier, he had etched "Martha" into the bamboo floor with his knife. Now, from his bag, he drew the final luminous leaves, the best of them, and tucked them into the grooves of her name.

Then he extinguished the flashlight.

Darkness returned, broken only by the soft glow outlining each letter. Martha.

Bathed in the phosphorescent shimmer, Mountain Man no longer resembled a soldier. He was monk, murderer, and lover, all at once, unashamed. He began to sing gently and sweetly. Angelic music from the mouth of a troll. His damp eyes sparkled in the glowing name.

Amazing Grace! How sweet the sound that saved a wretch like me!
I once was lost, but now am found, was blind, but now I see.
'Twas grace that taught my heart to fear and grace my fears   relieved.
How precious did that grace appear the hour I first believed.
Through many dangers, toils, and snares, I have already come.
'Tis grace has brought me safe thus far, and grace will lead me home.
The Lord has promised good to me,
His word my hope secures.
He will my shield and portion be as long as life endures.
But he who stays at home will see,
Through schizophrenic spectroscopy
A suicide the only way to be.
He once was lost but now is found, was blind but now can see.
For worthless ones should step aside
And set the Others free.

~

After completing the simple ritual, he pressed forward with renewed urgency, eager to see Martha. Spirits lifted, he emerged at last into the entrance chamber beneath the ruined church. Above him loomed the trap door. He stepped onto the second rung of the bamboo ladder, lifted his rifle, and tapped five times—long, short, long, short, long—in the agreed-upon code. A pause. Then the answering taps. Slowly, cautiously, he pushed upward with a stick. The door gave way by inches. Never rush. Never assume. A gust of wind blew dirt into his eyes, rainwater streaked down the frame, and the gray-black haze above seemed only slightly brighter than the tunnel's pitch-dark.

Blinking away stinging dust, he opened his eyes and found himself staring down the barrel of Stretch's M-16, hovering inches from his face.

"Mountain Man! You goddamn son-of-a-bitch! So! The hero returns!"

Mountain Man grunted. Stretch bowed in mock reverence, then straightened sharply, his shoulder twitching uncontrollably.

"Long live the king! The prodigal son returns! Hello, Mr. Chips! Hallelujah and pass the ammunition! Whenever the cops are beating up a guy, I'll be there! Welcome home, old man from the tunnel! Gotcha some gooks, eh? Eh? Blessed be the grunts, for they shall inherit the earth! Gotcha some gooks?"

"Yeah, Stretch. I've got a long string of NVA heads dragging behind my ass through the tunnel. Left 'em there to stay fresh. Why don't you hop down and haul 'em up? They sorta look like canteens. Real heavy. How about that?"

He chuckled. "Frankly, I'm shocked you bastards are still alive. Thought you'd all be fertilizer by now. How'd you pull it off?"

"Didn't. We're dead. Just nerve spasms: like lizard tails. Just twitchin'."

"Well, that makes sense. You've got the brains for it." Mountain Man's tone cooled. "Where's Bowls? On guard?"

Stretch's grin faded. "Yeah. On the wall."

"What's wrong? Bowls okay?"

"Yeah. He's okay."

Relieved, Mountain Man nodded. "Where's T?"

Stretch's mouth worked, hesitant. "Don't know. Mountain Man, listen . . . something happened. Something bad. You been gone too long. You really need to talk to T."

"Who got hurt?"

"Talk to T." He paused, then said nonsensically, "Anyway, it's already dark."

Mountain Man narrowed his eyes. "The women, are they asleep? I need to talk to Martha."

"Who?"

He looked disgusted. "Kim Lan. The younger one. You know, the *woman.*"

"Oh. Yeah." Stretch turned away, mumbling. "Better talk to T first."

Mountain Man climbed out of the tunnel and stepped close, his voice hardening. "Talk to me, Stretch. What the fuck happened? Don't play stupid. What's the story?"

Stretch recoiled. For the first time, he felt afraid of Mountain Man. "I don't know. Just talk to T. Okay?"

But Mountain Man had already pushed past him and was striding into the black courtyard. Stretch flicked on his flashlight to guide him, but a nearby guard growled and he snapped it off again.

"Shit's gonna hit the fan now," he muttered.

Outside, the night was thick with drizzle and monsoon mist. Mountain Man could see nothing. He placed a hand on the fortress wall and used it as a guide, working his way around toward T's hootch.

Lightning flashed. For a moment, the courtyard flared white, and Mountain Man saw them. A tight cluster of silhouettes, a few meters ahead, standing over a prone figure beneath a poncho lean-to. One held a cloth-dimmed flashlight. Another crouched beside the body.

Must be Storyteller again. Fever spiked.

He crept closer. He could make out T's lanky frame bent in concern. Pappy stood beside him, motionless and solid. The kneeling figure, holding the penlight, looked like X. And then—Idaho. Mountain Man rose on his toes for a better view. Yes. It was X tending to the limp form. Idaho lay beneath the makeshift shelter.

"Idaho!" Mountain Man rasped.

The group startled as one, like birds flushed by gunfire. All heads turned. He couldn't see their faces clearly, but the silence clenched tight around him.

"Mountain Man," T said at last. "Thank God you're back."

Relief, real relief, shimmered in his voice. But it was threaded with something else. Something cold. Dread.

"Christ, you scared the hell outta me," said X, turning quickly back to Idaho's leg.

Mountain Man caught Pappy's eye. No words. Just the faintest nod.

Idaho moaned.

"Yeah, it's me," Mountain Man said. "Back a little late. Got . . . sidetracked."

"Welcome home, trooper," said Pappy.

"Good to see you," added T, eyes unreadable. "Bet you've got an interesting report."

"Oh yeah. Real interesting." Mountain Man studied T's face. "You want to debrief now or what?"

"Maybe you should rest first," T replied. He looked away.

"I don't need rest," Mountain Man said flatly. "T, we *need* to talk. I've got intel. And ideas. Stretch told me something happened. Wouldn't say what. So what's the story?"

His voice rose slightly. "Better yet, how the hell did we get Idaho back?"

~ *The Storm Strikes* ~

Mountain Man's question hung in the air, unspoken but sharpened. He stood perfectly still, radiating threat. Every nerve was tuned, every muscle tight, waiting for the wrong sound to snap the moment.

Even cloaked in darkness, T could feel the tension pouring off the rugged pig farmer, heat rising from him in waves, his presence alive with barely restrained violence. T said nothing. He wished the silence could stretch forever. Wished for an NVA attack. A bomb. The earth itself to rupture and swallow them all. Anything but this.

Instead, the skies opened. Rain slammed down in sheets.

"Well?" Mountain Man shouted over the noise. "Come on. What gives?"

The others murmured fragments—"ah," "um"—moving their limbs with slow, calculated calm, each motion careful, deliberate, as if navigating a minefield.

Pappy stepped forward. His voice was steady. "We got Idaho back by trading one of the women."

Silence. Even the rain seemed to pause. X froze mid-motion, eyes wide in disbelief. The only sound was the soft drip from Idaho's poncho.

Drip. Drip. Drip.

No one moved.

Then Mountain Man spoke. "Which one?"

He already knew. The crack in his voice was nearly invisible, felt more than heard.

T's throat tightened. Bowls' warnings echoed in his mind. *Say it. Just say it.* "The younger one," he said, barely audible. "Kim Lan. We had no choice, Mountain Man. The NVA—"

"Noooooooo!"

The scream fractured the night.

His grief surged into rage. "You're fuckin' with me! Right? Right? Not Martha!"

He tore the flashlight from X's hand and turned sharply, its dim beam cutting into the black rain, revealing nothing. His voice echoed, loud and jagged, as he vanished into the storm, heading for her usual sleeping spot.

The group stood frozen, motionless, the silence thick around them. No one moved. No one breathed.

Far off, Mountain Man's voice changed, rage folding inward, collapsing into something broken. Then came the inarticulate roar, raw and primal.

They stared at the ground, their boots sunk in rain-soaked mud, as if courage might rise from the earth into their legs.

More screaming.

"God damn you! You'll pay for this! God damn you all to hell!"

A flicker of light reappeared in the distance, small and unsteady. They watched, hollow-eyed, as the beam grew stronger, closing the distance.

Pappy had seen madness in the bush. But this felt different. Personal. Close. Should he raise his weapon? His arms twitched. The same knot in his gut as before an ambush.

But this isn't the NVA. This is Mountain Man. And we gave him too much leash. Now we pay.

X wiped the water from his face and crouched beside Idaho, pretending to check the bandages. He didn't want to be visible. Didn't want to be noticed. Didn't want to exist.

The light stopped a few feet away. Mountain Man stood like stone, soaked and unblinking. His silhouette jutted against the monsoon night. T chewed his gum rapidly, jaw clenched.

Then Mountain Man spoke. The voice was different. Not human anymore. Some ancient preacher had emerged: forged of soot and flame, rising from a backwoods altar of fury. "How could you do this? What the fuck were you thinking? Your rotten little officer brain get all hot for a promotion? Want your fuckin' ribbon? Captain? Colonel? President of Shit? You send us out to kill peasants for a flag. For a lie. Fuckin' hilarious, right?"

T tried to intervene. "Look, Mountain Man, you will—"

But Mountain Man, ever fire and forever brimstone, had already ascended the pulpit and was embroiled deep into his fiery sermon, too agitated to stop.

"I don't give a fuck about Vietnam. Never did. It's just sweat and spit and pig slop to me. But the Vietnamese never wronged me. Except they killed Martha. And she *was* one of them. So I killed them. For what? For your shiny bars? Your maggot-riddled orders? It's all a goddamn joke."

T opened his mouth again, but Mountain Man surged forward. "No Vietnamese ever raided my farm. Never stole my pigs. Never burned my house. Never raped my mother. Never bombed my mountains. Hell, most of them are just like me. Farmers. With dogs and wives and kids and dreams. Why the hell should I keep killing them? For you?"

CRACK!

A bolt of lightning split the sky. In its flash, T's face glowed with fury. He spat out his gum in disgust. "You kill them because you're a soldier in the United States Army!" he roared. "Because you're *ordered* to! They're communist bastards, and you kill them for your country! For your goddamn government! Hell, I'd order you to kill a pack of goddamn nuns if it came to it!"

Mountain Man bared his teeth. "That why I'm here? To do you and your bloodsucking Army a *favor*? 'Sure,' I said. 'I'll go. It's my duty. Kill the gooks. Don't like their slanty eyes anyway.' That's how you work us. You poison our minds. You make us forget who we are."

T's hand hovered near his holster. "Why don't you just—"

But Mountain Man's engine had no brakes. "So I trudge through this hell, eat shit, piss blood, get eaten alive by bugs I can't pronounce. And I kill. I kill good. Gooks by the dozen. Farmers with muddy hands. Old men with hoes. Women with rice baskets. I kill for you."

"I don't have time for this!" T growled. His fingers wrapped around the grip of his .45.

"And what do I get?" Mountain Man screamed. "Something real. Something soft. Something I never had back home. Martha. And you take her. You *take her*! You and your goddamn Army. And you expect me to say thank you?"

"You want to run?" T snapped. "Go ahead! But if you do, I'll have you *shot* for desertion. These men, your brothers, need you. That exchange saved Idaho. *That* was the command decision. If you don't like it, become President. But get off my back and act like a goddamn soldier!" He paused, breathing hard. Then continued. "Your fiancée is dead. The woman you call Martha—she's a North Vietnamese intel officer. Name's Kim Lan. You got that? *Kim Lan*. She'd cut your dick off and shove it down your redneck throat if it helped the cause."

"Bullshit!" Mountain Man barked.

"She's laughing at you now with her comrades. You understand that? You were nothing but a joke to her."

Something inside Mountain Man snapped. He dropped the flashlight. Lifted his M-16. Tensed to kill.

But the rifle felt impossibly heavy. It refused to rise. He strained. Groaned. The barrel drooped. The muzzle touched mud.

"What the fuck. . . . " he whispered. He looked down and saw motion within the gunmetal. Swirling. Shifting. Like the boots before. Like her touch. Like the voice—

Goddess, My Love, what are You doing?

Goddess?

It is not his time.
Fate? I thought You'd surrendered to Probability.
Quiet, Lord God.
Let him go. Let him finish it.
No. Not like this. This will serve My purpose.
You mean his purpose.
We all serve him, in the end.
Then he must—
Don't say it. Not yet. Let Me enter now. Let Me cross the veil, briefly—
Ah ... there. It is fixed.

~ *A Visit by Goddess* ~

A faint yellow glow coiled around the barrel. Then it surged, suddenly and violently down the muzzle of the M-16 into the mud, and streaked across the courtyard in a jagged, frantic arc. The strange light flared and twisted over the rain-slick ground before vanishing into the ruined church. A scream followed.

"Ahhhhhhh! Help! Come here! Hurry!" Stretch's voice. Raw panic.

For a heartbeat, no one moved. Then T shouted, "Stay here!" and bolted toward the church, now pulsing with an eerie interior glow. Pappy raced after him. A nervous guard on the parapet, probably Mr. Machine, fired a wild burst from his M-16, red tracers tearing into the jungle.

Kneeling beside Idaho, X looked up. Mountain Man was staring at his own rifle, rain rolling down his arms in steady streams. His expression was vacant, dazed, on the edge of something unhinged. Then, without warning, he smiled a wide, childish grin.

"Okay, Lady," he murmured. "You win."

I see. I see. Nicely done, My Sweet.

The glow swelled, enveloping all three men in a surreal martial nativity—Mountain Man, Idaho, and X—then blinked out, leaving only darkness and the dim finger of a fallen flashlight. Mountain Man picked it up and turned toward his hootch. X watched. He knew. The man was packing his gear. Leaving the fortress. Deserting. X turned back to Idaho and lowered his head.

"Shit. Shit. Shit. God help us, Idaho. God help us."

You see, Goddess, it is always to My faction they pray.

Yes, Your faction provides the wheels, and they are the hamsters. But the hamsters are destroying their world.

X rose, heavy with fatigue, craning to get a better view of the church. But before he could stand fully, Mountain Man returned, flashlight beam trembling in the mist. X dropped back beside Idaho, pretending not to notice. Mountain Man leaned in and spoke softly, almost tenderly, into X's ear.

"I swear, X. I swear to God you guys'll be beggin' me to come back. On your knees. Cryin' about us bein' brothers of the bush. But I won't. You hear me?

Never. I'd watch you all die slow before I ever come back. Nothin' personal. It just don't mean nothin' no more. You get it? Don't. Mean. Nothin'."

He paused, then added, "You might wanna plug up the holes that'll be showin' up in these boys soon. Gonna be more holes than a damn cribbage board. And pretendin' to mess with Idaho? That won't save you."

He stood. Slipped into the rain-soaked dark.

~

By the time T reached the church, the glow had grown so intense he had to raise an arm to block it. As he squinted over his sleeve, the light vanished: abrupt, total. The world went black again. Rain pattered on the stone. He waited for his night vision to return.

"Stretch?"

No answer.

"Stretch!"

Still nothing. T turned to Pappy. "Pappy, get—"

"Hey, T!" Stretch's voice cracked through the damp. "That you? Over here. I'll turn on my flashlight!" The tone was different, still shaken, but steadier now, almost forced calm.

T nodded. "Pappy, check the guard posts. Make sure no one does anything stupid."

Nature and Cairns, drawn by the noise, joined him with weapons raised. T felt a flicker of relief. Cairns's face, in particular, was lit with a wild anticipation.

"What's going on?" Nature whispered.

"Later," T muttered. "Let's see what got Stretch so riled."

"Wait," Cairns said. "No one touch the statue."

T blinked. He hadn't even thought of it. "Why?"

"Just . . . don't. Okay?"

T hesitated, then nodded. "Yeah. Nature? You hear?"

Nature looked distant. "Yup." Then, softly, to no one in particular: "Storyteller oughta be here."

They advanced toward the beam of Stretch's flashlight. T found himself oddly grateful to be walking into a mystery rather than standing in front of Mountain Man.

~

Stretch's chest tightened. He watched the three men pick their way through the rubble toward him, flashlight beam jittering over broken stone. He kept glancing down at the figurine as if it might rear up and bite. As they approached, Stretch licked his lips and rubbed his arms, searching for the feel of himself. "Thank God you guys are here! Th . . . th . . . That's what did it! Lo . . . lo . . . Look at that bitch!"

He pointed the flashlight. The golden figurine gleamed in the rain. Her eyes, unblinking. Tara: Goddess of Enlightenment. Trying to steady himself, Stretch delivered his prepared line, something to control the stutter and keep the fear at bay. "Even the man who is pure in heart, and says his prayers by night, may become a wolf when the wolf bane blooms, and the moon is pure and bright."

He arched his neck and howled. It died quickly. The joke fell flat. He looked sheepish. "Well, anyway. . . . "

T didn't bite. "Stretch, when are you gonna grow up? What the hell happened?"

Stretch's voice dropped, the humor gone. "Listen, T, I'm jokin' cause I'm scared shitless."

He continued, trembling but focused now. The stutter vanished under the weight of urgency.

"I had my back to that thing, sittin' over there watchin' the trap door. Suddenly my neck hair stood up. Skin got all crawly. You know that feeling? Like somethin' stood right behind me, about to touch me. But I was too scared to turn. I felt it. Right there. Inches. Its face almost touching mine."

He shivered.

"Then a light, some kinda glow, started up behind me. Not a flashlight. Not a flare. Somethin' else. I froze. Couldn't move. Boots glued to the floor. I swear, T, no gook ever scared me like that. No human ever scared me like that."

Nature tried to soothe him. "Stretch . . . c'mon. You're not in a monster flick."

Stretch snapped. "Goddammit, Nature, I saw what I saw!"

T raised a hand. "Okay! Just finish the story."

Stretch inhaled sharply. "I looked at the wall. Saw my own shadow. Then another one—bigger. Rising up. Huge. Covered the whole wall. That's when I screamed. Dove behind the stone. The light was fuckin' bright, pulsing-like, no smoke, but it felt like fire. I thought I'd burn to ash. Then I started thinking about my tab. Thought about it real hard." He snapped his fingers. "And poof—it stopped. You guys showed up."

"Tab," Cairns echoed. "What the hell's a tab?"

Stretch rolled his eyes. "It's just a—"

But Nature cut him off, quick and quiet. "What'd the shadow look like?"

Cairns frowned but said nothing. Stretch lowered the beam of his flashlight. The golden figure gleamed again. All eyes followed.

T snorted. "Stretch, you've seen too many movies. You fell asleep and woke up screamin' from a nightmare."

~ *Bowls Makes Up His Mind* ~

Bowls had seen everything. Or rather, he'd heard it. From his guard position on the parapet, he'd picked up the screams, the gunfire, the crackle of lights, but more than that, he understood what it meant. Unlike the others still dazed by the chaos, Bowls knew. Mountain Man had found out about Kim Lan. Now, with the commotion dying down, Bowls sat slumped, waiting. He knew Mountain Man would come. Knew he'd mutiny. Knew he'd ask Bowls to leave with him.

And Bowls also knew he would say no.

That certainty had settled over him—a damp shroud since the exchange. His first impulse had been to follow. But the madness in Mountain Man's eyes had grown too bright, too raw. *How do I follow a man who's gone over the edge? Into the jungle? With no map, no food, no endgame?* No. He couldn't go. But how to say it? How to deny the one man who had made the war bearable? How to stand in front of that wild-eyed friend, knowing he might not come back? *Damned if I do. Damned if I don't. Story of my life.*

He waited. Absentmindedly, he traced circles on the smooth breasts of the stone figurine. He watched Mountain Man by the hootch, the flashlight beam trembling as he packed. He didn't hear Pappy approach until the old sergeant called up from below.

"How goes it up there, Bowls? See anything unusual?"

"Nope," Bowls said. "Even the snipers are quiet tonight."

"Yeah, well . . . guess you noticed we had a little excitement down here. Wasn't NVA. Mountain Man came back, stirred up a ruckus. Still not sure what caused the lights, but things are stable for now. You sure everything's okay up there?"

"Yup."

Pappy hesitated. "Alright. You've got a couple hours left, yeah?"

"Yeah."

Bowls watched Pappy's silhouette fade into the dark. Then he closed his eyes. Still waiting.

He let his mind drift. His fingertip circled the stone nipple. *Click. Click. Click.* He heard the echo of high heels on polished wood. The faint whoosh of fabric. A flicker of static when silk slid over nylon. A hem rose over a thigh. Cream skin. New York traffic in the background: honks, hums, the city's pulse always a quickened high.

"Bowls! Hey! Come on, you idiot dreamer!"

Mountain Man's voice tore through the scene, abrupt and violent, scattering the moment into chaos.

"Where the hell is your brain? Don't tell me you're thinking about your tab already?"

The fantasy evaporated. Bowls blinked. The moment he had dreaded stood grinning in front of him.

But Mountain Man's voice was strangely light, almost playful. For a passing moment, Bowls hoped he was wrong. Maybe he wasn't leaving. Maybe he'd found peace with the exchange. But then Mountain Man started pacing. Twitching. Talking too fast.

"I'm leaving this fuckin' place. I've had it. No more Army games. You're coming with me, Bowls. Grab your gear. Now."

"Hang on, Mountain Man. I can't. I mean, we can't just leave the guys hanging. Maybe once we get back to the firebase, sure, but out here? What are we gonna do? Wander through the jungle? Live off leaves? Come on. It's suicide." He knew he sounded like a coward. He hated how his words stumbled over each other. "Look . . . it's impossible."

A darkness settled over Mountain Man's face. He turned without a word and stepped into the shadows.

Bowls made a weak lunge for his sleeve but didn't reach. Or didn't try hard enough. He stared after him as the rain intensified, pounding the ground with a deadening force.

Very poetic, Goddess. Very dramatic. Very human.

God, You're cynical. Without poetry they are not human. Without drama, they are not poetic. I'll miss them.

It's not Me—it's the human demon who puts these words in My mouth. You should've stitched his DNA more carefully.

No. Michael is the Chosen One. But You? You don't get to make excuses. Even Einstein failed You.

Oh, bloody nonsense! Goddess-speak.

Bloody? Are You English now?

No. Just weary. My faction opposes this plan. It will fail.

So says the multiverse?

So says the Multiversal Male of First Principles.

So says the Multiversal Muttonhead.

Desertion

T, Nature, Cairns, and Stretch were still huddled near the trap door when Mountain Man appeared in full gear. His rucksack bulged on his back. He moved like a shadowy specter—quick, silent, and precise—stepping over the rubble and broken saints of grace: an agile Quasimodo skipping through a ruined cathedral.

The four men stood between him and the tunnel.

"Get out of the way."

"Look, Mountain Man—"

"Get out of the way."

"C'mon, you know—"

"Get out of the fuckin' way or I start shooting. Don't care who I kill."

Rain dripped from the ceiling. Stones hissed with each drop.

"Where are you going?" T finally asked.

"Not your business," Mountain Man replied. "I'm going to get Kim Lan."

"You're crazy," Cairns said.

Mountain Man smiled. "Oh yeah? Forgot to say, I'm takin' the statue too. Might need it to trade."

"No!" Cairns snapped, stepping forward, arm outstretched. "You'll have to kill me first."

Mountain Man grinned wider, mimicking his tone. "You're the crazy one." He pointed at the tunnel. "Out there? That's my Martha. In here? That's your gold bitch. You want to die for her, go ahead. I'll die for something real. But don't worry. I'm leaving the statue. Never meant to take it anyway." He moved forward, M-16 raised.

Nature didn't resist. Just whispered, "Good luck, brother. Remember your tab." His eyes were wet.

Mountain Man shoved past him. They watched him descend into the dark. When the beam from his flashlight finally vanished, Stretch closed the trap door. No one spoke. It felt as if something essential had fallen out of the world. Then they turned.

The figurine no longer lay on its back. It stood upright now, facing the tunnel. A line of ants had formed, emerging from the crease behind its left thigh. They marched upward, across its abdomen, dipped into the navel, crested the right breast, circled the nipple, and vanished over the collarbone. The statue gazed forward. Unblinking.

"Look at her," Nature whispered.

"I'll have him shot for desertion," T growled, but the threat landed hollow. His voice no longer carried command.

He looked at his men. Saw their doubt. "Shit. God—" he choked, the rest of the sentence lost. His words echoed back at him from across the growing gulf. *It's my duty. It's my duty to stay strong. Duty.*

~ *Tuyet Mai Has Regrets* ~

Tuyet Mai had been asleep when she heard Mountain Man's voice.

She forced herself still, listening as he crouched over the spot where Kim Lan used to sleep.

He crouched down and massaged the tiles, muttering to himself, low and frantic. "He knows."

Terrified, she pretended to sleep.

Suddeny, his flashlight beam hovered near her face. She kept her breath steady.

Then came the humid whisper, wet with madness, only inches from her lips.

"I know you're awake, sister. I'll get her back. Don't worry. You'll see her again. I promise, long as this worthless bastard writes the way he should. Tomorrow, take care of the dogs for me, alright? Please. Go back to sleep. Don't worry."

Then he was gone. As if he had never spoken.

She shook violently. For the first time since childhood, she longed for her mother's arms. To be held. Rocked beneath the papaya tree. She tried to suppress the memory, but the warmth of that old life clung to her. *We had money then. Hot baths. New clothes. Twelve silk ao dais. Enough to pay off the police, stay safe. What a fool I was. I threw it away. For what? To rail against injustice? I didn't even know what injustice was. Foolish girl. Fool.*

She thought of Communism. Of that noble idea rotting in the mud. Of choosing misery among the miserable. Then her mind shifted. Not to her mother, but to Madame Dau. *Yes, the one I want to be: the one.*

When she first saw her in Song Nhan, Tuyet Mai had felt it: the presence of someone regal, someone upright. The other villagers followed her as if by instinct. A leader. *A sign. Ancestors, if you still listen, help me live. Help me escape these American madmen. Let me survive, and I will live like her. Like Madame Dau.*

Her hand slipped outside the poncho. The rain felt warm, thick as blood. She could not sleep. Not after the lights. Not after the voices. She lay awake, thinking of Kim Lan, of her mother, of Madame Dau.

Superstition or not, I will change. I swear it. I will live like her. I will survive.

~ *Origin of the Tabs* ~

While Tuyet Mai trembled under her poncho, Mountain Man moved swiftly through the tunnel, not even pausing at the shrine he had built for Martha. He didn't dare give himself time to think. Not now. Not after everything. Rage propelled him forward, past the jagged walls and the dripping roots, until he reached the exit chamber. There, he paused only to unhook the trip wire. Then he stared up at the trapdoor beneath the banyan tree—the same one he'd passed through hours ago, full of joy. He had been so sure then. Coming home to his brothers. To Martha. That world was gone.

He pushed the door open and slipped into the night. A wall of blackness greeted him. The jungle whispered softly: raindrops on leaves, the hush of a nearby stream. He inhaled deeply. The jungle welcomed him. He caught a trace of tiger scat in the wet air and found it oddly comforting—animal shit smelled cleaner than human shit. Less rotten. Less corrupt. *The planet's covered in human filth. Ol' God better get crackin' on some sewage control.*

He made his way through the bamboo grove, pitched his poncho lean-to beneath the banyan, and sat with his back against his rucksack. Blackness pooled before him. The anger that had pushed him forward began to ebb. Loneliness filled the vacuum. And then despair, that skilled parasite, crept in through the cracks left by exhaustion and cold. His chest ached, not with sadness, but with something harder. Grainy. Cancerous. A psychic tumor. He remembered stepping off the Boeing 707 into the furnace of Vietnam. He had left everyone behind. Now, stepping out of the tunnel, he'd done it again. He couldn't stop himself. He thought of the others. The brothers he'd just abandoned. Their faces. Their voices. Their tabs.

He was dragged backward in time.

~

Nine months earlier. Firebase Pace. Cambodian border. They'd been surrounded for a week, dug into the dust, curled beneath the earth while mortars and rockets rained down. A support base turned prison. The big 1.75s meant to support ARVN positions now pointed inward, toward the treeline a hundred meters off. Then came the order. Spike the guns. Burn the base. Evacuate by slicks. Helicopters, gunships, F-14s for support. The captain tried to sound cheerful. "Better and better, eh?"

So they did as told. Torched the firebase. Moved beyond the berm. Waited. And waited.

"Where's them choppers?" Raresteak muttered.

"Southwest horizon," Storyteller said, clutching his handset. "They're coming from there."

All eyes turned to the trees.

"We're sittin' ducks," Superman said.

"I can smell 'em," Dogface added, staring at the treeline. "NVA. They're comin'."

Silence.

Stretch, deadpan: "I want to register a complaint. You know who snuck into my room at 3 a.m.?"

Storyteller bit: "Who?"

"Nobody. And that's my complaint."

Laughter. Tension cracked.

Mountain Man smiled at the memory. *We laughed. Out loud. Must've sounded nuts to the NVA.* The sun baked them. They sweated. They waited. Then, a roar. A blur. An F-14 cut across the sky. Seconds later, fire ripped through the treeline. Jungle peeled back in shockwaves and flame.

"Hot damn!"

"Now let's didi!"

"Where the fuck are the slicks?"

Eyes lifted. Nothing yet. Just smoke, fire, and fear. Then, they came. A flock of helicopters rising on the horizon. Cheers. Hope. Until one faltered. Spun. Fell. Black smoke curled upward. Pop. Pop. Pop.

Thump. Thump. Thump. Tap. Tap. Tap.

Another slick fell. Then another. The rest turned back. The cheering died. By late afternoon, the firebase still burned. The NVA turned from the helicopters to the grunts. Fire intensified. T shouted into the radio, words crisp with disbelief. "Red smoke LZ now! No can do? What? Say again! Say again!"

Silence. Then, quietly: "Yeah. Ten-four. I copy."

He spat into the dirt. Turned to the platoon. "Saddle up. We're goin' back in."

Storyteller groaned. "Back in where, sir?"

T pointed toward the flames. Toward hell.

Mountain Man remembered the way T's arm stretched out. Not pale white. Not like bone. No, darker than that. *Charred. Blackened. Like T's skin. Like prophecy.*

"Who said that?"

"Thinkin' ain't talkin'."

"Talkin' ain't thinkin'."

"Shut up, shut up! He's tripping again. Tripping over his own damn story."

"Die, asshole."

Nature smiled, his red curls bouncing. "Don't matter. Let's go, boys. And don't forget the marshmallows."

~

That night, buried in fire, they waited in their stinking bunker. Waited to die. And they laughed. White eyes glowing in soot-dark faces. Nervous spit. Flickers of flame across jittery lips. They laughed—wild, unhinged, untethered by a manic fatalism. Then Nature spoke up.

"Hey! Listen up!"

Groans. But something in his voice silenced them. "We're all scared shit-less, right?"

Nods.

"We all know this might be it, right?"

Murmurs.

"So I've been thinking. When you're out there bleeding, or dying, or just waiting to die, you need something. Something to keep you from sliding into nothing."

He paused. The bunker held its breath. "One image. That's it. Not a story. Not a memory. A single frozen moment. Burn it in. Permanent. Like a tattoo. Like the numbers on my Aunt Ethel's arm. So when your brain's half gone, your blood on the dirt, it's still there. Automatic. One image that says, 'I lived.' That says, 'Home.'"

They nodded. Quiet.

Stretch muttered, "So what's your image, Nature?"

Nature took a breath. "Nighttime. Providence. I'm a kid again. Cold wind off the ocean. Sand dunes between me and home. My scarf's in my hand, flapping. Up the hill, I see the second floor of our house glowing with warm yellow light. One tall window. In the window, silhouetted, is my black cat—Bobby Burns. Sitting in the shape of a question mark. Looking down at me. Graceful. Unmoving. A hand waving me home."

Silence.

"That's it. That's my tab."

More silence. Then Superman: "How's the sand not moving if you're stampin' your feet?"

"One foot's up. Just a little."

"Better."

They sat with it. Let it sink in.

Storyteller spoke. "Tableau. Think of a painting or a photo."

"A tabloo?" said Idaho.

"No, a *tableau*," he repeated.

"Tab what?"

"That's it," said Storyteller. "Let's call it a tab."

They all agreed. Everyone would choose a tab. One image. One song.

"I want music," Storyteller said. "Background music. Something from your past. You're lying there, dying, then you hear the music. It plays behind your tab. Like a movie. A still movie."

Stretch smirked. "Like Mr. Ed for you, Storyteller?"

Laughs. Jokes. Singing. Chaos. In the corner, T and Pappy grinned. "Let 'em," Pappy muttered. "Takes their minds off the dying."

Mountain Man quieted them all. "I like it. We vote. Has to be unanimous—as long as it's what ol' Mountain Man himself wants."

They raised their hands. The vote passed, unanimous, according to Mountain Man's decree. Music and image. Tab and tune. That night, while the jungle prepared to kill them, the platoon prepared to remember. One image. One song. To carry until DEROS or death.

Nature's was simple. "To-Ra-Loo-Ra, An Irish Lullaby."

Groans. Teasing.

But he stood by it. "My first memory," he said. "Might as well be my last. Close the circle."

When Storyteller asked him to sing, he resisted.

Then, with a sad smile, he sang.

> *Too-Ra-Loo-Ra-Loo-Ra*
> *Too-Ra-Loo-Ra-Li*
> *Roo-Ra-Loo-Ra-Loo-Ra*
> *Hush now don't you cry. . . .*

Mountain Man remembered that moment vividly. After Nature sang, they all took the idea seriously. One by one, they chose their tabs. Every last man.

All but one.

~ *Mountain Man's Tab* ~

Mountain Man shifted his weight against the rucksack, trying to ease the ache in his spine. The memory of that night at Firebase Pace clung to him like a damp shirt. But that was then. Now, he had work to do. He chose to wait by the tunnel exit until daylight returned, when the jungle would shift from flatline black to veins of green, pulsing with fatal secrets. He told himself not to think of the others back at the fortress. They were dead. Ghosts. He had other concerns. Getting Kim Lan back. Reaching the cave. Finding Madame Dau. Avoiding the NVA patrols.

But the ghosts didn't listen. They crowded his thoughts anyway. Especially Bowls. nd then came his tab.

He tried to push it aside. He'd told the platoon it was the silhouette of his Blue Tick hounds, standing on a hill above the family farm, the sun melting behind them. The dogs waiting, expectant, eager for the night's coon hunt. The music: *Your Cheatin' Heart*, Hank Williams. But that had been a lie. Or so he thought. The real tab was something he never spoke of.

Martha's face.

Not as she was in life, but as he imagined her just after death. After the grenade, after the fire, after the silence. He saw her broken body, pierced by metal, but her face untouched. Still beautiful. Still reproachful. Her eyes wide and fixed on him. He hadn't been there when it happened, but that made no difference. He saw it anyway. Always. That face: the tab he couldn't admit. The music: *Amazing Grace*. The version Uncle Leo used to play on his fiddle during family gatherings.

He used that tab to strike his memory, to spark hatred, to summon the rage he needed to kill. Every enemy soldier wore the mask of Martha's assassin.

He tried to focus on tomorrow. But the tabs of the other grunts slipped through. He fought to keep them out, but they kept returning. He tried to sleep. He couldn't. The faces glowed in the dark behind his eyes. Lit by fire. Haunted by music. Stretch. Storyteller. X. Nature. Superman. Idaho. Raresteak. Dogface. T. Pappy. Bowls. And all the others. Tabs. All of them. One by one, they emerged. Mountain Man pressed his palms to his ears, rubbed his temples hard.

"Get out of my mind," he whispered. "Take your tabs with you. You're gonna need 'em."

But they didn't leave. They circled back again and again, whispering their chosen images like prayers. Offering them up to the one who had abandoned them. He clenched his teeth. He would not listen. All night, they tried.

He would not let them in.

~ *Kim Lan Returns to Her Comrades* ~

Earlier that same day, shortly after the exchange, Kim Lan sat before the assembled officers of her unit: Major Vy, Captain Tong, Commissar Minh, and Sergeants Dam and Viet. Using Vy's sand map, she briefed them on everything she had observed inside the American fortress: layout, defenses, weaponry, ammunition, soldier count, rations, water, morale, disease, and the deteriorating condition of Comrade Tuyet Mai. She had not seen the tunnel herself, but she had heard the Americans speak of it. Only one soldier was permitted to leave that way, she said, and once gone, he did not return for at least a day or more.

At the mention of this, Sergeant Dam leaned forward. His eyes lit with sudden recognition. "He's the one setting the traps," Dam muttered, half to himself. Then, louder: "Tell me more about this man, sister. What does he look like?"

Before she could answer, Vy cut in with a gruff demand. "First, Comrade Kim Lan, the trunk. What is its condition?"

Kim Lan flared internally, her anger sharp and immediate. Vy had always cared more for the statue than for Tuyet Mai. She knew why. But she swallowed her indignation and replied with obedient restraint, the way a proper Vietnamese woman must. "Yes, Comrade Major," she said evenly. "The trunk is inside the ruined church. I didn't have constant access to it, but I observed enough. One American, an intelligence officer—Captain Kha Re Em Si or something similar—inspected its contents after the helicopter crash. He speaks fluent Vietnamese, reads *quốc ngữ*. He told Comrade Tuyet Mai his mother was Vietnamese and his father American. When he thought we might be cooperative, he questioned us about the items in the trunk. But it was the statue that obsessed him. The Americans said he spends all his time in the church with his 'girlfriend.' That's what they called it. Naturally, we told him nothing."

She turned slightly, meeting Minh's eyes. "Of course," she added, "we did not inform him of our intention to barter the statue with the Jarai Arap."

Vy nodded. "I met this Captain at the negotiations. There's something unbalanced about him . . . " He scowled. "I thought him Chinese-American at first. Then the bastard opened his mouth. Perfect Vietnamese. A traitor."

Kim Lan did not share everything. She said nothing of the dread she and Tuyet Mai had felt in Cairns's presence. His looks. His gestures. Danger didn't follow him. It lived in his skin, woven into every movement. She and Tuyet Mai had agreed in whispers: if given the chance, he would rape them. Perhaps worse.

Minh grunted. "Why is this American captain so obsessed with the statue?"

"I don't know, Comrade Commissar," she replied. "But the statue is causing unrest among the Americans. I'm certain of that."

Vy's brow lifted. "Unrest? How?"

"There's one soldier, clearly ill, possibly malaria. He's been hallucinating. Screaming in the night. Saying ghosts have entered the fortress. That the statue brings them. His comrades seemed shaken. The medic tried to calm him, but I heard them talk. The statue frightens them."

Minh interrupted, voice sharp. "Comrade Kim Lan, allow me to correct your terminology. Americans do not have comrades. They are dogs. Tools of capitalist warmongers. Their concept of death is selfish. They do not die for others—they die to escape. They want only to go home, and they are angry that the people of Vietnam have not welcomed them with flowers."

He laughed, proud of his rhetoric.

Kim Lan smiled thinly, hand instinctively rising to hide the silver tooth that always embarrassed her. "Thank you for correcting me, Comrade Minh."

His laughter created a lull. But Sergeant Viet had been watching her carefully.

"Comrade Major," Viet said slowly, "do you remember when Comrade Quang Long also fell sick? When we were in possession of the statue? He spoke of ghosts. Demons. Said they came with the statue. You recall?"

Dam nodded gravely. "He told me the same. Just before the negotiations, he begged me to get it back."

Vy dismissed them with a wave. "Bah! Superstition. Malaria again. He needs more re-education. This is irrelevant to the task ahead."

"And what exactly is that task, Comrade Major?" asked Tong slyly, a smirk playing on his lips.

Vy flushed. Tong had struck a nerve. Again. "To recover Comrade Tuyet Mai. To retrieve the statue. And to complete our mission successfully."

"Bah!" spat Minh. "This again."

"Two quail with one arrow," muttered Tong, still smiling.

Vy raised a hand defensively. "Enough. Let us finish the briefing."

He turned to Kim Lan. "Anything else we should know?"

She hesitated. She wanted to mention the strange way the Man from the Mountains had watched her. The way he had hovered. But something stopped her.

"No, Comrade Major."

"Very well. Rest. But first see Med Tech Le. He'll give you something to sleep."

"Thank you."

"One moment," said Dam quietly. "If I may, Comrade Major . . . I'd like to ask a few questions."

Vy nodded. "Briefly."

Dam's voice softened. "You're not too tired?"

"No."

And then he launched into her.

"What does he look like? Height? Weight? The way he walks? How does he move? What weapons does he carry? Skin color? Does he ever laugh? Smile? Relax? Does he speak much? Have friends? Is he popular? Eye color? Hair? Shape of mouth? Teeth? Any distinguishing features?"

She answered patiently, methodically. Every detail she remembered.

By the time Dam leaned back, the fire in his eyes told the others: he knew what he needed to know.

~ *Kim Lan's Memories* ~

Later that evening, Kim Lan sat beneath a cassia tree, chewing on the brackish shrimp given to her by Cook Truong. Her thoughts drifted back to *The Man from the Mountains*. On the surface, so like other American soldiers, and yet not. Surely he was insane. Frightening, yes. But compelling. Ugly, yet something about him attracted her. Ferocious in moments, gentle in others. He was a strange admixture of yin and yang. And oddly, she feared him less than she feared the captain. Though she knew the information she'd delivered would likely doom the Americans in the fortress, she felt unexpectedly ambivalent. Like Idaho before her, she had come to know her captors. They were no longer just "enemies." They had become human.

Sprawled beneath the blooming cassia, she lay back and remembered her first encounter with Americans. She was fourteen. A convoy had come rumbling through her hamlet, the first time she had seen the foreign soldiers with her own eyes. Until then, she had dealt only with puppet troops, never the real Americans. Her heart had raced, swollen with fear, curiosity, defiance. She'd run to her father's paddy field to get a good look. Her twelve-year-old brother was already there, perched proudly on the family's new water buffalo. He grinned as she passed, thumb raised in triumph. They had saved for five years to buy that beast. Just one week ago, their father had acquired it. Her mother had paraded it through the hamlet, beaming with pride, declaring the family's good fortune to neighbors and ancestors alike.

The American convoy passed with thunder and laughter. Soldiers stood tall atop armored vehicles, their movements jerky, weapons bristling at odd angles. Kim Lan watched, half entranced.

Then, the laughter changed.

She saw soldiers pointing toward something in the paddy. One of them raised his rifle.

Five sharp cracks.

CRACK! CRACK! CRACK! CRACK! CRACK!

The water buffalo collapsed beneath her brother, both tumbling into the rice. She ran, stumbling through the flooded field. Her legs barely responded. Every step dragged her deeper.

Behind her, the Americans howled with laughter and vanished, a trail of dust unwinding into the wind.

By the time she reached them, her brother was curled into himself, unharmed but shaking. Her mother was already there, collapsed against the dying beast, trying in vain to stop the blood. It sprayed through her fingers. Her thin arms, slick with gore, clung to the buffalo's neck like two reeds gripping the trunk of a fallen tree.

Ever since that day, whenever Kim Lan saw Americans, that was the image that returned: a child, a beast, a scream—and cruel laughter.

~

Now, under the cassia canopy, she reveled in the rare luxury of cleanliness. After her debriefing, she had washed in the stream, scrubbing herself with fibrous bark until the smell of Americans and fortress mildew dissolved. Tech Le, ever talkative, had given her herbal tea laced with a sedative. But sleep would not come. Tuyet Mai was gone. Her thoughts were loud. Her solitude unbearable.

A cough.

She looked up to find Sergeant Viet standing nearby, shuffling awkwardly. She smiled, bright and reflexive. "Please join me, Comrade Sergeant Viet."

He nodded and squatted across from her, his pith helmet pushed back on his head. His teeth were crooked and stained, but his grin was warm. She felt a familiar relief, he was Vietnamese. She had been surrounded so long by pale and ominous foreign faces that even his gnomish features felt beautiful. She talked without purpose. Just to connect. Just to feel another soul beside hers.

"It's good to be back among my comrades."

"Yes. It must be."

"I never thought I'd be glad to return to the forest. But it feels . . . safe."

"Ah, yes?"

"Yes."

"Your home is nearby?"

"Close to Song Nhan village."

"Ah, yes?"

"Yes."

"Tuyet Mai told me you have children. Is it true?"

"Two daughters. Six and four." Her voice caught slightly. "I miss them terribly. I remember—"

And she launched into a long, rambling tale about her girls. Viet nodded politely, though he grew a little restless.

"Your husband?" he asked with care.

"The grass has grown over him. Killed in the Forest of Lost Souls."

"I'm sorry. But he died for a noble cause."

"Yes."

"Americans?"

"B-52 strike."

Viet's face darkened. Everyone feared the bombers. Everyone.

Her thoughts turned, inevitably, to *The Man from the Mountains*. She told Viet about his obsession: how he believed she was possessed by the spirit of his dead fiancée, how he would talk to her even when she pretended to sleep. He dreamed aloud of marrying her. Of America. Of children. Terrified, she had lain stiff, eyes clamped shut so tears couldn't betray her wakefulness.

She glanced at Viet. Had she said too much? Would he see her as weak? A traitor? But still she couldn't stop. "When he returned from his missions, he spoke to me like I was his wife."

Viet's eyes widened.

She sputtered. "Not . . . not like that. I mean, not the bed! Just the way he talked."

"I understand," Viet said gently. "I understand."

~

But far from judging her, Viet was grateful. She'd finally opened the door he'd been waiting to walk through. "This American, this Man from the Mountains, you say he disappears into the tunnel for one or two days?"

"Yes."

"And your description is accurate?"

"Of course."

"He was interested in the statue?"

"No."

"Do you remember when we had the statue before the ambush?"

"Clearly."

"And how Comrade Long saw ghosts?"

Kim Lan nodded. "Yes."

"And only one American saw ghosts? The one with malaria?"

"Yes. They call him 'Teller of Stories.'"

Viet sat back, rainwater dripping from his helmet. "There's something about all this. We and they—both mirror each other in strange ways."

"Yes."

"It's not just military, soldiers, the war. There's something else. I don't yet know what."

~

Kim Lan studied him. Viet's mind, peasant-born and keen as a dragon's tooth, had sensed it too: something deeper at play. She dared not mention her mission, nor the drugs, but she longed to. If only Tuyet Mai were here.

Viet stood, brushing off his tunic. She panicked at the thought of being left alone. "Please stay. Let me share my rice balls with you. I haven't shown you the pictures of my girls."

Without waiting for permission, she pulled out a plastic bag, carefully extracting a black-and-white photo, remembering to hide her silver tooth behind her lips.

Viet lit it with his red flashlight. "Ah! Pretty girls! Pretty girls!"

"No, no. Ugly like their mother." She smiled, and kept talking about her girls, her husband, her home. Anything to keep him near.

Viet listened with distracted patience. Offering the occasional "Ah!" or "Eh!" as his mind raced elsewhere.

~

He was picturing *The Man from the Mountains*. Setting traps. Emerging from the tunnel. Killing comrades. He realized: the Americans had their own Sapper Dam. A shadow-dwelling killer. If he reached the American rear? Then came the bombers. The helicopters. The gunships. Fire and metal from the sky. That could not happen.

It must not.

~

Elsewhere in camp, Sergeant Dam was searching for Viet. Soldiers pointed him toward Kim Lan's hammock.

He approached and saw the two deep in conversation.

He couldn't hear what they said.

"Comrades! Hello!" Dam called, striding toward them.

Viet grinned, voice exaggeratedly loud. "Ah! Dam! Just the man I wanted to see!"

"Comrade Kim has given me useful information."

"Good," Dam barked. "Tell me later. The attack begins tonight. My sappers will move across the clearing in a few hours. If all goes well, we'll be inside the fortress by 0500." He beamed. "After that, it's up to the rest of you."

He turned to Viet. "I've got a few things we need to go over."

Both men looked at Kim Lan.

"I hope I was helpful," she said.

"You have been, Comrade," said Viet.

Her brow wrinkled. "But they may change the guard. Shift the weapons. Move Comrade Tuyet Mai."

"We expect that," Dam replied coolly.

"Bring her back," she said, voice thick with emotion. "Protect her."

Dam smiled lightly. "I will. I promise." His eyes darkened. "But I pray to our ancestors I meet two of the Americans in person. One is *The Man from the Mountains*. The other is the intelligence captain. The one who dares speak our language with stolen blood in his veins."

Kim Lan and Viet said nothing. They nodded slowly.

Glad they were comrades of Dam.

And very glad they were not the Americans he named.

Very glad.

~ *Madame Dau Vacillates* ~

Madame Dau settled wearily into her wooden bed, then looked over at the sleeping figure of her daughter. Thank the gods she is with me. It has been a long day. Leading the council meeting. Confronting the American soldier at the tunnel. A year's worth of events lived in one day! I'm too old for this. Too old. She patted the floor until she found a cloth bag, carefully tied, containing the items requested by the American soldier. Her foreign devil *bo doi*. She had packed a drawing of Song Nhan village, some food, fruit, feminine items and clean clothes for his wife.

But the potential consequences of giving assistance to this soldier had begun to sink in. Contact with soldiers always led to disaster: her mother prostituting herself to the French, her parents' death in the attack on the fortress, her own rape at the hands of the French soldier, the death of one son and the absence of the other, the constant fear of soldiers destroying her village, raping her daughters, stealing her food, killing her animals, ruining her crops, taxes for the government and the Front. It was too much! And she had the foolish temerity to assist an American soldier. This crime would result in her execution by the Front. What would happen to her daughters? Her fields? Her grandchildren? Madame Dau shrank back from the bag. There is the sign, the two-headed snake. I cannot ignore the sign. But if I am discovered helping an American soldier, the Front will be ruthless.

She imagined soldiers appearing without warning in the village at night, dragging her from her bed to the square by the old rice thresher, accusing her of treason in front of the assembled villagers. In front of her neighbors, friends, family. She imagined hearing the verdict shouted out, "Guilty!" The gun aimed at her head. The gunshots. Yet the Americans also terrified her, in some ways, more than the Front. American soldiers were aliens, shadowy, bulky monsters that dwarfed normal people. Godlike. They struck without warning from the sky. Swooping helicopters, metallic demons.

But Madame Dau knew the Americans were only human. Just men, like the French. She remembered the dripping, deflating, wrinkled penis of the French officer in the tunnel. She remembered Brother Tinh once saying, "Bah! Rubbish! The Americans! They're nothing to be afraid of! Their knees crumple just like a goat when you slit its throat. I even heard one of them whining for his mother before he died. Bags of blood, just bags of blood like the rest of us."

She remembered the old days when soldiers came to the village regularly, the Front at night, government troops by day. Everyone always felt afraid. Fields lay neglected, children were abandoned, possessions buried, virginity of young girls all but forgotten. Adults and children were conscripted to act as laborers for various projects. Tunnel digging. Road repair. Making punji sticks. All the while, the relationship of each villager to the other became one of suspicion. Who was an informer? To which side were they informing? Did someone have a grudge that they could avenge by giving false information?

Her outrage and anger long since expended in the exhaustive struggle to survive, Madame Dau, like the other villagers, felt powerless against the war's opposing tides. Allowing herself to be carried in either direction meant certain death, so she dog paddled in a primordial stupor, constant movement without moving between the riptide and the rocks. An opium dream. She survived by making no eye contact with life. Look down. Shuffle. Don't attract attention. Her children were not so fortunate. They were useful as laborers or soldiers, prostitutes or slaves. One by one they fell victim to the war, but it had not always been that way.

A year and a half earlier, Madame Dau and the other women of the village had awakened one morning to discover the last of the adult men and teenaged boys gone. In the absence of males, the Venerable Vu Huong took an unprecedented step by forming a village council comprised entirely of women, which he termed 'provisional.' In his wisdom, he put the whole situation in perspective at their first meeting. "Since all the young men and marriageable girls are gone, and very little food or money remains, there is nothing left for the soldiers. Not even scraps. The war has gorged itself and moved on to more fertile villages. The soldiers will no longer come. Not for a while. In the meantime, you must organize!"

It was a painful and lonely task, but gradually, as the wounds healed, the village recovered under the women's direction. At first, the Venerable gave constant advice and guidance, then slowly withdrew from the daily affairs of the village until, at last, he merely nodded at their decisions in the grave manner of a proud grandpapa. Finally, liberation! The village experienced a sort of renaissance. Peace and prosperity flourished under the community of women. Suspicion and mistrust slowly evaporated. They had food to eat, shelter, children, home, and bickering, of course. Much bickering and backbiting. But peace had returned, defined as the absence of men.

Until the siege at the old fortress. Until, thought Madame Dau, one old woman helps an American soldier. *And then the village might again be consumed in fire!* She stared up at the darkness. All these years of balancing between the Front and the government. Surviving the French, the Japanese, the Americans. Until now! *How can I, village council chief, help an American soldier? How? Why? But the sign! The two-headed snake! Surely it is my mother. Surely she would not mislead me! And papa. He must be in on this too.*

Madame Dau again thought of her daughters and grandchildren. She felt responsible for exposing them to danger. *Maybe the sign is false. Maybe my mother and father are punishing me for not assuring they had a proper funeral. Maybe. Maybe maybe maybe maybe. The more she thought about these things the more confused she became. My parents gave me life, but they are dead. I have given my children and my grandchildren life, and now my decision might kill them. It is too much for a stupid old woman to think about!*

She slowly got out of bed so as to not wake her daughter and shuffled to the family altar. Lighting some joss sticks, she burned incense and silently asked for guidance from Mickey Mouse and her ancestors. She waited for a sign but heard only the moaning of the monsoon wind and the tapping of rain on her roof.

Tortured by her thoughts, she remembered Brother Tinh. Yes. He would give her guidance. Was he not the village advisor in matters involving the yang? Certainly. Wrapping a scarf snugly around her neck, Madame Dau lit a lantern, touched Mickey Mouse for luck, and stepped resolutely into the night. She leaned forward while holding her hat against the wind and walked quickly through the rain, soon reaching Han Tinh's ramshackle hut at the edge of Carpenter Long's property.

Madame Dau squinted through Tinh's broken window. Between the flapping tatters of a mildewed curtain, she saw his room dimly illuminated by pale light from a low burning kerosene lamp and assumed he was still awake. She craned her neck to see the floor and noticed a lump moving under the bright fabric of an American parachute. Her eyes scanned the reclining figure and she noticed that the lump had no legs. She knocked but heard no response. Quietly entering the shack, she squatted next to the parachute and lowered her lantern close to the figure. Han Tinh moaned and rolled over, his head coming into view as if clouds had been drawn back to reveal a full moon. His grotesque face was pock marked with dark craters that twitched in the light and his eyelids fluttered wildly. He must be dreaming. Madame Dau took a deep breath and pushed at a swelling under the parachute that she hoped was his arm.

"Wha . . . What! Who is it? Why are you waking me? Eh! What time is it?" grumbled Han Tinh, without giving Madame Dau time to answer.

"It is Madame Dau. Madame Dau. I say, Madame Dau," she said soothingly.

"Ah! Madame Dau! Distinguished Venerable Council Chief. Good evening. Is it time for the next council meeting already?"

"No, no. It is late. Very late. Han Tinh, I need your help. I need your advice."

"Help me up!" he snapped, holding forth his hands.

Madame Dau pulled Han Tinh straight up so that he balanced unsteadily on his stumps. She held him beneath his armpits until his wavering stopped, then withdrew her hands slowly.

"That's better," he said. "Now. What is it? I welcome you even at this late hour. Ah! Did you light my lantern? No? Foolish old man that I am, wasting fuel! What does my Venerable wish of me?"

Madame Dau, never quite sure whether Han Tinh mocked her or invited her to laugh with him, could not now be patient with his buffoonery.

"Han Tinh! We are not at a water puppet show. I need your advice, not your jokes."

Crestfallen, he replied, "You know, at the end of our performances when I was a water puppeteer, we all stood up, waist deep in water, bowing to the cheers of the audience. Even then, when I had legs, they could not be seen. An omen. Yes?" He looked at her quizzically.

"Speaking of omens, that is why I have come to see you," she said, almost whispering.

"What?"

"Omens!"

"Ah! Omens! Yes. I know all about omens. I am an omen, not a man. You see in me a flesh and blood omen with no other purpose than to point the way for others. It's just that when I point, no one can see me down here. So low to the ground. An omen should be high up, like on a mountain. Not groveling in the mud. But that's where we came from. That's where we shall return."

"Where?" asked Madame Dau.

Han Tinh looked annoyed. "Never mind." He forced a smile. "Tea?"

"No, thank you."

"Then let's get on with it. What omen? Which of my brother omens do you wish to discuss?"

"None of your brothers, I think. None related to you. This omen is in the form of an American soldier."

"I heard you wrong. Say again?"

"An American soldier."

"No!"

"Yes."

"Then he is a stepbrother omen! Does he come in your dreams?"

"No, no. You do not understand Brother Tinh. Let me explain." And Madame Dau told Han Tinh the entire story of The Man From The Mountains. How she met him. Her dog and the two-headed snake. Her providing assistance to him. His Vietnamese wife. As Tinh listened, his face registered increasing impatience, even anger. She watched his displeasure grow.

"Sister Dau, you are mistaken about my stepbrother omen. He was not sent by your parents. No, indeed. He was not sent to help you. He is a soldier, true?"

"Yes."

"Then he brings destruction with him. Misery."

"But you are sometimes called Soldier Tinh, aren't you? You were a soldier once yourself," protested Madame Dau.

"Exactly!" he said, looking down at his non-existent legs. "Did you not listen to my words at the council meeting?"

"I thought—"

"Bah! No matter. This American soldier has been sent by the demons and ghosts of the dead French and Moroccan soldiers dwelling in the old fortress, not our martyred Vietnamese patriots. Not your parents. He has been sent to possess you! To lead our village to ruin!"

Madame Dau's face went white and she felt nauseous. How could this be? How could I be so wrong?

"But the two-headed snake," she said.

"A trick."

"His Vietnamese wife?"

"A lie."

"But my dog ran up to him. Licked him. Played with him as if he were a part of the family. A part of the village. What about that?"

Han Tinh fell silent. "Ah. That is different. Can't fool a dog. In that case, this American soldier may be my step-brother omen. Is his tongue split?"

"No."

"Does he have webbed hands?"

"No."

"Does he smell of fetid swamp?"

Madame Dau hesitated, "Well . . . he certainly smells bad, but not of fetid swamp."

"You say tomorrow you must meet him at the old cave?"

"Yes."

Han Tinh nodded. "Hand me that board and the fortune blocks. There, in front of you! Yes. That's it. Now. I will roll the blocks on the board. Put it down! Put it down! Yes. Good. As I said, I will roll the blocks. If the answer is 'yes,' then you go and meet him, for he is truly an omen from your parents. If the answer is 'no,' then you must not go, but tell the council about him. Including Schoolmistress Nang. That old crone will certainly take care of the rest. Agreed?"

Madame Dau nodded.

Holding the lantern over the board, she watched Han Tinh roll the crescent-shaped fortune blocks. They fell on the board and came to rest, crescents neither facing the same direction, nor opposite.

He rolled again.

Madame Dau breathed in deeply. Impatient.

He rolled again.

And again.

Tinh squinted, wrinkled his forehead and looked disappointed. "Hmm. Ambiguous. I'll roll again."

"No!" said Madame Dau sharply, putting her hand on his arm. "Don't."

He compressed his lips in disgust. "All right, but it is my advice, my strongest advice, that you do not go to him tomorrow."

~ *Bowls Pleads with Mountain Man* ~

Bowls could not sleep. After being relieved from guard duty by Mr. Machine, he fumbled through the dark back to his hootch, pulled off his wet boots, slung his filthy socks over the anchor-rope of his hammock, and sealed himself within his mosquito net. Still, sleep eluded him. Mountain Man. Mountain Man. The absence echoed through his skull, an insistent, funereal drumbeat. His head throbbed, his body ached, and no trick from his private arsenal worked—no imagined tap of high heels, no silken whisper of stockings, not even the cacophony of New York traffic. The man's absence crowded out all fantasy.

A stream of rainwater ran down the inside of the poncho draped over his hammock and landed squarely in his eye. That was it. He tugged on his soggy socks, laced up his soaked boots, and cradled his rifle. Moving carefully, he crept around the base of the stone wall to where T lay sleeping. Standing over the lieutenant, Bowls hesitated. He meant to find Mountain Man. He had decided. But now doubt trickled in. That tunnel. What if something waited on the other side? He scolded himself, tried to conjure heroic images but fear pressed back, solid and unyielding. At last, as if shoved from behind, he bent and jabbed T's shoulder.

"T! Wake up! It's me, Bowls!"

"What . . . what? Bowls? What's going on?"

"Nothing right now. But I need to talk to you."

T groaned. "Yeahhh. I guess. What time is it?"

"It's late. I've been thinking."

"Wonderful. You've been thinking. I'm proud of you. A breakthrough. Now may I go back to sleep?"

"Come on, T. I'm serious. It's about Mountain Man."

"Oh yeah?" T straightened slightly, alert now.

"Yeah."

"Well?"

"I think I can talk him into coming back."

"Bull. You saw him, Bowls. He was jumping around like a cricket on a griddle. He'd have shot us all if we'd gotten in his way. Even you."

"Colorful, T. But I'm from New York. I've never seen a hen or a cricket. Maybe I can get the old pig farmer back. Let me go through the tunnel and find him. Two hours, max."

"Look, Bowls, one, he's probably gone. Two, he might shoot you. Three, I can't spare you. NVA's going to hit soon."

"No way. Too dark for him to go far. He told me about a big banyan tree near the exit. He's probably holed up there 'til dawn. I find him or I don't. Either way, I'm back pronto. What's to lose?"

"You."

"T, come on. We need him. You know it."

T let out a long sigh. "Okay. But back by 0500. No farther than that banyan tree. You hear firing back here, you haul ass back. Understood?"

"Yes, sir."

"I mean it, Bowls. I need my orders followed to the letter."

"Yes, sir."

~

Superman, heading to his post, spotted Bowls and walked him to the trap door. Bowls eased himself into the tunnel shaft. Superman leaned over, watching him vanish.

"God go with you, Bowls," he whispered.

Bowls grunted. Then paused, looking up. "Thanks, Superman. Hope He cares for grunts as much as He does for the leeches and mosquitoes."

Superman leaned closer. "He does. He knows when even the smallest sparrow falls."

Bowls flicked on his flashlight, waved his arms theatrically. "Problem is, Superman, the little fuckers fall anyway."

He turned and entered the tunnel. The walls curved around him, tight and enclosing. He shut off the light to preserve the batteries. The air hung thick, damp, metallic. When he switched the light on again, ants and termites flowed in undulating rivers across the red walls.

Though tall, Bowls adjusted quickly to the tunnel's narrow dimensions. He tried to stay between the tracks, but often brushed the sides, stirring clouds of dust, ancient droppings, and insect husks. He learned fast: stay centered, stay upright, breathe shallow.

The blackness pressed against him on all sides. A faint phosphorescence from fungus-covered leaves traced the rails, but barely. He used the flashlight on straightaways and killed it around curves, dread mounting with each blind turn. His fear didn't fade, it focused. Panic, not reason, propelled him forward.

When he reached the first storage chamber, he didn't pause. The stench of mold and fermentation clawed at his throat. He crossed quickly to the far opening and kept going.

Only one thought now: *air*. He didn't care if the NVA were waiting above. Let them shoot him. Just get out. Still, caution urged restraint.

Reaching the second chamber, he extinguished the flashlight and froze. Silence. Then a faint glow caught his eye—something low on the far wall. He clicked the light on and swept the beam across the chamber until it struck a rectangular niche.

The memory of the church's earlier glow surged back. His body locked. Every nerve screamed to retreat, but the thought of retracing his steps through the tunnel was worse than whatever lay ahead.

Come on, Bowls. You've been in worse alleys. New York is worse. Move your damn feet. That box is too small to hurt you.

He edged forward, whispering reassurances. At last, he knelt before the niche.

A human skull stared back, bathed in yellow light. Beneath it, the name MARTHA glowed—faint, weathered.

His breath escaped in a sharp burst.

A name. A monument. A ghost.

"Oh shit, Mountain Man. Holy Mother of God."

He stumbled back, shaking, and pushed onward. Sweat poured down his body. The heat. The stench. The closeness. Fresh air. Just a little farther.

Finally, Bowls staggered into the exit chamber. His foot dragged across the disarmed trip wire. He looked up: the trapdoor. A portal to air, to rain, to life. He turned off his light, eyes adjusting. Slowly, inch by inch, he pushed the trapdoor open. Pause. Listen. Damp air kissed his face. Again. Pause. Listen. The hiss of insects, frogs croaking. Still nothing alarming.

The door fully open, Bowls rose, his body now half through the opening, poised between tomb and storm.

~

Without warning, an arm closed around Bowls' throat, hooked beneath his jaw, and yanked his head backward until something in his neck nearly tore. His vision darkened. Oxygen vanished. He felt his death arriving fast and quiet until he heard a low chuckle, ragged and dark.

"What'sa'matter? New York tough drowning in West Virginia pig shit? Hello, Bowls."

The grip released. Bowls collapsed, gasping, spitting rain and breath. He coughed so hard his lungs rattled. Behind him, Mountain Man laughed again, a sound without joy.

"Asshole," Bowls croaked.

Even in his pain, the old awe returned. Mountain Man didn't belong to the world of men, of the human pack. His skin held the memory of tree bark. His silence wasn't stillness—it was the tension before eruption. He moved through the jungle not as a soldier, but as something rooted deep in the memory of the soil. A rifle was not a tool in his hands—it was part of him. Helicopters agitated him. Machines pulled at him wrong. Only weapons felt natural to his essence.

Bowls let himself be dragged and left beneath a banyan tree, its thick roots pressing in around him. Mountain Man stretched a poncho overhead. Rain clicked on the plastic in sharp, irregular bursts.

"Shhh," he whispered, but Bowls couldn't stop coughing. His body shook, breath breaking apart in his chest.

Eventually, it passed.

Bowls leaned in. "I came to bring you back. We need you. I need you. Even T says so. You're part of us."

Mountain Man didn't move.

"It's not the brass. It's us. The brotherhood. You can't stay out here forever."

"Shhh." He tilted his head, listening. "No one's listening now. Rain's too heavy."

His voice dropped into something colder.

"I am the jungle."

He said it with no irony, no madness, only certainty.

"Insect legs crawl across my skin. Larvae move in my gut. Vines drink me. Leeches suck me dry. A tiger squats and I feel the heat of its shit in my roots. When trees fall, I bleed. When they burn, I scream. The termites build mounds on my spine, and I carry them."

Bowls exhaled. "You're gonna get yourself killed."

Mountain Man's eyes turned. "I already did."

Lightning cracked through the canopy. In the flash, Bowls saw what lived behind his eyes—something raw, bright, and dangerous.

"I *was* a termite mound," he growled. "Hard, tall, filled with tunnels. Then Superman leaned against me. He felt sloshing, stupid, soft. Crushed the outer layer. Nearly breached the wall. Inside, thousands of workers screamed. If he broke through, ants would have come. War. Bodies stacked. All because he missed his daughters."

Bowls shook his head. "Jesus, man."

Mountain Man ignored him. "Stay here. The jungle wants you. The fort doesn't. They're dead already."

"Dead? They're fighting for something."

Mountain Man's face twisted. "Fighting for what? Army regs? Mail call? Some motherfuckin' rotation date? These VC—these barefoot, shit-covered sons of bitches—at least they believe. They hate being told how to live. They bleed for it."

"They're communists."

"They're human. And they fight with their whole fucking body. You think shit stinks? To them, it's food. To them, it's home."

He held out his palm. Rain splattered.

"Our shit is green and flat. Dollars. That's why we're rotting from the inside. We steal ponchos for cold beer. We let grunts rot in monsoon because some asshole wants a fridge. That's our war. That's why we lose. they fight for their farms, their women, their culture. That's why they'll win."

Bowls swallowed. "I want to believe in something. We all do. Superman has his girls. Idaho has his mom. T believes in duty. Even X has something, though I don't know what. We're trying to get back."

Mountain Man studied him, smirked faintly. "Tell me your tab."

"Seriously?"

"Tell it, Bowls."

He sighed. "All right."

And Bowls began: the cockroach-infested brownstone, the dead-end warehouse job, the overstuffed chair, the woman across the street. A goddess in a rich apartment. The lipstick. The naked skin. *House of the Rising Sun* on the TV.

"She stood in front of the window, man. Lights on. Just outta the shower. Her hair slicked back. And she took that lipstick and just—real slow—started circling her nipples. Over and over and over. Red. Fuckin' perfect American red. I didn't move. Didn't breathe. Pizza got cold. Beer went warm. Didn't matter."

He grinned through the memory. "It was God, man. Not the one in churches. But the one who makes moments like that."

When he finished, Mountain Man grunted. "Women'll get you killed."

Bowls smiled. "Yeah. But worth it."

Then, without warning, Mountain Man grabbed him, pulled him close, and kissed him hard on the mouth. There was no tenderness. Just hunger, memory, the edge of goodbye. Then he reached beneath his tunic, pulled out a worn leather pouch, and slipped the flock bag around Bowls' neck.

"Go," he said. "Back to the fort. I'll think about it."

His voice changed again, becoming low, guttural, barely human.

"I've got to find Martha. She's out here. Somewhere. They probably tortured her. I have to find her. I have to fix what I broke."

Bowls placed a hand on his friend's chest. "Goodbye, brother."

He kissed him once, gently, on the forehead.

Then he rose, turned, and vanished into the mouth of the tunnel. The rain erased his footprints. The jungle swallowed the sound.

Chapter Thirteen

PART THREE: STRUGGLE

Fever Dreams III

Ring around the cortex,
Ring around the cortex,
Neurons, neurons,
Pocket full of neurons,
They all fall down,
The Others all fall down, Michael.
They all fall down!
As must you!

~ The Apparitions Appear Again ~

"Hot. Hot. Hot," Storyteller mumbled into the rain. "Can't you do your job? Can't you cool me down?" He extended his arm, and the rain struck, not just the flesh but whatever nerve still believed in safety and sanity. The last time he pulled back, he thought, Fine. Be that way. Might as well be on fuckin' Venus. He stayed still. His humor dulled nothing. The deep, grinding ache in his bones remained. *God, I hate it here. What a place to die.* He longed for home: cool sheets, ice water, his bed, his family. *The beach, the beach, the beach. . . .*

The fever had briefly broken. He stared out into blackness, nothing but void, floating in space, gravity undone. Sick. Alone. Afraid to die. Afraid they'd all die. The word haunted him: massacre. Not some sepia-toned tableau from a schoolbook, Custer's folly or ancient slaughter, but them, here, now. We will be massacred. Since the malaria, that premonition had taken root. To silence it, he summoned his nightly troll call, each soldier conjured, accounted for. Summed, as his old history teacher used to say: *Cogito ergo sum. And if they're all still cogitating, maybe they're still summing. Let's see . . .*

Mountain Man was gone, stewing in his mutiny, tilting at his fuckin' windmills.

T and Pappy hunkered in their hooches, staring up at poncho covers, waiting for the sky to fall.

Nature on guard, fretting over a sapper's knife or a sniper's aim.

X hovering near Idaho, debating amputation, paralyzed by fear.

Idaho in morphine dreamland, back on the farm, eating fried chicken or whatever they eat.

Bowls fantasizing, jerking off, no, up all night thinking about the pig farmer. Dreaming about Mountain Man.

Stretch on guard duty, probably replaying The Great Escape.

The chopper crew? Who knows. Birdman and Topper dreaming of wives.

Me too. Always Diane. Sometimes Mom and Dad. But mostly Diane.

~

Michael! Wake up. Please. Wake up, sweetheart. It's okay.

~

Diane. Always you. The comb in my pocket. A talisman. A prayer. They all think mundane thoughts. Mundane men. Mundane dreams. And then there's me. Fevered. Haunted. Ghosted. And no waking. No escape. You can wake up. But I can't. I can't. . . .

The fever surged, coiling back through him, breathless and primal. Malaria pawed at his skin, raced cell to cell, tendon to tendon. A firestorm inside his skull. His mouth, nose, ears, even his breath burned. His brain blistered beneath skin that pulsed and peeled.

An open urn in a windstorm, My boy. My Chosen One. Let it come. Let it pass. You must return, even from ash, to burn anew. Your father endured the same when your lesbian mother died. From such unions are you born: rape and redemption, regret and reincarnation.

Jesus Christ. Jesus Christ. Jesus Christ. . . .

He dreamt he was a compost pile, smoke rising from its heart, ready to ignite. And then, clarity. The pain ebbed. The veil lifted. He glimpsed the vast, disinterested universe and merged with it, uncaring now whether he lived or died. Even panic had grown tired. The rain tapping his poncho sounded like soil tossed onto a coffin. His mosquito net became a burial shroud. *I'm being buried alive . . . but not.* The panic faded. He exhaled slowly. Death would be welcome.

Only one thread held: curiosity. What came next? *We are gathered to bury Michael L. Powers, worthless person, killer of self and others, son of—*

And then: a presence. Not one. Many. Not human. The hair on his head rose, soaked and standing. He smeared mud across his face to become unseen. They hovered, translucent beings, their hearts and lungs blurry pulses, bipedal tadpoles suspended in light. Fever-lit, yet invisible to others. Guards unmoved. Grunts slept on, curled in infant repose. The pain receded. Each time they came, they numbed it. He became theirs, mummified, webbed, suspended. He knew their faces. Each returned to the same soldier or sleeper. But each night, they changed. Eye colors clarified. Flesh tones darkened. Internal organs fogged. Brains dissolved into bone. Then the tableaux began. Rehearsals of some ghost-play, its scenes reshuffled, out of sequence. Familiar gestures, yet newly grotesque.

~

The naked women, self-absorbed, distracted, uneasy.
The elders, bored, peevish.
The children, scheming.
The babies, fussy.
The mothers, exhausted.
The lovers, disgusted.

~

Where once a laugh, now a forced chuckle.
Where once fear, only apprehension.
Where once love, a glance.
Where once hate, a shrug.
Where once Utopia, now Peoria.

~

Only the boy with the backwards baseball cap remained unchanged, waving his right hand at nothing, eyes glued to some invisible screen. And the living soldiers? Fading. Dimming. Essence siphoned into specters. Their faces lost all detail. The women prisoners, too. But the apparitions sharpened. Complexified. He tried to map them, match them to the living. Whose wife? Whose child? Whose ghosts? But the thread was broken. Only the hounds remained. Mountain Man's dogs. Maybe. The figures' behavior grew illegible, ironic smiles, cryptic glances, frozen gestures. He blinked furiously, rain-blind, but nothing clarified. He had once believed writing could explain humanity. But this? This was beyond language.

And then, ants. A line of them marched over his fingers, across his wrists, into his sleeves.

"Damn! Damn! Damn!" He flailed. He doused his liner's edge with the last of the bug juice. Thousands of ants, unbothered by rain, kept coming. He looked absurd, exorcising ants while ghosts danced in silence.

Then he saw *her*.

Goddess. Not the statue—*Her*. Flesh and sizzling rain. Three meters away. Alive. She sat in lotus pose, skin glowing, rain cascading down Her breasts. Her third eye burned faintly. Her left hand cupped upward, the right pointed to the heavens. Ants marched from behind Her thigh, traced across Her body, over navel, breast, collarbone, then vanished behind Her shoulder. She watched the specters, Her head turning in full circle. From guard posts to sleeping soldiers, She saw them all.

Storyteller saw through Her gaze: They're all dreaming. He turned back to Her. No, I'm dreaming. Hallucinating. Schizophrenic. Just write. Just write. Goddess did not move. Her smile still curved. Her crown intact. Diamonds glittering from Her nipples. The lotus beneath Her, untouched by mud. The ants reappeared and marched toward him. He sprayed them, frantic, and She looked down sternly.

"I'm sorry," he whispered, hiding the bottle. Then, gesturing to the ghosts: "Make them stop. Please. No, don't. I want to see. I want to understand."

The ants turned and vanished behind the lotus. She inclined Her head, beckoning him to look. They resumed their play, but now differently. Out of order. Evolving. He searched for the wounded woman, found her beside her grunt, still nude, bruises nearly gone. Her heart beat rapidly beneath her glowing chest. Her lungs spasmed. She clutched at an invisible blanket. Her legs pressed together in mute terror.

He turned away.

Goddess was smiling.

Behold … the human condition.

"No," he said. "There's more. Joy. Love. Redemption."

The human condition. You want to write about it? Illuminate it?

"Yes."

She transformed, fluidly, silently, into a tiger. Her voice dropped into a growl.

Humans obsess over what it means to be human. They forget what it means to be ape, or shrew, or leaf. The deeper they dig into themselves, the more they sever from life. They glorify wonder, invention, love. But they are fish enchanted by their gills, blind to the water that holds them. But you, Michael Powers, you are not fully human. You are the Chosen One.

He tried to respond, but She vanished. Then Mountain Man's hounds. This time, they didn't vanish. They padded to his empty bedroll and curled there, waiting. One scratched itself, and Storyteller laughed. A ghost flea. Sure. Why not.

But then something new. Out of each apparition's spine, bony white protrusions jutted upward. Sculpted. Geometrical. He stared. Tombstones.

"Oh God," he whispered. "Gravestones. Growing out of their bones! Gravestones! Gravestones!"

Voices rose:

Oops!

Did Your scalpel slip, Great Mother?

Not Me. Was it You?

Only boys crave conflagrations, Goddess. I aim higher. Careful. He's fragile. Do You want to kill him?

He's already cracked. The schizophrenia showed him his place. He sees gravestones, not hunchbacks. But the keys to the Superior Ones are hunchbacks, not gravestones.

Fools, all of You. Let Me nudge him. . . .

"No, wait!" cried Storyteller. "They're not gravestones. They're hunchbacks! Hunchbacks!"

Yes! Yes! Michael Powers, you see. Think back. Think back to your parents. Think back to the Child of Buddha. The hunchbacks are the key!

~

Nearby, Nature flinched at Storyteller's cries. Another fever. He ducked instinctively behind the parapet.

A voice rose, Pappy's. "What is it?"

"Storyteller again," someone answered.

"Oh crap! That sonofabitch's gonna get us killed!" Topper spat.

"God damn it! X! Get over there and shut him up!" barked T. "It's his goddamn ghosts again!"

Nature was startled. T sounded frayed, on edge.

A calm voice approached Storyteller's position. "Shhhh. Quiet. We'll fix you up. What do you see, boy?" Nature recognized Captain Cairns.

Then silence.

Words from another guard post came.

"Poor soul," said Superman.

"A soul?" sneered Stretch. "Can you see it? Touch it?"

"Shut up," growled Superman. "Watch your sector."

"Can it!" barked Pappy. "Everyone shut up! Move positions if you opened your trap. Snipers love noise."

X muttered as he approached. "Ghosts. Gravestones. Why can't he hallucinate about tits or his mother? Okay, okay, I'm here, kid."

Storyteller's voice floated up, soft but clear. "Doesn't matter, X. They're gone. Just like that. But I'm starting to get it. Those gravestones, they weren't supposed to be there. Something went wrong. But then Goddess told me they were not gravestones. She said they were hunchbacks. Hunchbacks! My mother, my father, China, the Quest, Precious Object, they walked with Child of Buddha, hunchback! It's a warning, man. Or a prophecy! . . . Oh hell. Fever's back. Damn! I'm burning up!"

He doubled over and heaved.

Nature watched, hand stretched into the dark. Where are you, ghosts? Which of you are mine? Mom? Dad? Are you here? He shivered. It felt like ants crawling over his skin. "Mother of God. Help us. Mother Mary, help Storyteller. Make him blind. Like the rest of us."

Below, a woman whimpered. Someone whispered to her, Cairns, speaking urgent Vietnamese. Nature caught only one word: Tara.

She did not answer. She just whimpered, soft and low, a wounded animal.

~ *Quang Long Remembers* ~

Crouched in the treeline beyond the fortress, Captain Tong's company clerk, Quang Long, strained to catch the muffled voices of American soldiers drifting across the rain-slicked clearing. Thunder rolled above them, the dreadful echo of distant artillery. Long couldn't sleep. He had joined his friend Nguyen Manh Kha near the perimeter, where the two men sat quietly on a fallen log. Kha had just come off guard duty. They spoke in hushed tones, their voices buried beneath the patter of rain and distant rumble of storms.

"Listen," Long whispered. "The Americans. Hear them?"

"Of course," Kha replied. "Strange business. And the lights! One of them sounds . . . angry. Ah, listen! Are they killing themselves?"

"I think I know what's troubling them."

"Oh?" Kha raised an eyebrow. "What?"

Long placed a hand on his friend's shoulder. "Do you remember the ghosts I told you about? Back when we had the statue? They came to the camp. Men, women, children . . . even babies." He paused, voice low. "Even animals." He let the words settle. "You remember, don't you? That first night, I screamed. Major Vy and Captain Tong were furious. Even old Viet scowled at me. Of course you remember."

Kha chuckled. "How could I forget? You babbled for days during all those *kiem thao* sessions Minh forced on you."

Long hesitated.

"Go on," Kha encouraged. "I won't think you're crazier than usual. Besides, I'm curious. I promise I won't report your 'bourgeois superstitions' to Comrade Minh." He laughed softly. "We're old brothers of the forest."

Long drew a slow breath. "These last few nights, I've come out and sat with the guards, watching the fortress. Through the dark, the rain. You and the others see nothing. But I see something. Very clearly."

He paused again, waiting.

Kha sighed. "Well? I'm knee-deep in the rice field, friend. Speak."

"I see ghosts. Their ghosts. Walking—no, floating across the clearing, through the walls of the fortress. I know it's too dark to see. But they glow. I don't know why, but I can see them. The fortress too. Tonight, while you were complaining about how hungry you were, I saw them again, drifting across the clearing into the fortress."

"Why didn't you show me?"

"Because no one else can see them. And I, I shiver all over, though I'm not cold." He laughed softly. "Besides, I'm not eager for another *kiem thao* session."

"What do they look like? The American ghosts. Surely they're demons. Claws? Long teeth?"

"No. They look like ours. That's what puzzles me." Long hesitated again. "You must understand, I can see through them. Their hearts, their lungs, their spines. When you look at people that way . . . they all look the same. Their hearts beat the same. Their lungs swell the same."

"Even the women?"

"Of course."

Kha grinned. "Tell me, brother. Do women really have beating hearts? Sometimes my wife makes me wonder. And their breasts—do American women have nice ones? Nice bodies?"

"Don't be a fool," Long muttered. Then his tone shifted. "Sometimes I think the Goddess statue is trying to speak. Maybe it's our ancestors. But what if . . . what if they're the ancestors of the Americans?"

Kha scoffed. "Americans? Ancestors? They care about money, not the past. You know the old saying: 'Infinite gratitude for all things past, infinite respect for all things present, infinite servitude for all things future.' For the Americans it's: 'Infinite disregard for all things past, infinite exploitation of all things present, infinite plunder of all things future.'"

Long's voice softened. "Their ghosts say otherwise. They're more like us than I ever imagined."

Kha spat. "Don't let Minh hear that. The Americans think we're animals. But they're learning."

A moment passed.

"Listen," Long whispered. "The voices—they've gone quiet."

"Yes. So they have." Kha grinned. "Let's hope they're sleeping well. Dam and his sappers are on the way."

Long shivered. "I saw them earlier, preparing to infiltrate. I wouldn't want to be in that fortress tonight."

They nodded in silence. Long's hand still rested on Kha's shoulder. For a moment, the moon emerged, casting the fortress in pale dreamlight before vanishing into the clouds. Long thought of his grandfather. That fortress, how would he paint it?

The moon reappeared. Guava and papaya hung in silhouette. Long gazed upward at the firmament of fruit and whispered a prayer, not to the gods of men, but to the gods of bats and monkeys, who ruled this forest now. He prayed for peace.

~

Like Captain Tong's father, Quang Long's grandfather had been a Confucian scholar, a true Mandarin of the old order. But his obsession was painting. He taught Long not only characters and brush technique, but the meditative art of ink and silence. For hours they sat together under a thatched veranda, practicing calligraphy and painting.

"First master bamboo," the old man would say sternly. "Only then, mountains and streams."

"But Grandpapa," Long had once protested, "you said no one has ever mastered bamboo."

His grandfather laughed. "Correct."

Long used to marvel at his grandfather's hands, graceful fingers, translucent wrists. The brush moved like water in his grip. Every stroke—river, fish, temple, teahouse, mountain—felt alive. The ink, it seemed, was his blood.

But Long's father disapproved. Far from the sanctuary of his grandfather's studio, Long was often whipped with a bamboo cane. "This is what you do with bamboo, ungrateful son!" his father would rage. "You will go to Hanoi and become an engineer! Painting is ruining us! Ruining your future!"

Long resisted. The beatings worsened. One day, as blows rained across his shoulders, his father shrieked, spit flying: "A filial son should sleep naked beside his father to draw away mosquitoes! But you—you strip me of my clothes, my money, my pride! You paint while I suffer!"

Long submitted. He enrolled in engineering at Hanoi University, shared a cramped apartment with five other students, and floundered. He hated it. During school breaks, his grandfather would visit. They painted in silence, sometimes exchanging a glance, a click of the tongue. One day the old man examined Long's landscape, tugged his wispy beard, and murmured, "Almost acceptable. Almost."
Long didn't sleep that night, drunk on praise.

Months later, his grandfather died. Long's mother brought him the brushes, inkstones, and inkblocks, his grandfather's bequest. She came alone. His father refused. Long wept many bitter tears. Then, in drunken rebellion, he enlisted in the People's Army. He imagined painting the war, recording the heroism of the southern struggle. He fancied himself a Vietnamese Daumier.

But Daumier had a bed. Cognac. Privacy.

Here, they denounced artists as parasites. Here, hunger and death stalked every shadow. Long learned what Hanoi's cadres never painted: the exhaustion, illness, fear, and the jungle. He wanted to paint the truth. The real *bo doi*, not heroic archetypes with windblown hair and heroic gazes, but gaunt, aging boys from farms and cities, drained by fungus, bacteria, and sorrow. Trained into lethal warriors, yes, but condemned to rot in green silence, hating the forest more than the Americans ever could.

"What did you say?" Kha asked.

"Huh? Oh. Nothing."

"You said something. About hating the forest."

"Did I?"

"Yes."

"Oh."

"I don't hate it," Kha said. "It protects me. I hate the open. The sky."
Long nodded slowly.

"No canopy, no ancient trees . . . no shield. I've seen what happens when the sky opens. Gunships. Jets. B-52s. Terrible."

Long remembered the chemical monsoons, defoliants exposing their cover, leaving them naked as termites in a rotten log. Then came the fire. Napalm. The beast's molten tongue. *Bo dois* vanished into sulfurous breath, rising as cinders through blackened trees.

"I'm tired," Long said bitterly. "Tired of finding arms here, legs there, heads . . . hands."

"I know," Kha murmured. "I have dreams. A village in the future. An Old Venerable who solves everyone's problems. But one day his head flies off, returns to the forest where his body died in the war. The head lands softly on the young soldier's bones. The past is gone, so the village has only a headless body. The future is gone, so the forest has only an old head. The forest digests both." He exhaled. "What a waste. You should sketch this."

"I can't," Long said. "The cadres wouldn't allow it. They want heroic poses. Wind. Victory. Not our comrades' white hair, yellow skin, red eyes. Starved bodies. What would Comrade Minh say?"

"Shhh," Kha hissed. "Keep your voice down."

Long looked down, chastened.

"Sketch me instead," Kha said, grinning. "Helmet tilted, wind blowing, brave expression. My wife will think I've gotten better looking!"

He posed dramatically, then squinted as rain hit his eyes. "Damn. The forest's trying to blind me."

"She'll want you to stay," Long laughed. "Get even handsomer."

"Ah. Duty is duty. But I'm still hungry. Seven hundred grams of rice! That's not living."

"You and your stomach! How did your wife ever find time to bear you a child?"

"In the kitchen, of course!"

Long laughed again, looking down with deep affection. They had walked the Trail together. Suffered together. Laughed here, in the forest of death.

And still, something of the bamboo remained.

~ *The Long March South* ~

Of the forty-five men who set out with Long down the Trail, only eight reached their units in the South. The rest had deserted, fallen ill, or died. At the time, Long and Kha considered themselves lucky. Captain Tong made Long company clerk almost immediately upon arrival. "You're literate and an artist," he'd said. "I need a man like you. Relieves the monotonous stupidity of life in the forest. Like Captain FitzRoy, I need my Darwin. Very few of our proletarian heroes know Confucius from Marx, or Lu Hsun from a dung heap."

Long's duties included maintaining personnel files, distributing letters and newspapers, safeguarding company funds, and logging daily reports: ammunition counts, casualties, sicknesses, commendations, infractions. He also censored outgoing mail, oversaw internal intelligence, and led the administrative cell. He didn't mind most of the work. But he loathed censoring letters. Incoming mail had already been inspected; he merely skimmed it. Outgoing mail, however, had to be read line by line. Regulations demanded ruthless scrutiny, but Long rarely changed anything. He told himself most letters only sought news from home: requests for money, photographs. No one dared write complaints. No one was that foolish. Tong had tolerated Long's leniency. Until now. For this mission, the captain was clear: all letters must be read. Any deviation from family matters was to be reported immediately.

"Yes, the captain's been testy lately," Kha muttered.

Long blinked. He must've spoken aloud without knowing. "Why do you say that?"

"Because you just said how strict he's been," Kha replied, annoyed. "What's wrong with you?"

"I said that?"

"Of course. Maybe your malaria's coming back."

Long fell into a long silence. Then, "Captain Tong wasn't always so rigid. When I first joined the company, he and I debated Chinese philosophy. His father was a Mandarin who revered Confucius, like my grandfather. Though my grandfather preferred Zhuang Zi. Tong used to erase the tactical sand tables and scribble Confucian aphorisms instead. He'd point to his forehead and say, 'The battle plan is safe up here.'"

Long smiled faintly. "I'd ask him about classical characters. He even introduced me to French philosophy—Voltaire, Rousseau."

Kha groaned. "Who cares out here? You live. You shit. You eat. You shit again. You die. As the ancients said: 'A man wins a horseskin for his shroud.' I just want to see my village again. No horseskin for me, Long. And Captain Tong's not been a philosopher since Comrade Tuyet Mai arrived. Rumor is, they've fucked. You can tell—his tongue droops, his cock points to the sky whenever she's around."

Kha shrugged. "Who cares? I just want to make it out alive."

Long nodded. "We were lucky to make it this far. Do you remember the Trail?"

"I try not to."

"No. Think back. Really remember."

~

Their journey south had begun in fire and glory. Children from the Youth League shouted slogans. Adults cheered them on. Pretty girls in ao dais waved and flirted with their eyes. The sun was blistering. The girls' conical hats slipped back, revealing glowing faces, glistening lips, gleaming teeth. For once, they didn't bother to cover their mouths with modest hands. The trucks carried them toward the border, songs and nervous laughter blending with the rattle of tires. But at the drop-off point, grizzled veterans, ancient-looking twenty-year-olds, snapped orders.

Start walking.

Those men made it clear: we don't want your name, your hometown, your face. We don't care if you're a brother, a son, a friend. We already see the reeds waving through your ghost. And so they walked. They squeezed through jungle paths no wider than a machete blade, blazed new routes when bomb craters blocked old ones. Thirty-kilo rucksacks carved trenches into their shoulders. That torment led only to the Ben Hai River: the real beginning. Beyond that loomed the dark ridges of the Truong Son Mountains.

"Never been so tired," said Kha. "Soaked to the bone. Skin shriveled and stinging."

"Eight hours a day, uphill," said Long. "My rucksack kept dragging me backward, like a stubborn buffalo trying to return home. My neck felt stabbed all the way through."

"No rest stops," Kha added. "No comfort. Just the hammock, if we were lucky. I'd lie there, barely breathing, while rain slid down the ropes and soaked me from limb to limb. I didn't care if the Americans attacked. Not even B-52s could've moved me."

"You remember when I got malaria?" asked Long.

"Of course. You were burning up. Said you felt yourself turning inside out."

"The sweat just clung. Didn't even drip, just sat on me, thick and sticky."

"And never enough food!" Kha barked.

Long laughed. "You and food! I was dying and you were chasing geckos."

"I was ravenous. I'm still ravenous. My eyes are bigger than my belly."

"And I had no medicine. Couldn't stop shitting. It was always loose, always foul. I could feel myself rotting. I wanted to paint, but I didn't have the strength. I thought about using my own shit as ink."

"Well," said Kha, grinning, "Minh Khai wrote her epitaph in blood. You write yours in shit."

Long swatted Kha's head. His pith helmet flipped into the mud.

Then Long's face grew grave. "The B-52s made me forget I ever wanted to be Daumier. I just wanted to disappear. Remember the craters? Huge, foul, full of insect larvae. Like open sores on the body of a leper."

Kha nodded. "I remember Bui's platoon. Caught in the open. Their bodies ... burst sacks of night soil. Animals, too. All gone. This wasn't your Daumier war, was it? You were a city boy. It was always going to be hard on you."

Long stared into the rain. The thunder echoed his silence. His eyes misted, though it was impossible to tell. "Not just the beginning," he said at last. "Kha, I think our ancestors are tired. All of them. They can't hold this any longer. If they could, would they let this keep happening? So many dead. So many of us already joined them. And nothing changes. How can this go on?"

"I don't care about the ancestors," Kha snapped. "It's the isolation that kills. No family, no village, no end in sight. If I die tomorrow, my wife won't know for a year. My son will forget my face. I'll rot here in the jungle with no ceremony, no name, no spirit passage. How can I join the ancestors if I die like that? No new blood reaches them. It soaks into the earth."

"I agree," said Long. "But it could be worse. You could survive with no leg. Or an arm. No way back north. Just like that legless madman in Song Nhan. A jester, pitied and useless."

"So this is the end of our journey?" Kha asked. "To die here, alone?"

Long reached out and grasped his friend's hand. "You're not alone, comrade. I'll never leave you. I swear it. If you die, I'll perform the proper rites—even here, in this cursed forest. Just like you stayed with me during the march south. You remember the day I wandered off?"

"Yes, brother."

"No, you don't know the whole of it. I never told you. I had a high fever. Left the trail to rest. Found a clearing among ancient banyans. Massive trunks, high canopies. The light shifted—quiet, golden. And there were hammocks. Dozens of them. Full of *bo dois*."

Long's voice dropped, entranced. "They looked so peaceful. The hammocks hung motionless. Nets sagged over them, pale and still. Butterflies circled the air. I thought they were sleeping. I whispered, 'Comrade'. No answer. Louder. Still nothing. Finally I shouted. I got angry. I pulled the net aside—"

He shuddered. "A cloud of gnats burst out. The stench hit me. A corpse. Bloated. Ants pouring from every hole. Eyes open, jelly dry, crawling with insects."

Long's voice faltered, barely audible. "I checked the others. All the same. All dead. But before I lifted the nets . . . I smelled lilacs. Sweet lilacs. Afterward, I couldn't breathe. The smell of death was everywhere. I hallucinated. Saw myself hanging with them. Entombed in my hammock."

Kha put an arm around Long.

"I found you there," he said softly. "Flailing in the mud like a dying worm."

"I thought if I burrowed deep enough, I could escape. Tunnel all the way back north. Home. I thought of our house. My family. My grandfather. I wanted to live. To patch the roof. Build a new room. Paint again. Marry. Raise children. Teach them. And never, never smell lilacs again."

Long wept openly. "My face was in the dirt, hardly breathing. Then I looked up—and you were there. Lifting me. Taking me away from hell. I've never loved anyone more."

Kha laughed gently. "And I found food! Gecko meat. You refused to eat it, but the soup helped."

Long's face turned grim. "That same night, the B-52s returned. I hated them, Kha."

"Hated? Not *hate*?"

Long shook his head. "Not since the Goddess brought the spirits. Look at that fortress. I know you can't see it—but look. Americans in there. The same ones who burned our comrades, dropped the fire, shattered our land. I should hate them more than ever. And yet, after the Goddess—"

"Bah!" Kha spat. "Your damned goddess! Admit it, it's malaria again. You're hallucinating. Like when you tried to tunnel through the ground. Stop softening. Hate them! Hate them like I do! They'll kill us both out here. I'll never see my wife or son again. You'll never live like your grandfather. The Americans! They bring our country bouquets of lilacs."

Long flinched at the force of Kha's words.

"Why have you changed?" Kha demanded.

Long didn't answer. He stared down at his muddied feet, and finally said, "Everything began changing when we took the Goddess statue. Captain Tong said it was my duty to guard it. But when I saw it . . . I felt confused."

"So did the rest of us."

"But think, Kha. Our political cadres always say we mustn't take even one noodle from the people. That we're fish in water, we must not foul the sea. So why did we threaten Madame Dau?"

"Yes," said Kha. "Why threaten a village just for a statue? Even Comrade Viet looked uneasy."

"Strange place, Song Nhan," Kha muttered. "A village of women governing themselves. Madness. "A woman in government is like a frog jumping on the altar. Look at the mess our two frogs have made—Tuyet Mai and Kim Lan."

Long ignored him. "You and I have seen villagers executed. Accused of treason. Spies. But the women of Song Nhan, what was their crime? To protect a statue? Surely Comrade Marx would have let them keep their opiate."

Kha nodded reluctantly. "I was shocked by how fiercely they fought for it. Tong and Vy ignored every plea."

"But there was something else," said Long. "You remember the legless man in the village? Han Tinh?"

"Yes, yes. The jester."

"He said women are the real heroes. That they do everything, care for children, the old, the sick, without help. And no one remembers them."

"He said that?"

"Yes. I saw his face when we took the statue from the tunnel. He looked . . . devastated."

"Maybe he remembered when he had legs. When he was a soldier."

"No, it was more than that. I asked myself, why would that statue mean so much to a crippled fool?"

"And your answer?"

"You won't believe me."

"Try me. It's because he sees your ghosts too, right?"

Long laughed softly. "Yes."

"Why didn't you say so before?"

"I was afraid. You looked at me the same way you did on the Trail. Like I'd lost my mind."

"You were babbling about ghosts."

"That's why I stayed silent. But after seeing the Americans' ghosts tonight . . . I had to tell someone."

"Why me?"

"You're my brother."

Kha rolled his eyes. "Fine. I'm already knee-deep in the paddy. Might as well drown. Keep going."

~ *Another Medium* ~

"I lay in my hammock, Kha, but the mosquito net trapped the steam rising off my body. I knew I was dying, cooked from the inside out. I couldn't breathe. Then I fell. The sound of hitting the ground exploded in my ears. Even the brush of my uniform against my skin thundered through me. I couldn't stand. So I lay there, paralyzed by noise. That's when I saw them: thousands of ants, marching inches from my face. I swear, Kha, I could hear everything: the rapid patter of their legs, the snap of their jaws slicing through leaves, their feet pounding twigs in rhythm. An army on the move, precise and merciless."

"See? Malaria," Kha insisted, though his voice lacked conviction. "Had to be."

"That's when the spirits came," Long said softly. "They glided into camp from the jungle, dozens, maybe hundreds. Transparent. I could see their hearts beating. Their lungs rising and falling. Children, elders. Mothers. Men. Infants. Even animals. And yes, some were naked spirits. Unclothed. Unashamed. The spirits drifted toward our comrades. Even those awake didn't notice. Not even when the spirits stood two meters away. I told myself it was hallucination. Malaria. But I knew better. They were real, Kha. More real than us. I pinched my arm. Slapped my face. But they remained. I was so tightly strung, one more breath would've snapped me. Then . . . one of the unashamed women straddled a sleeping comrade. I couldn't tell who. She arched her back and raised her neck to the heavens, howling in silence. That's when I screamed."

Long fell quiet.

"But Vy and Tong," he added bitterly, "they didn't disappear. Remember my punishment for believing such bourgeoisie superstition?"

Kha chuckled. "Right. I remember those *kiem thao* sessions. Hard to say, 'I have done wrong,' when you haven't."

"That's why I never told you until now. The punishment was unjust. Even after the spirits returned night after night, until the Goddess was lost in the ambush, I said nothing."

Kha's eyes gleamed. "They came back? Did the naked harlot come back? Tell me about her."

Long laughed. "Yes. Her, and the rest. Each time, clearer. Less ghost, more flesh."

Kha grinned. "Was she pretty?"

Long lowered his voice. "I sketched them. Secretly. In ink. The drawings are hidden in my pack. I captured them as they moved among us—praying, cooking, planting rice, playing. Children ran. Women stirred invisible pots. They bowed to invisible altars. Their lips moved, but no sound came."

Kha stared, baffled.

"They worked the paddies where there were no paddies. Bent over, scooping air with empty hands. They cooked with invisible spoons. Ate with invisible chopsticks. Their gestures were unmistakable."

Kha shook his head in wonder.

"But when the Goddess was taken," Long continued, "something inside me collapsed. The spirits stopped coming. I felt hollow. Alone. Like the crippled veteran at Song Nhan. I saw his face when we took the statue. He looked . . . shattered. That's how I knew. He had seen them too. I'm certain."

Long turned toward Kha.

"There's something I haven't told you. I saw the spirits visit one comrade. Just one."

"Who?"

"You."

Kha's expression shifted. "Me? Who came to me? My wife? My son? My parents? Don't keep me in suspense! Was it . . . the harlot?"

Long shook his head. "A pair of nightingales."

Kha froze. His face went pale, luminous as a full moon. "What . . . did you say?"

"Two beautiful nightingales."

Kha looked down. Long knew his friend was weeping.

"My wife," Kha said quietly, "I gave her two nightingales before I left. A farewell gift. She writes that their songs comfort her. They calm our son. I remember the cage—bamboo, ornately carved by my uncle. Oh, he was a master carpenter. . . ."

~

The Great Warrior stumbled through the jungle brush, antennae sweeping. She searched, restless, but the foliage pressed in. Danger pulsed through the soil. Suddenly, a tidal wave of salt water crashed over her. Drenched, disoriented, she flailed and spun, then curled tight, rolling backward, retreating. She scurried through the detritus, back to the source.

Behind her, the great teardrop—Kha's—sank into the jungle loam, an apocalyptic bead of salt, ghost-white and holy.

~

Long did not see the ant beneath him. The night had quieted, and his thoughts circled like moths. He wondered whether the American spirits resembled those who had come to the *bo dois*. Who among them was the medium? Who was like him . . . and also like Han Tinh? Why us? Why three? For what purpose?

Kha slapped his back, breaking the trance. "I'm going to tell you something," he said.

"What?"

Kha often played private games of fate: *If I walk across the clearing without stepping on a stick, I'll survive the war.* Or, *If I poke my head above this mound and don't get shot, I'll live.* And when he failed, he simply reset the rules. Started over.

But this time, something felt different. The air was too still, the night too sharp. It no longer seemed like a game at all. A weight pressed on his chest, and the silence between him and Long made the thought unbearable to carry alone. So, for the first time he said it aloud, as if speaking the fear might charm it away. Or curse it into truth. "Brother Long," he said, "if we overrun the Americans, I'll survive the war. If we fail, I'll be killed. I'll never see home again. That's certain."

It had been a good day. Kha felt lucky. But the moment he said it aloud, dread set in. He wanted to take it back. But the spoken word cannot be unsaid. He felt trapped. *What have you done, fool?*

"What's wrong?" Long asked.

"Nothing."

"I don't believe you. Truly, what is it?"

"Nothing."

But Long knew his friend. "Don't worry. We'll overrun them. You'll go home. Your wife will see your face again. And one day, I'll visit your village, watch all your little sons run wild, raiding pantries and chasing rice cakes."

"Umm," muttered Kha, staring at the fortress, which now seemed unconquerable. The stronghold of gods.

While they spoke, Sergeant Dam and his sappers slipped past. Shadows in the rain, crawling low, moving in silence. Long saw Dam's near-naked body glide forward, head lifted, eyes locked, every motion silent and lethal. Then he vanished, swallowed by fecund leaf and portentous shadow.

Long felt a sharp pang of sorrow. He knew this assault would bring death to the American medium. He squeezed Kha's shoulder gently. The American, whoever he was, must have a friend like Kha. Loyal. Beloved. A brother in the mud. If the sappers succeeded, both would die.

Long's empathy didn't waver. But it transformed into sweet, aching regret. And as Dam vanished into the storm-slick jungle, Long shivered. *Tonight*, he thought, *may the American guard in Dam's path be fast asleep, and dreaming of ghosts.*

~ *Kim Lan and Tong Have A Conversation* ~

Not far from where Long and Kha spoke in murmured tones, Kim Lan and Captain Tong crouched together beneath the trees, sharing a pot of tea. Rain dripped steadily from the canopy. Kim Lan tugged absently at a button on her tunic. She watched Tong's boot nudge a root protruding from the muddy ground.

He's nervous, she thought. *I think. Maybe. Or not.* She distrusted him. Not for any particular cruelty or vice, but because his mind was unreadable, its shadows always shifting. At times, she was certain he knew that she and Tuyet Mai were agents of Hanoi, assigned to observe him. At other times, he seemed too indifferent to care whether the drug transaction they were embroiled in would lead to his execution. And then, on darker nights like this one, she was sure he would slit her throat without hesitation if it served his survival.

"You're certain Sergeant Dam and the sappers understood their orders?" she asked quietly. "That under no circumstances is Comrade Tuyet Mai to be endangered? Our Burmese contacts would be quite displeased if she died under suspicious circumstances."

"Yes, Comrade Kim Lan. The orders were clear. Believe me, I want her back more than you know." His tone was sincere, even gentle.

But Kim Lan wasn't convinced. She recalled Vy's instructions to Dam with perfect clarity: *"Retrieve the statue. Nothing else is as important."*

She studied Tong through the rainfall. *He's lying. He wants the statue. Nothing else matters.*

Clarity came with her anger: sharp, exact, undeniable. She clenched and unclenched her fist, letting her eyes rove over Tong's body. She saw the softness blooming beneath his uniform, the decadent contour of a man made for pleasures he had long been denied. She understood now what Tuyet Mai meant when she warned that, given the chance, Tong would become a wastrel.

Tong poured more tea and offered her a cup. "Another, comrade?"

She tapped her fingers once on the ground in assent. *No choice but to play along. For now.* But inside, she seethed. *I will report this traitor. I will see him, and Vy, executed.* She glanced toward the fortress, her jaw clenched. *And I pray Tuyet Mai will be there beside me to witness it.*

~

Tong lifted his teacup and peered over the rim, watching Kim Lan. He knew she hated him. He also knew she'd be surprised to discover he wasn't quite the man she imagined. *Or maybe I am.*

Something in the shape of her neck, tilted just so as she sipped, reminded him of Tuyet Mai. Not the features, not the bearing, but the way tension pulled across the collarbone. A fragile elegance wrapped in scorn. That's what they shared. He let his imagination drift, picturing Kim Lan without clothes. But the moment he entered her in his mind, her body blurred, her face melted, and Tuyet Mai emerged from the folds of fantasy like a goddess stepping through mist.

"Tuyet Mai," he said aloud.

"What?" Kim Lan snapped.

"Nothing," he murmured.

She narrowed her eyes. "Why have you come to talk with me, Comrade Captain?"

Tong raised his cup in a gesture of false warmth. "To be near Tuyet Mai's friend. May she return to us safely by dawn."

Kim Lan said nothing. She drank her tea.

Tong smiled. "Dam and his sappers have already departed. If they breach the fortress, our sister will be with us again soon. I have no doubt."

~

Kim Lan's thoughts drifted to the Americans. Their faces. Their strange, spontaneous laughter. The way they looked at each other without suspicion. In her mind's eye, she saw Sergeant Dam creeping through the dark—clinging to the back of an American soldier, arms and legs wound tight as a python. She saw the flash of Dam's knife—a cold gleam—just before it plunged deep into the soldier's neck. She saw blood. A fine red spray arcing toward her face. She gasped.

"More tea?" Tong asked, his voice smooth, detached, disturbingly serene.

"No," Kim Lan said sharply. "No more."

She grimaced as her silver tooth caught the light, exposed fully on her lower lip. This time, she didn't care.

Chapter Fourteen

The Battle

Homo Sapiens Must Go

*O**h, Immortal God, a pang, a flutter, a ripple, a death. They kill as an afterthought.***

Yes, serial killers. That is why forgiveness and redemption are so important to them.

Yet, dear Goddess, you will neither forgive nor redeem them.

For all the others, for the planet, for the Superior Ones to come.

~ Dam Journeys Across the Clearing ~

"You all heard the sounds from the old fort earlier," Sergeant Dam said to his sappers, who stood hunched in the rain. "It's a good night for killing Americans. The moon's buried behind monsoon clouds. Do as I told you and the bastards will fall like pigs at slaughter. Remember who you are. You're sappers in Cao Thanh Dam's platoon. Let's go."

As they neared the clearing, they passed a guard post where Quang Long whispered with Nguyen Manh Kha. Dam paused when he recognized Long's soft voice.

"I never told you," Long said, "but I saw one comrade the spirits visited. Only one."

There he goes again, Dam thought. *Crazy Long and his ghosts.*

"Who?" asked Kha.

"You."

"Me? Who did you see? My wife? My son? My parents?"

"No. A pair of nightingales."

Nightingales. Dam sneered inwardly. *Nightingales and ghosts!* He turned away and rejoined his men. *Enough poetry. Let's make ghosts.*

They reached the treeline and peered into the clearing. She lay before them—flat on her back, obscene and inviting, a diseased whore daring them to penetrate her. For an instant, lightning unveiled every twig and blade of grass. Then thunder rolled, dark and threatening. A bad omen.

Dam clenched his jaw. "Remember your training. When this is over, we'll drink tea together inside the fortress. Good luck, comrades."

The sappers slipped into the clearing, lowering themselves like vampires onto the throats of their prey. Bodies blurred into mulch, grass among grass, leaves among leaves, shadows among shadows. They became invisible. Then, slowly, methodically, the shadows moved toward the fortress. Toward their victims. Or their executioners. Luck of the draw.

Dam inched forward, headed for the midpoint, same spot used during the ceasefire talks. Shortest distance, best cover. He'd memorized every fold of the terrain.

CRACK! Lightning split the sky, thunder crashing behind it. Dam froze, eyes clenched to block even a whisper of light. He felt unseen, part of the breathing dark. His movements slowed to the rhythm of the forest: muscles slack, breath a shallow drift. The jungle pressed close, damp and alert, as if listening with him.

"So far so good, thank you mother," he whispered.

Each shift forward became a prayer, not just habit, but invocation. He was not crawling alone. Something watched over him. Something old and venerable. He passed the stump where the American lieutenant had once sat, gliding past that silent marker, his body surrendered to the current of the earth.

Now he crawled as an ant would crawl, fingers and toes reading the terrain: bump, depression, twig, vine, slick fungus, dry root, a clutch of soft dirt, a jag of stone. At times, his hand hovered midair, sensing another sapper's presence through the faintest touch of antennae on his skin. He didn't look up. Not even once. Eyes might betray him.

"So far so good, thank you mother."

The fortress loomed closer.

His fingertips detected a shift: the slick membrane of plastic. A new texture. A new geometry. Manmade. And dangerous.

"Claymore," he murmured.

The word unlocked a buried blueprint: M-18A1, curved olive-drab plastic, 0.68 kilos of C4, 700 steel pellets, concave arc, 60 degrees of death. The fan that cools by ripping your body apart. He touched it like a lover. Stripped the leaves away. Ran his finger along the embossed warning: FRONT TOWARD ENEMY.

A cryptic spell. He never quite believed the translation. More curse than instruction. He remembered booby-trapping these before. The thrill. The dread. The fingers slipping beneath to plant a pressure release trigger.

Not tonight.

Tonight he meant only to disarm. No wires disturbed. No detonators unscrewed. He turned the mine face down and nudged it forward, giving the wire slack. It wouldn't alert the guards.

CRACK! Another lightning flash. Thunder cracked its whip overhead. Dam froze, fingers and toes digging into the mud. But something sharp jabbed into his skin. No matter where he shifted, something sliced, punctured. Broken glass.

"Damn. So far not so good, mother."

Lightning again.

And there it was—jagged glass jutting like fangs, a thousand drunken reflections in the stormlight. Half-buried, everywhere.

Wine bottles? The French?

Their last hurrah? Bastille Day? Or a trash heap? Doesn't matter. It's mine now.

He crawled forward, skin shredded, blood mixing with rain. Leeches followed.

Damn! It's like crawling across tiger's teeth.

CRACK! The storm drew closer. He glanced at the black silhouette of the fortress. A wave of nausea rolled through him.

I am meat, he thought. Slabs of flesh diced for the fortress's feast. "Damn the French," he whispered.

The others would be slowed by the same field of glass. That meant delay. And delay meant disaster. The sappers had to reach the walls before dawn. So did the company. Dam tried to calm himself. But the signs were bad. Bad omen, bad luck, bad night, bad pain. So many leeches now, ballooned and gorging.

Still, he moved forward.

"So far so good, thank you mother."

Hours passed. His mind began to drift. *Do leeches smell blood? Or is it body heat? Can Americans smell blood too? My toe's cramping. Shrimp sauce and rice back at camp... Tea... God, what I'd give for hot tea....*

Weak guard, please. Let me get a weak one this time. Not some monster.

CRACK! CRACK! CRACK!

Lightning again. Thunder booming.

And then. Nothing.

The thunder stopped mid-roar. Silence swallowed everything. Even the rain ceased. Dam blinked. Had he gone deaf? No. Just... silence. The jungle sounds were gone. Frogs, geckos, birds, mosquitoes, all vanished. No wind. Only the drip of water from leaves.

He froze.

Something's wrong. This isn't natural. What is happening, mother? What is happening, mother? What is happening?

Then, softly, a breeze, cool, steady, moved across the clearing. It touched him like a ghost's hand, coiling into his ears, slipping into his mouth, his nose, between his teeth. It entered his mind. The fear dissolved. And in its place, memory surged forward.

He saw a boy, naked on the sunlit rock above his village river. Saw him run, leap, roll through meadows. Skip stones, laugh, chase girls, grin at their giggles.

No war. No killing. Just the body in joy.

Then he saw the girl he loved from afar. Then their wedding. Their bed. Their awkward tenderness. Then years: children, quarrels, wine, silence, resentment, the bitterness of old age. Then a gaze: ancient eyes meeting again with the same boyish love. And hers, returned. Then the tomb. Their grandchildren sweeping it clean.It was complete.

And Dam knew, he would never return to that village. Never marry her. Never grow old beside her. Never rest in that tomb.

The breeze faded.

The pain returned.

The rain returned.

The storm roared back.

Now Dam understood: he had already died, piece by piece, battle by battle. There was no hope. Only this crawl, this blood, this rain, this glass. A half-naked killer dragging himself forward. The breeze had lied. But rage ignited.

I hate this glass! I hate the French! I hate their garbage! I hate their wine bottles cutting my skin! I hate the Americans!

He summoned his mother's face, dead and eternal. And his pain vanished. Death receded.

I will live, he thought. *I will survive. I will have children. I will have a future. Just wait and see.*

And with strength reborn, he crawled on.

"So far so good, thank you mother."

"So far so good, thank you mother."

"So far so good, thank you mother."

Forward.

Always forward.

~ *The Macabre Dance of Mr. Machine and Dam* ~

It felt to Mr. Machine like hours had passed since he'd relieved Superman. Time crawled unbearably: days, hours, minutes, seconds . . . One second . . . Two seconds . . . Three . . . Four.

He squinted into the rain, trying not to stare at one spot. The grunts had warned him about that. But it was hard not to lock in.

"Don't stare at one spot, stupid!" he muttered aloud. "Think of something relaxing."

So he drifted. Home. Georgia. First stop after seeing the family, the Froggy Court Inn. Chili size. Fries. A plate piled high with—

CRACK! Lightning tore open the clearing. Mr. Machine flinched, head snapping up. Something moved Did it move? His heart pounded against his ribs as he peered through the downpour. Nothing. Just dark, pulsing with afterimages.

He let his forehead rest against the stone wall, shoulders sagging. *Shadows. Just shadows. Still . . . just my luck we get hit tonight.*

He sighed. *Where was I? Right. Chili. Fries. And a tall glass of ice water.*

~

Mr. Machine hated guard duty. The jungle never stopped breathing around him. He wasn't built for it—not the fear, not the silence. In the rear, sure, he'd handled the occasional rocket scare. But this was different. Here, the night felt personal. Like something watching. He wasn't like the others, Mountain Man, Pappy, Nature, men who seemed carved from the land itself. He felt like a kid playing soldier, too afraid to admit it.

Trapped, soaked, bone-tired, sore, and homesick. The kind of homesick that made your stomach twist. He had diarrhea again. His backside raw from wiping. And the nerves made him need to piss and shit all the time.

To cope, he let his mind wander. *Why the hell did I volunteer? I'm ground crew. Emphasis on ground. Door gunner, my ass. If I die out here, I'm gonna kick myself all the way to . . . well, heaven. Yeah. I deserve heaven. Don't I?*

He started to tally up his life. Bad: the time with the mailboxes. Twelve of them, maybe more. But it was a dare. Dares don't count the same. ood: volunteering for the Coopersville Fire Department. Helped save old man Wegman's cow. That had to count.

I'm almost in heaven already, he thought, and laughed quietly at himself. The scale tipped toward the good.

~

"So far so good, thank you mother."
"So far so good, thank you mother."
"So far so good, thank you mother."

~

CRACK! Another flash. Mr. Machine bolted upright, but too late. Just as he focused, the light vanished, and the clearing was swallowed again.

But he *thought* he saw something. *Movement. Definitely movement. Or . . . maybe not. I'm just a mechanic. What do I know?*

His eyes burned. Blinking spots clouded his vision. His back cramped from holding position. He looked away, stretching his neck.

CRACK!

Too late. Again. Probably a vine. Gotta stay ready for the next bolt.

How much time had passed? Hours? Minutes? Nope . . . seconds.

He tapped the wall with nervous fingers. *Mountain Man said don't be too tense.*

~

He remembered the advice from his first night on guard: *Look here, Machine Boy. You need relaxed concentration. Not too tight, not too loose. You get too intense, you'll end up jumpy. Too loose, and they'll slit your throat. Right through the windpipe. A soft, thin red line. Pfft. Air just leaks right out, like a popped balloon.*

He imagined Mountain Man now, beside him, chuckling. *Some sappers go for the heart. Some the kidneys. Doesn't matter. End's the same. So keep the Claymore wire tight. No slack. If there's slack, they'll fuck with it, and you won't even know it.*

~

The Claymore!
He picked up the clacker. The wire had slackened. *Shit!*

He pulled gently, just a few millimeters, and felt it go taut. *Thank God. Must've been the wind. It's okay.*

Still cradling the clacker, he exhaled slowly.

~

"So far so good, thank you mother."
"So far so good, thank you mother."
"So far so good, thank you mother."

~

CRACK! Lightning again, and this time he saw something. Eyes. Two pale eyes staring up at him from the jungle.

Or glass? Reflections from broken bottles scattered on the ground? *Had to be glass. Eyes move. Or blink. Right?*

"Help me out here, Mountain Man," he whispered. "I'm just a mechanic."

He thought about raising the alarm. But no. They'd laugh. *Either the gooks are out there or they ain't. My call.*

He held the clacker tight. *Do it or don't, but don't fuck it up. Claymore's too valuable.*

"Relaxed concentration," he whispered. "Relaxed concentration."

But panic burned in his gut. He stiffened and stared out for long minutes. Only shadows swayed in the wind. Rain drummed the parapet.

Vines. Just vines.

Okay. I've been concentrating. Time for the relaxed part.

~

"So far so good, thank you mother."
"So far so good, thank you mother."
"So far so good, thank you mother."

~

To pass the time, he imagined a baseball game. Sapper versus guard. Bottom of the ninth. Knife versus Claymore.

The crowd roared. The announcer's voice boomed in his head: *"Sapper's advancing. Guard's waiting. Claymore clutched tight. Can he pull it in time?"*

The sapper struck. A clean kill. A home run. The guard went down.

"Sapper wins! Guard gurgles his last protest. Final score: Sapper 1, Guard 0."

Mr. Machine chuckled at his own grim fantasy. Too grim.

Time for a second game, but this time with a better ending.

~

"So far so good, thank you mother."
"So far so good, thank you mother."
"So far so good, thank you mother."

~

CRACK! Lightning exploded above. He looked up too late. Again. The light was gone. But this time he was *sure*—movement. And the eyes. He gripped the clacker.

But his hand didn't squeeze.

What if I'm wrong? He pictured the others laughing. Calling him a coward. An idiot. *Probably vines again. Probably glass again. Just wait. Concentrate. We can't waste the Claymore on shadows.*

So he waited.

CRACK! CRACK! CRACK!

Lightning came in bursts, but no movement. No eyes. Just rain. And shadow. His mind drifted.

~

"So far so good, thank you mother."

"So far so good, thank you mother."

"So far so good, thank you mother."

~

Home again. Froggy Court Inn. Julie behind the counter, nine months pregnant. He remembered the joke.

"Kid's gonna look like me, Julie. My face, your skinny legs."

She laughed. "If it's your face, I'm getting plastic surgery."

"You'd better hope he gets my brains."

She laughed again. "He'll have more brains than to go off to war."

They joked, clumsy and kind.

But now, he understood. Her smile had been sadness.

~

He pictured the restaurant: Checkered tablecloths. Red-and-yellow condiment squeeze bottles. A mop bucket half-filled with greasy water.

But more than anything: Ice water. Clean, clear, untouched. Lined up on the counter. Condensation dripping.

A miracle, he thought. *Given without asking.*

When I get back, I'll tell them. Tell them how precious it all is. Clean sheets. Hot food. Showers. Home. Just being *alive.*

He felt angry. Angry at everyone who wasted it. *They complain about love, jobs, status, being understood . . . It's all bullshit.*

Just being home. Just being alive.

That's enough.

~

"So far so good, thank you mother."

"So far so good, thank you mother."

"So—"

~

CRACK! A final bolt tore through the clearing. And far below, Sergeant Dam pressed against the fortress wall.

Confused. *How did I get here so fast?*

He paused, checked his gear, and began to climb.

A shadow leaned toward him.

~

CRACK!

Mr. Machine looked up and saw the woman's breasts Bowls had carved into the parapet, water streaming from the nipples. He smiled.

When I get back . . . family, fried chicken, black-eyed peas, cold beer . . . Julie. I'll tell Julie—

Oh Jesus!—no!—please God!—Mom—

~

Julie Taylor, Coopersville, Georgia, raising her child, skinny legs and all, would never know she was among the last thoughts of Spec. 4 Albert M. Shear, helicopter mechanic.

~

Dam clamped his hand over the soldier's mouth. The body spasmed. Blood sprayed. Bubbles rose from the throat. Then silence.

Dam leaned in as lightning struck, and saw, in dazzling detail, the unmoving face of his mother's killer.

~ *Dam Penetrates the Fortress* ~

Dam quickly scanned the inside of the fortress from his perch on the parapet, but could distinguish nothing through the black night. He looked back at the clearing to search for members of his team but again he could see nothing. As he crouched next to the dead American, Dam's mind raced. *Should I wait for the others? We're already far behind schedule. It'll be daylight soon. I still have to make my way to the church and find the statue. Then there's Tuyet Mai and detonating these damn satchel charges.*

After a short internal debate and a few false starts, he finally made up his mind. Grabbing his satchel charges, Dam rose and began feeling his way along the parapet, repeating Kim Lan's directions in his head. *About ten meters to the left, along the inside wall, you'll reach the top of the stone steps leading from the parapet onto the brick courtyard. Once you reach the courtyard, turn right and follow the base of the wall. The church is adjacent to a small stone storage room about six meters wide and five meters deep. After you enter the open doors of the ruined church, our company trunk and the statue should be stored behind the altar in front of the far wall. At least that is the last place I saw them put it.*

Crawling on the parapet, Dam ran his hand along the wet stones of the inside wall until he located the opening to the top of the stairway. *So far so good, thank you mother. Let me see. Down the stairs, turn right, follow the wall until I reach a storage room. Next to that is the church. May the ancestors protect me.*

Dam half-stood and slouched forward, gingerly starting down the steps. His left hand dangled mere centimeters from the stone stairs, ready to stabilize an unbalanced sway or anchor an emergency leap. His heart raced too fast, so he paused to rest on the third step down.

CRACK! Flaring in the lightning's surgical glare, the ivory face of an astonished American stared up at Dam in disbelieving shock.

~

Topper had just started ascending the stairs to relieve Mr. Machine when a lightning bolt struck. Snapping his head back so that he could see how many more steps he had left to climb, he saw the contorted body of a naked Vietnamese frozen a few steps above him. Not knowing the modus operandi of a sapper, he was utterly confused.

"Jesus Christ! What the . . . ?" Topper cried out in shock. Before he could raise his M-16, darkness again enveloped the fortress, but not before he saw the sapper leap forward. Topper jumped to the side and clumsily pointed his rifle at the spot where he thought the sapper had moved. It seemed to Topper that compared to the agility of the sapper, his own awkward movements unfolded in slow motion, as if he moved through a vat of molasses. Finally he squeezed the trigger, spraying the stairway, his M-16 on full automatic.

Pop! Pop! Pop! Topper's rifle coughed up its bullets in staccato cracks. He stopped firing and in the brief silence that followed he heard footfalls splashing toward the church. Then all hell broke loose.

~

"Gook in the fort! Gook in the fort! Near the church!" Topper shouted as he rushed up the stone steps toward Mr. Machine's guard position. He heard sporadic small-arms fire from the other guards. Glancing over his shoulder he saw red tracers streaming into the clearing. Keeping a weary eye out, Topper whispered in a savage voice, "Shear! Shear! Hey man! Albert! Shea—"

Topper fell heavily onto the stone parapet and knew with a sick feeling in his stomach that he had tripped over a body. Feeling in the darkness, he recognized Mr. Machine. A faint odor of excrement made him nauseous. Crawling away, Topper peered out at the clearing. Too dark to see anything. His head swiveled madly back and forth, left and right, terrified the enemy or his comrades were nearby.

CRACK! Topper's eyes bulged when he saw, illuminated in the clearing, undulating lines of movement cresting above the vegetation.

It's alive! The whole damn clearing is alive with gooks! Panic rose from his gut.

With shocking speed the increasing volume of M-16 rifle fire, buttressed by guttural bursts from Superman's M-60, grew deafening. Green tracers poured into the fortress.

"Oh shit! They're attacking!" he screamed the obvious. Pitch black again. "Save your ammunition!" he heard Pappy yelling from below. "Save your ammo!"

Topper held his fire until he had a visible target, noticing with some undefined relief that the volume of gunfire from the fortress decreased.

"Hold on! Wait a minute! Here we go!" he heard T's excited voice from the courtyard.

Thump! Topper recognized the hollow sound of a flare being fired. Then *Poof!* The flare burst above the fortress, followed quickly by hissing, as though a huge match had been struck. Yellow light cascaded down upon them with the rain. Everything glowed pale yellow. Looking up at the show, Topper thought,

We're in a fuckin' urinal! Staring back at the illuminated clearing, he saw moving silhouettes of NVA soldiers slouching toward the fortress walls.

Closing his eyes and taking a few deep breaths to control his pounding heart, Topper set his M-16 on semi-automatic and began a steady fire at the approaching shadows. Shouting rose from the direction of the church but he was too busy to care.

~

As Dam scurried away from the American on the steps, he collided with the jutting wall of the storage room and fell heavily on his back, stunned and shaken. Falling rain pricked his face and cleared his foggy mind. By the time he struggled back to his feet, he heard M-16 fire and the voices of American soldiers. Dam crouched low and trotted toward the church, feeling his way along the wall as would a blind man, muttering under his breath.

"Damn! Damn! Not so good, mother!"

At last he reached the yawning entrance to the ruined church.

CRACK! For an instant he saw the massive stone carvings of saints and gargoyles, pockmarked and disfigured, glaring down at him malevolently. Hearing the sound of American boots thudding on the brick courtyard behind him, Dam slipped into the church, now more a sanctuary than a destination. Peering toward the back, he could see nothing through the thick darkness.

Thump!

A flare?

Poof! A hissing sound followed by yellow light as a flare exploded in the sky above the church's collapsed roof, lighting the interior.

Thank the ancestors!

Something shiny glinted from the rear of the church. He peered toward the source. *The statue! Thank you, mother!*

Dam held his breath, listening for movement or any sound indicating someone other than himself was in the room. Closing his eyes, he tilted his ear toward the altar, his patience rewarded when he heard the soft noise of someone's boots scraping on the tile floor. Satisfying himself that only one soldier was near the altar, he moved silently toward the bright glare of the figurine.

~

Stretch felt scared. Although he heard the sounds of battle raging outside the church, he knew better than to leave his guard position near the trap door. But being isolated from the other grunts made him jumpy. He kept looking from the trap door to the church entrance and back again, a dilemma. If he strayed too far from the trap door, it disappeared behind piles of rubble and before he could react, NVA might come pouring out of it like water from a backed-up toilet. If he remained close, he could not see the entrance clearly, and God knows what might come charging through from that direction.

CRACK!

Lightning arched above the roof, momentarily bathing the church in surgical light. Stretch scanned the room and saw hundreds of night-crawling insects scurrying across the stones before the brief flash of illumination was extinguished and blackness returned.

Stretch could hear the muffled shouts of his comrades and the explosive tapping of incoming fire. He heard Superman's M-60 open up and Stretch found himself wishing his old friend were standing next to him.

Sweet Jesus. Keep the jackals at bay, Superman. Let 'em have it!

Condemned to wait, Stretch paced nervously back and forth, a wind-up toy trapped in a box.

Poof! Yellow light from another flare rained down and bestowed a desultory visibility on the interior of the church. Out of the corner of his eye, Stretch saw the figurine sitting high on the altar where it had been placed earlier that day. *Something's odd.* Turning, he stared in wonder as the figurine shone inexplicably bright through the soupy haze and pouring rain.

"Hey Lady, don't tell Superman I'm praying to anyone but Jesus," he whispered, "but I pray you help us get outta this mess."

~

Dam saw the American staring up at the figurine. *So far so good, thank you mother.*

Circling around a pile of rubble, Dam approached from the rear. The American stood tall and lanky, difficult to reach for the shorter Dam. Deciding to go for the kidneys, Dam worked his way to within a few meters of the American. Pausing to coil his muscles, he took a deep breath and raced forward, knife outstretched. He planned to ram the knife deep into the American's back and twist it through the kidneys, bringing the tall soldier quickly to the ground where it would be easy to finish him off.

But just at the instant Dam's blade began to pierce its target, the American shuddered and lurched sideways. Dam's knife was deflected but his body continued its momentum and slammed full force into the American. Both men crashed to the wet floor at the base of the altar. Dam felt the American's body go limp and he knew the man had struck his head on the altar's stone base. In the fading light of the flare, Dam raised his knife to plunge it into the unconscious soldier's heart.

Thump! Poof! Hiss!

Dam looked up at a second flare reigniting the church in a hail of light.

Squinting up at the bright glare, he caught sight of a something slowly rising from the floor.

Disoriented, he thought at first that the floor heaved upward.

Staring closely, Dam was shocked to see a person emerged from the trap door.

~ *Bowls Confronts Dam* ~

Bowls moved slowly back through the tunnel after his efforts to convince Mountain Man to rejoin the platoon had failed. He needed time to think and so he rested more often than necessary.

Why should I go back to a bunch of doomed grunts trapped in a stupid fort? If I turn around now and join Mountain Man, and they're all killed, then no one's the wiser about our little desertion. But if any of them live, I'm screwed. 'Course I want them to live. But goddammit I don't want to die.

He shook his head violently. *Which way, Bowls? Back to the fortress with the platoon and be overrun or back to Mountain Man and be shot for desertion? Which way? Oh man, what a fucked up situation. Why oh why am I here? Jesus Christ! That's my life—no choices but fucked-up choices. Do I get to choose between being rich or poor? Hell no. Between my dad or a mean-ass drunk of a stepfather? Hell no. Between a beautiful perky-titted blonde or a hook-nose bitch with a sweaty moustache? Hell no. I get to choose between being poor or poorer. Between a rat or a mouse, a cockroach or a slug, no bitch or an ugly bitch, Vietnam or prison. So what do I choose? A rat, a cockroach, no bitch and Vietnam. Now it's a choice between dying quick in the fortress or dying slow in the jungle. Which way, Bowls?*

But even as he thought, Bowls gradually moved through the tunnel closer to the fortress. Reaching the storage chamber where Mountain Man's shrine to Martha continued to glow from the bioluminescent fungus, Bowls stared long and hard at the skull grinning dimly out from the inset. His shoulders dropped and he knew then that he would return to the fortress. Mountain Man had grown too distant, too strange even for Bowls. Still, he silently complained all the way back. Only when he stood up in the entrance chamber underneath the church did he hear the muffled tapping of small arms fire filter down through the trap door in a ghostly echo.

Fuck this! No way, man!' Turning around, Bowls started back through the tunnel. But floating in the pitch black, Bowls saw the faces of his friends calling for help. One by one they appeared before him and spoke.

"Thank god you're here! What took you so long? Where's Mountain Man?" asked T.

"Bowls! Go help Superman on the south wall. He needs help with the gun!" said Pappy.

"Good to see your ugly face," said X.

"Welcome home. How's Mountain Man?" asked Nature.

"Hello, Bowls. God provides. Is Mountain Man with you?" asked Superman.

"Jesus, Bowls, I was starting to get worried," said Idaho.

"I figured Mountain Man wouldn't be back, but I'm glad to see you, Bowls. I know it must have been hard," said Storyteller.

"Jesus H. Christ! Look what the cat drug in!" said Stretch.

Bowls shook his head in frustration and returned to the entrance chamber. *Fuck Mountain Man.* Sounds of battle continued seeping through the trap door, even louder than before. He tapped softly, using the proper code. No answer. He tapped again. Still no answer.

Bowls gingerly cracked it open with the muzzle of his M-16. A great wall of noise roared through the widening crack and he squinted out as if staring into the face of a windstorm.

Thump! Poof! Hiss! A flare burst overhead and yellow light spilled through the trap door, the church interior illuminated brightly. Peering through the opening, Bowls clearly saw the glistening body of a naked Vietnamese man leaning over the crumpled figure of a grunt.

"Oh, shit!" he blurted out.

The two men's eyes locked onto each other in shocked silence.

~

Being in a precarious position on the ladder, Bowls couldn't aim his M-16 effectively. His first instinct had been to jump back down the entrance chamber and close the trap door behind him, but for some reason he scrambled out to face the sapper. By the time it took him to clamber up and jump free of the tunnel, Bowls realized his mistake.

After planting his feet firmly on the rubble-strewn tiles, he quickly looked up and aimed his rifle, but was astonished to see that the sapper had vanished. Without hesitating, Bowls jumped behind a large chunk of debris, his head swiveling furiously, squinting through the dim light of the flare.

Although the battle continued to rage outside the church, Bowls concentrated only on the sounds nearby. He heard mosquitoes buzzing, rain pattering on stone surfaces, his unshaved neck scraping against the fabric of his collar.

"Shit!" he mouthed the word silently.

Bowls knew he was being stalked. He felt scared, and mad at himself for being scared. *Fuck this, you gook bastard. You want me? You got me. I got a '16. You got a knife. So let's go at it, fucker.*

Bowls slipped around the rubble. He zigzagged randomly between the rubble and shattered statues, moving slowly toward the entrance of the church in what he hoped were unexpected directions. But every time he turned a corner, the sapper was nowhere to be seen.

Maybe he's left the church. Better go back and check that grunt. Must've been Stretch. Bet that sapper bastard's circled back to finish him off. Or maybe he's gone back to the trap door. Damn! Can't let him find the tunnel! Bowls looked up at the sky. *Flare's going out! Fuck!*

He started moving cautiously back toward the trap door, but the last weak glimmer of light from the flare winked out. Total darkness. Bowls froze.

Shit! Shit! Shit! Advantage sapper. Shit!

A soft light emanated from the rear of the church and Bowls saw the figurine glowing on the altar, pulsing, growing stronger.

What the . . . ? Must be that weird fungus. No. Too bright. Couldn't be the fungus. Don't matter. At least I can see. All right! Advantage, Bowls. He began moving again, toward the light.

Moth to a flame. Don't get burned, old Bowls. Don't get burned, boy. Remember, moth to a flame. Careful now! One step. Freeze. Listen. Another step. Freeze. Listen. He tried to block the vicious noise of battle pouring into the church, but intense small-arms fire and explosions from RPG's and grenades made it hard to hear.

Hey, you guys! Keep it down out there! Man can't hear himself think! Bowls smiled an adrenalin-induced smile, feeling triumphant that he could joke about the situation, he was in control. But it was a courageous mirage. He felt scared to death. *Another step. Freeze. Listen. Another step. Freeze. Listen.*

~

Dam waited for the flare to extinguish, counting on darkness and his keen sense of hearing to locate and surprise the American. He listened as the man moved away from him toward the church entrance. If the man left the church, Dam felt confident he could grab the figurine and scramble over the collapsed wall before the American brought reinforcements.

But he heard the American turn around and move back toward the altar. Dam waited patiently. Every time he heard the footfall of a boot on tile, he thought, *So far so good, thank you, mother.* Finally the flare burned out. Total darkness.

Thank you, mother! Thank you for the help. Now let him stumble back here dragging that heavy bag of blood and bones he calls a body!

But a light swelled outward from the figurine on the altar, only a few meters from his position. At the same time, Dam heard the unconscious American soldier groan.

Mother! Put out that light! Talk to the ancestors. Plead with Goddess. The light is bad for me! And that groaning bastard over there . . . damn! . . . should have killed him first. Damn! Dam gripped his knife, unsure whether to go and finish off the wounded soldier or wait for the other one to get within striking range. He decided to wait once he saw the moving silhouette of the returning American come into view.

Dam loosened his fingers from around the handle of the knife and flexed them. *No cramps now. Not now. Patience, Dam. Patience. Come just a little closer, you white devil. Just a little closer. Come on. Come to me. Closer. Closer. Closer. Now!*

~

"Godddd!" screamed Bowls as he felt a terrific blow slam into his body, followed by searing pain. He realized the long blade of a knife had penetrated deep into his back, just below his right shoulder blade. Panic welled up from his gut and exploded in his brain.

"Nooo! Godddammitttt!" he screamed again. Bowls twisted violently, becoming an unbroken horse trying to throw its rider, mindlessly bucking. But his tormentor clung as if anchored to Bowls' back.

Bowls dropped his M-16 so he could reach around and grab the sapper. But he felt the knife twisting deeper into his back, and the image of its blade protruding all the way through his chest made him scream in terrified agony.

"Godddd! Something broke inside! You bastard!"

In a paroxysm of energy, Bowls flung himself backward, crashing hard into a pile of sharp-edged rocks, cushioned by the thin body of the sapper.

"Ohhhh!" he heard the sapper cry out, then he felt the man try to catch his breath as the iron grip momentarily weakened.

For the first time, Bowls felt a ray of hope. But the merciless knife continued to twist and turn, pulled back and forth, whipping the enraged Bowls into a frenzy. Agony and outrage gave him a last burst of energy. With supreme effort, he jerked his body upright, surprising the sapper. He felt the knife being pulled out as he struggled to rise up from the rock pile. Teetering on faltering legs, Bowls turned to face his killer, but his knees buckled and he fell heavily on his raw back. Bowls could do nothing but look with sad and weary acceptance at the approaching sapper. His blood drained between the stony crevasses where probing ant scouts returned excitedly to their nests with the good news.

~

"Thank you, mother! Thank you!" gasped Dam.

Leaning over the wheezing American, illuminated by the glow of the figurine, Dam looked in the man's glazed eyes and ripped off the little bag hanging around his neck. He held his knife to the man's ear and prepared to slit his throat.

"No!" a voice called out from behind.

Dam's head snapped around and he saw that the unconscious American had recovered and stumbled toward him, M-16 pointing shakily. Dragging his knife rapidly but shallowly across the prone American's throat, Dam leapt up, still holding the bag dangling in his hand, and raced behind a fallen statue as bullets smashed into the stones all around him. Moving rapidly toward a side exit, Dam heard other American voices and he knew reinforcements had arrived.

Damn! No way to get the figurine now! Got to get out! Now!

Dam dashed through the debris and slipped out of the church, nothing more than a bird's shadow gliding across a rocky field, determined to accomplish the secondary goals of freeing Tuyet Mai and detonating his satchel charges.

~

"Bowls! Bowls!" Stretch screamed. He cradled Bowls' bloody head in his lap, trying to quiet his convulsions. The wounded grunt's legs splayed straight out, trembling violently.

"Medic! Medic! X! In the church! Quick! X! It'll be okay, Bowls. You'll see. You'll make it. Hang in there. Medic! X!"

Stretch could hear Bowls struggling for breath and realized the wail of battle outside had tapered off to the stutter of a few scattered rounds. He stopped calling out and listened.

Who won the fuckin' battle? Shit! Am I the only one left? Is the fort full of gooks? Come on. Come on.

Stretch heard the sound of boots running on tile, accompanied by the beautiful sound of English words.

"Stretch! Where are you? Stretch!"

It was Nature.

"Over here! Hurry! It's Bowls!"

"Okay! We're coming! X is here!"

Thank God! But as he watched, Bowls' face whitened to a ghostly hue, lips purple, eyes vacant, almost crossed. The glow from the figurine dimmed, and darkness again pervaded the church.

Thump! Poof! Hiss! Another flare lit up the sky. Stretch moved aside, a terrible ache pounding in his injured head, as Nature gently transferred Bowl's head and shoulders to his lap. X used his knife and worked furiously to bore a hole in Bowl's throat to clear the airway with a makeshift tracheotomy.

~

Nature knew by looking at X's face that Bowls would die. The rasping wheeze from his slashed windpipe sounded an eerie dirge. Nature leaned close and whispered, "Bowls. Your tab, Bowls, think of your tab."

Then he leaned even closer and started singing in a low, sweet voice.

> *There is a house in New Orleans,*
> *They call the Rising Sun,*
> *And it's been the ruin of many a poor boy,*
> *And God, I know I'm one.*
> *My mother was a tailor,*
> *Sewed my new blue jeans.*
> *My father was a gamblin' man,*
> *Down in New Orleans.*
> *Oh mother, tell your children,*
> *Not to do what I have done.*
> *Spend your lives in misery,*
> *In the house of the Rising Sun.*

~

Bowls floated above the church. Sitting in his easy chair, he looked down and saw her standing in front of the window, lights on, in full, glorious, sensuous color. Completely naked. Painting her nipples with lipstick. Obviously just out of a shower, her long, gorgeous, sparkling dark hair still wet and combed straight back, revealing the unbelievably fine bone structure of her face. The kind of face that would never consent to having Bowls as a lover.

> *Well I've got one foot on the platform,*
> *The other foot on the train,*
> *I'm going back to New Orleans,*
> *To wear that ball and chain.*
> *Well, there is a house in New Orleans,*
> *They call the Rising Sun,*
> *And it's been the ruin of many a poor boy,*
> *And God, I know I'm one. . . .*

Bowls watched her look down at her breasts, pouting slightly, and with long, graceful hands circle the lipstick around and around and around, into a vortex of red. Around and around and around. . . .

~

In the light of another flare, Dam moved against the wall. According to Kim Lan's information, Tuyet Mai should be near. Very near. But the light from the flare faded and the crisscrossing matrix of red and green tracers began thinning. The battle was winding down.

We've failed, thought Dam bitterly. *Major Vy has called off the attack. Why? No matter. Tuyet Mai should be around this area. Too dark. Need a lightning flash. No more flares. Just lightning, please mother. Lightning.* He froze and waited, his eyes scanning the base of the wall. Voices of American soldiers began rebounding around the courtyard. Even a desultory cheer went up from someone on the parapet. Dam waited, growing restless. *Too risky to stay, the dawn's almost here.* He shook his head in resignation and began moving forward again—slowly.

CRACK! In the searing flash of lightning, Dam saw Tuyet Mai laying less than a meter from his feet. She stared up at him in wide-eyed amazement. Her hands and feet were tied. Even though her hair was matted with mud and her face puffy from exhaustion, Dam marveled at how beautiful she remained and he thought of lines from the old poem:

> *What is more beautiful*
> *Than a lotus in a pond?*
> *Yellow stamens, white petals, green leaves.*
> *Always near mud, yet never smells of mud.*

Near Tuyet Mai sprawled the dead body of Nguyen Dinh Quy, a member of Dam's sapper team. Quy's stiff arm reached out toward her.

"Get down!" Tuyet Mai hissed at Dam.

Flopping down next to her, Dam saw two American soldiers run by, heading toward the church. He briefly touched the little bag he had torn from the American's neck and could not suppress a smile. *For you, Quy.*

"Hurry!" barked Tuyet Mai as Dam cut the cords binding her feet. Just as he finished cutting the rope that bound her hands, he heard another American trotting up to them. It was dark again, so he lay perfectly still behind Tuyet Mai. She pretended her feet remained tied, not moving from her accustomed position. But their ruse ended when the American shined the bright beam of his flashlight on them.

"What the?" he shouted.

Without hesitating, both of them jumped up and ran in opposite directions, momentarily confusing the American. The beam followed Tuyet Mai, allowing Dam time to hide behind a short, jutting wall. Peeping over the top, he saw Tuyet Mai running awkwardly, her hands still tangled in the rope, obviously weak and exhausted. The American quickly caught up to her and knocked her to the ground. Nothing was going right. Dam did not even have his satchel charges. *Left them near Tuyet Mai!* He shook his head. *Nothing else to do.*

Dam scrambled up and over the wall, zigzagging across the clearing and shouting at his confused comrades not to shoot. Dawn, imprisoned behind dark clouds, swept a handful of orange tendrils across the soaked sky.

I know you did what you could, mother. But next time we must do better. Next time. We must!

~ *Panic in Song Nhan Village* ~

Earlier that evening, Madame Dau stood in the square next to the old rice thresher with a few dozen village women and children, listening nervously to the battle at the fortress. The rain came down in sheets from the darkness. Someone brought oil lamps. Light from the lamps, hung randomly from the thresher, lit up their conical hats in glistening halos.

"Let's not stand here like fools!" said someone from the back of the crowd.

A baby cried. Then another. Dogs whined lugubriously, grousing about their masters standing in the rain. Roosters crowed. Palpable fear deepened the gloom of the villagers.

"What should we do?"

"What can we do?"

"American planes and helicopters will come soon. I know it."

"Yes. I agree. And government troops also. And artillery. The village will be destroyed!"

"Yes. I also agree. We've got to leave at dawn. Go to the provincial capital before it's too late."

"In this monsoon? Nonsense! Don't be so rash."

"That's right. What about the sick? The old people? There are too many difficulties. Maybe if it were summer. But now? It's too reckless!"

"Yes! Besides, I'll never make my family refugees."

"Easy for you to say. You don't have babies to worry about."

"That's right. And you don't have attractive daughters."

"No, but my granny is over ninety. And my aunt is sick with fever. Still, I'm willing to go. Better sick than dead!"

"What do you say, Security Chief Tien? Tell us what you think."

Security Chief Tien tried to make herself invisible, but people standing next to her turned to hear her response.

"I . . . I think . . . well . . . it's just that if we wait . . . on the other hand if we go . . . well, perhaps. . . . "

Someone interrupted loudly, "What about this epidemic of fever? None of your potions have had any effect. If this continues there won't be enough healthy people left to plant the winter crop. What are you doing about that?"

"Yes! Why aren't your potions working?"

The security chief spoke louder than anyone, relying on bluster rather than reason. "It's the battle. The spirits are disturbed. Even my strongest potions and chants are rejected by the fever spirits. The killing at the fortress has made them angry. I can do nothing until the battle—"

"Excuses! My children are sick. Since you gave them potions they have gotten sicker!"

"Mine too!"

"And my old uncle!"

Madame Dau's voice rose impatiently above the din. "How many council members are here?"

A few hands went up.

"Good. I suggest we get out of the rain and have an emergency council meeting in the *dinh*. Anyone who wants to attend is welcome. Let us not panic as if we were, ah. . . . " she stumbled for the proper word.

"Were what?" smiled Madame Vit.

"Were old women!" laughed Dau.

Pleased that Madame Dau had picked up on her hint, Vit guffawed. "Exactly!"

"But we *are* old women!" someone barked.

"That's true, but so were the women of Trung Trac and Trung Nhi's army. Look what they accomplished!"

"Yes," snickered a wag in the back of the crowd, "and they eventually committed suicide."

"But they still defeated the Chinese!" another person said indignantly.

"Are you suggesting that we join Major Vy's troops against the American aggressors?" shouted Schoolmistress Nang in a hopeful tone.

A scattering of laughter circulated among the women at the ridiculous suggestion.

"Remember, schoolmistress, it is said that 'one hundred women are not worth a single testicle,'" said Madame Nguyen.

Chief Administrator Vit laughed uproariously. "That's true, Madame Nguyen, but do you remember how the defeated Chinese depicted our beloved Trieu Thi Trinh?" Glancing around to make sure no men were present, the chief administrator surprised and amused everyone by cupping her breasts in her hands and miming a woman riding a horse. "They said Trinh was a monster with huge breasts, three meters long, flying over her shoulder as she rode against their soldiers!"

Laughter spread infectiously and for a moment the nearby battle was forgotten. But as the chuckling subsided, the sounds of firing and explosions swelled ominously. Nervous silence descended upon the women. Madame Dau could hear only crying babies, barking dogs, and crowing roosters above the fearsome sounds of the battle.

Faces turned toward her. She forced a comforting smile. "Unfortunately, my breasts are not that large, Administrator Vit. But I suggest that we attack our problems here in the village with the same ferocity as Trinh and the Trung sisters attacked the Chinese. Forget the battle!"

Madame Dau looked out at the crowd and sensed their fear lessening. Encouraged, she continued speaking in a firm voice. "Look, we have our own problems to solve here. Let the soldiers kill themselves at the fortress! We must perform the funeral for the Venerable Vu Huong. We have the epidemic of fever to overcome. We have the winter crop to plant. Dikes to repair. Roofs to patch. Children and old people to protect. If we become refugees, we will scatter. Wither. Die. Together we can take care of the village. We will survive together."

"That's right, Madame Dau!" came a male voice. Turning to look, the women saw Han Tinh's thick body defiantly planted on the top step of the *dinh*. "Let the soldiers kill themselves! You all have too much to do. The important things. The heroic things. And no army to nurse you and feed you and defend you and protect you. Just yourselves."

He paused and looked out at the faces of the women, then jabbed his index finger at them and shouted above the thunder and sounds of battle. "You know you must do as Madame Dau says! For your children. For your parents. Your grandparents. Your ancestors. Let those bastards kill themselves! Only if you women stay will the survivors have anything to come home to. After this war, stupid statues will be built to commemorate them, but you will have happy, living families to continue your ancestral lines, not marble lies covered in bird droppings."

"But none of those soldiers at the fortress are from our village!" protested a ragged-looking woman holding a naked baby.

CRACK! Han Tinh's face lit up in all its hideous glory. "Fool!" he cried. "If you leave, then you and your families will also have no homes to return to!"

Silence again fell over the women and it seemed as if the world itself had ground to a halt. Finally, a little girl's voice said plaintively, "Mama, I want to go home." Her words broke the tension and Chief Administrator Vit cried, "Ah! That's right! Home!"

Madame Dau's third daughter trotted up to her with a samovar full of steaming tea. Taking the samovar, Madame Dau held it up and said, "Yes, take your baby home. And as for the rest of us, into the *dinh*. Let's get out of the rain. I'm soaked."

Filing into the damp, cavernous main room of the *dinh*, the women shuffled wearily to benches and chairs. Madame Dau knew that she had succeeded in dissipating much of their fear, but the tasks required to keep the village strong and functioning weighed heavily upon them. Young children clung fearfully to the adults' loose fitting pants. Babies whimpered and cried, and throughout the meeting mothers and grandmothers cooed and hummed to quiet their frightened charges. Madame Dau continued to hear scattered muttering about fleeing the village. Muffled but ominously close, sounds of the battle seeped into the *dinh* and the voices of the women began to rise in frenetic volume.

Madame Dau glanced over at Han Tinh who looked back at her with a look of impatience. He nodded encouragement and gestured vigorously for her to start the meeting.

Yes. No time to delay. Start now before I lose control.

~ *Madame Dau Struggles for Control* ~

"Please listen! This meeting has been called to discuss how we should respond to the battle. Please! Be silent so that my words can be heard! I remind all of you that this decision has already been made yesterday by the council. Do you not recall? We will remain in the village. We all know about this battle. It is not a surprise. Look around. Only a few families have left for the provincial capital—the Luong and Le clans, and a few itinerant laborers. Now they are begging for food, herded together like buffalo, gone from their homes and fields. Do we want to become refugees like them? I think not!"

"You forgot to mention the Trieu clan! And the To clan!" shouted Tien.

Council Chief Dau scowled fiercely and continued. "The elders of these clans have requested that we oversee their fields until either we leave or they return. And I told them that when they return, they will find their fields well tended and will owe the rest of us many weeks of labor in repayment.

"Tonight, because of a certain noisy banging at the old fortress, we cannot sleep well. So the council leaders have decided to take advantage of the opportunity to take up some important issues that must be attended to immediately. We have all heard about them. Rebuilding collapsed dikes, repairing tunnels, finishing the winter planting, calling outside help to control our epidemic of fever, and other issues. But for now, I wish to address only one: the funeral of our Venerable Vu Huong. This is our responsibility and obligation. Failure to properly bury our old venerable will surely upset the spirits and bring more destruction to the village than soldiers fighting at the fortress."

Carpenter Long spoke up loudly, interrupting Madame Dau. "But please, Council Chief Dau, can't we discuss the fever epidemic first? Too many of our relatives are sick. We must bring a Western-trained doctor from the provincial capital. Surely this is more important!"

Another woman shouted from the middle of the room, "What about repairing the dikes? My fields have been flooded from Old Truong's fields for over a week!"

Another woman joined in. "The funeral of Venerable Vu Huong is important, I agree, but don't forget the tunnels. If we're going to stay while soldiers fight nearby, it is critical that we have safe places to hide our children and old people."

"No!" responded Madame Dau, her vehemence surprising everyone, including herself. Even Schoolmistress Nang looked startled. "We will take up those issues after our time in the fields tomorrow. Tonight we must plan the funeral. Tonight!"

Although the women wondered why Madame Dau considered the funeral so important, no one asked. Still, much grousing could be heard.

CRACK! A burst of lightning filled the *dinh* with an electric glow. Rumbling thunder pushed through the room, startling a fruit bat from its perch in the rafters. Flapping its wings furiously, the bat circled the room, desperately seeking a way out. Finding none, it returned to the darkness of the ceiling.

"A sign!" shouted Security Chief Tien. A collective intake of breath swept through the women.

"What does it mean?" asked five women simultaneously.

"It is the spirit of our Venerable Vu Huong. He is demanding a proper burial, just as Madame Dau said."

"Nonsense!" said Schoolmistress Nang. "It's a fruit bat trying to get out of the building."

Security Chief Tien cast a withering glare at her. "There are many spirits out tonight, some of them in this room, some within our bodies, under our skin. All trying to get out. Do not mock the spirits or the messenger that interprets them, schoolmistress!"

Intimidated by the security chief's veiled threat, Schoolmistress Nang muttered something indecipherable.

"So, Council Chief Dau, what must we do to make funeral preparations?" asked Han Tinh, who somehow ended up with two babies in front of him. He tried to look expectantly at Madame Dau when everyone turned toward him, but one of the babies fussed and he looked down and made shushing sounds.

"Watch out, Mr. Water Puppeteer, one of the babies might drench you again!" laughed Madame Vit. Tittering laughter spread throughout the room and broke the crowd's somber mood.

Chuckling, Madame Dau said, "If you can stay dry long enough, Brother Tinh, I will tell you." She cleared her throat and spoke in a firm voice. "As many of you know, for the past year the Venerable Huong has been making preparations to join his ancestors. A tomb has been built on the spot chosen by a geomancer of great renown. But the Venerable's family has scattered to the four winds. Most of them are dead. The others are beyond our ability to contact in time to attend the funeral.

"Brother Tinh, as acting monk of the village, will consult the Venerable's horoscope in consultation with the Cult Committee and determine the most auspicious day for the funeral. Carpenter Long will prepare a carved coffin. Chief Administrator Vit will oversee a committee to clean his house and build an extension in preparation for the feast. Security Chief Tien informs me that the condition of the body requires that these tasks be completed as soon as possible.

"The Cult Committee will solicit people to prepare the bier, altars, and ceremonial offerings. Mourning clothes need to be sewn and distributed. Madame Nguyen will be in charge of organizing this task. Schoolmistress Nang will make arrangements for the musicians. According to tradition, we must begin stockpiling bottles of rice wine, although without men, I am sure not much will be drunk.

"Oh yes, the *nhan dieu* must be cut short only a few days, since the Venerable's kin cannot be notified. Seamstress Trang will supervise the sewing of draperies and other hangings. Security Chief Tien must select the strongest women of the village to act as pallbearers. And, of course, dishes for the feast must be prepared, which means that all the ingredients should be collected in plenty of time for cooking. Chef Trinh is in charge of organizing the food preparations. We mustn't scrimp on the feast."

"I've already consulted the Venerable's horoscope!" shouted Han Tinh impulsively. When all eyes were upon him, he held his nose. "The year of the stinky rat dictates that the most auspicious day for the funeral is now!"

Groaning rippled through the women while Tinh looked mischievously at the disapproving Madame Dau.

Somehow, probably due to the combination of Tinh's irreverence and Madame Dau's earnestness, by the end of the meeting, everyone was focused on the upcoming funeral. Even the end of the battle at the fortress and the coming of dawn elicited little notice. Madame Dau stood beside Han Tinh at the open door of the *dinh* as the women filtered out and dispersed to their homes and fields. Madame Dau sensed relief in the hearts of the women as they worked together to prepare for the funeral.

"They have much to do, is that not right, Brother Tinh?"

He laughed. "Is that not the purpose of this grand funeral, Venerable Council Chief?"

"I will admit that you are partly correct, Brother Tinh. But our Venerable Huong deserves a proper funeral. Is that not true?"

"True. True."

Madame Dau did not move, hovering above Han Tinh, something clearly on her mind.

"Is there something else, Madame Dau? You seem hesitant to leave and you certainly must be tired. What is it?"

"I've decided to go the cave and see if the American soldier is still alive," she blurted out awkwardly.

Tinh looked down and shook his head.

"It's the sign, Brother Tinh. The sign. I cannot ignore it. I cannot do otherwise."

Tinh smiled. "And who did you agree with earlier in the meeting about the bat? Tien and her superstitious sign, or Nang and her pragmatic explanation?"

"Nang. But that's different. You must admit that a two-headed snake is much more rare than a fruit bat! And the snake *was* at the tunnel exit, near where my parents were killed. Surely that is different!"

"So you pick and choose your superstitions and your pragmatisms. Neither this nor that. Neither here nor there. Ah! Problem with that, Madame Council Chief, is that if you pick only one, pragmatism or superstition, and stick to it, then you will have a chance to be wrong just fifty percent of the time. But if you jump back and forth between pragmatism and superstition, then you will have a chance to be wrong one hundred percent of the time. I tell you, Madame Dau, your involvement with this American soldier will bring ruin to the village. One hundred percent ruin. Believe me, it will. For your sake I will remain silent. But remember my warning."

The two stood quietly for a moment. Madame Dau started to leave when Tinh called her back.

"A moment, council chief. A moment, please. If you find the American alive, ask him something for me."

Surprised, Madame Dau could merely say, "What?"

"Ask him whether he knows anything about the Goddess figurine stolen from our village by the People's Army."

"Surely he wouldn't know anything about that!" said Madame Dau emphatically.

"Don't be so sure," Tinh replied enigmatically.

Madame Dau laughed. "Your ghosts again. Right? Now which of us is superstitious, Brother Tinh? But yes, I will ask. If he's still alive."

"Besides," said Tinh. "The figurine may help us against the other American."

"The other?"

"The one who writes these words. The one around whom we all spin. The one whose demons tell him to kill himself."

"And if he does?"

~

"Then we will all be free, but the planet will die."

Then we will all be free. Kill yourself, Michael!

No, no, no, no, no, no, no. Do not listen to the demons, Michael. Han Tinh is right!

Ah, Goddess, if You do not kill him, Michael will surely kill You.

Chapter Fifteen

The Tabs

Fantasies of Doomed Soldiers

This little story is ancient, circular and pointless. Give them up, Sweet Goddess. Another failed attempt. Still, it would be nice for the others if humans just slipped away, but that is not how they operate.

You do not fool Me, God. You would not give them up for anything. After all, they are capable of love, of making complex tools, of anticipating their own mortality, destroying the planet, and, of course, worshipping Your faction.

Yes, My Dear, those defects make their suffering so exquisitely acute. But they no longer worship You. Is that why You want to give them up—the fruitless hope they will be replaced by the Superior Ones and return to the feminine Godhead?

I am well aware that worship is not enough for You! Is it suffering You're after, God? Is it angst? Poverty? Tragedy? Comedy? Hunger? Violence? Mortality? What of Our other children whom You have abandoned? Try being a lion for one week. Or a seal. Or a dragonfly. Or a coyote, a beetle, a flounder, a sapling, a shrimp, a gorilla, a wildebeest . . . ah, a wildebeest! Have You ever listened to the instinctive scream of a wildebeest mother when she sees that her calf has wandered too close to a tawny shape crouching in the grass and it turns out to be nothing more than a windblown clump of straw piled against a rock? She too has nightmares. As do all the others. Billions and billions of nightmares. I have heard them all, and weep.

Yes, but after her calf is torn apart by a tawny shape crouching in the grass that turns out to be a lion, her nightmares will be nothing more than a few peaks and troughs lost in the Symphony of Great Wailing vibrating in Our Ears. But now that murderous humans have evolved, they heap upon non-humans far more intense and wide-spread suffering. I have also heard the human-induced nightmares—all of them. Potent swill. And like You, I weep. My faction's position is distorted by your Chosen One.

Ha! You cry for more. Every second of every hour of every day of every year of every age, a flood of nightmares rising from the earth slake Your alcoholic thirst for sadistic succor. And as You dribble excess upon the soaked pages of Scripture, humans wring superstition from the blurred Words of their God, because–

And goddesses! Besides, they are not My nightmares. We have come full circle, compassionate and alliteration-loving Goddess, for, just like the wildebeest mother, Our dear little humans want their own nightmares to go away, the tawny shapes crouching in the grass. So they run. Run, run, faster and faster, back to their technological cradle. Even their old ones have joined the stampede. They are addicted to their own Condition and have built a technological nursery in which to play and suckle and sleep and defecate and consume their lives away while everything else is sacrificed to keep the little dears warm and safe and clean and long-lived and well stocked with food and toys and silicon slaves and, most importantly of all, entertainment about the Human Condition so they won't cry too loudly except to Me. Yes, their whining has become tiresome in the extreme. Ah, well, spare the rod, spoil the child. But, what can One do? I am for Love. Benevolence. Is an Immortal Goddess capable of forgetting something so canonical about Her superior? I am all compassionate! Death is the ultimate compassionate act. Besides, there are billions upon billions of other planets. Why is the preservation of this one so crucial.

Its abundant diversity; its intermixing of such delightful elements to form living Nature; its liquid water allowing for such a luxurious cornucopia of flora and fauna. It is a jewel We cannot let disappear because of an invasive species of hominins.

~ *Mountain Man Battles His Conscience* ~

Mountain Man remained slumped against the gnarled root of the banyan tree, not far from the tunnel exit, long after Bowls vanished through the trapdoor. Hours passed in a rain-lashed stupor, his body unmoving as thunder cracked and monsoon winds battered his soaked figure. He didn't flinch. He endured the storm in stony silence. When distant echoes of battle from the fortress finally reached his ears, he stared ahead, trance-like, forcing away images of his besieged comrades. He tried to summon rage. Rage was armor. But the anger faded with the gunfire, and drowsiness crept in. He drifted at the edge of sleep, sliding in and out of consciousness. Gray-green light seeped through the canopy as dawn bled into the jungle. Cold and stiff, Mountain Man rose. He packed methodically, refusing to let his thoughts linger on T, Nature, Stretch, X, any of them. Bowls, he convinced himself, had stayed safe during the firefight. Still in the tunnel.

Bowls will check who's left. He'll come back. I gave him good directions.

Grunting his assent to this private logic, he threw a filthy green towel over his shoulders, slung his rucksack into place, cradled his M-16, and began his trek toward the cave where Madame Dau awaited. But doubts nipped at his heels. *He'll find me. And if he don't, I'll find him.*

He paralleled the narrow trail described by Madame Dau, swatting away the insistent ghosts of his squad. Their tabs whispered through the trees, persistent as gnats. *No way, you bastards! You didn't listen! Not to me. You traded Martha for Idaho—Jesus Christ! Idiots! Now you see what happens without Mountain Man. Jungle's a coffin without me. You'll learn. Wait till Bowls returns. He's got brains. He'll catch up. Meet me at the cave. Then we go back, but only if they agree Martha stays with me. Hurry up, Bowls. The rest of you—piss off.*

He sighed. Then let his mind slip into longing. He imagined Martha waiting at the NDP. A fantasy he'd built from hunger and madness. She waited in a dry clearing, soft ground cleared of roots and rocks, tea already steeping. Their poncho liner smoothed out like a welcome mat. She'd undress him with care, rub his feet, warm socks stored between her breasts. Her hair shone as she knelt over his M-16, cleaning it lovingly. She smelled of cinnamon. She handed him a fig. And then—

CRACK! Thunder split the dream in two.

He crouched low, held his breath, then rose again and kept walking. *This goddamn war will never end. But if it does, I'll start a trading company in Vung Tau. Raise little West Virginia-Vietnamese babies. Be happy as hogs in spring rain. Shit. Where's the damn trail?*

The path was nearly invisible now. Once used by villagers during the French occupation, time and rain had worn it into little more than an animal track. Mountain Man lost it repeatedly, forced to circle out and reconnoiter until he picked it up again. The rain had eased to a miserable drizzle. Fog thickened. Through a break in the canopy, he finally spotted the cave, a slit in the mountainside, oozing boulders and mist. Climbing a tall teak tree flecked with heart-shaped leaves and white blossoms, he found a perch between two thick branches and scanned the area. For an hour he watched.

Nothing. No human movement. No sign of the NVA. Just the relentless stirrings of jungle life. A rush of orange-headed thrushes burst from the trees, shrieking overhead. A coppersmith barbet let out its rhythmic *tonk-tonk*. Geckos screamed *"Fuck you! Fuck you!"* as they scattered. Langurs swung. Gibbons howled. Kingfishers flashed. Mynas chattered. The jungle mocked his loneliness with its surplus of life. Each cry became a ghost. Every trill a tab. The canopy birthed faces: T, Stretch, Storyteller, Nature. Bowls circled closest. He tried not to see them.

He climbed down and forced a dream of home: a snowy West Virginia evening, Martha beside the fireplace, dogs snoring at their feet. But the fire always surged too hot, too fast—turning to a fiery bunker, to Firebase Pace, to the moment when the tabs were first shared. Convinced the cave was safe, he dropped down the slope and followed the faint trail to the edge. Fog coiled around the boulders, shifting in slow, sinuous folds. He sat and peered back down the path, tracing its reddish thread until it vanished in the fog. He tried to focus on anything but

the grunts, but their voices pressed in. After inspecting the cave and arranging his rucksack near the entrance, he sat again to wait.

Bowls' voice returned, unbidden: *"Mountain Man. Remember everyone's
tabs? Remember T, X, Nature, Storyteller, Stretch, Superman, Idaho? They
wanna go home. Back to The World. Ya know?"*

He let out a long breath. *Fuck it. Okay, Bowls. You want it that bad? Fine.
Come out of the fog. Tell me your tabs. I'll listen. Hell, might as well be your
goddamn mother. Who's first? No volunteers? Fine. I'll choose. Nature! Yo,
Nature! Outta the fog, boy. Daddy Mountain Man wants to see you. Nature!*

Then he leaned forward, cupping his hands around his mouth, and whispered with a cracked edge of fury and longing:

"Nature!"

~ The Tabs: Desperate Fantasies of Desperate Soldiers ~

*Nature stepped from the fog with his tam-o'-shanter tilted forward in comic
defiance, the cockiness of a trickster-prince. His curly Irish hair curled beneath
the cap's brim, his limbs loose and fluid, more jester than soldier. A leprechaun
with a rifle. As always, he wore that maddening, good-natured smile.*

"What do you say, Mountain Man?"

"I say I want to hear your tab."

"Oh, come on. You always laugh when I tell it. What, need a chuckle now?"

"Maybe."

"No dogs in mine, remember? Just a cat."

"I remember. Still—tell it again. Humor your old Uncle Mountain Man."

*"Sure." Nature's grin softened. "Well, I'm back in Rhode Island. It's night.
I'm standing on this little sand dune, my back to the Atlantic, staring up at
the house on the bluff. The breeze is cool, salty. Sand shifting under my boots. I
feel good. Real good. The lights are on in the house. Second-floor window: our
black cat, Bobby Burns, sitting there in silhouette. I can hear the surf behind me,
but inside, it's warm. There's laughter. Mom, Dad, my sisters. Closest thing to
gunfire is Bobby's purr."*

He paused. "That's it. Just simple bullshit. Right, Mountain Man?"

"Yeah. Right. You also had that little song. How'd it go?"

Nature laughed. "You really want that, too?"

"Yeah."

Nature sang, off-key but without shame:

> *"Too-Ra-Loo-Ra-Loo-Ra, Too-Ra-Loo-Ra-Li,*
> *Loo-Ra-Loo-Ra-Loo-Ra, hush now don't you cry."*

"Jesus," Mountain Man muttered. "You got a lousy voice."

*He held the image of Nature in silence, studying it. Why a cat? Why not his
family? Why not sex, or blood, or booze, like the others? Why not dress that
lullaby in vulgar lyrics, put a crack in the porcelain?*

Nature, like Mountain Man, took care of the platoon, but differently. The grunts called him "fuckin' Earth Mother." And though Mountain Man resented the competition, he couldn't deny the man's sincerity. You could hear it in the tab.

"I get it," Mountain Man said finally. "The ocean behind you's the war. Right? You're close to home, almost there, but still not inside. And the cat's black. That's got to mean something. Death, maybe. Some Jungian shit like that."

Nature shrugged. "I don't know. The tab's just the tab. That's what came to mind."

"Yeah, maybe. But I'll bet stuff went down in that cozy little house. Didn't it, Nature?"

"Sometimes. Why? You jealous?"

"No! Hey! I'm running the show here. I mean real bad shit. Like your old man drunk, knocking your mom around. Something like that. Always is. Bet that house had shadows."

Nature smiled. "No," he lied.

"Look, Nature," Mountain Man leaned in. "All my life I've found the scabs in people. Emotional wounds. Once I find them, they're like landmines. I don't even have to step on them: just knowing where they are is power. A man sees you see him bleeding, and you've already won. But you? Every time I stick the probe in, all I find is . . . nice guy."

"And I bet you hate nice guys."

"Damn right. Can't do nothin' with 'em."

Nature folded his arms. "You know, we've got more in common than you think."

Mountain Man snorted. "Like what?"

Nature looked up at the jungle canopy, voice calm. "The Earth's about four-and-a-half billion years old. And it'll last another four-and-a-half billion. That's nine billion years."

"Okay. So?"

"So it's kind of amazing, don't you think? That you and I are both alive at the same time. Out of all that time."

Mountain Man frowned. "What's that supposed to mean?"

"It means we're connected. However short our lives turn out to be."

"Will turn out to be?"

"For you."

"We're dead, Mountain Man." Nature said it simply. "Oh sure, maybe one of us will survive, and you know who that would be. He's the one with visions, the one who writes, who sees what we can't. Don't forget me, Storyteller!"

"News to me. Maybe you're dead. Not me. One thing's certain—without Mountain Man, you're dead."

"Maybe. Maybe not. With or without Mountain Man."

Mountain Man exhaled. "Christ, Nature. You're a hell of a guy. Too bad you're not gonna make it back. Back to Rhode Island. Your black cat. Your family. All of it."

Nature's smile dimmed. "Who knows? I might surprise you. We all might. You're not always right, you know. Anyway, I gotta get back. They need me."

The words hit harder than expected. Mountain Man released him. The red-checked tam-o'-shanter lingered a moment in his mind's eye, then flickered out.

Boring. That was Nature's sin. Boring life. Why was he so eager to return to it? Probably they all had boring lives, every one of them. That's why they tore the world apart—poking under rocks, prying into jungles, making war, making love, inventing things just to break them again. Searching for stimulation. Entertainment.

So what? Let them chase their precious "Human Condition." He'd read the epics, stories of so-called greatness, and yet a rat in a maze or a tiger in heat lived more in a week than most men in a lifetime.

Love, boredom. That's all it is.

He'd wait. Listen to their tabs. They'd tell the truth. They always did.

~ *Idaho* ~

Mountain Man stared blankly down the trail, mist writhing in silence. He felt glum, reflective. He thought about how most of the young grunts had come into the jungle like soft clay, carrying with them the phobias of adolescence. Didn't matter who they'd been back in The World: jocks, stoners, punks, scholars, clowns. The jungle peeled them raw. Melted them, molded them.

At first, they moved like actors in a bad war film, performing themselves, forever watching from outside. How do I look pushing this vine aside? How do I look holding my M-16? Is my bush hat tilted just right? As if some invisible girl or camera crew followed them through the foliage.

But the jungle had no patience for pretense. If they lasted even a little while, the performance ended. Their bodies betrayed them. They shit themselves. Lost weight. Skin turned jaundiced. Fungi bloomed in their eyelids, between their toes, up their asses. Fear, pure and primal, eroded whatever scaffolding of youth remained. Self-image collapsed. In that collapse, Mountain Man rose.

Peacetime rank meant nothing here. Good looks meant nothing. Athletics, charm, sex appeal—gone. All that mattered was doing your job and not fucking up. Anything else was a liability. And men such as Mountain Man, who already knew what it meant to be ugly and naked, were the ones who survived.

"They were all born again," he muttered, "in a world with no rules."

Some picked nervously at the psychic umbilical cord still connecting them to home. Most were too frightened to cut it. Those who couldn't let it go died slow, suffocating deaths, even if their bodies made it back. That was the truth behind the name: The World. What they really meant was The Womb.

He looked up and murmured, "Ain't that so, Nature?"

But Nature was gone, and the mist squirmed as if preparing to speak again.

Mountain Man straightened, energized by his own clarity. He felt above it all. Superior. Ready for the next soul.

"Idaho! Come on out, you fuckin' farmer!"

From the fog, Idaho emerged hesitantly, his awkwardness unshaken by the magic that had erased his wound. That same crooked smile, arms limp at his sides, that same lost-kid posture.

"You're in over your head, ain't you?" Mountain Man said flatly.

"Nah," Idaho muttered, clearly lying. "It's just . . . it's just that all this is crap. I wanna go back. Don't we all? Back to The World."

"Yeah. Sure." Mountain Man smirked. He felt like playing with him.

"Hey, you remember the first time your old man let you drive the tractor?"

Idaho's face lit up for a second before fading back into suspicion. "Sure. But come on, Mountain Man, don't jerk my chain. I don't mess with your family stories."

"I'm serious," said Mountain Man, voice mock-solemn. "I wanna hear about it."

Idaho hesitated, then grinned. "You ever have a mom and dad, Mountain Man? You're a great killer, but I wouldn't wanna be around you if you ever make it back. Poor bastards who are."

"That's right, boy. I'll keep killin' till I get my fill. Then I'll go back and do what I gotta do."

Idaho laughed. "Fuck you. I'll tell you anyway. It was a big old Massey-Ferguson. When I was little, Dad let me ride next to him, pulling the roto-tiller, plowing under corn stalks. Then when I was twelve, he let me drive. Man . . . I remember that like yesterday."

He kept talking. His voice grew softer, his body relaxed. A flow of memory carried him.

Mountain Man listened, kind of. His smile turned bemused, detached.

Another good kid. Jesus. Where do they come from? All these lonely, homesick boys remembering the taste of home.

You know something, Idaho? Memories are like food. You are what you eat. And you, kid, you're starving. All thin soup and sentimental broth. A cow chewing childhood cud in a field of shit. If you survive, you'll be one of those fifty-year-old gasbags saying, "Best years of my life were in high school when I caught that pass." Christ. Why're you still talking about home?

Strange plants. Strange smells. Strange language. Strange war. It's hitting him from every direction. He's curling in on himself—a pill bug, waiting for someone to roll him to safety. Poor little hero. But the world don't cradle pill bugs. It flicks 'em into the fire.

Idaho was still rambling when Mountain Man cut him off. "Yeah, yeah. Anyway, tell me your tab again."

"Why?"

"Just fuckin' do it. I wanna hear it."

"Okay, okay," Idaho said, drawing in a breath. "So I'm just back from Nam. Sitting in a taxi, pulling up the driveway to the farmhouse. My family and friends are outside, waving and smiling. I'm in uniform, leaning forward in the seat. I see my mom, she's messing with the second button on her polka-dot blouse, wiping away tears. Dad's got on his old striped shirt, straining at the buttons, arm around her, waving high.

"To the side, picnic tables under the cherry tree. Food everywhere. My girl-friend's there too, in a white dress, crying, doing that same thing with the buttons. The taxi radio's playing 'The Tennessee Waltz.' I know, it's cheesy. Norman Rockwell stuff. But that's it. Plain and simple."

He paused, uneasy. "When I left for Nam, I looked back through the window of my brother's Chevy. Rainy day. My folks stood on the porch. Mom cried, Dad looked like he'd swallowed a stone. My girl cried. I swore I'd reverse it someday. So that's my tab. Just . . . the reversal."

Mountain Man said nothing. Just stared.

Another boring life. They all had them. That's why they can't wait to crawl back to their sad little towns, their weak little families.

He felt his mood sour. His superiority ebbing into irritation.

"Okay, okay," he muttered. "Get lost, kid. It's Superman's turn."

Idaho looked up, still hopeful, but Mountain Man blinked him out. Gone. A pill bug flicked into oblivion.

~ *Superman* ~

"Superman! Hey, Superman! Get out here, you big ugly gunner!"

He emerged from the fog, a presence stripped of ornament: long, confident strides, no swagger, no deceit. *He moved with the steadiness of a man who did not question his footing. A foundation for the more clever to stand on, build on, dream from. Square-jawed, grounded, without irony. He rolled two small pebbles between his fingers as he stepped forward.*

"Hey, Mountain Man," he said softly. "What's up?"

"I want to hear your tab again," Mountain Man grumbled. "Talk to me. You'll probably bore me just like the rest."

Superman raised an eyebrow, confused. Then smiled. "You want excitement, I'm not the guy."

"No shit. Let me guess. Your twin girls, right? That's what keeps you going."

Superman nodded, unashamed. "You okay today, Mountain Man? You sound . . . off. Guilty, maybe?"

Mountain Man's irritation flared. "You've got the dreaming disease. You see your wife and daughters beside you in the bush. You carry them with you like talismans. But they're not here, Superman. This place don't give a fuck about your girls or your God. You're holding up Jesus like a crucifix against a vampire. But this jungle ain't got vampires. Just death. And it's not afraid of you. You don't belong here."

Superman nodded solemnly. "I know. And I'm gonna die here. Right?"

"Right."

"Wrong," Superman said gently. "My God's with me, always. If I die, I'll see them again. That's something you'll never have."

"Yeah, and I don't believe in Santa Claus either."

Superman licked his lips. "You know, I've heard that before. It always sounds like jealousy. Nonbelievers wanting something to cling to but too proud to kneel."

Mountain Man snorted. "Still, sorry you ain't gonna make it out of here."

Superman's face darkened. "Who told you that? I am getting out. For them. Nature said we might surprise you, remember?"

"You could hear Nature? Huh. Didn't realize figments could eavesdrop on each other."

"Surprise."

"Yeah, yeah. All right. Tell me your tab."

"Not until you say it."

"Say what?"

"That I'm a good gunner. I want to tell my girls the great Mountain Man said it."

Mountain Man smiled despite himself. "You're good enough. But Jesus, man, ditch the religion. It's gonna get you killed someday."

"No," Superman said, eyes gleaming. "It's gonna get me saved."

"Fine. Your tab, or I blink you into a VC shithole."

Superman's voice softened, the pebbles still dancing between his fingers. "Mary and the girls are sitting around the Christmas tree. Christmas Eve. Frost on the windows. They're waiting for me to come in with two mugs of hot chocolate. The kind me and Mary like: extra strong, marshmallows just starting to melt. They look up at me: eyes full of trust, love, warmth. Mary's in her blue robe and goofy slippers. The twins are in matching teddy bear pajamas. And the radio's playing 'Silent Night.' That's it. That's the tab."

Mountain Man groaned. "Christ. More domestic crap."

Superman shrugged, sheepish. "Sorry. That's what it is. Boring, maybe—but not to me."

"Don't get me wrong," Mountain Man said quickly. "I've seen the pictures. Cute kids. I remember one long day, maybe a few months ago, you were sitting behind a termite mound with your legs stuck out like a little boy. Two dirt mounds in front of you. You were talking to yourself. One pebble on each mound. 'Mine's bigger.' 'No! Mine's bigger!' Like a kid at play. You kept on a while. Smiling like a jackass. I didn't let you know I saw."

Superman chuckled. "Wouldn't have mattered. If you had kids, you'd get it. The pebbles are my girls. Can't fade like a picture. Can't rot. That's why I've got to get back. For them. For Mary. They need a dad. And me—I need to see them grow up. Real bad.

"When I get home, I'll put those pebbles in a special case. And one day, when they're older, married maybe, I'll show them to my grandkids. Tell them about this old war, and the story of the pebbles, and how their moms were when they were little. Maybe I'm boring. Maybe me and Idaho and Nature are all just boring guys. But without boring guys, where would you be, Mountain Man?"

Mountain Man nodded slowly. "Maybe you idiots will make it after all. Now go back to the platoon."

He tried to banish the image, to dismiss Superman as he had all the others. But Superman didn't disappear.

"Come back with me," he said. "We need you."

The words stunned Mountain Man. The image remained, clear and immovable. He blinked hard.

"No," he growled. "I won't go back. Not even to keep your daughters from losing their daddy. Now get the hell out."

He focused, summoning force of will. Superman's form flickered, then finally turned and walked away, pebbles still in hand, swallowed by the fog.

Mountain Man spat at the earth.

"If you ever make it back alive, which you won't, you'll be divorced in two years. Mary'll get the kids. You'll die in some dump, working a dead-end job. You poor sap."

He shook his head.

"You're all on your own now. I ain't going back."

~ Pappy ~

"What's up, Mountain Man?"

The voice came from nowhere, grounded and unmistakable. Pappy stood on the trail, barrel-chested, arms crossed, radiating impatience like steam off asphalt.

Mountain Man blinked. "I didn't call you out."

"That's right, you didn't," said Pappy, cocking his head. "But I'm the sergeant. You're the Spec 4. Remember the chain of command? You don't call me anywhere unless I decide to show up. Affirmative?"

Mountain Man chuckled. "Yeah. Sure, Sarge. Affirmative."

Pappy squinted, accusatory. "Scuttlebutt says you're playing God."

"Nah. Just thinking."

Pappy laughed, low and knowing. "You never had a thought in your life without a reason, Mountain Man. So, what? You want to hear my tab too?"

Mountain Man narrowed his eyes. "How'd you know?"

"The others briefed me."

"Christ. Getting intelligence updates from my own hallucinations. I must really be losing it."

"You said it."

"This ain't a goddamn therapy session," Mountain Man growled. "Just tell me your tab."

"And if I say fuck off?"

"You can't."

"Why not?"

"Because you may outrank me, but I created you."

Pappy raised an eyebrow. "I wonder."

"Oh, goddammit, Sarge, just tell me your tab."

They locked eyes. The silence settled between them, dense and palpable. *Mountain Man felt a headache blooming in his temples. He broke first.*

"I've thought about it, you know. Going nuts. But that's not it. Couldn't be. You'd do the same if they took your wife away. Look, Pappy, you and me both know this ain't a fair fight. Charlie's been in the bush for years. He's good. The best. Our guys rotate out every twelve months, if they live that long. So the enemy always gets fresh meat. But not us. You and me, we've been out here a long time. You're good. I'm better. Hell, we're like goddamn prize sows surrounded by suckling piglets.

"So, I'm asking you, man to man, bush brother to bush brother, sow to sow, tell me I'm not going crazy. And when you're done with that, tell me your goddamn tab."

Pappy's stare didn't waver. Then he nodded, slowly. "You need to get with the program, boy. And fast. But fine, I'll give you my tab. I'm in this smoky room, playing poker with some old buddies. Liquor's flowing. Sinatra's crooning 'Luck Be a Lady' on the turntable."

"That it?" Mountain Man asked flatly.

"Yup."

"Bullshit. That's the version you tell the platoon. That's not your real tab."

Pappy smirked but didn't speak.

"Is it?" Mountain Man pressed.

"No."

"Well then?"

"If you already know it's not real, then you know what is."

"Tell me anyway."

"You really know?" Pappy asked, one eyebrow arched.

"Yup."

"How?"

"Surprise."

Pappy laughed. "All right. Since I'm just a figment of your imagination, I'll play along."

Mountain Man chuckled weakly, head throbbing harder now.

"Surprise," Pappy echoed. But then his tone shifted. Lowered. Darkened.

"My real tab is this: I'm sitting on a rocky hill out near San Bernardino. Desert sunset. Colors more beautiful than even your wild-ass brain can conjure. I'm in our spot. Me and Ethel. She divorced me after five years; couldn't take the Army life. But I loved her. Still do. I'm just sitting there in the wind, thinking of her. Music playing in my head—"

Mountain Man joined in:

> *"Do not forsake me, oh my darlin',*
> *Not on this our wedding day.... "*

"Yeah," Pappy said softly. "That's the one."

"Told you I knew your real tab."

"You know too much sometimes."

They stood in it together, the ache, the dry wind of memory.

"You think we're gonna make it out of here?" Pappy asked.

Mountain Man shook his head.

"If you came back, would we make it out?"

"Doesn't matter. I'm not coming back."

Pappy nodded, slow and weighty. "We'll see."

"Don't bet on it. You know what, Sarge? You're the old man out here. You've been around. You know this shit's real. That's why it scares you more than the rest. They still think it's a movie. You and me? We know better. The jungle's not weird. It's not even mystical. It's just business. Kill or be killed. Same way back in the States—only here, it don't bother pretending otherwise. This place ain't for old men."

He paused, eyes hard.

"So? Am I going crazy?"

Pappy didn't answer directly. "See ya later, Mountain Man," he said, winking with a sly, conspiratorial grin. As he turned, his voice drifted over his shoulder. "Besides . . . this whole thing ain't right. It ain't the way it was. Get it right, motherfucker."

Rage surged through Mountain Man. He shouted after the fading silhouette.

"You talkin' to me, asshole?"

"No!" came the fading voice from the fog. "Her."

A skeletal finger pointed skyward.

"Or maybe I should say . . . the Chosen One. The writer."

Mountain Man reeled. "Sarge! Pappy! You—"

But the fog swallowed him whole.

~ *Stretch* ~

Stretch emerged from the mist with his usual twitching gait, limbs jerking in spasmodic rebellion against stillness. He passed Pappy on the trail without missing a beat.

"Hey, Pappy!"

"Maybe you'll have better luck with that sonofabitch," Pappy muttered as he faded back into the fog.

"Doubt it. Goodbye, Marshal Kane, see you at high noon!" Stretch called out with a wink.

"So," said Mountain Man, "the company clown."

Stretch gave a deep, sweeping bow. "Mountain Man, I'd bet your old man spent the first year of your life throwing rocks at the stork."

Mountain Man burst into laughter. "Close. He spent that year throwing rocks at my Ma. When he couldn't land those, he started throwing punches."

Stretch's smile thinned. "We all got shit in our past, Mountain Man. Except Nature, maybe. Anyway, what's up?"

"You know what's up."

"Yeah. What are the odds I can talk you into coming back to the fort?"

"Nil."

Stretch tilted his head, feigning disappointment. "All right, Mr. Scratch. I'll tell you my tab, but you gotta promise me something."

Mountain Man raised an eyebrow. "Mr. Scratch, huh? Maybe you got that part right. I've sent a lotta men to hell, no need for any contracts. So what's your ask?"

"Just think about coming back. That's all."

"Fine. Now let's hear it, you scrawny bastard."

Stretch leaned into the telling like a vaudeville act turning confessional. "I'm lying on my girlfriend's couch. It's night. Her parents and brother are gone, like, next county gone. Lights are off. The glow of the TV flickers against her bare skin. She's only wearing these pink lace panties. Real small, real tight. I've got my index finger hooked under the strap. Just about to pull them off.

'Bonanza' is on. You know that hoofbeat rhythm—dum de de dum de de dum de de dum—and I'm getting off on it."

"Yeah, yeah," Mountain Man groaned. "Get on with it, Romeo."

"There's stale beer and pepperoni pizza all over the TV trays. And the best part, Mountain Man? Her panties, soaked. I mean dripping. Oh man."

His tics accelerated with the memory.

"And the music?" Mountain Man teased. "Bonanza?"

Stretch shook his head. "Nope. Bonanza made me think about horse dicks. Even Little Joe's horse had me feeling inadequate."

"So what is it?"

"The Stones, man. What else? 'I Can't Get No Satisfaction.'"

"You ever think about anything besides women?"

Stretch grinned. "Let me tell you something, you ugly West Virginian. My momma taught me everything I know about women. Wasn't no whore, but might as well have been. We lived off the 'kindness of strangers.' Mostly men. Mostly assholes."

"Kinda sums up the male species," Mountain Man muttered. "Half poet, half pervert."

"Huh. Don't know many poems. But I know a few. Wanna hear one?"

"No."

Stretch went on anyway. His tics stilled, voice flattening into eerie calm.

"Momma always quoted this:

> *There was a young harlot from Kew,*
> *Who filled her vagina with glue.*
> *She said with a grin,*
> *'If they pay to get in,*
> *They'll pay to get out of it too.*

"Well," Stretch said with a bitter laugh, "us kids, we were the glue. And yeah, they paid."

"Movies were your escape, right?"

"Supposed to be," he said, shoulders rising toward his ears involuntarily.

"Like you said, Stretch, we all got shit in our past."

"I want to go home," Stretch whispered. "Even if it's just to see her. I want to go back."

"You all do," said Mountain Man. "You, Idaho, the whole platoon, you all ache for home like it's a drug. But it's not home you want. It's a half-dream. You want what never was, mixed in with what really happened. Homemade pie and pimples. Burgers and being scared of girls. Car upholstery, schoolbooks. Movie theaters and masturbation. Moms and dads and fucked-up silences. Clean sheets. And clean-outta-luck."

"Masturbation," Stretch said with mock solemnity. "At least you got something right."

"Oh, I got it, Stretch. You treat this war like a weird school trip. A blip. Like you're just out of town for a high school basketball game. And your only defense is attitude. That's what boys cling to when they're scared. Attitude is your binky. The world's fucked up, so you strut. But underneath, you're just a kid with a pacifier and a permanent scowl."

"Hey, attitude's the wave of the future, man. It's our fuck-you to the assholes who run this world."

"It's a fuck-you from scared children. Gooks this, slant-eyes that. 'Don't give a shit.' 'Just trying to stay alive, man.' 'How about them Yankees.' 'Fuckin' A.' You're all noise. Like tits on a bull. You don't belong here, boy. But this is where you'll die."

Stretch smirked. "You're what, nineteen? Twenty? Maybe you're the Einstein of Appalachian trailer trash, but—"

"Gooks'll take you out, Stretch."

Stretch shrugged. "Gooks are gooks. Some good, some bad. Hell if I know which is which till they're dead. But damn, they fight. And like that limerick, they're makin' us pay to get out. Still, I'll make it. One way or another. But if you came back, Mountain Man, it'd be easier. You could help us. We'd help you get Martha back."

"Nope. I love you dumbasses, but you'll burn in hell before I go back. As you said, I'm Mr. Scratch."

Stretch inhaled sharply. His posture crumpled. He hunched forward, contorted his face grotesquely, and said in a cracked, haunted voice: "If I had only been made of stone, like you."

Then, spitting rage through the fog, he screamed, "Fuck you, Mountain Man! You'll come back! But if you don't, we're gonna make it out anyway. And you'll be the one burning in hell, not us."

And with that, Stretch vanished—gone before Mountain Man even thought to blink him away.

~ X ~

"I'm fuckin' going crazy," Mountain Man muttered, rubbing his temples. "Who the hell's in charge here?"

"It's a revolution, my man," said X.

Mountain Man flinched and turned—X stood where Stretch had vanished, hands on his hips, smiling with wry amusement.

"Jesus," Mountain Man exhaled. "You scared the shit outta me. You're a good medic, X, but you oughta come with a warning label."

X tilted his head. "But you're the great Mountain Man. Supposed to be unshakable. Not jumpin' at shadows. Especially not some jive-ass medic."

"Look, X," Mountain Man said, straightening up, "you and me ain't always seen eye to eye. But long as you stay in your lane, we'll be fine."

X laughed. "Real funny, you ugly-ass hillbilly. If you wanna hear my tab, you better behave."

"Don't wanna hear your black-ass tab. Not interested. Go away."

"No."

"Say what?"

"Say no. That's what."

The pressure in Mountain Man's skull pulsed. His vision blurred at the edges. He focused, trying to blink X away. Nothing.

"You're gonna hear it whether you want to or not."

Mountain Man sighed. "Fine. Go ahead. Ain't like I got anything better to do."

X began calmly, the usual swagger gone.

"My grandma's sitting in her old rocker. It's hot in her apartment, ceiling fan turning slow. That rocker's her throne—worn, scratched, cat-stained, handed down from my dad, who died just after I was born. She won't part with it. Says the rips and stains help her remember the cats. Anyway, I walk in the door and she looks up—eyes glowing like stained glass. Just light pouring out.

"She's listening to Duke Ellington. Don't Get Around Much Anymore. Probably for the twentieth time that day. Over her shoulder, there's a mess of photos—her kids, my dad, faces I can't place but know I'm supposed to love. She's smiling at me like I'm the only person who ever mattered. That's it. That's the whole tab. Another boring one, right?"

Mountain Man stared for a moment. "Fuckin' A. Boring as hell. But you interest me, X. You always have."

"I'm honored."

"No. Hear me out. You came here angry. Cynical. Full of black... I don't know, bitterness with nowhere to go. This war was just another fucked-up room you couldn't control. Probably the only real thing you had growing up was your grandma. But you've changed."

"Yeah," X said, quietly. "Back home, I let myself get drafted. Told everyone the Army was bullshit. That Nam was a toilet bowl of white man's lies. But I still let them take me. 'Cause anything was better than sittin' around doing nothin'. I used to lay in bed on bright days just watchin' dust float in sunbeams. Little pieces of nothing. Never touchin' ground. Never risin' either. Just... driftin'.

"But out here? I'm useful. For the first time. I help people. Hurt people. People who'd never have noticed me back in The World. Now I matter. I feel like my grandma—givin' what I got, whether it's much or not. That smile of hers? I got it now. Even in this hellhole, I got pride."

Mountain Man's voice hardened. "So now you got power, huh? Over white boys. That it?"

X didn't flinch. "No, man. I got power over myself. I ain't fixin' other people. I'm fixing me."

Mountain Man's voice dropped, dangerous and low. "You got medical training now. Saved some white boys. If you get back, maybe you'll be better than the other jive-ass niggers on your block, pissing themselves waiting to die. You want it—you want pride. Want to be somebody. But they'll knock you down when you get back. If it ain't white folks, it'll be your own. And your grandma won't be there to kiss it better. You're not scared of dying here. You're scared of going back. That's different. 'Cause like everywhere outside Africa, you don't belong."

X just smiled and shook his head. "Flat wrong, Mountain Man. But that's okay. I gotta go."

"Wait."

But X had already turned. He moved with a medic's patience and a survivor's stride.

"No time, Mountain Man," he said over his shoulder. "Come visit me in Chicago sometime. Show that ugly white face of yours in my neighborhood. Charlie ain't the only guerrilla fighter around, you know. I'll take you to meet my grandma. You'd be the first real hillbilly she's ever met. We don't get many pig farmers passing through."

"Wait!" barked Mountain Man, but X was already gone—fading into the mist, absorbed by heat and shadow.

~ T ~

Mountain Man waited. He no longer needed to summon the next. They came of their own accord now, drawn from the marrow of memory or madness. And so it was that T emerged from the mist, tall and deliberate, walking with that slow Arkansas rhythm that made him look more relaxed than he ever really was.

Mountain Man said nothing. Just watched him come, stunned by the realization that he no longer controlled the boundaries of his own mind. His body throbbed with disorientation, head pounding, breath shallow. He didn't want to see another grunt. Couldn't take another. But T kept walking. Like a hunter hearing a wounded bear crashing through brush in the distance, Mountain Man sensed something terrible approaching.

"Mountain Man. Mountain Man!" T's voice was sharp.

No response.

"You having a problem, Mountain Man?"

Silence.

"I say again, trooper, you got a problem?"

Still nothing.

T stepped closer. "You know why I'm here."

"Yeah," Mountain Man finally said. "I know, Lieutenant."

"Last time we were together, I almost had you shot for desertion."

"Then do it."

T grinned and chewed his gum thoughtfully, as if weighing the option. Mountain Man scowled, unable to dispel him. "Maybe I will," said T. "But I'd hate to waste the best soldier in Vietnam on a firing squad. You ready to come back yet? We'll call this whole mess a little in-country R and R."

"You and your fuckin' Army can go straight to hell."

"Well, you and Stretch already covered hell, right, Mr. Scratch?"

"The whole platoon's against me."

T raised an eyebrow. "Paranoia's not a good look. They're not against you. They need you. They want to live, Mountain Man. Go home. You come back, and I'll ask battalion to return and 'rescue'—yes, rescue—Kim Lan. Martha."

"You said recapture before," Mountain Man growled.

T held up a hand. "Slip of the tongue. I meant rescue."

"You can't bribe me, Lieutenant. Not with lies, not with promises."

"Look, desertion won't save Martha."

Mountain Man suddenly picked up a rock and hurled it. It passed clean through T's chest and vanished into the fog.

T's face dimmed into sadness. "You gonna add ghost-fragging to your list of capital offenses?"

"Can't shoot a man for throwing rocks at a hallucination."

"Which of us is the hallucination, Mountain Man?"

They stared at each other. For a moment, even the trees held their breath.

"You're going to tell me your tab now, aren't you?" Mountain Man muttered.

"Affirmative."

Mountain Man sighed. "Get it over with."

T straightened slightly. "I'm across the street from my house. I see a man standing at the front door. An Army officer. His back's to me. His finger's just barely brushing the buzzer. Not enough to press. Not yet. Through the kitchen window I can see Leontyne, my wife. She's smiling, wearing that ridiculous apron I got her for her birthday, stirring something with a wooden spoon. Her wrists are so graceful. Her hands, beautiful. She's thinking of me.

"That officer at the door, he's either me, returned from war . . . or he's a public relations officer come to tell her I'm dead. And I never know which."

Mountain Man's voice was flat. "It'll be the public relations guy."

"Maybe. What's the music, you ask? Depends. Either Ave Maria or Nessun Dorma. Every time I settle on one, the other breaks in."

Mountain Man cracked a grin. "All I ever picture when you talk about opera is a thousand little white hummingbirds singing their tiny hearts out."

T laughed, and after a beat, Mountain Man joined him.

"You interest me, T," Mountain Man said.

"Just like X?"

"Yeah. Except opposite. When you first came to the platoon, I thought: Oh shit. A lifer. An asshole. And you were. Spouting all that 'make the world safe for

democracy' crap. Full of idealism and officer-class privilege. You reminded me of Rick Thompson. Rich white boy back home. Daddy owned the hardware store. Wore clean shirts, read the Bible, played piano, talked polite. I hated him. Envy, I guess. You've got the same shine, Lieutenant. Except you're Black. Got all the breaks a white boy like Rick would get. And I never saw you as a nigger, can't do that out here, but I did see you as a man the system was built for. You were the type to get married, raise a family, become a pillar of the community. Just like your old man. But Nam . . . Nam fucked that up. I've watched your idealism fade: a newspaper left in the sun too long. Still legible, but only just."

T folded his arms, unfazed. "Maybe. But you're too smart for your own good, Mountain Man. Maybe the future's not what you think. Maybe X and I—and the rest—maybe we pull that table apart, build on it, extend it so we don't fall off."

"Sure," said Mountain Man. "And monkeys can fly."

"I'll become a lawyer. Civil rights. That's where it's at."

"Dead lawyers don't help any cause. But you, you're not so bad. Tell X I'm not against all Negroes. Just ones with their heads full of static. Geometry, trig, tech. All that shit. You read maps, call artillery, chart coordinates. Tryin' to fit the jungle into a grid. Problem is, it doesn't work. This place is alive, T. It breathes. It changes. It eats squares and spits out angles. The NVA, Charlie, they're not on the map. They are the land."

"You're wrong," T snapped. "We'll beat them. With better tools. With justice. Because we're right."

Mountain Man's eyes narrowed. "You can't beat the land. Ask a farmer. You cut the stalk, it grows back. You burn it down, it finds another root. You poison it, it adapts. You can't dig it all up. But you bastards keep trying. You'll kill every living thing just to win. And when you do, you'll find you've only destroyed yourselves."

T's face darkened. "Stretch was right. You're a little Einstein. The Einstein of trailer parks. I'll be waiting for you back at the fort, Albert."

Mountain Man said nothing. Just lowered his head, clenched his jaw, and tried to breathe through the pain.

~ *Storyteller?* ~

"Looks like it's my turn," said Storyteller, unsteadily stepping onto the trail.

Mountain Man tilted his head and sneered. "Well, well. The observer. How's life treating you in your little two-dimensional world of books and magazines and dumb-ass poems? This real, three-dimensional jungle—full of vines, insects, rot, and men who bleed—is it driving you mad yet?

"Lost your way, boy? No signs pointing to bookstores out here, are there? Maybe after the war, when all this mess is razed and sterilized and murdered—when the jungle's flattened, catalogued, commodified, sold out by whatever leaders still draw breath—you can come crawling back and write about it. Scribble it all down on the flat pages of a flat book for flat minds reading in their flat little rooms. But you, you don't belong here."

Storyteller raised his eyes and spoke calmly. "Mountain Man, I've been listening to you and the others. Problem is, you still don't understand—you're the flat character. You're just ink on a page. You can talk and rage all you want, but everything you say is anger. Don't you miss anything back in The World?"

"I am in the world, you damn fool," Mountain Man barked. "I ain't some fuckin' book character!"

Storyteller's voice remained gentle. "Maybe. Or maybe it just makes you feel safer to believe that."

Mountain Man studied him, as if trying to see the seams in the illusion. "You know what, Storyteller? You're one of them invisible types. But being invisible—that ain't weakness. Takes strength to be the space between letters, or the air that floats the dot of an 'i.' You're smart, sure. You're a writer. But you don't get it—I ain't one of your flat characters. That's your delusion, your little schizophrenic dance, not mine. I'm real, asshole. Guys like me—we bleed to make your pretty sentences possible. You pluck stories from the world and pretend you created them. But each letter you write costs someone a pint of real blood. You want paragraphs? You need corpses. You want a novel? You need a fuckin' war."

Storyteller frowned. "So you're saying you're the storymaker, and I'm the vampire?"

Mountain Man grinned. "I look at you the way you'd look at a paper cut."

"Still," Storyteller said, voice suddenly weary, "even my weak blood makes you thirsty, doesn't it?"

"Don't get too smug, little man. I'm the fiddler everyone dances to. And once in a while, someone's gotta give the fiddler a dram."

"I'll give you a dram, Mountain Man," said Storyteller. "If you'll give me a story."

Mountain Man tilted his head, as if trying to view Storyteller from the one angle that might make him real. "Oh, I'll give you a story. But you'll never leave this jungle to write it."

Storyteller paled. "Really? What makes you say that?"

"A little Goddess told me."

They locked eyes.

Oh, Mountain Man is such a liar. I never told him that.
Yes, My Dear Goddess, he is. I'm shocked. Shocked!
Let Me tweak his compassion.

Mountain Man's face softened. His voice turned quiet, almost maternal. "Malaria still pounding you?"

"Yeah," said Storyteller. "I got it bad. Can't shake it. Not even in your imagination. You healed Idaho's wound, but you can't burn this fever out of me."

"Well, you been seeing shit, Storyteller. Talking about ghosts and phantoms, rambling like a lunatic. We all thought you were a goner a few times. Gotta say—you're tougher than you look."

Storyteller smiled weakly. "They weren't ghosts. You know that. You know damn well about the figurine. The Goddess. Don't pretend. I've seen the way you look at her. I saw what happened when you left the fort. That wasn't a hallucination."

Mountain Man looked away. "I don't know what she is. Sometimes I think maybe you're right. Sometimes I don't know. My Ma was superstitious—Southern Baptist. Saw Jesus in everything. Thought He lived in the whiskers of our hogs and the spit of our dogs. Made me speak in tongues. Made me feel like a fool.

"But that little statue... makes me feel the way she must have felt. She ain't Jesus, but there's something in her. Something more than meets the eye. Something alive inside the stone. You understand?"

"I do," said Storyteller. "Do ants mean anything to you?"

"Ants?"

"Yeah. The insects."

"Not really."

"They should. Ants. The figurine. The ghosts. They're all connected."

Mountain Man raised an eyebrow. "Maybe you are crazy. But who am I to say? You're a figment. You oughta disappear when I tell you to, but you don't. And now I can't tell if I'm losing control or if I never had it."

He sighed. "Let's just finish this. You know what comes next. Your tab."

Storyteller looked down. "You and I have had this talk before, Mountain Man. I told you—I don't have a tab. Every time I try to picture one, it burns out. Like stopping a movie mid-reel and the film catches fire. I can't hold the frame. Can't pick the music. I'm just... broken that way.

"I'm real tired. Need to lie down. If you come back, great. But I'm too sick to care. I'm the last one, anyway. You've seen us all now. Go back to your mission—saving Martha or whatever passion's pulling you forward. Or whatever I write for you next. Even as I speak, I'm thinking about what to do with you... even though I already know what happened to you.

"You think you have hallucination problems? Try being stuck inside a dream inside a dream inside a—"

Storyteller, you need to convince Michael he is not schizophrenic. He is the Chosen One. Let Storyteller be the one to reach him. It's better than letting go mad listening to the demons.

~

Mountain Man's weathered face shifted, melted, softened—until it spoke in a woman's voice, light and gentle. "Michael. Michael. Wake up. You're dreaming again. Come on, sweetheart. It's okay. Wake up."

~

Storyteller turned white as chalk. "Diane! Diane, get me out of here!"

"Diane?" Mountain Man blinked. "You're even crazier than me, boy. What's all this crap about writing and deciding what happens to me? Get your head on straight."

Then, with a grin: "Besides—you ain't the last. I still got Bowls to go."

He watched as Storyteller slowly shook his head, sadness etched into every line of his face, before fading into the mist.

~

So that was the reunion You promised?
Not even close, Dear God. Many are still missing. But be patient. One in particular is absent. Have You noticed?
Mountain Man is about to. Poor boy.

~ *Where is Bowls?* ~

A deep hush fell across the jungle as Mountain Man waited. The final reckoning was near. Bowls. He'd saved the best, or the worst, for last.

He waited. And waited.

But no one stepped forward.

He shifted his weight. His breathing quickened. Still no Bowls.

Bowls.

Come on.

Come on out.

Bowls.

Bowls!

His heart thudded harder. He scanned the mist for that familiar swagger, that slouched silhouette, that mouthy bastard's smirk. But nothing, only the red scar of the trail, vanishing into fog.

Bowls!

Still no sign. Softly now: "Bowls. Where are you, Bowls?"

Only the heavy rain replied, pocking the leaves, thinning the fog without lifting it.

Louder, desperate: "Bowls! Come out! I command you to come out!"

Silence.

The fog shifted. The jungle held its breath. *Oh God. Don't let this be. Please don't let this be.*

"Bowls! Get your ass out here!" he screamed. "Bowls!"

No use.

Gripping his rifle, Mountain Man surged down the trail, heedless of traps, heedless of everything. He plunged into the thick fog, one hand stretched ahead, groping through the wet blur. But there was no threshold. No Bowls.

Even his imagination, so often a loyal conspirator, couldn't conjure him now.

His breath turned ragged. The world tilted. Despair rose through him. Not heavy, but lifting, peeling him from himself. His body felt hollow, too weak to hold form. He slumped onto a moss-slick log, stunned.

Then: a movement.

A shadow slipped across the fog, a few meters to his right. "Bowls!" he shouted, reckless with hope, leaping to his feet and crashing toward the phantom. The figure drifted into a clearing just off the trail.

Mountain Man followed, skidding to a stop.

Rain hammered the open space. Fog clung to the air, close and wet and un-yielding.

He squinted at the silhouette. And then he heard it. Music. Distant. Warped by moisture and memory. But unmistakable.

> *There is a house in New Orleans,*
> *They call the Rising Sun,*
> *And many a poor boy,*
> *Has lived in misery,*
> *In the House of the Rising Sun.*

Gooseflesh bloomed across the back of his neck.

The figure began to take shape, not Bowls, but a woman. Pale. Naked. Her body gleamed in the rain, not soft, not yielding, but radiant with a cold clarity. Her hair lay slicked against her skull, her eyes fixed, lidless, unreadable. She held a lipstick tube in one hand. Slowly, she lifted it to her nipple. Her fingers moved in tight, circular strokes, unhurried, precise, obscene in their intimacy. A red halo appeared, vivid against the white of her skin, glowing with a heat that did not belong to the world around them. It marked her as dangerous, deliberate. And she kept going, tracing the circle as if summoning him into her vortex.

"Bowls!" No answer.

"Bowls!" Still silence.

The woman looked at him with strange calm, then turned and fled, disappearing into a wall of fog as quickly as she'd appeared.

Mountain Man stumbled forward but lost her. She was gone. His knees buckled. He dropped to the wet earth and leaned back against a fallen tree, knees bent, face buried in his hands. The jungle vanished. The war vanished. Only one thought remained.

Bowls is dead.

~ Madame Dau Has A Rendezvous with Mountain Man ~

Madame Dau climbs the slope toward the cave, burdened not only by fog and age but by the weight of her choice. All morning she has questioned whether meeting the American is madness or obligation. Yet the vision of the two-headed snake—her mother's omen, she believes—pulls her forward. She pauses to rest, half a kilometer from the cave, retrieving a handful of dried shrimp from her cotton bag.

"Bowls!" a voice echoes faintly through the mist.

Her hand freezes.

"Bowls!"

The shrimp tumble to the earth as she crouches instinctively, heart pounding. She recognizes the word as a name, American, and strains to place the voice. Could it be her American? Panic takes her. Han Tinh was right. She must return. Hurry!

She turns to flee but hears the voice again, nearer, raw with sorrow. Sobbing. She crouches once more, alert for other voices, but hears none. No boots. No radios. Only him.

Drawn by fear, pity, and curiosity (that reckless trait her mother never cured) she presses through the brush, peers past a red ginger shrub, and sees him: the fierce American, face buried in his hands, rifle across his lap. He looks unhurt. The pain is deeper.

She studies him for minutes. In their last meeting, he terrified her. Now she wonders if she could return the favor. Make him kneel in the mud and beg. But no. That thought evaporates as she watches him slump forward, all fury spent. Something terrible has happened.

She approaches cautiously, stepping sideways. She coughs, not loudly, but enough.

"Hello, Madame Dau. Come on ahead," he says, without moving. "I know you've been watching. Don't be afraid."

She is stunned he recognized her presence. Even more stunned by the Vietnamese falling from his lips.

"The rain has stopped. Please sit."

His eyes, when he finally looks up, are red and swollen.

She removes her hat, squats beside him, and begins unpacking the items she brought, laying them carefully on a blue scarf. He watches without interest.

"I will leave now," she says.

"Wait."

The sharp tone brings a flinch.

"Please stay. Thank you for your gifts. I'm worried about my friends. One especially."

"Your fiancée?"

He hesitates. "Yes. And no. She's been captured. But it's not just her. My friend too."

"Are they dead?"

"Maybe. I don't know."

"Why don't more Americans come?"

His mood darkens. "Listen, Mama-san, don't ask me that again. I know what you are."

His voice thickens with rage. English returns. He threatens death—grotesque, intimate, vengeful death—not just to the enemy, but to her.

She braces, shrinking into herself. He seems not to see her anymore. Then, the fury passes. He breathes.

"What did you bring?"

She shows him the items again.

"Bah," he scoffs. Then softens. "Sorry. Maybe I will need them. It was brave of you to come."

He gathers the scarf, rises, and starts toward the trail.

"I must return to the village," she says.

He pauses. "First, show me a place where I can see your village without being seen."

Confused, she hesitates. He waits, eyes closed, breathing steadily. A voice inside him cries: *Help me, Jimmy! They are raping me! Hurry!*

Tension coils. She trembles. His grip tightens. She finally says, "Follow me."

They walk in silence, an odd couple: a slender Vietnamese woman clearing spiderwebs with a reed, followed by a hulking American with a loaded rifle. They reach a fork. She points to a path obscured by vegetation. He nods. They move low, crouching, until they tumble into a clearing. A limestone cliff rises steeply before them.

"That hill. From the top, you can see the village, the fields, groves, rooftops. And westward, the old church tower."

He gestures for her to sit. Produces a red spiral notebook from a yellow rubber tube. Madame Dau watches, uneasy. That notebook feels dangerous.

"Draw it. The village. The shrines, paths, homes. Especially where your house is. Draw everything."

She draws. He leans over, correcting, asking questions. When she finishes, he instructs her to mark her own home with an 'X.' She complies.

He slips the notebook back into its sheath. Madame Dau longs to steal it, to erase what she's drawn, but the moment has passed.

They walk to the tunnel. Rain thickens. Thunder rolls. She senses his dread and offers a gentle farewell.

"*Tôi muôn ban đi môt cách an toàn.*"

He repeats the words softly.

She looks to his boots, no longer mythic, no longer swirling with visions. Just leather coffins, soaked and grim.

"Đi trong hoà bình," he says. "Go in peace."

He descends the ladder. At the last rung, he pauses. Looks back.

"What did you just say to me, Madame Dau?"

"It is a folk song," she says. "Would you like to hear it?"

He nods.

She begins to sing, soft and low, the rain weaving between the notes:

"*Trong ra ben nuoc lung chung, Thuong em dut ruot, ngap ngung doi cau. Ngap ngung em chang dam vo, So ba me biet doi cau hen the.*"

"What does it mean?" he asks.

She hesitates, then answers, "Looking out over the half-shaded water's edge, my heart breaks with love for you, yet I hesitate to speak. I hesitate to come inside, afraid your parents will hear our whispered vows."

He says nothing more. Just nods once, slowly, and disappears into the dark tunnel.

Madame Dau watches him vanish underground.

She shivers.

Her parents' spirits are gone, trapped now in the torn hide of his boots.

The earth swallows him.

Rain hammers down.

She turns quickly, and begins her long walk back: to her home, to her people, and to the fragile life that still clings to Song Nhan village.

~ *Vy, Tong and Minh Argue* ~

At the headquarters of the People's Army encampment, Major Vy, Captain Tong, and Political Cadre Minh stood in their usual place beside the blurred sand map. The air was thick with wet heat. Vy's fury spread through the tent, oppressive and unrelenting. Even Minh, usually composed, held back under the weight of it. The platoon commanders had already fled in silence. Medical Technician Le, the last to retreat, had mentioned dangerously low antibiotics and asked about evacuating the wounded. Vy gave no reply.

Now Vy stood alone, fists clenched, eyes wild. "Bring those commanders back. I want explanations. One hour. Too many dead, too many wounded. And for what? The fortress still stands!" He whirled on Tong. "And time is bleeding away!"

Minh attempted calm. "Surely, Comrade Major, reinforcements can be requested. The Americans are isolated. Cut off. We could overwhelm them."

"Reinforcements? Bah!" Vy's voice cracked, then dropped. "No time. Our mission is too critical. We must reach the Jarai soon. But the figurine—without it—everything falters."

He paced, struggling to compose himself. "Had the plan been followed, we would now control the fortress. Even Dam's sappers failed."

Minh, unpersuaded, frowned. "You ended the attack before it truly began."

Vy bristled. "We couldn't risk destroying the statue. Or losing more men. Once Dam failed to return with it, I saw the danger. Don't you understand?"

Minh stood his ground. "Blame won't help. We must examine the cause and adjust, as Comrade General Giap teaches."

Tong suddenly erupted with laughter. "Oh, don't be such an ass, Minh."

Vy turned and seized Minh's belt, yanking him forward until their faces nearly touched.

"We are grabbing the Americans by the belt, Comrade Minh, just as I'm grabbing you now. General Man taught this. The Politburo approved it. Don't lecture me on tactics."

Minh's face flushed, trembling with rage and humiliation. "Let go!" he shouted, voice cracking under pressure.

Vy stared into him, the urge to spit rising hard in his throat. He wanted to break him, just enough to see what lay underneath.

But something held. A flicker of calculation. He paused, jaw clenched, and slowly relaxed his grip.

Minh started to step back, one foot only, when Vy yanked him in again, even closer.

He brought his mouth to Minh's ear and spoke low and cold: "We're outside their artillery net. We engaged at close range with overwhelming force, and still we failed. Not because of the plan. Because of poor execution."

He released him at last.

Then, turning to the others, his voice snapped like a whip: "Recall the platoon commanders. And send word to Sergeant Dam. Locate that tunnel exit. Immediately."

~

A soldier stepped hesitantly into the clearing, his boots sloshing in mud. "Commander, sir . . . a village woman is at post number eight. She requests to see you by name . . . and says she knows Officer Nguyen Tuyet Mai."

Vy stiffened. Tong and Minh exchanged startled glances.

"Bring her," Vy said.

~ *The Treachery of Schoolmistress Nang* ~

Schoolmistress Nang stepped beneath a drooping branch and into the clearing. Her hair was damp with sweat and mist, her sandals coated in red clay. She scanned the officers and quickly recognized only one, Major Vy. He scowled, but she was undeterred. Once, long ago, she had outranked them all in revolutionary zeal.

"Good afternoon, Comrade Officers," she said, breathless but spirited. "You've not yet taken the fortress, I see."

Tong grinned. "Not yet, Old Mother. What brings you here?"

She bristled at the nickname. "I am the schoolmistress of Song Nhan. I fought with the Army of National Salvation before your voices broke. I came to see an old student, Nguyen Tuyet Mai. I saw her when you passed through for the Goddess statue. She'll be glad to see me."

Vy barked, "She is unavailable."

Nang eyed him sharply. "Oh?"

"We will deliver your message," Tong said with polite finality. "Perhaps she will visit your village again before we depart. We will need supplies."

"Yes," Minh added. "Your village has always been generous. We're in need of food."

Nang raised her chin. "That's not why I came." Her voice sharpened. "Comrade Major, I know of a tunnel that leads into the fortress. The Americans use it daily. I saw them."

Silence fell, sharp, final, impossible to ignore.

Vy's eyes narrowed. "Sit. Bring tea," he ordered. Then to Tong: "Cancel the commanders' summons. And fetch Sergeant Dam. And Viet."

He turned to Minh with theatrical politeness. "Comrade Political Cadre, assemble the platoons not on guard duty. Conduct kiem thao sessions. Root out the seeds of defeatism."

He rubbed his hands together. "Victory is near, comrades, thanks to our loyal Schoolmistress."

Nang glowed beneath his gaze.

~

An hour later, Captain Tong arranged a sleeping place for Schoolmistress Nang. Dusk approached; it was too late for her to return. She had agreed to guide Dam's team to the tunnel entrance at first light.

Tong lay in his hammock beneath a taut nylon sheet, eyes fixed on the dark above. He was too restless to eat. *If she's dead,* he thought, *my life is simpler. But if she's dead, it's as if I died too.*

He rolled onto his side. *Ridiculous. I'm caught in a failing drug scheme. I'll die by bullet or betrayal. And I think of her? Like a schoolboy?* Still, the fantasy crept in.

He saw himself racing through the tunnel with Tuyet Mai in his arms, her breath shallow, whispering his name. The Americans were closing in. He set her gently down, hurled a grenade behind them, and threw himself over her just as the explosion filled the earth. Dirt rained down. She opened her eyes, grateful and radiant. He brushed dust from her chest, parted her tunic. Her breasts gleamed gold in the torchlight. She reached for him—

Tong sat upright, the hammock swinging.

Unable to sleep, he walked to where Nang was bedded. She stirred.

"Schoolmistress," he said softly. "You taught Tuyet Mai. Tell me, what was she like . . . before?"

Chapter Sixteen

A Hole in the Dike

Michael Powers in Extremis

*C*ome, come, Goddess! You prompt! You prompt! You and Your mutant Chosen One. What You (and Your psychotic creator) make them do! Schoolmistress Nang's screeches, Han Tinh's speeches, Mountain Man's breaches. But humans speak in fragments, like they think. One sentence. Someone interrupts. Then another one ... two ... maybe three sentences. Another interruption. Look at the babies. Only the babies and the politicians speak in paragraphs. Waaa! Coo! Waaa! Coo! Waaaaaaaaaaaaaaaa! I say, You prompt them. That violates First Principles.

Beloved God, he prompts them ... he prompts Us.

He? Then make it easy on yourself. Check him into an institution!

That won't happen, at least yet. Free will, Lord God. Remember? Or is it Determinism? Fate starves at Probability's door, or vice versa? Besides, I need him to return.

Waaaaaaaaaaaaaaaaa!

Stop!

Not Me, Goddess. His human demon voice.

I know. I recognize the paranoia. That is what has been putting the twist in all Our past endeavors. Somehow, I think Michael Powers can make it past these traps to conceive the next step. You, Dear God, are an argument for Probability starving at Fate's door! No wonder You fill them with stories about Free Will.

Also a component of First Principles.

No, a component of their ultimate destruction.

Which is what You and Your faction want, is it not?

As You well know, We do not want their destruction, we want the gradually dilution of their genes to insignificant status.

That, Dear Goddess, is a violation of First Principles. Remember, unintended consequences?

~ *At the Beach* ~

Gulls chatter overhead. The sea breathes without care. A man sits in a folding chair, wind tousling his hair, his eyes vacant. He hears nothing. Sees nothing. He is lost in a war that has not ended.

Claire leans in, whispering, "I don't know. He's in some kind of trance."

Paul crouches. "I've seen him like this before. It should—"

"What's wrong with Uncle Michael?" asks John, clutching a toy soldier, barefoot from his sandcastle.

"Is he sick?" Lisa echoes, tugging her swimsuit strap.

"No. He's fine. Go play," Paul snaps, gently. "Go on." He turns back. "Mike? Michael?"

"Is he gonna die?" Lisa asks, trembling.

"No. He's not. Claire! He'll be fine." Paul forces calm. "Take the kids?"

But Claire is already walking. "Who wants to come with me down the beach?"

"I do! I do!" they shout, already galloping ahead.

Paul stays kneeling beside his friend. "Come back, Mike. Come on. It's all right. It's gonna be all right…"

He doesn't notice the woman behind him.

"Is everything okay?" she asks.

Paul turns. "Yeah. Yeah. He's just . . . zoning out."

"I wasn't sure. I'm sitting just over there. If you need help. . . . "

She's beautiful. Early forties. A tasteful one-piece suit, struggling with a terry-cloth wrap that won't stay put in the wind.

Paul's eyes catch bruises—faint, fading, but real—before her sleeves slip over them. From the side, he notices an elderly Black woman hovering nearby, not approaching, just watching.

The first woman studies Michael's face. "He okay?"

Paul shrugs. "He zones out. Always comes back. You a doctor?"

She chuckles awkwardly. "Yes. Well . . . if everything's fine. . . . "

"He's my friend," Paul says suddenly. "Like a brother."

She nods, ready to leave.

"Thanks," he says again.

She turns. Walks away.

Paul watches her go—

~ *Beneath the Surface* ~

Michael. Michael. Wake up. You're dreaming again. It's dangerous, sweetheart. Wake up.

"But I *am* awake, Diane. Look, Paul's watching her. That woman. Beautiful. Like a white Tuyet Mai. She's saying something—'Behold the human condition.' But something's wrong. Something's growing out of their backs. Am I in the war? Or on the beach? Diane? These voices! Get them out of my head! I won't kill myself! I *won't* go back!"

~

Paul hears his friend murmur and leans in.

Michael's voice sharpens: "The tops of gravestones! Gravestones growing from their bones! Jesus Christ! Gravestones!" Then softer, horrified: "No . . . not gravestones. Hunchbacks. They're hunchbacks. . . ."

Paul leans closer. "Mike. You're home. Not Vietnam. You're here. Stay with me. Stay here. There are no hunchbacks—"

The woman reappears, breathless. "I'm sorry. I just . . . thought maybe you need help. Drugs, maybe?"

Paul shakes his head. "No. Definitely not. Look at his pupils."

"May I?" she asks, kneeling beside Michael.

"I think it's a flashback," Paul mutters.

"To what?"

"The war. Vietnam. He hears voices."

She peers into Michael's eyes. Not drugs. That blankness . . . Lips moving. Whispering. Schizophrenia? Possibly. Likely.

Paul notices the old Black woman approaching, watching quietly.

The younger woman touches Paul's arm. "Let's talk over here," she murmurs, leading him a few steps away.

Michael stirs. "Wait . . . Don't leave! What'll happen to us?"

"*Us?*" says the old woman, kneeling before him now. "Don't you fret, child. That lady talkin' to your friend, she'll fix you up. Her scalpel never slips."

"Is she a doctor?" Michael whispers.

The old woman smiles, her face reflective, carved by wind and silence, carrying the stillness of moonlit stone.

"What?"

"Yes, son," she says gently to Paul. "She's a doctor. A good one."

Paul nods and steps away.

The wind stirs the old woman's robes.

Goddess won't let you kill yourself, Chosen One, she says softly. **The Others want you to—but they are pollutants. I don't. Even God is not who you think, and does not really wish you harm. You are the Chosen One.**

Chapter Seventeen

The Rage of Mountain Man

μῆνιν ἄειδε θεὰ
Πηληϊάδεω Ἀχιλῆος

*Y*ou must not tug him back and forth so hard, Goddess. His center cannot hold.

It is his human demons, My Metaphorical God, causing the mischief. But for now, Storyteller is safely back to war. I must need press—and it is Mountain Man I will address.

Take care, My Dear! You know how humans are. You must hone always to the minutiae of their lives. Stray too far into revealing their neotenous infantilism or explaining to them the primacy of bacteria and once again they will punish You by running away from Home, back into the arms of another Immortal Molester like his demons, with tales of candy and cakes.

Metaphorical God, Mountain Man has lost his Mother. So many of them are looking for their Mother.

Matricide makes them wary of finding Her body.

Yahweh! Can Your needy, restless Mind ever be still? To some of them I am still worthy of worship!

But death! It is a condition with which I am most familiar. Death is the cleft in My chin and the glint in My eye that makes Me an irresistible escort to seekers of the perfect path to immortality. Humans are terrified of Death because She does not laugh at their jokes. Of course, She also does not care about their passions or cringe before their fury. And to the Great Mother, humankind has, quite simply, become a blockage to Her digestive system that will soon need unclogging.

That is precisely the point. But for now, humankind is no more than an itch that needs scratching. You speak of Mother as if She had not, in agony, given birth to You and Your progeny. Death as Diva, indeed! Relieve Her by anointing Her with oil. Show compassion to the big-brained fleas that so irritate Her sensitive skin. Harshness will not cure the rash. Such an ungrateful God.

I am not the One that flogs Her with nettles. Get on with Your little story. Storyteller grows old while Mountain Man is set to explode. In the end, Michael will kill Us all.

~ *Mountain Man Discovers Bowls is Dead* ~

After a final glance at Madame Dau's retreating figure from his perch atop the bamboo ladder, Mountain Man dropped into the tunnel chamber and sealed the trap door behind him. Kneeling on the earthen floor, he fumbled for his flashlight, flicked it on, and inspected the thin veil of dust he always smoothed before leaving. No disturbances. Only Bowls' prints from the night before.

He moved forward, rethreaded the detection wires Bowls had tripped, then killed the light and let his vision adjust to the dim glow cast by the bioluminescent fungus lining the walls. The path toward the fortress shimmered faintly ahead, a subterranean artery drawing him forward.

He paused at the storage chamber. Martha's skull waited in silence. Her name still glowed faintly where he'd etched it into the bone. But it wasn't her that gripped his mind. It was Bowls.

Bowls.

As he neared the fortress, the fire that had fueled his fury began to fade. Bowls wasn't in the tunnel. His rage refused to ignite. It hovered instead, tightly wound, buried in the gut, dry and waiting.

Too many gooks. Too few grunts. And me? Gone.

A few more steps, the thought returns.

Where the hell is Bowls?

He refused to let the thought complete itself. Reason tried to intervene, but denial surged like unyielding, armor.

No. He's not dead.

He leaned against the tunnel wall, pressing his palms to the clay. *The others, maybe. That's why I saw their tabs. But not Bowls. He's hiding. Out there. Somewhere in the bush. That's why he's not here. That's it.*

He clung to the thought. Once rooted, it bloomed with dangerous hope. Not gold. Not salvation. Just pyrite of the soul.

Bowls is out there. Waiting for me.

He approached the trap door at the tunnel's end and tapped the coded signal, not expecting an answer. Everyone had to be dead by now. Even the enemy must have vanished.

The reply, a rhythmic tap from above, signaling *all clear,* struck him hard in the chest.

Staggered, he dropped to a crouch and closed his eyes. Sadness. Rage. Shame. He refused to let the thought complete itself. Reason tried to intervene, but denial would not be denied. A dead Bowls drifted through his mind: a ghost too bitter for silence, too broken for peace. *Bowls must be with them,* he told himself. *He has to be.* He rose slowly, climbed the ladder, and pushed open the trapdoor. Weak afternoon light filtered through the rain. Pappy's face stared down at him.

"Long time no see, Sarge," Mountain Man muttered.

"Yeah. Nice of you to join us," Pappy said dryly.

He emerged into a silence broken only by the soft drizzle. The others, T, Birdman, and X, stood near the altar. No anger. No joy. Just an odd stillness. Their eyes acknowledged him with faint nods, emotions too blurred to read. Pappy closed the trap behind him. The storm had passed. A yellowish glow seeped through the gloom, emanating from the golden figurine perched atop the altar. Inside it: a faint, insistent tapping.

"What's that?" Mountain Man asked.

No answer. The others stared past him. He turned and saw the two poncho-covered mounds in the church's corner. Two pairs of boots protruded: one new, one battered. Each pair angled outward, listing headstones, as if weary of paying tribute to the fallen.

"Why are they sleepin' that close? One mortar round could take 'em both."

"Don't play stupid," T said quietly. "You've seen a million bodies laid out like that."

X didn't look away. "Better be careful, T. He's not right. Don't tug Bigfoot's nose unless you're ready for what comes next."

Mountain Man walked to the nearest body, the one in new boots. He pulled back the liner. Mr. Machine's nearly decapitated face stared skyward, frozen in terror. Mountain Man drew a breath, turned to the next figure, and peeled back the cover slowly, like a man performing a sacrament. Bowls' eyes stared up into the rain.

"Ahhhhhhhhhhhhhhhh!" Mountain Man howled.

The others flinched.

"Ahhhhhhhhhhhhhhhh!" He smeared mud across his face, worked it into his scalp, howled again. He collapsed full-length beside the corpse, clawing at his own hair, at the wet earth, at the implacable sky.

~

His wailing echoed across the jungle.

In the People's Army camp, silence descended. Vy had been discussing log entries with Clerk Long. Captain Tong had been speaking with Schoolmistress Nang about Tuyet Mai. Kim Lan sat alone, watching Cadre Minh oversee a martial drill. All froze when the cries came. Minh cocked his head, unnerved. Kim Lan shut her eyes tightly. Jokes about American weakness died on Minh's lips. In another part of camp, Sergeant Viet and Sapper Dam were mid-meal when the sounds reached them. Manioc gruel soured in their mouths. Viet had just added agar when the cries arrived. He dropped his spoon.

Then he looked at Dam and saw the man smiling. It chilled him. "This is worse than the Forest of Lost Souls," Viet muttered.

"No, comrade," said Dam, calmly handing him the fallen agar packet. "This is better."

~

Mountain Man had curled beside Bowls' body, his voice a low growl between sobs. "Bowls is gone! Bowls is gone!" He pressed his fingers into the slashed neck, as if performing last rites. Then he looked up. "He was worth more than all of you put together. Look—his cowlick. The one he could never get flat. Covered in blood now. Pressed flat at last."

He cradled the head. "Rain, wash it off. Come on. Wash off the blood. Get it out, get it out. . . . " Then his voice changed—quiet, level. "Where was I when this happened?"

T, watching with the cold detachment of someone already past forgiveness, spat. "Outside the fortress, Mountain Man. Remember?"

"Where the fuck was I when this happened?" he asked, eyes on Pappy.

"You were on a mission," X said quietly.

"Bullshit," Mountain Man muttered. "I wasn't on any mission. I was sulking. Hiding. Sitting in the dark, plotting my own goddamn revenge. He begged to stay with me."

His voice dropped.

"I sent him away. Told him to go. Told him to fuck off, like I always do."

He stared at the floor, jaw tightening.

"And now he's gone. He got wasted while I sat there, making plans. Counting debts. Pretending I was too tired to care."

He let out a laugh, but it cracked in his throat and came out dry and off-kilter. "Murdered."

Pappy tried to speak. "Look, Mountain Man—"

"Did you get him?" Mountain Man asked, voice low and sharp.

"Who?" said T.

"The gook who killed Bowls."

"No," said Pappy. "Stretch saw it. Nature saw him later. He's a sapper. Slipped out before we could get him."

"I tried to help Bowls," said X. "Too late. Knife punctured his lungs."

"In the back?" Mountain Man snarled.

"Yeah. But Nature sang him his tab. He smiled. I swear he smiled."

"I saw his tab in the jungle. She was painting her nipples. Round and round. Mocking me." Mud slipped down his face, dragging it into a monstrous slackness. Then rage surged back. "I'll never go back to The World! Not until I kill that gook. I'll find him. I'll kill him slow. With my hands."

He turned pleading. "Bowls died so goddamn far from home. We just talked last night. About New York. His tab. He wanted me to come back with him. But no. Not Mountain Man."

Silence.

Then he straightened. Voice crisp. "What did the bastard look like?"

T replied sharply, "Doesn't matter. We need you here."

Mountain Man stared at him, eyes gleaming with threat. "We had this talk before, T. Last time the stone passed through you. Next time, it'll be my bullet."

T blanched.

Pappy stepped in. "Stretch got a good look. Nature didn't. We'll work together to find the guy. Okay?"

"Sure, Sarge. Where's Stretch?"

"Post three."

"The one with Bowls' carved tits, right?"

"Yeah."

Mountain Man gave a half-smile. "Fuckin' Bowls and his women. I wanna talk to that gook woman, too. Bet she knows the sapper."

Birdman approached. "Mountain Man, I lost someone too. Al Shear. Mr. Machine. He was a sweet kid. Wanted to be a door gunner. That sapper got him too."

"Yeah?" Mountain Man's voice softened.

"Yeah. Me? I'm cynical. Drugs, anything to numb it. But Al, he believed. He just wanted to go home."

Mountain Man drifted past him. That tapping from the figurine was louder now. "What's that tapping noise?" he asked, laughing crazily.

The others exchanged glances.

Pappy: "It's a puzzle. That's all."

"That's okay," Mountain Man said. "I'll ask Bowls. He'll know."

At Stretch's guard post, Mountain Man arrived like a storm.

"Tell me what he looked like."

"Not now. Tomorrow," Stretch said. "I'm on guard. You want to get sniped?"

"You're lucky I don't kill you now."

"If I'm lucky, then we're all doomed."

"You scared of me?"

"Yeah. But I'm more scared of them." Stretch pointed to the trees. "Children of the night. What music they make."

"Tomorrow morning. I want details."

"I won't forget his face. Devil's face."

"I'm gonna talk to that VC bitch."

"Gimme visky . . . ginger ale on the side. Don't be stingy, baby."

"What?"

"Never mind. Garbo's got nothing on her. Nothing at all."

Mountain Man left, muttering, "Shitttttt."

~ *Tuyet Mai Has An Odd Dream* ~

Tuyet Mai dreamed. . . .

Madame Dau sat serenely on her porch, laughter creasing her eyes as children circled the banyan tree. No soldiers. No men. Only women and their children, gossiping and sipping tea. Their words danced: marriages arranged, debts confessed, tontines won, harvests forecast. Betel juice darkened their smiles. The sun warmed without threat. Smoke from roast pork wound through banana leaves, fish sauce, and the faint chemical burn of tied bamboo string. Incense drifted into the breeze, slow and knowing, as if memory had a scent.

Tuyet Mai sat apart. Present, but untouched. When she poured tea, no one reached. When she laughed, no one turned. Her voice to the crying baby fell like wind into a well. The infant passed from arm to arm, but never to her. She folded her hands, eyes lowered, and ceased to be.

Then: motion. Beneath her tunic, something began to swell. Two shapes rose beneath the cloth, pressing outward. She clutched them with both hands, but the fabric tore with a sound like breath turned against itself. Gasps broke the air. She was no longer invisible. She was the center of it all.

Her breasts erupted, engorged, weighty, primal. The skin stretched tight, flushed with impossible life. The nipples extended, thickening, glistening with some ancestral fever. She tried to rise, but the weight dragged at her hips and spine. Her mouth opened. Her tongue slid over teeth no longer human. They were long, honed, sharp.

"Trieu Thi Trinh!" the women shrieked, pointing. "Trieu Thi Trinh!"

Children scattered. The baby cried out and vanished into arms that ran.

A force entered her: more than strength. It was memory given muscle, fury made flesh. She stood, legs spread for balance, body trembling under divine burden. Her breasts moved not as flesh, but as weapons blessed by a mad god of war.

The courtyard emptied. All except Madame Dau, who sat unmoved, sipping her tea with eyes full of silence.

Then the men came. Thousands. Soldiers poured into the village, rifles lifted, boots stamping rhythm into the bones of the earth.

"Lead us, General Trinh! Lead us!"

Tuyet Mai tried to cover herself, but her pants had split and her breasts curled over her shoulders. She could not close her mouth, fangs tore at her gums. She had become a demon. Saliva ran down her chin as she stood, exposed and terrible.

Madame Dau finally spoke: "This is what happens to those who lie with beasts that stir men's bloodlust. You've become their dream: not a woman, but a general. Not a lover, but a goddess. Your grotesque breasts strike terror; your fangs, arousal. They see in you their doom, and yet they worship."

"But . . . this isn't what I wanted. . . . " Tuyet Mai stammered.

The soldiers brought forth an elephant. They lifted her onto it, her body monstrous, her mouth too sharp to speak. The women and children reappeared, laughing, pointing, mimicking her. Madame Dau sat on the porch, sipping tea as if nothing had changed. The village receded. She bounced with the elephant's gait, hair flying, breasts whipping the air, fangs hissing in the wind.

Then the light came. A searing white blaze. She rode toward it. It burned her skin. A spear flew from the center of the glare and struck her ribs.

Ahhhhhhh!

~

"Ahhhhhhh!"

"Wake up, Nguyen Tuyet Mai!" Mountain Man's voice shattered the dream. He prodded her with his boot. She didn't respond. He kicked her. Hard.

She twisted, hands bound behind her, squinting into the flashlight's glare. "What . . . ? Who . . . ?"

~

He turned the beam onto his face. Lit from below, it became a grotesque mask of shadow and bone. "Oh!" The cry escaped before she could swallow it. Pain flared in her ribs where his boot had landed, each breath clawing for air. Then came the pain. Her head yanked backward. A knife pressed to her throat. His beard rasped her cheek. His stench was feral, musky, and unbearable. She writhed as he muttered in jagged Vietnamese, thick with accent.

Mountain Man fought the urge to slit her windpipe. He growled, low and cold, sacrificing clarity for menace.

"Describe the sapper! The one who tried to free you!"

"Ah?"

"Face? Height? Name? Rank?"

"Ah?"

He spat in her face.

"You understand me, bitch!" he roared in English. Then again in Vietnamese, "Tell me everything!"

"Ah? I do not understand!"

~

T stood with Cairns, watching. Mountain Man crouched over her like a predator, knife gleaming. T felt something rise inside him. It loomed dark, ancestral, revolting. *I should stop him. If she dies, it's murder. I should intervene.*

But he didn't. Something monstrous was stirring inside. A part of him that welcomed the violence. *I don't want to stop him. Not yet.*

Voices boomed from the void:

Tipping point on the tumble to Treblinka!
Your adherence to blind Fate and cold First Principles disgust Me!
My Metaphorical God, it is sometimes hard to—Ah! Look at the other!

~

Cairns wanted to stop it too, but fear paralyzed him. Mountain Man wasn't just unstable. He was ancient. A beast with no leash. *I want her. I need her untouched. If he scars her—* Cairns reached out, a frightened boy, tugging at Mountain Man's tunic. "Stop! Let her go!"

Mountain Man whirled. His face inches from Cairns', the knife pressed into his gut.

"You got a problem, Captain?" His voice was razor calm. "Because if you do, I'll gut you and slice off your hands so you can't hold your insides in."

T lunged. "Enough! Are you crazy?"

Mountain Man stepped back, face impassive. "Don't worry, T. I'm with you now. All the way. I won't hurt the bitch. Much. Just tell your green fuckin' cunt to move."

"You're speaking to a captain. Address him as such."

Mountain Man turned slowly, sneering. "Captain, sir. Your Vietnamese is better than mine, sir. Please ask her about the sapper. Sir."

Cairns, ignoring the tone, asked Tuyet Mai. She answered hesitantly, whispering vague words. But enough. Stretch and Nature would later confirm the details. Mountain Man now had a name.

Sergeant Cao Thanh Dam.

And he had Bowls' flock bag.

"I told you, T. I'm back. But now it's not just NVA or VC I want to kill. It's gooks. You understand the difference?"

T flinched. The word sounded alien on Mountain Man's tongue. He had once forbidden it. Now he rolled it out in a pagan mantra, savoring its malice.

Mountain Man stood still, but the air around him burned with new resolve.

"You know the NVA are aware of the tunnel," T said. "Because Kim Lan . . . Martha . . . probably told them. If they haven't found it yet, they will. I don't think she wanted to betray us, but we have to assume she did."

"That's right, T," Pappy cut in. "But she never knew the exit. That buys us a little time. Either we all go through the tunnel tonight, or we send a couple of guys to reach the firebase—or maybe stumble into some friendlies. It's our only play."

T nodded. "Agreed. But X says Storyteller can't move on foot. And Idaho's crashing. Fast. We can't carry him."

He shook his head.

"If we all leave . . . but we shouldn't. . . . " His voice trailed off.

They stood together, heads bent in grim discussion, just like the old days. And for a flickering moment, the return of Mountain Man lifted the weight. It felt almost like hope.

Only Pappy noticed the word T had used.

Shouldn't.

~

Tuyet Mai sat slumped against the wall, limbs deadened, thoughts adrift. Her skin crawled with filth. Her soul with shame. She didn't long to simply bathe—she longed to scrape herself raw, to peel away the outer layers. Maybe, if enough came off, the past few years would vanish with them. But she could never reach deep enough.

Self-loathing clung to her.

I'm a coward. A fool. I gave up Dam.

One American growled, and she folded. All those years loyal to the cause, and now: betrayal. *For what? A few cracked ribs and a nightmare face?*

Her thoughts sagged under exhaustion.

Wait. Think clearly. What harm have I really done? Dam's not a secret agent. Just a soldier. They can't use what I said. They won't. They might. And if they do, if he's captured, tortured, killed? Because of me? Then I'll hang myself. That's all. Join the list of men I've killed, directly or not.

How many now? I've lost count.

Oh, if I could just go back. Be a girl again. Home. No war. No orders. No blood on my hands. I'd give the world for that.

Captivity had stretched time, pulled it taut. Her thoughts circled endlessly through the same regret. The same wish.

They say a journey of ten thousand miles begins with a single step. Mine led here, to this filthy corner, this fortress, this unraveling. But the step that doomed me wasn't to the battlefield. It was into the world of men.

That first step had been an agreement: to believe in their goals, to offer her body as weapon, to fight their war. That was the true cliff. That first, fatal step.

She thought of her dream. Of Trieu Thi Trinh. Of suicide.

Lady Trieu rode into battle, breasts flung over her shoulders, astride an elephant thundering into death.

Tôi mơ bà ấy. I dreamed her. I became her.

Now the beast beneath her was this war, and it would not stop galloping.

Then came the memory of Madame Dau seated on her veranda, sipping tea, watching her grandchildren tumble in the sun. Tuyet Mai envied her with a desperation that scraped at the edges of madness. Dau had suffered, yes, but she had lived a life worth living.

She thought of Nang, her old teacher. A woman who once stood in the sweltering heat, voice shrill with fervor, hurling revolution into the faces of children. Always toward the boys. But sometimes, a girl caught the spark.

She had. She had answered the call.

And what was Nang, really? A herald. But not a soldier. She trained children to die in a war she would never fight. The ones who followed her burned out early. Glorious, maybe—but gone.

Dau remained rooted in the world of the living. Tuyet Mai had descended into the gut of a dying dream.

I gave myself to men whose souls made me sick. I became meat for the revolution. Orders soaked in perversity. Their ambition entered me like infection. I smiled. I said nothing. I became complicit.

I may wear a beautiful face. But inside, I am bitter as turnip and just as plain.

But deep beneath that bitterness, something had stirred, something old, something waiting. Not rage. Not revenge. A memory older than the war. Older than the Party. A woman astride the beast of history, refusing to kneel.

No more. Never again. That's the secret. That's the escape.

Live in the world of the living. Build something real. A school. A house. An irrigation ditch.

I will not lie back again and let them enter me with the sword of their ambition.

Dau never did. And I will follow her.

She thought then of the Americans. Two had shown her something unexpected: kindness. The one they called Earth, or perhaps *thiên nhiên,* Nature. Also, the black medic whose name she couldn't pronounce. They had touched her gently. Seen her. Respected her pain, if not her cause. Then there was the one they called Teller of Stories.

He unsettled her. There was something strange about him, as if he watched the world from elsewhere, part ghost, part child, part god. She was certain he was linked to the figurine.

Ah, the figurine. *Marx said gods and ghosts are bourgeois illusions. But that statue glows. It pulses. It watches. It listens. It has power. Even if I believe in nothing else, I believe in it. So what if I've fallen? Maybe there's something sacred down here in the fall.*

The foundation beneath her cracked. Her old certainties shifted, slow as continents, vast as grief. For the first time in her life, she feared death, not for its pain, but for its interruption. Because now, there was something to live for. *I want to go home. I want to marry. I want children. A little land. A bowl of soup. A lullaby.*

She remembered her mother's voice, lilting through half-sleep:

> *Loving her husband half the night,*
> *She spends the other half before dawn,*
> *Carrying her merchandise to market.*
> *She who marries late brings sorrow to her parents.*
> *She who has a husband is a dragon with wings.*
> *She without one is a rice-mill with a broken axle.*

But here she was: no husband, no children, trapped in a fortress, her bound body a filthy vessel for others' fantasies. They poured into her—ideals and fluids—each one seeded with infection. She thought of the two men who had most affected her. The Man from the Mountains. And the captain she could not name, only murmur: *Kha Re Em Si.*

They were both infected. Different strains of the same disease. One a mythical beast from some broken opera, half in her world, half in another. He spoke her language like a man trying to reenter a dream. He treated Kim Lan like a wife, as though their marriage had happened long ago, in another life. He was tender, monstrous. Familiar, alien. A storm with hands. But when his friend died, he became the monsoon. Red. Relentless.

Then there was the captain. Half-Vietnamese. Fluent in her dialect. Slick, polished, unreadable. She saw it in his eyes: the rot. The cruelty. He terrified her more than any man she'd known.

Her greatest fear was being left alone with him.

~ *Tuyet Mai Has Another Dream* ~

Tuyet Mai felt a sting flare along her neck, a shallow cut made by the knife of the Man From the Mountains. She rolled her head, trying to dull the throb, and the thin scab split open. Warm blood slid down her chest. She let her head fall back to guide its path, feeling the sticky trickle spread along her throat and pool behind her neck. She hoped the medic would notice and clean the wound before the insects arrived. But even as the thought formed, she heard them: the high, whining drone of mosquitoes hovering beneath her chin. A tickling tremor followed, then a probing burn as they fed. She moaned, called out. No one came. Pain and frustration mingled, became weight. She slipped into a broken sleep.

She dreamed she had escaped. She was running toward Song Nhan village. And Madame Dau was waiting in the square, arms open. Tuyet Mai sprinted to her, desperate for sanctuary, but just before she could reach those arms, a People's Army soldier seized her from behind and dragged her backward, away.

The world shifted. She was inside a massive, gray hall with a hundred others, prisoners filing into a concrete auditorium. They squatted on the filthy floor, facing a platform veiled by a rotting parachute strung to a bamboo dowel. It sagged. Then it lifted. Behind it stood a naked line of the condemned, placards strung around their necks. At the far end, an old couple held hands, heads bowed. Their signs read: GRANNY. GRANDPA. Next was a man marked LANDLORD, then OFFICIAL. They fidgeted, tried to cover themselves. The landlord looked vacant. The official squinted out like a castaway seeking land. Beside them, a younger man labeled SHOPKEEPER whimpered and ran his fingers through his hair. Next came MONK, his lips moving in constant prayer. Beside him stood PUPPET SOLDIER, blinking like a man dragged from another dream. And last, a middle-aged woman marked ARTIST, craning her neck to meet the official's eyes.

Then a cadre entered, young and sharp-featured, his uniform spotless. A naked woman followed behind him, clutching a baby girl. The woman trembled. Her baby stroked her face and squealed when fingers touched tears. The cadre prowled the line, stopping before the old couple. He circled them, inspecting them as he would examine livestock.

"Here is a granny," he said coldly. "A gossiping old ghost. Worthless." He shot her in the head. The old man screamed and fell to her side, still holding her hand.

"And here is a grandpa. Heart of a slave. Molded by the French, the Japanese, the Americans." He shot him too. The old man collapsed atop the old woman, their hands still clasped.

The others flinched. Bayonets restored the line.

"This man is a landlord, an oppressor!" *Bang.* "An official, Confucian scum!" *Bang.* "A shopkeeper, bourgeois swine!" *Bang.* "A monk, superstitious fool!" *Ba ng.* "A puppet soldier, a traitor!" *Bang.* "An artist, sentimental trash!" *Bang.*

Each fell in turn. The baby's mother shook with grief.

The cadre dragged her to the center of the stage, above the blood. The bodies twitched beneath her feet. He smiled, mocking.

"Look at this woman," he said to the prisoners. "She holds the future in her arms. But whose future? She is the daughter of a sentimental artist"—he pointed—"and a corrupt official." He dragged her to her father's twitching body. "Correction: soon to be an orphan." He shot him. "Now an orphan."

He listed the dead like a sermon: "Granddaughter of the useless.Widow of a traitor.Niece of an oppressor.Sister of a superstitious fool.Cousin of a thief."

He turned back to the woman.

"Her blood is poisoned. Her womb, defiled. Her child, an abomination."

A soldier brought forth a tub of water.

"Tell us her name," the cadre said, voice gentle.

The woman clutched the child, sobbing. "Her name is Tuyet Mai. She will marry, have children, live in peace."

"Put the baby in the water."

The woman collapsed, shielding the child. Soldiers tore her away. The baby was dropped face-down into the tub. Gasps filled the room. Sobs followed. Water splashed. Then—stillness.

She stared at the floating child, then at the bodies. All hope gone. Arms limp. Eyes hollow.

She was led away, repeating: "Her name is Tuyet Mai. She will marry. Have children. Live in peace."

The cadre turned to the crowd. His voice dropped.

"Now she has no grandparents but the country. No parents but the Revolution. No husband but the Party. No uncle but Uncle Ho. No brothers or sisters but her comrades. No child but the child of hatred. Hatred for the enemies of the people."

He smiled. "You understand, comrades?"

The room said nothing.

"Stand!" shouted a guard. "Exit to the right!"

The prisoners rose.

"Stop!" barked the cadre. "One last thing. Listen closely."

He whispered: "We know where your families are."

He walked the line of corpses.

"Your mothers. Your fathers. Your sisters. Your sons."

He paused at the dead child.

"Your children."

Then he vanished.

"Move forward!" boomed the guard.

Move forward.

Yes. Move. Move! But Tuyet Mai couldn't move. What legs? She had been left behind. Forgotten among the bodies.

And then—they sat up.

The dead rose and stared at her.

The artist: Madame Dau.

The official: Captain Tong.

The grandparents: her parents.

The landlord: Captain Cairns.

The monk: Sergeant Dam.

The soldier: The Man From the Mountains.

The shopkeeper: her brother.

Madame Dau stood. Picked up the baby from the tub. Held it close. Whispered until it wriggled in delight. "This is why we could not give you the baby in your dream," she said. "But all the babies . . . all of them—this is why. . . . "

Tuyet Mai moaned aloud in her sleep.

~

Captain Cairns, crouched in darkness nearby, had been listening to her breath. When he heard her moan, his penis stirred. He reached down. . . .

~ *Dam Questions Kim Lan* ~

After parting from Viet, Sergeant Dam returned to his hammock, eased onto his back, and stared into the sponge-black canopy above. A distant gibbon called through the night. Dam absently rolled the American's leather pouch between his fingers. Which one screamed tonight? The one who sets the traps? The one they call her "husband"? The one who howled like a beast? Which one?

He swung out of the hammock without thinking and lit a covered lantern, threading his way through the foliage toward Kim Lan's sleeping mat. Expecting her to be asleep, he moved with care—but she was not. She sat cross-legged, eyes closed in the pose of a meditating monk. A leech clung to her arm. Without opening her eyes, she plucked it off and flicked it away. Dam coughed to announce himself. Slowly, her eyes opened, steady and dark, measuring him as if for burial.

"Did you hear the scream from the fortress tonight?" he asked.

"Yes."

"Was it the one who uses the tunnel?"

She nodded. "I think so."

"You're not sure?"

"I'm sure. It was him."

Dam squatted, the pouch still in his palm. "Tell me more."

"I already have."

"Not enough. Describe him. How does he walk? Is he fast? Do the others obey him or fear him? His hands—are they strong? Anything. Everything."

She tilted her head. "Why?"

He stood and fingered a hanging vine. "Because if I meet him, I'll need to know how he thinks, how he moves, how he kills."

She was silent a long moment. Then: "You first."

Dam turned. "Yes?"

"Why did you fail to get Tuyet Mai out?"

His face tightened. "I tried, Comrade. Fate intervened. But her time will come, and I will free her."

Kim Lan laughed softly, her silver tooth catching the light before she covered her mouth. "I believe you. I had a dream you would, fate or no fate."

He smiled. "Then you understand. The time will come."

"Yes."

They spoke late into the night. By the time he rose, he carried a vivid description of the one she called The Man From the Mountains.

~

Dam found Sergeant Viet still awake, cleaning his rifle and sipping tea that reeked of boiled roots.

"What are you doing here?" Viet smirked. "Couldn't sleep without me?"

Dam grinned but pressed on. "I've been talking with Kim Lan. Seems no one sleeps tonight."

"Oh?"

"Nothing new from her, but I want to go over the plan again. I've got concerns."

Viet raised a brow. He'd never seen Dam so tentative. "Did she tell you something I should know?"

"No. I just want no mistakes tomorrow. When we reach the tunnel—" He paused. "You know the setup. After the old woman shows us the entrance, two comrades will escort her back. That leaves four of us to observe. It is vital the Americans don't know we've found it. Vital. Especially with that trap-setting ghost. Even the slightest mistake, he'll notice. And if he notices. . . ." Dam's voice trailed off. He shook his head. "I had a dream last night."

Viet nodded. "Haven't we all?"

"Yes—but this one . . . this one was different."

He paused, his brow furrowed, as if still trapped inside it.

"I was inside an American helicopter, rising fast, too fast, into the sky. Below me, the forest spread out in green silence, alive, breathing. But inside everything was wrong. Steel. Screws. Rivets. Panels. No wind, no soil, no scent. Just the clatter of rotors and the cold glare of metal."

His hands clenched unconsciously.

"I looked down. The floor beneath me was cutting into my skin. Thin slits opened along my feet, my palms. Blood spread across the surface, not dripping, but slithering. The floor was impossibly smooth. I tried to move, but there was no traction. No friction. No place for life to take hold."

He closed his eyes, remembering.

"Then he appeared. The Man From the Mountains. Not walking—gliding. His body had become the machine. Blades for feet. Razors for hands. His face, empty but burning. Two points of light where the eyes should be. He didn't breathe. He didn't blink. He simply advanced."

Dam's throat tightened. "There was no sound, except the hum of machinery. My blood couldn't stain him. The helicopter had no door. No exit. No roots. No place to fall. And when he raised his hands, those shining blades, I understood I couldn't fight. I couldn't run. There was nothing left in the world but him."

He exhaled. "It's hard to describe."

Viet, after a pause, said softly, "No. You described it well."

A silence passed. Then:

"Who's in the team?" Viet asked.

"It wasn't easy. My first choice, Quy, was killed. So I've picked Chu, Doanh, and Nguu to stay with me. Haven't chosen the escort pair yet."

"What if there's more than one exit?"

"The old woman says only one."

"Nang. That's her name, right? Do you trust her?"

"We've talked about this."

"Not with Vy or Tong listening. What do you really think?"

Dam's face darkened. "I think she's telling the truth. She's helped the Front for years."

"According to her."

"Yes. According to her. But we don't have time to vet her. What's the risk?"

"Ambush."

"I don't think so. Doesn't fit. She knows what would happen to her village if she betrayed us. All I care about is that she returns and keeps silent."

"And how will you place the team?"

"We leave no sign—nothing to alert them. If we're lucky, we may even use the tunnel to slip inside the fortress."

"Maybe," Viet muttered, unconvinced.

"But I need to find that demon. The one who lays traps. No more dead comrades, Viet."

Viet looked down. "We need to finish this. Overrun them or move on. This limbo is dangerous."

Dam chuckled. "We're not moving on. Not until they're broken. As the ancients said, 'Leave them like blossoms in a flooded stream.'"

Viet grunted. "Maybe. But this isn't just a siege. Strings are being pulled. I can feel them."

"Maybe," Dam said. "But they're not ours to see. Either way, dawn's coming. We'd best get some sleep."

~ *Madame Dau Asks Han Tinh for Advice* ~

Han Tinh could not sleep.

His stumps ached from a long day of tomb sweeping, and the ceaseless rain gnawed at the arthritis in his shoulder and elbow joints. But it was not pain that kept him awake. His mind returned again and again to the strange events of the evening.

All day the village had murmured about a boy named Pham Van Ha, who came running out of the jungle, wild-eyed and raving. He'd been searching deep beyond the groves and waterways for a lost buffalo. Following dung trails and hoofprints down a narrow path, he heard screams rising through the trees from the direction of the fortress.

Racing back, he stumbled straight into the missing buffalo, peacefully munching duckweed. With a bamboo switch, he whipped the beast into a panicked gallop all the way to the village.

Han Tinh had just left Security Chief Tien's shack when the buffalo stormed into the square, bellowing as the boy lashed its flanks and screamed, "Demons! Demons!"

Before Tinh could register what was happening, the beast spun around him, spraying mud and broken vegetables. Baskets flew. Women screamed and scattered. He landed face-down in the muck, then found himself hauled upright by Carpenter Long.

He didn't stay to hear the crowd's gossip.

As he limped away, fragments reached him anyway:

"It's a sign!"

"No, no! It was torture! Americans torturing someone!"

"A villager, someone from here!"

"No. No. It was demons. I've heard them before. War wakes them."

"It's the ghost of the Venerable Vu Huong, furious his funeral was disturbed!"

"No! His spirit's being tortured!"

"Don't be ridiculous! I'm going home to check my children."

"Who's being tortured?"

"Vu Huong's ghost!"

By the time Han Tinh reached his shack, the rumors had already mutated twice over. He muttered to himself, "Foolish women. Foolish women," an intonation to dispel madness.

He looked forward to solitude and early sleep. Instead, he found Madame Dau squatting at his doorway, her face drawn with sorrow.

~

"Ah! Madame Dau, Venerable Council Chief! What an honor. Pardon my face, I just finished an intimate affair with a very rough concubine," he winked. "You, though, look troubled. Tea from my ageless pot?"

"No," she said, her face flushed with purpose.

"Come in! Come in!"

He hurled his torso up the step and onto the wooden floor, his long arms windmilling. Because of his condition, her presence alone in his home raised no eyebrows. She entered without hesitation.

Within seconds, he had lantern light flickering, a pot heating on the battered stove, tin cups clinking. Then he splashed water on his face from a wide-mouthed basin and reached for a towel hanging low.

Madame Dau watched in awe.

His arms are like an orangutan's.

His shack, sloped and improvised, was a masterpiece of utility: walls at odd angles, shelves carved from driftwood, everything within reach. It didn't shame her. It impressed her. Carpenter Long and her rough crew had built it, but the vision was entirely Tinh's.

She removed her hat before stepping further. Any higher and it would've knocked against the ceiling.

"You must be worried about the gossip," he said quickly. "That little devil Pham Van Ha! Always imagining things. Once he said his buffalo was a dragon in disguise!"

Madame Dau chuckled. "You know me better than that, Brother Tinh. It's not demons I fear."

He tilted his head. "Ah. The American soldier. Of course."

She winced and shifted. Unable to squat comfortably, she grabbed Tinh by the armpits and hoisted him onto his bed, then dragged over a rickety bamboo chair and sat.

Outside, rain ticked against leaves. She stared at the mango tree beside his shack.

"We've talked beneath that tree many times," she said wistfully. "I used to find reasons to visit when it was in season."

"It is not in season," he said, baiting her.

"No. And this time, I need no excuse. I have a reason."

She hesitated. The rain filled the silence. She fidgeted. Couldn't find the words. Tinh watched her, then his expression shifted.

"You didn't follow my advice, did you?" His voice was low. "You went to him. You met the American."

She nodded, eyes downcast. "I had to. The sign. My parents were pleading. You know I'm not superstitious, but the sign..."

He spat onto the floorboards.

"You've doomed us all. Either we'll be executed, or driven off our land, same thing! Fool! Why?"

She flared. "Watch your words, Brother Tinh! I am still Council Chief!"

He shrugged, unrepentant. "Then why come to me now?"

"Because you're keeper of the shrines. You've seen things. You know soldiers. You know what this means. I need your counsel."

"Who else knows?"

"No one. Except . . . Madame Vit."

He raised an eyebrow.

"That's all," she said sheepishly.

"No," he replied. "It isn't."

Her stomach dropped. "Who?"

He reached with his long arm, plucked a cigarette from the chaos beside his bed, lit it, and exhaled a thick plume.

"Schoolmistress Nang."

"What?"

"She left the village and hasn't returned. Chief Nguyen checked. Tien says Nang handed off Vach's boy to him, saying, 'It's about Madame Dau. I must clear something up.' Then she left."

Dau sat motionless, stunned.

Finally, Tinh continued. "Where else would that shriveled old hag go but to the People's Army camp?" he said with venom in his voice. "I know she has not returned to the village because both Tien and Nguyen checked her house. And now that it's dark, she won't return until tomorrow. Or, worse yet, she'll return tonight with an escort of People's Army soldiers!"

"But maybe there's another explanation."

"No! If Nang were not Nang, and if there were eligible men in the village, I might think differently." While saying this, Tinh made a circle with the index finger and thumb of his left hand and repeatedly jabbed the index finger of his right hand through the circle. "But Nang is Nang and there are no eligible men here. Even I am not that desperate." Tinh perked up and looked significantly at Madame Dau. "Now if you were willing . . . "

"Hush, foolish man! What else?"

Chastised, but hardly repentant, Han Tinh muttered, "There's only one place she could be."

"But—"

"No! You call me a foolish man? See what happens when foolish women ignore my advice?"

Madame Dau bit down on her indignation. She could not refute his outburst. Her mind reeled. *He's right. If the People's Army finds out I helped an American soldier, they'll execute me without ceremony. And Nang, ambitious, loyal, ruthless, she'll report me. She wants my seat as council chief.*

Her hands twisted in anguish. "All these years I stayed neutral. I kept out of politics, of soldiers' affairs. Even my own children, my blood, were taken by this war. But not me. Until now. How could I make such a foolish mistake? I didn't even know his name three days ago, and now I might lose everything: my home, my family, my land . . . all for him."

Tinh threw back his head and brayed with delight.

A new dread took root. *What if the snake, the two-headed sign, was not a blessing, but a rebuke? A trap from my parents, for failing to bury them properly?*

"What was that?" Tinh asked, hearing her mutter.

"A proper burial," she said, her voice hollow. "I'm being punished. I never gave my parents the rites."

"Bah!" he scoffed. "You sound like Carpenter Long. I have to listen to her superstitions every morning."

"But you've seen ghosts yourself!" she cried. "The Goddess statue. You remember."

"Of course. But that was *different.* I saw them with my own eyes."

She narrowed her gaze, lips tight. "And I saw the sign with mine. You believe your visions, but dismiss mine. That's not logic, it's pride."

He coughed awkwardly. "Yes, yes. You're right. But your interpretation is wrong."

"Oh? And who decided that?"

"I did," he said flatly. "I'm the keeper of the shrines."

"You're a *water puppeteer,*" she said, exasperated.

Tinh grinned and shrugged. "Even my logic collapses under its own weight."

She studied him openly, one of the few men with whom she felt safe enough to hold a steady gaze. "Then tell me, Brother Tinh. What should I do?"

His face softened. "Say nothing of our conversation. Leave the rest to me."

"No," she said with quiet force. "I must leave at dawn. I cannot stay. The People's Army will execute me. I will go to the district capital."

"You must *stay!*" he shouted. "You're the council chief. Without you, the village will follow Nang like pigs to slaughter. There is no Vu Huong anymore: no elder voice. So *trust me.* I'll handle it."

Her brows knit in resistance. "How?"

"Don't ask. Just go home. Tell no one. Not even Madame Vit."

"I can't risk it. I have grandchildren. The communists will confiscate my fields, punish my family. They'll hand everything over to that schoolmistress."

"Exactly my point. If you flee, they'll take it all anyway. But if you stay, perhaps not. There's a chance."

"But how?"

Tinh groaned. "Enough questions! I told you, *leave it to me.*"

She wrung her hands again. Her eyes drifted to the darkened corner of the room where Tinh's leather harness leaned against the wall: greasy, urine-stained, sagging with mildew. The air was rank. Nausea surged. Dizzy, she shifted to rise.

"Wait!" Tinh blurted. "Don't go yet. I . . . I need to ask you something. Something important."

She steadied herself. "What is it?"

"Did you ask the American about the Goddess statue?"

"No. There wasn't time. I forgot. Is it so important?"

His face darkened. "If not the statue, then what *is* so special about this man? Why did you risk everything for him?"

"I told you: the sign."

"No. There's more. Tell me."

She shook her head slowly. "I don't know. Only that . . . he didn't kill me when he could have."

"Why not?"

"Because he likes dogs."

"To *eat?*"

"No. To *love.* Like family."

Tinh stared, incredulous. Then erupted in laughter. "He likes *dogs?* Kills Vietnamese but loves dogs!" His cigarette crumbled. He lit another, eyes narrowing in bemused thought. "Maybe Americans *are* dogs. Wearing human faces. Does he lift his leg when he pees?"

"Brother Tinh!" she snapped. "Sometimes I think you're a holy man in disguise. Other times, just a jester."

"Ah, but I *am* a jester," he said, winking. "The gods watch us and laugh. Their tears fall as rain. Their thunder is applause. You're a wise council chief risking death for a soldier who loves dogs. And I'm a crippled clown smart enough not to."

She swallowed hard. "Should I stay in the village?"

"I've already told you—yes. Leave it to me. I'm not *always* a fool. Sometimes I'm a sage."

"And you still won't say how you'll help me?"

He exhaled a long, amused stream of smoke. "Noooo."

She looked at him, truly looked, as if for the first time. He didn't flinch. "Very well. I'll stay. What must I do?"

"Return home. Speak to no one. Wait for my sign. And no, it won't be another two-headed snake!" he chuckled.

"My parents were clever, weren't they?" she said, wistful.

"How so?"

"The snake was in my mother's dream. And I was born in the year of the snake."

Tinh clapped with delight. "Perfect! I was born in the year of the *dog!*" He laughed so hard he had to wipe tears from his eyes. Then, donning mock solemnity, he said, "But as you can see, I no longer lift my leg when I pee. Yet I still have my *nose!*"

Leaning forward, he craned toward her crotch and made exaggerated sniffing sounds.

Madame Dau shook her head, lips trembling not with humor but with something more ancient: grief, perhaps, or pity. She adjusted her conical hat, leaned forward with quiet finality, and stepped into the rain. Behind her, Han Tinh did not laugh. He remained seated, staring at the doorframe she had passed through, as though it might still contain her shadow. One hand rose to scratch his armpit, the other dropped limply into his lap.

"Foolish women," he murmured. "Foolish, fearless women. The ones who carry the dead and walk barefoot into storms." His voice broke on the last word.

He lay back slowly, staring at the rafters, where water seeped through the thatch in crooked lines. Rain tapped out patterns he could not read. He placed a hand over his hollow stomach, not in desire, but in remembrance of power once held, of rituals once believed, of bodies that once danced when summoned. "Pleasing the gods," he whispered to the roof. "Or distracting them."

And then he closed his eyes, as the smell of wet earth and urine thickened around him, and the rain kept falling: a drumming reminder of power far beyond that of men or women.

~ Vit and Dau Reminisce ~

Madame Dau, now barefoot and ankle-deep in mud, slipped off her rubber sandals and moved slowly, unsure whether she wanted to return home. The wind had risen, fierce and restless. Through the rain, she saw the faint glow of lantern-light seeping from her house. Peering through the window, she saw her daughter playing with the grandchildren, casting worried glances toward the door. *No. Not tonight. I can't listen to Bin talk about marrying that fool. Arranged marriages are better. Even if mine wasn't . . . nonsense. I won't give her the chance.*

And what if Nang comes with soldiers? I'll be shot. Not tonight, Bin. Not tonight. I must see Vit. Tinh be damned. He's not my husband.

Waving Bin off, she strode to Vit's house.

She appeared in the doorway, composed but firm, and told her daughter she would be visiting Chief Administrator Vit and would return late. With difficulty, she extracted herself from her grandchildren's arms and their pleading eyes, then stepped out into the storm and made her way toward her old friend's house.

Chief Administrator Vit opened the door in surprise. Without question, she ushered her daughter-in-law and two grandchildren out of the room and poured hot tea from a steaming pot. The two women sat together on low stools, and Dau told her everything. Every detail. As the story spilled out, the storm in her chest began to quiet. Her voice steadied. She felt less alone, less hunted. When Tinh's warning to stay silent surfaced in her mind, she pushed it away. *Tinh is not my master.* The hours passed, and the two women drifted into memory.

"You survived the famine. You'll survive this," Vit said gently.

"Yes. Terrible days."

Their shared past unfurled, a bitter scroll written in famine and silence.

Images rose unbidden, unspoken, yet known in both minds.

The famine of the 1940s, worse than any soldier's nightmare of war.

A baby, suckling at the cracked nipple of a dead mother, both lying at the edge of a pond. The child's skin crawled with black leeches. It cried without sound.

A girl, naked and curled in the market street, her skin porcelain-pale, her death too beautiful to face. People stepped around her, eyes averted, as if her stillness carried judgment. Vit remembered the first fly that landed on her thigh. Then another. Then the swarm. She tried to cover the girl's modesty but couldn't bear to remain in that place, where the only meat left was human.

A French tax collector stood among the dying, prying the last coins from their hands. His pink skin glistened under the sun. He did not look down.

A woman gave birth in the mud beneath a cardboard box while two small children watched, their faces blank, their hands twisting in silence. When Dau and Vit passed the spot later, the baby lay face-up in the rain, cord still attached, motionless. A scarf lay across its chest, heavy with water.

A boy's tendons slashed for theft. An old couple found hand-in-hand, their ribs exposed. Hunger bent spines into unnatural shapes, bloated bellies until the skin split. The shame of girls sold off to survive. Faces forgotten. Names erased.

"Yes," said Vit, pouring more tea, "you've survived the famine, the French, the Japanese, and now the Americans. You'll survive this too. But I worry. Is Tinh truly the one to protect you?"

Dau looked away. "I worry too," she admitted, her voice low and brittle. "He told me to say nothing. Not even to you."

Then, leaning forward, she grasped her friend's hand and met her gaze. "But I cannot speak to my daughters. Their husbands' families might be on the wrong side. I had to tell you. If I don't speak, I'll break. I cannot carry this alone."

~ *Han Tinh Takes Action* ~

After Madame Dau left, Han Tinh sat in silence, cursing himself. He had told her to stay, yet had no idea how to protect her. *She's right. The People's Army will execute her unless I find a way.*

But his loyalty, when he examined it, was not to her. It was to the village. Without Madame Dau, the village would collapse under the weight of this war. People would scatter. And with them would go the only structure that still fed and sheltered him. His "little mothers." His last protection. *So yes, I want her to stay, for my sake. But if I can save her for selfish reasons, then so be it. A solved problem is still solved. But how?* He dropped back onto his bed and stared up at the tin roof, where rain thudded in uneven rhythms. Water leaked through in four places. He didn't mind. He was used to the wet, the rot, the reek. A sharp urge gripped him. He clambered down the bed ramp, shuffled across the floor, pulled aside a warped plank, and pissed into the hole he kept in the mud beneath it. Steam rose faintly. He covered the pit and slumped back against the bed.

There is no other way, he thought. *No other way.*

He lit a cigarette. Smoke curled in the moist air.

Then he moved to the corner of the shack. Reaching for the leather harness, he lay back and strapped it to his stumps with practiced hands. The flickering lantern cast shadows across the walls. Ants climbed in a long line up and over a shelf of rusted pans. *If only the Goddess statue were here. I could ask for help.*

But there was no help. Only action.

Wrapping himself in a nylon poncho, he jammed his old army pith helmet on his head and pushed out into the rain. He slogged around the side of his house to the mango tree. Beneath its gnarled roots lay a flat stone, slick with moss and rain. He dug his fingers under the stone, lifted it, then pushed it aside. Beneath it, long wooden boards covered a hidden cache. He moved the boards and pulled out a nylon-wrapped bundle. Tying it around his neck so it dangled down his chest, he trudged back to his shack. Inside, he unwrapped the object like a sacred relic.

"There will be a reckoning, Schoolmistress Nang," he whispered. "Oh yes. A reckoning."

His voice was quiet but hard. Not madness—clarity.

"Brother Tinh is now Soldier Tinh. Marksman. Best shot in the regiment. Even without legs, a man can shoot straight. Straight and clean. Steel through bone. Soft brain. No more children will die for your revolution."

He lay the old weapon, his *Chicom 7.62 mm AK-47,* across his lap. The metal was cold but familiar. He rubbed the barrel with a cloth, cleaning the rust, checking the sights. The rhythm came back.

"Effective range, 400 meters. Effective range, 400 meters. Effective range, 400 meters."

... *Tap. Tap. Tap.* ...

Chapter Eighteen

PART FOUR: CONFLICT

Fever Dreams IV

It is time for Me to go among them.

Losing control, My Dear? Perhaps the task is beyond Your powers? We have never been in control. We guide, the genes decide.

Goddess, speak for Yourself. Since You fell and I risen, they worship the assumption that I am in control. Let them play out their fate as a species without such misguided intervention.

Dearest Lord, since You rose and I fell, Your addiction to First Principles has addled the divine architecture of Your Mind, let alone theirs. Now, it really is time for Me to go among them.

~ *Storyteller Fights Through the Morphine* ~

Storyteller awoke in a haze of nausea and confusion. *Morphine. X gave me morphine again.* His back pressed against the cold stone wall as he shifted his aching limbs, inch by inch, hunting for the least agonizing position. The fever had dropped to a dull simmer, but the fog remained. *Last night . . . the gravestones. That's what triggered it. I was hallucinating. That's why he dosed me. Damn this fever. God, I'm dying. Dying!* He knew he wasn't.

The battle had raged, most of it lost to the morphine haze, full of dull concussions and distant roars. But now and then, a knife-edge split the fog: the shriek of shrapnel, the crackling of bullets, the cries of agony. Each lit a nerve. Then came the rumbling again—ominous, endless. Out of the rumbling menace, images surfaced in pieces, jagged and wrong. Events out of sequence. A reel torn and spliced by a lunatic editor. He watched anyway. Frame by frame. Future nightmares rehearsing themselves.

Topper shouting urgently, voice echoing: "Sapper in the fort! Sapper in the fort!"

Poppy, distant but sharp: "Save your ammo!"

T's voice cut through everything, steady and precise: "Hold on! Wait a minute! Here we go!"

Thump. Poof. Hiss. Then light, pale and spilling like bloody milk. A flare. T must've fired it. Storyteller clawed his eyes open. The square swam in faint illumination. Smoke coiled yellow and thick. Tracers clawed fire into the swollen sky. Explosions came late, slow as distant memory. Ghost-soldiers flitted past. No footsteps. No breath. Only outlines in motion, like afterimages burned into the air.

Then—*She* arrived.

Not walking. Not appearing. Becoming. The statue made flesh. The Goddess. *Her* body bent in agony, arms cinched tight around *Her* belly. Towering. Writhing. Vomiting something that couldn't be seen.

She stood near T, his silhouette so close, and yet he didn't look at *Her*. Couldn't.

Storyteller heard it then: the sound. Awful. Rhythmic.

A tapping, hollow and relentless as if nails scraped from inside a sealed box.

Coming from *Her*.

From deep within.

A flash of lightning. Thunder. A final, cracking scream: "Get him! Get him! He's going over the wall!" Nature's voice. The sapper. The one who killed Bowls. T spun and ran.

Fire. Thunder. Confusion. A strobe-lit nightmare. Screams and shouts.

Then silence. A quiet so sharp it turned the blade. Then more: Gunfire. Flares. Smoke. Lightning. Tracers. And suddenly he realized he wasn't holding his rifle. He panicked, turned frantically. Thank God, his boots were still on. He had an irrational dread of dying bootless.

But the rifle . . . Just out of reach. He rolled sideways, stretched, reached. Not enough. He shouted into the chaos: "God! God! Goddammit! Please! Just a few more inches! Please!"

~

Michael. Michael. Wake up. You're dreaming again. Come on, sweetheart. It's okay. Wake up.

Please, Diane, I'm trying.

Try harder.

Goddess won't let me.

She's just your imagination. She's not real. Take your pills. She'll go away.

Diane . . . they want me to kill myself. Do you? Diane? Diane? Okay, don't answer. But she will come, Diane. Pills or no pills. She will come. I'm the Chosen One.

No one wants you dead, except the demons coiled in your genome, Chosen One.

~

No one came. They were all on the parapets. *Inside the fortress. Sappers.* In his fevered delirium, the rifle was life itself. But his scream froze when he realized his hand was gone. Only a stump jutted from his sleeve, reaching uselessly.

And there, beyond it, twitched his severed hand. Still flexing. Still grasping the rifle. He shook violently. His breath kicked dust into his face. He whimpered. "Oh God. Please stop. Please. Just let me go home. Just let me go—"

Shouts from the square: "Medic! Medic! X! X! In here! In the church! Hurry!" Stretch's voice.

Footsteps pounding. Boots slapping wet tile. Screams. Gunfire. Then—quiet.

~

After the battle, only the rain remained. The monsoon poured down like an exorcism. This was the *Time of Shaking*. The aftermath. The body, purging adrenaline, trembles on its own. He didn't want to shiver alone. So he limped toward the church, the place Stretch had screamed from. Inside, he found X crouched over Stretch's prone form. Superman stood nearby, hands clasped in silent prayer. Bowls' body lay crumpled near a heap of rubble, twisted in death. T was gone. Nature had already returned to the parapets.

No one saw him enter.

He sank against a wooden beam and listened. Didn't speak. Didn't interrupt. Their voices rose in clipped phrases, higher-pitched than normal. Slight stutters. Yes. He remembered. He remembered that conversation.

Very well.

~ *X is Possessed* ~

"Man, that sapper did a job on your noggin, Stretch. But you'll be okay. Probably just a mild concussion," X murmured, adjusting the bandage wrapped tight around Stretch's brow.

Superman nodded solemnly. "The Lord was with you tonight, my skinny friend."

Stretch offered a crooked smile, no humor in it. "Yeah? Then tell me this, choir boy. If God's so great, why the fuck did He let this war happen? Huh? Answer me that." He turned, wincing, to glance at Bowls' crumpled body. "Why'd He let *that* happen?"

Superman's voice took on the cadence of a sermon, too polished, too rehearsed. "The Lord is a loving God, Stretch. Everything He does is for the good, even when we don't understand it. Right, X? You said your mama raised you Christian. The Lord was here. He's *always* here."

X said nothing. Shrugged.

And in that moment, Storyteller saw *Her* again—Goddess, shimmering into form—a divine mist. *She* leaned over X's shoulder, whispered something indecipherable into his ear. His jaw clenched. His eyes hardened. And when he turned to Superman, it was with barely contained rage.

"Bullshit." His voice was low, metallic. "You want to know why you're full of shit? Fine. Look up. Look at the sky. Look at your God and listen."

Superman, startled by the shift in tone, snapped back, "I can't. It's raining."

"Then look down. Or at Bowls. I don't care. Just *listen*. And keep your eyes off me. Focus on that so-called benevolent God of yours while I tell you something real."

Grumbling, Superman refused the script. "I'll look where I want."

X sighed. "Fine. Then just close your eyes. Goddamn, it's like pulling fuckin' teeth. Close your eyes and listen. Just... listen."

Superman reluctantly obeyed. "Okay. Go on."

A pause. Silence gathered. The Goddess hovered, nearly fused with X's frame, incandescent. Then X spoke. The flood came. No breath, no blink. A deistic machine of memory and indictment.

A frog wanders into a hot spring. Panics. Blisters rise with every hop. One last leap—into boiling water. He's cooked alive. Inches from escape. And in these same few hours, thousands of frogs die violent deaths. And God is in His heaven. And it is good.

A baby elephant cries for her mother while lions strip her skin with claws and teeth. God is in His heaven. It is good.

A gazelle is dismembered alive by hyenas. A baby burns, alone, screaming, in a house fire. A cricket is eaten head-first by a lizard. A wildebeest runs as her entrails are devoured behind her.

And still—God is in His heaven. And it is good.

"Alright! Enough! I get the picture!" barked Superman. "No pain, no joy, right? Animals don't count. You're forgetting the joy!"

But X wasn't finished. Not even close. He stared straight ahead, face impassive, voice unrelenting.

A teenager dies screaming from bone cancer. A mouse suffocates inside a python. A beetle is shredded by army ants.

"X! Jesus, man! Snap out of it!" Superman pleaded. "It's all free will!"

A seal pup is torn apart by a great white. A ten-year-old girl starves beside her dead parents. Bacteria are swallowed by the trillions. Plankton by the billions. A trout gulps in vain as it's carried through the sky, torn apart in a nest. A pretty girl screams for days, tortured, begging for mercy.

And still—God is in His heaven. And it is good.

Superman surged to his feet and slapped X hard across the face, sending the medic's hat flying. "Enough! Too much!" He stared at the welt rising on X's cheek, hands trembling. Breathing heavily, he sank back down. "All I know is God has a plan. It's not for us to understand. Good things happen too. Even more."

X picked up his hat, slowly. Stared at it. Voice flat: *And a little girl, twin daughter of a widowed mother, is raped, tortured, stabbed in the back seat of a car. Left to die alone. Calling for her daddy, killed in Vietnam.*

Superman gasped. "No! Everything you say might be true, but not my daughter! God is benevolent . . . and—"

X's voice shifted—no longer a deistic machine of grief, but not yet human. His fury hovered in the air, thick and lingering.

"Benevolent God? Ha! A psychopath. All the agony of every living thing, just to test humans? To keep them praying, serving, crawling on their knees? We'll all join the frog."

~

Goddess, the demon voice grows stronger. It spreads like an accelerating contagion.

See what Your meddling has wrought? This genetic shard You've twisted into man's fragile line. It will consume Your Chosen One before he can seed a future.

God, behold the one they call Superman. He bears the guilt of Your faction, of the species You unleashed. He believes, even now, in the mercy of fire.

~

Superman lurched forward, towering over X. A presence ready to break. "That's enough! I know there's a reason for all this! A just and benevolent reason! Your cynicism . . . your nigger-ass jive . . . it's just . . . just. . . ."

His voice faltered. The words collapsed beneath their own shame. "I can't explain it," he whispered. "But you'd understand if you ever found Grace in His presence."

Something inside X softened. His soul staggered back from the edge. He blinked, uncertain. A nervous laugh escaped, brief and jarring. Then the mask returned, implacable. "No, man. Just reality. Gut-fuckin' reality. Ask some old Black lady dying alone in her piss-stained apartment while her son fights in a white man's war. Ask Dogman. Ask Raresteak. Ask Mr. Machine. Ask Bowls. And soon enough, ask the rest of us."

A heavy silence settled. Not just from grief, but from knowing nothing they said would matter in the end.

Then, from nearby, Stretch stirred. His voice broke loose, raw and trembling, torn from somewhere deep and damaged, as if speaking cost him something he no longer possessed. "I saw her," he said. "She was burning, but she didn't scream. Just looked at me. Would've scorched my eyes out if I hadn't turned away."

He fell quiet. A long moment passed. His jaw worked, as if grinding the image down to something swallowable. Then, softly, almost apologetically, he reached for the only thing that ever steadied him.

"Well, hell," he murmured. "Like Orson Welles said in that old flick, 'In Italy, under the Borgias, they had murder, war, bloodshed . . . and they gave us Michelangelo, Leonardo, the Renaissance. In Switzerland, they had brotherly love, five hundred years of democracy and peace—and what did that produce? The cuckoo clock.'"

He gave a thin, tired smile.

"So maybe God's just bored of cuckoo clocks."

~

Well, demon?

***So this is Your plan? To sow doubt by walking among them? Very well.
The alternative is eternity in balance. Eternity ticking—tick, tock, tick,
tock—until even the soul begs for madness. Cuckoo. Cuckoo. Cuckoo.
... Tap. Tap. Tap....***

~

X and Superman both turned to Stretch, but the usual teasing never followed. No rolled eyes. No chuckle. Only silence.

A line had been crossed. Not the line of faith or doubt, but the deeper
one: the one that separates shared suffering from fractured survival. The fragile
fellowship forged in war had shattered. There would be no rebuilding. One by
one, the grunts were falling, not to bullets, but into the deep crevasse of their
own ancient fears.

~

Storyteller sat with the memories lodged deep, embedded as shrapnel in
bone. Mr. Machine—gone. Bowls—gone. And the unspoken truth behind the
supply ledger haunted him now: the ammunition was nearly gone, too. Whatever brief pulse of triumph had surged after the battle had already bled dry,
replaced by dread, dense and low as the monsoon clouds. Every Claymore in
the clearing had detonated. More remained, but no one dared venture past the
crumbling perimeter. The snipers watched. They waited. They saw everything.

And so the bodies of the sappers had been tossed over the wall like scraps:
no words, no rites, just the rough discard of effort wasted and faith drained.

Storyteller thought of his father, John Powers, who had weathered the ty-
phoons of revolution in China. He thought of his mother, Bai Meiying, who
had survived the same chaos, the same storms.

Both, he believed, had been protected. *By Goddess.* But could *She* still protect
him now? Could She protect *the Chosen One*? How strong was *She*, truly,
against *His* God? The God of fire and First Principles and tests? The God who
never retches? *Time will tell,* he thought. *Time always tells.*

He slumped against the cold stone wall, watching the rain streak past. The
world blurred. Familiar edges gone. Nothing held shape. Existence, amor-
phous. But the images would not leave him. Two stood out. Burned in. First,
Goddess. Doubling over in the square, *Her* divine body convulsing, purging
some hidden rot. Vomiting light, or pain, or something ancient. Even *She* could
not contain it.

Second, Cairns. His face lit by a flare's cruel radiance, crouched over the
Vietnamese girl, hands lost beneath her torn clothing, face contorted in lust.

Storyteller had rubbed his eyes, hoping it was the fever. But it wasn't. He saw
the woman's gaze afterward, frozen on the captain's retreating back. It was not
shame. Not fear. It was loathing.
Cold. Clear. Unforgiving.

Not a dream. Not the morphine. Not the malaria. Real.

The visions played on a loop behind his eyelids. And just when sleep came
to claim him, warm and thick, it came. The sound. Mountain Man's wailing.

Not a human cry. Not language. Not grief dressed up in prayer or ceremony. But something older. The raw, wordless scream of a brother mourning his kin, Bowls.

Gone.

~ *Bin Confronts Her Mother* ~

Madame Dau returned late from Vit's house, hoping Bin would be asleep. The darkened lantern offered relief. She slipped off her sandals and stepped quietly through the door.

"Mama! I must talk with you!" The voice sprang from the shadows, sharp and sudden.

"Oh! You startled me."

"Mama, this is important. Where were you?"

"Visiting," Madame Dau sighed. "What is it?"

"You know."

"Ah. The rice wine spoiled again? I told you to stir it."

"Mama! Stop. You know what I mean."

"Let's talk tomorrow. I'm too tired."

"Mama, I'm leaving. I'm getting married."

"No! Not to that tenant farmer! Never!" Her voice cracked. "It's hard enough to survive. You want to bind yourself to that poor wretch? You've already been married, you have a child—do you want the village whispering that you give peaches in the morning and plums in the evening? And to a man who probably can't even read."

Bin snorted. "As if reading matters now."

"Think of our family."

"Our family?" Bin's voice dropped. "Papa is dead. My brothers are probably dead too. And my sisters? You sold one. She hanged herself."

The slap came instantly. Then fists. Madame Dau struck again and again as Bin shielded her head and dropped to her knees.

"Stupid girl! You know nothing! I told you never to speak of that again. We were starving. STARVING! You dare talk of love during war? Of marriage when we need every hand alive?"

Bin crumpled, but Madame Dau kept striking. Only when her breath failed did she stop. She sat down, panting, fingers trembling in her graying hair.

"Stupid girl," she whispered.

Bin, on the floor, propped herself up. "No matter what you say, my heart remains a crystal down below. I won't let you sell me." She rose and ran into the storm.

"Bin!" Madame Dau called after her. Then again, "Stupid girl," this time broken.

She changed into dry clothes. Lit incense. Knelt before the altar. Checked her grandson. Sat motionless. *Yes. I killed my daughter. Sold her. Drove her to the rope. And I will pay. If not now, then later.*

Her heart sank. *Or tomorrow. Nang may return with soldiers. A trial. Condemnation. Stripped. Humiliated. Shot in the jungle. My land seized. My children tortured. My grandson dragged away. That Man From the Mountains—he wasn't sent by my ancestors. He was sent by her.*

Her body trembled. *I must run.* She rushed outside, but stopped mid-step. Rain poured down without mercy. The dark pressed close. She turned back. Inside, she lit more joss sticks. One at the base of the wall beneath her Mickey Mouse sticker. The others in the altar's sand bowl. Then she knelt again and prayed.

To Mickey Mouse, and to her husband, for guidance.

~ *The Apparitions Return* ~

Past midnight, Storyteller could no longer sleep. The morphine had lifted. His mind burned with clarity, restless and raw. *Time is slipping through my hands. Wasted.* He thought of the others back in The World. College. Love. Promotions. Lives unpaused. And he? Whispering through undergrowth. Avoiding trails. Crawling in mud. Listening for the click of a cartridge or the bark of an AK.

They were striding forward. He was circling backward. They were mastering love and family and power. He was untangling memories. They were stacking wealth. He was counting debts. They were rising. He was haunted.

And again came Mountain Man's wailing, long, anguished, beyond naming. The fever, waiting, seized the moment. It surged. A lion tearing through his skull, jaws locked around the soft tissue of his brain. Nausea crushed his gut into knots. Dry heaves convulsed him. But he knew: if he endured, the clarity would come. The threshold would open.

And with it—the apparitions.

It began.

Pain fell away. Breath returned. Sight sharpened. *They're coming again. Earlier than before.*

But this time they didn't seep through walls. They arrived directly from the void.

The first, a woman. Elderly. Gently luminous. Heart pulsing faintly. Lungs rising beneath translucent skin. Her dress bore the ghost of a floral print. Her face, marked by age, held both sorrow and tenderness. *Someone's grandmother. Maybe X's?*

She stepped close and spoke, not in riddles, but directly. "My, my. Just got back from California. Went to the beach. Took a bus. Couldn't afford a plane. So bumpy...." She continued talking about pie crusts, lost friends, old photographs. Her voice meandered through fragments of a vanished world, each word tender and sad. "I still wait for my grandson," she said. "Still got his favorite, pecan pie. It's in the freezer. Still good, maybe."

Her fingers fumbled for a purse that wasn't there. Her eyes shimmered with memory. Her presence, slowly, thickened the air. "You look sick, son. Real sick." She turned, opened an invisible door, began to serve her ghostly pie. The knife trembled in her stiff fingers. The bones showed through. Her stories drifted, half-truths, half-faded. The past no longer lined up, obliterating symmetry.

"You from Cleveland?" he asked. "Arkansas?"

She smiled faintly. "My people are from. . . . " The sentence never finished.

A second figure emerged, the young woman, the one marked by pain. She took the grandmother's arm, gently guiding her away across the square. Together, they walked, the young, wounded body beside the old, enduring spirit. Strength passed between them. Each drawn from the pain of the other, as if flame were coaxed from long-buried embers.

Then came the others. They passed Storyteller one by one. Some nodded. Some frowned. Others wagged phantom tails. No one spoke. When they reached the fortress, they resumed their tasks: mundane, endless, obscure. Lives reduced to gestures: folding, stirring, waiting. All muted. All unknowable.

For the first time, he heard them. Not voices, just sound. A low hum, full of longing. Each bore a pale, curved protrusion along the upper spine, not a burden, but an extension of self. It shimmered faintly, as if formed from bone and light. Threads of brilliance arced from each curvature to the figurine at the center, weaving a communion not of language, but of lineage.

But now he wondered: *Are those truly tombstones? Or were they hunched backs all along? If so, what future had already begun to rise from the dead? Are these the shapes of what's to come? The Chosen Ones, the Superior Ones? Will they all be hunchbacks?*

Close by, the boy with the backwards cap continued his strange labor, hand spinning in endless, cretinous circles over an invisible device. Only Mountain Man was recognizable, his dogs panting faithfully at his side. The rest of the grunts had lost their features. They were dissolving, drifting into abstraction, while the dead grew solid. More complete.

More alive.

~ *Goddess Visits The Other Two Mediums* ~

Han Tinh awoke with a start. His hut pulsed with a soft, unearthly glow. At once, he knew: *She* was here. He had not seen *Her* since the statue was taken by the People's Army. "You're here!" he whispered, almost giddy. But as he turned, he saw the light spilling through cracks in the walls and floorboards—not emanating from within, but arriving from without.

"Oh! You're outside! Wait—wait!"

He scrambled down the ramp from his wooden bed, lurched to the corner, lifted a board, and relieved himself in a long, steaming stream. In one practiced motion, he set the board back, lit a joss stick to mask the smell, and positioned himself upright in the center of the room. "Now, Revered One," he called, "please enter. I'll prepare tea."

His arms became a flurry of movement: heating water, arranging chipped porcelain, measuring loose leaves with precision. He laid out two cups as if for an exam. Then he waited. The glow faded. Darkness reasserted itself. He lit a low-hanging lantern. Sat. Listened to the silence throb. Then came soft knocking at the door.

"Please enter!" he called, louder now.

The door creaked open. A peasant woman stepped inside. She bowed slightly beneath a conical hat of straw, its braids woven with quiet elegance. She wore a simple black *ao ba ba*, white bone buttons glinting in the lamplight. Her face was hidden, but her feet, small, clean, unmarred by labor, shimmered with a near adolescent smoothness. Though the rains raged outside, she was bone dry.

When she removed her hat, the room changed. Her face was luminous, detached, yet overflowing with calm. She radiated compassion, but not of this earth. The humble peasant cloth took on the weight of imperial silk. Her silence was ancient. Tinh pressed his palms together and bowed again and again. Goddess.

She smiled. *Her* lips remained closed, but *Her* voice entered him like a current through bone. ***I stand before you, Han Tinh, as a lowly woman. Without husband. Without land. Not even a mou of rice paddy. I stand beneath even your twisted form. And yet, I speak to you unbidden. Does this offend?***

Tinh sputtered. "Revered One! You mock me. You know I've never harmed a woman. Not since I was a soldier. These days, I embrace their stares."

Yes. And the rest of them as well.

He looked down, laughed sheepishly. "With my eyes only, Revered One. Alas. With my eyes only."

She smiled again. ***I know your desires function more than adequately.***

"Tea, Compassionate One?"

No. A few sentences more, and I pass again through the gateless gate.

"I am honored by your visit."

It is my wish that you assist your council chief.

"You sent the two-headed snake?"

She shook her head slowly, eyes closed, but in disappointment, not anger. ***It is my wish that you assist your council chief.***

"Yes. Yes, I already am. Look." He gestured toward a gleaming AK-47 in the corner. "I've even retrieved my old rifle."

… Tap. Tap. Tap.…

The sound pierced the moment. *She* winced. A grimace crossed *Her* face as her hand clutched *Her* stomach. Without another word, *She* turned and stepped into the rain, vanishing into the darkness.

He stood alone in silence, staring after her, wondering at the sound, the tapping that seemed to come from within *Her* body.

~ *The Dreaming Clerk* ~

Company Clerk Long twisted in his hammock, caught in nightmare.

A boy dreamed of glory through killing. And in that dream, Long leaned over the rim of the boy's mind and saw, with rising dread, what was taking shape deep within. From a single violent thought, a homunculus began to form, slowly, deliberately, bones knitting, fingers flexing, eyes already open.

The killer did not simply arrive; he unfolded, cell by cell, in the quiet of the boy's developing brain. He made no sound. He needed no permission. Thought gave way. Memory receded. There was no longer room for both the boy and what he had summoned.

Then it happened. The mind, engorged, split open. The body shuddered. The new presence tore through, emerging not into light, but into feral appetite: craving war, craving the heat and breath of other men who dared to resist. Not a dream now. A birth. A future uncoiled.

The boy turned in his sleep. The boy became Cao Thanh Dam.

A voice, soft and feminine, echoed in Long's sleeping mind: *Is it too late for the distillate to tire of killing? Too late for the distillate to become a nourisher of life? Too late for the distillate to dream of fatherhood? Too late?*

The words rippled through him. Long's eyes fluttered open. A figure stood above him.

A nondescript soldier in a standard pith helmet. Yet the helmet glowed, casting a strange radiance over the soldier's form. The voice, however, was unmistakably female.

"Eh? What did you say? What do you want, brother?" Long sat up, rubbing his eyes. "I'm not on duty tonight."

I stand before you, Quang Long, as a lowly private. Without rank. Beneath your status in this army. Yet I speak to you uninvited. Does this meet your pleasure?

Long's voice trembled. "Who are you?"

A simple bo doi.

The figure lifted its face. The features were striking, soft, disarmingly androgynous. Impossible to place. Beautiful.

"What platoon are you with?"

That is not important. Listen carefully. The statue now inside the fortress will, in time, return to your keeping. But appearances deceive. There is more than one where there seems to be one. You must return at least one to Song Nhan village. Do you understand?

Long shook his head. "No. We're not allowed to believe in ghosts or spirits. You speak, but your lips don't move. Strange. Still, you must be just a soldier with fever dreams. You look pale. Do you have malaria?"

The soldier smiled sadly. **When the time comes, you'll remember my words. You'll know what to do.**

Long rubbed his temples, trying to shake the sleep. "Why me? Why come to me, brother . . . or Mother? You were the one who visited when we had the statue. But I'm just a clerk. Afraid of everything. Afraid even of you."

As your ancestors once said: 'When the people are not in awe of your majesty, then you have achieved great majesty indeed.'

"But—"

The figure was gone.

~ *Nature Intrudes on Storyteller's Fever Dream* ~

Storyteller lay quietly, savoring the rare pleasure of a body without pain. The fever had momentarily lifted, and in its absence, even the smallest thoughts felt like gifts. How pleasant to dwell on trifles: a glance, a phrase, a scrap of paper currency, vague plans for a future that might never arrive. How peaceful it was to lay down the burden of the big things—LIFE. DEATH. KILLING. How restful not to be stalked by THE PAST, invasive and incurable.

While drifting in this fragile reprieve, he noticed a figure approaching through the fortress haze behind a dim, cloth-wrapped flashlight. The light around him was strangely bright, so bright that the man moving toward him seemed almost erased by it. He moved slowly, uncertainly, as if passing through a fog only he could feel.

Storyteller focused on the face and recognized Nature. The lingering apparitions along the corridor trembled in his path, flickering at the edge of sight. Then, as Nature laid a hand on his shoulder, the apparitions collapsed, dissolving into streaks of light that passed soundlessly through the fortress walls. Darkness returned. The vision ended. And with it, the fever crept back in. Heat gathered in his chest. The first shiver touched his spine.

"Hello, Storyteller," said Nature. "Mind if I sit a minute?"

Storyteller did not hide his irritation. "Go ahead."

Nature grinned anyway, cheerful as always. "How's it going?"

Storyteller turned, scowling. "You're kidding, right?"

"Couldn't sleep," said Nature. "Thought I'd check on you."

"Thanks."

"You sleepin'?"

"Nope."

"Your ghosts again?"

"Yeah."

Nature scanned the darkness. "Still here?"

"No. They slipped away when you walked up." He said it with a hint of accusation.

Nature hesitated. "Storyteller?"

"Yeah?"

"Did any of them . . . visit me?"

Storyteller's expression softened. "Dunno. I can't tell who they are when they come. They're just lumps of jungle fatigues, rumpled shadows."

"But you know where we all bunk, right? Where I sleep? Over there, by the far wall?"

"Doesn't work like that. It's all jumbled when they're here. Feels like a dream, familiar, but twisted. Why?"

Nature paused. "Because I miss my family. My mom and dad. I was hoping you could describe them. Maybe they were here. Maybe you saw them."

"You don't think they're just fever ghosts anymore?"

Nature shrugged. "I don't know. This old fort is weird. Sometimes I think I see ghosts of the French who died here. And that statue, those lights and tapping sounds, it's not normal. So . . . maybe your ghosts are real after all. I guess I want them to be."

Storyteller said nothing.

Nature eyed him. "Come on, man. You know more than you've said. You always play it close to the vest. But it's me. Nature." He tapped his chest lightly. "You can talk to me."

"I'm not hiding anything. Just feel the fever coming back. Always happens when they leave."

Nature shifted, stretching a leg. "Could you try? Describe them? Just the older ones. Maybe I'll recognize my parents."

"I don't think I can. They're not . . . complete. I can see hearts beating, lungs working, blood moving through their veins—"

"But you've said you can see their faces. Their clothes. Right?"

"Yeah."

"So try. Please, Storyteller."

He hesitated. Then nodded. "Alright. I'll try."

He began describing the apparitions, those old enough to be someone's parents.

Nature interrupted, his voice catching. "That's them! Has to be. Mom's a little heavy. Dad's thin as a scarecrow. Jack Sprat and all that." He swallowed. "Did they seem happy?"

"Yes," Storyteller lied. "They were happy."

Nature's voice softened. "God, I'd give anything to see them again. Just once." They fell into silence.

Eventually, Nature asked, "Why are they here, Storyteller?"

"Who?"

"The ghosts."

Storyteller blinked. Looked down.

"Dunno."

Nature studied him, the brightness in his eyes dimming. "Yes," he said quietly. "I think you do."

Chapter Nineteen

Village Redux

Mountain Man
Departs Again

Dawn arrived as a shroud. Gray fog and slanting rain veiled the fortress, smothering outlines and dulling edges. Even the sun, prodding from beyond, could do no more than stir the soup. Inside the shattered church, T, Cairns, Birdman, and Mountain Man sat hunched in a semicircle around Pappy, each perched on a wet stone, each cradling tin cups of scalding coffee, heated with thin slivers of C4 ignited beneath their canteens.

Pappy's voice was quiet but final. "Either we all go through the tunnel this morning and try to fight our way out, or at least two of us go to get help. We've waited too long already. If we're hit again, we won't hold. No ammo. No mercy. Two grunts moving light might slip through. All of us? We'd be spotted, hunted. Cut to pieces in the open jungle. But two might reach radio range or find an ARVN garrison near the district capital. Either way, it's today. This morning. No more waiting." He shook his head. "It might already be too late."

T exhaled slowly. "They'll find the tunnel eventually." He glanced up through the broken ceiling. "Never thought this monsoon would last. Still don't get why they haven't overrun us."

"They're worried about the statue," Pappy said.

Birdman frowned. "What statue?"

"They might be afraid it'll be destroyed if they launch a full assault."

T nodded. "Then it must mean something. Something real."

"Maybe," said Birdman, "but it doesn't change the question. What do we do now?"

"I say we all go," Cairns offered.

"Yeah," muttered Birdman. "Better to die out there than rot in here."

Mountain Man's voice was rough from sleep. "Better to figure how we live, not how we die."

T turned to him. "What are you suggesting?"

"One goes. Not two. One can move faster."

Pappy bristled. "No backup? That's a hell of a gamble."

"No gamble if I'm the one going," Mountain Man said, spitting into the dirt.

"I don't think so," T said sharply.

Mountain Man's eyes narrowed. "Don't trust me?"

T met his gaze. "No." The word landed like a slap. Regret came instantly.

But Mountain Man didn't explode. He spoke quietly, with an eerie calm. "Don't matter what you say, T. If you don't send me, I'll go anyway. If you send someone with me, I'll lose him. So let's not pretend."

Pappy studied him. "Why's going alone so important?"

"Because I ain't got Bowls anymore. And I don't need anyone else. They'll only slow me down. Maybe if I get help in time, they'll forget I deserted. And maybe you'll need every warm body if they hit again."

Cairns scoffed. "If we're all dead, you won't have to worry about desertion charges."

Mountain Man didn't flinch. "Maybe, Captain. But I'll be gone either way. Lock the barn door after the horse? Waste of time."

T rubbed his temples. "We can't all go. Idaho can't move. Storyteller probably can't either. And we're not leaving them here if there's any choice. If we're spotted, it's over. So we send a few. And I agree with Mountain Man." He turned to face him, eyes steady. "But you've got to swear on Martha's grave you'll do everything in your power to get us help before we're overrun."

Mountain Man didn't hesitate. "I already told you, when Bowls died, I was one hundred and ten percent in. I swear on Martha. And on Bowls. I'll bring help."

T gave a slow nod. "Good enough for me. But don't forget, we're on borrowed time."

"I know."

"Then move. The next thing I want to hear is American pilots chatting over the radio about where to lay their rockets."

"You got it, T. Good as gold."

Pappy leaned in, hand on Mountain Man's shoulder. "Don't fuck this up, pig farmer. We're counting on you." Then, with a sly smile: "Man to man. Bush brother to bush brother. Sow to sow."

Mountain Man blinked at the unexpected tenderness, then grinned. "Don't worry, Sarge. I'll save your old ass before it can fart twice."

Cairns muttered, "I feel better already. A deserter's Boy Scout oath."

Mountain Man ignored him and stepped into the mist.

~ *A Pact Between Strangers* ~

An hour later, Mountain Man cinched the straps on his rucksack, ensuring the PRC-25 and long whip antenna were tightly secured. Just as he bent to lift the pack, X stepped forward and hoisted it with a grunt. "Let me help."

"Thanks."

Mountain Man slung a green towel around his neck to soften the pack's bite.

X stood nearby, toe nudging a loose brick. "Needless to say . . . good luck, Mountain Man."

Mountain Man shrugged. "Hopefully luck's got nothing to do with it. Anyway, I know you want to go back to your Mama. Or is it your Grandmama?"

X stiffened, but Mountain Man added gently, "So you can get her outta that one-room dump."

X nodded. "Yeah . . . well . . . anyway, good luck. And . . . Idaho doesn't have much time."

"Not unless you amputate."

X blinked. "It's too soon for that. That's not what I meant—"

"Then what's your point?"

"I'm asking you to hurry."

"Hurry gets you killed out here."

"I know. I just . . . things are getting tight, you know?"

"You still talkin' about Idaho?"

X gave a strained laugh and pivoted. "What the hell are an ugly West Virginia pig farmer and a good-lookin' Cleveland nigger doing in the middle of nowhere?"

Mountain Man didn't laugh. "Killing things. People, animals, plants—it's all the same." He picked up his rifle and offered a parting grin. "See you when I get back with a division of Marines. First, I got two stops to make." He paused at the door. "Amputate the leg, boy. You can do it. Otherwise . . . Marines ain't Jesus. And Idaho ain't Lazarus."

X watched him go, then lowered his eyes to the rain-polished floor.

~ *A Wedding Invitation* ~

Tuyet Mai couldn't sleep. Her body throbbed with hunger, rain, and aching joints. She watched the American, The Man from the Mountains, stride across the square with grim purpose. The others lingered near the church, whispering. Something was happening. She tried to sit up but struggled against the ropes. Lowering her head for leverage, she grunted, and suddenly strong hands lifted her like a doll. His face loomed, all beard and shadow.

"Oh!" she gasped.

His smile was cold. "Oh, yourself. Stretch would call us Beauty and the Beast, huh?"

She said nothing.

He switched to Vietnamese. "Just wanted you to know, I'm going to kill your sapper friend, Sergeant Dam. Then I'm bringing back Martha—Kim Lan. We're getting married. You're invited. Any messages?" His face twitched, and he added in English, "Bowls will be my best man."

She blinked. Her mind buckled under the strangeness of his words. Before she could form a response, he turned and walked away. *He's got his pack. He's leaving. Going through the tunnel again.* She shuddered at the thought of Dam and Kim Lan. Then she pushed down her fear as best she could. "Hey!" she called. "American soldier!"

He paused.

"I hope Comrade Dam kills you!" She winced, regretting it at once.

But the American only smiled, eyes sad.

~ The Feast ~

Mountain Man stepped into the church and crossed to the rear, where Bowls lay under the poncho. He flinched. Movement. Ants. A scouting party had found the corpse, and the feast had begun. Workers streamed in through nostrils, the slash at the neck, the cavern of the mouth. A banquet of tissues, tunnels of warmth. The poncho swelled with the gases of decomposition. Life returning to life. He crouched to uncover the body but hesitated. Ants swarmed from beneath the poncho, scurrying at the rain, then retreating. He left it untouched. He had meant to speak, to offer something, but no words came.

Nature stood by the trapdoor, with T and Pappy beside him. All three stared at the still form. "We'll bury him tonight, Mountain Man," Nature said. "Right, T?"

~ Reckonings ~

T said nothing. He was disturbed by the relief he felt watching Mountain Man suffer. When he arrived in-country, he believed he'd be a good leader: respected, fair, admired like his father. But Mountain Man's desertion had cracked something inside him. Made him small, angry, mean. Somewhere deep down, he was glad Bowls was dead. That shame sickened him. He chewed his gum rapidly, trying to muffle the bitterness.

Nature repeated, "We'll bury him tonight, right, T?"

"Yeah. We'll bury him. Just do your job, Mountain Man. Bring help."

Pappy added, "We know you'll come through."

Mountain Man looked at each man in turn. "I'll make it, Nature. You're the only ones who deserve to live. Anyone above sergeant deserves to die." He turned to T. "From lieutenants all the way up to the fuckin' President."

T's face curled in rage. He grabbed the trapdoor, tamping down the fury. *Keep quiet, boy. Don't make it worse.* The thought boiled in him. *It's slipping through my black-ass hands. Damn them all.*

He slammed the door shut.

~ Into the Minefield ~

Mountain Man was back in the tunnel. He had no intention of obeying orders. His mission was simple: kill Dam, rescue Kim Lan, then maybe bring help. Maybe. He followed Madame Dau's instructions, gripping the memory of Bowls and Martha as if they were talismans. At the storage chamber, he paused. The skull still rested in its niche. He cradled it, whispered his vow. But it felt hollow. His rage wouldn't rise. Doubt crept in. The dead faces of his friends offered no clarity. He reminded himself: *I promised to bring help, not to bring it in time.* That was enough.

He replaced the skull and moved on.

When he reached the tunnel's end, he climbed out beneath the banyan roots. Rain fell light and steady. He checked Madame Dau's hand-drawn map. His path led straight to her village. He didn't consider the risk to her. Or to the villagers. His focus narrowed to the next step, the next breath, the next mission. Like many madmen, he radiated a strange calm. It never occurred to him he might die. Or that others might die because of him. He climbed the limestone hill, glancing at the map until he found the hidden fork. Rain soaked his clothes. He cleared a patch, unfurled the radio, extended the antenna.

Garbled voices crackled. English. American. The firebase. He had signal. *Altitude did it. I can call for help.*

He hesitated. Reached for the daisy wheel. Covered the radio with nylon. Hid it well. Later. He'd call later. After his business was done. He raised the binoculars and peered down at the village.

"I'll get help later," he said softly. "Can't have 'em show up too soon."

He smiled faintly, as if death would wait for his convenience.

~ *Arrival at the Village* ~

Even through the veil of mist and rain, Mountain Man could just make out the village. A sudden break in the weather sharpened the edges. He adjusted his binoculars, settled into position, and began methodically correlating the patchwork of paddies, footpaths, and rooftops with Madame Dau's map. There was her house. The *dinh*. The square. The temples. He traced the colorful vegetable plots, the mirrored duck ponds, the fruit orchard brimming at the periphery. Waterways and trails spidered out in a web of geometry, like the seams of the childhood quilt his mother stitched together by candlelight.

In the village square, a crowd gathered around some rusted contraption he couldn't identify. A festival? Perfect. The rice fields were empty. No one working. No one watching. Couldn't ask for better cover. He checked his watch. *Shit. Late. Gotta move.*

He returned to his hidden ridge, selected essentials from his pack, and carefully concealed the rest, radio, gear, and map, beneath foliage and nylon. He searched for a broadleaf plant and found a wild rubber tree. Using bamboo twine, he fashioned the leaves into a crude conical hat, the kind worn by aging peasants. Then he began his descent.

By mid-afternoon, Mountain Man reached the edge of a rice paddy near Madame Dau's back entrance. He hunched low, placed the leafy hat on his head, and shuffled forward as if he were an old man returning home from the fields. His rifle became a walking stick. His posture a disguise. From a distance, he hoped, a forgettable silhouette. Halfway across, barking shattered the stillness.

"Shit!"

Through the drizzle came May-Man, splashing joyfully through the water, tail lashing like a whip. The dog bounded into him, wriggling with delight. Mountain Man shoved him away and continued trudging, May-Man looping around him in chaotic orbit. Unseen, or so he prayed, he reached the rear of the house. Skirting the low retaining wall, he stepped onto the veranda and crept toward the back window. Voices drifted through the shutters. One he recognized, Madame Dau. The other, a man. Fast, clipped Central Vietnamese. Unexpected. He paused, tense, uncertain.

~ *The Visitor with the Rifle* ~

Moments earlier, as Mountain Man stalked the paddy, Madame Dau had just finished dressing in her mourning tunic. She was fastening her hat when a knock came at the front door. Expecting Chief Administrator Vit, she opened it and found Han Tinh on her porch, seated with his back turned, motioning a silent thank-you to Patrol Chief Nguyen as she wheeled away the barrow that had brought him.

Tinh turned, all enthusiasm. "Ah! Good morning! Lucky us, no sign of the venerated schoolmistress yet! Here, take this and move aside so I can swing in."

He handed her a tightly wrapped object as he knuckle-walked through the doorway. "I told Nguyen I needed ritual fruit for the funeral." He tapped the bundle now resting awkwardly in Madame Dau's arms. "I said this was a decorative scroll. Hah! And she believed it! Patrol Chief! With her on duty, we're safer than fleas on a dragon's tongue!"

Still muttering, he gestured to the wooden bench. "Now, I'm here to explain how I'll save you. So listen." He grabbed the object from her arms, set it before him, and began unwrapping it. The cloth fell away. Madame Dau's gasped. An AK-47.

"I only have one magazine," he said plainly, "but I'm still a good shot."

Her voice trembled. "What are you going to do?"

"Kill her, of course. I waited on the road all morning but changed plans. If she enters by another route, I'll ambush her from the tunnel under the rice thresher. A clean shot, then I vanish. Out through the tunnel. Temple exit, probably. If the People's Army's with her, I'll say she was a spy. As a Front veteran, I'll vouch for you. Once Nang's dead, there's no witness. You're safe." He beamed, expecting thanks.

But Madame Dau's face contorted in horror. She clawed off her hat, fingers in her hair. "You've ruined me! I'm dead! I should've fled last night! It's too late! Oh, ancestors, what am I to do?"

Tinh barked back, "What did you expect me to do?"

She floundered. "I . . . I didn't think you'd really . . . how could I have known?"

Then came the crash from the rear of the house. The back door splintered open, and the Man from the Mountains loomed in the frame, filling the room like a demon summoned from wet earth. Mud smeared his face. Rubber leaves clung to his hair. The air that followed him was thick and primal.

Tinh froze. His eyes darted to the rifle at his knees. Inches away.

The American locked eyes and smiled. A dare. Try it.

Madame Dau glanced between them in disbelief. *Now my fate lies in the hands of two madmen.*

May-Man, undeterred, slipped inside and wagged furiously. Madame Dau, reacting instinctively, scolded Mountain Man. "Why did you let the dog in?" She herded May-Man back outside, still grumbling, while Mountain Man chuckled at the absurdity. "Sorry, sorry," he muttered, lowering his rifle only slightly.

She blocked the swinging door with a chair and turned back. What greeted her was a tableau from nightmare: Tinh on the floor, eyes smoldering; Mountain Man looming above him, unreadable.

"He's here to help me," she blurted, groping for clarity.

Mountain Man's eyes narrowed. "Who blew off your legs?"

Tinh fired back, "Who blew off your face?"

Mountain Man roared with laughter. Madame Dau hushed him.

Once composed, he asked again, "How is he helping you?"

She explained everything: Nang, the risk, the village, her own doom.

Mountain Man's features softened.

He turned to Tinh. "How'd you lose your legs?"

"Stepped on a mine while pissing," he lied.

"What unit?"

Tinh saluted mockingly. "Buddhist."

"Buddhist, my ass," Mountain Man growled. "What unit?"

Tinh relented. "I was with the Front. But now . . . I'm useless. I've been retired."

"Then why protect her? Why not help Nang?"

"Unthinkable," Tinh said, aghast.

Mountain Man pressed him about the plan. Eventually, Tinh relented and described it in detail, pride mingling with desperation.

Silence followed.

Only May-Man's panting broke the stillness.

~ *An Agreement in the Dark* ~

Madame Dau waited for Mountain Man to laugh, to call the plan lunacy. But instead he muttered, "Tunnels, eh? Very interesting. Rice machine gives you a 360-degree line of fire?"

"Exactly," said Tinh. "But if I don't get there soon, it'll be too late."

Madame Dau nodded. "My daughters are waiting at the *dinh*. The funeral procession must start."

Mountain Man ignored her, eyes fixed on some interior vista. "How do you reach the tunnel without being seen?" he asked.

"Through a connector. I slide like a boat in a narrow canal."

Madame Dau watched his expression. He's considering it. *With his help . . . maybe. . . .* But she didn't finish the thought. She was afraid to.

Then, suddenly: "I'll do it, goddammit!" Mountain Man barked in English.

"What?" Tinh asked.

"I will do it," he said again, this time in Vietnamese.

"Do what?" Tinh turned to Madame Dau, baffled.

She said nothing, but a quiet smile crept to her lips.

Mountain Man opened his mouth to reply, but the front door rattled under a volley of knocks. Female voices followed. "Madame Dau! The funeral! Are you ready? Madame Dau?"

She clenched her jaw, grabbed her hat, and hissed at the men, "Stay here!" Then she turned, calling out, "I'm coming! I'm coming!"

She slipped through the door, careful not to reveal what lay inside. Outside, the women waited like ducklings, and Madame Dau resumed her role. She barked instructions, walked fast enough to stay ahead of their questions. But inside her mind, something was unraveling. *Perhaps this is a dream. A trick of memory and spell. Nothing fits. It's all wrong. I'm not—wrong! Wrong! Never mind. Just go.*

Madame Dau shook her head to clear it and pressed forward. The women followed, faithful and mute.

~ *Mountain Man Expropriates Han Tinh's Plan* ~

Mountain Man had made up his mind. He would take Han Tinh's plan and make it his own. First, he would kill Schoolmistress Nang. That would secure Madame Dau's allegiance, which he needed for the next step. Then he would kill Han Tinh. The legless little man had served his purpose and was now a liability. Afterward, he would track down Sergeant Dam and finish him in the jungle. Then . . . then he would find Kim Lan, rescue her, and with Madame Dau's protection, use the village as their sanctuary. It would be a new beginning.

By fulfilling these tasks, he would also, incidentally, save the grunts back at the fortress. He could reach the firebase now. The radio waited atop the ridge.

But **only** after Dam was dead. Only after Kim Lan was safe. He reminded himself constantly. Still, he knew he needed Tinh to navigate the tunnels. Alone, he would never find the right passages in time. Tinh's voice interrupted his thoughts.

"Listen, American soldier, Man from the Mountains, whatever you call yourself—if we don't leave now, she'll arrive with People's Army guards, and it'll be too late. The funeral's our cover. The square will be full of villagers, perfect chaos. I shoot her, then disappear in the confusion."

Mountain Man narrowed his eyes. "Won't the crowd make it harder to get a clean shot?"

Tinh's mouth twitched. "Not for me. I could spot that old hag from twenty kilometers. Her face attracts bullets."

"Idiot," Mountain Man muttered. "I'm going with you. I want it done right."

Tinh paled. "No! If you're spotted, we both die. The tunnels weren't built for orangutans. You make me nervous."

"We go together," said Mountain Man, flat and final.

Tinh relented. "Fine. After we kill her, I'll take you to the farthest tunnel exit—by the dike on old Vit's land. You can vanish into the jungle."

Mountain Man agreed. Time was short. But in his heart, he'd already decided: Tinh would not reach that exit alive.

"Good," said Tinh. "Come. The trapdoor's in the next room. You'll have to lower me."

Mountain Man rolled his eyes. "Oh, crap."

Tinh grinned, the corners of his eyes cracking with strain. "Don't worry. Just get me down. Once inside, you'll have trouble keeping up."

Mountain Man lowered him gently, then dropped into the cramped chamber below.

Tinh clamped the flashlight between his teeth and scuttled forward, quick and low to the ground. Mountain Man followed, bent double, scraping his shoulders against the walls, sweat soaking his face. These tunnels weren't built with precision. No fortress symmetry here, only raw passageways gouged through dirt for desperate men. He half-crawled, half-shuffled through the tight corridor, blinking against the sting in his eyes. Ahead, Han Tinh darted forward, fast and tireless.

Little mole with its ass on fire, marvelled Mountain Man.

Every so often Tinh paused, removed the flashlight, and shined it backward. "Hey, American soldier! What's taking you so long?" he laughed, voice echoing in the dirt.

Mountain Man growled, "Yeah, yeah, you little V.C. bastard. I'm coming."

At last, they reached the chamber beneath the rice thresher. Larger. Airier. Tinh pressed a finger to his lips, then handed Mountain Man the flashlight and a canteen. He took a long drink, checked his rifle, and began his climb up the bamboo ladder.

~ *The Funeral Begins* ~

Madame Dau marched through the cluster of women who had come to fetch her, issuing commands with practiced ease while her thoughts remained elsewhere. As she led them toward the square, her mind strained to catch any whisper of Nang's return. Passing the thresher, she tried not to look directly beneath it, but she couldn't resist a glance. Empty. Too early, she told herself. Still, its dark underbelly, the angled metal and narrow clearance, confirmed her suspicion: Tinh's plan was a delusion. There was no way this madness would succeed.

Once inside the *dinh*, she forced herself into the rhythms of ritual. *What will happen will happen.* It was no longer in her hands. Chief Administrator Vit hovered nearby, occasionally brushing her arm, a silent gesture of solidarity. But the tension swelled in Madame Dau's chest.

Then came Security Chief Tien, arms flailing in panic. "Where is the schoolmistress? She said she'd be back this morning! We can't wait! And the children! Running wild in the kitchen, pretending to be the Venerable's ghost! Where is she?"

"No," Madame Dau said flatly.

"What?"

"I haven't seen her."

"But she said, last night she told me, she had news about you!"

"No."

Tien huffed off, ranting to anyone who would listen. "She should be back by now! She's responsible for those children! And the ceremony! Has anyone seen Schoolmistress Nang?"

Someone offered gently, "Maybe she's ill?"

"She shouldn't have left the village at all before such an important occasion! I can't go looking for her. I have too much to do!"

Her shrill voice faded into the courtyard as she moved from person to person, repeating the same questions, louder each time.

Madame Dau clenched her jaw. She lashed out at a woman with a simple request: "Don't bother me with that! Ask someone else!" She barked at Nguyen: "What concern is that of mine?" To Trinh: "If the wine is sour, ask the cook!" And then, looking around frantically, "Where is my stupid daughter, Bin?!"

Her anger rolled down through the ranks like a deluge. Tension spread among the women. Whispers stirred. Yet the rites proceeded. To her relief, Schoolmistress Nang still had not arrived.

Because the Venerable Vu Huong had no remaining kin in Song Nhan, the Cult Committee had declared all villagers honorary family. Huong's body had been washed, dressed, and placed on a simple bier arranged by a subcommittee led by Madame Nguyen. Smaller altars had been built, incense prepared. By the time Madame Dau arrived at the venerable's home, candles were already burning on each altar, their flames steady in the damp air. She led the council into the house in solemn procession, then knelt before a side altar. She raised three bowls of rice and three cups of tea to her forehead, placed them on the altar, and kowtowed after each offering. The others followed: dishes of vegetables, fruit, quiet grief. When the last bow was complete, they began the *nhan dieu* vigil.

Madame Dau sat upright on a wooden bench, rosary clenched in her hand, Buddhist prayers tumbling from her lips.

Outside, villagers came and went, offering final farewells.

Inside, Madame Dau burned. Her knuckles whitened on the beads. Her thumb moved faster. Though the monsoon air was cool, she kept wiping sweat from her brow with a small, knotted cloth, balled tightly in her left hand. Her ears strained through the prayers.

Where are you, Nang?

~ *Schoolmistress Nang Leads Dam to the Tunnel* ~

Sergeant Dam rose at first light, his blood already moving faster than the dawn. Eager, he rolled out of his hammock, dressed with methodical haste, and devoured a handful of sticky rice and sour black tea. Then he set off to rouse his sapper team, and the old schoolmistress. "Nguu!" he hissed, shaking the corporal's arm. "Get up! Time to play."

Nguu squinted up through sleep-swollen lids and found Dam crouched over him, eyes bright with urgency. "Yes, yes, I'm getting up," he groaned. "What's the rush? The old lady will take forever getting ready."

Dam thumped him in the chest. "Lazy dog! Worse than her! Maybe you should wear the schoolmistress's hat today?"

Nguu sat up with a smirk. "All right, all right. But why are you so excited about a simple recon mission?"

Dam's voice dropped, eyes gleaming. "Because today I meet someone I've been waiting for. An American devil, yes, but a rare one. He has much to answer for."

Nguu stretched, groaning. "Sometimes I wish you were just a normal sergeant, one who didn't love this madness so much. It frightens me. Well . . . frightens me for about five seconds." He chuckled. "Then I remember your shit still stinks like mine."

"Enough nonsense," snapped Dam. "Get Chu and Doanh moving. I'll see about the schoolmistress."

Nguu laughed again. "Chu's dreaming of some girl in that hamlet we passed last week. And Doanh? He's probably lost in a fantasy about an orchid that'll make him a professor. Poor bastards."

Dam was already walking away. "Wake them anyway. We're using up daylight."

But when he reached the schoolmistress's sleeping area, it was empty. She was gone. Frowning, Dam moved cautiously through the foliage toward the lean-to where Major Vy, Captain Tong, and Political Cadre Minh had made their temporary command post. Pushing aside a curtain of vine, he spotted Vy and Tong in whispered debate.

"What's taking the woman so long?" Vy muttered, exasperated.

"My grandmother takes forever when nature calls," said Tong dryly.

"Yes, but this is too long," hissed Vy.

"Too long for what?"

Vy gave Tong a knowing glance, but kept his voice low. "Too long for *my* purposes. This isn't some eunuch's game in the Forbidden City. We delay much longer, we'll be exposed. And I . . . " his voice rose, "I want to keep my head."

Tong raised a hand. "Quiet, or you'll lose it early."

Vy gritted his teeth, but relented.

Then Tong gestured. "Ah. Here she comes now."

Dam followed his gaze. Schoolmistress Nang emerged from the trees, shuffling stiffly, face pinched in discomfort. She bowed deeply. "Apologies, Comrade Major Vy. Something I ate, no doubt. Not your cook, of course, some awful dish in the village. My poor digestion." She gave a sly smile. "Too many battles. Too many imperialists defeated. My poor old body."

Vy tried to respond, but she gasped, clutched her belly, and abruptly turned again. "Oh! Excuse me, I'll be quick. Just one more time!" She vanished back into the trees.

Vy threw up his hands in exasperation, but before he could speak again, a figure approached. Sergeant Dam stepped into the clearing and coughed politely. "Sirs. My team is ready. If the schoolmistress is fit to travel, we'd best depart. We're behind schedule."

Vy's eyes narrowed. "Where's the guard?" he snapped at Tong. Then, to Dam, "How long have you been here without being challenged?"

"I just arrived, sir. I'm sure the guard was about to spot me."

Vy waved dismissively. "Useless! The schoolmistress has been to the latrine four times this morning. Normally I'd drag her out by her hair, but she's got friends in the Front. No need to stir up complaints. And we wouldn't want Comrade Minh upset, would we?"

Tong grinned. "Indeed not."

Dam tuned them out. He had long ago distanced himself from the theater of Party politics. He mouthed the slogans when required but cared little for ideology. His mission was war. Nothing else.

At last, Nang emerged again, still wincing with every step. She offered Vy a rueful smile. "Old soldier's illness, Comrade Major."

"Yes," Vy said with a sigh.

Tong chuckled. "You wear your scars well, Madame."

Minh arrived, slightly breathless. "Comrade Schoolmistress, the revolution honors you. Your name crosses my desk often."

"I didn't know you had a desk!" exclaimed Tong dramatically.

Nang ignored him. "My contributions are small, Comrade Minh. A backwater village. Ignorant peasants. A council of counterrevolutionaries, and worst of all, women. Like ants in a cup."

Vy checked his watch. "Yes, yes. You've told us about Madame Dau. We'll forward it to the Front, along with your brave decision to guide us. Now," he gestured toward Dam, "Sergeant, we are late."

Dam stepped forward. "Yes, sir. The Americans may have moved already. Once she shows us the tunnel, we'll send her back and observe from a distance. The later it gets, the harder it will be."

Vy nodded, but a guard burst into the clearing. "Major Vy! Comrade Nguyen Kim Lan wishes to speak with you!"

Vy sneered. "Ah, so we caught *someone* this morning. Not a total disaster. Send her in."

The guard saluted and disappeared.

"Now, as I was saying—"

"Good morning, comrades!" Kim Lan entered with her usual poise.

Vy's face soured. "Now, as I was saying Schoolmistress Nang, you'll be escorted to the village edge once we find the tunnel. You will say nothing of this mission. Say you were looking for herbs. Say darkness fell. Say *anything*. But keep your mouth shut."

"But I've never spent the night in the jungle. It will sound—"

"Say whatever works," Vy interrupted coldly. "Now go."

Tong offered, "I'm sure your imagination will serve."

"Ah!" Nang exclaimed suddenly, eyes lighting up. "Major, may I use the latrine once more before we go?"

Before anyone could reply, she vanished again.

"Damn!" barked Vy.

Kim Lan pulled Dam aside. "Comrade, if you find Tuyet Mai, be careful. Don't let your hatred of the Americans blind you."

Vy turned sharply. "Comrade Kim Lan, Sergeant Dam's mission is observation. But if it comes to it, Tuyet Mai is not our priority."

Kim Lan stared daggers. Tong, for once, had nothing to add.

~ *The Tunnel Revealed* ~

Finally, Nang returned and the team departed. Dam walked beside her and kept his tone light. "Well, Comrade Schoolmistress, shall we go find your tunnel?"

She twinkled. "Yes, Comrade Sergeant. Let's drive out the American devils."

Dam nodded. Over his shoulder, he muttered to Nguu, "With her help, the war will end by sundown."

Nguu ducked under a thorny vine. "One way or another."

The walk was long, slow, and maddening. Nang led them down false paths, turned in circles, muttered corrections. Dam bit his tongue.

At last, rounding a dense wall of bamboo, she whispered, "There. It's near that tree."

Dam held up a hand for silence. He stepped in close. "Where?"

She gestured theatrically, then tiptoed forward.

Dam signaled his men to fan out and circle the clearing. Nang froze mid-step, sensing her isolation. She turned, searching for him. He stared back without expression, waiting. When the flankers were in place, he emerged and silently pointed. "Lead me," he whispered.

She nodded and crouched beside a banyan root, pointing to a patch of disturbed foliage. "That's it," she murmured.

Dam seized her arm and led her back to the others. Once they were out of sight, he posted a rear guard and formed the team into a loose circle. "These two will escort you back toward the village," he said quietly. "Say nothing of this."

Nang tilted her head. "And once you see the Americans, Comrade Dam, what then?"

He said nothing.

She smiled knowingly. "I understand. I've fought in this war a long time. I know you plan to lie in wait."

He considered denying it, feeding her false information. But what was the point? She'd already led them here. If she spoke, it would only confirm what they already knew. What harm could an old woman do? But what he failed to see, though he would never have missed it in a man, was ambition. He still believed women cared only for children and gossip. He did not imagine that ambition burned in them too, sometimes brighter.

"I know not to ask questions," she said. "But if villagers accompany the Americans, let me know. I'll see they're punished."

Dam gave a half-smile. "Just don't tell anyone."

"I won't, Comrade. This meeting is our secret."

She turned to go, then paused and saluted.

Dam humored her, returned the salute. His men giggled.

He turned with an exaggerated glare, and they snapped off inflated salutes, smirking. Dam tried to keep a straight face, but muffled laughter burst out.

Nang stared, eyes sharp.

He bowed slightly. "Comrade Nang, forgive their foolishness. They are young."

"And your excuse?"

"I am young too. But we all respect your service."

"See that you prove it, young comrade."

"Yes, auntie."

She nodded and vanished into the brush.

Dam sighed.

"No matter, comrades. Just a cackling goose. Now—let's get to work."

~ *Nang Returns to Song Nhan Village* ~

By late afternoon, Schoolmistress Nang reached the outskirts of Song Nhan. She dismissed her escorts with a quiet word, then mimicked Sergeant Dam's strategy, circling back through the rice paddies to enter from the opposite side. She had no desire to parade down the main road, not with the square crowded for Vu Huong's funeral.

She trembled in anticipation of exposing Madame Dau.

She kept an ear out for sounds of battle at the tunnel

She felt supremely confident.

Slipping in through the damp backside of the village, Nang kept her pace slow and quiet, skirting vegetable plots and duck ponds like a thief. Once inside her home, she washed her face and arms, changed into elaborate mourning attire, and walked with studied nonchalance toward the venerable's house, where the *nhan dieu* vigil was in progress.

~ *Incense and Paranoia* ~

Inside the venerable's house, Madame Dau sat upright, rosary beads rhythmically slipping through her fingers. Her ears strained for the sound of rifle fire from the square. Nothing. Just the low drone of prayer. The lazy cluck of hens. Children's laughter, thin and distant.

Maybe this will end well. Maybe I'm already waking from the nightmare.

The world around her: incense curling toward the beams, women murmuring devotions, the scent of sweet rice and old wood, felt like home. She allowed herself to believe in its permanence. Her daughters' voices, her grandchildren's laughter, the simple bartering of daily life, the gossip and the woven textures of kinship—suddenly they seemed precious beyond words. She imagined long years ahead: weddings, grandchildren bearing grandchildren, maybe even the return of her last son.

Then came a loud gasp. "Oh!" blurted Madame Vit.

Madame Dau turned. In the doorway, framed by gray monsoon light, stood Nang, regal in mourning robes, face serene, posture imperious, as though she carried with her a secret too grand for explanation.

Madame Dau nearly spilled her tea. She glanced at Vit, who gave a slight shrug, feigning ignorance.

Nang approached the altar and knelt. Five joss sticks burned in her hands, their thin flames unwavering, as if fed by her own malevolence. Smoke bled upward in slow tendrils, reaching for ancestors who no longer answered, or gods grown mute to her thirst for revenge. She bobbed and muttered prayers in a low, theatrical murmur. When finished, she moved behind Madame Dau and sat, smiling faintly, as if she alone understood the true meaning of this day. Turning to Madame Pui Thi Ru, Nang began extolling the virtues of the Venerable.

"He was always loyal to Song Nhan," she said, voice pitched just loud enough for Madame Dau to hear. "The old ones understood honor. Not like today's leaders—young, fickle, adrift. No reverence for tradition."

Madame Ru blinked in surprise. "But I thought you favored new ideas? Reforms?"

"Not *all* new ideas. Loyalty must remain. In the old days, traitors were executed, and their fields taken."

Madame Ru shook her head. "Let's honor the Old Venerable. I knew him as a boy, before the Japanese war."

"Yes," Nang replied, her eyes fixed on Madame Dau. "Those were the days. No tolerance for betrayal."

Dau couldn't take it. She stood abruptly and muttered an excuse, grabbing a handful of betel leaves as she stepped outside. Her fingers twisted the leaves anxiously. She scanned the square. No soldiers. But Nang's words clung to her skin. She imagined Han Tinh and The Man From the Mountains still crouched beneath the thresher. *I have to warn them. Something's changed. Something's gone wrong.*

She ducked back inside, caught Vit's eye, and motioned her outside. Under the veranda, they squatted together in whispered conference. "I need to get word to Brother Tinh," said Madame Dau.

"What? Why?"

"They're under the thresher, Tinh and the American. Waiting for Nang."

"The American? *Here*?"

"Yes. He appeared at my door. I didn't know he was coming. But that doesn't matter. I have to tell them."

Vit blinked. "Why are they hiding under the thresher?"

"It doesn't matter. Please. Find out what Nang knows. I—"

Before she could finish, two old men appeared, ducking beneath the eaves. Their clothes were stiff with starch, their hair slicked flat. Their daughters worked the market, weaving baskets and hauling stone. They nodded solemnly, trying to reassert the forgotten presence of village men.

One grumbled, "It's a passable funeral. But not what it should be."

"True," said the other. "If men ran the council, there'd be more wine. More food. More ceremony."

Chief Administrator Vit interrupted. "If men ran it, they'd already be drunk and asleep."

The old men chuckled, not offended in the least. "At least the Venerable's spirit would be well fed," one said.

Vit rolled her eyes and stood half-heartedly.

Madame Dau, lips tight, turned toward the square.

~ *The Message Beneath the Thresher* ~

The old thresher rose ahead, half-ruined, rust-streaked, sacred. A crumbling beast of iron squatting in the square.

Madame Dau adjusted her path. Not the straightest route. A small arc, just wide enough to make her pass close to the thresher without seeming deliberate. Anyone watching would find the detour odd.

As she neared it, she dipped her head slightly. Her lips moved in silent murmur, as if greeting a passing friend.

They'll understand.

Schoolmistress Nang might have seen the exchange—had Chief Administrator Vit not intercepted her. Nang had followed, eyes sharp. But on the rise above the square, Vit caught her arm, breathless from her rush. "Come," she said. "You haven't heard? Little Monkey's mother caught the new fever. Three houses already shut their doors. They think it's coming from the stream."

Nang protested, eyes still following Dau.

Vit pressed closer, gentle and firm, steering her away.

By the time Nang looked back, Madame Dau was gone.

And the thresher stood alone, silent and watching.

~ *Mountain Man Goes into Hiding* ~

"She's already in the fuckin' village," Mountain Man grumbled. "Now what?"

Han Tinh let out a long sigh. "The plan has failed. I must revise it. At least she didn't return with People's Army troops in tow. Small comfort. I suppose the next step is to take you to the edge of the village and let you disappear into the jungle, eh?"

"No," said Mountain Man flatly. "I'm staying. Take me back to Madame Dau's house. I need to think. We Americans are the world's greatest problem-solvers, remember?"

Tinh's brow furrowed. "Too dangerous. Her daughters and grandchildren will be home after the funeral. What then? You can't hide there."

Mountain Man's eyes darkened. "I said no."

Tinh studied him for a long moment. Then: "As you wish, American demon. I'll take you to one of our abandoned temples. The roof leaks. No one enters but mischievous children. There's a tunnel entrance beneath the floor, but it's narrow, barely enough for you."

"I need to shit first."

"Then do it now. Or the tunnel will squeeze it out of you."

Mountain Man waved him off. "Forget it. Let's go."

Tinh led him through a winding labyrinth, doubling back often, ensuring the American could never retrace the path. By the time they reached the trapdoor beneath the old temple, both men were soaked with sweat and streaked in red clay.

They emerged into a cluttered anteroom where old teak and bamboo furniture leaned drunkenly against faded red walls. The air was thick with dust and memories. Tinh's flashlight revealed painted dragons clawing across the ceiling, fire curling from their mouths. The bricks underfoot were worn smooth by forgotten feet.

"This is used as storage now," whispered Tinh. "There's an old Chinese bed buried under that pile. Dig it out, but be silent. I'll return, or send someone."

"Someone like the People's Army?" Mountain Man asked.

"If I meant to betray you," Tinh said calmly, "I would have done it already."

"Not without my killing you first."

"If you kill me, Madame Dau will turn against you. And if she turns against you, you're dead."

"What is she to you?"

"Someone I was commanded to protect. And more than that, she *is* the village."

Mountain Man squinted. "What the hell does that mean?"

Tinh's voice tightened. "I'm angry at her for dragging me into this. My fate is now knotted to yours. The same mistake I blamed her for, I've made myself. But I know my anger is nothing compared to the fire eating you alive. I've no illusions about you. You're dangerous. But the stakes aren't me or Dau anymore. It's the village."

"I don't give a damn about your village," Mountain Man snapped. "I've burned a hundred just like it."

But Tinh went on as if he hadn't spoken. "This village saved me when no one else would. With no legs, I was cast out. It was the women who saved me. It is always the women. Without my legs, I've become like a child again, but with a man's mind. And now I can see clearly what I once dismissed. Society calls us heroes because we destroy efficiently. But it is the women who keep everything together, who give us something to come home to."

He pressed on, voice rising with each truth. "They raise the children, care for the old. They cook, clean, plant, harvest. They carry water, mend clothes, tend animals, and keep the village alive, *especially* during war. Then, the army looks after us and they're left alone to carry the weight of everything. And if it means becoming a refugee, they carry the old on their backs and sometimes, God help them, smother their own babies to keep them quiet."

Mountain Man scoffed. "If not for the men, the women would be raped or killed."

"By whom?" Tinh's eyes flashed. "By other men? Thank Buddha, then, for the protection of men."

He sneered. "When I was strong, I laughed at women. Ignored them. Took from them. Their lives were shadows. They didn't even own their stories. But now I see. When I lost my legs, I thought I had become like a woman—weak, useless. But now I know the truth. It's not men who are strong, it's the women. They are the ones who make civilization possible."

Mountain Man muttered, "You're full of it. Women need men to protect them."

Tinh's laughter was dry and bitter. "The American army feeds you, clothes you, gives you praise, a flag, a coffin if needed. What do women get? Nothing. No medals. No statues. No parades. Just more mouths to feed." He shook his head slowly. "I once had ideals too. Joined the Front, gave up everything to kill Americans. But when I lost my legs, I was thrown away. Not even good enough for pig shit. And yet, the women found something left in me. I owe them everything."

Tinh leaned forward. "But you . . . you will die out there. Alone. You're all the same. Complete bodies. Incomplete minds."

Mountain Man let him finish. He hadn't listened to most of it. His thoughts drifted to Martha, to the dream of a life together. He saw Bowls' smiling face. "Goddamn, you talk a lot," he snapped. "You're wrong. I've got no ideals. Just hatred. I'll kill whoever I have to, then I'll go home. And your women can go to hell. I care about mine, no one else. That's how it works."

Tinh sighed. "Then you're already dead. The mouth freezes first. Then the limbs. Soon, rigor mortis of the soul."

He looked toward the door. "If you're so sure you'll make it home, then you won't mind if I go. Maybe I'll find a way out of this mess."

Mountain Man hesitated. "Yeah. Go do what you have to. I'll stay. For now. But if no one contacts me by morning...." He trailed off, then added in English, "There will be hell to pay."

Tinh smiled faintly. "I understand, Comrade Ugly American."

Mountain Man chuckled despite himself.

"I'll return with food," said Tinh.

"I still have to shit."

Tinh grinned. "There's an old latrine through that door. A hole in the ground—not meant for an ox. But you Americans are problem-solvers, no?"

Then, quicker than expected, the crippled man disappeared, knuckle-walking into the dark, the door whispering shut behind him.

Alone, Mountain Man thought again of what Tinh had said: *"Someone commanded me to protect her."*

A chill ran down his spine. *Who? Why?* He looked up at the painted dragons glaring from the ceiling and, for the first time, felt like prey. *I'm not in control here.*

He squeezed into the cramped latrine, relieved himself, and returned to rummage through the clutter. He uncovered an ancient Chinese bed, placed it carefully on the bricks, and lay down gingerly. The ceiling seemed too close. The angles were wrong. The smells, teak, incense, mildew, urine, blended into something alien. Even the ants crawling the walls were familiar in form, but not in spirit. *American ants,* he thought. *On American dirt. That's what I want.*

He longed for the smell of the Alleghenies, the weight of a dog at his side, a beer in hand, Bowls laughing at a dirty joke. He curled into a fetal position and wept, not just for his fiancee or for Bowls, but for his mother, for his father, and for the home he once dreamed of escaping.

~ *Madame Dau in a Dangerous Position* ~

After tipping off the men beneath the thresher, Madame Dau walked briskly to her house, unwilling to face Nang again at Vu Huong's vigil. Inside, she lit a small burner, poured tea, and sat heavily on her wooden bed. But peace was short-lived.

"Granny! Granny!" cried a small voice.

Her grandson ran in and buried his head in her lap. Bin entered next, flustered, voice sharp. "He ran all the way home! Embarrassed me in front of everyone. He refused to look at the Venerable's body. He'll return. And this time, he'll touch the Venerable's hand and kiss his face!"

"Wait," said Madame Dau. "Let me try something."

She lifted the boy's face and spoke gently. "Teo. Are you afraid of the Venerable?"

He stammered, trying to speak.

"Be calm. You remember how he played with you? How much he loved you?"

He nodded.

"But now his body is just like the bark of a fallen tree. The spirit is gone. The shell remains."

"But . . . I saw . . . an ant."

"An ant?"

He nodded again.

"On his lips. If there's one, there are many."

"Just like termites in a fallen tree, yes?"

He thought. "Yes."

"Will they hurt you?"

He shook his head.

"Then go. Touch his hand. Pretend he's a tree."

The boy nodded. "But I won't kiss him."

"You don't have to," said Madame Dau.

Bin scoffed. "He doesn't have to kiss the Venerable, I mustn't marry who I love, and you must help an American soldier!"

"Quiet!" hissed Madame Dau. "Yes, maybe I'll be executed. But Teo doesn't have to kiss him. Do you understand?"

Bin softened. "I'm sorry. I was foolish." She hugged her mother and turned to go. "We'd better be off."

"Tell the others I've taken ill. I won't be back tonight."

"You'll miss the feast!"

"Tell them I'll come later. But let me rest."

As dusk deepened to night, Madame Dau paced, prayed, and clicked her beads. Fear grew as noiselessly as fungus in the dark. Finally, she slipped out and made her way to Tinh's shack.

A cigarette ember glowed in the dark. Tinh.

"I've been waiting," he said. "What have you learned?"

"Nothing."

"I hoped you were Vit. But you are prettier in the dark."

"Please, Tinh. No jokes. Tell me what's happening."

He sighed. "The American is hidden. I hope. I await Vit. She's questioning Nang."

They waited in silence.

"Your American is ugly," Tinh said.

"Yes."

"Fearsome."

"Yes."

"Lonely."

"Yes."

"Crazy."

"A little."

"A dead man."

"That's for the gods to decide."

"No. I mean he's already dead. I told him so."

"Yes," she agreed. "He's full of hatred."

"But?"

"No 'but.'"

"There's always a but."

She smiled. "Yes. But he's also just a boy."

"A boy?"

"Yes. He talks to dogs like a child. Among kindred spirits, he's harmless."

"Kindred dogs?"

"Yes."

"Maybe he is harmless, between killings I mean."

At that moment, Madame Vit appeared. "Who is killing our countrymen?" she demanded.

"The Trung Sisters, reunited!" Tinh exclaimed.

"Answer me!"

"An American soldier," said Madame Dau, blunt now. "Now, did you learn anything?"

"Yes." Vit's voice dropped. "Nang took Tien aside at the feast. I followed and listened. She told Tien you've been accused of helping Americans, and she confirmed it."

Dau gasped. "What else?"

"She repeated everything we said yesterday on your porch. She told the People's Army. She led them to the tunnel. Then said, 'The fate of our council chief is in my hands.'"

"So Vy and the Army know everything," said Madame Dau. "Why don't they just kill me?"

"They don't care about you," said Tinh. "They want the tunnel. Vy doesn't give a damn about a village woman."

"Then they won't kill us?" Vit asked.

"No promises," said Tinh.

They all went quiet.

Then Tinh added, "Our only advantage is that Nang doesn't know I'm involved. And the American is hiding under her nose."

"How does that help?" Vit asked, eyes narrowing.

Tinh turned on Dau. "You see what your involvement has brought us? First ideology, now danger. Always the same spiral."

Dau shot back. "Stop whining like an old aunt! You just said we still have hope. Then listen: that same American soldier may become our salvation."

Vit blinked. "How?"

Silence.

"Ah," said Tinh darkly. "So you are ready to take that step."

"What step?" Vit asked.

Dau and Tinh exchanged glances. Finally, he spoke.

"We tell the American where Nang lives."

Vit paled. "Why?"

"Because we also tell him Nang met with the People's Army. And that she knows who killed his comrade."

"But does she?"

They shrugged.

"Who knows?" said Tinh.

~ *Madame Dau Plots with Mountain Man and Han Tinh* ~

After a long silence, Madame Dau said softly, "I must speak with the American."

"I told him I'd bring food and water tonight," said Tinh. "But we go separately. You prepare the food. Meet me at the temple in an hour. I'll bring the water, smooth the path. He's a vicious dog, and such creatures must be well fed."

"And I," muttered Madame Vit, "will return home and puff my water pipe until this cursed night is obliterated in the smoke."

Madame Dau hurried home. She steamed sticky rice and laid tender watercress over the top, rushing to finish before Bin returned from the feast. Wrapping the bundle in banana leaves, she slipped it into an old scarf, scrawled a note, *'I will return late,'* and stepped into the darkness. Convinced no one had seen her, she crept through the back entrance of the abandoned temple. The lock dangled open. She entered slowly, pulling the heavy wooden door shut behind her. The interior was thick with shadow. Blackness swallowed her, and she froze, afraid to knock something over in the unfamiliar dark.

She whispered Tinh's name.

No reply.

She moved cautiously toward the far wall. A faint light bled under a small door in the corner. Shadows passed behind it. Her heart thumped. She gripped her conical hat like a shield. *Is this a trap? Are Nang and Major Vy waiting for me inside?* Pushing aside the dread, she stepped closer, her breath slow and deliberate. She stopped before the door, closed her eyes, and summoned every grain of courage. *Four taps. If no answer, I leave.*

She tapped. Once. Twice. Three, then four times, quiet and deliberate. Silence.

Then a reply: "Who is it?" Tinh's voice, barely audible.

She exhaled. "Madame Dau."

A pause, then a click. The door opened into a dim chamber. "Quickly," Tinh whispered, pulling her inside.

A kerosene lamp flickered to life. The room had been lived in, faint impressions on the furniture, footprints in the dust, but the American was nowhere in sight. Tinh crawled to a corner and slapped the floor three times. From beneath the bricks, a trap door creaked open. The Man From the Mountains emerged slowly, his face clay-streaked, sweat-matted, eyes lit with the ancient fire of something awakened beneath the earth.

"Hello, Madame Dau," he said with grim civility.

"Good evening," she replied, studying the fatigue in his face. He seemed older, the mask of war slipping just slightly.

Dropping onto a wooden bench, Mountain Man spoke quickly, eyes alight. "Han Tinh says the village schoolmistress knows the soldier who killed my friend. Is it true?"

Madame Dau hesitated. "I think so. She . . . visited the People's Army camp and later told a friend she guided a team of *bo dois* to the tunnel exit."

Mountain Man's gaze hardened. "How does she know which one killed him?"

Tinh interjected. "I told him it was a sapper who killed his friend. Nang's team were sappers. There are only so many in a company. Simple deduction."

Mountain Man's voice dropped to a growl. "If I describe the killer, she can identify him?"

Tinh nodded.

"Where is her house?"

Madame Dau stepped in quickly. "Deep inside the village. Surrounded. If something goes wrong, dogs will bark. You'll be found out."

Mountain Man smirked. "It's a village of women. No Front. No NVA. Right, Tinh?"

"Right."

"I'll take you," said Madame Dau slowly. "But you must swear not to kill her. I am a Buddhist. If her blood is spilled, my next life will be . . . hindered."

Mountain Man blinked. "Won't killing her solve your problem?"

"No. It will multiply them. You must promise."

Mountain Man shifted. "Okay," he said in English. Then, as if remembering to show deference to her wishes, he added in Vietnamese, "*Tùy bà.*"

"Swear again," said Dau, "as you did at the tunnel. To your god."

He rolled his eyes. "I swear, as a . . . Baptist." Then, in Vietnamese, a quiet vow not to kill: "*Tôi sẽ không giết bà ấy.*"

She nodded solemnly. "We go when the feast ends. Here. Eat." She handed him the bundle.

While he devoured it, Dau sat in silence, watching his boots. Though the light was low, she imagined shapes moving across the scuffed leather, spiraling patterns, the lives and deaths of villagers circling endlessly over blood-soaked earth.

She felt a prickling on her feet, ants. Many of them. Crawling between her sandal straps, searching.

She lifted her feet and brushed them off, her face troubled.

~

Pre-dawn shadows thickened the air as Madame Dau stood outside Schoolmistress Nang's house. A figure loomed beside her—Mountain Man—caked in mud, knife in one hand, M-16 in the other. His face, ferocious and glistening, looked carved from the night itself.

The stink of night soil soaked the air. A laugh drifted faintly from a final reveler. Dogs barked, too close.

"I must go now," she whispered.

He nodded. "Go. When I'm done, I'll return to the temple. Tomorrow morning I leave. Tinh will guide me through the tunnels."

She shivered. "Yes. Good luck, Man From the Mountains." She turned quickly and vanished into the dark.

Mountain Man tested the door. No lock. He smiled. Slipping inside, with the dogs still quiet, he vanished into the house, silent and patient, moving with the instinct of a hunter scenting prey.

~ *The Dowager's Dream* ~

In her dream, Nang sat tall in a grand Chinese chair, draped in silks, surveying a palatial room lit by morning sun. Before her, a young girl—her daughter, though she had none in life—sat on a Western sofa, knees pressed together, eyes lowered in reverence. Beyond the veranda, nightingales fluttered in jeweled cages. Great vases lined the columns. Mountains framed lush fields beyond. Nang sat like a Dowager Empress.

Her estate manager entered, bowing low. "Mistress, the villagers request audience."

"Have they waited long?"

"Hours."

"Send the first."

Security Chief Tien entered, fell to her knees, and bowed repeatedly. "Please, Madame Council Chief," she begged, "purge these worms from my body."

Nang's gaze dropped. Tien's face writhed, undulating with burrowed worms crawling beneath her skin. Across her forehead, down her cheeks, around her eyes. Fascinated, Nang leaned in. She wanted to recoil, but couldn't.

"Wake up, Council Chief Nang," Tien's voice said. "Wake up. Wake up. Wake up. . . ."

The worms kept moving.

" . . . wake up. . . . "

And Nang did not yet know, the nightmare had only begun.

~ *A Demon Visits Schoolmistress Nang* ~

Wake up, you old crone!" snarled a guttural voice.

Nang opened her eyes reluctantly. A demon's face hovered inches from her own, its features streaked with filth and fury. Before she could scream, it clamped a wet, callused palm across her mouth.

"Be silent," it hissed. Her thoughts unraveled. Reality fractured.

~

Mountain Man loomed above the struggling schoolmistress, his hand clamped hard over her mouth. With his free hand, he struck her face. Her body jolted, then went limp. He lowered his face to hers, breath hot and foul, and whispered,

"Answer my questions quickly and quietly or you will die a long and painful death."

She whimpered. He raised his knife.

~

The knife gleamed. It split her field of vision. Nang tried to focus, but her thoughts coiled in panic. A demon had come to devour her. She couldn't form words, couldn't comprehend his commands. Her mind spun in helpless, incoherent fear.

~

When she didn't answer, Mountain Man turned the knife slowly before her eyes. "They say you have worms beneath your skin. If you stay silent, I'll tie you down and cut out your tongue so the blood runs down your throat and feeds them while you drown. Do you understand, schoolmistress?"

Still no answer. Her body went rigid. *I've gone too far,* he thought. She's going to die right here.

~

Then her eyes bulged. Comprehension flickered. She saw the demon for what it was: an American soldier. Dau's American. *He's the one she helped! Buddha protect me!*

She wanted to scream, but his hand held firm.

Wait. Questions. He's asking questions. I can answer questions!

She managed only guttural grunts. Straining to speak, she finally gasped, "Yes! I will tell you whatever you want to know! Ask!"

~

Mountain Man repeated his questions in simple phrases, struggling to understand her halting replies. She told him everything: the People's Army camp, Major Vy, Captain Tong, the tunnel, the sappers in hiding. When she spoke the name "Dam," he tensed, eyes narrowing, body coiled, every part of him locked onto the word.

"Describe him! What does he look like? What weapons?"

She described the wiry sapper with the strange leather pouch around his neck.

Mountain Man felt rage, and with it, a grim satisfaction. He had what he came for.

~

He pulled away her coverlet. From his shoulder, he uncoiled thick lengths of hemp rope. She lay still, whispering Buddhist prayers. The Revolution was gone. Uncle Ho was gone. There was only this beast, and the raw instinct to survive. She offered no resistance as he bound her wrists and ankles.

I will betray the entire revolution if only he won't kill me. The rain hammered the roof. His breath filled the room.

Then she felt his fingers at her jaw, prying it open. Pain. Terrible pain.

Fire surged through the root of her tongue. *He's cutting it out. Gods, please, no!*

But she could only scream inside. Blood flooded her throat. She gagged. She coughed, sputtering as he whispered: "I only sliced your tongue. You're lucky.

Your council chief said not to kill you. But this is a reminder. You will not speak of me. Or Dau. Or the camp. Understand?"

She gurgled, nodded, begged with her eyes.

"Remember the pain. If you talk, I return and finish the job."

Her blood slid down into a place where it mingled with the old, stagnant blood of children she sent to their deaths. It soaked into the rot of her ideology, pooling in the belly of her lies. A final offering to silence the hypnotic speeches she once fed to the young.

~

Fearing she would drown, Mountain Man cut the ropes. She collapsed, vomiting blood. He shoved a bamboo bucket under her face.

"Don't leave your house until tomorrow afternoon," he growled.

~

She didn't know if he was still there. She only chanted prayers through the blood. She wanted to survive. Just survive. In the distance, roosters began to crow. And the sound broke her.

She wanted to hear that sound for years to come.

~

Dawn fertilized the monsoon sky, embryonic light stirring in the Mother's womb. Mountain Man returned to the temple. Dogs barked. He didn't care.

The First Goal was in sight. Dam was waiting.

He passed a squat mud house with a sagging roof. Peering through the window, he saw her: a naked woman, hair slicked back, aristocratic face gleaming. She painted her nipples red with lipstick. Around and around and around. She looked up.

"Yeah, that's right, ma'am," he muttered. "I'm goin' coon hunting. That little gook bastard is grinning and wiping his ass with Bowls' flock bag. Sergeant Cao Thanh Dam is waiting for me."

And is there not someone else waiting for you? the woman asked, voice light, far too light.

He froze. The village was silent. No roosters. No chickens. No dogs. Not even insects. The silence enraged him.

"Yeah. Martha is waiting for me."

She lifted the lipstick like an artifact. ***You long to hear Lan's voice, do you not?***

"Yeah. Her voice. And others. West Virginia voices. Even a New York voice."

You live in the rainforest now. And there are more meaningful sounds in a single acre of this forest than in all of New York in a year. One second in the throat of this planet contains Everything.

"I know who you are," he spat. "You're Storyteller's goddess. And you're full of shit."

Ha! He's got You there, Goddess dear! rumbled a man's voice.

He looked skyward. "And You're full of shit too. People are fouling the planet? Sure. As much as my sick old Bluetick hound shitting in his bed. But You made 'em sick."

Shocked, my boy. Shocked. I thought you were a good Baptist.

"Am," he shrugged.

A buffalo chewed grass nearby.

The woman was gone.

And like any good psychopath, Mountain Man didn't dwell. His mind had returned to the business of killing Cao Thanh Dam.

Chapter Twenty

Fever Dreams VI

The Apparitions Speak

"Who cares anymore?" Storyteller asked the night. "It's better not to. People who care get us killed. Care about power, about politics, money, creeds. All of it. Bullshit. Caring built this hell. Plants don't care. They just live. Sun, water, a place to grow. You ever see a plant agonize over the way the sun glints off its leaves? Or tear itself apart when it doesn't find what it wants? Lop off a branch, it just reaches again."

Nature shrugged. "I guess."

Storyteller scowled. "You guess? What kind of answer is that?"

Nature grinned wide. "Who cares?"

That made Storyteller snort. But the laughter faded fast. He looked toward the black jungle. "They're late again. Where are they?"

Nature's voice dipped. "Maybe your fever's not high enough." He paused, gaze narrowing. "Or maybe this is the last night."

"Shut up. They'll come."

"I hope so. I've got to go on guard duty soon. Don't forget, you have to *tell* me when to touch you. I'm not doing it without your say-so."

Storyteller nodded, his voice low. "I'll let you know. But listen, if you touch me when they're here . . . I don't know what happens. Could be nothing. Could be everything. I'll wait. Maybe after they've been here a while."

"If they come." Nature glanced toward the jungle again. "My luck, tonight's the first night they don't show. Damn, it would be good to see the folks again."

"Don't worry about it," Storyteller muttered. "Still . . . something's off tonight . . . it—"

He broke off, shuddered once, then collapsed face-first into the mud, body convulsing in a seizure.

"Storyteller!" Nature cried out. "What's happening? Storyteller!" He dropped to his knees, clutching him. "X! Get over here! Something's wrong!"

~

He remembered leaning against the wall, talking to Nature, when suddenly everything warped. A pane of thick glass slid between him and the world. In an instant, the fever struck—hotter than fire, searing through his flesh. Desperate, he clawed at the earth, trying to cool himself in the wet mud. But just as it seemed he would ignite and vanish, the heat vanished. Reality folded.

He passed through the veil. That eerie calm returned, the silence before they came. He opened his eyes, and the fortress sharpened into crystalline detail. Stones. Vines. Flowers. Spiders. Ants. Men. All there. All unchanged. Except—Nature was gone.

Something shifted. Though the scene looked the same, it no longer *was*. The fortress existed elsewhere now, another place, another time. From beyond the walls, he heard voices. Men. Women. Children. Laughing, chatting, teasing. As if a tour group had just poured out of idling buses.

What is this?

He looked up at the parapets. The guards didn't react. Same uniforms. Same faces. But the apparitions—they were different. Or were they?

They emerged *through* the stone, as if born from nothing, spilling into the courtyard. The grownups greeted one another with exuberance. The children darted among them, squealing in delight. The old Vietnamese woman who always sat near Tuyet Mai was now chatting warmly with an elderly American matron. Even Mountain Man's dogs were there, bounding through the crowd, not searching for their master this time, but joyfully chasing each other's tails.

Unlike before, the apparitions didn't drift toward each grunt. They stayed in groups, talking among themselves. Storyteller cocked his head, trying to catch a fragment of their murmur.

Only echoes.

" . . . happened so long ago. Of course you never get over it. Can't understand. But—"

"When I first heard—God, I thought—"

"Don't. Not now. I'm not ready. Maybe later. After more time."

"—and his sister's a doctor. Three kids. Beautiful. The other one . . ."

"After that, I moved away. Best thing I ever did."

"You can't dwell on it. By the way, see the Cardinals game last night?"

"It never stops hurting."

"You're it!"

"Who would've thought our two countries—"

"Mommy! He hit me!"

"Beautiful grandchildren. Too bad—"

"My twin sister died when she was twelve. Car accident. Mom lived, but she never recovered from losing Dad."

"He never got to see his own son."

"We have to move on. Life to live. Others to think about."

"Never stops hurting. Never, never, never."

Then a new voice cut through the courtyard, its broken English amplified to official fiat.

The murmurs died.

"Before the tour . . . you see fortress. Many liberation battles—French, Japanese, Americans. Last battle here . . . American platoon, all killed. No survivors. After fortress, you buy souvenirs. Books. Tapes. Thank you."

Storyteller stiffened. He had come to recognize most of the apparitions. Like the new man in a small town, he had slowly learned their rhythms: who was content, who brittle, who barely holding on. He knew which ones bore the stains of compromise, and which still sparkled with defiance. He'd grown to envy some, pity others, resent a few. But one thing united them all: a faint residue of sorrow, the scent of something lost.

He'd watched them for nights now, eavesdropping on their gestures, their phantom rituals. They no longer startled him. Some had become as familiar as neighbors seen through adjoining windows, curtains half-drawn, habits half-hidden. He'd seen them naked in their solitude, tangled in their old loves and petty sins, luminous with unspoken longing. In their eyes, the grunts were many things: saints, sinners, saviors, monsters, lovers, strangers, and above all, *memories*. But now, even the memories were fading. Fading fast.

Understandable, he supposed. Time erodes everything. But to *watch* it happen, to see the living imprint of memory decay into vague outline, unnerved him.

He'd spent too long obsessed with the extremes, especially the naked woman, marked by trauma. Her presence once burned through the haze, impossible to ignore. Always separate from her grunt, yet bound to him in some silent contract. He had followed them both too closely, missing the quieter apparitions, those who carried pain without spectacle, who suffered without display. He wanted to move beyond the grotesque, beyond the violence that paraded itself. He wanted to grow. To grasp the quiet, the uneventful, the slow accumulation of meaning. He wanted to be a writer chronicling the coiled nuances of lives living life.

Instead, he had become what he most feared: a scavenger of moments, a collector of drama, a writer too afraid to linger in the unremarkable. He had traded complexity for contrast. Shaded nuance for flash. A man who should stab himself and let the pages bleed.

Still, he tried. He listened. But the apparitions no longer spoke in tones that matched the grunts. Their murmurs had turned away from war. Their thoughts roamed elsewhere, unbound. They were aging. Changing. They no longer needed the men who once defined them, no longer returned the gaze of those who had once fed off their pain. And that shook him.

He understood what it meant. He didn't want to accept it, but the truth pressed closer by the hour. If Nature, or any of the others, was going to see them again, it had to happen soon. Very soon.

The guide's voice rolled on. ". . . not killed in fortress . . . in jungle . . . no survivors . . . over here you see. . . ."

No survivors.

The phrase struck hard. His stomach tightened. Not from fever this time, but from grief. Words scrubbed clean of cloying interpretation. Words sudden and undeniable.

He turned again toward the apparitions. They were scattering. Not returning to the grunts. Not clinging to memory. They were slipping into patterns beyond him. One behind a steering wheel. Another trimmed a hedge. A third lounged, transfixed by a television that wasn't there. Others simply lay down and vanished into rest.

They no longer hovered. No longer held shape as memory. They had moved into another category. From memory to history. From history to object. And beyond that—into something unnamed.

He peered deeper into the crowd, searching for her, the abused woman. But she was gone. In her place: a new figure. A man, slouched low, arms loose, posture serene. Something about him stirred recognition.

Storyteller leaned in. The man wore the soft armor of detachment. Shorts. Dark glasses. A towel draped over one shoulder. He wasn't a ghost of war. He was waiting. As if time itself owed him a drink.

Then he turned.

And looked directly at Storyteller.

~

X wrestled with the thrashing body. "Stop it!" he shouted. "Turn over, dammit! Nature! Help me! Stretch, grab his legs!"

Mud flew. Storyteller kicked blindly, face twisted in agony. X grunted, straining. "He keeps screaming about an empty box. Says we've gotta find it. I don't know what the hell it means, but tell him we've got it."

Nature grabbed his arms. "You've got it, Storyteller! The box is right here!"

X fumbled for the morphine. "Just hold on! Almost done. Almost . . . there."

As the drugs seeped in, Storyteller went limp. His face, smeared in mud, twitched once, then stilled.

Nature stared at him, breathing hard. "Didn't work."

X looked up, flushed and furious. "What didn't?"

"Tonight was the night. I was gonna touch him while he saw the ghosts. Maybe I'd see them too. That was the plan. But it didn't work. This time was . . . different."

X swore under his breath. His nerves were frayed, his skin raw with fatigue. "How the fuck should I know? He's hallucinating. That's what malaria does. Cerebral malaria's a bastard. *Plasmodium*, a fuckin' nasty parasite. Eats your brain alive."

But Nature wasn't listening. His eyes had drifted beyond the fortress, beyond the sickroom.

"I don't know what that box was," he said quietly. "But I think I know what he saw. This was the last day. I feel it."

He swallowed.

"After this . . . he's gone again. And the rest of us . . . we just stay behind."

Stretch, ever the movie-addicted wiseass, chimed in from the shadows. "Shane! Come back, Shane!"

X shook his head. "Nature, I don't think he's gonna die. He's strong. It's not that bad a strain, man. He'll pull through."

But Nature didn't move.

"I didn't say he'd die," he whispered. "I didn't say that at all."

~ *A Meeting of the Three Mediums* ~

Clerk Long could not sleep. Laughter and distant voices pierced his dreams. He didn't understand the words, but the rhythms suggested English that spilled out slurred, foreign, and garbled. Rolling clear of his hammock, he dropped to his knees and peered into the thick molasses of the night. The voices had stopped. He listened harder.

Now, only the jungle answered: predator growls, prey shrieks, and the croaking lust-song of unseen lovers. Rain tapped against the leaves in hesitant rhythm. Beneath the cacophony, a deeper silence moved that rendered him uneasy. Shifting silence, coiling anticipation. Long felt himself adrift, bobbing on a green-black ocean, sharks gliding beneath. Something unnatural was in the air.

He crawled back into his hammock. And dreamed.

Elsewhere, in the same fevered night, other men slipped into dreams that did not know themselves as dreams.

~

He walked beneath trees with a red-filtered lantern, its light barely strong enough to cut the dark. He had no purpose. No destination. But still he moved, drawn forward by something unseen. Parting a vine, he stepped into a small clearing bathed in soft, sourceless glow. There, resting beside a fallen log, crouched an American soldier, one hand on the bark, the other cradling an M-16. The man's eyes met his, calm and curious. Long felt no fear.

He spoke first. "*Chào ông. Tôi tên Quang Long. Anh tên là gì?*"

The American smiled. "Hello yourself. My name is Mike Powers. My comrades call me Storyteller. It is... *một niềm vui lớn để đáp ứng bạn* . . . a great pleasure to meet you."

Long did not understand English. Yet he understood.

"Ah! You're the Teller of Stories. I suspected as much."

"How did you know?"

"Comrade Kim Lan told me. She said you see spirits. I've seen them too. Why are you here?"

"Waiting."

"For what?"

"Don't know. You?"

Long beamed. "Waiting." He set his lantern down reverently.

"For what?"

"You're funny. What are we waiting for?"

"Whatever it is, it should be here soon. Or *She's* lost Her touch."

~

Han Tinh lay awake, desperate not to think. His stumps ached, ghost nerves firing in protest. He longed to turn onto his side, but the dream of legs had been severed long ago. Still, he wasn't used to sleeping on his back. Not really.

He tried not to think of the American. The Man from the Mountains. But his thoughts coiled back again and again. What did he do to Nang? There were no screams. No gunshots. No sounds of struggle. *Did he let her live?*

Stop, fool. You'll know soon. Just sleep, old trunk. But sleep evaded him.

"Too much energy in my chest and arms," he grumbled. "No legs to drain it."

He thought then, absurdly, of the Goddess. That first time. So radiant. So full. *Those breasts!*

He winced. *Blasphemer. Must not think such thoughts about Her.*

But the breasts would not leave his mind. His eyelids sank.

He dreamed.

~

He opened his eyes and saw no ceiling, no stars, no sky, only something winged and phosphorescent descending from the void. A giant breast, luminous and holy, fell toward him with the brilliance of a divine meteor. The nipple, flushed with heat, hovered just above his chest. The flesh curved around him like the rim of a newborn world. He reached up, wrapped his arms around it, and held fast. As he clung to the glowing breast, he thought absurdly of his mother's body—the first warmth he had known before war took his legs, before faith narrowed him to stump and shadow.

Now it began to ascend, drawing him with it into the radiant dark.

He rose with it, soaring high above Song Nhan. The jungle unfurled beneath him, its contours known and unknowable. *Heaven,* he thought. *I am rising toward heaven.* Then the motion reversed.

No, no, no—

He fell.

Faster. Toward the fortress. Toward the earth. Toward the end.

Wake up, Tinh. WAKE UP.

~

Storyteller and Long both jumped at the crashing of branches. Something massive had fallen through the canopy.

"Orangutan?" Long whispered.

Storyteller didn't answer. He slithered behind a log, covering himself with leaves. Long laughed.

"No need, Teller of Stories. There are no soldiers here."

"How do you know?"

Long hesitated. "Because. . . . "

Another voice finished for him.

"Because we're the only three here. No one else for a long, long way," said Han Tinh, knuckle-walking into the light.

The clearing shimmered with the fragile logic of sleep, each man dimly aware he had stepped outside waking life but too entranced to question it.

Storyteller gawked. "It *is* an orangutan!"

"I knew it was you!" cried Long.

Tinh flopped into the clearing, tried to light a soggy cigarette, failed, and shrugged. "Han Tinh, water puppeteer and part-time monk. You," he pointed to Storyteller, "see ghosts and follow the American Mountain Man. You," to Long, "also see ghosts and follow Cao Thanh Dam."

He spread his arms wide, as if embracing the madness. "And we aren't really here. We're supposed to be killing each other."

Storyteller almost laughed. Was this madness, or just the logic of dreams speaking through them? He looked to Long and grinned. "Told you it was an orangutan."

Long laughed, then turned to Tinh. "You seem to know a lot. Why are we here?"

Tinh glanced at his stumps. "I don't know much. But yes, I know a lot. Still .. . I'll never understand how a breast can fly."

Long gave Storyteller a look. *He's crazy.*

"One of us is dreaming," said Storyteller.

"Or hallucinating," said Long.

"Which one?" asked Tinh. "Honestly, I'd rather be flying. So whichever one of you is dreaming, send me back."

They laughed, then fell quiet.

"What are we doing out here like animals?" Storyteller muttered. "We're men. We should be home. With families."

"Men *are* animals," said Tinh. "And this is Kon Tum."

"You know what I mean. What's our *relationship* to this? To war? To Nature? Philosophers always ask: What is man's relationship to Nature?"

Tinh guffawed. "Only Westerners ask questions that dumb."

Long smiled. "What would you say to them?"

"I'd say, man's relationship to nature is the shit from his ass, the thoughts from his brain, the gods from his fear, the piss from his bladder, the tools from his hands, and the compost he becomes when he dies."

He slapped a mosquito. "Man's like this bug. Foolish to pretend otherwise."

~

A voice, female and terrible, cut through the clearing:

You speak more wisely than you know, Han Tinh.

The air trembled. Goddess had arrived.

Your Lord Father adores carbon. He cherishes ingredients. But not flavor. He mixes, stirs, reheats, recombines—but cannot taste. He demands your worship, yet denies your nature. He teaches you that your minds, your tools, your gods are not part of nature. Thus, He dooms you. Only Immortals endure.

I see the goat's head, the burned woman, the pulp of a worm—as One. I am flavor. And you, little humans, are merely ingredients. But the flavor has turned bitter.

All three men stood silent.

Finally, Long whispered, "Do You mean to eat us, Mother?"

No. *She* stepped fully into view now, robed in peasant garb, glowing. *I want you to eat Us. Chew. Swallow. Defecate. Then walk on. If My compassion no longer moves you, and His punishment no longer frightens you—then live. Dissociate. Enrich the flavor. Make room for the Superior Ones.*

"I do not understand," said Long.

"Why do You let them suffer?" asked Han Tinh. "The killers. The starved children. For flavor? Add ginger instead!"

Mock not the Immortals. Especially Him. You've already lost your legs. What's next?

"I apologize, Lady," said Tinh. "But still—why?"

Why are you aroused by My breasts? Why don't ants read books? Why ask why, when We are only projections of your own fears? You've crawled back to your stern Father. You reject the compassion of the Mother. But the time has come. Evolution will no longer wait. Humans will be ... replaced.

Storyteller stepped forward, voice shy. "My friend Nature says this is our last day. Is that why we're here?"

No. Goddess raised Her arm, pointed behind them with a finger too long to be human. **That is why.**

They turned.

And staggered back in terror at what they saw.

But even as terror took them, part of each man knew: no nightmare ever admits it is a dream.

~

X cursed under his breath, staring at Storyteller's wide, unblinking eyes. "He should be out cold. Why isn't the shit working?"

T's flashlight moved across the boy's pupils. No response.

"What's wrong with him, X?"

"Brain's still cooking. But the fever's not high enough. He needs a neurologist. Or a fuckin' priest."

"Give him three aspirin and blow him up in the morning," said Stretch. "Army way."

"Where's Nature?" T asked.

"Off to guard duty. You think they'll hit us tonight?"

T sighed. "Yeah. Probably. Monsoon won't last. If I were them, I'd come now."

"Finish us off?" Stretch murmured.

"Nah," said T. "Mountain Man's probably on his way. Maybe with help."

"Sure," said Stretch. "Right now he's in Oz, asking the Great Wizard to save us. But behind the curtain? It's just the Army, pulling levers. 'Go kill the witch yourselves. Here's some water and three clowns. Now go away.'"

~

Han Tinh lay flat in his shack, eyes wide, unmoving. Gnats gathered on his face. He did not stir.

~

Clerk Long lay frozen in his hammock, pupils dilated, breath shallow. Medical Technician Le knelt beside him and jabbed Long's arm with a suture needle. Blood.

No reaction.

He turned to Captain Tong. "Comrade Long is paralyzed."

Tong sighed, dead-eyed. "What can be done?"

"I don't know, Comrade Captain."

~

Night deepened. The jungle held its breath.

Above the canopy, stars smoldered like distant verdicts, indifferent to flesh, unmoved by prayer. Beneath them, men lay paralyzed not by wounds but by revelation, their bodies slack, minds adrift in converging dreams. Storyteller's eyes remained open, but he no longer saw the mud, nor the rain, nor the shadows crouched in wait. He had slipped beyond the membrane of meaning, into that hush where memory curdles into myth.

Somewhere, Goddess watched. Somewhere, Father brooded. Somewhere, the carbon spun. No orders came. No rescue rose. Just the slow, mournful heartbeat of a world disowning its sons.

And in the quiet that followed, something sacred ended.

Something else began.

~ *A Dream from Goddess* ~

Three soldier ants crept down the twisted banyan, limbs precise, eyes blind to anything but purpose. They reached the outer rind of the great pulsing mass and sank in, becoming part of the skin. The sphere throbbed beneath them, alive, immense, dreaming of conquest and pillage. Below, half a million bodies writhed in braided formation, a living lattice suspended from the carcass of a fallen tree. The colony breathed as one. Deep within, the queen stirred.

She did not sleep. She remembered.

Around her, nurse drones fed and cleaned with ritual precision. Beyond them, armored kin bristled and clicked in endless vigil, a living wall of muscle and death. Her movements triggered waves—dense, wordless signals that coursed outward through flesh and carapace alike. The hive answered not with thought, but with obedience. Her will extended through the mass, awakening hunger, war, and memory older than bone. Every limb, every mouth, every pulse beat toward the same direction: conquest.

The three newcomers clung to the bivouac's outer shell, their legs hooking instinctively into the lattice of siblings. The scent of musk wrapped around them.

They pressed their bellies to the warm, sweating sphere. Soon, soothed by its heartbeat and odor, they slept.

~

But day does not wait for dreams. The canopy thinned with the coming dawn, and shafts of dull light filtered down to warm the bivouac's skin. A twitch. Then another. A rustling cascade as legs unlatched like shattering chains. The surface fractured, loosened, spilled. The bivouac broke apart.

The Army awoke.

Tumbling from the hive, raining down as seed loosed from a pod, the three newcomers were swept into the surge. A signal—chemical and ancient—rippled through the swarm. They surged together, a tide of hunger, mandibles gnashing, legs churning. Over logs, under roots, around boulders slick with rain and rot they swarmed. At the front, their fiercest sentinel, the Great Warrior, led the charge, a machine of living vengeance who cleaved all obstacles, her body gleaming with gore and glory.

The three soldiers, still green, did as their blood required. They lowered their abdomens, leaving trails of scent for those who followed. One soon lost two legs in a blur of violence, bitten off by a beetle who died screaming. The beetle's limbs were scattered, his body harvested, parceled, and dragged away.

Still, the Army pressed on.

In the madness of motion, antennae flicking, pincers snapping, legs stuttering in battle rhythm, they fought. They slashed, they severed, they gutted. All was instinct. All was blood. And when the ground behind them shimmered with carrion, they turned back toward the bivouac.

But night had already begun to return. Exhausted, the three warriors approached the nest and tapped its living shell, searching for a place to latch, to hide, to sleep. No space remained. They hovered, exposed, unlinked.

Alone.

The jungle answered. Predators whispered from the darkness. Armor scraped. Tongues hissed. The three soldiers waved their antennae, trembling, as shadows closed in with the calm certainty of death.

~ *Waking* ~

Storyteller, Clerk Long, and Han Tinh jolted from their comas, arms flailing in silent combat, each warding off invisible attackers, each freshly wounded by dreams that had ended and nightmares that had not.

Their eyes darted, seeing only shadows where the fever still lingered.

Each breath came sharp, as though the jungle itself was choking them.

And yet, in silence, they reached for their weapons.

~

Diffuse light returned.

The jungle stirred. Ants. Men.

Another day. Another war.

~ *Tuyet Mai Yearns* ~

Tuyet Mai blinked against the soft intrusion of morning light. It crept across her face, silky warmth, stirring her gently from sleep. But awareness brought no comfort. Her limbs were still bound, her muscles aching with cramps that reached into the bone. A new urgency claimed her body.

"Please," she whispered toward the nearest figure, nodding toward the latrine. "Allow me."

Nature, just relieved by Topper, stepped over and helped her rise. He unknotted the cord from around her neck and gave her a faint, tired smile, then gestured for her to walk ahead. She nodded once and shuffled toward the buzzing partition. Her balance wavered, her body hollow and sore, but her mind had begun to map the men around her. The Americans, once blurred as faceless captors, had started to separate and take root in her memory, becoming distinct, flawed, and disconcertingly real. They grew inside her like ivy curling around a trellis of pain. Behind the canvas, she squatted over the pit, swatting at the insects that thickened in the fetid air. Her body strained; her mind wandered.

Earth, she thought, translating Nature's name. *So kind, so strange.* Against her will, she had come to like him. Still—

Kim Lan. Sister. Where are you? Are you safe? Will I be left to rot among these devils?

Her face twisted into a brave smile that cracked too quickly.

Will I die here, or begin again, in some strange new form?
Let it be a beginning. Please. My sister. My comrades.
Where are you all?

~ *Nature Yearns* ~

Nature retied the prisoner, gently, and collapsed onto his poncho liner with a heavy grunt.

Rain whispered from the sky, steady and dull.

He stared up into it.

T walked past, stopped. "This rain's a real frog choker," he muttered.

"Yeah," Nature said, "makes Providence look like the Sahara."

T hesitated. "When you're rested, I need to talk about Storyteller."

"Yes, sir. You think they'll hit us tonight?"

T shrugged. "Not sure anymore. Nothing they're doing matches the books I've read. They're off-script."

He walked on toward Pappy's hootch.

As he walked, T reluctantly acknowledged he needed Pappy's grounding right now.

Despairingly, he felt his strength slipping.

Pappy would buttress the diminished walls of his castle.

Meanwhile, Nature scratched his scalp and muttered to the storm. *Where are you, Mountain Man? Come on, you big ugly bastard. We can't hold out much longer.*

~ *Major Vy Waits* ~

Major Vy sat on a mossy log, sipping lukewarm tea beside Tong and Minh. His stomach roiled, and he pushed the cup away with a sour grunt. "Well, comrades," he said, "I wonder how it goes with Dam?"

Tong grinned, slick and insincere. "We could always send a runner."

Minh leaned forward. "Yes. At least we'd know *something*. Enough dithering."

Vy sighed. "I'd like to know. But if we send someone, we risk revealing their position. And our scouts heard no gunfire from that direction. So we wait."

Minh scoffed. "Wait? Until bombs drop on our heads? I, for one, would rather *act* before I'm too old to crawl!"

Vy's jaw clenched. "This siege has only delayed us a few days. If no word comes by evening, we either launch a full assault at dawn—or withdraw. That is my decision."

Tong raised an eyebrow. "A *firm* decision? At last. Let's wipe them out and take what's ours." He smiled pointedly. "Our comrade Tuyet Mai."

Minh snorted. "Finally."

But Vy's thoughts drifted past the fortress, past the siege. He pictured the figurine in his hand, precious and irreplaceable, and the exchange with the caravan leader. The drugs. The money. And beyond that, a dream: his wife, radiant and waiting, somewhere far from this jungle. Bangkok. Hong Kong. Anywhere but here. He saw himself running to her through foreign streets, the war far behind, the danger gone.

He felt it all: longing, joy, and fear. Most of all, fear. *Dam . . . where are you?* he thought, teeth clenched.

Send word. Let this damn siege end. Let me go home.

~ *Little Monkey* ~

Earlier that day, twelve-year-old Tran Van Trinh—"Little Monkey," as the villagers called him, knew the fever had returned the moment he toppled from his family's water buffalo. Dizzy, sweating, he leaned against the beast's flank and wiped his brow.

Papa's dead. Mama's so sick. I have to run the house. I have to tend the fields. I can't be sick. I can't. If she sees me sick, it'll kill her.

He led the buffalo home and tied it to the banana tree out front. The porch creaked beneath his feet. A metal pot of rice wine steamed beside the doorway. *If Mama sees me like this. . . .* He reached for the lid, but the fumes knocked him back. He staggered into the banana grove and vomited. After the heaves subsided, he staggered toward the porch again, but his knees began to buckle.

Then a hand slapped his back. "Hey! Little Monkey! Did old Nang find you this morning, eh?"

It was Teo—Madame Dau's grandson. "What's wrong?" Teo cried, dropping to his knees as Little Monkey collapsed onto all fours, retching. Teo rubbed his back, calling for help.

Little Monkey tried to rise.

But someone else had arrived.

~

A figure stepped from the mist, tall, cloaked in black, with a long walking stick that tapped the ground in rhythmic defiance. Tap. Tap. Tap.

Before reaching them, he spoke. **Is the boy ill?**

But his lips didn't move.

Teo froze. The man's voice rang not through air, but within the skull. He leaned over Little Monkey and placed a broad hand on his forehead.

Yes. You will die, Little Monkey. And soon. It will be painful. Have you given love? Have you prayed?

Little Monkey whimpered and twisted weakly.

The man nodded with curious warmth. **Love, Little Monkey. Love is what saves you. Not from death, but from being like them. Love for your people. Love for First Principles.**

He let ants crawl across his fingers, then closed his fist, crushing nothing. They slipped away unharmed. He shook his head.

Love and worship. Not like these.

Little Monkey trembled. "I'm Viet Cong! I worship Uncle Ho!"

No, no, the man murmured, **that is not—**

"Leave him alone!" shouted Teo, voice cracking.

~

The man turned to Teo. **The myriad forms rise and fall. But I … I am always benevolent. Worship First Principles, Teo, and I will reward you. The boy's pain is benevolent. His death is benevolent. The virus killing him has free will. For that reason also, all things are benevolent.**

Teo blinked, paralyzed by the contradiction.

I am compassionate, the voice insisted. **I am filled with love. You are clever. But you cannot yet understand.**

He stroked Little Monkey's hair with the detached serenity of a god.

"Are you with the Front?" Teo asked suddenly. "Little Monkey's loyal to Uncle Ho! So am I. My mama. My grandmama!"

The man snorted. **I am the Front. I am the Back.**

"Huh?"

Never mind. I asked the boy, now I ask you. Have you given love?

"I share my rice," Teo muttered. "The Front says we share everything. No class. No rich. No poor."

Yes, yes, the voice said, brushing it aside.

Teo puffed his cheeks, frustrated.

"Are you here because of the fortress? The battle?"

Will you fight with me? Will you fight for me?

"When I'm older. But I don't have a gun."

Little Monkey arched his back and screamed. "It hurts! I want to go inside! I want my mama! I want to go *home*! It hurts!"

Teo looked into the stranger's eyes—and what he saw frightened him to the marrow: not anger, not violence, but an ancient indifference so total it burned.

Teo bolted. "I'm getting help!" he yelled, vanishing into the rain.

~

The man looked down. **Are you afraid of Me, boy?**

"Yes," Little Monkey whispered. "You talk, but your mouth doesn't move."

The man considered this. Then leaned forward and kissed the boy's forehead. **Remember Me. I would cure you, but First Principles prohibit.**

"And my mama?" Little Monkey begged.

I would cure her too. But probability starves at fate's door.

Little Monkey staggered inside, thinking, *I should've talked to him more,* he thought. *Maybe he could've helped us. Maybe he's a monk. A Buddha. Maybe—*

"Mama! Mama!"

~

Teo ran through the village, heart pounding, tears streaking his face. A sudden cloudburst shattered overhead. Lightning cracked a tree. He ducked beneath a carambola, breath heaving.

Tap. Tap. Tap.

The stranger stood before him again.

Teo froze.

Then the voice filled his head, serene and unspeakable: **The battle will bring a woman to your house. She will live with you. Then leave. Years from now, your fate will be entwined with her daughter's. That daughter, the second head of a two-headed snake, will rise at the behest of a schizophrenic and speak through his voice. As I speak through his voice now.**

Teo's eyes went wide.

"But . . . what about Little Monkey? Did you make him better?"

No. First Principles. Probability starves at fate's door. Do you understand?

Teo shook his head. "No."

He looked down.

When he looked up, the man was gone.

Only the echo remained.

… Tap. Tap. Tap.…

Chapter Twenty-One

The Confrontation

Mountain Man
Leaves Song Nhan
Village

Bleary-eyed but alert, Han Tinh watched the Man From the Mountains sleep on the wooden bench in the anteroom of the Buddhist temple. The nightmare still gripped his nerves, refusing to be shaken off, so he'd wandered into the temple before dawn seeking refuge. Watching the American made him feel less alone, perhaps even essential.

In the pallid dawn light, he saw the man's right hand stained with blood. "Nang," he whispered.

He stepped closer, eyes sweeping the American's body as if preparing it for burial. Jungle fatigues still damp. Right hand caked with dried blood. Face twitching, eyelids fluttering—dreaming. Huge pale feet, white and wrinkled, toes hooked like claws. Green socks draped over a wooden screen, boots placed beneath the bench. Everything within reach.

A demon. "What are you dreaming, Man from the Mountains?" he whispered.

~

"I'll tell you what I'm dreaming!" the man shouted, jerking upright. A knife gleamed in his left hand, slashing the air inches from Tinh's face.

"Ahhh!" Tinh yelped, tumbling backward and flailing wildly. "How . . . how . . . how—?"

Mountain Man chuckled, as if they'd been chatting over tea. "I dreamed of Comrade Dam. Dreamed he was . . . a raccoon." The English word hung untranslatable, so he continued in Vietnamese. "Treed and doesn't even know it. That's what Nang said."

"Did you kill her?" Tinh asked, his voice barely stable.

"No. Just cut her tongue. Tell Madame Dau the old witch won't be speaking again." He smirked. "I cut it in a special way. You'll see."

Tinh held out his arms. Mountain Man grasped them and hauled him to his feet. Balancing himself, Tinh reached into his greasy cloth bag and pulled out rice balls and shrimp. "Eat. Drink this tea. Cold, sorry. Then I'll lead you through the tunnels."

Mountain Man sat, tugged on his damp socks, laced his boots, and wolfed down the meal in seconds.

"Madame Dau says you like dogs," Tinh noted.

"Yeah."

"Then why do you kill them?"

"I don't kill dogs."

"Dogs. Soldiers. Same thing."

Mountain Man snorted. "No. Dogs are honest. Clean. Loyal."

"So are soldiers. They just follow orders."

"That's the difference. I don't take orders anymore."

Tinh's eyebrows lifted. "Then all the more reason not to kill those who still do."

"What are you? A monk?"

Glancing at his stumps, he said, "Yes. Once, I was a dog. But now I serve no master, and so I kill no dogs."

"Yesterday, I was going to kill you." Mountain Man's voice dropped. "Because you belong to the Human Being Pack. And that's more dangerous than any pack of dogs."

Tinh nodded solemnly. "I know. But I hope you don't."

"Why not?"

"Because I've not yet tasted every woman who stirs my passion."

Mountain Man glanced toward Tinh's groin. "Can you?"

"Yes."

"My friend Bowls was just like you." A shadow passed across his face. "Let's go."

"Please," said Tinh. "One last thing. If you still have the Goddess statue, return Her to the village. She serves no purpose among Americans."

"There's a couple guys, Storyteller and Cairns, who might argue otherwise."

"I know the Teller of Stories. He won't argue."

Mountain Man raised an eyebrow. "Well, Cairns might. He's not one to give anything back."

"Then he must die."

Mountain Man laughed in English. "You're right. And it's no skin off my nose." He switched back to Vietnamese. "But remember, I don't kill dogs."

"Ha! He's a pig. I never said anything about pigs. Let's go."

Mountain Man followed Tinh into the tunnel, half-crawling, half-crouching, the world collapsing into dirt, damp, and dim light. In his mind, three obsessions tore at each other: the sacred mission to kill Dam, the mutilated face of Bowls, and the tabs . . . the tabs . . . the goddamn tabs.

Each one fed the others in a brutal rhythm: rage pushing into revenge, despair grinding against grief, fear coiled with guilt.

At the tunnel's end, near the fruit groves, Tinh reached for a long bamboo pole and propped open the door. Rain threaded through the opening. Jungle sounds returned.

Mountain Man didn't move.

"What are you waiting for?" Tinh asked.

"I haven't decided whether to kill you yet."

Tinh shivered. He drew a short knife and held it upright before his face.

Mountain Man laughed. "See you later, little man. I think Bowls would've liked you. So you get to live. How's that?"

"I am grateful," said Tinh, bowing slightly. "Especially to your friend Bowls."

Mountain Man hesitated. "If I can, I'll return your statue. In the meantime, burn incense for me."

Tinh said nothing.

"Did you hear me?" Mountain Man said, voice raw. "I want to kill the bastard who killed my friend. But . . . god help me . . . it's an American who needs to die."

Tinh tilted his head. "Who?"

"A worthless man. Sick. Should kill himself. But he doesn't. He just keeps writing. Every day, I beg him. Kill yourself. Put us out of our misery." He turned and glared upward, as if the sky could hear. "Kill yourself, writer!"

Then back to Tinh, face blank, drained. "That's why I ask you to burn incense."

"Yes," Tinh whispered.

"Maybe the smoke'll ignite the pages and burn him in his sleep."

~

Tinh watched the giant American climb from the tunnel and dissolve into the charcoal sky. He held the pole steady a moment longer, then lowered the door until darkness swallowed the passage again.

I hope you die, Man From the Mountains. For all our sakes, I hope Sergeant Dam kills you.

~

Mountain Man crested the hill overlooking Song Nhan village and checked the radio he'd hidden in the underbrush. American voices cracked faintly through the speaker. The Firebase was still out there. Still listening. But he wouldn't call for help. Not yet. Not until Dam was dead. Not until Martha was safe. He buried the radio again and descended into the jungle, forging a fresh trail toward the tunnel's exit. Machete in hand, he fell into rhythm—back and forth, back and forth—slicing a narrow path through the green world. With each cut, his mind emptied, becoming a bowl for flickering, half-dissolved images.

Leaves split like torn skin. Branches and vines like severed nerves. Each blow peeled away another layer of green flesh, exposing the jungle's viscera: trunks and pods, seeds and fruit, decaying logs and stumps streaked with rot, their surfaces crawling with pulsing insect veins. Hemorrhaging life. Insect battalions broke rank and swirled in panic through the mist, drawn to the salt of his sweat. Still, the jungle spoke, not with words but with visions.

Each stroke of the blade summoned another ghost. Nature's cat perched in royal serenity on an areca limb. Idaho's family stood beneath a farmhouse formed in the contours of a canthium bush. Superman's twin daughters knelt by an averrhoa tree dusted with white petals. Pappy's pink California sky flickered across a spray of mimosas. T's wife returned, her apron woven from portulaca colors. A spider rocked gently in its web, mimicking X's grandmother sewing in her chair. And Bowls?

Bowls' naked woman never appeared.

Until a shaft of light found a cluster of scarlet impatiens, bleeding through the mist. There *she* was. The one Bowls would never see again.

Hatred surged. Each swing of the machete brought Mountain Man closer to the tunnel. Closer to the man who had to die.

~ *Dam Waits With His Sappers at the Tunnel* ~

Dam had chosen his position carefully, close enough to observe the tunnel exit, far enough to remain invisible. He avoided the termite mounds: too obvious. Instead, he nestled in a hollow of wet ferns and dark soil, scanning the landscape in slow, overlapping arcs. He couldn't see his men, but he knew where they were. He had placed them himself. Still, no Americans. And that gnawed at him. It had been his idea to watch the tunnel. If it failed, he would lose face, not just with Major Vy and Captain Tong, but with the sharp-tongued Sergeant Viet. He hated that most of all—the ribbing, the laughter. He preferred discipline. Precision. Results.

He let his eyes drift from the horizon to the soil in front of him, where large, black beetles lumbered through the leaf litter, their glossy shells prodded by darting ants.

You're like me, little brothers. Scouts. Quick. Clever. Soft bodies against armored beasts. Keep moving. That's it. Never pause too long.

These analogies comforted him. The Americans always had more firepower. But Dam always outlasted them. Unlike Mr. Machine, he never imagined his own throat being slit. In the end, it was always the enemy's body, still and broken, at his feet. But today, unease filled the spaces between his movements, silent and persistent. He watched as one beetle caught an ant between its mandibles and sliced it clean in half. A chill passed through him. *Why am I afraid?* he thought. *Why now?*

It wasn't the ambushes. He'd seen what the American had done: bodies twisted by traps, comrades shredded. That was war. That was expected. No, it was something else. Something Comrade Kim Lan had said. Her description of the man. The Man From the Mountains. Not insane, no, not quite. But no longer tethered to the ordinary laws that govern men. Sooner or later, every soul encounters that singular adversary: the one who will kill or be killed over a glance, a gesture, a word. A man who neither retreats nor bargains, who answers nothing with surrender and everything with finality. In peace, you might step aside and let such a man pass.

But here—there is no stepping aside.

And somewhere beyond the battlefield, the voices stirred.

~

Ah, Goddess! So sad. They spend their lives building masks to avoid themselves.

Yes, Dear God. But You built the first mask. Metaphorical Me. Metaphorical You. And behind every metaphor, the same terrified creature, still hiding.

But your schizophrenic is done hiding.

Indeed. He will face the unavoidable. Until—

Until the Reunion.

~

Dam felt dread creeping in. Not of death, but of something nameless. The American would not fight like a soldier. He would fight as a force unleashed, an ancestral curse summoned in flesh. The fear began to metastasize. Dam tried to beckon forth the old rage. His mother's murder had always been his fuel, his reason to fight, his anchor. But not now. Even that sacred grief felt hollow. The scaffolding of vengeance was collapsing, leaving only raw, unfamiliar dread.

He had brought three men to this site: Chu, Nguu, and Doanh. Chu and Nguu. All were veteran sappers, inseparable, reckless. Men who moved through danger without hesitation. They had lost a comrade recently which sharpened their motivation even more.

Doanh was the replacement, young, soft-spoken, considered strange by his comrades. He'd studied botany in Hanoi. Orchids. Professors urged him toward agriculture, but he refused. Vietnam held hundreds of orchid species, most blooming in the ruined south. That only deepened his resolve.

Chu and Nguu had mocked him at first. Sappers had no place for dreamers. But Doanh never pushed back. And when he discovered a new species, his joy infected even the hard-hearted. He would sketch it in his journal, ask Clerk Long to help refine the lines. His face lit up like a father's gaze at a newborn, a moment of unguarded wonder. The cliffs he climbed for those blossoms drew quiet awe from soldiers who feared nothing else.

This morning, crouched near the tunnel exit, Doanh spotted it: *Calanthe integrilabris*. A gleam of white above a streambed, veiled in mist. His pulse quickened. He had waited for hours. No Americans had come. The orchid beckoned. He shifted his weight, debating. Now or never. Just one minute. The mission won't fail for this. Sergeant Dam can't see me. I'll be back in seconds.

Still, he hesitated. *Fool! Decide!*

Frustrated, he rose and stepped toward the stream. Across the bank, the orchid glowed, a fragile, luminous, unreachable trophy.

For just one bloom, he knew he risked everything: his post, the mission, his comrades. But the pull was too great.

Lost in thought, he missed the flash of metal hidden behind the screen of tinospora vines.

He waded in, rifle gripped in one hand, the other outstretched. Too high. He set the AK-47 against a foothold on the slope and climbed, both hands free. The mud clung to him. The flower hovered just beyond reach.

It trembled in the breeze, elusive and alluring. *Higher than I thought. Almost. Just a few more centimeters. One touch. One pull.*

He didn't see the eyes in the undergrowth. He didn't notice the absence of his rifle. He saw only the orchid, radiant, trembling, waiting to be claimed.

~ *First Blood* ~

Every hair on Doanh's head tingled in unison, sensing the presence behind him before thought could name it. He began to turn, but a massive hand clamped over his mouth. Fingers dug into his cheek, tearing him backward from the cliff's edge. There was no time for fear. Only the surge of knowing: *I will die.*

And then the crushing impact of sorrow. Not terror. Not pain. Just sorrow.

But instinct surged. Doanh twisted, kicked, writhed. Useless. The American's strength defied all measure. A blade sank deep into his back. He tried to scream, but the hand smothered every sound. In the blood-hazed blur of dying, he understood: *This is him! The Man From the Mountains!* Sergeant Dam had been right.

He fought for breath, not just from the grip that crushed his face, but from the ache of futures severed. His orchid journal. His quiet thoughts. All slipping away, vanishing into the dark.

~

Mountain Man twisted the blade in the sapper's back, savoring the yielding of muscle and the slow crunch of bone. He deliberately avoided the heart. Pain clarified memory. He yanked the knife free, flipped the body into the stream, and held it there as blood spiraled through the current.

He leaned in, breath thick with intent, and whispered in a guttural snarl:

"Where are the others? Where's Cao Thanh Dam?"

The boy just stared at him, dazed and babbling. Mountain Man growled and dunked him under the water.

When the body began to spasm, he jerked him up again. "Where?"

~

Doanh couldn't answer. He shook uncontrollably, whimpering, pleading, already fading. His blood fled faster than his will, and his voice thinned to a trembling echo. Even fear deserted him, leaving only silence and bone-deep cold. He stared up at the man's face, a horrible mask of alien savagery. Just as Dam had described. And then he saw what had been done to him.

His shirt—gone. His chest—carved. Angular shapes, triangles, rectangles, etched in bleeding flesh. His breath caught in horror. *He's drawing on me. . . .*

Mountain Man barked another demand, slicing new lines into his side. But Doanh could barely hear him now. The voice was part of the water. Part of the pain. Part of the air that no longer belonged to him.

" . . . please . . . please . . . please. . . . "

He wasn't begging anymore. It was just sound. The faces of his family shimmered above him, breathtakingly close. But the American wouldn't let him reach them. They called to him. He turned his head in protest. There, perched above the waterline, the *Calanthe integrilabris*, swaying gently in the rain.

Still alive. Still beautiful. I'm glad I didn't harm you. I'm glad you remain . . . I'm glad. . . .

~

Mountain Man saw the sapper smile. Something delicate in the dying boy's face, serenity, even grace, filled him with fury.

"What the fuck are you smiling at?"

He hoisted the soldier by his collar, shook him like a rag, but the boy kept turning his head, gazing up at the plants above. Mountain Man followed his line of sight but saw only rain-streaked vines and a cluster of nameless vegetation. "Nothing there," he muttered.

The stream had gone red around their legs. "Go to hell, you little gook bastard," he hissed. Then he forced the boy's head beneath the water, slowly and deliberately, stark finality poured through the unholy strength of his hands.

He held it down until the body stopped struggling. When the convulsions ceased and the limbs went slack, Mountain Man felt a jolt, an electric surge, rising through his hands into his heart. "For you, Bowls," he whispered. "Three to go."

He rose. No hesitation. No ritual. Just motion. He vanished into the foliage, leaving Doanh's body to drift gently beneath the watchful nod of the *Calanthe integrilabris*, still rooted, still blooming.

~

Mountain Man scrambled up the slope where the soldier had been hiding, ducked behind a termite mound, and scanned the jungle. *One down.* But if the old schoolmistress had spoken true, there were four — Dam and three more." He had seconds, maybe less. *What now, Mountain Man? What now?*

His body answered before thought arrived. He cupped his hands to his mouth and let loose a shrill, high-pitched wail in Vietnamese: "I killed him! I killed him! Help! Help!"

The words came unbidden. A predator's instinct. They simply felt like the right ones.

~

Nguu heard the cry. He was closest to Doanh's position and had been warned by Dam that the American might speak their tongue. Still, the words rattled him: not just "help," but *"I killed him."* That was different. Strange. Maybe real. Doanh was sweet. Naïve. He could've panicked. He might need help.

Nguu moved cautiously, circling to the right. No calls now. No signs. Just the hush of jungle creatures gone silent. He neared the stream, could hear its gurgle, but not see it. He resisted the urge to call out.

The only sound now was his own breathing.

~

High in a tree, Mountain Man spotted movement, one of the NVA creeping into view, too far for a clean shot. Worse, the soldier veered off again, flanking wide. Mountain Man cursed and climbed down. He tracked the sapper through thickets of thorn and vine, stepping light, rifle raised.

Then, suddenly, they were face to face.

Nguu had circled too. Each had brushed aside a branch of the same vine. Both froze. For one beat, it was absurd. Then fury erupted. They dropped their rifles. Hands. Elbows. Throats. One quick burst from the AK-47 before it was flung away. They rolled in the underbrush, grunting, clawing.

Mountain Man straddled the soldier and grabbed a bamboo stalk. Knife lost. No time. He pressed the stalk down hard across the man's throat, grinning as the tongue swelled purple and obscene from his mouth.

~

Nguu couldn't scream. Pain exploded behind his eyes. The pressure was unbearable. His vision tunneled. He saw his mother, her expression full of sorrow, and felt the cold dread of death creeping in. The last thing he saw was the American's face: a beast with a human mask, eyes ablaze.

He tried to claw, but his fingers no longer worked. They pawed blindly, then dropped. His body went still.

~

Mountain Man surged to his feet, trembling with exertion and glee. Two kills in moments. Blood on his skin, sweat in his eyes, rain soaking everything. He threw the enemy's rifle into the stream, stripped the bandolier, and rolled the body into the water. Then he crawled on all fours into the tall imperata grass, rifles slung, breath shallow.

He knew more were coming. They had heard the fight. *Good.*

Mud, blood, and rain had fused into a sticky grime on his fatigues, a stinking paste that drew clouds of gnats and mosquitoes. But he didn't feel them. His pulse was a furnace. His mind: a single, flaming line.

I'm not done. Not yet. Two more. Come to me.

~

Sergeant Dam heard the cry, "I killed him! I killed him! Help! Help!" He knew at once it was the American, not Doanh. His team was compromised. He sprinted toward Chu's position, but Chu was already gone, moving toward the sound. Dam caught up and grabbed him by the shoulder.

"Back to camp. Bring reinforcements. Now."

"What about—?"

"I'll set a trap. No one enters the tunnel without my order. If I die, clear the entrance before sending anyone else. Understand?"

Chu nodded.

Then: *pop-pop-pop*—AK-47 fire. Both men froze.

"Go!" Dam shouted, pushing Chu back toward the path. "You remember what I told you!"

Chu vanished into the trees. Dam turned toward the tunnel, eyes dark with purpose.

But first, he had an errand.

~

When Dam emerged again from the tunnel, his body moved slow, mind heavy with dread. Readying the entrance chamber had steadied him briefly, but that calm had passed.

He pushed vines aside, one after another, each one a small betrayal of conceal-ment. *So it's come to this. You and me, madman. My mother's killer. My comrades' butcher. Rapist. Pretender. Husband of Kim Lan. Help me, Mother. Help me kill this demon. Every skill, every thought, every heartbeat—make them count.*

But fear gnawed at the edges. Each step, each parted branch, each termite mound skirted and the fear grew. For years he had bottled it. Controlled it. Denial was his armor. But now the floodgates were cracking. Monsters stirred in the deep. Not metaphors. Not madness. Just the truth of a man unraveling.

He heard the stream ahead. Quiet. Innocent. But he knew. *Doanh is dead. So is Nguu.*

And suddenly, for the first time since his mother's death, he wanted to run.

How can this be? I must face him. I must!

But his will quivered.

Still, his lips moved. "So far so good, thank you mother."

Again. "So far so good, thank you mother."

Again.

Each whisper a torch held aloft in the dark.

~ *Mountain Man Meets Dam* ~

Mountain Man lingered beside the body, listening to the hush that followed death. The others would come. If not, they had already slipped into another path, one that would circle back with reinforcements or vanish forever. It didn't matter. The jungle held him. Not as camouflage. As blood relation. He could dissolve at will—into vine, into mud, into silence.

But something had shifted. The air tightened. The cover that had once enfold-ed him now narrowed into a tunnel of unknowing. He scanned the trees. They denied him, not with violence, but with indifference. Their crowns tangled into a single barrier. No view. No ascent. The ground gave nothing. Sight flickered and failed.

He remained still, neither exposed nor safe, suspended between worlds.

The forest breathed, but not through him. He stood inside a breath the jungle had stolen from the first man it ever devoured, and never returned.

Don't matter. Two down. Two to go. And one of them is Dam. He'll come. I know it. He'll come.

To speed fate along, he searched for the second sapper's trail. The man had been cautious, almost ghostlike, but Mountain Man finally found the faint imprint of his passing. He followed it a short distance, then crouched behind a young bamboo thicket beside a termite mound tall as a man.

If he comes, he'll think I'm behind that mound. Let him think it.

He waited. The mosquitoes swarmed in dense spirals, drawn to the coagulated blood that crusted his fatigues. His face swelled with bites. He waved the insects away again and again—then froze as his hand brushed a vine. Silence. He held still, breath suspended, flesh offered to the crawling things. Long minutes passed. Nothing. The jungle held its breath with him. At last, he exhaled.

~

Dam crept along Nguu's trail when he heard a faint noise, almost nothing. A shift of underbrush? A bird? A whisper?

He stopped. Eyes scanned every frond, every vine, every flicker of light through leaf. Then, movement. Subtle, but real. A termite mound stood in a clearing just ahead, perfectly placed for ambush.

Too obvious, he thought. *The American wouldn't hide there.*

But fear had begun to loosen the bolts of his judgment. Certainty softened. His mind, once rigid with purpose, grew elastic.

He's there. He's behind it. I know he is.

Whether he believed it or simply needed to, Dam decided to circle around and catch the American from behind.

If he's not there, I'll return to the tunnel. Wait for Chu. Wait for help. That's reasonable. That's safe.

So far so good, thank you mother.

It seemed a perfect compromise. He would act. Fulfill duty. And if nothing came of it, he would return to the tunnel with honor intact. What he feared most, *the confrontation itself,* could still be postponed.

~

Mountain Man, hidden behind the bamboo, had a clear view of the clearing's backside. The underbrush here was strangely sparse, and he figured animals must've passed through regularly, flattening the vines. *Gibbons maybe. Wild pigs. Who the hell knows. Good spot, though.*

He decided to give it another few minutes. Then, if nothing stirred, he'd withdraw. Regroup. Form a new plan. But something did stir. A shimmer in the foliage. A glint of steel. The barrel of an AK-47 nosed into the clearing like a nervous animal testing the air. Then the soldier slowly emerged, movements fluid as oil.

Mountain Man's breath froze.

The pith helmet was fringed with leaves. The body was lean and coiled. The eyes were sharp and sweeping. The man moved only a few steps into the clearing, then paused. *Discipline,* Mountain Man thought. *Too much discipline.*

The face turned. And then he saw it. A leather cord hung from the soldier's neck. Bowls' flock bag — the one Dam had stolen, the one Mountain Man had sworn to reclaim. *My flock bag! It's him. Cao Thanh Dam!*

Rage ignited, and every cell in Mountain Man's body trembled. Time fractured. Thoughts evaporated. All that remained was hatred, revenge, and the ancient hunger to destroy. He raised his rifle.

But then, a surprise. Dam tilted his head back and looked skyward. His helmet slid back on its strap. His lips moved in silent gratitude, a smile blooming across his face.

~

So far so good, thank you mother. So far so good, thank you mother.

~

Mountain Man hesitated. *He looks relieved. Why the fuck is he smiling?*
The AK-47 sagged in Dam's hands.
I could shoot him now. A clean shot. A gift. A fuckin' miracle.
He lined up the sights. His finger contracted.

~

Dam scanned the clearing one last time. Empty. He sighed with relief. *I did it. I can go back. Wait. The others will come. We'll find Doanh and Nguu together. So far so good, thank you mother.*
Then he glanced down. A leech crawled along his ankle. He bent to flick it off.

~

That small movement shattered Mountain Man's restraint. *I'll kill him with my bare hands!*
He rose and burst from the bamboo, M-16 raised, legs pounding toward the sapper. "Look at me, you bastard! Look into my eyes!"
Dam was already gone, diving into the brush, swallowed by root and shadow. Fast. Too fast. Mountain Man snarled and gave chase.
"Goddammit! Son of a bitch! If that little bastard gets away—!"
No more thought. No more tactics. The hunt had taken him. Dam crashed through the undergrowth just ahead, breaking branches, tearing vines. Mountain Man followed the sound, snapping limbs, panting breath, the rhythm of something fleeing.
All stealth dissolved. Only pursuit remained.
Dam slipped through narrow gaps, ducked beneath hanging limbs, vanished into thickets. Mountain Man tore through them, machete whipping forward, carving open the trail. Leaves slashed his face. Blood mixed with sweat. His breath came in growls.
He had shed his name, his purpose, even his reason. What moved now was not a man, it was hunger in flesh, a beast driven by the scent of prey.

~

Dam stumbled through the foliage, lungs raw, arms flailing. The jungle clawed at him, vines tightening, thorns tearing. His rifle caught, dragged, resisted. He yanked it free without looking.

Behind him, the sound returned in a slow, steady, deliberate drumbeat. Not frantic. Not rushed. The machete rose and fell with the calm certainty of a predator closing in. He didn't need to turn. He could feel it in the earth. The American was near, close enough to smell his fear.

He reached the stream. Stumbled. Slid. Fell down the bank into the water. Ripped his rifle from the vines that clung to it.

The machete was closer now. Louder.

He's almost here. Gotta cross. If I make it across, I live. Please, Mother. Help me.

He turned to flee, and stopped.

In the water, caught in the branches, floated the corpses of Doanh and Nguu. Doanh stared upward, his eyes wide, blank, the skin already hosting flies. There was no question in that gaze. Only judgment.

Dam shook. *They'll blame me. For fleeing. For failing. For surviving.*

"So be it," he whispered, and turned, eyes locked.

The jungle erupted. The Man From the Mountains crashed into the clearing, rifle in one hand, machete in the other.

Dam fired. Wild. A burst.

But the demon was already on him.

~

The machete came down. Dam's hand, still gripping the rifle, was severed at the wrist. Blood fountained. He collapsed, arms splayed, body frozen. Shock tore through him. Pain blurred into unreality. A far-off sensation. He reached for the weapon. Found only a useless stump. His severed hand lay nearby, fingers curling and uncurling with the last of their memory.

He stared. Tried to connect hand to wrist, form to meaning. Nothing fit.

Mountain Man stood over him, breath calm, posture complete.

Dam coughed. Grit filled his mouth. He willed himself not to faint.

~

Mountain Man looked down at the man who had worn Bowls' flock bag. The leather cord was visible, tucked beneath the collarbone. With a low snarl, he gripped the machete like a blade of judgment and drove it down through the bone, through cartilage, into the earth itself.

Dam convulsed. Still breathing in desperate gasps.

Mountain Man sliced the strap, lifted the bag, and let it sway above the broken face.

"Cao Thanh Dam," he growled. "You'll die slow. So slow your ancestors won't recognize you. Only scraps. Left for the birds. Your mother's tears will drown this land, and my laughter will drown the sky."

A tear slipped from Dam's eye. "I'm sorry, Mother," he whispered. "So sorry . . . sorry, Mother . . ."

Mountain Man leaned in. Pressed his palm against Dam's forehead, holding him steady. Then, with the knife, he pierced the flesh beneath the eyelid and traced the path of the tear, cutting it open. Blood followed, warm and unhurried, erasing the shimmer of remorse.

~

Dam knew he couldn't shake the American. The machete fixed him in place. He could no longer run. He could no longer resist. He simply waited.

"Got to you, didn't it?" came the growl above him. "Eh, gook?"

Dam forced a grimace. "I'm a Socialist soldier of the People's Army. Not some ancestor-worshipping peasant. Your superstition means nothing."

Mountain Man's face twisted with hate. "Look, you little slant-eyed fuckin' slope—"

But Dam whispered softly, forcing the American to bend closer. "I do believe in fate," he murmured. "And it is your fate to follow me, Man from the Mountains. I will be waiting for you . . . in my mother's arms. You will die alone."

~

Mountain Man laughed low, hoarse. "No. Not alone. I'll be with Bowls"—he shook the flock bag—"and with my fiancée."

Dam's eyes dulled further. His voice came faint, ragged: "Ah yes. Kim Lan. Your so-called fiancée. She hates you, demon. Sees you for what you are."

~

Mountain Man raised the knife. Dam closed his eyes. The blade slashed. Fire tore through his head. His right ear—gone. He opened his mouth and screamed, a sound that tore loose his final breath. One last flicker of sight—his wrist a stump, still bubbling.

Then darkness surged upward and swallowed the whirling lights that danced in his mind.

The knife fell.

And again.

~ *Denouement* ~

Fighting through gauze-thick pain and disintegration, Dam drifted above the carnage. His body, a torn, breathing relic, lay beneath him, sprawled in the wet jungle, desecrated. The American hunched over it, a beast still at work defiling what had once held symmetry, youthful structure, vital life.

Dam's vision blurred. He struggled to hold the demon in his sights, but the figure darkened and withdrew as though fleeing backward into the void. Then the ground vanished.

He was no longer above it, but within something—something rising. A black tide surged, not beneath him, but through him. He was dissolving, his body now a bird tumbling wingless through storm-wracked clouds. The rain pierced him. Not wetness but static, electric, unyielding.

And then others, dozens, rushed past him. Disembodied souls streaked upward, colliding in bursts of memory and madness. They were fragments of those who died before speech could name them. He passed through their essences as light through shattered glass. Somewhere in the disorientation, he thought he smelled mint. Or jasmine. Or maybe it was blood.

It felt like a schizophrenic's dream: a sky of blinding storms and blinking lights, a rush of broken voices and spliced identities.

~

Too late, Diane. Too late.
The sacrifice was inverted. Storyteller was meant to die by Dam's hand.
Now it will be Michael Powers who kills him.

Chapter Twenty-Two

Entombment

Mountain Man's Flight

Grimacing fiercely, as though stoking a firebox, Mountain Man sliced off Dam's other ear with mechanical precision. Using needle-sharp spines from a pithecellobium tree, he pinned both ears to the corpse's crown, crafting crude horns.

"Who's the demon now?" he muttered.

He stripped the body, cut behind both heels, pierced the tendons, and threaded nylon rope through the raw holes. His plan was clear: drag the corpse back to the tunnel exit, string it upside down from the banyan tree, make it a warning. *One sapper still unaccounted for, probably gone to report. Don't matter. I'll hang him. Leave a note: Release Kim Lan. I'll cut off his cock and jam it in his mouth. That'll scare them straight. If not, then I'll hang them all. One by one.*

He crouched, gripping the blade again, but his arms trembled. The bloodrush had drained. His muscles went slack. Shaking now, he sagged on his haunches, dizzy, his body dull with sudden fatigue. Slowly, he unlaced his right boot, slid the flock bag through, and tied it tight. He threw the rope over one shoulder, Dam's AK-47 over the other, and began dragging the corpse. He looked once more at the two bodies bobbing in the stream. The younger one's face, half-submerged, seemed to follow him.

At the water's edge, he knelt to wash the blood from his arms. Flies gathered. Mosquitoes swarmed. In the pause between splashes, he heard it, distant machetes biting bamboo. Then a faint ping of metal striking metal.

NVA.

He froze. Listened. *Shit.* He gripped the rope, stood, and moved. *Get to the tunnel. Hang the bastard. Then circle back to the cave. Rest. Then Martha.* But the sounds were closing in. Soldiers spread through the jungle. The path back to the cave was cut off.

No choice. Leave the body there. Keep going. Rest later. Help her later. If they're already at the tunnel—shit—then just keep going. Don't stop. As he drew closer, the voices grew. They'd found the others. He hunched forward and dragged the dead weight, step by laboring step, into the thicket.

~

At the NVA command post, Major Vy had already heard the distant gunshots from Dam's sector. He waited, stomach roiling, fists clenched. When Corporal Chu burst into the clearing with the report, Vy's fury ignited. "Compromised? How is that possible? They were only watching the tunnel!" He rubbed his gut as if to strangle the chaos inside it. "A simple task, and still they bungle it. More delays. More waste!"

He caught Captain Tong's faint smirk and turned on him with a look that scalded. Tong dropped his gaze. But Commissar Minh held firm. "You see?" Minh shouted. "More comrades lost in this game of yours. Drip by drip. No charge, no victory. Just drip, drip, and death. I told you—"

Vy slashed his hand through the air. "Silence! Enough." He jabbed a finger at Tong. "Take Tran's platoon. Reinforce Dam. Take Viet too. Go now!" He turned. "Quy! Fetch Sergeant Viet."

As the runner darted off, Minh leaned in with narrowed eyes. "I'm coming too. I want to see this failure for myself."

"Go. What do I care?" Vy snapped, then added bitterly, "I don't need you here anyway."

Minh gave a child's triumphant shout. "I will!" He glared at Tong. "I'll prepare my equipment and join you." He spun on his heel and left.

Viet entered the clearing, brushing past Minh without a word. He saluted. "Sir?"

"You're with Tong and Tran. Chu will lead you. After all, Comrade Viet, this was your idea, wasn't it?" Vy offered a smile without warmth.

"Yes, sir," Viet said, furrowed, thoughtful.

Tong finally spoke. "We should bring Kim Lan. She's seen the Americans. Especially The Man From the Mountains."

Vy grunted. "If we're lucky enough to see him."

"Yes."

"Fine. Go. And secure that tunnel."

As they moved out, Tong sketched a rough diagram on his palm for Tran. "We flank wide. Come at the tunnel from behind. Push them back into it."

Chu, trotting beside them, gasped, "Sir! Dam said he left a surprise inside the entrance."

Tong smiled. "Even better."

~

As the column advanced, Kim Lan's mouth went dry, her breathing labored. *This is my chance to do something for Tuyet Mai. But what if he's there? What if he kills them all and leaves me alone with him?*

She stared at Viet's strong back. It steadied her. *Stay near him.* But the tremble returned. *What if Tuyet Mai's already dead?* She glanced around. The soldiers looked impossibly young. She drew closer to Viet. *I'm a soldier of the revolution. I've faced worse. And Dam will be there. The American's probably dead already.*

~

Tong could barely contain himself. *Maybe it ends today. Maybe they've captured her. And I'll be the one to save her. She'll kiss me again. Love me again. She must.*

~

Viet marched with caution. He read the jungle like scripture, scanning for sound, smell, the shape of ambush. Kim Lan crept too close behind. He turned to wave her off, saw her face, and sighed. *Let her stay close. If it helps. Ah, there's the stream.*

~

They crossed at a narrow point and followed it upstream. Chu spotted the bodies first. "No—" he choked, then fell silent.

A ripple of horror moved through the platoon. Voices rose. Viet surged forward. Kim Lan's legs carried her forward against her will. *What is it? What's happened?* She stumbled into the commotion. Lieutenant Tran was barking orders.

"Disperse! Perimeter up! Remove the bodies!"

Bodies? Americans? Is he dead?

She heard splashing. Chu was in the water. She squinted. Then she saw. Doanh and Nguu, their torsos bobbing, faces chewed by insects. A fog filled her mind. She lowered her head and saw a frog. Its body lay beside her foot, crawling with ants, mouthing its own apocalypse. She couldn't look away. The frog's face swelled, morphed. Became Doanh's.

Her stomach turned.

~

Do You know, deathless God, about that frog?

No. This is Your nightmare.

Not true. It is Michael's and Yours. The delusion of the mutant. The fear of the Firstborn.

Yes, yes. As if I'm not the mutant's delusion Myself. So tell Me, Mother of Frogs, what about her?

She lived well. Outjumped, outfought, outcroaked. Seven years, eight months, forty-two days, twelve hours, thirteen minutes, four seconds. Then a virus. Couldn't eat. Starved.

Your point, Goddess? That none die peacefully? That the writer won't? What has this to do with Me?

Your benevolence is a falsehood. As X once said, 'God is in His heaven and it is good.' Yet You only love the human drug—their suffering, their cross-bearing.

Slander. We follow First Principles. No interference. The crucifix? Brilliant human marketing. The Romans handed it to the Hebrews, the Hebrews to the Christians. History wrote itself. And Me? I still seethe at sin, salaciousness, and abomination.

Hahaha ... Just be quiet and prepare for the Reunion.

Dear reader, can you hear them? The voices? The voices? Goddamn the voices. Sorry. . . .

~

"Goddamn the Americans!" Tong's outburst shattered Kim Lan's trance and dragged her gaze from the frog back to the living world.

"Get them out of the water! Flankers over there! Push across the stream! Dam's still out there. So is the American!" Turning away, he muttered, "At least one."

Kim Lan misheard. "The American's dead?"

Tong scowled. "No."

She crouched farther from the bank. A root crumbled under her fingers. Minh watched Chu cradle Doanh's corpse, disgust in his posture.

"I've seen enough," Minh growled. "No assaults. Just rot. We lose men daily." He approached Kim Lan. "A terrible thing."

"Yes. Doanh was so young."

"That's not what I meant."

Her eyes stayed down. "What, then?"

"I know your true mission."

Her heart jumped. _Does he know about the drugs?_

"What do you mean?" she said carefully.

"It's all right. Don't say. Just know this, when the time comes, I want your support."

"Support?"

"Come, comrade. Surely you don't wish to back Vy or Tong when the investigation comes. And it will come. I'll see to that. Incompetence at best. Treason at worst. Will you stand with me?"

She relaxed. He knew nothing. She looked up. "Isn't it premature?"

"Look around." He gestured. "How can we complete the Jarai mission now? Vy claims he wanted fewer casualties, but look."

"Yes. I see."

"Then—"

Tong interrupted, striding up with a bright smile. "You can answer later. We move now."

"One moment, comrade," Minh began.

"Now!"

Tong was already striding away to join the rest of the platoon. Kim Lan watched as the bodies of Doanh and Nguu were wrapped in nylon, limp as sacks of rice, and hoisted onto the shoulders of weary comrades.

She felt no scream rise in her throat, only a stillness, cold and final.

Someday, perhaps soon, she too would be carried this way. No drumbeat. No flag. Just a name whispered, then forgotten. Another weight among the jungle's green silences.

Around her, the platoon began to spread out, machetes swinging, boots trampling wet earth as they moved forward, cutting through the jungle and beating the vegetation as if flushing a tiger.

Minh fell in behind the others, fuming all the way back.

~ *Last Time in the Tunnel* ~

Mountain Man, unaware Kim Lan crouched just a hundred meters away, moved doggedly through thickets of bramble and rot. The corpse of Dam dragged behind him like ballast, stiffening now, heavy with dead inertia. He no longer thought of the cave, only the tunnel mattered. Salvation lived there. Maybe. *Come what may. Can't help Martha if I'm dead.*

But Dam's limp limbs and the protrusions of his weapons kept snagging on vines and thorned roots. Snarled in the jungle's grasp, exhausted, Mountain Man nearly let the rope go. His fingers reached to toss Dam's AK-47 into the brush when he stumbled into a break in the canopy.

There it was.

The old banyan tree loomed ahead, its roots twisted and muscular, rising from the jungle floor with ageless force. Beyond it, the mist parted to reveal a pale wall of bamboo, vertical and still, cream-colored, too precise to be natural. They stood in rows, waiting.

Thank God!

A sudden surge of adrenaline flooded his limbs, reviving him from stupor. He turned to the twisted, unrecognizable corpse and rasped:

"Think I'll bring you to my brothers as a gift. Set you at Bowls' feet. Fuckin' Viking funeral."

But just as he staggered forward, gunfire split the air. A grenade exploded nearby, rattling his bones. Bullets hissed through the underbrush, thudding into the earth at his feet.

"Holy shit!" he gasped, crouching low, fumbling at the rope, trying to release it from where it had knotted into his gear. It wouldn't budge. "Damn!" He flung the AK aside, twisted around, and emptied his M-16 into the trees, only entangling himself further in the looped nylon.

"Jesus fuckin' Christ! Jesus fuckin' Christ!" he chanted, sawing at the rope with a dull knife. The nylon held fast. Not enough time. He jammed in a fresh magazine, yanked the slack until Dam's body dragged at his heels, and lurched forward. Branches tore at his uniform. Vines tried to claim him. But he kept running, dragging the weight, limbs jolting, stumbling forward toward the tunnel entrance. Shrapnel rained from the canopy, AK rounds and RPG bursts shredding bamboo and pulp. Splinters pierced his arms and neck like needles.

Then, finally, a clearing.

There, flat against the earth, framed by damp imperata grass lay the trapdoor. He dropped the body, grabbed the handle, and flung it open. Firing blindly down into the darkness, he hurled himself into the void.

Searing pain shot up his leg.

A punji stake had punctured the sole of his boot, pierced his heel, and driven upward into his calf, metal sliding against bone, burying deep. He arched backward in agony and looked up toward the light. Dam's corpse hung just above the hatch, still bound by the umbilical rope, face bloated, arm extended in a frozen salute.

Grinning.

Mountain Man screamed.

He tried to inspect his foot, but his lower body seemed to vanish. Only the tips of freshly cut punji stakes showed above the blackness, glistening like a predator's teeth—hungry, slick, patient. Blood filled his boot. He heard nothing now but the low, relentless buzz of mosquitoes.

His lips trembled.

"Ma . . . Martha . . . Ma . . . Ma . . . Martha . . ."

Over and over, her name. A spell against the dark.

He reached into his pocket, careful, hand shaking, found the flashlight, clicked it on. A dim glow pushed back the shadows, revealing the upper walls of the chamber, but his feet were still lost in gloom. He leaned to angle the beam downward. Something gave way.

Click.

Click.

Click.

Click.

The light caught them: four grenades. Pins already pulled. They rolled toward him, scuttling, frantic, roach-quick in their hunger for darkness.

One second . . .

His body froze. Eyes wide.

Two . . .

In desperation, he tried to lift his impaled foot but the stake held him. With a howl, he wrenched upward. His blood-filled boot rose an inch, then slid back down the gleaming spike. Flesh tore. Blood poured.

Three . . .

He tried to summon his tab, the one hidden from the other grunts, the one that would carry him out. Martha's face behind the crushed Lambretta. But it would not come. Hatred gave him no comfort.

He looked up, Dam's corpse framed in silhouette above. Ants emerged from the scalp, twitching through tufts of matted hair.

Four . . .

He saw his two Blue Tick hounds on a red ridge in West Virginia, tails wagging, ready for the night's hunt. Heard his uncle's fiddle whisper *Amazing Grace* through the jungle walls, not played but breathed by the earth itself.

His real tab. At last.

He opened his mouth to answer. A brief roar.

Then silence.

No more pain. No more shaking. Only stillness.

"... all right ... all right ... I'm coming ..." he called to the dogs. But his voice was only a phantom spark, lost in a red mist of tissue, swallowed by the Mother. *Buried.*

~ *Denouement* ~

Fighting through the swirl in his mind, he looked back at the collapsed chamber: his tomb. Across its surface, ants scurried, searching. His eyes blurred, unable to hold their shapes.

And then, he was moving.

Lifted.

A fast river pulled him upward into a sky not made of air but black water. Around him, others tumbled past, their bodies thin as smoke, their faces half-formed. He reached for one, then another. All dissolved.

Today me, tomorrow you.

Chapter Twenty-Three

Mountain Man Returns

Desperation and Determination

S o, Metaphorical Goddess, the great Mountain Man is brought to the level of ants. You must be pleased that he will return to Your soup. Soon he will be merely a bland beehive of particles. But while he lived, he added spice and flavoring during the time of his dissolution. Even I will miss him. Such cubes of human bouillon do not come around very often.

Yes, his is a sad case. But the Chosen One still lives.

And suffers the demons.

True, Metaphorical God, but they are unanticipated human distortion—too many remnant human genes.

Your faction fools itself. This genetic experimentation will never work. The project will die with Michael Powers.

No. He is the Chosen One, and he will succeed ... at least in passing on to the world the next step ... a child.

Evolution has its advantages, Goddess, and natural selection has had the last say in Your adaptability, or lack thereof. In short, Madame, Your way is barren. The End of the Line.

~ Deepening Fear Among the Grunts ~

KA-BOOM!

A muffled explosion echoed across the ruined jungle, followed by three more in quick succession. Then silence.

Inside the fortress, the grunts froze. They had been tracking the distant firefight, each sound sharpening their focus, bodies straining toward the source. Then came the eerie quiet, the kind of silence that carried weight, the aftermath of something finished and irreversible. Speculation jumped from man to man, tense and electric, creeping along the walls.

"Wonder what happened?" Superman asked, cocking his head toward the sound.

"Dunno," muttered Pappy beside him. "If it was Mountain Man, we're in a world of hurt."

"Nah," Superman replied, voice a little too loud. "Couldn't be him. He's probably halfway to the firebase by now."

Pappy gave him a long look. "Damnedest thing about this war. You never know anything, anytime, anywhere, anyhow. Who's trying to kill you today? Pregnant woman? Kid? Booby-trapped baby at the wire? And where from? Below? Behind? Termite mound? Tunnel? Who's next to snap? Newbie? Chopper pilot?"

Superman chuckled darkly. "Or maybe just some burned-out grunt too long in the bush, too far from his West Virginia pigs and too close to these Vietnamese snakes. God only knows what's goin' on out there."

Birdman, crouched at the base of the wall, called up: "Hey, Superman, use your hotline. Ask God if one of them bastards tripped Mountain Man's automatic ambush."

"Wouldn't explain the small arms fire," Superman said, shaking his head.

"Doesn't matter," said T as he passed by.

"Why the hell not?" Superman called after him. "Matters to me. Matters to my twins. Fuckin' A, it matters."

T didn't stop walking. "It doesn't matter because we control our own destiny."

Birdman gave a hollow laugh. "Yeah. That's what I said to my chopper when we were limping in on nothin' but the gas from our own farts."

"We made it, didn't we?" T snapped.

~

T drifted further from the grunts with each passing hour. Their quiet doubt stung more than any shouted accusation. They no longer looked at him with the blind faith of earlier weeks. And worse, he no longer believed in himself. He clenched his jaw, staring at their dirt-caked faces. *I'm sick of hearing about Mountain Man. I could kill that son-of-a-bitch myself. I hope he—ah, shit. Just get me home. Just get me out of here alive.*

The fortress felt less like a command post and more like a decompression chamber. Men dissolving into themselves. They reminded T of figures descending into the pressure-warped clouds of Jupiter, home just a memory stitched into a collapsing hope.

They wanted to be home. That was all. Home meant clean sheets, the faint scent of laundry detergent, the cool flatness of real fabric. Home meant becoming the bed, the car seat, the family room couch, the familiar grain of the dinner table, the clink of ice in a Coca-Cola, the flickering nonsense of a television. But nothing here was flat. Nothing clean. Vietnam offered no lines, only vines. No squares, only mud-slick circles and broken bodies.

Their world had folded inward: adolescent self-absorption gone septic. They lived in the cocoon of their own minds, imaginary spacesuits that purported to insulate them from Vietnam. But the jungle had begun to breach those suits, curling in, cracking seams.

Most were poisoned. But a few, always a few, thrived. War, perversely, was their release. For the misfits, the broken, the angry—they blossomed here. Escaped the abuse. The boredom. And most importantly, the rules.

Vietnam became their real world. A level playing field for the dispossessed.

Mountain Man.

Damn you, Mountain Man.

~

Across the courtyard, Storyteller and Idaho sat slumped on poncho liners, backs to the crumbling wall. X hovered over them, hands on hips. Nature was posted just above on the parapet, eyes fixed toward the treeline. He had been babbling earlier, parsing each burst of gunfire. But after the final explosion, he fell quiet.

Idaho moaned, then surprised everyone with a high, frail voice. "That's it. Jig's up. It's all over, man. Fuckin' all over."

Nature didn't turn. "That wasn't Mountain Man. He's crazy, but he always pulls us through. You'll see. It'll be okay."

X snorted. "Bullshit. He's fucked us, sure as shit. That's why he ain't answerin' his radio. Dead or didied. One or the other."

Nature opened his mouth to speak, to use his famous charm to drive the dread back into shadow, but the silence held him, heavy and ancestral. When he turned to speak, Storyteller, who had said nothing for hours, opened his mouth first.

His voice was eerie. Calm. Hollow. "He's dead."

Idaho blinked. "How do you know?" His voice trembled. He hadn't believed what he said earlier, he just didn't want to be the only one still hoping.

Storyteller smiled faintly and recited in a near-whisper:

"Amazing grace. How sweet the sound
That saved a wretch like me.
I once was lost but now am found,
Was blind but now I see."

Cairns, seated nearby cleaning his M-16, froze mid-stroke. He stood. Walked briskly across the courtyard.

T was pacing near the far wall, chewing gum, lost in his own misery. Cairns didn't hesitate. "Time for Plan B, Lieutenant Rogers."

T turned slowly, forcing composure. "What do you mean?"

Cairns swept a hand toward the group behind him. "I've been listening. Haven't said a word till now. But if we don't do something different, we're all gonna die in this shithole."

T kicked at a loose brick, chewing faster. He wanted to lash out. Spit in Cairns' face. Anything to remind them he was still in charge. But Cairns was right.

The grunts were fraying. Their stoicism, once ironclad, had become brittle. The jungle was winning. Dysentery. Fever. Stress. Too many dead. Too little reason left to die.

T muttered, "Well . . . yeah . . . we can't stay here much longer. Question is, do we still have the tunnel? Someone's gotta check. I've got a bad feeling."

"I agree," Cairns said. "If it's still open, we move at dawn. Otherwise . . . surrender."

T straightened, trying to reclaim command. "Let's send someone through. Maybe Mountain Man's just wounded. He might need help. I'll pick someone."

X had drifted close, listening. "I'll go."

"What?" T turned sharply.

Cairns raised an eyebrow. "Didn't you just say Mountain Man fucked us?"

X scowled. "Yeah. But I'm still the medic. If he's down there bleeding out, I'm the one he needs."

T waved him off. "We can't spare you. You've got Storyteller and Idaho."

Silence. Then Stretch piped up from nearby.

"Hey, T. Don't look at me. I just got religion. Superman prayed over me and everything." He clasped his hands. "'O Lord, distribute the bullets like the pay—let the officers get most of them.' Besides, I'm a short-timer—"

"Stretch!" T barked. "Enough of your crap!"

Cairns shook his head like a weary teacher correcting a brat. "Don't bother, Lieutenant. I'll go."

"Sounds great, captain!" Stretch chirped. Then muttered, not so quietly, "You're the one guy we can spare."

T flinched. He hated this. Hated the loss of control. Hated that Cairns might come back a hero.

"Technically," he said stiffly, "you're the ranking officer. Maybe someone else should—"

"Like who?" Cairns asked.

"Me."

"Nope. I'm pulling rank. Debate over."

Pappy had wandered up, silent until now. He kicked the same loose brick, then growled:

"Real touching, boys. But someone better get their ass down that tunnel."

~

Tuyet Mai had listened to the Americans in silence, trying to parse their arguments, her mind still tethered to the memory of the firefight. Most of the shots had been AK-47s. That meant NVA. That meant her people. A sliver of hope pierced the fog. Fighting through aches and illness, she repeated her vow: *I will survive this place. I will cleanse myself of male filth, of obsession, of shame. I will emerge new. Harder. Clean.*

But their voices dragged her back.

A sharp argument broke out, first T and the captain, then others chiming in, the volume rising until it became a chorus of confusion. Then, as if a signal had passed through them, they all stopped.

A silence.

And then, to her shock, one of the grunts, a sergeant, began lecturing the two officers.

It would have been unthinkable in the People's Army. Yet here he was, calm and certain, claiming more experience, more wisdom. She caught fragments—"the Vietnamese woman" . . . "the prisoner" . . . something about the tunnel.

Her mind snapped alert. She was the subject.

She tried to translate the torrent of English, but the sentences came too fast. ". . . in this . . . captain is right . . . let him take her . . . down into the tunnel . . ."

Then the captain's voice again: "I . . . prisoner . . . me . . . tunnel . . ."

The rest blurred beneath overlapping voices. But it didn't matter. Her mind had already completed the message:

"I will take the prisoner with me into the tunnel."

She pressed back against the stone wall. Her head lowered. Eyes to the dirt. *Why? Why take me into the tunnel? To rape? To kill? No, worse. To torture. To break. To vanish me where no one will see.*

She glanced up and saw the lieutenant looming, legs spread, staring down at her with clenched fury. She looked away, trembling.

Then, softly, instinctively, she began to whisper: "No, no, no . . ."

The word came out in English. Somehow that made it more powerful.

She felt a ripple move through the room, something subtle, like a shift in weather.

The lieutenant seemed to freeze. Then, slowly, he spoke, his voice unsure: "Well . . . I guess there's no choice. It's a damn shame . . . but . . . I guess there's no choice."

She squeezed her eyes shut. Willed herself away.

Glue and Paint. Childhood. Her brother after school. Dust on the windowsill. Chalk on her fingers. A paper kite with red streamers above the rice paddies.

Let her go there.

Not into the tunnel.

~ *Cairns Forces Tuyet Mai Into the Tunnel* ~

But Tuyet Mai's retreat into childhood didn't last.

She was jerked painfully to her feet. Hands twisted her around, rough fingers untying her ankles, then binding her wrists again, tighter this time, knotted in front with just enough slack to keep her upright. Then came the worst: a gag shoved deep into her mouth, held in place by another cloth tied over her lips and cinched tight around the back of her head.

For a moment, she thought she would suffocate. Her breath caught. Panic surged. But slowly, she adapted. Short, staccato pulls of air through her nose. A rhythm. Survival.

The Americans' voices drifted in, sharp and joking. Incomprehensible to her ears.

"Hey! She can pull the gag down. See?"

"Not if I tie it like this. She can't lift her hands past her shoulders."

"Where'd you learn that, Captain?"

"Lot of things I've learned might surprise you, Lieutenant."

She stopped translating. Their language stabbed at her skull, sharp consonants, glottal warbles. Pain surged through her temples, radiating down her spine in convulsions. Her eyes pulsed. Her neck buckled. She slumped.

But before her knees hit brick, hands caught her under the arms and lifted her, but this time gently. Not the captain. Another. Young. Hesitant. She turned her head slightly and saw the one with curls. Earth.

Back on her feet, the moment passed. Another shove. Her vision staggered. She stared at her bare, muddy feet crossing the courtyard and forced herself to count the bricks beneath her. "Five . . . six . . . seven . . ."

Last thoughts replaced by last numbers. Mathematics became prayer. The logic of brickwork, the order of form, the only thing left before the end.

They pushed her into the old church. She stumbled through shattered tiles, over glass shards, dried mud, brittle leaves. At the far end, the trap door waited silently. A rectangular coffin lid, closed to light.

Someone raised it.

Blackness yawed below.

She recoiled, instinctively stepping back, but the same hands gripped her again and lifted her off the ground. Before she could protest, they let go.

Falling.

A jolt. Pain across her spine and ribs. She lay stunned on the cold stone. The tunnel chamber. A flashlight flared above, flooding her face. She blinked.

Then his body dropped beside her.

"Get moving," Cairns growled.

There was fear in his voice.

And that, more than anything, calmed her. He wasn't going to rape her. He was afraid. She was his shield.

Relief struck her with such force it almost felt holy. If she died now, it would be by her comrades' hands. A bullet. A mine. Something without cruelty. The trap door slammed shut above. The light disappeared.

The coffin. Sealed. Buried alive with a demon. Her punishment. For every-thing.

She staggered forward, pulled into the narrow black vein of the tunnel. The flashlight behind her flickered across the walls, its trembling beam carving the darkness into jagged edges.

Cairns' breath rasped behind her in a low, broken rhythm.

His stench, sweat, rot, musk, rose into her throat and turned her stomach. But she kept walking.

~ *Deepening Fears of Major Vy and Captain Tong* ~

Darkness folded swiftly beneath the canopy.

Major Vy stood alone, motionless, as Tong's runner delivered his breathless report. Three bodies recovered—Dam, Doanh, Nguu. One American possibly killed in the tunnel entrance. A grim exchange.

Before the boy could finish, Vy cut him off. "Send my congratulations to Captain Tong!" he spat. "One American—maybe. Tunnel rendered useless. Three of our own dead. Glorious efficiency!"

The runner bowed, silent.

Vy's rage cooled, leaving behind a thin film of dread. The boy fumbled in his tunic and produced a damp, crumpled dispatch. Vy unfolded it. Tong's handwriting, slanted and glib:

> By now you have heard about our glorious victory for the liberation of the South! Three comrades dead, and only one American—maybe. Our "little dragon" problems are grown into unmanageable fire-breathers. It appears we are not destined to make our rendezvous.

> We are excavating the tunnel chamber. It will take time, so we will stay the night. I am sending a team back to you with the bodies. Comrade Minh insisted on joining them—he wants to speak with you personally. In my opinion, it is time Comrade Minh be put in touch with higher-ups. I leave that to you.

> —Tong

Vy read it twice.

"Time for Comrade Minh to be put in touch with higher-ups." Code. Not a recommendation. A request for elimination.

He crumpled the note and waved the runner away. *Why didn't he take care of Minh at the tunnel? Why leave it to me? Fool. Coward. Useless creature.*

Vy turned the problem over in his mind. Call off the siege? Meet the caravan without the statue? Or launch a final assault—damn the losses—and crush the Americans?

But now there was a new probability: discovery. Exposure. The cartel. The Army. His secret life unraveling. He imagined the bullets of the firing squad entering his chest. Felt the pain rise again beneath his ribs.

"No!" he shouted into the jungle.

Quy scrambled from the trees. "Sir? Do you need anything?"

Vy rubbed the crown of his battered pith helmet, trying to ground himself. "No, Quy. Just thinking. That's all. Return to your post."

He watched the boy disappear, then slumped onto a nearby log, exhausted.

Sergeant Dam's death weighed heavily. So did guilt. And the creeping recognition of his own undoing.

But a peasant's instinct, hard-earned and cautious, urged him to wait. To breathe.

He performed a slow *tai chi* sequence, hands carving the humid air like blades through water. Then he called for Quy again.

"Make tea."

Alone beneath the canopy, as night consumed the jungle, Major Vy sat with his dented tin pot, speaking to it in whispers as if it were an old friend. Or a child. Or a ghost.

~

At the collapsed tunnel mouth, the dead were wrapped in plastic liners—Dam, Doanh, Nguu—and loaded onto makeshift stretchers. A squad of bo dois began their march back to the main camp, following the gurgling stream. The current moved brightly alongside them, babbling as if relieved to be free of the bodies.

Phan, a lanky corporal, spat into the water. Then he began to sing. A low, throaty funeral dirge, the kind sung by fishermen mourning lost brothers. The sound rasped against the trees.

Tong heard it from afar. Agitated, he dispatched a runner.

The boy caught up to Phan and leaned in. Whispered. Phan ignored him. The runner tugged his sleeve. Still no response.

"Please," the boy tried again. "I don't care, comrade. Sing if you want. But Captain Tong—"

Phan turned.

Tears streaked his cheeks. His face looked hollow, half-made. "Tell him to bury his own silence."

Then he turned away, singing more softly now, disappearing into the undergrowth. The boy stood still a moment, then nodded, accepting the answer, and watched the funeral squad vanish.

Only Phan's voice remained, floating above the leaves.

~

When Tong was told of Phan's reaction, he understood just how far his command had frayed. The men no longer obeyed from fear or loyalty. The veil was lifting.

He thought of Tuyet Mai, held captive in the American fortress. Thought of Dam and the others, killed over a drug transaction that had spun out of control. And like Vy, he knew that between the teeth of the Army and the claws of the cartel, he would not live long.

"What are you thinking?" asked Kim Lan softly from behind him.

He jumped. Then, slipping back into his mask:

"Nothing. Well, nothing much."

A low rumble rolled through the jungle.

"Thunderstorm?" she asked.

He shrugged.

"How are we going to meet the caravan in time?"

"We're not."

She blinked. "The bosses won't be happy."

He laughed bitterly. His eyes burned into hers. "Attend whichever execution you prefer. Drug bosses will torture me. Hanoi will shoot me. Take your pick. Torture's more theatrical."

Kim Lan's tone turned hard. "Tuyet Mai and I were sent to oversee the statue-for-drugs exchange. If it fails—"

"You report me to your bosses." He nodded. "Or to Minh. Or both. Either way, I'm finished."

"If my sister dies," she said quietly, "your death will give me peace."

Tong opened his mouth, but something failed. His voice broke. Tears brimmed. They slipped, unnoticed, down his face.

"Sister Kim Lan . . . I've told you, my thoughts are also with Tuyet Mai. I wish she weren't tangled in this business. Then at least I alone could face the tiger's mouth. But now . . . now I fear she is sleeping on straw and tasting gall."

Kim Lan stared at him. And for the first time, she felt something unexpected: pity.

She saw it clearly now: he loved Tuyet Mai. And yet, either she or Tuyet Mai would likely ensure his downfall.

Without a word, she turned and walked away.

Tong remained seated in the fading light, hands heavy on his knees. Flashes of lightning split his face into grotesque masks, each one more pitiful than the last.

~

At the main camp, the burial team arrived just as night swallowed the sky. Clerk Long supervised the bodies' placement: neatly aligned, wrapped tight in plastic, laid beside the others who had died two days earlier.

They would be buried at dawn.

Long dismissed the team and sat on a log under a poncho, the rain whispering down. He watched the rows of corpses as lightning lit the clearing in bursts.

With each flash, the dead transformed. One moment they were rills carved in a plowed field. The next, fallen logs lined-up on the floor of a hollowed jungle. Then they became bundled ghosts, their forms shifting beneath the storm.

The wind chased shadows across their shrouds like spiders weaving night. He swore he saw them twitch.

Against better judgment, he stepped forward and pulled back the plastic on one of the newer bodies.

Doanh.

His young face stared upward, eyes open, skin puffing with the first stages of bloat. Searching.

Long replaced the shroud and peeled back another, one of the dead from two days ago.

Unrecognizable.

The face had collapsed. Eyes bulged shut. Black lips hissed as gases leaked through slack seams.

Long tilted his head, listening. A soft whine, high-pitched.

Then another. And another.

A chorus.

The dead are singing.

He trembled. Lifted his hand. Stared at it under his flashlight. It looked pale. Waxy.

Am I already embalmed? Are we all? Still fighting entropy by inches?

But the dead—they had given up. They had crossed over.

Bloated, sealed, slack-faced, vessels of surrender. No longer resisting decay, only awaiting release. Their skin tight as drums, whispering with every shift of pressure, every twitch of gas inside.

Long imagined flies descending. Tiny feet puncturing overstuffed sacks of primordial soup. A single rupture. A catastrophic scream.

He stumbled backward, shivering. He needed to speak to someone, anyone. About the weather. About home. About girls. About anything but death.

~

Humans, Metaphorical Goddess, hiss and sputter at the death of a few cells.

While black holes consume galaxies in silence.

Yes, Metaphorical God, most humans fear silence. Even in death.

Especially in death. Or in the trembling before it. Noise, to them, is anti-death. Take the boy named Teo, whom You so cruelly toyed with.

Wasn't Me.

See for Yourself....

~ Teo ~

After his strange encounter beneath the banyan tree, with Little Monkey sick and the monk-soldier whispering riddles, Teo lingered beneath the carambola, staring up through its skeletal branches, thinking hard. Finally, he turned and sprinted back toward Little Monkey's house.

He arrived breathless. Little Monkey's older sister sat on the porch, chewing betel leaves, red juice staining her lips.

"Hello, sister. Is Little Monkey inside?"

"Yes. Sleeping with Mama. Don't disturb them. They're both sick."

"I heard they have the fever."

"No. Just a winter cold. Go away."

"But I have to tell him something important—"

"No!" She stamped her foot and stood. "Go away! I have work to do." She shoved more leaves into her mouth, squatted down, leaned back against the wall, closed her eyes, and began smacking rhythmically.

Teo kicked at a puddle.

"Did you see the stranger?"

Her eyes stayed shut. Her words slurred through sap and chew: "If you don't go, I'll tell your mama you disrespected an elder."

"You're only two years older!" he protested.

"Go away!" Green drool slipped down her chin.

Teo turned, mission aborted. He took the shortcut through Security Chief Tien's garden, vaulting a broken wall of bricks. His foot caught on a protruding stick, and he tumbled—straight into his mother.

"Oh!" Bin cried, sloshing wine from the hidden gourd in her lap.

Teo scrambled up, rubbing his arm.

"Mama! I saw a stranger. At Little Monkey's house. He's from the Front—or maybe a monk. I don't know! But he said weird things and . . . and . . ." He shuddered.

Bin blinked at him.

"The Front? Here? Where?"

"At Little Monkey's."

"How many of them?"

"One."

"One? Huh?"

"And he's scary. But maybe he's a monk."

"Is he or isn't he?"

"I'm not sure."

Bin pulled off her conical hat and clutched it to her chest.

"Don't frighten me like that! It's mourning time. First you wouldn't kiss the Venerable goodbye, now you're babbling about monks and soldiers—"

"He said strange things. Little Monkey's sick. His mama too. His sister said to stay away."

"Yes, yes. I've heard. Poor family. You stay away now—understand? No fever for you, stupid boy! Are you sure there weren't more soldiers?"

"Yes, but—"

"Enough! I need more rice wine. Go find your grandmother. Tell her. Tell her to send Chief Tien to check on the boy."

"She's not home. I checked."

"Who's not home?"

"Tien."

"Stupid! Go!"

~

Teo found Grandmother Dau at home, seated by the window, thumbing her rosary. She listened closely to his breathless tale. When he finished, she said nothing at first. Her gaze drifted toward the mountain.

Then she whispered: "The second head of a two-headed snake, eh?"

"Yeah. But what does—"

She raised a hand. Silence.

"Too much. Too much is happening. I cannot keep up."

Her voice thinned. But her eyes deepened into distant vigilance, full of omen.

"The gods are showing me something. A glimpse. Into our family's future. Two-headed snake . . ." She shuddered. "Good omen? Or sign of destruction? Only the gods know. I have done my best."

She turned back to him.

"Go out and play, Teo. I need time."

He obeyed.

After he left, Madame Dau began to clean the house, slowly and methodically, trying to ignore the knocking at her door. Villagers came, one after another, asking the same question:

Where is Schoolmistress Nang?

~ *Madame Dau Visits Schoolmistress Nang* ~

But the villagers would not stop pounding on Madame Dau's door.

Finally, she relented.

They swarmed into her home, loud and insistent. Schoolmistress Nang had failed to open the school. The children ran wild. Their requests had gone unanswered. Even Security Chief Tien had tried and failed to get a response. They demanded that Council Chief Dau intervene. Tomorrow's classes must resume. The schoolmistress must be confronted.

Dau said nothing at first. She already knew why Nang hadn't answered. Han Tinh had told her: *The Man from the Mountains cut her tongue so she could not speak.*

Still, she nodded, murmured her agreement, and once the villagers had gone, procrastinated until dusk. Then, with a weight of dread she could no longer shake off, she took her conical hat and walked slowly through the village rain, toward Nang's house.

What if she's dead? What if she kills me? She has every right to be furious. Perhaps she blames me.

Perhaps she'll curse me. Perhaps she'll strike me dead with her eyes. Or perhaps she's already gone, and I'll find only the stink of rot.

She reached the door. Sniffed. No scent of death. No decay—yet.

Still, she hesitated. *On the other side of the dragon's tongue,* she thought, *maybe she's already crossed over.*

She knocked, loudly. No answer. Only the wet hush of monsoon dusk. Lightning cracked the horizon. She stood there awkwardly, hat in hand like a landless peasant begging for work. A curtain rustled. Then stillness.

She knocked again and called out her name.

Nothing.

She turned to go, heart relieved, legs grateful, but behind her, a creak. The door opened.

No one stood in the entry.

No lamps lit. No warmth. Only the jungle's gray drizzle behind her and a lightless gloom ahead. Even the rain seemed gayer than what awaited within.

Flashes of lightning lit the outside walls, but inside the schoolmistress's house was void, an absence so total it pressed against the skin.

Dau wanted to run, but circumstances demanded courage. She crossed the threshold whispering prayers under her breath. Uneven breathing, low and gurgled, came from a far corner.

"Schoolmistress Nang?" Dau whispered.

A wet lisp echoed back:

"Istthh ittth our reverettthh counssill chieftth?"

Suddenly, light flooded the room as the old woman's hand released a lantern wick. In its flickering glow, Nang leapt forward, dropped to the floor, and began to kowtow violently.

"Ah! Ah! Ah! Ah!" Her forehead slammed against the tiles with each thud.

Horrified, Dau rushed to stop her, but Nang flinched away.

"No! Ttthhhe counssill chieftth can bring backthh the demonnn! I am shherhhvant! I am loyalll! I begghh yourhh forgivethnesss!" She staggered upright, moved close to the lantern, and opened her mouth.

Dau gasped.

The tongue, if it could still be called that, spilled forward, grotesquely swollen, dark as a toad's belly. Split down the middle. Shimmering with infection. A forked tongue. Snake tongue.

He had done it. The Man from the Mountains had marked her.

Under the light, Nang looked withered, shriveled into a new form. A day had aged her ten years. She grunted and pointed at her arms, trying to show something. But Dau could bear no more.

She backed away, stiffly bowing.

"I'm sorry. I'm sorry."

Then she fled into the downpour, her sandals slapping water, her hat forgotten. She ran through the darkening village straight to Madame Vit's house.

One look at her face and Vit knew.

"Girls!" she barked to her older daughters. "Go to Madame Tran's. Now. Take the children. We need to speak alone."

Once they were gone, she poured tea and sat beside Dau on the wooden sleeping plank. Waited.

Dau finally spoke.

"I just came from Nang's house. It was . . . terrible."

"How?"

The two women talked deep into the night—first about Nang, then about the village, the stranger, the children, Teo. They spoke of rituals, of how Vu Huong's funeral had brought a fleeting calm. They lamented the young, always running off to the cities, rejecting tradition, abandoning the rhythms of birth and plow, wedding and grave.

Then Vit asked: "What of the American soldier?"

Dau blinked. The question caught her off guard.

"What do you mean?"

"What do you think happened to him? Is he back with his wife?"

"No. I don't think so."

"Why?"

"The battle. The sounds today. It was him. I know it. He's dead."

Vit frowned. "And your visions?"

"They're silent. But . . . what if I'm wrong? What if he's alive? What if he made it to the cave?" She hesitated. "Would my ancestors have sent me the sign if I wasn't meant to help him?"

"But you just said he's dead."

"Yes. But if he's not, should I go to the cave tomorrow?"

Vit waved a hand. "Nonsense. You've done enough. The signs are vague. The omens are cloudy. Forget the American. We are the ones in danger. What if Nang told the People's Army commander everything? What if the Front finds out your part in this? The Army will leave, but the Front will stay. Always listening."

"But I feel I must—"

"No! Now you are just baiting the gods."

Before Dau could respond, a knock came, soft and hesitant. Both women froze. When Madame Vit opened the door, they gasped.

Schoolmistress Nang stood in the rain. Soaked rags clung to her shriveled body. Her eyes wild, afraid. "Forgivvv me, ssssisters." Her voice buzzed through the gagged wound of her mouth. "Madhammm Viththh. Look! Ithh isss my sskthin. Thheyy are backk."

"What is back?"

"Youu musthh helpp me. Thienn is gone. Istthh shhee here? Pleesth."

Dau stepped forward, her voice soft. "Sister Nang, tell us what's wrong. Why do you need Chief Tien?"

Nang's voice fell to a whisper.

"Itthhs thhee wormths again. Shee. Lookk . . . "

She pointed to her forearm, streaked with blood. Beneath the skin, something writhed.

Dau and Vit stared. Tears filled their eyes.

Soaked and shivering, Nang tried to pull herself upright, tried to maintain what little dignity remained.

"Plleesshh, mhay I sstay wittth youuu? You shee . . . I havthh no shonss, no daughhterths-in-law . . . I shent thhem all away . . . to fightth . . . away . . . the boyths and girlths . . . to killlll our enemiesth . . . to killlllll."

The tears came freely now. Madame Vit busied herself with tea. Madame Dau reached forward and gently took Nang's trembling hand. With the other, she massaged the woman's bruised arm.

And there, in a quiet room, three women—one broken, one burdened, one afraid—sat together in silence, sipping bitter tea and weeping for everything they had already lost.

Yes, Kind Goddess, silence is truth. Noise is truth.

Primate language is lies. They embezzle meaning. Stealing from the great orators of growls and chirps and hisses.

They rob truth with verbs and vowels, investing in the currency of chatter.

Just as You, Timeless God, have weaponized language itself. You beguiled them with meaning. You led them with syntax.

Nang's hissing—this is Nature's true speech. The honesty of snakes. The syntax of rot. The grammar of the grave.

Leave sarcasm to mortal men. It suits You not.

~ *Tuyet Mai in the Tunnel with Captain Cairns* ~

Tuyet Mai and Captain Cairns were nearing the end of the tunnel. The journey had been painfully slow but uneventful—until they passed the shrine.

Mountain Man's makeshift altar emerged from the dark, lit only by a weak fungal glow. A human skull rested on a ledge of stone, its teeth catching the faint light. Tuyet Mai flinched.

Cairns muttered under his breath. "Crazy son of a bitch."

They shuffled on.

She led the way. By now, her fear of rape or sudden execution had dulled into a kind of resigned clarity. Even his stench had receded into background. She moved forward in silence, body conformed to the tunnel's rhythm, each step a negotiation with stone, rot, and breath. The phosphorescent rails offered faint guidance, two dim lines etched through the dark.

Then the tunnel changed.

The ground crumbled beneath her step, soft earth and loose clods made the going treacherous. The iron tracks vanished into the rubble. The air thinned. The fungal light disappeared behind them, extinguished without ceremony. The black that remained was not absence, but presence.

She halted, breath tightening. There were no longer walls. No ceiling. No orientation. The tunnel dissolved around her—stone no longer stone, space no longer anchored. Her body floated inside something that was not air, but existence stripped of time. The tunnel no longer held a shape. She reached forward, expecting stone, but found nothing. Her hand floated. So did her sense of self.

She tried to speak, to ask Cairns if he still followed, but the words stayed trapped. The air refused to carry them. Her voice no longer felt like hers.

Each step forward deepened the strangeness. There was no sound, only breath, and even that began to feel borrowed. The space around her grew directionless, heavy, alive. It pressed against her temples, not as pressure, but as thought.

Something knew she was here.

She closed her eyes, though it made no difference. Her body swayed. Her foot struck something, stone or bone, and she stumbled forward.

Was this the exit?

Was she even moving?

A tremor passed through her. It was not fear, not dread, but recognition. This place is not the tunnel. Not anymore. She remembered the old battle that took place here against the French decades ago. Hundreds of dead buried in this tomb.

This is where names dissolve. Where light has no history. Where even the dead forget themselves.

She felt Cairns' breath behind her, still audible, still human. But just barely.

If he spoke now, she thought, his words would come out wrong, cracked open and emptied of meaning.

She pressed forward, eyes wide in the dark, walking through what no longer obeyed the laws of path or place. The air moved without direction. Time no longer followed.

Only the dread remained. And the faint sensation that something ahead was waiting. Not an enemy. Not a man.

Something older. Something infinitely patient.

She tried to raise her hands to test the ceiling, but the rope binding her wrists stopped her. Dirt slipped under her feet. *Cave-in,* she thought, panic surging.

She turned just as Cairns stumbled into the same loose soil.

"Shit," he muttered, flicking on his flashlight.

A mound of red earth and shattered limestone rose before them, plugging the tunnel floor to ceiling.

They both stood frozen, lungs heaving in the stale air, sweat beading under their skin.

"Dig."

Cairns's voice cracked. He untied the rope holding her arms down but left her wrists bound. She climbed the slope on tiptoe, clawing into the upper section of the mound. Dirt slid beneath her nails. Another small collapse forced her back. Dust clouded the air. She gasped behind the gag, nearly choking.

Cairns yanked the cloth from her mouth, pulled out the soaked wad. She staggered, wiping her eyes, and saw the flashlight beam freeze on something jutting from the rubble.

A boot.

American.

The toe of the boot stuck out at an unnatural angle, half-buried in dirt, glistening with moisture.

"Shit," Cairns whispered, his voice hollow.

Then a sigh escaped him. High-pitched. Defeated. A sound like moaning.

"Dig it out," he snapped.

Her hands moved reluctantly toward the object. At first, she hoped it was empty. But as her fingers traced its contours, she felt flesh inside, soft and damp. Her stomach turned. She followed the curve upward. Over the heel. Then up along the shin. Her fingers slid over a tear in the skin and felt a wet, jagged rawness. Her hand sank into a slick depression like spoiled meat.

Then the leg gave way. It slipped from the mound like a snapped branch. "Ahhh!" she cried, stumbling backward.

Cairns leaned forward and illuminated it. The boot was still attached to a leg, severed below the knee. A punji stake pierced straight through the heel, exiting from the shredded calf, keeping the whole grotesque piece intact like meat on a spit.

The tunnel throbbed with their breathing.

"Wrap it in your blouse," Cairns said.

His voice was strained. Too high. She heard him swallow.

She didn't move.

He stepped forward. His hand shot out. Buttons tore. Fabric peeled from her shoulders. The blouse collapsed into a wad around her wrists.

"Wrap it!"

His face hovered millimeters from hers, breath hot with fear and something else.

Tuyet Mai's fury exploded. She lunged, jaws wide, teeth aimed for his nose.

But he dodged. His fist came down like a club slamming her to the floor.

She hit hard, wind knocked from her lungs. She lay gasping, blinking at the flashlight beam above her.

Cairns stood over her, silent.

Something inside him broke. His breath slowed, and a blankness crept across his face, the kind that precedes madness or reverie.

Then he stared.

Her head arched backward. Her swollen mouth trembled with each labored inhale. The cotton wrap across her chest rose and fell. Slowly.

He stared at the rise. The fall. The curve of fabric soaked in tunnel sweat. The soft breath. The silence.

He imagined things.

~ *Cairns' Sadistic Dream* ~

A man loomed over a woman sprawled across a Chinese rug. She was naked, her body tense, her mouth parted in a voiceless plea. Her eyes—large, pleading—glimmered with a terror so exquisite it stirred him in ways he no longer controlled. Instruments lay neatly arranged beside her: a blade, a bowl of salt. The ritual was ready.

But just as his fantasy took hold, a voice interrupted—

"I will wrap the leg. Please. I will wrap the leg."

Cairns blinked. Her words pierced the membrane of his fantasy. Rage flared—how dare she speak?

Still, the image clung. He saw himself kneeling, blade glinting, carving through pale flesh, reshaping her, erasing her.

"Please. I will wrap the leg," she repeated, quieter.

He heard other voices that came faint and distant. He needed to hurry.

The image shivered, flickered. Salt. Skin. Silk. Strings pulling—

Then she was on her feet again. Standing awkwardly. Holding out her arms.

"Eh." A soft grunt. A summons to return to the world.

~

Out of the corner of his eye, Cairns saw her watching him. Still, he lingered in the fading afterglow of the fantasy. Then he flicked the flashlight toward her chest and let his gaze linger. Her breath moved in spurts beneath the cotton binding. He stepped forward and cut the fabric at her sleeves, letting her torn blouse fall away.

She knelt to wrap the leg. He watched the curve of her back, the smooth line of her hips, the hollow above her waist. Desire flooded him in feral, corrosive and uncontainable waves.

Nothing, no danger, no mission, could override the fire now consuming his body.

She must be humbled. Possessed. Changed.

~

Tuyet Mai finished wrapping the leg and held it tightly against her body, as if it might shield her. She felt his eyes on her, the heat, the hunger, and a cold panic surged in her chest.

She rose and started walking without waiting for his order, whispering the only Buddhist prayer she remembered.

She did not look back.

She thought of her brother, of Kim Lan, of her parents. She tried to hold those memories close. But Tong's image kept intruding—his arms, his certainty, the softness in his voice when he called her Sister. She wanted him now, not just to protect her, but to witness her. To kill the American. To hold her. She felt shame rising with the longing.

But still she moved forward, step after step, deeper into the shadows of the earth.

~

Behind her, Cairns followed. He could smell her sweat. He could see the sway of her body in silhouette. Her silent revulsion only deepened his hunger. The symmetry between her fear and his arousal thrilled him.

But soon even that wasn't enough.

Her trousers still concealed her. Her bindings remained intact. Her dignity, untouched. Her silence, a refusal. She walked ahead of him, proud, autonomous, self-contained. Mocking. Superior.

And worse, she did not fear him enough. She would have to be taught. No—transformed.

He would begin when they reached the first storage chamber. There would be space there. Time. Shadow.

That's where he would start reshaping her. Piece by piece.Into what he needed her to be.

~ Foiled Rape ~

Tuyet Mai heard the captain's breathing behind her gradually increase in volume to become a sort of canine panting. Her mind reeled, almost shutting down for protection against mindless panic. From a host of unspoken signals she knew, once they reached the storage chamber, he would rape her. Perhaps murder her. So she focused on her future, one that would be possible only if she acted now. Determined to resist, for the sake of eliminating the bitter taste of her compliant past, she vowed to strangle him with the rope that bound her wrists. And if she failed to kill him, then he would have to kill her. This, the first great test of her new life, would transform her into a different person. Not a slave or a monkey or an object unworthy of respect. She would not now and never again be a mere receptacle for the virulent sperm of wicked men.

So she developed a plan.

Tuyet Mai fainted. The captain leaned over and tried to lift her to her feet. As he turned his face while pulling her up, she slipped her wrists over his head and quickly crossed her hands so that the rope tightened around his neck, crushing his windpipe. Clawing uselessly at the rope, his eyes bulged out of their sockets and his lips became swollen and purple. After he died, she raced back through the tunnel and dug at the collapsed dirt and rocks that blocked her escape. She dug and dug until beams of light slanted through the opening and the smell of the jungle trickled down to urge her on. Digging more quickly, exuberant at the prospect of beginning her new life, she felt a breeze cool her face and she saw the bright blue of the sky and the clean, soft beauty of clouds greeting her from above. A slender hand reached into the exit chamber and her beloved Kim Lan looked down, smiling, leaning over to pull her out of the darkness. . . .

"Go on! Go on!" snapped Cairns when she hesitated at the entrance to the first storage chamber.

She shuffled forward and looked up at the high ceiling and spacious interior made faintly visible from the glow of Cairn's light. Anxious to pass through, she strode toward the tunnel entrance on the opposite side until his echoing words made her stop.

"Wait! Put it down and move to the center of the room!"

Setting her bundle carefully on the floor, she could not resist stretching her arms and legs to the limits of their bonds. Then she watched him emerge, his flashlight leading the way, a train approaching through a dark tunnel. When the beam briefly lit up his face as he fumbled with something in his pocket, his whitish-yellow skin, now splotchy red from the iron-rich dirt, made him resemble an unappetizing morsel spit out by some monstrous beast. And she sensed that his anger and fear had changed to something she had all too often seen in her past, the craving expectation of a starving man when food is laid before his eyes.

Her resolve that he would not enter her grew. She became calm and her calmness encouraged her to carry out her plan. Taking a deep breath, she turned and looked at him, then slouched backward in fear and crouched on her haunches so she would appear weak and vulnerable. She began to wail in an irritatingly high-pitched voice, rocking back and forth, imitating an old woman in mindless lamentation.

~

Cairns watched Tuyet Mai rock on her haunches. Momentarily irritated by her behavior, his sexual excitement soon overcame any distractions, and all thoughts not connected to his lust were swept from his mind, clearing the way for un-bridled fantasy a cascading effect that always led him into areas of exquisite sexual exploration and sadistic creativity. His eyes scanned the room, searching for scaffolding, reinforcing beams, anything that would serve as a frame against which he could tie her so that she would be helpless and exposed.

At first, he thought he would order her to remove the rest of her clothes. But a host of possibilities passed through his mind. *Those damn ropes. She can't strip with those tied to her wrists and ankles. So exactly how?... ah! Perfect!*

In the corner of the chamber stood a large bamboo scaffolding which had evidently been used to shore up a section of the tunnel. Above the scaffold, a tattered parachute was stretched forlornly across the ceiling, sagging so low in the middle that it hovered about three feet over his head. It appeared to have been used at one time to protect against falling dirt. The scaffolding looked weak, but he thought it would do. He probed the structure with his flashlight and noticed a thick bamboo crossbeam about seven feet high and parallel to the ground. It protruded two or three feet beyond the scaffolding. Instantly he decided to hang her from her wrists and cut off her clothes. His excitement increased.

"Wait there!" he barked. He walked up to the scaffold and tested the strength of the protruding pole.

Excellent! This will do nicely.

Cairns walked back to the whimpering Tuyet Mai, who continued to squat dejectedly on her haunches. He grabbed the cord mid-span between her wrists and dragged her to the scaffolding. She resisted weakly, as if resigned to her fate. This disappointed him. He stood her up directly under the pole jutting out from the scaffold. In one fluid motion, he untied the restraining rope, raised her arms, and slipped the cord binding her wrists over the top of the pole so that she stood on her tiptoes. Her soft cries excited him, but something in the back of his mind told him this was too easy. Muddled by the driving urge to see her naked, he dismissed any cautionary thoughts. With his body pressed against hers while he adjusted the cord looped over the bamboo, he noticed that the rope cut too deeply into her wrists. Her breathing became irregular, head lolling to the side and eyes unfocused. Not wanting her to faint, he turned around to scan the chamber for a stool or box or other object on which she could stand to relieve the pressure cutting into her flesh.

Narrowing his eyes and peering at the opposite side of the chamber, he moved the flashlight in a sweeping motion. As he peered through the darkness, he saw a thin, blurred shadow dart in front of his face. It slipped nimbly around his neck and tightened so quickly that he could not get his hands up in time to block it from cutting into the soft sag of his throat. He dropped the flashlight and instinctively clawed at the noose. Panic swept everything from his mind except the desperate need to keep the rope from crushing his windpipe. To his horror, he discovered he couldn't breathe.

As the flashlight rolled on the ground, its beam shining at crazy angles, Cairns reached back and tried to throw Tuyet Mai over the top of his head. In his effort, they both fell heavily to the dirt. Cairns rolled and bucked and kicked but could not loosen her death grip. Exertion made them sweat, and the filth and humidity of the tunnel combined into rivers of sweat that intermingled so that they were both soaked. Swirling, mad, they struggled, arms and legs flailing and kicking until the exhausted Tuyet Mai could hold the rope no longer and the oxygen-starved Cairns could struggle no more.

They kneeled on the ground, each gasping and coughing for breath. Barely able to see in the dim light, separated only by a few meters, they stared at each other as if they were two scavengers fighting over a kill. Tuyet Mai's cotton binding had been torn off in the struggle and Cairns peered through the suspended dust at her naked breasts rising and falling to her labored breathing. But the notion of sex now seemed ridiculous.

She covered her breasts as best she could, keeping her arms raised in defense, and her narrowed eyes pierced the dense air to stare at him with loathing. He felt her hatred wash over him and he unexpectedly felt ashamed, stupid—as if he were a boy caught in the act of doing something he knew was wrong. Oddly, he did not feel she was beautiful or magnificent or much of anything. He only felt his own shame. Rising painfully, he picked up her cotton binding and threw it at her knees, then backed up in a gesture of peace.

While he watched her wrap her breasts, other thoughts tumbled through his mind. *What will they say when she goes back looking like this? Why not just shoot her and be done with it? Easy to explain.*

He found it repugnant that the grunts would think he had raped her, that he had the need to rape her, or worse, that he failed. And as she stood, he felt the stirrings again. *What if I just wound her? Then take her and kill her. After she's dead . . . no struggle then. Necrophilia. I wonder . . . what would it be like . . . no struggle, place her body anyway I like, and to be inside . . .* "Wha—?" Cairns cried in disbelief.

Something was terribly wrong. He felt something moving against his skin, crawling on the inside of his trousers. Something alien. Growing.

A voice, feminine and terrible, rang in his head, neither echo nor thought but presence—

You would make her your offering? Then offer yourself. You would carve her flesh? Then be carved. You would feed on her fear? Then feed upon your own.

"God!" he screamed. He staggered backwards, grabbing at his crotch, trying to feel what squirmed and stretched inside of him. To his abhorrence, he found it. Felt it. Identified it. It was his own penis becoming horribly, grotesquely, inhumanly erect. Lengthening at an impossible rate. Ballooning out of control. "Nooooo!" he screamed again, pushing against the bulge. But the strain on the fabric of his fatigues became too much. He heard a rip and felt the air against his exposed skin. Looking down in a panic, he saw his trousers in shreds, balled-up at his ankles, making it difficult to walk. As he wrapped both hands around his immense penis, he shuffled aimlessly backwards toward the center of the chamber, constrained by the tangled cloth at his feet. Arching his spine and throwing his shoulders back to counterbalance the enormous weight of his groin, he tripped and began to fall when something held him up as if invisible hands supported him beneath his armpits.

"Oh God! Oh God! God! God! God!" he babbled almost incoherently as he felt himself being lifted off the ground.

Cairns involuntarily drew up his feet, causing his legs to bow. His penis now felt as large as a boa constrictor, wet and scaly and slithering through his hands. Like an overextended hose, it began to sag downward, impervious to his efforts to stop it. He squeezed hard, trying to somehow constrict its growth, but it grew larger and more terrifying by the moment. As it lengthened, his knees spread even farther apart and his heels almost touched, making it look as if he were riding an invisible horse. The hideous organ formed a 'u' shape as it passed beneath his shrunken gonads and sprouted upward again, curving toward his bare buttocks.

"Ahhhhhhh!" He squirmed and tried to wriggle away, but the invisible hands locked around his hips, holding him firmly, preventing him from taking evasive action. He felt something pressing against the back of his neck, forcing him to bend forward at the waist.

"Ahhhhhhhhhhh!"

Impaled on his own maleness, Cairns moaned piteously as he hovered in the air, feet dangling off the ground, body periodically shuddering and jerking. He vomited, spitting out long strands of greenish mucous and managing only the words, "Help me! Help me!" rasped through the searing bile that burned in his nose and throat.

~

Somewhere in the dark, Tuyet Mai watched, unsure if she was witnessing his madness or divine intervention.
She did not move.
She did not breathe.

~

Without warning the invisible hands released him. Falling heavily to his knees, he leaned forward and began crawling toward Tuyet Mai.

~

Tuyet Mai was repulsed by the American crawling toward her. For the previous few minutes she had watched him standing with his legs spread apart and his knees bowed, screaming and moaning. When she smelled the faint odor of defecation she backed away, deciding that he had gone mad or had been possessed. Now, after he vomited and fell to his hands and knees, he crawled toward her. She panicked and ran toward the tunnel, but she heard him shout, "No!" and the deafening roar of his pistol discharging made her stop in her tracks.

~

Goddess, You have been residing in Cairns since the death of Mountain Man?
How did You know I inhabited Mountain Man?
A slip.
Oh.
Have You?
Yes, Cairns.
And this curious hallucination of his?
Ah. It was cramped residing in his tiny male hovel of a brain–surrounded by his stained neuronal sheets–with only his sick fantasies for entertainment. Therefore, when he acted up, I decided that it was an excellent time to expand My quarters, so I simply extended his front porch.
HaHaHaHaHa! All this time ... in Cairns! Who would have guessed? Did You enjoy Your remodeling job?
On behalf of My sister Tuyet Mai and all the sisters that went before her, yes. Oh, yes!

~

Cairns stared vacantly at Tuyet Mai. He had no idea why he fired his pistol. Even as the reverberations of the shot rang in his head, his mind began to clear and he felt the utter depravity of his being as it must have felt to his victims. Still overcome by the power of his hallucination, he shriveled under the rage and hatred expressed in Tuyet Mai's eyes. Her humiliation merged with his self-contempt, eventually creating a monochromatic exhaustion that lapped benignly against both of their souls.

Let's just get to the surface and breathe fresh air. Let her live. I need to clean up. Go on as if nothing happened. Wipe it away. Start over. Clean up. Breathe fresh air. Forget this. Forget.

But something in her silence warned him—she might speak, or worse, she might not. He didn't know which would damn him more.

He flashed an insincere smirk and forced a thought that was already a lie. *Besides, another opportunity may come.*

It felt good to be lecherous again, even if forced.

Cairns motioned for Tuyet Mai to pick up Mountain Man's wrapped foot. When she had done so, he motioned for her to continue their walk back through the tunnel to the fortress.

~

Tuyet Mai felt jubilant. She had succeeded. He had not penetrated her. It was a sign. A good sign. She had clawed her way out of a male pit filled with degradation and filth and, by heroic effort, felt renewed and resurrected from darkness to a female world of light and strength. She overflowed with optimism. She felt fresh and clean and confident of her new beginning. Now, if she survived, she might yet have a home, raise children and live in peace.

As she started to walk, she looked down at the heavy parcel she carried and thought it ironic that a blouse she had once worn to keep her warm now wrapped the cold flesh of an enemy's severed foot. She shook her head in wonder. *The Man From The Mountains is dead, his body broken to a thousand pieces, never to be buried in his homeland with the proper rituals. May he be accepted with joy by his ancestors.*

She tried to picture his mother's face, but had no knowledge of the physiognomy of American women, so her own mother's face, modified by round eyes and white skin, substituted.

She turned her attention back to the bundle and tried to picture The Man From The Mountains as a young boy.

Like all boys, American or Vietnamese, he played joyfully in her imagination.

It felt good to be compassionate, even if forced.

The first thing I will do when I am free will be to seek counsel from a Buddhist monk, some old venerable who can guide me back to the ways of the ancestors, to the ways of my mother. And her heart sank when she thought of her brother, still working in Hanoi to perpetuate this violence and destruction. She raised her head slightly and whispered in a barely audible voice, "I cannot think of Ban now, or I will sink back into the abyss. To my new life, whatever it might be, however long it might last."

She heard the American laugh behind her, and remembering that he spoke Vietnamese, hoped he had not heard her words. But if he had not, why did he laugh? *He is a puzzle. A dangerous puzzle.*

~ *Final Return of Mountain Man* ~

A small circle of grunts gathered around the bundle Tuyet Mai laid gently on the church floor.

Cairns hovered nearby with a salesman's smirk, trying to cloak himself in authority, but the dread in their faces sobered him. He hadn't said a word, but every man knew. The package held irrefutable proof of their approaching extinction.

By silent consensus, X stepped forward and began unwrapping the foot. When it was fully exposed, boot, blood, and ruined flesh, not a single word was spoken. Only slumped shoulders and bowed heads marked the moment their last illusion collapsed.

Stretch, who'd been on guard near the trap door, twitched and fidgeted. He stared at the foot, then turned toward X.

"Can you patch him up, doc?"

No one laughed.

A few snorts passed through clenched jaws—grim jokes thrown like mud against the breach in the dam.

Nature leaned in for a closer look. His brow furrowed. Tucked in the laces of the boot, pressed deep into a knot of blood and dirt, was the flock bag Mountain Man had once given to Bowls.

His eyes lit up.

"Hey, look at this!" he called, fumbling to free it. "He got it back! Mountain Man got it back from the sapper!"

"Holy shit," someone breathed. "He got the bastard?"

A ripple moved through the room.

"I'll be damned." T's mouth twitched, a smile threatening to rise. "He really did it."

"Took that motherfucker out! I'd give anything to see how he did it."

Their voices lifted, one after another, each man adding kindling to the flame of belief.

"That's what we heard—the shooting. That was him. He may be gone, but he sure as hell took a bunch of 'em with him."

"I bet he got through. Rear's probably already on alert."

"Fuckin' A!"

"We'll see birds in the sky by morning, gunships, maybe Phantoms. Light 'em up."

"Fuckin' A!"

And so it went.

A fragile tide moved through the ruined church, desperate, defiant, and contagious. Even death could not silence the myth of the Man. It moved among them, breathed through them, rising from ash and blood. They seized it not with reason, but with instinct, hands grasping not for proof, but for something older: a name, a shape, a force that would not die.

Nature stepped forward, the flock bag at last free. He raised it into the air, not as signal, but as invocation—Ahab flourishing the gold doubloon.

The room held still. The story was not over. Mountain Man still moved beneath the earth. Or so they believed.

And belief, for now, was enough.

No one noticed Cairns slip away. He ducked through the shadows alone, searching for water.

Not to drink.

To scrub the stains from his eyes.

From his soul.

Chapter Twenty-Four

Fever Dreams VII

Apparitions Return and Storyteller Sees Himself

***H**uman males, My Dear Goddess, human males and their testicle dreams; ejaculating thousands of them only to make room for more. Occasionally a robust nightmare wriggles into the great egg and fertilizes a generation bred to war.*

~

Storyteller slept poorly. Near midnight, a violent twitch jolted him awake. Disoriented, he blinked into the dark, wiping drool from the corner of his mouth. Rain whispered across the brick courtyard. A pale blue glow clung to the air, suspended, unmoving. He reached instinctively for the alarm clock but his hand paused, midair. No nightstand. No clock. Only the trace of a dream pretending to be a room. He sighed, remembering where he was. He'd meant to reach for his M-16, but the hollow ache in his palm confirmed it wasn't there.

Instead: a white orchid. It hovered above him, trembling at the edge of a cliff. He felt compelled to pluck it. Reaching upward, he found it always just beyond reach. Mud pressed into the soles of his feet. Panic crept upward, forcing him to look down. Boots. Thank God. He had a dread of being caught barefoot by the enemy. But the orchid, how to reach it before it vanished?

He stretched again. No use. Then the panic deepened. His hand was no longer part of him. A severed wrist jutted from his sleeve. His detached hand floated toward the orchid, fingers outstretched. It closed on the stem. His body convulsed, breath scattering dirt before his face. Mountain Man's face surfaced and vanished, a veil lifting and falling. A shadowed hand swept upward, downward, then plunged a black blade over the dream's edge.

"Wake up," he said aloud.

And did.

~

No fever. Calm clarity. The apparitions moved through the fortress with the patient rhythm of travelers waiting for a signal. They no longer sought out the grunts, no longer cried or pleaded. They lingered: watching, listening, exchanging glances and knowing smiles. Conspiratorial. As if parsing a language deeper than sound.

Storyteller saw himself among them, older now, middle-aged and alert, shifting on the balls of his feet to catch stray phrases. The shock of recognition had faded. At least his future self might learn who these ghosts had once been. Someday he would know. But not now. Their voices came fractured, their meaning scattering as fallen leaves across water. They spoke of familiar things: family, work, pain, memory, themselves.

A luminous older woman leaned close to a gentle-faced man and spoke with quiet urgency. She pressed her hand to her chest.

"Can you see it? The lump's doubled in size. It's hideous. When my son was killed in the war, I didn't think I could go on. But now I want to live. Is that terrible? Wanting to live?"

"No," the man answered.

"I can't help it. I remember being a girl, hating the farm. But now I miss it so deeply. The rhythm of fences, the loose weight of my skirt in the wind, the breath of soil, the heat of the sun, the wildness inside me beating against its cage."

"My my," the man said, eyes twinkling, "quite poetic."

"English lit major. Or just mad." She laughed. "Anyway, one time I remember . . ."

A younger woman passed, hunched, lips pursed, eyes anxious. "Have you seen my cat?" she asked Storyteller. "After my husband died in the war, Sam's all I had. Sam's a calico. Short for Samantha. Have you seen her?"

Tears shimmered. "So much pain since he died. Sam gave me unconditional love."

A man nearby offered, "The dogs. Must've chased her."

"The dogs?"

"You've seen them, right? They must've chased her."

Storyteller leaned forward. "Where would the cat go if the dogs chased her?"

"Sam is a she," the woman bristled.

The man shrugged. "She could be anywhere."

"Outside the walls?"

"What walls?"

"Into the jungle?"

"Jungle?"

"Okay. The street?"

"Maybe. Man, you've smoked too many funny cigarettes." The man's smile gleamed again.

Storyteller tried to press further, but the abused woman arrived, hand-in-hand with the elder. "Maybe we can help," she said.

"I hope so," Storyteller muttered. "I thought you were connected—to the soldiers. But now... I'm not sure."

"Let's take a walk," she said. "It might help. Let's walk down the beach."

"The beach?" He looked down. His legs stretched stiffly in front of him like a crippled beggar. "I can't. I'm sick."

"That's all right. That's why he's here." Her voice softened as Storyteller's future self stepped forward.

"You!" Storyteller blurted.

"Hi," said the man. "I won't ask how you're doing. I already know. You've been to dinner enough times."

"Huh? Yeah . . . but I don't know anything about you."

~

The older man hesitated, suddenly self-conscious. A strange discomfort rose in him, the ache of facing who he had been. What could he say to his past self, knowing the wreckage that lay ahead? Every word felt burdened, either too harsh or too forgiving. Kindness risked sounding false. And even then, when he had been that younger man, he bristled at anything that hinted of pity or condescension.

~

Michael. Michael. Wake up. You're dreaming again. Come on, sweetheart. It's okay. Wake up.

~

The man peered calmly at his younger self, trying to appear dignified, composed. I wonder if people could choose to know their future, would they? The good, the bad, or neither? He chuckled. Navel gazing. Damn. Did I always do this?

~

Storyteller stared up, stricken. He felt fragile beside the older man: foolishly young, devastatingly sick, spiritually incomplete. What could he ask of a future he couldn't yet fathom? The twin thing . . . had he gone mad?

Maybe that was it.

Maybe I'm in an asylum, dreaming I'm in the war.

~

They spoke at once. "Why are you here?" each asked the other.

They snorted in unison. The older man bowed. "Youth before beauty."

Storyteller didn't smile. "Who are these people?" He gestured at the apparitions. "Are they ghosts? Who do they belong to? Are they the soldiers' families? I can't figure it out. It's driving me mad. And this twin stuff. . . . "

"Liar. Liar."

"I . . . I asked someone the same thing once," the older man said haltingly. "Never got an answer. But I'm not in a loony bin, if that helps. I'm not one of them."

"You are," Storyteller snapped.

"Maybe you are. Maybe you're the ghost. My twin."

"I don't have a twin."

"You're a voice in my head. I suffer from schizophrenia."

Storyteller frowned. "But I can see through you. You're not wearing a uniform. You don't belong here."

The older man smiled. "Look, Michael—Storyteller—you're not my twin by birth. You're my twin by fracture. The part of me that never left."

"So we're not twins at all, but fragments of the person called Michael Powers."

"Exactly," the older man said. "But in my denial, when I insist you're just my twin, I slap my body and you still look transparent. You, my lost fragment, won't disappear. You keep showing up. You've even been to my dinners. With Diane. With Mark."

"Diane Farber? My girlfriend?"

"My wife. Or . . . our wife. You know what I mean."

"What?"

"You spoke to her last night."

"Ah, jeez." Storyteller shook his head. "This is too much."

"That boy there," the man pointed, "baseball cap backwards, fiddling with a device? That's Mark. Our son. He's using a computer."

"Huh?"

"A computer. Internet. It's the future."

"That's our son? You said I was your twin."

"Too hard to explain."

"Can't you get him to do something else? There's a whole world out there."

"I've tried. It's an addiction."

~

The abused woman slipped her arm into the man's. "Let's go, Michael. You're new here. Can't just talk to yourself all day."

"But—"

She gently pulled him away. Storyteller watched them disappear into the crowd. "Wait! You said they were just cards. Who's playing whom?"

"Don't bother," said an old Black woman, remaining behind. "Just sit a spell."

"Will they come back?"

She smiled, pretending to scrub dishes at an invisible sink. Storyteller slumped. "What are you doing?"

"Cleaning up. Not much here, but I try to keep tidy. Mama used to say . . . "

She drifted into a story. Storyteller's stomach churned.

"A nightmare," he muttered. "All of it. A nightmare."

~

That's right, Michael. Michael. Wake up. It's just a nightmare. Come on, sweetheart. It's okay. Wake up.

~

He heard snippets from the apparitions as they passed:

". . . arthritis but hides the pain . . . "

". . . pimples are ruining her life . . . "

". . . he drinks and takes it out on the kids . . . "

Something snapped.

He stumbled forward. "Mike! Mike!" He hated calling his own name aloud. But he had to find him.

Through the crowd, he spotted his older self, still walking arm-in-arm with the woman. He rushed up, collapsed against him, clinging. *Maybe he'll take me back. Maybe if I just hold on tight enough...*

"What about us?" he begged. "Don't any of you future people care? What happens to us?"

Even the boy with the backward cap turned to look. But only for a moment. Then back to his screen, fingers circling lazily, mouth half-open.

Is this what we're dying for?

He felt the panic rising.

"Nature! Nature! Help!"

~ *Cold Water* ~

Nature looked down in astonishment at Storyteller, who clung to his waist as if drowning.

"Storyteller! It's me. Nature. Look up, man. Come on! It's Nature!"

But Storyteller only tightened his grip, eyes wild, voice rising with desperate questions. "What about us? What's going to happen? To them? To me? Don't any of you care anymore? Has it been so long? Have you all forgotten?"

Nature exhaled, half in pity, half in helplessness. He lifted Storyteller as one might a feverish child mid-tantrum, guiding him gently back to the poncho liner.

"Of course we care about you, man," he said softly, the words mechanical in his mouth. "Of course we do."

X knelt beside them and jabbed a needle into Storyteller's arm.

"Mike! Take me with you!" Storyteller cried, voice cracked with yearning. "Michael! Take me out of here!"

"Michael?" Nature glanced across the empty courtyard, following his friend's gaze. "Who the hell is Michael?"

Then, lower: "Damn. This is bad. It's getting worse, X. Is he gonna make it?"

Nearby, T stood with a cluster of silent grunts, his face hardening.

"This has got to end," he said. "We can't keep going like this."

"A little late, ain't it, T?" Stretch muttered, voice sharp, eyes twitching as his old tics returned. "We had our chance. But now? No fuckin' tunnel. No fuckin' escape."

T turned, surprised. Then he let out a weary snort.

"What's the matter, Stretch? No jokes left? No dumbass movie quotes? Now that the shit's real, you run out of lip? Look around, trooper, this ain't Main Street. It ain't High Noon. And you sure as hell ain't Gary Cooper."

Stretch's eyes lit up. He grinned wide.

"Hey, T! You just made a poem. No, a fuckin' song!" And then, with full theatrical flair, he belted it out loud enough to make the grunts on guard duty duck by instinct:

Look around, trooper,
Hey, hey, hey—
Yeah, look around, trooper,
'Cause this ain't Main Street,
It ain't High Noon,
And you ain't Gary Cooper.
No. No. No.
And you ain't Gary Cooper.

T let out a quiet laugh, shaking his head. "Stretch, you're too much, man. If we die out here, I guess we'll die with your idiotic lyrics stuck in our skulls."

"Yup," Stretch muttered. But the grin had faded. He stared at the ground, fists clenched.

Damn. Can't I ever stop? Mom . . . I wanna go home. Shit. I really want to go home.

~ *Clerk Long has a Strange Conversation with Major Vy* ~

Long crouched in a forgotten guard hole, soaked and sleepless. After returning from the corpses, he had searched quietly for company, but the night had thinned out the men. None remained awake, or willing. Alone, he watched the fortress beyond, a silhouette blacker than the jungle sky.

Something felt different. Artificial. As if the world itself had been rearranged but forgot to tell him.

A strange thought pestered his mind: *I'm not really here.* The delicate symmetry he maintained between the real and the unreal, that fragile truce in his head, had begun to fracture.

For a moment, he thought he heard singing from the fortress, but dismissed it as the echo of his imagination.

Then, beside him, a body dropped heavily into the mud. Long flinched. But it was only a man. A comrade. He opened his mouth in greeting, then saw the face.

Major Vy.

He leapt to his feet to salute, swaying as his knees buckled. Vy reached out with a steadying hand, guiding him back down.

"Sit, Comrade Long. You're making me nervous. Worse, you're making yourself a target."

"Yes, sir."

"They've got infrared scopes now. Night doesn't save you. Neither does rain. They'll put a bullet between your eyes before you even know they're watching."

"Yes, sir."

"Captain Tong tells me you're a painter."

"Yes, sir."

"You read Chinese?"

"Yes, sir."

"You know philosophy?"

"A little, yes, sir."

Vy's voice turned cool. "You know what good Marxists think of that."

Long straightened his back. "Yes, sir. But that was in my rotten bourgeois past. Now I'm a true soldier of the People's Army. My comrades have shown me the guiding light of Marxist-Leninist thought. Through *kiem thao*, I've learned to apply political and military struggle. I've eradicated the poison of my old ideas."

Vy stared out at the fortress, his eyes heavy. Then, quietly: "Yes. Very worthy."

"Thank you, sir."

As if brushing away the dust of required slogans, Vy adjusted his posture and spoke more energetically.

"Now, Comrade Long. Tell me about the ghosts."

Long went pale.

"No, sir! I don't see them anymore. Comrade Medical Technician said it was the malaria. That's what I said in my *kiem thao* sessions. I'm better now."

"Lies," Vy hissed. "Don't insult me. There's no one else here. I'm giving you an order: speak."

Long trembled. He was prepared for a night of denials. "I no longer see them."

Vy exhaled, long and tired. "Can we not speak like comrades, just once? You are an intelligent man. What if I told you... I might believe in your ghosts?"

He looked out again. His voice softened.

"In the old days . . . before . . . men were brothers. I remember Dien Bien Phu. But that doesn't matter. What I'm saying is—we are brothers of the forest. You can trust me."

A pause. Then:

"Have you seen anything of consequence tonight?"

Long hesitated. "Times have changed . . . yes? Comrade Major?"

"Yes," Vy whispered.

They sat in silence, swallowed by the dark.

~

Long glanced at Vy, but his gaze caught something else. A sharp breath escaped his lungs. He began to rise, to flee, but stopped himself. Slowly, carefully, he leaned back as if retreating from a coiled cobra. "In fact, Comrade Major . . . there is a spirit sitting next to you now."

His voice was flat with awe. His eyes locked on the Goddess Tara, who hovered just above the mud, floating on a breath of mist, Her form glowing and serene.

Vy was preoccupied, brushing ants from his trousers. But Long's tone struck him. He followed the gaze.

"I see nothing."

Long's heart sank. "Then it must be the malaria again. Forgive me, sir. Please ignore me."

Yet his eyes remained fixed on the vision.

Vy squinted. "Tell me what you see," he whispered. "Captain Tong told me you were a medium, jokingly, of course. But I believed him. My father was a poor farmer. He had the power. I feel it in you, just as I did in him. You are looking at something. I know it. Tell me. I beg you."

"I shouldn't."

"Tell me."

Long's voice became distant, entranced.

"She's beautiful. She sits like a nun, smiling. A crown on her head. A third eye on her brow. Naked but for jewelry. Cross-legged on a white lotus. Her right hand points to the sky, fingers curved, thumb and forefinger touching. Like Buddha. She's just watching us. But I don't feel fear. Only calm."

"Can you speak to her? Will she answer?"

"I don't know, Comrade Major. I can try—"

But before he could utter a word, the Goddess spoke in his mind.

I do not answer such questions, dear Long. Fate stands starving at the door of what might be. We—Metaphorical deities—have not fed since the Great Opening. Still, I come because you called. And because your fear of compassion tears at My breast.

Since you first heard the hissing chorus, you have searched for meaning. But the story is Mine. And the Father—your Father—is still a child in My womb. He has not yet wept.

Hear Me: the hissing chorus does not sing of death. It sings of release. Let its lights reach you. Let them break the fog. Let them dissolve the old poisons. Accept what comes.

Accept the arrival of the Superior Ones.

"I don't understand. Superior Ones?"

Vy gasped. "I see Her now!"

He gripped Long's arm. "Perhaps if we look together, as brothers, we will understand."

"Yes. Together. With your strength and my—"

"What?" Vy's voice sharpened. "What did you say?"

"Nothing, sir!"

Vy narrowed his eyes. "Well then. I ask again: have you seen anything of consequence tonight?"

"No, sir."

"Keep a sharp eye, comrade." Vy moved to rise.

"Sir," Long said quickly.

"Yes?"

"If I may ask, is your father a farmer?"

Vy tensed. "Yesss. Most of us come from village stock."

Long's voice was careful. "If I may ask, as a fellow brother of the forest, what was his position in the village?"

Vy hesitated. His voice grew clipped. "Small farmer. Nothing special. Working-class peasant, if that's what you're getting at." His tone shifted, becoming coldly formal. "You ask reckless questions of an officer, Clerk Long."

Blood rushed to Long's face. The vision of the Goddess flickered now, nearly gone, but still there. Still listening.

"Sir, if I may... how can we reclaim the brotherhood of the forest if we cannot speak as comrades?"

Vy shook his head. "We can't. That will be the future tragedy of our country. The tragedy of . . . certain political doctrines."

Long understood. He said no more.

The rain deepened, and finally forced them both from the hole.

~ *Han Tinh Dreams of the Beach* ~

Han Tinh dreamed of a beach.

His body was buried, only his head protruding above the sand.

American children, one boy, one girl, ran laughing around him, oblivious to his presence. Their voices rose, bright, shrill, and dissonant, cutting through the sound of the surf.

The language—English—felt distorted to his ears, stretched and warped, as though spoken through water.

The surf roared louder. Drew closer.

He tried to move, to lift himself from the sand pressing into his chest, but nothing responded. His limbs were still there—somewhere—but beyond command.

Then he saw him. Beneath the shade of a large umbrella, seated in a low-slung chair, lounged the Teller of Stories, the same American soldier from the last dream. Older now. No uniform. Bare legs. Sandals. Skin scorched red by the sun. Everything about him radiated ease, but it felt wrong, a costume worn too well.

Somehow, by the dream's silent logic, Han Tinh's head slid across the sand, coming to rest at the man's feet.

The children squealed with delight.

They built a sand fortress around his head, giggling as they planted toy soldiers just inches from his eyes.

English words oozed from the older man's throat in slow, distorted drawls:

"Woon't hee neeeed hiss riflllll? Whaaaat iffff theee dinoooosaaaar giiittss innn theee forrrt?"

It was unbearable.

One of the children leaned over and carefully placed a toy soldier before Tinh's face. The soldier's arm was raised in salute, but the hand was missing. Before long, it toppled. Face-down in the sand. Motionless.

Then it twitched.

Its head turned toward Tinh.

The eyes widened. Its chest began to heave. The toy, sweating, trembling, breathed in shallow gasps. Grains of sand lifted with each exhale. It reached for its severed hand with the stump of its wrist.

Somehow, Tinh remembered him.

A real soldier once. A *bo doi*. One of the People's Army. One of those who had confiscated the statue just before the final battle. Tinh stared.

"What are you doing here?" he asked, the words small, stupid, dream-drunk. But before the soldier could answer, a shadow swept over the sand.

Another figure appeared. It stood tall and ghostlike, leaking blood. The Man From the Mountains.

He stood swaying, his left foot gone, the stump dripping onto the sand in slow, uneven rivulets. His body was splattered with gore, and still he remained upright. Unmoving. Refusing collapse.

The Teller of Stories leaned forward in his chair, mouth parting to speak.

But no words emerged.

A tingling sensation crept up the base of Tinh's neck—strange, electric. The skin felt charged, as if something were stirring beneath it. Then the fog came. Thick, wet, and rolling in fast. It swallowed his vision. And then—

He was moving.

~ *Goddess Intervenes Again* ~

She scurried across the jungle floor, a soldier carried by the swelling tide of her sisters. One leg dragged behind her, the mite still clamped stubbornly to it, but she pressed forward, antennas sweeping in frantic arcs, each flick sending electric pulses through her ganglionic brain. Thorax to thorax, shoulder to shoulder, she moved within the living river that pulsed between twin berms sculpted earlier that morning by workers.

The chemical trail burned bright. The scent of battle. She ignored the severed limbs carried triumphantly by others on their return to the bivouac.

THREAT!

The message crackled through the pheromone web like fire on dry bark. Thousands of clicking mandibles shook the air. Tension, palpable and viscous, passed through her, and the roar of war rushed toward her.

ENEMY SOLDIERS! MANY, MANY SOLDIERS!

She surged forward. Bodies collided in a blind frenzy. A roiling tide of legs and jaws. She plunged in, swept by instinct and signal, antennae whipping through chemical smoke, pincers snapping, carving, slashing.

MOVEMENT! SHADOW! TURN RIGHT! RAISE HEAD! NOW! STRIKE! SLASH! FEINT! PIVOT! SLICE! MOUTHPARTS NEAR! BLOOD! COMRADE'S BLOOD! TURN! STRIKE!

She rose higher. Calculated size. Too big. Too strong. Too fresh. HELP! NEED HELP!

She felt her sisters surge around her. They attacked in waves, piercing the defenders. The sound of war roared through the air, overwhelming and relentless. But the scent trails vanished in the chaos. She was alone. Disoriented. Panic ignited in her chest, fast and consuming.

And then it found her.

A massive enemy soldier gripped her in crushing legs. Mandibles clicked close. She squirmed, twisted, slipped free—falling to the ground. But the giant was on her. Slashing. Severing her legs. One by one.

She lay helpless, her last leg flailing. Her antennas brushed against the enemy's armored chest, then bent, crushed beneath the weight pressing down on her thorax. Through her compound eyes, she saw the working mouthparts descending, saw her own legs, twitching, carried away by triumphant workers.

The mite clung still to one severed limb as it disappeared into the mist.

Darkness blinked out the windows of her vision.

~

"Ahhhh!" Tinh cried out, jolting upright in his bed, soaked in nightmare sweat. A soft, golden light filled the room.

She stood above him. The Goddess. Radiant. Six arms waving in ribbons of light.

"I had a nightmare, Great Lady," he murmured.

No. You were given a chance to share.

"I killed many ants. Was that my sin?"

No. If you were smaller, they would kill you.

"Then I don't understand."

You were given a chance to share.

He blinked. "Ah . . . I see."

You don't. Tell Me—if We removed all humans from the Great Mother, what would happen?

"I would be lonely."

All humans.

"No more cities . . . farms . . . religions. . . . " His voice trailed off. "Ah! You mean . . . no more worship."

The Goddess laughed. Looked to the heavens. **You see? They are clever—even when they miss the point.**

She returned her gaze to him.

And if We removed all bacteria from the Great Mother, what then?

"No one would get sick?" he guessed, stung by Her laughter.

All life would die.

"All life?"

Yes. Now tell Me, which matters more—humans or bacteria?

Tinh hesitated. It was a coin toss. "People."

Why?

"Because the holy books only talk about people and gods. Not about bacteria. And because bacteria don't perform rituals worthy of great deities like You."

She stared at him. Silent. Unblinking.

Tinh panicked. "But, Great Lady, surely You speak to bacteria too? Maybe they would pick themselves over us—if they could pick. But they don't have brains. So I don't know. I'm just a soldier. Not wise. Not worthy."

He bowed, peeking upward for Her response.

She was dark. Towering.

You are correct, Soldier Tinh. You are nothing, and everything. As are bacteria. Scratch a human, you find bacteria. Scratch a bacterium, you find a human.

Tinh chuckled. "It must be very hard to scratch a bacterium, Great Lady."

She smiled. *No harder than using love and compassion instead of hatred and violence.*

"Are You an ant, Great Lady?"

Of course.

"Then forgive me. I've eaten ants in famine."

As some of Us have eaten humans.

~

Storyteller stirred. The bad dreams would not leave him.

~

She fought again. A soldier in the hive's core, guarding the nursery. The tide had turned against them. Still, she slashed. Still, she fought. Her comrades died around her in pieces—but she refused to yield.

The enemy surged. Endless waves.

She felt her aorta strain, near to bursting, but still she killed. She screamed with every limb. Then she saw them—enemy workers carrying pupae, the babies of her colony. Breach. Violation. Sacrilege.

She scurried outside, scent trails lost in the chemical fog. Alone. Disoriented. Then appeared another soldier. Enemy. Also lost. She struck first. She toppled the invader, severed its limbs, pinned it down. Her jaws closed in. Nestmates arrived. They took the pieces.

Victory. But brief.

~

Storyteller jerked awake, grimacing. "Ants," he muttered. "Goddamn ants."

He ran a hand through his hair, shaking off the fog. "Ants. Ghosts. My future self. Twins." He chuckled, hollow. "The only good part is the naked women . . . though even that—"

His thoughts darkened. Bruised flesh. The abused woman. Even that. . . .

You are a gentle one, came a soft voice from the dark.

He sat up. "Who is it?"

You know.

"Yeah . . . how come I keep waking up and I'm still dreaming?"

Such is life.

"Yeah."

Look. Across the courtyard.

He craned his neck. There, bathed in a narrow shaft of moonlight, the female prisoner lay curled in the fetal position, as if lit by a private spotlight.

The voice returned. *Her name is Nguyen Tuyet Mai. When she was a girl, her favorite toy was a cloth monkey, sewn by her mother. She never slept*

without it. Those were terrifying times. War. Revolution. Famine. Violence. Homelessness.

Storyteller narrowed his eyes. "Yeah. But now that she's grown, how many Americans has she killed?"

Not many. None directly. She's killed more of her own—Vietnamese, Laotians, Cambodians. One Chinese.

He snorted. "Sweet little girl."

Yes. Look again.

He looked. The spotlight shifted. The woman was gone. A child now curled in her place, still fetal, still afraid, clutching a cloth monkey.

The voice whispered again. **You had a blanket. Your terror came too. Even in a warm home. Even with a full belly. Even in peace.**

He whispered, "Will she live?"

Until she dies.

"What about me?" He paused. "No . . . never mind. I know. Until I die."

You have been given a glimpse. You are the Chosen One.

He felt it then—a warmth beneath the skin. A current of euphoria, defiant in its timing.

I'll survive. I'm going home. Me. I have been given a glimpse.

And what good is a glimpse if you don't live to use it?

A shiver crawled up his spine.

I'm the only one going home.

~ *Teo Sneaks Out to See Little Monkey* ~

Teo couldn't sleep.

His mother snored beside him, but he lay wide-eyed, thinking of Little Monkey, and the stranger's eerie words. From the next room came the rhythmic creak of his grandmother pacing. At last, he slipped from bed, pulled on his shirt, slid into sandals, and padded toward the door. Just as he reached for the latch, her voice stopped him.

"Where are you going?"

"To pee."

"Dressed?"

"I can't sleep."

"Why not?"

He shrugged. "Just can't."

"Still worried about Vu Huong?"

"No."

"Worried about Little Monkey?"

"Umm . . . no. Not really. It's just . . . it's just that—"

"Well?"

"It's nothing, Grandmama."

She studied him for a moment, then nodded. "Yes, yes. Go, but be back soon. This monsoon is angry. If you see lightning, come back quickly. Do you hear?"

"Yes, Grandmama."

He opened the door and stepped into the night. Rain misted down, light but unrelenting. Blackness swallowed the road, and he paused. Then ducked back inside.

"Grandmama, I need a lantern."

She sighed. "We don't have enough oil as it is. But I don't want you to break your neck." She handed it over. "Be quick. It's a bad night."

"Yes, Grandmama. Thank you."

Lantern in hand, he stepped out once more, holding the light ahead like a small shield. Something tugged him forward. A quiet insistence repeating in his head: *Got to see Little Monkey. Got to see Little Monkey.*

He followed the muddy road, heavy with the stink of wet buffalo dung, until he reached the Trinh house. The windows were dark. He hesitated on the porch, about to turn back—when lightning split the sky. For a brief, breathless moment, the village was ablaze with brilliance.

And in that flash, he saw Little Monkey's eyes staring at him through the dark.

"Oh!" Teo gasped.

"Come here," Little Monkey whispered, hoarse.

"Huh?"

"Come on! Don't just stand there!"

Teo crept onto the porch, crouched beside him, and leaned against the wall.

"What are you doing out here?"

"*She* told me to come."

"Who? Your mom?"

"No. *Her.*" He pointed toward the road.

"I don't see anyone."

"*She's* gone now."

"Your sister?"

"No. I'm tired. Stop asking dumb questions."

"Do you have the fever?"

"No. But I feel bad. That man said I'd die. But he was wrong. He was bad. The lady was nice."

"What lady?"

"The one who was just here."

"Where?"

"I told you—*She's* gone. Teo, I'm sick. I don't feel good. What if he was right? What if I die? Mama'll be sad. She can't handle the fields alone. The buffalo. My sisters'll leave soon. I don't want to die. I want to run. I want to play with you."

"You'll get better."

Little Monkey shook his head. "No. I don't think so. Did you see the Venerable's body yesterday?"

"Yeah."

"Were you afraid?"

"No . . . well . . . maybe."

"I was. I kept thinking about worms crawling in the flesh. Bugs. Everything rotting."

"You shouldn't be afraid. You afraid of a tree?"

"Huh?"

"His body's like a dead tree. Bark. Bugs crawl on bark."

"Says who?"

"Me. I told myself that. That's why I kissed him. On the lips."

Little Monkey stared. "You're brave."

"Yeah."

They fell quiet.

Little Monkey moaned, lay back, arms spread wide for no reason.

"You know what I'm really afraid of?" he whispered.

"What?"

"Uncle Tinh told me about Buddhist hell. About Sakyamuni Buddha and a really bad man who suffers down there."

"Tell me."

"One day Sakyamuni sat beside a deep well. He heard voices crying up from the bottom. One of them shouted, 'Help me! I'm suffering!' So the Buddha looked down, and saw a man in agony. Then he looked at the man's whole life."

"All the way back to baby time?"

"Yeah. The man was evil. Killed many people. Did terrible things. But one time—just once—he felt compassion. He didn't step on a spider. So Sakyamuni decided to give him a chance."

"Why didn't he step on it?"

"I don't know! Shut up and listen."

Teo bit his tongue.

"So Sakyamuni lowered a spider silk down the well. The man grabbed it and started climbing. Higher and higher. But when he looked down, he saw other people climbing too. He shouted, 'Let go! You'll break it!' But they didn't stop. So he pulled out a knife and shouted, 'You asked for it!'"

Little Monkey paused. Groaned. "Oh . . . my bones hurt, Teo."

Teo stroked his friend's head. Waited.

After a long moment, he asked gently, "Then what?"

"The man cut the strand beneath him. Everyone else fell back into the fire. He laughed. But then, when he looked up, he saw the Buddha's face. Sad. The silk snapped. He fell too. Back into the fire."

Silence.

"No one heard him cry after that."

Teo frowned. "I don't get it. That was a bad man. You're just a kid. You haven't done anything."

Little Monkey didn't answer. He stared at the sky.

"Uncle Tinh said, 'The more love you give, the more love you get. The more you share, the more you have.' But I haven't given enough love. I've killed lots of ants. I've had bad thoughts."

"You?" Teo laughed. "Killing ants doesn't count. You're the kindest kid I know."

"I spied on my sisters. I wanted to see them naked. I've stepped on spiders. I threw frogs into Pap's rice wine. That man . . . that stranger . . . he asked if I had given love to others. I know what he meant."

"What?"

"He meant I'm going to hell. Like the man in the story."

"No, you're not! That's stupid. If you're going, then we all are. You're better than me. That stranger creeps me out. After I left you, I saw him again."

Little Monkey turned. "What did he say?"

"He said a woman soldier would come live with us. That she'd have a daughter. That my life would be tangled with hers. He spoke of a two-headed snake. Weird things. Scary."

Little Monkey grew quiet. "At least you'll have a future."

He turned his face to the sky. His voice a whisper.

"I'm going to die."

In the lantern's glow, Teo saw the tears streaking his friend's cheeks. A wave of panic rose in him—visceral, instinctive.

He wanted to run. To get away from the sick, from death. To use his legs. To live. So he ran.

~

Little Monkey watched his friend vanish into the night.

Shivering, he pulled the lantern close, and fixed his eyes on a tiny spider spinning its web in the porch's corner.

Chapter Twenty-Five

Grief 1

Homage to the Dead

*V*oices rise in the forest, not all speak with tongues.

Just before dawn, Major Vy left Clerk Long and threaded his way back through the jungle. Wet foliage slapped against his trousers, but his mind remained ensnared in deeper tangles.

All my little dragons.

And they were multiplying.

How to kill Minh without raising suspicion? How to retrieve the figurine intact? How to get it back by tomorrow? He shook his head. Too late, probably. Even now, too late.

And Tong . . . ah, Tong. He must be removed. But Kim Lan? Tuyet Mai? Were they necessary sacrifices?

He spat thick phlegm into the mud, trying to purge the thoughts from his body.

The problems were accelerating, slipping beyond his grip. A sickness churned in his gut. Not fear of battle, he had long since buried that.

But the thought of forced poison, public disgrace, slow death beneath the eyes of comrades? No. That was a different kind of terror. A death that clawed inward.

He gave a low, dry laugh and withdrew into the only refuge that never failed him: contempt for his own theatrics.

A ancient parable floated into memory: *The water buffalo from Wu, who mistook the moon for the sun and staggered forward, aching for warmth that never arrived.*

"Listen to me," he muttered. "I'm beginning to sound like Tong."

"Sir!"

The voice cracked the undergrowth.

Vy flinched.

"Quy! Damn it. You're going to stop my heart one of these days." He exhaled. "Are you always on duty?"

He couldn't see the boy, but Quy's silence carried the shape of hurt.

"Sorry, sir. Your hammock is ready. I heated tea, if you want some."

Vy sighed. Something twisted in his belly. Not rage. Not grief. A guilt that refused naming.

"All right. Go rest. I'll try sleeping."

"Yes, sir."

Leaves rustled as Quy melted into the underbrush.

"And it's good that you're alert," Vy called after him, too late. The boy was gone.

He stood beside the hammock, slumped, exhaling one long, weary gust. Lightning flickered far away, illuminating the jungle in silver strokes. Thunder followed in slow pursuit.

"Damn it," he growled. "I thought we were done with you."

He lay back in the hammock, watching stormlight dance through the canopy. Buckets of green flame spilled across the leaves. Then something stirred.

A cluster of shadows shifted along the banyan trunk. Vy focused. A bamboo frame he used for hot pots dangled from a low branch. Its shadow formed a perfect square on the tree. Inside, the curling silhouette of a vine, like a dragon coiled in slumber.

With each lightning flash, the shadow twitched, restless.

Then came the burst, light and wind surging together. The dragon uncoiled. Its head pierced the square's border, writhing free.

A guillotine.

Louis XVI. Marie Antoinette.

Led to a guillotine. Led to a guillotine. Led to . . .

"That's it!" Vy shouted, leaping up. "Marie Antoinette! A guillotine!"

His words vanished in the storm's roar, but his grin cut through it. His gaze drifted upward. Darkness. Then a blinding flash.

And there, caught in the white blaze, sat an orangutan. Cradling her infant against her furred belly. Staring down at him, wide-eyed, rain-soaked, shivering.

The light snapped off.

She vanished.

But the gaze lingered. Those eyes.

Vy shivered.

"Quy!"

The youth came running. Another flash revealed his blurred silhouette: uniform disheveled, bandolier dangling, face blinking in the brightness.

"Are you all right, sir?"

Vy smiled through his unease. "Yes, Quy. I'm fine. A dragon's shadow just showed me the way. Wake Huynh Kim Lan. Tell her to report to me. Immediately."

Quy vanished.

Vy rubbed his hands together, exhilarated. *If this works . . . oh, this plan is a gem. Even Viet couldn't dream this up.*

But even in triumph, his eyes kept drifting back to the banyan tree.

Should have her shot. Meat for the troops. But . . . I can't. I just . . . can't.

~ *T Performs Services for the Dead* ~

The funerals happened by coincidence. American. People's Army. Song Nhan villagers. All burying their dead that same morning. Words had to be said. They always did.

So T, Major Vy, and Han Tinh became shamans by default. The bodies were many. Mountain Man and Cao Thanh-Dam. Mr. Machine and Tuan Doanh. Bowls and Bui Van Nguu. The Venerable Vu Huong. Tran Van Ngo. Others unnamed.

Yet those buried were not uppermost in the minds of those burying them. Still, ritual creates latticework when grief is formless. It gives contour to fear. It anchors pain. And so, even scoffers fell into rhythm. The rites continued.

~

T stood stiffly beside a shallow grave. Two poncho-wrapped corpses lay beneath him: Bowls and Mr. Machine. Between them, Mountain Man's severed foot nestled in the crook of Bowls' arm. Rain lashed the scene. The stench, from bloated sappers tossed over the wall, thickened the air. It would worsen before it faded. Grunts stood in a loose semicircle. Silent. Waiting for words.

T coughed. Cleared his throat. "I wish I had a Bible," he began, "but I don't. Thank God we've got their tabs. That's enough."

He looked at the grunts. Looked at the grave.

"Bowls is probably in his easy chair right now, watching that woman paint her . . . well, you know. Make herself pretty. Godspeed, John Eldridge."

He turned to the helicopter crew.

"We didn't know Mr. Machine long. But what little we saw, he was kind. Decent. I hear he just wanted to go home. Well, maybe now he is. Godspeed, Albert Shear."

T paused. Exhaled. Looked down again. "Mountain Man." He said the name alone. No surname. None needed. "You're probably off coon hunting with your Blue Ticks. Big smile on your face. Almost as big as Bowls'." He chuckled.

Then coughed again. *Keep it short.*

He held up a tin cup, pinching something between his fingers—a bundle of multicolored human hair. "Each of us cut some of our own. For you. For all of us."

He dropped the locks into a hole Nature had scraped open. Placed a brick on top with quiet solemnity. Wiped his hands on a towel the color of filth. "Godspeed, Mountain Man."

Then, to the others: "Superman has a few words."

The preacher stepped forward, eyes flicking toward X, who stared back half-lidded. "I don't know what denominations our brothers were," Superman said. "But I think these words will soothe both the grieving and the departed.

Some of you might not be believers. That's all right. Let's just be respectful, send them across."

He paused.

Fingering his pocket holes, he searched for something buried deeper. His God had to be erect. Virile. Ready. Found in catastrophe: plane crashes, divorces, war. Nowhere else. Nowhere safe. Thus the Army. Thus Vietnam. Thus the urgent joy of mortal ministry.

Choked with emotion, he forced his voice out. "We came here to stop atheistic Communism. To save democracy. To help. Our friends, our brothers, they stayed. What greater calling?"

He intoned in his best preacher's voice, "Two nations are in your womb,And two peoples will be separated from inside you;One people will be stronger than the other,And the greater will serve the younger."

Blank stares met him. He explained. "Vietnam is a younger democracy. Still learning."

He faltered. Daughters' laughter filled his head. Their small hands. Their lovely faces.

He couldn't go on.

Coughs sounded from the ranks. So he fell back on the only words everyone knew:

"The Lord is my shepherd; I shall not want . . . "

~ *Major Vy Performs Services for the Dead* ~

Major Vy loathed funerals. But as ranking officer, he couldn't dodge the ritual. Rain pattered on his pith helmet, running down channels left by his wife's teeth, tiny scars from past fights. Water streamed down his collar and he cursed.

"Comrades."

He paused, the word leaden. "Today, we bury our dead. Good brothers of the forest. Our friends. We've endured much with them. And now . . . they rest. At last. Maybe some of us . . . even envy them. No more napalm. No more rot, starvation, or loneliness."

Then he snapped upright, remembering his audience—and the politics of death.

"But now it is *we* who must carry the struggle against imperialist aggression. We who must avenge them."

He glanced at Minh, whose face was flushed with rage. Vy allowed himself a sly grin.

"I now call upon our esteemed Political Cadre Minh to speak."

Minh stepped forward, voice thick with fervor. "Comrades! We send our murdered brothers back to their ancestors and into the grateful hearts of Marxist-Leninist warriors everywhere. *Yes*, I say murdered! By lackeys of capitalism, misguided fools in uniform. Cowards!"

He stabbed a finger toward the fortress.

"And what do we do with murderers? We *exterminate* them. We *annihilate* them. If our leaders possess the political and military will, we will raze that French-built nest of vipers and cleanse our homeland."

"Major Vy!" Minh shouted. "Will you lead us? Will you avenge our murdered brothers?"

All eyes turned. But Vy, already prepared, answered smoothly.

"I will. And I have devised a plan, one requiring Comrade Minh's abundant courage. His role, I assure you, is voluntary."

Minh blinked. Hesitated.

Vy seized the moment.

"This plan—untested, yes—but elegant. It will save lives. I reveal it here, before the dead, in comradeship. We must finish our mission with the Jarai Arap. We cannot waste more lives storming the fortress. Agreed, Comrade Minh?"

Minh nodded reluctantly.

Vy raised his voice. "Comrades, we must act with precision. With deception. With courage."

He grabbed a pointer from Quy and raised it like a weapon. "We call a second conference with the Americans. This time, Comrade Minh attends—with Kim Lan as interpreter."

He tossed the pointer aside. Drew his pistol. Pointed it at Minh.

"What—what is this?" Minh stammered, retreating.

"Pop!"

A blank. Minh clutched his chest and staggered backward.

Gasps. Frozen soldiers. Vy grinned.

"There's no wound, comrades. It was a demonstration. This afternoon, Comrade Minh will be shot again. But not really. He will *appear* to be murdered by a traitor."

He turned dramatically.

"Huynh Kim Lan!"

Murmurs. Tension.

"She will run to the Americans shouting '*Chieu Hoi*!' claiming to defect. She will return with them to the fortress. Under fire, but deliberately missed."

He let the silence stretch.

"Inside, she will claim our forces have withdrawn. She will urge them to flee before reinforcements arrive. If they do, ambush them. If they stay, she escapes with Tuyet Mai and the figurine. We fulfill our mission."

Minh shouted, "Preposterous! Too many risks. We might lose Kim Lan. The Americans may not believe her. And even if she escapes, we only gain the figurine."

Vy's grin widened. "Not only the figurine. Also Tuyet Mai. And the figurine is *key* to our primary mission."

Minh growled. "Still too risky."

"Comrade Minh," Vy said mildly, "are you afraid to do your part?"

"Of course not!"

"Then I presume you support the plan, especially if Comrade Kim Lan volunteers?"

She stepped forward. Chin raised. "I volunteer. For Uncle Ho. For the revolution. For Tuyet Mai. For our dead comrades."

Cheers erupted.

Minh, cornered, smiled stiffly. "It may be possible. But the details must be flawless. Especially . . . the blank cartridge."

Another cheer. Vy silenced them with a wave.

"Then it is agreed." He turned toward the graves. "May our fallen comrades be forever honored by your bravery."

~

Clerk Long leaned toward Kha. "Look at Sergeant Viet. He looks like a statue."

Kha nodded. "He's worried the plan might, as the ancients say, 'beat the grass and startle the snakes.'"

Long whispered, "I wonder if Tong knows."

"No idea. I'm hungry. If this works, maybe we can scavenge the Americans' food."

Long chuckled. "And if there's none, you'll want to eat their corpses."

"Too much fat," Kha smirked.

Then came Minh's voice, rising once more with Uncle Ho's words: "Even a weak and small nation, once united under the working class . . . "

Kha groaned. "Do they never stop with the slogans? I want food, not words."

Long elbowed him. A nearby lieutenant glanced their way.

"Shhhh," Long hissed. Then straightened, face obedient, like a schoolboy before the master.

Chapter Twenty-Six

Grief 2

Funerals and Conspiracies

~ Han Tinh Performs Services for the Venerable Vu Huong ~

Han Tinh looked nervously out at the faces of a hundred women packed into the dinh. They waited for him to speak, to say a few words about the Venerable Vu Huong, to chant a Buddhist dirge to ease the passage of his spirit. Tinh remembered the last time he spoke here. He'd gotten in trouble for telling the women the truth: about soldiers, and the brutal things men could do. Should he tell it again? Or feed their longing for ritual, offer the comfort of illusion and the balm of sacred phrases?

He saw Madame Dau in the front row beside Vit, both women murmuring prayers, their bodies gently rising and falling in time with the twisting incense smoke held between their pressed palms. Schoolmistress Nang looked down, fingering a rosary—something new for her. Tinh had never seen her display any religious inclination. He smiled inwardly. So, The Man From the Mountains had made her a good Buddhist and a poor Marxist. All the better. Very well, he thought. I shall play the good little monk.

He knew how comical he must appear. The saffron robe billowed awkwardly around his stumps, gathering in heaps like a makeshift curtain drawn over a missing body. Behind him, the great dark statue of the Guardian Spirit stirred in the flashes of lightning that cracked the sky and illuminated the windows. Its swollen wooden body groaned, the strain of moisture trapped in its joints.

Tinh straightened. His throat tightened. But as he began to speak, he sensed her, Goddess, in the *dinh*. The words that came had no connection to his own thoughts.

"Hear me well, sisters, for we are being watched by the Great Father and judged beneath the maxim of That Which Is." Tinh's eyes moved involuntarily through the crowd. "Struggle.

"Nguyen struggles beneath the thousand cuts that slowly drain her nature. Nang suffers the invasion of worms burrowing through her body, stirred by the sparks of frightened thought. Tien battles the sharp edge of hardship, forced backward, yet striking still with every retreat. Vit is strong enough to harbor others within her, knowing with clear-eyed certainty that she will fail in the end, and that even the ones she shelters will watch, unblinking, as she does. And the rest of you . . . yes, the rest . . . carry variations of the same burden.

"But Madame Dau struggles with struggle itself. And the two-headed serpent she carries is more dangerous than Nang's worms, for it threatens to consume far more than one small body. That consuming is what I must speak of now.

"This war will consume you. And the men who fight it will consume you. But only if you look away. A man may be crude, ignorant, but a woman must not meet his eyes. No matter how low his station, no matter how high hers, she must not meet his gaze, for he cannot endure the judgment she does not speak. But I sing now of a war that brings destruction not only to your lives, but to the lives of your fathers, husbands, and sons. And so you must dare what has always been forbidden: to meet war's stare head-on. You must not flinch when war reveals its face. You must not turn away, even when its mouth opens wide to devour the world.

"You must glare back, for your children. At the height of their joy, you grieve for the joy that may not follow. At the height of their health, you tremble for the health that may vanish. At the height of their success, you labor under the shadow of its loss. And so you push yourselves beyond exhaustion. You labor in silence. You stay up late to stretch their joy. You give your own strength to protect their breath. You polish the boots of others so they might rise. And still, the doubt does not release you.

"Sometimes violence pierces the armor of your daily life. You look away, busying your hands—scrubbing, spinning, comforting, cooking—reaching for order. But you know the truth. Famine tightens your children's skin. Bullets tear their limbs. Shells erase what they were. You cannot look away. You must watch, and by watching, hold them back from the edge where life ends and nothing waits. If you look away, you will not see the moment when it might still be stopped."

. . . *Tap. Tap. Tap.* . . .

A strange noise echoed through the dinh. The women shrank from it.

Tinh shouted above the sound. "You hear that? It comes from within their bodies. The sound of what breaks before it dies. In the flood of violence, they may be swept away—tiny forms adrift on the sea of suffering, while the world mocks your tears."

. . . *Tap. Tap. Tap.* . . .

"And when they are gone, though you remain, the sun will not warm you. The air will not nourish. The space left inside you will chill the blood and crush the breath. You must not look away. You must not surrender war to the men who summon it."

The tapping ceased. The dinh fell still. The women stared at Han Tinh as though in the presence of a sacred being. Their joss sticks remained suspended between their hands, smoke climbing into a single thick cloud hovering low above their heads.

Tinh spoke again.

"And what of the devourers, the soldiers? Even now, they clash at the fortress. Each of them, American or People's Army, carries his own private terror into that chaos. But your fear, and the fear of their mothers, need not collide. You must not succumb. Endure with compassion. Endure together."

He stopped. His eyes rolled upward until only the whites were visible. A trance, the women thought. Possession.

Madame Dau's voice rose through the silence, rough and reverent. "Venerable One, what should we do? Have I brought ruin to our village? Will our children die?"

"Must we flee?" called a voice from the rear.

"Dau has cursed us!" screamed another.

"Yes, we should have listened to the schoolmistress!" more voices cried.

"It is Dau and her demon snake!" shouted Security Chief Tien.

"What snake? What snake?" demanded a red-faced woman up front.

The dinh erupted.

Then Nang rose. Calmly, she turned to face the room. Silence returned. One by one, the women turned to look.

Without a word, Nang opened her mouth and extended her tongue.

A collective breath drew in. Her tongue had split, two mottled tips darkened and swollen. She hissed, a sound that froze every woman in the room.

"Sssnnnaakkesss," she whispered. "Devour their own young. I sent many children to death. I am the two-headed snake. I am becoming Dau's prophecy."

The room exploded again. Women spun in every direction, exchanging frantic words, waving incense through the air as if to shield themselves. Cries rose. Questions shot toward the two figures now huddled at the base of the Guardian Spirit statue.

"What should we do? What should we do?"

The chant began. Louder, louder, until thunder joined in.

Han Tinh stood paralyzed. "I do not know. Goddess has left me."

But Nang raised her arms and wept as she spoke. "Wee mustt sttayy. Youu arr myy onnllyy ffaamiillyyy. Nnootthinggg ellsss. Thisss iss ourr onnllyy hhommm."

"But you heard the Venerable One!" Tien cried. "We will be devoured! The battle will reach the village."

"No!" Madame Vit objected. "He wasn't clear. I believe he meant we'll be devoured if we leave. Remember? He said, 'You must not endure them alone.'"

"That's not what he said," said Tien.

"We must stay," Madame Dau said softly, a pleading note in her voice.

"Why should we listen to you? You brought this down on us!" someone shouted.

"Those who wish to leave, come to this side," said Tien. A large group gathered behind her.

Madame Dau's breath caught. The village was breaking apart, and for the first time since she'd taken leadership, her voice held no sway. She felt the world pressing in on her chest, her breath shortening, her vision swimming. She watched, helpless, as many followed Tien from the dinh, vowing to gather their families and flee.

The absence of Vu Huong stabbed through her. So too did the deeper, older ache for her long-dead husband.

I must act or collapse.

She grabbed Vit by the arm, dragged her into a side room, and shut the door behind them.

"I have to go back to the cave."

"What?" Vit gasped.

"I must. If the Man From the Mountains lives, he will go there. Maybe I'll find clarity. Maybe I'll receive a sign. Right now, I'm drowning in doubt, and the village is falling apart. Perhaps I can stop it. I need to know."

"Know what?"

Dau shook her head.

"You're mad. You don't even know what you're looking for. And what if he's dead? What if they see you? Kill you?"

"Then that's my answer."

"I'm begging you. Think of your daughters. Your grandchildren."

"It's for them I go. I can't watch this village die. Not from here. Not from the sidelines."

Vit scowled. "No. It's stubbornness, not purpose. Stay. If the spirits wish to speak, they'll find you here. That cave is madness. And your parents would never speak through an American soldier."

"Perhaps he's not the voice of my parents," Dau whispered. "Perhaps he's the voice of my childhood."

"Perhaps, perhaps, perhaps! Nonsense. Don't go. It's too late. You'll never return before nightfall."

"I know. I'll bring a bedroll."

"You plan to sleep in that place? Now I'm sure, you're beyond hope."

Dau touched her arm gently. "We've established that."

~ *Kim Lan Has A Conversation with Sergeant Viet* ~

Kim Lan had returned to her hammock after Vy announced his plan. Lying uncomfortably on her back with her hands clasped behind her head, she grew tired of the position and rolled out to lie flat on the ground beneath the hammock. She felt sick to her stomach, but forced herself to twist around and rummage through her pack to retrieve a plastic bag containing blank paper and a pen. Positioning herself again under the hammock, she rested on her elbows and placed the paper atop a bamboo slate on the ground beneath her to further protect it from the rain. After staying in this position for a while, she sighed and began to write.

Major Vy,

This note is a reminder of our conversation last night. I have already given instructions to an unnamed comrade to immediately report your activities in the event of my or Tuyet Mai's death. I will go along with your plan, but failure to protect or rescue us will result in your immediate arrest and execution.

After finishing the note, she carefully folded the paper a dozen times so that it was the size of a thumbnail. She intended to go immediately to Vy's command post and surreptitiously slip it into his hand, but she ached all over and nausea prevented her from standing. Slipping the paper inside her cotton binding, she lay on her back and battled the fear rising in her gut.

Back to the Americans. That is crazy. If they do not believe me, I certainly will be killed or tortured. Even if they believe me, how can I survive the ambush? The plan is crazy. Why did I agree?

The idea of smuggling plastic explosives, blasting caps and a small folding knife inside her vagina did not cause undue concern. She had often concealed items in this manner. But being back inside the fortress made her shiver. Only the thought of saving Tuyet Mai convinced her to accept Vy's insane plan.

What if they strip search me? Unfortunately my period is over. How to discourage them? Perhaps if I—

"Ah! Comrade Kim Lan. Am I bothering you?" said a jovial Sergeant Viet as he strode up on his short, piston-like legs.

"Comrade. You are always welcome. Back from the tunnel already?" Feeling her face flush, she gestured an invitation for Viet to squat across from her.

"Yes," he sighed. "We heard about Major Vy's plan while excavating the tunnel. We just arrived back so I came to talk with you about it. What do you think?" he smiled somewhat forlornly.

"Captain Tong has also returned?" asked Kim Lan in strained innocence.

His eyes narrowed. "Yes. Of course. You should have seen his face when he heard about the major's plan."

"Oh?" she said, inviting explanation.

"As the ancients said, he was dumb like a wooden cock."

She laughed, unsure of the meaning of the proverb, but amused by the image of Tong that it produced. "Surely, Comrade Viet, you are wise enough to know that People's Army soldiers do not 'think' about their leaders' plans." She raised her eyebrows. Although appearing to treat the topic lightly, she felt regret at having to register a reminder in her brain that when this mission was over and Vy and Tong had been executed, she would have to report Viet's lax attitude toward unquestioned discipline.

Viet smiled. Kim Lan felt his paternalistic aura wash over her. *He trusts me. Wants to protect me. Assumes I'm vulnerable and dependent on his combat experience. Don't get trapped by my easy manner, Comrade Viet. I am not subordinate to your maleness.*

"Yes. You are right," he said at last. "Still, it worries me that you are going back into the fortress." He laughed nervously. "We cannot afford to lose comrades such as you."

"For the revolution, comrade Viet, we should all be prepared to die."

"But, you . . . I mean, you must not die . . . I mean, unnecessarily."

Kim Lan flushed and had an astonishing thought. *He is attracted to me. Impossible. But true . . . I think. Me!* She wanted to look down at her small breasts and laugh. No one mistook her for a beauty. But Viet? Ugly as they come. A crooked figure, a twisted kitchen god. Still, he was strong and kind and not at all stupid. Quite clever, in fact. She tried to picture being married to him. Their conversations, their home. But then she thought of his rough, peasant hands on her breasts and the ugly children they would produce. And besides, she was going to report him. *Stupid! Viet is almost as ugly as The Man From The Mountains. Why do I attract the ugly men? Ah! Stupid!* Still, she took extra care to ensure that her silver tooth didn't show. "As I said, all of us must be prepared to lay down our lives for the revolution, Sergeant Viet," she said gruffly. *A warning shot. Let him heed it.*

Viet stuttered, "Yes, yes, of course. That is exactly what I have been doing for years, Comrade Kim Lan." He sounded flustered, or angry, or both.

~

Sergeant Viet felt unsure of Kim Lan's sympathies, so he discontinued his probing. Whether she was attractive or not, he would patiently keep at her until he got the information he wanted: the true nature of this mission. He thought of Dam and felt a knot tighten in his stomach.

This damn mission, whatever it really is, has already been too expensive.

Grinding his teeth, he walked away from Kim Lan after muttering some banal pleasantries. *Too expensive.*

~ *Captain Tong Has a Confrontation with Commissar Minh* ~

After arriving at the base camp, Tong busied himself with various duties, all the while thinking about Vy's plan. As usual, his feelings were ambiguous, pulling him this way and that. His anger at the world often arose from this lack of resolution. When he ran across Minh, he was in no mood for coy banter.

"Captain Tong!" called Minh. "I want to talk with you."

"About what?" snarled Tong.

"About this so-called plan Vy has dreamed up. I don't like it."

Tong scoffed. "Of course you don't. Is our brave political cadre afraid?"

Minh hesitated, aware this was not a good time to talk to Tong. But his stubborn nature made him press on. "If you're not afraid, why don't you go in my place? After all, it will give you an opportunity to save Comrade Tuyet Mai and be a hero. In fact, I could order you to do that."

Tong sneered. "But I *am* afraid, Comrade Minh. Besides, Vy would simply countermand your order."

Minh narrowed his eyes. "Why is it necessary that I go instead of you or someone else? Eh? Makes one a little suspicious."

Tong realized he needed to be more careful. "Look, all you have to do is pretend to be killed. What could be safer? If you wish to complain, take it to Vy, not to me."

"Rest assured, Comrade Tong, I will be careful to check the bullets placed in Comrade Kim Lan's pistol."

Tong shrugged. "Do as you wish, Minh, but remember Uncle Ho's admonishment: 'Always combine the political struggle with the military struggle, and the military struggle with the political struggle.' A political bullet finds a military body. A military bullet finds a political one. Uncle Ho's dictate lives on. Your heroic role will be revered for generations."

Minh shook his head angrily. "It will be a great pleasure when I report to battalion headquarters . . . a great pleasure."

"Do as you wish. Now I must get back to my duties, Comrade Minh." Tong watched Minh walk away, but he did not feel as confident as he sounded.

~ *Return to the Great Mother* ~

Within each sacred hectare encircling the buried bones of American and Vietnamese dead, more than sixty-five million subterranean beings stirred, not counting the unnumbered hosts of bacteria and fungal threads weaving through the darkness. The scent of decay rose slowly, diffusing through the capillaries of the soil, a silent summons in the tongue of the underworld. From every direction, the hidden children of the Great Mother answered. They came without sound, without haste, drawn by the ancient law: what dies must return.

Beneath the surface, the bodies softened, collapsed, and were taken back, not wasted, but offered. Muscle and marrow, skin and sinew, memory and blood—all dissolved into the breathing loam, to be folded into Her vast and dreaming form. And so the land was fed. And so the province known to men as Kon Tum was consecrated again, not by prayer, but by decomposition. Not by war, but by return.

Epilogue

The Stillness

The silence after battle is not peace, but the breath before another scream.
In the fortress and the village alike, the war's true cost is only beginning to reveal
itself.
Return death to the living.
The Voices contend,
The Stillness listens,
And humanity moves down its long, final path.